THE BEST OF
SUBTERRANEAN

THE BEST OF
SUBTERRANEAN

EDITED BY

WILLIAM SCHAFER

Subterranean Press 2017

First Edition

ISBN
978-1-59606-837-7

Subterranean Press
PO Box 190106
Burton, MI 48519

subterraneanpress.com

Table of Contents

For Gretchen,
with all my love

Perfidia

BY LEWIS SHINER

"That's Glenn Miller," my father said. "But it can't be."
He had the back of the hospital bed cranked upright, the lower lid of his left eye creeping up in a warning signal I'd learned to recognize as a child. My older sister Ann had settled deep in the recliner, and she glared at me too, blaming me for winding him up. The jam box sat on the rolling tray table and my father was working the remote as he talked, backing up my newly burned CD and letting it spin forward to play a few seconds of low fidelity trombone solo.

"You know the tune, of course," he said.

" 'King Porter Stomp.' " Those childhood years of listening to him play Glenn Miller on the console phonograph were finally paying off.

"He muffed the notes the same way on the Victor version."

"So why can't it be Miller?" I asked.

"He wouldn't have played with a rabble like that." The backup musicians teetered on the edge of chaos, playing with an abandon somewhere between Dixieland and bebop. "They sound drunk."

My father had a major emotional investment in Miller. He and my mother had danced to the Miller band at Glen Island Casino on Long Island Sound in the summer of 1942, when they were both sixteen. That signature sound of clarinet and four saxes was forever tied up for him with first love and the early, idealistic months of the war.

But there was a better reason why it couldn't have been Miller playing that solo. If the date on the original recording was correct, he was supposed to have died three days earlier.

⁂

The date was in India ink on a piece of surgical tape, stuck to the top of a spool of recording wire. The handwritten numerals had the hooks and day-first order of Europe: 18/12/44. I'd won it on eBay the week before as part of a lot that included a wire recorder and a stack of 78s by French pop stars like Charles Trenent and Edith Piaf.

It had taken me two full days to transfer the contents of the spool to my computer, and I'd brought the results to my father to confirm what I didn't quite dare to hope—that I'd made a Big Score, the kind of find that becomes legend in the world of collectors, like the first edition *Huck Finn* at the yard sale, the Rembrandt under the 19th century landscape.

On my Web site I've got everything from an Apollo player piano to a 1930s Philco radio to an original Wurlitzer Model 1015 jukebox, all meticulously restored. During the Internet boom I was shipping my top dollar items to instant Silicon Valley millionaires as fast as I could find them and clean them up, with three full-time employees doing the refurbishing in a rented warehouse. For the last year I'd been back in my own garage, spending more time behind a browser than trolling the flea markets and thrift stores where the long shots lived, and I wanted to be back on top. It wasn't just the freedom and the financial security, it was the thrill of the chase and the sense of doing something important, rescuing valuable pieces of history.

Or, in this case, rewriting history.

⁂

On the CD, the song broke down. After some shifting of chairs and unintelligible bickering in what sounded like French, the band stumbled into a ragged version of "Perfidia," the great ballad of faithless love. It had been my mother's favorite song.

My father's eyes showed confusion and the beginnings of anger. "Where did you get this?"

"At an auction. What's wrong?"

"Everything." The stroke had left him with a slurping quality to his speech, and his right hand lay at what should have been an uncomfortable angle on the bedclothes. The world hadn't been making much sense for him for the last eight months, starting with the sudden onset of diabetes at age 76. With increasing helplessness and alarm, he'd watched his body forsake him at every turn: a broken hip, phlebitis, periodontal disease, and now the stroke, as if the warranty had run out and everything was breaking down at once. Things he'd done for himself for the five years since my mother's death suddenly seemed beyond him—washing dishes, changing the bed, even buying groceries. He could spend hours walking the aisles, reading the ingredients on a can of hominy, comparing the fractions of a pound that separated one package of ground meat from another, overwhelmed by details that had once meant something.

"Who are these people? Why are they playing this way?"

"I don't know," I told him. "But I intend to find out. Listen."

On the CD there was a shout from the audience and then something that could have been a crack from the snare drum or a gunshot. The band trailed off, and that was where it ended, with more shouts, the sound of furniture crashing and glass breaking, and then silence.

"Turn it off," my father said, though it was already over. I took the CD out and moved the boom box back to windowsill. "It's some kind of fake," he finally said, more to himself than me. "They could take his solo off another recording and put a new background to it."

"It came off a wire recorder. I didn't pay enough for it to justify that kind of trouble. Look, I'm going to track this down."

"You do that. I want to know what kind of psycho would concoct something like this." He waved his left hand vaguely. "I'm tired. You two go home." It was nine at night; I could see the lights of downtown Durham through the window. I'd been so focused on the recording that I'd lost all sense of time.

Ann bent down to kiss him and said, "I'll be right outside if you need me."

"I'll be fine. Go get something to eat. Or go to the motel and sleep, for God's sake." My father had come to North Carolina for the VA hospital at Duke, and Ann had flown in from Connecticut to be with him. I'd offered her my guest room, 25 miles away in Raleigh, but she'd insisted on being walking distance from the hospital.

In the hallway, her rage boiled over. "What was the point of that?" she hissed.

"That's the most involved I've seen him since the stroke. I think it was good for him."

"Well, I don't. And you could at least have consulted me first." Ann's height and big bones had opened her to ridicule in grade school, and for as long as I could remember she'd been contained, slightly hunched, given to whispers instead of shouts.

"Do you really need to control my conversations with him now?"

"Apparently. And don't make this about me. This is about him getting better."

"I want that too."

"But I'm the one who's here with him, day in and day out."

It was easy to see where this was headed, back to our mother again. "I've got to go," I said. She accepted my hug stiffly. "You should take his advice and get some rest."

"I'll think about it," she said, but as the elevator doors closed, I could see her in the lounge two doors down from his room, staring at the floor in front of her.

⇥⇤

I had email from the seller waiting at home. Her initial response when I'd written her about the recorder had been wary. I'd labored hard over the next message, offering her ten percent of anything I made off the deal, up to a thousand dollars, at the same time lowballing the odds of actually selling it, and all the while working on her guilt—with no provenance, the items were virtually worthless to me.

She'd gone for it, admitting picking everything up together at one stall in the Marché Vernaison, part of the vast warren of flea markets at Saint-Ouen, on the northern edge of Paris. She wasn't sure which one, but she remembered an older man with long, graying hair, a worn carpet on a dirt floor, a lot of Mickey Mouse clocks.

I knew the Vernaison because one of my competitors operated a high-end stall there, a woman who called herself Madame B. The description of the old man's place didn't ring any bells for me, but the mere mention of that district of Paris made my palms sweat.

My business gave me an excuse to read up on music history. I already knew a fair amount about Miller's death, and I'd gone back to my book-shelves the night before. Miller allegedly took off from the Twinwood Farm airfield, north of London, on Friday, December 15, 1944. He was supposed to be en route to Paris to arrange a series of concerts by his Army Air Force Band, but the plane never arrived. Of the half dozen or more legends that dispute the official account, the most persistent has him flying over on the day before, and being fatally injured on the 18th in a brawl in the red light district of Pigalle. Pigalle was a short taxi ride from the Hotel des Olympiades, where the band had been scheduled to stay, and the Hotel des Olympiades was itself only a short walk from the Marché Vernaison.

I walked out to the garage and looked at the wire recorder where it sat on a bench, its case removed, its lovely oversized vacuum tubes visible from the side. I'd recognized it in the eBay photos as an Armour Model 50, manufactured by GE for the US Army and Navy, though I'd never seen one firsthand before. The face was smaller than an LP cover, tilted away to almost meet the line of the back. Two reels mounted toward the top each measured about four inches in diameter and an inch thick, wound with steel wire the thickness of a human hair. More than anything else it reminded me of the Bell & Howell 8mm movie projector that my father had tortured us with as children, showing captive audiences of dinner guests his home movies featuring Ann and me as children and my mother in the radiant beauty of her 30s.

The wire recorder hadn't been working when it arrived, but I'd been lucky. Blowing a half century's worth of dust off the electronics with an air gun, I'd found the broken bit of wire that had fallen into the works and caused a short. That and replacing a burnt-out power tube from my extensive stock of spare parts was all it had taken—apart from cleaning the wire itself.

The trick was to remove the corrosion without affecting the magnetic properties of the metal. I'd spent eight hours running the wire through a folded nylon scrub pad soaked in WD40, letting the machine's bailers wind the wire evenly back on the reel, stopping now and then to confirm there was still something there. Then I'd jury-rigged a bypass from the built-in speaker, through a preamp and into an eighth-inch jack that I could plug into my laptop. With excruciating care, I'd played it into a .wav file and worked on the results with CoolEdit Pro for another hour, trying to control the trembling in my hands as I began to realize what I had.

❄

When I got to the hospital in the morning, my father was reading the newspaper. Ann was still in the same clothes I'd last seen her in; she'd already had circles under her eyes, so it was hard to say if they were deeper. "You're here early," she said, with a smile that failed to cover the implied criticism.

"I'm on a plane to Paris tonight."

"Oh really?"

"You going to find out about that tape?" my father asked.

"That's the idea. My travel agent found me a cheap cancellation."

"How lucky for you," Ann said.

"This is business, Ann." I stifled my reflex irritation. "That recording could be worth a fortune."

"Of course it could," she said.

"Don't give those French any more of your money than you have to," my father said.

"Oh, Pop," I said. "Don't start."

"We had to bail their sorry country out in World War II, and now—"

"No politics," Ann said. "I absolutely forbid it."

I sat on the edge of the bed next to him. "You're not going to die on me, are you, Pop? At least not until I get back?"

"What makes you so special that I should wait for you?"

"Because you want to see how this turns out."

"I already know it's a fake. But there is the pleasure of saying I told you so. You'd think I'd get tired of it after all these years, but it's like fine wine."

I leaned over to hug him and his left arm went around my back with surprising power. He had two days' growth of beard and the starchy smell of hospital soap. "I'm serious," I said. "I want you to take care of yourself."

"Yeah, yeah. If you bag one of those French girls, ask if her mom remembers me."

"I thought you were only in Germany." His unit had liberated Dachau, but he never talked about it, or any other part of the war.

"I got around," he shrugged. His left arm relaxed and I pulled away. "Don't take any wooden Euros."

Ann followed me out, just as I knew she would. "He'll be dead by the time you get back. Just like—"

"I know, I know. Just like Mom. It's less than a week. The doctors say he's out of danger."

"No, he's not." She was crying.

"Sleep, Ann. You really need to get some sleep."

⇥⊹⇤

I myself slept fitfully on the way over, too cramped to relax, too tired to read, but my spirits lifted as soon as I was on the RER from DeGaulle to the city. There was no mistaking the drizzly gray October world outside the train for the US, despite billboards featuring Speedy Gonzales, Marilyn, Disneyland, *Dawson's Creek*. The tiny hybrid cars, the flowerboxes in the windows, even the boxy, Bauhaus-gone-wrong blocks of flats insisted that excess was not the only way to live. It was a lesson that my country was not interested in learning.

I'd been able to get a room at my usual hotel, a small family place in the XVIIth Arrondisement, a short walk from the Metro hub at Place de

Clichy and a slightly longer one from Montmartre and Pigalle. I stopped at the market across the street to pick up some fresh fruit and exchanged pleasantries with the clerk, who remembered me from my previous trip. The hotelier remembered me as well, and found me a room that opened onto the airshaft rather than the noise of the street.

The bed nearly filled the tiny room, and it called to me as soon as the door closed. If I stayed awake until 10 or 11 PM I knew my biological clock would reset itself, so I forced myself to unpack, drink a little juice, and wash my face.

"Hey, ho," I said to the mirror. "Let's go."

The number 4 Metro line ended at Porte de Clingancourt, the closest stop to the markets. I walked up into a gentle rain and a crowd of foot traffic, mostly male, mostly black and/or Middle Eastern, dressed in jeans, sneakers, and leather jackets, all carrying cell phones, talking fast and walking hard.

I headed north on the Avenue de la Porte de Clingancourt and the vendors started within a couple of blocks. These were temporary stalls, made of canvas and aluminum pipe, selling mostly new merchandise: Indian shawls, African masks, tools, jeans, batteries, shoes. Still, it was like distant music, an invocation of the possibilities ahead.

I passed under the Boulevard Peripherique, the highway that circles the entire city, and the small village of flea markets opened up on my left, surrounded by gridlocked cars and knots of pedestrians. The stalls here were permanent, brick or cinderblock single-story buildings with roll-down metal garage doors instead of front walls, and they were crammed with battered furniture, clothes, books, and jewelry. Deeper inside, in the high-end markets like the Dauphine and the Serpette, the stalls would have glass doors, oriental rugs, antique desks, and chandeliers.

I walked north another block, then turned left into the Rue de Rossiers, the main street of the district. A discreet metal archway halfway down the block marked the entrance to the Marché Vernaison in white Deco letters against a blue background. Twisting lanes, open to the rain, wove through a couple of hundred stalls, some elaborate showplaces, like my friend Madame B's, some dusty, oversized closets piled with junk. As in any collector's market, the dealers were each other's best customers; I watched a man in a wide polyester tie and a bad toupee hurry past with a short wooden column in each hand and a look of poorly concealed triumph on his face.

Madame B's emporium was in the center of the market, a corner stall with sliding glass doors, pale walls, and a thick, sand-colored carpet to show off the filigreed wood cabinets of the Victrolas that were her specialty. She was talking to an official-looking man in a suit and black raincoat, so I stayed outside and admired a beautiful 19th century puppet theater until he was gone.

"*Bonjour,* François," she said, almost singing the words, and I looked up to see her in the doorway. She was somewhere in her 50s, a little older than me. She kept her black hair trimmed to shoulder length, with severe black bangs that matched her black-framed glasses, long black vintage dresses, and black cigarette holder.

"Problems?" I asked, nodding toward the man in the raincoat.

She shook her head and offered her hand, palm down. "What a lovely surprise to see you. You are buying today, or just looking?" She talked to me mostly in English and I answered as best I could in French.

"Looking for a person." I showed her the photos of the wire recorder while we exchanged a few pleasantries. Her business was doing as badly as mine—no one had any money, and thanks to September 11 and the war in Iraq, American tourists had all but disappeared.

Eventually she pointed a long, red fingernail at one of the photos. "And this item," she said, falling into eBay slang like so many in the business, "it is not one of mine."

"They tell me it comes from somewhere in the Vernaison. An older man, perhaps, with long gray hair?"

"It is familiar, I think. When I see it I am interested, but it is maybe a little pricey. I go away for a day hoping the man will come to his senses, *et voila,* the next day it is gone."

"You remember who it was?"

"I think maybe Philippe over in Row 9? Let us look."

She locked up and set a brisk pace through the rain, ignoring it, as most of the locals seemed to do. There were only nine rows in the market, running more or less north and south, but I still had trouble remembering where specific vendors were, and more than once had gotten badly turned around.

Row 9 was the slum of the Marché Vernaison, where old and broken things came to their last resting place before the landfill. I had to wonder how some of these vendors paid for their stalls, what pleasure they found in sitting all weekend amid a clutter of useless and ugly objects, their glazed eyes not even registering the few customers who hurried past.

At the bend where Row 9 curved east and emptied into the market's café, a man in his 60s sat with his eyes closed, listening to a scratchy LP on a portable phonograph much like the one I'd had in high school. He had long graying hair, aviator-style glasses, a checked flannel shirt, and an ascot. The booth matched the description the eBay seller had given me, down to the worn carpet and the Mickey Mouse memorabilia. There was some electronic gear as well: a cheap reel-to-reel deck from the early 60s, walkie-talkies, an analog oscilloscope, a pocket transistor radio.

"*Bonjour*, Philippe," Madame B sang again. He gave no indication that he'd heard. "This is my friend François," she said in French, "and he wants to know about something you might have sold."

"To a woman from the United States," I said, laying the photos out on his nearly empty desk.

Philippe seemed to live at a completely different pace from Madame B. He slowly picked up each photo and stared at it, as if searching for something in it that might cheer him up.

"It's a recording device," I said, hoping to hurry him. "It records on a spool of wire." I didn't know the French name for it.

"I must get back to my shop," Madame B said. "Good luck with your quest."

I kissed her on both cheeks, and as she rushed out she seemed to take the last of the room's energy with her. Philippe eventually sighed, set the last photo down, and gave an elaborate shrug.

"So," I said, struggling for patience, "this was perhaps yours?"

"Perhaps." His voice was barely audible over the music.

"I'm not with the authorities," I said, thinking of the man in the black raincoat. "I don't care whether you pay your taxes or how you do your accounts. I just want to know where this came from. I'm a dealer, like you, and it would help me very much to have the provenance. Is that the right word? *Provenance?*"

He nodded slowly. "Many things come and go from here. It is difficult to keep track of all of them."

"But this is very unusual, *non?* I think you have not had many like it."

He shrugged again. It felt like we'd come to a stalemate, and I looked around his stall for a couple of minutes, trying on a pair of sunglasses, paging through the postcards, trying to think of a way to reach him.

"You like Jacques Brel, yes?" I pointed to the record player.

"Of course. You know of him?"

"A little. I like that he quit performing when he got tired of it. And that he didn't want to play in the US because of Vietnam."

"You are American, or English?"

The implied compliment was that I hadn't immediately given myself away. "American," I said, "but not proud of it these days."

He nodded. "You have another Vietnam now, I think." He pointed to the record player. "You know this record?"

I'd recognized the voice, but nothing more, and risked the truth. "No," I said.

"You wouldn't. It was his first, only out in France."

"Do you have the radio broadcasts from 1953?"

"I have them. They are interesting, but they are on CD. The CDs are too cold, I think."

I myself didn't understand why having pops and hiss made a recording more desirable, but I also understood that plenty of others disagreed. "They are also on LP, a—what's the word?—'bootleg' in English."

"We say 'bootleg' too. You have this record? I have never heard of it."

"I have a friend who does. If you give me your address, it would be my pleasure to send it to you."

"Why?" The question wasn't hostile, but the skepticism surprised me. "Is it because of this information you want?"

"Because it would mean more to you than it does to the person who has it. And this person owes me a favor. It is a small thing."

He was quiet for a moment and then he pointed to the record player and said, "Listen." On the record Brel was suddenly angry, spitting words in a theatrical fury. It didn't touch me, particularly, but I could see Philippe was moved.

When the song was over, he said, "I have been listening to this record for more than 35 years now. It is still incredible to me to hear a man be so… plain and direct with his emotions."

"Yes," I said. "I know exactly what you mean."

He took a yellow wooden pencil from a can on his desk, looked it over, then used a thumb-sized sharpener to put an exact point on it. On a blank index card from a wooden box, he wrote his name and address in an ornate longhand, then tapped the card on its edge as if to get rid of any stray graphite before handing it to me.

"Enchanté," I said, reading it, and offered my hand. "My name is Frank. Frank Delacorte."

He gave me a firm handshake. "Come back on Monday, in the afternoon. I will find out what I can."

⇥⊹⇤

It was already getting dark when I came out of the Metro at Place de Clichy. I called the States on my cell and arranged to have the Jacques Brel bootleg expressed to Philippe. When I was done, a wave of fatigue hit me so hard I nearly passed out. I knew if I went back to the hotel I'd be asleep within minutes, so I walked down the Boulevard des Batignolles to Le Mont Leban, my favorite neighborhood restaurant. I'd never had the heart to tell them how wonderfully inept the English translations in their menu were: "Net of raw lamb, spied on," "Chicken liver fits in the lemon," and my favorite, "Girl pizza in meat, tomatoes."

They put me at a two-top in the window. I was thinking about a time right after college when I'd been working ridiculous hours at an electronics firm. I'd liked eating alone then, but now that I was pushing fifty, three years on from the breakup of a long marriage, it seemed more of a stigma. I liked my job, especially when I was busy enough to feel like I was reversing entropy in a substantial way. But I also knew I wasn't bringing anything new into the world. No new music, no kids, no world-changing inventions. A life like mine would have been plenty for my father; he'd been a soldier and then a salesman, paid his debts, and was going to leave the world a better place for who he'd been. And I was generally happy enough. What I missed was a sense of significance, which may have only been another way of saying I wished I had somebody to share it with.

I feasted on Foul Moudamas, Moutabal, Falafel, and Moujaddara ("Puree of lens with the rice in the Lebanese way") and thought about how much my father would have loved the place. We'd traveled to Europe twice when I was a teenager, and my father had attacked each native cuisine with curiosity and appreciation, while my mother had nibbled Saltines and begged for a plain hamburger.

The memory made me impatient to talk to him, so I paid the bill and went out into the night. The locals were walking their dogs, or hurrying toward the Metro in evening clothes, or headed back to their apartments with a bottle of wine or a paper-wrapped baguette. The subtle differences from home—the melody of the barely audible voices in the background, the tint of the streetlights, the signs in the windows of the shops—were liberating, intoxicating.

I showered and got in bed and called the hospital. My father sounded weak but cheerful, and Ann tried very hard not to sound put upon. I was too tired to react, and I fell asleep within seconds of hanging up.

It felt odd to have come so far and not be in pursuit of my mission on Sunday. My alarm woke me at seven and I took the number 13 Metro line all the way across town to Porte de Vanves and spent the morning in the flea market there. I didn't find anything for myself, but picked up some wine labels for my father, who had been trying to develop pretensions in that direction ever since he retired.

By one PM the antique dealers were packing and the new clothing vendors were setting up. The sun had burned holes through the morning's ragged clouds and I gave in to a sudden urge for the Seine and the Ile de la Cité.

Cynics say it's only a myth that Paris is full of lovers, but I saw them everywhere. A girl on the Metro to Saint-Michel had her arms around her boyfriend's neck and leaned forward to kiss him between every few words. I had to make myself look away, and when I did I saw a woman across from me watching them too. She was about forty, with very short blonde hair and a weathered, pretty face. She smiled at me in embarrassed acknowledgement and then looked down at her lap.

The sun was fully out on the Boulevard Saint-Michel, and locals had crammed in next to the tourists at the tiny café tables. I crossed over to the Ile de la Cité and saw more windblown couples holding hands in the gardens along the south side of Notre Dame, where the leaves were just starting to turn.

I wandered out onto the Pont Saint-Louis, which was closed to cars on Sundays, and stopped to hear a clarinetist and pianist who'd rolled a small upright piano out onto the bridge. The view was spectacular: the width of the Seine and the ancient Hotel de Ville to the north, the thrusting spires of Notre Dame behind me, the ancient, winding streets of the Latin Quarter on my right, the elegant 17th century mansions of the Ile Saint-Louis straight ahead.

A crowd of thirty or forty tourists listened from a discreet distance. I saw the blonde woman from the train there, closer to the musicians than the rest. She'd piled her coat and handbag at her feet; her short dress showed off a slim body and strong legs.

It was her feet that held my attention. She was moving them in an East Coast Swing pattern, rock-step triple-step triple-step, covering just enough ground to make her hips sway. I recognized it as a sort of international distress signal that meant, "Dance with me."

I was still deciding whether I should answer when the musicians wrapped up "New York, New York" and started the Benny Goodman classic "Don't Be That Way." It was more than I could stand. I walked up and offered her my left hand. She held up one finger, stashed her purse and coat next to the piano, then came back and took my hand and smiled, revealing a faint, ragged scar on one cheek. I turned her to face me, put my right hand on her back, and danced her out to the center of the bridge.

She was lively and responsive, picking up my leads but also feeling the music, shifting effortlessly between six-count and eight-count patterns, never losing her smile. It was one of my favorite songs, and the sun sparkled on the river and gulls circled the bridge, crying out in pleasure, and I recognized it as one of those rare moments that you know are perfect even as they're unfolding.

"I'm Frank," I said, when the song ended. "You're a great dancer." Then I caught myself and asked, *"Est-ce que tu parle anglais?"*

"Sandy," she said. "And I *am* English."

"Manchester?"

"Originally. London now. Good on you—most Americans can't tell Scots from Welsh. And you're a good dancer, too."

"Thanks." The band laid into "Moonglow."

"You want to try again?"

After "Moonglow" they played "In the Mood," maybe the Miller band's most enduring hit.

"Why are you laughing?" Sandy asked.

"Glenn Miller," I said. "I'll tell you later."

Two other couples were dancing now, and the musicians hammed it up for us, the clarinetist pointing his instrument straight up at the sky, the pianist kicking away his stool to play standing up. They stretched the song for extra solos, but I still wanted more. When they finished I dipped Sandy low and held her there for a second or two, and then we were all applauding, and I threw a five-Euro note in the clarinet case, and then they rolled the piano away and it was over.

"Wow," Sandy said. "That was fantastic. Do you fancy a coffee or a drink or something?"

We crossed over to Ile Saint-Louis and I had to resist an impulse to take her hand. "What are you doing in Paris?" I asked.

"A week's holiday. Ending tomorrow, sad to say. Then it's the train and back to the Oxford Street Marks and Sparks." She looked over at me. "That's—"

"I know. Marks and Spencer. I've been in that very location."

"You're quite the world traveler, aren't you? Here on business?"

I told her about the wire recorder and Glenn Miller while we stood on line for takeaway hot chocolate at a hopelessly crowded café. I was still feeling the intimacy of the dance and saw no harm in talking about it. When I got to the part about the prostitutes and the drunkenness, I could see her expression change.

"But that's perfectly awful," she said. "What do you mean to do with this thing?"

"Auction it off, probably."

"Wouldn't there be a scandal? I mean, the man was a war hero."

My romantic fantasies were fishtailing away, and I was angry at myself for losing my head so easily, for assuming that moving well together meant anything more than that. "Our government lied about Glenn Miller, just like they lied about the weapons in Iraq."

She shook her head. "I can't abide hearing people talk about their leaders that way. It's so disrespectful."

I felt myself losing my temper. Political arguments always ended up reminding me of my own helplessness. What was my one vote compared to the power of PACs and big money special interest groups, to corporate campaign contributors and the media? I drank off my hot chocolate and threw the cup away.

"It was great dancing with you," I said, and meant it. "I've got to go."

I started to walk away, but she grabbed my arm, her fingers remarkably strong. "Wait."

I stood with my hands shoved in my pockets. She ignored my defensive posture and put her arms around my waist and buried her face in my chest. I could smell the sweet scent of her hair.

She said, "I've got to go back to my miserable, dull life tomorrow and I don't want this to be over yet. Please? Could we just go to dinner and pretend a little? Maybe go dancing? We don't have to talk about politics or Glenn Miller or anything important. We could be two different people entirely, just for tonight. Couldn't we?"

Without any conscious decision, my arms went around her. "Yes. Sure. Of course we can."

She looked up at me with eager gray eyes and big smile and kissed me quickly, so sweetly and unexpectedly that it vaporized whatever will I might have had left.

She took me to the pet market at the entrance to the Cité Metro stop, where vendors were selling everything from hamsters and cockatiels to chinchillas and prairie dogs. True to the spirit of our bargain, I ignored any qualms I might have had about the cages and focused on her delight. From there, we crossed the Seine to the giant toy waterworks of the Pompidou Center where we watched a clown juggle fire on an enormous unicycle, then walked through the tiered gardens of Les Halles, holding hands as the sun set. We ate dinner at an Indian restaurant near my hotel, shying quickly away from topics that threatened to go sour, like our differing tastes in films, and struggling to stay with the ones that seemed harmless, like our distant pasts, or the places I'd been that she'd always wanted to go. The shared effort brought us closer, like a kind of training exercise.

When we stepped back into the street, the wind had picked up and the temperature had dropped. She nestled under my left arm for warmth and I opened my coat to bring her inside it, then turned her face up and kissed her. She tasted of cardamom and wine. Her lips were tense at first, then opened in surrender.

"Do you have someplace we can go?" she whispered.

"My hotel is just up the street."

"And do you have, you know—"

"Condoms? Yes. I didn't think I'd be using them, but—"

"But you never know."

Once in my room the mood turned awkward again. There was nothing there but the full-sized bed, two small end tables, and a half-size refrigerator. The TV hung from the ceiling and the closet was small and without doors. I went to shut the window to the airshaft and Sandy said, "It's freezing in here."

"I know," I said. "Sorry." I shed my coat and took hers. "Get your shoes off and get into bed. I'll warm you up."

The plastic mattress cover under the sheets made crinkling noises as we got in. I pulled the covers over us and held her for a minute or two, fully clothed, without saying anything. I listened to the rhythm of her breathing, both alien and comforting, and felt the muscles of her back slowly begin to relax. I buried my nose in her neck, inhaling the warmth of her skin, and then I was kissing her neck, her ear, her mouth. We slowly worked our way out of our clothes and pushed them out onto the floor, and then I had a condom on and was kissing her breasts and their small, clenched nipples, and moving down to taste between her legs. It had been so very long.

"Mmmmm," she said. "That feels wonderful, but if you're trying to make me come, I should warn you it's not going to happen."

"No?"

"Not with a man. Not even with a man present, if that was going to be your next question. I appreciate your thoughtfulness, but you should carry on and enjoy yourself."

"What's in it for you?"

"Don't fret, it feels lovely. Oh, don't let's talk. Just make love to me, will you?"

I had been seesawing between desire and irritation all night, but at that point I suspended all judgment and let my body have its way. As I entered her she said, "Yes. Oh, yes."

Later, I asked her about the scar.

When she finally answered, it was in a firm, affectless voice. "I was coming home late from the clubs about four years ago and a man in a balaclava—what is it you call them?"

"Ski mask."

"Yes, one of those. He had a broken bottle and he dragged me into a car park. I was so startled at first I didn't think to scream until it was too late and he had the glass at my throat and was tearing my tights off. He never said a word, and when he was done he twisted the glass into my cheek, like he was disgusted with me."

"Christ. I'm so sorry."

"I had a mobile, and I called the police even as he was walking away. I was lucky—they caught him, and sent him up, though it was only for two years. That was when I left Manchester. I know the odds of it happening again were no worse there than in London, but I just couldn't feel safe there any more, you know?"

I didn't know what to do or say. We were both still naked and it seemed wrong to hug her, so I took her hand instead.

"It's easy to go from there to thinking men are just animals and all, but I didn't want to be like that. So I had to box it up and put it someplace, like it happened to somebody else. And in a way it did, you know, I mean, I wasn't part of it. And I know you're anti-authoritarian and that, but I will always be grateful there were authorities that night."

I resented her using her personal horror to score points in our ongoing hit and run political debate. She'd preemptively trumped anything I could say about the authorities having failed to prevent the assault in the first place, or their inability to keep her from living in fear afterwards. I hadn't been there, after all; I wasn't the one who suffered.

"And I don't blame men in general," she said. "There are nice things about them. Dancing. Sex, when it's sweet, like with you. You just can't trust them, that's all."

"What do you mean?"

"It's the sex thing. I mean, men cheat. It's the way they are."

"I don't," I said.

"Well. Perhaps you're the exception." She kissed my forehead in what seemed a very condescending way and turned her back to me.

I was still trying to find the words to answer her when she began to snore softly. I watched her for a while in the faint light from the airshaft and eventually I was able to work my way back to my first impression of her, one more lost and lonely traveler, not that different from me. I curled up against her back and felt her squirm slightly against me as she settled in, and then sleep took me too.

I woke at seven AM to Sandy sorting out her clothes in the half light. "You're not going?" I asked.

"I must. I have to pack and catch a train."

"Not just yet." I reached for her hand and showed her what I had in mind.

"Oh," she said. "Well…"

Afterwards, it felt as if we had wound the last eighteen hours back onto a reel and we were suddenly strangers again, with nothing to say to each other. She went to the bathroom, and then immediately began to dress.

"Can I come to the station with you?" I asked.

"I don't want you to even get out of bed." She bent to kiss my cheek and whispered, "Thank you. This was perfect."

"What about your address, or phone number? How can I get hold of you?"

She started to say something, then thought better of it. She wrote a phone number on a scrap of lined paper from her purse and handed it to me. "Bye now," she said, and slipped out the door.

I felt the way I did after a night of heavy drinking—back when I did that—minus the hangover. It was like I'd squandered something.

I tried to go back to sleep, but couldn't find a comfortable place for my mind or my body. The rain had returned, cold and steady, but I had warm boots and an umbrella, so I ate the hotel's continental breakfast and headed out to the Porte de Montreuil market, remembering to tuck a mini-cassette recorder in my pocket just in case.

The market was located in a faceless gray commercial neighborhood on the eastern edge of the city. It was mostly new clothing on Mondays, but deeper into the stalls there were always a few interesting antiques and collectables among the old tools and chipped plates. Nothing for me, though, not that morning.

I was nervous about going back to Vernaison. Philippe had meant well, I was sure, but too many times I'd come back to dealers like him and found only awkwardness and excuses. Once I'd turned around, though, I discovered I could hardly wait. I took the wet walk back to the Metro at nearly a run and hurried through two changes of trains.

When I finally got to Vernaison it was two in the afternoon and Philippe's booth was open, but deserted. I waited five minutes, pacing the narrow alley, and when I was about to give up, I noticed him coming from the front of the complex, head down, a FedEx package in his hands. My timing, I realized, could not have been better. He saw me, held up the package, and smiled.

I followed him into his stall. "You will forgive me," he said, and I waited while he carefully unwrapped the package, took out the record, and admired it. "Still sealed," he said. "Remarkable." He rubbed the edge of the album against the leg of his jeans with a practiced touch, parting the shrink wrap, and stopped to inhale the aroma of vinyl, cardboard, and glue before setting the record on the turntable and carefully cleaning it. I tried to picture him cooking a meal with the same deliberate speed, and imagined that he ate out a good deal.

The vinyl popped and hissed, an announcer made a brief introduction, and Brel began to sing, accompanying himself on guitar. "*Et voila*," Philippe said softly, then turned to me and said, in English, "I thank you so much for this gift."

"You're very welcome," I said.

He took another index card from his inside jacket pocket and handed it to me. I liked that he'd had it ready before the package came. "This is the man who sold me the recorder," he said in French. "Along with a lot of other things. He will see you this afternoon if you like."

"Thank you. This is very kind of you. If you don't mind, can you tell me what sort of other things you got from him?"

"They are mostly gone. A radio, a Victrola that our friend Madame B bought, some silverware. He had also some dishes and ladies' clothes that did not interest me. He is in the real estate business, he tells me. He comes across things from time to time in the houses he buys, and lets me know."

"He didn't say where he got the recorder?"

"I think from some old house. Maybe the owner died."

"Did you see the house?"

"The things were all in boxes, in the trunk of his car. I think maybe he lives in that car." He looked at me over the top of his glasses. "Seriously."

Just then a man in a black raincoat walked by. I didn't think it was the same man I'd seen at Madame B's on Saturday, but it made me unaccountably nervous. I thanked Philippe again and shook his hand, and as I left he was putting the needle back to the beginning of the album.

I called the name on the card, Vlad Dmitriev, from the street in front of the Vernaison. My nerves were still bad, and from the way I was looking around, people probably thought I was making a drug deal. I got a bad mobile connection and it took me a while to convince him that I was an antique collector and not trying to trap him into admitting anything. He finally agreed to meet me at the edge of the markets, where the Avenue Michelet met the access road for the loop. I was to look for a cream-colored Mercedes.

Half an hour later the car pulled into the swarm of traffic at that corner—pedestrians, bicycles, motorcycles, vans—and parted them like a killer whale. Vlad had his window down, yelling and shaking his fist at a gang of kids that had tried to cross in front of him. He was a bit younger than me, with long hair slicked straight back, a short beard, and a black leather jacket over a dress shirt and new blue jeans. He reached across to open the door for me and beckoned me inside.

"Where you going?" he asked. "I'll drop you." His French was slangy and heavily accented, and I could barely understand him. As I settled in, I noticed an open shoebox on the back seat that seemed to be full of American passports, and I had to fight off a moment of panic.

"I don't know where I'm going next," I said. "I was hoping you could tell me."

"The stuff from that old house, it's worth a lot, is it?"

"Only to a collector," I said. He didn't seem threatening, but things were getting a little out of control for my comfort.

He nodded, pulled into traffic. "It's okay. I don't do the detail work. I leave that to guys like you and Philippe. I'm strictly wholesale where junk is concerned."

"This place, what was it?"

"Just an old apartment house in Montmartre. Place was a wreck. Crazy old lady ran the joint, couldn't keep up with it anymore. I'm going to knock all the walls out, put in some offices."

"The old lady, she's still alive?"

"She's alive, but I don't think she'll talk to you. She hates the whole world. Living in some crazy past that never really existed. Doesn't sound like it was so great back then, either."

"Have you talked to her much?"

"Not really. Business, mostly, you know. She says the place used to be a whorehouse during the war, and that she worked there. I think she's making it up."

"You're talking about the Second World War?" Vlad nodded as if it were obvious. "I really need to meet this woman. I could pay for her time."

"She doesn't give a crap for money. Not like me. You say this is worth a lot?"

"If you've got a card or something, I promise I'll send you some money if I get rich from it."

He thought about it, then said, "No, it's okay. I'll take you to see her. Maybe she'll talk. Who knows?"

We were headed south and west, toward the center of the city, winding our way uphill into the artsy Montmartre district, the highest point in Paris. Vlad slowed the car and leaned across me to point out a narrow red brick building sandwiched between two others just like it. "See that? That's one of mine. You're not looking for something like that, are you?"

"Sorry," I said. "Just visiting."

"Maybe when you sell your whatever-it-is and you're rich, eh?"

The steep, narrow streets, the walled-in gardens, the parks and streetlight-lined stairways seemed both welcoming and saturated with history.

It was easy to picture myself living there, looking out one of those bay windows as I fixed dinner, Mingus on the stereo. Maybe when Pop finally goes, I told myself.

We turned down a cobbled alley and pulled into a narrow parking space. The building was plaster and wood, in poor condition, and Vlad led me up three flights of stairs to a peeling green door, one of three on the landing. He knocked, waited, knocked again. After a minute or so I assumed he would give up, but he said, "She's here, she's just making sure we're serious."

He kept knocking, and eventually I heard a faint *"je viens, je viens"* on the far side of the door. It opened on a chain, and the voice said, "Oh. Vlad," in vague disappointment.

She reopened the door without the chain, and while the door was closed I reached into my jacket pocket and turned on the minicassette recorder.

She wore a pink chenille bathrobe, which she held closed with one hand, and bunny slippers. Her face was striking—deeply lined, and yet with such clear skin that she didn't seem old enough to have been around for World War II. Her hair was white, with odd strands of gray and black, and came halfway down her back in a loose braid.

We followed her into the kitchen. "My good friend François has been begging me to introduce him to you. François, this is Madame Rochelle."

She took my hand and looked intently into my eyes. "So, you are a good friend of Vlad's? For this I am supposed to welcome you?"

I went with my instincts. "I just met Vlad a few minutes ago. I want to ask you about the wire recorder that he found in your house."

She pressed my hand and nodded. "Okay, Vlad, I will talk to François alone now."

Vlad hesitated, as if he didn't quite believe what he'd heard. Then he shrugged and took a business card from his jacket. "In case you are ever rich," he said. He squeezed the back of my neck in an oddly intimate gesture and let himself out.

"Come in," Madame Rochelle said. "If you insist on something to drink I expect I could find you some tea." Her French, like Madame B's, was musical, but in her case legato and husky. For my part, my own French was still ragged, but practice was bringing it back.

"I'm all right," I said.

She led me into the living room, which smelled damp and got a little second-hand light from the bedroom and a bit of filtered daylight through heavy orange drapes. She sat at one end of a faux Victorian couch with worn floral upholstery and I sat at the other.

"Talk," she said.

"I am here because Vlad found an old recorder in your house and took it to the flea market at Saint-Ouen, and eventually it ended up with me. There was a spool of wire with the machine that had a date of December 18, 1944. Do you have any idea what I'm talking about?"

"No, but I'm fascinated." She clearly wasn't. She lit up a cigarette and looked past me out the window.

"I think the recording contains the sound of someone being beaten to death. I think that person was Glenn Miller, the American musician."

"Not a very good musician, and he didn't die in my house. The military flew him back to the US, to Ohio, I think, and he died in a hospital there. This anyway is what a doctor friend told me."

The blood roared in my ears and I thought I might pass out.

"I forgot that my friend Louis had that machine going," she went on. "He wanted to record the great Glenn Miller playing with the band from the bar down the street. Everyone was much too drunk, especially Miller, and they sounded like a piano falling downstairs."

"Madame Rochelle, may I tape this conversation?"

"Why?"

"It is my only proof of what is on that recording wire. It makes it valuable."

"You are going to sell the recording wire?"

"I don't know yet."

"All right. You may tape."

I switched off the recorder surreptitiously as I took it out of my pocket, then set it on the coffee table and made a show of turning it on again. Madame Rochelle shot me a skeptical glance that told me I wasn't fooling her, but I felt better having it out in the open.

"How did the fight start?" I asked quickly. "Who was it that hit him?"

"That, my dear, is a much longer story. How much do you know about the black market here during the war?"

"Nothing, really."

"Okay. From the beginning, then." She took a deep drag on her cigarette and settled herself on the couch. "When the Germans came in 1940, they set our clocks ahead an hour, so we would be on the same time as Berlin. It brought darkness to our mornings and reminded us every day that we were defeated. That hour was the first thing they stole from us, but it was not the last.

"At first it did not seem so bad. We were already starving from the long siege, and when the first German tanks rolled into the city, the soldiers were tossing chocolate and cigarettes to us. Yes, like the way you Americans want to think of yourselves. We thought then the Germans would be bringing order, but they only brought *papier timbré*—you know, bureaucracy—and long lines. They helped the black market with their own stupidity. They hired local men to provides all their supplies, so of course the local men stole everything they could. That was right where your flea market stands now, at the Port of Saint-Ouen."

"That's amazing."

"What you call coincidence? That is just fingers."

I wasn't sure I'd heard her right. "Excuse me?"

She wiggled her fingers at me. "You see this finger and this finger and you think they are different things, but there is one hand that moves them both. You understand? Anyway. You know the word *se debrouiller?* It means to get by, to make do. From this we had *le systéme D,* the way of getting by. Everyone did it. These days, you can't find anybody who was not in the Resistance, but then it was different. We did what we had to do. We stole, we dealt with *le milieu,* the criminals, we traded our heirlooms, we got drunk or high whenever we could so we didn't notice how hungry we were. Or we were one of the *collabos horizontales,* a whore, like me. We were most of us whores then.

"You Americans came, but there was still no food. Then the American deserters moved in and took over the black market and it was bigger than ever. American soldiers were selling to them—that's how Louis got that wire recorder, from the American military. And Glenn Miller, he was friends with this Colonel Baessell, who was one of the worst. He would fly over from England with morphine he stole from the Army, hidden in cartons of cigarettes."

I knew the name Baessell, of course. He was the other passenger on the flight on which Miller allegedly disappeared. "Are you saying Miller was involved with smuggling morphine?"

"No. But everyone knew what this Baessell was doing, and Glenn probably knew too. He liked the things that Baessell could put his hands on. Booze and women. Glenn's appetites were enormous, and he was a very mean drunk. You know why? He was being eaten, from the inside out. Inside he was a great musician, but outside, his body could not play that well. He would have given everything he had if he could have been Jack Teagarden. You can't live like that, wishing you were somebody else."

My father loved Jack Teagarden, and used to lecture us on his awesome technique and control of the trombone. "So what happened on the night of the recording?"

"A man came in looking for Baessell, a boy, really, very young and nervous. He went right up to him at his table and pulled out a pistol and shot him, bang, in the face. Glenn came off the stage and knocked the gun out of his hand with his trombone, and they began to fight. People were running away now because of the gunshot. They knew the police would come and many of them should not have been there, deserters, black market traders like Louis. Still, someone could have stopped the fight. But there was no love here for Americans. They had not suffered the way we had."

I thought of the images I'd seen of the carnage at Omaha Beach and started to say something, but she cut me off.

"A few weeks of combat is not the same as years of hardship," she said. "And many of these men were like Glenn and Baessell, they had never seen combat. They came and took what they wanted—women, mostly, by force sometimes—and thought we should be grateful."

"What happened to Miller?"

"Like I say, he was a very mean drunk, and he was very drunk. Most fights I have seen have not lasted long, but this one—Glenn was crazy with anger and would not stop, and the boy, in the end, he was beating Glenn's head against the floor. I tried to stop it, finally, and then the Military Police came and took Glenn away. I was sure they would arrest us, but it seems they knew who the boy was who shot Baessell, and he left with them, and they said if we ever talked about it bad things would happen to us."

"Are you saying the US military was involved with Baessell's death?"

"Do I think it is possible that the US Army wanted to stop Baessell from stealing their morphine and didn't want the publicity of a trial? What do *you* think?"

"Have you ever told anyone else?"

"One time I told an American, after the war, and he was very angry with me and said I was lying. Then a few years ago a woman from England found me. She was doing a book about Miller, but then she went away and I never heard from her again or ever saw the book."

"Do you remember her name?"

"Sorry. I know these things are very important to all of you, but I don't care. They say life is short, but my life has been very long, and I am tired."

"You never thought of going to the newspapers when you saw the false reports of Miller's death?"

"Why? When your government decides to tell a lie, that is serious business. Like now, your President lies and nothing happens to him, but this man Wilson talks about the lies and the government sets his wife up to be killed."

I tried to find a polite way to ask if she could have been mistaken. "So you knew Miller well? He was a regular customer?"

"When I speak of his appetites, I do it from personal experience. He was not a bad person. He was not a wonderful trombone player, but he had a true gift as an arranger. He had a sense of humor. He was loyal to his friends, and he was brave enough to take on that boy with the gun. I don't understand your country. Your heroes cannot have appetites? You want to impeach Clinton for having sex, but you let Bush steal your election and carve up the country for his rich friends. All these soldiers who fought Hitler must be these brave idealists fighting the Good War. Well, the soldiers I saw, half of them had wine in their canteens and they wanted to know why they should be dying for stupid French people. But you never hear that now, just like you don't hear that Glenn Miller died drunk in a whorehouse. Your father, he was in the war?"

"The last part of it. He was very young."

"So many were at the end. Just children."

"He was with the group that found Dachau."

"Ah, yes, the camps. The Americans did many bad things at the camps."

"The *Americans* did?"

"Tortured and killed the guards. Shot German prisoners of war for revenge. Because they could not live with what they saw, and they were only human. Human like Glenn Miller." She looked at her watch. "I think you should go now."

And that was the end. Two minutes later I found myself on the street, dizzy from information overload, oblivious of the rain, clutching my recorder in one hand and my folded umbrella in the other. I sat on the steps of her building and rewound the tape for a few seconds to make sure I had her story. It was there, loud and clear.

"Holy Christ," I said.

I put the recorder back in my pocket and opened my umbrella and started walking. It was getting dark. At the end of the block I found myself on Rue Lamark, and followed it downhill past the stark white domes and towers of Sacré Coeur, then took the long flight of stairs down to Place Saint-Pierre.

It was the find of a lifetime, and now I had to decide what to do with it. My first instinct was to take it slow, send out a few emails to let key collectors know what I had, let word of mouth start the feeding frenzy that would doubtless ensue.

She'd stirred up a lot of different emotions, but most of what I felt was triumph. I'd waited a long time for this, and I was not going to screw it up.

※

My flight wasn't until Wednesday morning. I spent Tuesday at the Rodin Museum and the Gustave Moreau exhibit at the Musée de la Vie Romantique, then I picked up a few presents at the big Printemps department store, including a necklace with Russian-looking icons of the Virgin for Ann. I felt different, puffed up. No one was looking at me, but it was because they didn't know the secret I was carrying.

Afterwards, as evening fell, I walked around the Pigalle district. This was where Glenn Miller came to drink and let out his inner demons. It had changed, of course, since 1944. The Moulin Rouge now offered Vegas-style dinner-and-a-show, feathered-headdress nudity to busloads of tourists, and the shops were cluttered with sex toys and gag gifts—but there were still prostitutes and live sex shows and lonely men with their collars turned up against the night.

I dropped by the hotel around 7 PM to call and check on my father, and the night clerk stopped me in the lobby. "A man was here looking for you this afternoon, monsieur. He left this message."

It was a handwritten note, in English. "Urgent that I speak with you today. Please call me as soon as you get this, no matter how late." There was a local phone number and a name, David Smith.

I punched the number into my phone, nervousness edging toward fear. I had to remind myself that my passport was in order, my credit was solid, I'd done nothing wrong.

A woman's voice answered, and when I identified myself she switched to English with a colorless American accent. "Mr. Smith has been waiting for your call. Can you hold, please?"

When Smith came on, he too sounded like an American newscaster. "Mr. Delacorte. Thanks for calling back. If you can spare me half an hour tonight, I have some information I think will interest you."

"Are you trying to sell me something?"

"Quite the contrary. Do you know what a Missing AirCrew Report is? For example, if a military plane disappeared during World War II on a flight from a rural English airfield to Paris, there would have to be an MACR filed. Now do I have your attention, Mr. Delacorte?"

"Yes. Yes, I understand."

"I can be at your hotel in twenty minutes. Is that okay?"

"Yes, I guess so…"

"Great. See you then."

I dropped my packages in my room and washed up. Yes, I wanted to see a Missing AirCrew Report on Glenn Miller, but how would a stranger know that?

I was waiting in the lobby when he arrived, exactly twenty minutes from when I'd hung up the phone. He looked to be in his late thirties. He was wearing an expensively tailored gray suit, but his haircut and bearing both suggested the military. He had a quiet authority that went beyond self-confidence to intimidation.

He shook my hand firmly and said, "Is there someplace we can talk?"

"My room is a little small," I said. Ridiculous as it seemed, I didn't want to be alone with him.

He nodded toward a red vinyl-covered bench at the far end of the lobby. "Here is all right, I suppose. This won't take long."

We sat and he opened the manila envelope he was carrying and took out a single faxed page on plain copy paper. "You may read this here. I can't let you copy it or take any notes. When you're done I'll take it with me."

The form was crude, from a mimeographed original. At the top it said "R E S T R I C T E D" and beneath that "MACR No. 10770." The heading was "WAR DEPARTMENT/HEADQUARTERS ARMY AIR FORCES/WASHINGTON." I skimmed the report, which listed the command, squadron, departure, and destination points. The date was 15 Dec 44. Paragraph 10 listed the persons aboard the aircraft as John Morgan, the pilot, and passengers Lt. Col. Normal R. Baessell and Major Alton G. Miller.

The most interesting part was paragraph 5, "AIRCRAFT WAS LOST, OR IS BELIEVED TO HAVE BEEN LOST, AS A RESULT OF." There was an "x" next to "Other Circumstances as follows," and then the words: "Accidentally destroyed when aircraft strayed into Channel Bomb Jettison Area."

I read the whole thing again. "Are you serious?"

"The Norseman aircraft in which Major Miller was a passenger accidentally overflew an area in the English channel that was used for the disposal of bombs after aborted missions. Several observers on one of the bombers positively identified the Norseman."

"This is the Fred Shaw story that was in the tabloids in the 80s. There are a dozen holes in it. No one else ever came forward, there was no Mayday call, no wreckage—"

"And no MACR. Not available to the general public, anyway. It would have been a morale disaster if the truth had come out while our men were still in combat."

"I think this is a fake. For one thing, Baessell's middle initial was not 'R.' "

"No offense, Mr. Delacorte, but I think you're being a bit paranoid. The Army typist hit an 'R' instead of an 'F.' It's a simple typo."

"If this is the truth, why not admit it now?"

"If it were up to me, I would. But the military is a bit skittish about taking responsibility for past cover-ups at the moment."

Because of the current cover-ups, I thought. I didn't say it aloud because I was afraid of him.

"The important thing," he said, with what should have passed for a sympathetic smile, "is that anything else you may have heard is simply not true. There are rumors, for example, that he was murdered, or any number of other far-fetched scenarios. It was an accident, plain and simple. A piece of really lousy luck."

"You accuse me of being paranoid, but what am I supposed to think, with you showing up like this? Who are you? Who do you work for? How did you know I was investigating Miller's death? Who told you about me?"

"I'm sorry, Mr. Delacorte. I've told you all I can." He gently took the MACR from my hands and put it back in the envelope. "I will tell you that I have a legal background, and that both Major Miller and Colonel Baessell have living relatives. If you knowingly circulate libelous stories about either of them, you could find yourself—and your pertinent possessions—tied up in some very nasty litigation."

Smith, or whatever his name was, stood up. "I hope this was helpful to you," he said. "Enjoy the rest of your stay."

I couldn't eat, couldn't sleep. I sat in my room in the half darkness and replayed everything that had happened since I'd come to Paris. Had I been followed? What about the men in the raincoats at the Marché Vernaison? No one connected with the wire recorder—not Philippe, Vlad, Madame B, nor Madame Rochelle—knew where I was staying. Was somebody reading my email?

And what was I to believe about Miller? Madame Rochelle had seemed completely convincing, but she had a political agenda and the only evidence to support her was a handwritten label on a spool of recording wire, currently in my safe deposit box in North Carolina. If the recording had been made by anyone other than Miller, or at some earlier time, her story was no more than that. As for "David Smith," assuming he was military, he also had a motive to lie. American officers involved in the drug trade, and the Army implicated in a black market coup d'état, was far worse than his friendly fire scenario.

But it was the betrayal that came back to me again and again. Somebody that I'd been with in the last four days was deceiving me.

I had to do something. I called my airline and took a financial beating to change my flight to a Friday departure—from London.

I arrived at Waterloo Station just after noon on the train from Paris, and used a pay phone to call the number Sandy gave me. I got an elderly woman at a florist's shop who'd never heard of Sandy or anyone answering her description. "Sorry, love," she said. "You'll find someone else, I'm sure."

I wasn't surprised as much as curious to see how far the deception went. I took the tube two stops north to Charing Cross Road and wheeled my suitcase down the crowded sidewalks of Oxford Street and into Marks and Spencer. I found the cosmetics counter and was about to ask a sales clerk for Sandy when I saw her.

She caught my glance and something like panic flashed across her face. I went up to her, saw the name "Margaret" on her nametag, and said, "Which is it, Sandy or Margaret?"

"Keep your voice down, please. Please. It's Margaret."

"What are you so afraid of?"

"Please, could you pretend to be buying something? Everyone here knows me. I don't want them asking questions."

I picked up a lipstick, took the cap off, drew a blood red line on a scrap of paper. "What kind of questions?"

She looked down and whispered, "I've got a fella. They all know him. If word gets back to him that some glamorous older bloke was coming round to see me, I'll be in it for sure."

I thought the "glamorous" was a nice touch. "We have to talk."

"Not here. I've got lunch in a quarter hour. I'll meet you just inside the main doors of the HMV across the street."

"You're not going to stand me up, are you? "

"I'll be there. Fifteen minutes, I promise. Just go now, okay?"

I lurked inside the main doors of the giant record store, checking my watch when I wasn't looking out at Oxford Street. I knew she could easily slip into the crowds and disappear if she had a mind to, and it was with vast relief that I finally saw her hurrying up the sidewalk.

I stepped out to meet her and she said, "Let's walk. I don't want anyone to see us here."

We headed west toward Tottenham Court Road. "So your boyfriend is the violent type, is he?"

She walked on in silence for a long time and then said, "Yes."

"Is he the one that gave you the scar?"

"No, that part was true."

"Were you ever working on a book about Glenn Miller? Interviewing people for it?"

She gave me a sidelong glance as if evaluating my sanity. "No."

That left the tough one. "Did you talk to anyone about me? In Paris, or here? I mean anybody, a girlfriend, a stranger, a cop?"

"No. It's my secret." She stopped and looked at me defiantly. "Everything I told you is true except my name and the phone number you made me give you."

"You didn't tell me about your 'fella.' "

"You didn't ask. You just assumed." She started walking again. "I needed what you gave me. Maybe it'll eventually give me the guts to change my life. But if I tell anyone, it won't be mine anymore. I don't want to share it."

The sound of her heels against the concrete was like the ticking of an enormous clock. "It's really arbitrary, isn't it?" I suddenly said. "Who we choose to believe? It's subject to coercion, or habit, or wishful thinking."

"You're saying you don't believe me? Not that I blame you."

"No. I'm saying I do. Believe you."

"I'm really sorry," she said. "I didn't think I'd ever see you again."

After a minute I said, "I lied to you, too. When I said I didn't cheat? I did cheat. I had an affair, toward the end of my marriage. I hated the deception, even though I couldn't resist the sex part, for a while anyway. But I broke it off and swore I wouldn't do it again, and I would either make my marriage work or get out. I ended up getting out."

"It doesn't matter. I mean, in the circumstances, I'd be pretty much of a hypocrite to complain, wouldn't I?" She reached out and ruffled my hair. "Is that why you came all this way? To confess?"

"Something weird happened last night in Paris. It's nothing I want to talk about, but I had to know you weren't involved in it. I had to see you, face to face, to know for sure."

"And now what?"

I hadn't even thought about it until that moment, but once I did it seemed inevitable. "I want you to do something for me. Can you call in sick tomorrow?"

"I just got back from holiday."

"Tell them you picked something up in Paris."

She laughed, then turned serious again. "Listen. What happened in Paris…"

"It's not like that. I need to go to an abandoned airfield about 50 miles north of here. It's called Twinwood Farm."

⟫⟪

I called my father and told him about my change of schedule, then I spent the rest of the day arranging a hired car, finding the cheapest hotel I could, and reading at the British Library. Margaret met me at my hotel the next morning wearing jeans and a sweater, and I felt a pang of desire for her that I couldn't seem to shake.

We took the M1 north out of London, then the M6 on to Bedford. My head was too full for me to feel like saying much. Margaret talked easily about her boyfriend, her job, how envious her friends had been of her trip to Paris, and I was happy enough for the distraction.

I stopped at the post office in the town of Oakley and asked a man in his sixties if he'd ever heard of Twinwood Farm. "You're joking, son," he said. "Everyone knows of it now, what with the Glenn Miller festival just there in August."

We followed his directions and drove due east, through the tiny village of Oakley Hill and onto a well-kept tarmac road. We passed a sparse forest, then restored hangars and outbuildings as we pulled up to the control tower itself, a two story brick cube painted in broad vertical tan and olive camouflage stripes. I parked in front and we got out into a cold wind. Margaret went up to the building and looked in the windows. "It's some sort of museum," she called back. She read from a plaque: " '…opened on 2nd June 2002…contains a tribute to Major Alton Glenn Miller, who took his final flight from here 15th December 1944.' "

After a while she came back to where I stood by the car, hugging herself against the cold. "Don't you want to look?"

"I thought there might be something left of him here," I said. "But I'm too late. The myth has taken over."

"People need myths."

"We need the truth. But all we get is the amusement park version of it. And nobody cares."

"You care," Margaret said. "Isn't that enough?"

I dropped Margaret at a tube stop near the car hire agency. We had real phone numbers for each other this time, but I doubted we would ever use them. I slept poorly that night, and not at all on the long, long afternoon flight back to the States.

I went straight to the hospital from the airport and found Ann and my father watching the news. My father switched off the set as soon as he saw me; Ann looked like she was going to protest and then thought better of it. I hugged them both and handed out their presents and we made some small talk about the flight, how my father was feeling, the tepid meal he'd just eaten.

"So," my father finally said. "How was the wild goose chase?"

I sat on the edge of the bed and took his hand. "I've got somebody who says it was Miller on the tape. What you heard is the sound of him being murdered—murdered by somebody working for the US Army." Apparently, somewhere over the Atlantic, I'd made up my mind about who I was going to believe.

"You can't trust the French. They're all Communists." He smiled as if he were joking.

"I want to ask you something, Pop. I want you to tell me about Dachau."

"It was horrible. You've seen the pictures. You don't need to hear it from me."

"I do need to hear it from you. I want you to tell me what you did there."

He saw then that I knew, and that I wasn't going to let him escape. "I don't feel like talking about it," he said meekly.

"Francis?" Ann said.

I waved her off. "I learned some things in Paris, and then I read some more things in the library in London."

My father said, "I don't have to—"

"We have to stop pretending everything's simple, Pop." My voice was soft and I kept a gentle pressure on his hand. "Black and white, Greatest Generation and Axis of Evil. We have to take responsibility for what we do, and tell the truth about it. We can start right now."

I kept staring until he looked away. "Ann," he said, "could you leave us alone for a minute?"

She started to get up and I said, "I'd like her to stay for this."

I could feel her glare on the back of my head. "Francis, what do you think you're doing?"

"Sit down," I told her, still looking at my father. "Pop, tell me what you did."

He was motionless for so long I was afraid I'd given him another stroke. Then the tears started to run down his cheeks. "I've never talked to anybody about this," he said. "Not ever."

"Go ahead," I said. "We love you. Nothing you can say is going to change that."

"It might. It very well might."

I waited.

He sighed and said, "It wasn't a death camp, not like Auschwitz. Those were all in Poland. Dachau was a work camp. Not that there was a lot of difference, except they kept the prisoners alive longer. More or less alive. You've seen the pictures, you two have known about it all your lives. We didn't. We were kids, most of us, and we'd grown up in a sane, reasonable world. Until we went in that camp we didn't know why we were fighting that war in the first place. We thought it was about cleaning up somebody else's mess. We knew the Germans were brutal, inhuman, but nothing prepared us for what we saw.

"We went crazy, all of us. You couldn't look at those starved, brutalized remnants of humanity and feel anything but rage and hatred. Blinding, murderous rage."

"You shot the guards," I said.

"Lined them up and shot them."

"With no trial," I said.

"No trial, no questions, nothing. But that wasn't the worst."

"Tell me the worst, Pop."

"We had to search all the buildings. I was paired up with a Jewish guy from Brooklyn, a big tough kid named Schlomo. We found one of the guards hiding out in a latrine. Schlomo told me to keep him there, and he went out, and he came back...he came back with one of the prisoners. And we stripped the guard naked and..." He faltered.

"Go on," I said, and squeezed his hand.

"And we gave the prisoner a bayonet. I lost my nerve then, but Schlomo stayed and watched."

My father took a long breath and closed his eyes. "He told me later what happened. The prisoner…first he castrated the guard. Then he gouged out his eyes, one at a time. And then he started stabbing him, faster and faster, over and over. It wasn't until then that the guard finally started to scream, and then they were both screaming, and then it was all three of them, and I could hear them from outside."

My father opened his eyes. "I don't care about the guard. There was no torture, no punishment horrible enough for what he did. But I can never forgive myself for letting that poor bastard prisoner become a murderer too. It's like I took the last decent thing away from him."

I held my father and let him cry for a while. "Did you ever tell Mom about this?"

"No," he said. "She would have…"

"Say it."

"Some day, years later, when I was least expecting it, she would have used it against me."

"Never," Ann said, a whisper with claws. "She would never have done that."

I slowly let go of my father, stroked his forehead a couple of times, and turned back to face Ann. "Yes, Ann. She would have." Her eyes burned into me, hating me. "For five years I've stood by and let you turn her into a plaster saint. Whenever Mom got scared—like after those huge, screaming fights she and Pop would have—remember?—she would turn cold and vicious and spiteful. You used to know that. Now it's like you're turning into her, and I hate it."

"Get out," Ann whispered. "Just get the hell out of here."

"Not this time. You ran me off from Mom's deathbed and I'm not going to let you do it again."

"You don't know how to take care of people, Francis. You're too spoiled and too selfish. Mother and I made you that way, God help us, by giving you everything you ever wanted."

"I don't have everything I ever wanted," I said slowly. "I never did. Mom and Pop didn't have the perfect marriage. We're not the perfect kids. Neither of us."

I watched her anger overwhelm her, to the point that she could no longer speak. She jumped out of her chair and ran from the room.

"She's so angry," my father said. "I've never understood that."

"Mom's death hit her hard."

"Yeah. Me, too." We sat in silence for a while, and then he said, "What are you going to do with that recording?"

"I guess I'm going to play it for people. Starting with the *Washington Post*. If they don't want to write about it, I'll go to the *New York Times* and work my way down. I'll put it on the Internet and hand it out to strangers on the street. If I get sued, so much the better. The story has to get out. It's important."

"Okay," my father said.

It was after midnight in Paris and my body was aching for sleep. "You want the TV back on?" I asked him.

"That would be great."

I fell asleep in the chair almost immediately, and when I woke up the room was dark and silent. I went to the window and watched the stars for a while. My father made a noise and turned over. "Frank?" he said sleepily.

I sat down next to him and touched his shoulder. "I'm here," I said. "I'm here."

Game

BY MARIA DAHVANA HEADLEY

15 September, 1950
Nightfall.

I write this entry from my tent in Naini Tal, a village in the Kumaon Province of Northern India, shadowed by the snow-tipped Himalayas. I arrived here at 1300 hours, as the sun steamed the dew out of the forest like a laundress pressing an iron on a damp shirt. The whole place hissed, and I closed my eyes to inhale the cypress and cookfire smoke. Much has changed in my old hunting grounds, but were I to depend on my sense of smell alone, it would be as though I'd traveled backward thirty-two years.

A simple glance, however, reminds me of the landslip passage of time. Three years ago, the country dissolved its colonial status and departed from the reign of George VI. The time of the hunter is done, though I warrant that there is still a place for a man such as myself.

The children I met here in 1918 are now grandparents, but to them, I'm not the old man who sits before them. I'm an earlier incarnation, a warrior from a picture book, brought here at their request, a man with mystical powers over their enemy. They need me now, here in Naini Tal. I am their last resort.

My journey originated in Delhi, some four hundred rattling kilometers away. My bones ache despite the care of my porters, and of my colleague, the estimable Dr. K_____, but when the Kumaoni greeted me this afternoon, I felt my heart rise to meet my title.

"*Shikari*," they cried, all of them in unison. "Welcome, Shikari!"

Big game hunter. Usually reserved for the native men. For my kills, covered in international newspapers, my kills which inspired other kills, I was long ago granted an exception.

My old partner Henry, also a Shikari, and native to the Kumaon province, knew this place better than I ever could, but even I can see the changes. The trees were thicker the last time I was here, and the huts were roofed in woven branches rather than tin. Time has not been kind to this place, nor to me. The village now shines bright as a grub dug up slick and blind from beneath a rock, and another addition, a high fence made from a combination of thorn bushes and barbed wire, encircles it.

No one seems yet to have tunneled into the mountains, a mercy, nor taken their tops, but roads have been installed everywhere, and the locally manufactured automobiles known as the Baby Hindustan backfire and sputter their way toward the sky. With Henry, thirty-two years ago, I watched hawks wheeling high above these mountains, but now the air is streaked with machines. I notice a subtle depletion of birdsong. As likely caused by the creatures I come to hunt as by machinery, I know, but I imagine the tragedies to come in the near future, ornithologists aiming their glasses at the heavens in order to identify different species of aircraft.

Given these observations, I will note here that it is immediately clear what has spurred the tigers to their current behavior. Less than a century ago, the cats had limitless forest and limitless game. Now the wild is striated with roads and mines, and armed villagers have beaten the remaining tigers from Nepal into these hills, calling them all man-eaters. Every man and boy in the region has a weapon, a museum's worth of defenses, rusty swords and axes to rifles, but shooting to kill is a skill that must be learnt. Wounding is easier. A wounded tiger is a hungry tiger. Here in Naini Tal, trouble has been brought into town, all in an attempt to keep trouble in the trees. It is an old story.

Untwisting wire to enter through the gate today, I experienced a tremor in my thigh, no doubt caused by the climb, as unlike many men my age, I keep myself in fine form. A porter brought me the customary dish of metallic tea, lightened with buffalo milk and copiously sweetened with jaggery. Even as I sipped it, though, my cup chattered. An involuntary motion in my fingers, like that of a treetop in a fine breeze.

I've been softened by civilization, I admit it. It's been years since I last participated in this line of work, years I've spent writing and lecturing, years of domestic comfort in a house in Kenya, trees of my own, a bed, a wife. As I write this, I'm thinking of my wife's hair, falling straight and black to her knees. Evenings, she sits before me on the floor, and I wrap her tresses round my hands, succumbing, greedy as a nectar-guzzling bat, to this late-life pleasure. I think of how the strands feel running over my fingers, delicate, but when braided together they are strong enough to strangle a man.

Before her, I'd never thought of marriage. All my previous vows were to the creatures I hunted. I've done a good deal of seeing the world at grass level, my universe filtered through golden eyes, my world made of the pug marks of tigers, the tracks of *ghooral*, the mountain goats of this region, and the creamy camouflaged spots of the chital hind, my ears attuned to the barking of the *kakar* deer, and the hornlike belling of the *sambur*, to the chittering of monkeys and the churr of the nightjar. Before I met my wife, I'd never imagined anything of the world through the eyes of another human.

She's angry with me now. She doesn't want me hunting. She certainly doesn't want me hunting here. As I left our house, she stood in the doorway and shouted: "Old men need not go hunting for tigers! Tigers are already hunting for them!"

She's wrong about that. I'm equal to this, and Dr. Andrew K_____, my taxidermist colleague, is beside himself with excitement. This afternoon, he sat beside me on a stump near the cookfire, knees bouncing, his uniform crisply ironed and starched by his own wife back in New York City. I'd promised him a hunt. He'd read in his boyhood my accounts of the Monsters of the Mountains who'd dragged entire villages into the darkness, leaving only shards of bone behind for the poor Hindu funerary rites that required something to burn.

In certain cases, depending on how long the cat had uninterrupted possession of the dead, there'd be nothing left, the man-eater having devoured the entirety: skin and bones and bloodied clothing. On those occasions, I sometimes removed a fragment of ivory from my own baggage and presented it to the bereaved for burning.

My wife would say that with my substitutions, I've sent elephants to the afterlife, along with rhinoceroses and whales. That I've populated the sky with things that do not belong there. Therefore, I do not tell her. I consider myself to have been, at some moments in my time as a shikari, a minister of mercy. I spent my career in these forests. I have my own rules of conduct.

K_____, in contrast, has, according to the vitae he supplied me, spent the bulk of his own career in the bowels of New York City's Natural History Museum, his hands coated in glue, sinew and fragments of stretched skin, refitting the dead for display to the living. Having begged of his institution a paid procurement trip to India, he quivers in anticipation.

Naini Tal's man-eater will be taken to Dr. K_____'s museum and displayed there as a conservationary tale. The teeth and body will be examined for wounds caused by hunters. No tiger turns man-eater of its own instincts. We are not its natural prey. For one such as myself, who has long struggled to reconcile a history of violence with the world's shrinking spectrum of carnivores, the offer of any redemption was too tempting to resist.

Now that we are here in Naini Tal, however, I look at K_____, at his too-gleaming weapon, and at his tapping fingers, with no small degree of suspicion. There is something of the town-raised boy visiting the country in him. Something of the tourist. He carries sharp implements, chocolate bars, and gin in his case. I earlier apprehended a small transistor radio in his belongings, about which he hedged. In case of emergency, he insisted, but I forced him to relinquish it. I'm certainly not convinced he should be armed. The nervous man with his finger on the trigger is as likely to shoot the hunter as the prey, but a man without a rifle will likely need to be defended from the man-eater, given any proximity.

I have less tolerance than I once did. Since Henry's death, I've hunted alone.

Upon arrival, we were given a feast of roasted ghooral spiced with the local peppers, and warm cola coddled over rough roads from the city, the bottle recognizable even in the dark. I interviewed the villagers about their experiences of the man-eater, and they answered me vigorously. At first, the Kumaoni tried churchgoing, petitioning Christ and country, but prayer is an inefficient weapon, and the people in these mountains are finished with begging for miracles. Something is stalking them, and they mean to have its head.

There've been sounds in the forests, the villagers tell me, phantom noises of devils. Gunfire, and roars, but they swear no one from Naini Tal hunts tigers. I believe them. It is no longer in fashion, my profession, that of the skilled and specific tracker, that of the shikari. These hunters will be poachers. Everywhere now. Every forest, every jungle, the world over. Thieves of tigers and elephants, leopards and monkeys. Recently, an acquaintance of mine saw a tiger in the back seat of a car rattling through Delhi, the cat so recently slaughtered that blood was still seeping out, leaving a trail behind the sedan.

Pillbox hats made of wildcats and leopard skin capes over shocking pink taffeta dresses have lately appeared in Vogue Magazine, igniting a craze for fur. Couture demands man-eaters, and in truth, man-eater is no longer a reason to kill a tiger. *Tiger* is a reason to kill a tiger.

Everyone goes into the forests now, and a man with my history is every man on earth, or so you might believe if you sat down at a barcounter in Delhi and listened to men tall-telling about tigers. Pith helmets and Martini rifles. Waxed cotton tents. Triumphs.

I was, therefore, quite surprised to be personally summoned last month to Naini Tal, the request relayed first by the local version of the *cooee*, shouted village to village, and then by runner, at last arriving to me by phonecall, the villager's petition read aloud to me over the wires.

Dearest Gentleman,

We the public beg your kindly doing needful. In this vicinity, which is well known to you, and which has long suffered from famously troubles with tigers, we beg your help in hunting this demon that has turned man-eater since June of five years past. We venture and invite you, shikari, to shoot this demon, and save us from calamity, for she is no tiger, but an evil spirit, and no one of all the men who have tried to kill her has got near her heart. Please tell us of your arrival, and we will meet you with a cart to bring you to our forest.

I did not need to consider. I'd been haunted by this place, this village, these mountains long enough.

I've never ceased scanning the news for Naini Tal, even from afar. They've suffered more from man-eaters than other similarly situated villages, or so it seems to me, though I am possibly biased toward that perspective. Naini Tal and Pali, higher up the mountain, have long been plagued by a stream of bloodthirsting strangers walking out from the woods at night. That the village still exists is surprising. Superstition might long ago have caused the citizens to depart, pragmatic, their belongings on their backs. Who, after all, would choose to live in a place claimed by tigers?

From Kenya, I read of this man-eater's five year reign, a factory owner on an exploratory hunt being her most recent victim. The villagers showed me a list with some eight dozen names, the missing and the dead, and for every lost person, there is a story.

Initially, the tiger attacked only men, and those armed, typically game hunters, particularly those who'd come in from outside Naini Tal. Not two weeks ago, however, a young woman, just sixteen, was taken by the man-eater at midday as she gathered firewood, scarcely out of sight of her friends. Her silk sari was left draped on rocks, a trail of blood going up the mountain, and her hair spider-webbed from the bushes. That was when the villagers began counting their coins and mold-velveted paper money, begging their wives and mothers-in-laws for household funds that'd been secreted away, smashing their jars and tithing their tobacco rations.

The men here are gleeful at my presence. I declined a fee, unseemly for a man in my position, though they do not know my reasons. This man, ministering to this village. There is no pay for that. They saved their money for me despite my protestations, and brought it out to show. I complimented them on their hoard, and then ate heartily. In my early days as a hunter, I once found myself faint before a black leopard, having, due to gastrointestinal distress, eaten almost nothing for several days. Tonight, I noticed K_____ pushing his meat around his plate, and admonished him. He took a tiny bite, and swallowed abruptly and unhappily.

As darkness fell, I heard the call of a cat.

"It is a *shaitan* hunts here, shikari," one of the men said.

I listened to the tiger call, wondering at the sound of the roars, a scraping sharpened edge to them that I'd somehow forgotten, and I felt the familiar feeling in my stomach. It's an instinct I've long denied, the urge to curl myself into a protective position, and I suddenly found myself nearly not denying it. I am, suddenly, seventy-one years old. My father died at sixty, in his bed.

"The shaitan welcomes you home," said another man, and smiled at me, a kindly smile, even for the words he said.

The devil welcomes you home.

I stood and stretched, hearing my left shoulder crack, the bones themselves remembering my encounter with that leopard. My skin, as is true of any hunter who has truly hunted, is a Frankenstein's monster of a canvas, stitched together first with black thread, and now with scars, old wounds packed with chewed leaves, five claw marks stretching from right clavicle to left pubis, the mark of the Widower of Champawat, dead and gone these twenty years. Not the smallest tiger, and not the largest, but one who got close enough that I could see into his throat and feel his heartbeat as he savaged me. I felt that heart stop as I shot him. His shoulder, upon examination, housed an old bullet, suppurating, and his right front arm was darted with porcupine quills. Yellowed, soapy flesh beneath the balding pelt, a withered limb, and thirty-six quills, fat as pencils, broken off at the level of the skin.

I have never blamed him.

"Shall we?" I said.

K_____ radiated unease. "It's nearly dark," he replied.

I gave him the look that said *dark is how this is done*, clapped him on the back once, and then walked away from the firelight.

He needn't have worried. We were patrolling the perimeter for signs, but I did not intend to go deep into the trees. The cruelty of this commission was that it was necessary to await an attack. The tiger would have long since scented the roasting ghooral, and concluded that there'd be heavy sleep in the village. The man-eater would come to us.

The forest lay before us, black and singing. A hunter listens, and if a hunter does not, then he will not stay a hunter long. Any and all of the animals here will tell tales of a tiger. They'll explain where the cat is, whether it is still or in motion, how fast it moves.

Though I did not say it to K_____, though I would not admit it to anyone save these pages, mute as they are, I too hesitated to walk back into those trees tonight. The last time I entered this forest, I was carried out on a stretcher, mute with loss, the children surrounding me, my hands bloody. The last time I came down that mountain, I vowed I would not go up it again.

After that kill, there was nothing left to bury, nothing left to burn.

The birds are silent now, as I write these lines, and I feel observed. We've returned to our tents to wait for screams.

16 September, 1950
Dawn.

I woke three hours ago, blurred by nightmares, having been dream-stalking a man-eater, not the present tiger, but the one from 1918.

With me in my dream was Henry, his elbow in tattered cotton, his silvered beard and long hair, his skin a dark contrast to the yellowed whites of his eyes. I looked over at him once, and saw him open his mouth, but his lips moved, and I heard nothing.

The screams, when they came, seemed a part of the same dream. They were not. At 4:13 this morning, a young man of twenty-three was taken from his hut, and dragged through the center of town. A villager shot at the man-eater, and swears he hit her chest, but she leapt with her victim over the briars and barbed wire, twenty-five feet, a seemingly impossible height, and returned to the forest. Pitiful scraps of the man's clothing hang from the highest thorns.

Dulled by exhaustion from yesterday's travels, by the time I was on my feet and out into the main area, it was too late. In truth, I need not excuse my speed. If one hears screaming, rescue is already impossible. Those left behind can only hope that death will be quick. There's no possibility of pursuing a victim into the dark, not when they've bled so much that the dust is red mud, and the man's wife, having woken to the feel of something heavy and vividly alive brushing past her bed, is already keening in her doorway.

For twenty seven minutes after the attack, we listened to the tigress departing through the trees, heralded by a sound like a kennel of dogs readying for a feeding, though it was something quite different, the kakar barking their alarm, *tiger passing here, tiger coming.*

The man-eater scratched her victim's door, and the scores in the wood are deep. I showed them to K_____, who examined them with interest. There's a slight odor of alcohol drifting about the man this morning, that and a cloying floral cologne, for which I severely remonstrated him. He purged it with a gin-soaked handkerchief. Gin is better than lilies.

The tigress left pug marks in the dirt, and with them, I'll be able to identify her with certainty. K_____ dutifully cast them in plaster of Paris, and annotated his drawings with measurements. There is no blood trail. It is often the case that a tiger one shoots to kill, even as the bullet seems to have connected, remains strangely unwounded. This is the way things are here, even, in some cases, for a shikari.

K_____ has arrived with the cast and his rudimentary drawing, and I will examine them, taking notes here, as part of this entry.

Size: Extremely large, at least ten feet over curves, a nearly unprecedented size for a female, and her paws are strikingly unsplayed, unusual in a tiger so immense. Her claws are so sharp as to suggest daggers.

Age: She is, by her prints, young, though her intelligence would indicate experience. This is a tigress who's been terrorizing the villages in this region for over five years, a beast who certainly must at some point have been at least superficially wounded.

Tracks: The symmetry of her tracks shows almost no sign of such wounding. On her left front paw, there is an old scar across the pad.

A clean gash that clearly went deep. Can this—

Break in text

Later.

The shape of the scar stopped me as I sat looking at the marks by torchlight. It stops me now that K_____ has left, and I sit alone in my tent again. I can't—

After I came down from these mountains, I published a partial account of my exploits. There were photographs of my grin on newspaper front pages, a certain level of celebrity, a short film in which I demonstrated my stalking technique. I had no notion of what was coming for me, of the way this forest would stay with me. I had no idea.

After that film was screened, I borrowed a woman's fountain pen to autograph a photograph for her, and ink leaked onto the pad of my thumb. Without care for observers, for cameras, she took my thumb into her mouth and licked it clean, her tongue turning sepia.

"There," she said, when she was finished, still holding my hand, looking up and directly into my eyes. "Now you won't leave marks on me."

I took her to the coast. We fucked with the lanterns lit, bright enough that all the moths in miles flew to press their bodies against our tent. One night she ran into the dark, and I stumbled after her, calling her name, and waiting for her to show herself. I was tired of tracking.

"You might have found me by my footprints," she said, stepping out of the night, raising one foot to show me the scar on the right arch. "I stepped on a waterglass years ago, and didn't get it stitched. Look at that mark. Beautiful, isn't it?" I took her foot in my hand, and then stopped. The mark was a mark I knew.

She looked at me. Her eyes were not yellow, no. She did not change into anything but what she was, a beautiful woman with a broken footprint.

"You'll never forget me now," she said, and her tone was not quite playful. "Did you think you could? But you'll have to follow me, and if you don't, I'll follow you."

I fled the next morning before sunup. She opened her eyes as I pawed my way out of the tent, and said nothing, only smiled. I could see her teeth in the dark.

There were other women after her, and other nights like that, when I ran from imagined monsters. I knew there was nothing haunting me, and yet I couldn't seem to resist the narrative, the tracks of the tigress, broken prints, broken lines. I shunned my own hallucinations, but I kept looking.

I was a drunk, in those days. There are years of my life I scarcely recall. I will say that here.

I will also say that the tigress, the long-ago tigress, the dead tigress, was paw-scarred by Henry's knife. She'd surged up from below him as he leaned over a rock to peer at the place we believed she was lying up over a kill. He managed to roll from beneath her while she licked her wound, and I fired at her, but I missed. A few days later, he was gone, and I was broken.

No one emerges unscathed from my profession. The line between sanity and insanity is imperceptible until you cross it, a mere game trail on a hillside, unmarked and unnoticed, until one finds one's feet pacing that path, higher, higher, into the dizzying thinness of the air.

As I sit here, writing this, I shake my head.

The tracks—I can scarcely write these foolish lines—have appeared in various places over the years. In the dust of my stoop in Kenya, a woman's bare feet, scar in the arch. And padding in soft circles around the bed I share with my wife, a tiger's tracks, sliced cleanly across the pads by a knife. There've been times I've seen them everywhere I went. I know that guilt writes its own stories. These prints are true, though, the ones the tigress left here last night.

I leave this entry to page through all the pugmarks I've seen in the last forty years, recorded and coded in my notebook, searching for another explanation.

16 September, 1950
Later.

I find myself longing for my old partner. I should never have returned to these mountains. *Shaitan*, my mind tells me, but I should know better. Henry would.

The Best of Subterranean

In 1908, when I first met him, he was in his later 50s, but could easily spring shoeless straight up a mountain, fleet as a ghooral. I once saw Henry casually pluck a fish from a pool with his hand. I hadn't even seen the glimmer of it in the water. He was a far better hunter than I, for though I was young then, and strong, I was bound by strange decorum, intent upon differentiating myself from the beasts.

Henry's skills had been passed down through four generations, and he had himself functioned as the Kumaon region's chief shikari since the year I was born. The hunters did more than simply hunt. They catalogued the spirits in the trees and the devils in the waters, dispersed measured portions of the bodies of man-eaters to the villagers for their good luck charms. The rifles are lighter now, the bullets more destructive, and the ancient ways are being forgotten.

The old shikari could track a butterfly on the wing, by the breeze created in its flight. They could find a snake the size of a quill pen, slithering up from a trail, and chart its passage through the streams.

When Henry opened his mouth to speak, it was as plausible that a forlorn tiger's call for a mate would come from it as words in human language. He could mimic anything in these woods. Once, in a moment of triumph, having together slain a leopard after weeks of stalking, he smiled slightly at me, and gave a whistling trill, then another. Eventually, I counted thirty-seven species of birds flocking to us.

I would be remiss if I did not record here that Henry was also superbly mechanical, capable of combining two rifles into something better than either had been. Or of creating a precise and killing snare out of a length of silk thread drawn from a sari, a coil of spring, and razor blade. He mapped our prey with precision, and he knew which tiger might be near from the shape the creature's body left in the grass. For ten years, Henry and I hunted man-eaters all over India, surveying the trees for motion, listening to the sounds of warning coursing through the mountains like ripples on a gin-clear pond.

When Henry and I came to Naini Tal in the final days of 1917, it was our goal to deliver the residents of the monsters they'd made. If a plague strikes a remote place such as this one, and there are not enough villagers left to carry the bodies of the dead down to the water in procession, the rites of burial may be simplified. A live coal is placed in the mouth of the corpse, and then the bodies carted to a cliff, and thrown into the valley below, where the leopards and tigers find them, eat them, and develop their own desires.

We were summoned by a desperate rumor, a cooee call from ridgeline to ridgeline until it arrived at us. This place was far from the world, back then. There were no telephones, no telegrams. There were no cars. The village had lost their own shikari to a Himalayan bear six months before the plague began.

All the adults in the village were dead by the time we heard of Naini Tal, and only children remained. The tigers had taken over the town. They swept through the narrow passages between the huts, their golden bodies glinting in the starlight, their chins lifted to scent the air. It was as though the cats meandered through a night market, from stall to stall, sampling wares. There were twenty-six of them, and what had been a thriving village had become a place of terror.

Henry and I arrived to a place in shambles, tiger's marks before each door. The children were packed into one hut, and they'd left the rest of the village to the man-eaters. The pond where water was collected was half-dry, and all around it were the marks of claws.

When we arrived, the children came cautiously from the hut. They were all skin and eyes. There'd been no forage, and their livestock were dead. Each of the children had about their neck a locket containing a piece of tiger: red fur or black fur or bone or claw, but the charms had done nothing to save them. I argued to remove them from their village. I'd never imagined so many man-eaters in one location.

Henry, though, had grown up in the region. This was his territory. He knelt at the pond, treading on the tracks of the cats. He searched for a moment in his camp sack, and then brought forth an empty can, along with clockworks from my own recently smashed watch. I hadn't known he'd saved them.

After a few minute's work, he'd made of these materials a tiny creature. As the children came closer, fascinated by the toy he made, trusting him, he finished it, a sharp-edged bird made of metal. He twisted something beneath its wing.

It fluttered, and then, miraculously, took flight into the trees. It circled, swaying and wobbling in the air, and then landed again in his hand. The children looked at him as though he was a god, bringing animals to life out of broken things.

Henry shrugged when I asked how he'd made it, and told me it was nothing, a children's game. I never saw the bird again, though I thought of it often, the part of me that was still a child as enchanted as those children had been.

One by one, over the next months, we stalked and killed each of the man-eaters. At last, there was only one remaining.

I think of how I saw Henry last, his hand raised to protect his face, the choked sound he made—

He'd changed in the months we'd hunted those twenty-six tigers. Begun to drink in daylight, and sometimes at night. At the time, I didn't notice. I was killing tigers too. The night before he died, though, Henry looked over our fire at me, and asked if I thought the tigers deserved to win. I immediately answered that they'd developed a taste for humans, and killing them was all that could be done. I didn't want to talk about anything else.

After all of it was over, I convinced myself that Henry's death had been his own doing, that he'd been drunk, and endangered us both.

But in my mind, Henry looks at me again, mute as he was in my nightmare. I know what he wanted to say, I know.

He'd seen a glimpse of color. In places like this, anything red means tiger. Anything white means bone. Anything golden means seen, and seen means eyes, and eyes mean death, unless one is luckier than one has any right to be.

The tigress had watched as we placed ourselves, thinking we awaited her arrival, when in fact she'd been crouched patiently in her own blind, waiting for us all night.

In the book that was published all over the world, the book that inspired generations of hunters to come to these woods, I did not say that my courage failed me. When I felt the tigress coming close on me, I abandoned Henry and ran.

She didn't pursue me. No. She took him instead.

I regained my senses too late and followed the trail of her drag, but I found only a pool of his blood, deep enough to dip my hands in, deep enough to cover.

For another five days, I stalked her, sleepless, out of food, my rifle jammed in my flight from her. I talked to myself, and to Henry, talked to the tigers I felt but could not see. I was a coil of rope caught by something invisible and swift, my soul tight between its teeth. I unspooled into emptiness.

At last, I tracked the tigress around a crumbling mountain ledge, the only retreat back the way I'd come. She was there, sleeping in the open, confident in her size and speed, confident in my despair. Her abdomen was exposed, the fur around her teats matted down from suckling cubs.

I brought my pistol from behind my back, and shot her in the chest, my hands too unstable to aim at her head. She was awake and nearly on me then, but mortally wounded. The man-eater leapt over me, lunging through the trees. I shot her again as she retreated, and she lost her footing.

I witnessed her fall from China Peak, her body flipping, twisting, striped gold and black as a wasp, her back certainly broken as she flew.

Irretrievable, the bodies. The tigress fell deep into the straight-sided ravine, and Henry was gone.

I tracked the tigress' two cubs to the place she had hidden them. Not man-eaters. No. Mewling still.

After it was finished, I went down the mountain, eyes full of tears and blood, and I lied to them all about what had happened. I said that it could not be helped, that I had tried to save Henry, but even as I thought I was speaking, out of my mouth came something else, the cries of deer and the dying, the voices of birds and ghosts. One child wrapped my head in cotton while another packed my wounds and gave me, spoonful by spoonful, wild honey and herbs for my fever. They called from a ridge, and a message went forth to another village.

Some men of my slight acquaintance came and carried me from Naini Tal, hospitalized me in Delhi, and there I stayed for six months, convalescing, writing the book of lies that made me famous.

I wonder now if I'm still in 1918, and all I thought I saw and did since then a madman's dream, because the tigress I'm tracking now, the tigress whose prints I see in the dirt of this village, has been dead for thirty-two years. I killed her.

17 September, 1950
Nine in the morning.

"What is it you seek in those mountains?" my wife asked me just before I left. She'd found me at the table, my rifle out for cleaning. "What is it you seek that is not here? Everything is everywhere."

She poured red tea into my porcelain cup, white milk into the tea.

Blood, I thought. Bone. Tiger, I thought.

I thought about the footprints on our stoop. I thought about how every time they appeared, my wife came out with the broom, and brushed them away as though they were nothing. Perhaps they were nothing but dust.

She added an anthill of sugar to the cup, and then stirred it violently with a metal spoon, rattling the saucer.

"Do you want to kill every tiger in the world?" she demanded.

"Not all the tigers," I protested. "*This* tiger. In this village. In my village."

"That isn't your village," my wife said. "I'm your village. Do you see me?"

It was night, and a mosquito had landed on my arm to drink, its beak trembling. A calm came over my wife as she studied it. After a moment, she took the insect between her fingers and crushed its body, my blood smearing her fingers.

"This is a tiger," she said, and she didn't look at me as she carefully placed the mosquito in the flame of the candle, igniting its wings. "This was a tiger."

And now, I'm in Kumaon, making my way up and into the forest toward Pali. Whatever haunts me, I intend to find it. A ghost, a tiger, a woman, a hallucination. Maybe these tracks are left by the wind, but I pursue my old enemy today, and if she finds me before I find her, I deserve what she plans for me.

K_____ and I have been over the nearby parts of the forest, and now we prepare ourselves to enter it. K_____ has perversely overarmed himself, and his rifle is much too heavy. He carries eleven cartridges, far more than necessary, particularly considering that anything we shoot will be shot by me, not by him. Nevertheless, I can't convince him otherwise. I didn't bother to try.

Strapped to his back is a suitcase filled with powdered preservatives and skinning tools. The taxidermist is nervous as a cat, he told me, with some degree of humor.

"Tigers are never nervous," I informed him. "Tigers are nothing like us."

I looped the ropes for the machan around my arm. Aside from the pug and scratch marks, there's no other sign of the tigress in town, nor in the nearby trees. I'd expected to find scat, and other scratching, but I've seen nothing. All I see are her broken prints, familiar to me as my own hands, scarred pad, claws digging strangely unretracted into hard-packed dirt.

Several of the village men traveled with us this morning, and after six hours walk into the forest, we stayed with them to make camp. It is no small thing to have people waiting. A camp plays the role of a wife, tempting the parts of a hunter that do not desire a return home. It's too easy to choose to be lost.

I wasn't always so pragmatic about such things. When I hunted with Henry, we never set up camp. When he slept, if he slept, it was hunched in a tree. I'd be slung up in the machan, imagined man-eaters in my periphery, but Henry slept deeply, and if a tiger came near, he'd shoot. Nearly always, he'd kill his prey without aiming.

Henry's first hunt was when he was seven years old, a tiger that had killed two young sisters cutting grass. Later, their bodies would be found, naked and licked clean of blood, as peaceful as sleepers. Henry believed the tigress sought to replace lost cubs. I thought he was mad, imagining a tiger's heart as a though it were a woman's. Animals, I thought. Beasts. Heartless, I thought.

I wanted, I admit it, to kill every tiger, man-eater or not. I thought of the damage they did to men, and I wanted them to pay.

Henry went to great lengths to avoid targeting cats that had not turned man-eater. The killing of cubs was far astray from Henry's philosophy. He would have taught them about men by firing his rifle near them. He thought that without tigers the forests would disappear. We disagreed in those days. I saw the tigers as enemies. One killed enemies.

Whatever comes tomorrow, a hunter dies hunting.

Now, in our camp on China Peak, I feel observed, but no kakar call to warn us of creatures on the move. Only the trees watch us, I tell myself. And so, we sleep.

18 September, 1950

The forest was dark this morning and fragrant, the scent of needles and undergrowth, strangling orchids in bloom up a tree, a constellation of blossoms against a green sky. K_____ and I marched through it, he heaving with exhaustion and altitude, myself with unaccustomed activity. I'd forced him to change his leather shoes for a pair with thin rubber soles, and he was, at least, stepping quietly.

The temperature dropped as we ascended, and I saw a pugmark outlined in dew, another rimed in the light frost that lingers in the shadows long after sunrise. The marks taunted me, orphaned, one here, one miles onward, never two in proximity, not true tracks. High up a tree, a scratch, too high for a tiger, fifty feet, but I looked at it regardless, roped myself up into the branches to examine it more closely. I've never seen a mark like it before. Tiger, but impossible.

On a twig near the scratch, I found a scrap of blue cotton from the shirt of the man the tigress had taken from the village. I lowered myself, painfully stiff from the climb.

It is confirmed. This tiger is not a tiger. We are hunting a ghost.

The tigress walked a dotted line, dancing her way up into the heights, leaving her tracks and signs like breadcrumbs for me. And thus the shikari succumbs to fairy tales, imagining a tiger's ghost leading him not to heaven but to some airy hell.

K_____ knew so little about the habits of our prey he didn't think to ask what was wrong. Beside me, he struggled up the mountainside, heaving his bags miserably. He paused suddenly, paralyzed, his mouth a rictus of uncertainty.

"Hear that?" he managed.

I did not.

"That way. Roaring." I listened, and heard nothing, though K_____ heard it twice more. I wondered if I was losing my hearing, along with all else. My fingers ached, and my eyes, and my spine and my heart. Exhausted and too old for this.

He pointed waveringly to the west, and on his certainty, we shifted direction, the forest darker this way, no sun having yet reached this side of the mountain. I led, insisting on lightening K_____'s load by taking his weapon from him, though in truth I was keeping myself safe from any chance of his inadvertently firing.

I'd seen no sign of the tigress in hours. I, who'd tracked the progress of man-eaters by counting single broken blades of grass, by touching bent leaves. I couldn't smell her, couldn't hear her. Wherever she'd slept, there was no sign of it. But ghosts don't sleep.

K_____ stumbled behind me and I heard him retch, a despairing, scavenged sound. I spun, my rifle already cocked, but there was no tigress. No, something piteous instead. The taxidermist had tripped over the remains of the man she'd killed. Shards of ribcage hung with meat, spine crumpled, half his jaw, a few strands of black hair.

I knelt, unfolding the thin sheet I'd brought. We'd wrap him in it and return him to his family, that they might burn him. As I began to wind the sheet about the bones, though, I glimpsed something. I stood and aimed, squinting into the trees, as still as I could manage. Trembling fingers.

"We should go," K_____ said, his voice pinched.

I hissed him quiet. Red. No motion. *Tigress, waiting. Tigress watching.* My only hope would be to fire as she leapt.

My vision focused at last, revealing that the red was no tiger, no blood, but a small building, peeling paint. I let out my breath and stood. No smells of humans. No cookfire smoke. Abandoned. High in these mountains for a hunting cabin, but that, I thought, was certainly what it was. In the trees above us, I could see old bones hanging, their meat long gone. A stake pounded far into the earth, a chain, for what creature I did not know. A dog, perhaps, though a very large one. There was a circle worn in the dirt below the stake, a deep, claw-scarred track, which I chose not to examine. Some brave or mad man had lived here in tiger territory, and someone with a wish for oblivion, too.

I instructed K_____ to follow me to the hut. Door closed. Some part of my mind was certain the tiger would fling open the door and stand upright before me, her belly still stained with undrunk milk, the tooth-marks of the cubs she'd lost. I kicked the door open.

And stopped. K_____ gasped and then pushed his way past me.

The exterior of the cabin was wooden, but the interior walls shone. Flattened cans and springs, pendulums and gears, glimmering rocks and iridescent feathers. Rough tools, and some better, nail-hung on racks. Papers nailed up, drawings, writing, but too dark and stained to read. Claws were strung from the ceiling, garlands of teeth decorating the beams.

Against the far wall, a shape, bulky, striped. I shoved K_____ back, aiming my rifle.

"It's stuffed," he said authoritatively, and I realized, to my shame, that he was correct. The tiger was motheaten, its eyes replaced with chips of glass, its pelt dull and its pose stiff. "Someone who didn't know the modern techniques. Hadn't studied."

There was a bucket filled with rusting wires at my feet, another of white dust, another of black soil. Another filled with red, old red, dried to nothing now, but I knew what it was.

"A scientist working here," I said, remembering something of the kind. "Long gone, whomever he was."

K_____ was elbow deep in bones, piecing together a skeletal structure. Weapons and traps all over the room. Rifles soldered to other rifles.

Triple-barreled here, and here, something rusted and still lethal looking, a bayonet-barreled pistol attached to a chain. A hunting cabin, yes, but a strange one, inhabited by both science and old craft. I opened a jar and sniffed at the contents. Local alcohol of some kind, doubtless poisonous.

What fool had brought this stuffed tiger? I imagined the thing packed up the mountain by reluctant porters years before, the tiger standing on their shoulders, eyes staring at nothing, limbs leaking sawdust. The waste disgusted me, and the light was fading. I saw K_____ thoughtfully measuring the poor beast's ear between his fingers, tugging at the ancient leather.

"We will not be stopping here," I'd just informed him, when something glittered in a beam of sunset shining through the roof.

A metal bird. Perched on the stuffed tiger's back. I did not—

I still do not. Impossible. A plummeting certainty.

Thirty-two years spent in darkness, and now a blinding and horrible light shines on me.

Henry. Alive, Henry, and perhaps stricken somewhere on the forest floor, mere feet from me as I stalked his killer?

If you hear screaming, it is already too late. All one can do is track the man-eater. Henry's the one who taught me that. Was he in the cave where I'd found the cubs? Did he, bleeding, mute, watch as I killed them?

No. Surely not. My mind can only have lost control, ancient guilt mingling with memory. In my book, *I* was the one who'd killed all 26 of the man-eaters of Naini Tal. In my book, I killed the tigress that killed him, and I said nothing of how he'd saved me. I couldn't bear to write his name, and so I took his glory. No one knows. Not my wife, unless I've confessed it in my sleep. Not the world. Not the villagers.

But here I am, writing these words, and Henry. Oh, Henry.

I held my head in my hands, feeling my skull spreading in my fingers. In a pouch at my waist, I carry my lucky pieces, my own superstitious version of the lockets worn by natives. Tiger bones, one from each tiger I've killed. I've carried them to Kenya, and to America, and everywhere I've gone, they've kept me safe.

In Henry's house, I opened the pouch and spilled my luck out on the dirt floor. K_____ glanced at me, uninterested.

We found Henry under a coverlet on the metal cot in the corner. Skeleton undamaged, no bones taken, though one shoulder had been shattered and knit badly, the wound of the tigress. His long silver beard still clung to the last scraps of skin. Twenty years dead, longer.

And there, closed in the jaw of Henry's skeleton, a coal, burned almost away. Ash on the ivory. My mentor did his own last rites here, no river, no hymn, no strength.

"Did you know him?" K_____ asked, and I didn't answer. Why did he never return to Naini Tal? What was Henry doing here?

We sleep here, in this strange place, and we keep vigil over my friend's bones, though his soul is long departed.

I twisted the wing of the little metal bird tonight, hoping that it might fly. It opened its beak and sang a single rusting note. Then all was silent.

18 September, 1950

The tigress was waiting for us, as I knew she would be. We slept for three hours and rose in darkness this morning, K_____ protesting bitterly.

I didn't want to stalk her any longer. I'd dreamed of Kenya, and of my wife sitting at the kitchen table, her tea in hand. I thought about how I would likely not see her again.

I didn't expect to survive a tigress this large, to whom I'd already lost my courage once, to whom I'd lost my pride. A ghost made of hunger and air.

She was out there. The forest wailed her presence. I felt her intentions, her bulk in the trees. I took a small bone from Henry's hand, and placed it in my pouch. I'd burn it, and give him his true funeral, if I made it out from these trees again.

We walked, watched at every step. I felt her in the woods, moving parallel to us, but it was pointless to aim at nothing. One never heard a tiger if the tiger was planning an attack. One might hear a soft sound, as a tiger departed, having decided not to leap. K_____ looked around, uneasy, pale. He felt her too.

The forest felt brittle, each leaf frozen now, each twig K_____ tread on cracking like a shot, and we ascended still higher. At last, something I recognized, a tiger's call, but not that of a tiger.

Henry's version, a human voice, perfectly mimicking a tiger's roar. I heard him do it hundreds of times. It's nothing one forgets. I shook my head, trying to dispel the hallucination.

It was, of course, a tiger calling. A night spent in Henry's company. It was no wonder. Another roar, and this voice was Henry's as well, calling in the tones of a tigress, and a moment later, calling in the voice of a male tiger, and now another, an elderly cat, and a cub.

"Do you hear that?" I asked K_____ and his only response was quick breathing.

"How many are there?" he asked.

"Do you hear *Henry*?" The depth of my uncertainty had overcome me. I was queasy with it.

"I hear tigers," he said.

A flurry of calls, the startling bells of a sambur, like automobiles in traffic, squeezing horns. *Tiger here, tiger passing.* All in the voice of Henry. It was as though Henry had become the entire forest, and all its occupants.

I stood still, fighting that old urge, run, curl to protect stomach, meticulously checking my rifle instead. *Tiger running*, shrieked a peafowl, in Henry's voice.

Through the trees, I saw red. And more red. More than one tiger. How many? They were not leaping at us, but running for some other reason. A mass of tigers, in step, all moving at the same pace, flowing through the shadows faster than I could watch. This was nothing tigers, who do not hunt in packs, would do.

At last, I saw her, my old enemy, stepping out of the forest in front of us.

My rifle was already aimed as she leapt. I fired, but did not come close to hitting her. Her spring took her over our heads, and she landed, softly behind us. K_____ shook beside me, and I felt him considering a run.

"Don't move," I hissed. "If you move, she'll have you."

I scanned the trees for the other tigers, but they were invisible. She opened her jaws and roared to me in Henry's voice and I felt the tears of a madman running down my face.

Perhaps this was his last gift to me, I thought, this aural hallucination that reminded me what to do when a tiger had gotten this close. Call her closer. He'd taught me the call, and now I made it back to her. I roared at her, at Henry's killer, at this killer who hadn't killed him.

She stepped toward me, her pelt shining, her eyes golden and glowing, her muscles gathering, and as she launched herself, I fired into her throat, the rifle kicking my shoulder.

The tigress screamed in Henry's voice again, and threw herself into the trees as though they, and not I, were her murderer. I could see no blood on her pelt, but her madness was that of the wounded. The tree trunk cracked as she bellowed and threw herself at its branches, and slowly it toppled, tigress atop it, her growls quietening now, her motions slower.

I shot her once more, this time in the skull, just over her left eye, and she made a sound, a raw hissing, something beyond anything animal. I expected her to disappear, for there to be a cloud of smoke left behind, a ghost gone, but she did not. I edged closer, K_____ on my heels.

The tigress looked up suddenly, pupils fully dilated, and I knew that she was dying. How could a ghost die?

I could smell my own sweat, and a deep, metallic odor too, tiger's blood, I thought, though I'd long since forgotten the smell of it.

Above, the stars blinked on, one by one, and the bats began to hunt. Insects rattled their shells like shields.

The tigress' head dropped slowly onto her paws, and the light went out in her, as a headlamp on a train might go to black when pulled into its end station. There was a sound, a strange sound, which I attributed to bullets against stone, and then she was still.

"Shaitan," I said, quietly, a prayer to the devil I'd killed for the second time.

K_____ vibrated behind me. "Is it dead?"

"A man-eater for your museum," I told him, overcome by the sadness I always feel when I kill something large as her, and with this sadness, something more, something darker. Confusion.

"You must know she's not for a museum, old man," K_____ told me, his voice returning, more confident than it had been before. "A museum wouldn't pay for something like this."

I looked at him.

"Everyone wants a tiger," he said. "Everyone wants a man-eater certified by someone like you."

"Who's this tiger for?" I knew the answer already.

"A collector. Already has a table made of elephant legs."

K_____'s wry laugh sounded to me like something from a moving picture, overheard from far down the street, through walls and bodies. Hollow and cluttered, the laughter of something made of less than nothing. My own laughter had, on occasion, sounded the same.

He took his flask from his pocket, sipped, and offered it to me. I refused.

"Don't misunderstand me," he said, kneeling to unpack his case. "I read your book. That's why I do this. I show the world the things they want to see, but don't want to travel to. It's conservation, isn't it? People like that, here, they'd ruin things. You, though, you've killed what? Two hundred tigers? You know what you're doing."

With effort, he rolled the man-eater onto her back, and removed a scalpel from his pack.

"If I don't gut her soon, the skin'll spoil," he said, and then bent over the tigress, parting the fur on her chest.

"An old bullet wound." He jabbed her left shoulder, but I didn't look. I knew the wound. "There's another scar here," he said. "As old as the other."

He ran his finger down the man-eater's pelt, from chest to abdomen. I could scarcely keep myself from tearing the scalpel from his hand. I felt as though she was the only one on earth who'd known my past. I didn't dare think of how she could be here at all, thirty-two years later, did not dare imagine what this all might mean, for it *was* her. I knew her face, her tracks. It was her. A dead, mortal tigress.

"Peculiar," K_____ muttered, cutting into the scar. An echoing scratch. Scalpel on bullet, I thought.

"What in Christ is this?" K_____ whispered.

I wasn't looking at him, nor at the tigress. I was focused into the distance, imagining Kenya, when he shook my shoulder. I turned my head, reluctant to see what he'd done.

A gleam, straight down the center of the tigress' body. K_____ peeled back the flesh on either side of the incision.

There was no blood. No. Only skin, and beneath the skin, metal.

K_____ began tearing at the pelt, pulling it away from the structure beneath, breathing through his mouth.

"What is it?" he asked, looking suddenly, frantically up at me. "Is it a prank?"

I couldn't speak.

Henry, kneeling with a tin can and a watch spring. Henry, wounded, climbing down into that ravine to retrieve her body. Skinning her, hauling her back up the mountain, and bringing her back to life. He'd made a new kind of tiger, one that could resist hunters and poachers. One that could resist me.

K_____'s hands peeled the flesh back still further. I could see solder marks, where seams had been joined.

"The hide isn't dry. How did he get it to heal? What did he use? How does it move?"

He attempted haphazardly to slice into the tigress' chest, denting the metal. He pulled up the tigress' eyelid, his fingernail tapping at her pupil. Glass. I looked at her feet. The strange marks I'd seen in the village had not been made by claws. Henry had given her knives, forged into the shape of talons.

I felt myself half-smiling, an echo of the old enchantment, Henry's genius, Henry as a shikari.

"Whatever he's done, however he's done it," K_____ said, his voice scarcely under control, wobbling with joy, "We'll lead an expedition back here. Photographers. Film cameras."

He jabbed the scalpel into a seam between the metal pieces, levering at it. A dark fluid leaked out. Blood? Not blood? Henry never explained himself. I still had K_____'s rifle. I swung it slowly around to the front. When he heard the click, he looked up, entirely startled.

"What are you doing?"

I fired into K_____'s face, approximating the angle he himself would have taken had he stumbled over his own weapon in the forest, drunk on gin, and a fool. I left him where he lay, skull exposed. I used my handkerchief to polish his rifle and put it into his own hands. Took his scalpel.

Anyone who found K_____'s body would imagine he'd been attacked by a tiger, and inadvertently shot himself in the scuffle.

I chopped down two saplings, lashed the tigress to them with my machan ropes, and began a laborious drag. I'd drop her into that ravine. Everything was clear to me now. If the world learned of this tiger, they'd cut down the forests to find more like her, though surely there were no more. This would've taken Henry years to accomplish, however it was he'd done it. Magic. Gears.

Kumaon would be overrun. All the remaining living tigers would be taken, shot, opened like stuffed toys, left to dry in the sun, unused, unburied.

I hauled her through the trees, straining at her great weight, squinting toward the earliest light, toward the place I remembered from 1918. If I threw her off the cliffs here, she would not be found. Dead, I'd tell the villagers, and fallen, just as I'd told them before. My fingers were blue with cold despite the effort of hauling her, and my breath came sharply, each gasp painful.

At last, I found the place, and panting, unlashed her. My heart, by this juncture, was pounding inside me like something independent of my body, a metal bird flying for no reason other than someone else's will.

I pushed the tigress over the edge. I watched her fall for the second time, her golden face and fur, her gleaming, opened breast. I was not watching my footing. Is it any wonder I fell? Not from the cliff, as I might deserve, but over a small rise, and into a clearing, flat rock beneath me.

Hours have passed. I cannot stand. It's cold now, and the light fades again. My left leg, in my trousers, is bent in such a way that I know it would be useless to attempt to place it back in line. I've bled into the ice, and it shines like a glass ruby on an elephant's forehead.

I have this journal, and my pencil, and I write for comfort. What else do I have, after all these years wandering in the wilderness? Tomorrow, I'll burn these words. I write only to tell myself what happened, not to place the story into the world.

Out there in the sky I see each star again, and like every man dying from the beginning of his days, I regret the things I didn't do, and I regret the things I did.

19 September, 1950
Dawn.

All night, Henry's tigers paced around me, circling close enough to brush me with their fur. I couldn't count them, couldn't name them. There may be hundreds, or twelve, or a thousand.

Now, the sun is risen, and snow has fallen here at the top of this mountain, over me and around my body. If I could stand, I might look down again onto my own lost village, the teardrop lake at the center of the vista like the eye of a god, wide open for eternity, never freezing, never anything more or less than blue. No passage to heaven from that lake. One needs a river, one needs a fire, one needs bones.

Ram nam satya hai, sing the voices in my memory, a hymn to carry the victims away, shrouded and saved from further sorrow.

What will the tigers leave of me? Will there be bones to send to my wife? Who will find them here? The villagers await the sound of my fire, five shots to come and take the tiger from here, but I won't fire this rifle again. They will assume me dead, along with K_____, and the tigress escaped.

When I turn my head, all I can see in this clearing are pug marks, tracks circling over tracks, lines and circuits, loops and letters. Each of the footfalls, each of the places where a tail touched the earth, each spatter of blood, each piece of fur brushed onto a tree trunk tells me something.

Game | Maria Dahvana Headley

Coded lines left behind by Henry, placed in the tiger's metal minds, along with the calls he gave them, but I've no key to break them. When the cats move, I hear their machinery now, the sound of gears against gears, metal against metal.

All these years haunted by a ghost that wasn't. All these years imagining tracks around my house, when they were here all along. There are no ghosts but the ones you make.

I lay last night in the dark and heard the tigers dragging their claws through the snow, each one marking my name. That, at least, was mine, but it's become something the tigers use. I can't read it, but I know it belonged to me, just as one knows a book read long ago, the margins scarred with ink, the pages folded down. A possession. This book, this journal, I'd know anywhere. I sought to burn it, but my firestarter is wet, and I can't strike a flame. Perhaps the tigers will take it too.

In my hand, I have a penknife, given to me by Henry, the handle made of something's bones, the blade so thin now that it scarcely exists. Used on pelts, and on tin cans, and on apples, and on birds. Used on tigers and leopards, on man-eaters all over India. Used on tiger cubs. Two hearts eaten, and I thought it made me a man and gave me a vengeance on all the things that take hunters from their lives.

Over my head, high and far away, an airplane tears a line across the heavens, hunting some smaller prey, and I think about a sky filled with roaring ghosts. I feel displaced in time, a traveler returning home after decades spent in a place where years passed at a strange rate. If I came down from the mountains now, an old man, I might find the children I left in this village thirty-two years ago. I might find myself, walking into the woods. I might find Henry, twisting metal into life.

I am well-acquainted with the paths to heaven from this part of the mountains. I do not expect heaven.

Send my bones up in smoke along with those I killed, and let us hunt together, shifting between prey and shikari, stalking, killing enemies already dead. The bones in my pouch belong to the dead. Burn them.

A hunter hunts. We are all hunters here.

The Last Log
of the Lachrimosa

BY ALASTAIR REYNOLDS

W*ake up.*

No, really. Wake up. I know you don't want to, but it's import-ant that you understand what's happened to you, and—just as vitally—what's going to happen next. I know this is hard for you, being told what to do. It's not the way it usually works. Would it help if I still called you Captain?

Captain Rasht, then. Let's keep it formal.

No, don't fight. It'll only make it worse. There. I've eased it a little. Just a tiny, tiny bit. Can you breathe more easily now? I wouldn't waste your energy speaking, if I were you. Yes, I know you've a lot on your mind. But please don't make the mistake of thinking there's any chance of talking your way out of this one.

Nidra? Yes, that's me. Good that you're wide awake enough to remember my name. Lenka? Yes, Lenka is alive. I went back for Lenka, the way I said I would.

Yes, I found Teterev. There wasn't much I could do for her, though. But it was good to hear what she had to say. You'd have found it interesting, I think.

Well, we'll get to that. As I said, I want you to understand what happens next. To some extent, that's in your control. No, really. I'm not so cruel that

I wouldn't give you some influence over your fate. You wanted to make your name—to do something that would impress the other ships, the other crews— leave your mark on history.

Make them remember Rasht of the Lachrimosa.

This is your big chance.

⭒

"I'll find Mazamel," said Captain Rasht, clenching his fist around an imaginary neck. "Even if I have to take the Glitter Band apart. Even if I have to pluck him out of the bottom of the chasm. I'll skin him alive. I'll fuse his bones. I'll make a living figurehead out of him."

Lenka and I were wise enough to say nothing. There was little to be gained in pointing out the obvious: that by the time we returned to Yellowstone, our information broker stood every chance of being light years away.

Or dead.

That was what you got when you could only afford the cheapest, least-reliable information brokers. When your ship was falling apart around you and you were down to four crewmembers, of which one was a monkey.

"I won't fuse his bones after all," Captain Rasht continued. "I'll core out his spine. Kanto needs a new helmet for his spacesuit. I'll make one of out Mazamel's skull. It's fat and stupid enough for a monkey. Isn't it, my dear?"

Rasht interrupted his monologue to pop a morsel into the stinking, tooth-rotted mouth of Kanto, squatting on his shoulder like a hairy disfigurement.

In fairness, Mazamel's information wasn't totally valueless. The ship at least was real. It was still there, still orbiting Holda. From a distance it had even looked superficially intact. It was only as we came in closer, tightening our own orbit like a noose, that the actual condition became apparent. The needle-tipped hull was battered, pocked and gouged by numerous collisions with interstellar material. That was true of our own *Lachrimosa*—no ship makes it between solar systems without some cost— but here the damage was much worse. We could see stars through some of the holes in the hull, punched clean through to the other side. The engine spars, sweeping out from the hull at its widest point, had the look of ruptured batskin. The engines still seemed to be present when we made our long-distance survey. But we had been tricked by the remains of their enclosing structures. They were hollow, picked open and gouged of their dangerous, seductive treasures.

"We should check out the wreck," Lenka said, trying to make the best of a bad situation. "At least find the name of that ship. But there's something on the surface we should look at as well."

"What?"

"I'm not sure. Some kind of geomagnetic anomaly, spiking up in the northern hemisphere. Got some metallic backscatter, too. Neither makes much sense. Holda's not meant to have much of a magnetosphere. Core's too old and cold for that. The metal signature's in the same area, too. It's quite concentrated. It could be a ship or something, put down on the surface."

Rasht thought about it, grunted his grudging approval.

"But first the wreck. Make sure it isn't going to shoot us down the instant we turn our backs. Match our orbit, Nidra—but keep us at a safe distance."

"Fifty kilometres?" I asked.

Rasht considered that for a moment. "Make it a hundred."

※

Was that more than just natural caution? I've never been sure about you, if truth be told—how much stock you put in traveller's tales.

Mostly we aren't superstitious. But rumours and ghost stories, those are something else. I'm sure you've heard your share of them, over the years. When ships meet for trade, stories are exchanged—and you've done a lot of trading. Or did, until your luck started souring.

Did you hear the one about the space plague?

Of course you did.

The strange contagion, the malady infecting ships and their crew. Is it real, Captain? What do you think? No one seems to know much about it, or even if it really exists.

What about the other thing? The black swallowing horror between the stars, a presence that eats ships. No one knows much about that, either.

What's clear, though, is that a drifting, preyed-upon hulk puts no one in an agreeable frame of mind. We should have turned back there and then. But if Lenka and I had tried to argue with you on that one, how far do you think we'd have got? You'd have paid more attention to the monkey.

Yes, Kanto's fine. We'll take very good care of him. What do you think we are—monsters?

We're not like that at all.

No, I'm not leaving you—not just yet. I just have to fetch some things from Teterev's wreck. Be back in a jiffy! You'll recognise the things when you see them. You remember the wreck, don't you?

Not the ship in orbit. That was a wash-out. The fucking thing was as derelict and run-down as Lachrimosa. No engines, no weps. No crew, not even frozen. No cargo, no tradable commodities. Picked clean as a bone.

No, I'm talking about the thing we found on the surface, the crash site.

Good, it's coming back to you.

That'll help.

"It's a shuttle," Lenka said.

"Was," I corrected.

True: the shuttle was a wreck. But in fact it was in much better condition than it had any right to be. The main section of the shuttle was still in one piece, upright on the surface. It was surrounded by debris, but the wonder was that any part of it had survived. It must have suffered a malfunction very near the surface, or else there would have been nothing to recognise.

Around the crash site, geysers pushed columns of steam up from a dirty snowscape. Holda's sun, 82 Eridani, was rising. As it climbed into the sky it stirred the geysers to life. Rocks and rusty chemical discolouration marred the whiteness. A little to the west, the terrain bulged up sharply, forming a kind of rounded upwelling. I stared at it for a moment, wondering why it had my attention. Something about the bulge's shape struck me as odd and unsettling, as if it simply did not belong in this landscape.

Unlike the other ship, no misfortune befell us as we completed our landing approach. Rasht selected an area of ground that looked stable. Our lander threw out its landing skids. Rasht cut power when we were still hovering, so as not to blast the snow with our descent jets.

I wondered what chance we stood of finding anything in the other craft's remains. If the ship above had proven largely valueless, there did not seem much hope of finding glories in the wreck. But it would not hurt us to investigate.

But my attention kept wandering to the volcanic cone. Most of it was snow or ice-covered, except for the top. But there were ridges or arms radiating away from it, semicircular in profile, meandering and diminishing. I supposed that they were lava tunnels, or something similar. But the way they snaked away from the main mass, thick at the start and thinner as they progressed, gradually vanishing into the surrounding terrain, made me think of a cephalopod, with the volcano as its main body and the ridges its tentacles. Rather than a natural product of geology, the outcome of blind processes drawn out over millions of years, it seemed to squat on the surface with deliberation and patience, awaiting some purpose.

I did not like it at all.

Once we had completed basic checks, we got into our spacesuits and prepared for the surface. When Rasht, Lenka and I were ready, I helped the monkey into its own little spacesuit, completing the life-support connections that were too fiddly for Captain Rasht.

You may say: why did we all go out? Why did we all go down to the surface? The truth was, that was Rasht's way. If one or more of us stayed in orbit while he was down here, there was a chance of the ship leaving without him. If he sent one or more of us down here, while he stayed in orbit, he could not rely on our trustworthiness. We might find something and lie about it, keeping its secret to ourselves.

Rasht's way. And what Rasht wanted, Rasht got.

So our happy little party stepped out the lander, testing the ground under our feet. It felt solid, as well it ought given that it was supporting the weight of our ship. The gravity on Holda was nearly Earth-normal, so we could move around just as easily as if we were on the ship. The planet was about Earth-sized as well, enabling it to hold on to a thick atmosphere. Although the core was dead, Holda was not itself a dead world. Rather than orbiting 82 Eridani directly, Holda spun around a fat banded gas giant which in turn orbited the star. As it turned around the giant, Holda was subjected to tidal forces which squeezed and stretched at its interior. These stresses manifested as heat, which in turn helped to drive the geysers and surface volcanism. From orbit we had seen that most of Holda was still covered in ice, but there were belts of exposed crust around the equator and tropics. Here and there were even pockets of liquid water. Life had spilled from these pools out onto the surface, infiltrating barren matrices of rock and ice. According to *Lachrimosa's* records there was nothing in the native ecosystem larger than a krill, but the biomass load was enough to push the atmosphere away from equilibrium, meaning that it carried enough oxygen to support our own greedy respiratory systems.

In that sense, we did not really need the suits at all. But the cold was a factor, and in any case the suits offered protection and power-assist. We kept our helmets on, anyway. We were not fools.

It was a short walk over to the crash site. We plotted a path between bubbling pools, crossing bridges and isthmuses of strong ice. Now and then a geyser erupted, fountaining tens of metres above our heads. Each time it was enough to startle the monkey, but Rasht kept his spacesuited pet on a short leash.

The other ship must have been quite sleek and beautiful before it crashed, at least in comparison to our own squat and barnacled vehicle. Much of the wreckage consisted of pieces of mirrored hull plating, curved to reflect our approaching forms back at us in grotesque distortion. Lenka and I seemed like twins, our twisted, elongated shapes wobbling in heat-haze from the pools. It was true that we were similar. We looked alike, had roughly the same augmentations, and our dreadlocks confirmed that we had completed the same modest number of crossings. During port stopovers, we were sometimes assumed to be sisters, or even twins. But in fact Lenka had been on the crew before me, and although we functioned well enough together, we did not have that much in common. It was a question of ambition, of acceptance. I was on the *Lachrimosa* until something better came along. Lenka seemed to have decided that this was the best life had to offer. At times I pitied her, at others I felt contemptuous of the way she allowed herself to be subjugated by Rasht. Our ship was half way to being a wreck itself. I wanted more: a better ship, a better captain, better prospects. I never sensed any similar desires in Lenka. She was content to be a component in a small, barely functioning machine.

But then, perhaps Lenka thought exactly the same of me. And we had all been hoping that this was going to be the big score.

Our reflections shifted. Lenka and I shrunk to tiny proportions, beneath the looming, ogrelike form of our Captain. Then the monkey swelled to be the largest of all, its armoured arms and hands swinging low with each stride, its bow legs like scuttling undercarriage.

What a crew we made, the four of us.

We reached the relatively secure ground under the other wreck. We circled it, stepping between the jagged mirrors of its hull. The force of the impact had driven them into the ground like the shaped stones of some ancient burial site, surrounding the main part of the wreck in patterns that to the eye suggested a worrying concentricity, the lingering imprint of an abandoned plan.

I picked up one of the smaller shards, tugging it from its icy holdfast. I held it to my face, saw my visored form staring back.

"Maybe a geyser caught them," I speculated. "Blasted up just as they were coming in. Hit the intakes or stabilisers, that might have been enough."

"Kanto!"

It was Rasht, screaming at the monkey. The monkey had bent down to dip its paw into a bubbling pool. Rasht jerked on the leash, tumbling the monkey back onto its suit-sheathed tail. Over our suit-to-suit comm I heard Kanto's irritated hiss. In the time it had dipped its paw into the pool, a host of microorganisms had begun to form a rust-coloured secondary glove around the original, making the monkey's paw look swollen and diseased.

The monkey, stupid to the last, tried to lick at the coating through the visor of its helmet.

I hated the monkey.

"There's a way in," Lenka said.

I'm back now, Captain. I said I wouldn't be gone long. Never one to break my promises, me.

No, don't struggle. It'll only make it worse. That thing around your neck isn't going to get any less tight.

Do you recognise these? I could only carry a few at a time. I'll go back for some more in a while.

That's right. Pieces of the crashed shuttle. Nice and shiny. Here. Let me hold one up to your face. Can you see your reflection in it? It's a bit distorted, but you'll have to put up with that. You look frightened, don't you? That's fine. It's healthy. Fear is the last and best thing we have, that's what she told me.

The last and best thing.

Our last line of defense.

She? You know who I mean. We found her helmet, her journal, in the wreck. That's right.

Teterev.

Lenka fingered open a hatch and used the manual controls to open the airlock door. We were soon through, into the interior.

It was dark inside. We turned on our helmet lights and ramped our eyes to maximum sensitivity. There were several compartments to the shuttle, all of which seemed to have withstood the crash. Gradually it became clear that someone had indeed survived. They had moved things around, arranged provisions, bedding and furniture, that could not possibly have remained undisturbed by the crash.

The Last Log of the Lachrimosa | ALASTAIR REYNOLDS

We found an equipment locker containing an old-fashioned helmet marked with the word TETEREV in stencilled Russish letters. There was no corresponding spacesuit, though. The helmet might have been a spare, or the owner had chosen to go outside in just the lower part of the suit.

"If they had an accident," Lenka said, "why didn't the big ship send down a rescue party?"

"Maybe Teterev *was* the rescue party," I said.

"They may have only had one atmosphere-capable vehicle," Rasht said. "No way of getting back down here, and no way of Teterev getting back up. The only question then is to wonder why they waited at all, before leaving orbit."

"Perhaps they didn't like the idea of leaving Teterev down here," Lenka said.

"I bet they liked the idea of dying in orbit even less," Rasht replied.

We continued our sweep of the wreck. We were less interested in Teterev's whereabouts than what Teterev might have left us to plunder. But the two things were not unrelated. Any spacer, any Ultra, is bound to care a little about the fate of another. Ordinary human concern is only part of it. There may be lessons to be learned, and a lesson is only another sort of tradable.

"I've found a journal," I said.

I had found it on a shelf in the cockpit. It was a handwritten log, rather than a series of data entries.

The journal had heavy black covers, but the paper inside was very thin. I thumbed my way to the start. It looked like a woman's handwriting to me. Russish was not my strongest tongue, but the script was clear enough.

"Teterev starts this after the crash," I said, while the others gathered around. "Says that she expects the power to run out eventually, so there's no point trying to record anything in the ship itself. But they have food and water and they can use the remaining power to stay warm."

"Go on," Rasht said, while the monkey studied its contaminated paw.

"I'm trying to get some sense of what happened. I think she came down here alone." I skimmed forward through the entries, squinting with the concentration. "There's no talk of being rescued, or even hoping of it. It's as if she knew no one would be coming down." I had to work hard not to rip the paper with my power-augmented fingers. It felt tissue-thin between my fingers, like a fly's wings.

"A punishment, then," Rasht said. "Marooned down here for a crime."

"That's an expensive way of marooning someone." I read on. "No—it wasn't punishment. Not according to *this*, anyway. An accident, something to do with one of the geysers—she says that she's afraid that it will erupt again, as it did 'on the day.' Anyway, Teterev knew she was stuck down here. And she knows she's in trouble. Keeps talking about her 'mistake' in not waking the others. Says she wonders if there's a way to signal the other ship, the orbiting lighthugger. Bring some or all of the crew out of reefer-sleep." I paused, my finger hovering over a word. "Lev."

"Lev?" Lenka repeated.

"She mentions Lev. Says Lev would help her, if she could get a message through. She'd have to accept her punishment, but at least get off Holda."

"Maybe Teterev was never meant to be down here," Lenka said. "Jump ahead, Nidra. Let's find out what happened."

I paged through dozens and dozens of entries. Some were dated and consecutive. Elsewhere I noticed blank pages and sometimes gaps of many days between the accounts. The entries became sparser, too. Teterev's hand, barely clear to begin with, became progressively wilder and less legible. Her letters and words began to loop and scrawl across the page, like the traces of a seismograph registering the onset of some major dislocation.

"Stop," Rasht said, as I turned over a page. "Go back. What was that figure?"

I turned back the sheets with a sort of dread. My eye had caught enough to know what to expect.

It was a drawing of the volcanic cone, exactly as it appeared from the position of the wreck.

Perhaps it was no more than an accident of Teterev's hand, but the way she had put her marks down on the paper only seemed to add to the suggestion of brooding, patient malevolency I had already detected in the feature. Teterev seemed to have made the cephalopod's head *more* bulbous, *more* cerebral, the lava tubes *more* muscular and tentacle-like.

Even the way she had stippled the tubes to suggest snow or ice could not help but suggest to my eye rows and rows of suckers.

Worse, she had drawn a gaping, beak-mouth between two of those tentacles.

There was a silence before Lenka said: "Turn to the end. We can read the other entries later."

I flicked through the pages until the writing ran out. The last few entries were barely entries at all, just scratchy annotations, done in haste or distraction.

Phrases jumped out at us.

Can't wake the others. Tried everything I can. My dear Lev, lost to me.

Such a good boy. A good son.

Doesn't deserve me, the mistakes I've made.

Stuck down here. But won't give in. Need materials, power. Something in that hill. Magnetic anomaly. Hill looks wrong. I think there might be something in it.

Amerikanos were here once, that's the only answer. Came by their old, slow methods. Frozen cells and robot wombs. No records, but so what. Must have dug into that hill, buried something in it. Ship or an installation. See an entrance. Cave mouth. That's where they went in.

I don't want to go in. But I want what they left behind. It might save my life.

Might get me back to the ship.

Back to Lev.

"They were never here," Rasht said. "Teterev would have known that. Their colonies never got this far out."

"She was desperate enough to try anything," Lenka said. "I feel sorry for her, stuck all alone here. I bet she knew it was a thousand to one chance."

"Nonetheless," I said, "there *is* something odd about that hill. Maybe it's nothing to do with the Amerikanos, but if you're out of options, you might as well see what's inside." I turned back to the drawing. The mouth, I now realised, was Teterev's way of drawing the cave entrance.

But it still looked like the beak of an octopus.

"One thing's for certain," Lenka said. "If Teterev went into that hill, she didn't come back."

"I didn't notice any footprints," I said.

"They wouldn't last, not with all the geothermal activity around here. The top of the ice must be melting and re-freezing all the time."

"We should look into the cave, anyway," Rasht said.

I shook my head, struck by an intense conviction that this was exactly the wrong thing to do.

"It's not our job to find Teterev's corpse."

"Someone should find it," Lenka said sharply. "Give her some dignity in death. At least record what happened to her. She was one of us, Nidra—an Ultra. She deserves better than to be forgotten. Can I look at her journal?"

"Be my guest," I said, passing it over to her.

"Nidra is right—her body isn't our concern," Rasht said, while Lenka paged through the sheets. "She took a risk, and it didn't work out for her. But the Amerikanos are of interest to us."

"Records say they weren't here," I said.

"And that's what I've always believed. But records can be wrong. What if Teterev was right with her theory? Amerikano relics are worth quite a bit these days, especially on Yellowstone."

"Then we return to orbit, send down a drone," I said.

"We're here already," Rasht answered. "There are three of us—four if you include Kanto. Did you see how old Teterev's helmet was? We have better equipment, and we're not down to our last hope of survival. We can turn back whenever we like. Nothing ventured, nothing gained."

It took something to make our ramshackle equipment look better than someone else's, I thought to myself. Besides, we were inferring a great deal from just one helmet. Perhaps it had been an old keepsake, a memento of earlier spacefaring adventures.

Still, Rasht was settled in his decision. The orbiting ship had been picked clean; the shuttle held nothing of obvious value; that left only the cave. If we were to salvage anything from this expedition, that was the last option open to us.

Even I could see the sense in that, whether I liked it or not.

⁂

Don't mind me, for the moment. Got work to be getting on with. Busy, busy, busy.

What am I doing with these things?

Well, that's obvious, isn't it? I'm arranging them around you. Jamming them into the ice, like mirrored sculptures. I know you can't move your head very easily. There's no need, though. There's not much to see, other than the cave mouth behind you and the wreck ahead of you.

What are you saying?

No, it's not for your benefit! Silly Captain. But you are very much the focus of attention. You've always liked being at the centre of things, haven't you?

What?

You're having difficulty breathing?

Just a moment, then. I don't want you to die before we've even begun! It was lucky, what happened with the winch. I mean, I'd have a found one eventually, and the line. Of course it didn't seem lucky at the time. I thought I was going to die in there. Did you think of abandoning me?

I think you did.

Here. I'm making a micro adjustment to the tension. Is that better? Can you breathe a little more easily?

Wonderful.

❄

We went outside again. The monkey was having some difficulty with its paw, as if the contamination had worked its way into the servo-workings. It kept knocking the paw against the ground, trying to loosen it up.

"There aren't any footprints," Lenka said, tugging binoculars down from the crown of her helmet. She was speaking in general terms, addressing Rasht and I without favour. "But I can see the cave mouth. It's just where Teterev said it was. Must be about five, six kilometers from here."

"Can you plot us a path between these obstacles?" Rasht asked.

"Easily."

It was still day, not even local noon. The sky was a pale blue, crisscrossed by high-altitude clouds. Beyond the blue, the face of the gas giant backdropped our view of the hill—one swollen, ugly thing rising above another. We set off in single file, Lenka leading, Rasht next, then the monkey, then I. We were all still on suit air, even though our helmet readouts were patiently informing us that the outside atmosphere was fully breathable, and (at the limit of our sensors) absent of any significant toxins. I watched the monkey's tail pendulum out from side to side as it walked. Bubbling pools pressed in from either side, our path narrowing down. Every now and then a geyser went off or a pool burped a huge bubble of gas into the air. Toxins or otherwise, it probably smelled quite badly out there. But then again, we were from the *Lachrimosa*, which was hardly a perfumed garden.

I had no warning when the ice gave way under me. It must have been just firm enough to take the others, but their passage—the weight of their heavy, power-assisted suits—had weakened it to the point where it could no longer support the last of us.

I plunged down to my neck in bubbling hot water, instinctively flinging out my arms as if swimming were a possibility. Then my feet touched bottom. Instantly my suit detected the transition to a new environment and began informing me of this sudden change of affairs—indices of temperature, acidity, alkalinity and salinity scrolling down my faceplate, along with mass spectrograms and molecular diagrams of chemical products. A tide of rust-coloured water lapped against the lower part of my visor.

I was startled, but not frightened. I was not totally under water, and the suit could cope with a lot worse than immersion in liquid.

But getting out was another thing.

"Don't try and pull me," I said, as Lenka made to lean in. "The shelf'll just give way under you, and then we'll both be in the water."

"Nidra's right," Rasht agreed, while the monkey looked on with a sort of agitated delight.

It was all very well warning Lenka away, but it only took a few minutes of frustration to establish that I could not get myself out unassisted. It was not a question of strength, but of having no firm point of leverage. The fringe of the pool was a crust of ice which gave away as soon as I tried to put any weight on it. All I was doing was expanding the margin of the pool.

Finally I stopped trying. "This won't work," I said. By then I was conscious that my arms were picking up the same sort of furry red contamination that had affected the monkey's paw.

"We'll need to haul her out," Rasht said. "It's the only way. With us on firm ground, it shouldn't be a problem. Lenka: you'll need to go back to the lander, get the power winch."

"There's a quicker way," Lenka said. "I saw a winch in the stores locker, on the wreck. It looked serviceable. If it's no good, it'll only cost me a little longer to fetch ours."

So Lenka went back to the crash site, detouring around the pool in which I was still trapped, then rejoining our original path. From my low vantage point, she was soon out of my line of sight. Rasht and the monkey kept an eye on me, the Captain silent for long minutes.

"You think this is a mistake," he said eventually.

"I don't like that hill, and I like the fact that Teterev didn't come out of it even less."

"We really don't know what happened to Teterev. For all we know she came back to the wreck and was eventually rescued."

"Then why didn't she say so, or take her journal with her?"

"We're going into the cave to find answers, Nidra. This is what we do—adapt and explore. Mazamel's intelligence proved faulty, so we make the best of what we find."

"You get the intelligence you pay for," I said. "There's a reason other ships never dealt with Mazamel."

"A little late for recrimination, don't you think? Of course, if you're unhappy with your choice of employment, you can always find another crew." I thought he might leave it at that, but Rasht added: 'I know how you feel about *Lachrimosa*, Nidra. Contempt for me, contempt for Lenka, contempt for your ship. It's different now though, isn't it? Without that winch, you'll be going nowhere."

"And without a navigator, you won't be going much further."

"You're wrong about that, though. I can use a navigator, just as I can use a sensor specialist like Lenka. But that doesn't mean I couldn't operate *Lachrimosa* on my own, if it came to that. You're useful, but you're not indispensable. Neither of you."

"Be sure to tell Lenka that, when she returns."

"No need. I've never had the slightest doubt about Lenka's loyalty. She's emotionally weak—all this stupid concern over Teterev. But she'll never turn on me."

"Can you be sure of that?"

"We've covered that ground, Lenka and I. She challenged my authority once, before you joined the crew. It didn't go well for her, and she learned from that experience."

I had difficulty imagining the meek, submissive Lenka ever rising to challenge Rasht. I wondered what had happened to change her.

The monkey gibbered. She was coming back.

The power winch was a tool about the size of a heavy vacuum rifle. Lenka carried it in two hands. We had similar equipment, so there was no question of working out how to use it.

The winch had a grapple attachment which could be fired with compressed gas. Lenka detached the grapple from the end of the line, and then looped the line back on itself to form a kind of handle or noose. The line was thin and flexible. Lenka spooled out a length from the power winch and then cast the noose in my direction. I waded over to the noose and took hold of it. Lenka made sure she was standing on firm ground, turned up her suit amplification, and began to drag me out with the winch. The line tightened, then began to take my weight. It was still an awkward business, but at last I was able to beach myself on the surrounding ice without floundering through. I crawled from the edge, belly down, until I felt confident enough to risk standing.

"Your suit's a mess," Rasht observed.

"I'll live. At least I didn't dip myself in it deliberately."

But my suit had indeed suffered some ill effects, as became apparent while we resumed our trek to the cave mouth. The life support core was intact—I was in no danger of dying—but my locomotive augmentation was not working as well as it was meant to. As had happened with the monkey's paw, the organisms in the pond seemed to have infiltrated the suit's servo-assist systems. I could still walk, but the suit's responses were sluggish, meaning that it was resisting me more than aiding me.

I began to sweat with the effort. It was hard to keep up with the others. Even the monkey had no problem with the rest of its suit.

"Thank you for getting the winch," I told Lenka, between breaths. "It was good that you remembered the one in the wreck. Any longer in that pond, and I might have had real problems."

"I'm glad we got you out."

Perhaps it was just the flush of gratitude at being rescued, but I vowed to think better of Lenka. She was senior to me on the crew, and yet Rasht seemed to value her capabilities no more than he did mine. Whatever I thought of her lack of ambition, her willing acceptance of her place on the ship, it struck me that she deserved better than that. Perhaps, when this was over, I could break it to her that she was considered no more than useful, like a component that would serve its purpose for the time being. That might change her view of things. I even imagined the two of us jumping ship at the next port, leaving Rasht with his monkey. Perhaps we could pass as sisters or twins, if we wanted new employment.

The terrain became firmer as we neared the hill, and we did not need to pick our course so carefully. The ground rose up slowly. There was still ice under our feet, and we were flanked on either side by the steadily widening lava tubes, which were already ten or fifteen times taller than any of us.

Ahead lay the cave mouth. Its profile was a semicircle, with the apex perhaps ten metres above the surface of the ice which extended into the darkness of the mouth. The hill rose up and up from the mouth, almost sheer in places, but there was an overhang above the entrance, covered in a sheath of smooth clean ice—the "beak" of Teterev's drawing.

The tongue of ice continued inside, curving down into what we could see of the cave's throat.

"Still no footsteps," Lenka said, as we neared the entrance.

That the ice occasionally melted and refroze was clear from the fringe of icicles daggering down from the overhang, some of them nearly long enough to reach the floor. Rasht shouldered through them, shattering the icicles against the armour of his suit. As their shards broke off, they made a tinkling, atonal sort of music.

Now Lenka said: "There are steps! This is the way she went!"

It was true. They did not begin until a few metres into the cave, where sunlight must have only reached occasionally, or not at all. There was only a single pair of footprints, and they only went one way.

"That's encouraging," I said.

"If you want to remain here," Rasht said, "we can exclude you from your cut of the profits."

So he had gone from denial of the Amerikano settlement, to a skeptical allowance of the possibility, to imagining how the dividend might be shared.

We turned on our helmet lights again—Rasht leaning down to activate the light on the monkey, which was too stupid to do it on its own. The monkey seemed more agitated than before, though. It was dragging its heels, coiling its tail, lingering after Rasht.

"It doesn't like it," Lenka said.

"Maybe it's smarter than it looks," I put in under my breath, which was about as much as I could manage with the effort of my ailing suit.

But I shared the monkey's dwindling enthusiasm. Who would really want to trudge into a cave, on an alien planet, if they had a choice in the matter? Teterev had gambled her salvation on finding relic technology, something that could buy her extra time in the wreck. We had no such compulsion, other than an indignant sense that we were owed our due after our earlier disappointment.

The angle of the slope pitched down steeply. The ice covered the floor, but the surrounding walls were exposed rock. We moved to the left side and used the grooved wall for support as we descended, placing our feet sideways. The monkey, still leashed to Rasht, had no choice but to continue. But its unwillingness was becoming steadily more apparent. Its gibbering turned shriller, more anxious.

"Now now, my dear," Rasht said.

The tunnel narrowed as it deepened. All traces of daylight were soon behind us. We maintained our faltering progress, following the trail that

Teterev had left for us. Once or twice, the prints became confused, as if there were suddenly three sets, rather than one. This puzzled me to begin with, until I realised that they marked instances of indecision, where Teterev had halted, reversed her progress, only to summon the courage to continue on her original heading.

I felt for Teterev.

"Something ahead," Rasht announced. "A glow, I think. Turn off your lights."

"The monkey first," I said.

"Naturally, Nidra."

When Rasht had quenched Kanto's light, the rest of us followed suit. Our Captain had been correct. Far from darkness ahead, there was a silvery emanation. It did not seem to come from a single point source, but rather from veins of some mineral running through the rock. If they had been present nearer the surface, we would probably not have seen them against the brighter illumination of daylight. But I did not think they had been present until now.

"I'm not a geologist," Lenka said, voicing the same thought that must have occurred to the rest of us. We had no idea what to make of the glowing veins, whether they were natural or suspicious.

Soon we did not need our helmet lights at all. Even with our eyes ramped down to normal sensitivity, there was more than enough brightness to be had from the veins. They shone out of the walls in bands and deltas and tributaries, a flowing form frozen in an instant of maximum hydrodynamic complexity. It did not look natural to me, but what did I know of such matters? I had seen the insides of more ships than worlds. Planets were full of odd, boring physics.

Eventually the slope became shallower, and then levelled out until our progress was horizontal. We were hundreds of metres from the entrance by now, and perhaps beneath the level of the surrounding terrain. It would have been wiser to send a drone, I thought. But patience had never been the Captain's strong point. Still, Teterev would not have had the luxury of a drone either. Thinking back to her journal, with its increasingly desperate, fragmentary entries, I could not shake the irrational sense that we would be letting her down if we did not follow her traces all the way in. I wondered if she had felt brave as she came down here, or instead afraid of the worse fate of dying alone in the wreck. I did not feel brave at all.

But we continued.

In time the tunnel widened out into a larger space. We paused in this rock-walled chamber, leaning back to study the patterning of the veins as they flowed and crawled and wiggled their way to the curving dome of the ceiling.

And saw things we should not have seen.

We should have turned back there and then, shouldn't we? If those figures weren't an invitation to leave, to never come back, I don't know what could have been clearer.

What do you mean, Teterev went on?

Of course she went on. She was out of options. No way off this planet unless she found something deeper in the cave, something she could use to wake up the orbiting ship. To go back to the wreck was to die, and so she knew she might as well continue.

I doubt she wanted to go on, no. If she had a sane bone in her body by that point, she'd have felt the way the rest of us did. Terrified. Scared out of her fucking skull. Every nerve screaming turn around, go back, this is wrong.

Wrong, wrong, wrong.

But she carried on. Brave Teterev, thinking of her son. Wanting to get back to him. Thinking of him more than her own survival, I think.

You say we were just the same? Just as brave?

Don't piss on her memory, Captain. The only thing driving us on was greed. Fucking greed. The only thing in the universe stronger than fear.

But even greed wasn't strong enough in the end.

The Last Log of the Lachrimosa | Alastair Reynolds

The silver veins looped and crossed each other, defining the outlines of looming forms. The forms were humanoid, with arms and legs and heads and bodies. They were skeletally thin and their torsos and limbs were twisted, almost as if the very substrate of the rock had shifted and oozed since these silvery impressions were made. Their heads were faceless, save for a kind of hemispheric delineation, a bilateral cleft suggesting a skull housing nothing but two huge eyes.

The strangeness of the figures—the combination of basic human form and alien particularity—disturbed me more than I could easily articulate. Monsters would have been unsettling, but they would not have plumbed the deep well of dread that these figures seemed to reach. The silver patterns appeared to shimmer and fluctuate in brightness, conveying an impression of subliminal movement. The figures, bent and faceless as they were, seemed to writhe in torment.

None of us could speak for long minutes. Even the monkey had fallen into dim simian reverence. I was just grateful for the opportunity to regather my strength, after the recent exertions.

"If that's not a warning to go," Lenka said. "I don't know what is."

"I want to know what happened to her," I said. "But not at any cost. We don't have to go on."

"Of course we go on!" Rasht said. "These are just markings."

But there was an edge in his voice, a kind of questioning rise, as if he sought reassurance and confirmation.

"They could almost be prehuman," I said, wondering how we might go about dating the age of these impressions, if such a thing were even possible.

"Pre-Shrouder, maybe," Lenka said. "Pre-Juggler. Who knows? What we really need is measuring equipment, sampling gear. Get a reading off these rocks, find out what that silver stuff really is."

By which she meant, return to the ship in the meantime. It was a sentiment I shared.

"Teterev went on," Rasht said.

Her prints were a muddle, as if she had dwelled here for quite some time, pacing back and forth and debating her choices. But after that process of consideration she had carried on deeper into the tunnel, where it continued beyond the chamber.

By now the monkey almost needed to be dragged or carried. It really did not want to go on.

Even my own dread was becoming harder to push aside. There was a component to it beyond the instinctive dislike of confined spaces and the understandable reaction to the figures. A kind of unarguable, primal urge to leave—as if some deep part of my brain had already made its mind up.

"Do you feel it?" I risked asking.

"Feel what?" Rasht asked.

"The dread."

The Captain did not answer immediately, and I feared that I had done my standing even more harm than when I questioned his judgement. But Lenka swallowed hard and said: "Yes. I didn't want to say anything, but… yes. I've been wondering about that. It's beyond any rational fear we ought to be experiencing." She paused and added: "I think something is *making* us feel that dread."

"Making?" Rasht echoed.

"The magnetic fields, perhaps. It's strong here—much stronger than outside. What we saw before was just leakage. Our suits aren't perfect Faraday cages, not with all the damage and repair they've had over the years. They can't exclude a sufficiently strong field, not completely. And if the field acts on the right part of our brains, we might feel it. Fear, dread. A sense of the unnatural."

"Then it's a defense mechanism," Rasht said. "A deterrent device, to keep out intruders."

"Then we might think of heeding it," I said.

"It could also mean there is something worth guarding."

"The Amerikanos never had psychological technology like this," Lenka said.

"But others did. Do I need to spell it out? What did we come to this system for? It wasn't because we thought we'd find Amerikano relics. We were after a bigger reward than that."

My dread sharpened. I could see where this was going. "We have no evidence that Conjoiners were here either."

"They say the spiders liked to place their toys in caches," Rasht went on, as if my words counted for nothing. "C-drives. Hell-class weapons."

Despite myself I laughed. "I thought we based our activities on intelligence, not fairy tales."

"I heard someone already found those weapons," Lenka said, as if that was all the convincing Rasht would need.

But his voice turned low, conspiratorial—as if there was a chance of the walls listening in. "I heard fear was one of their counter-intrusion measures. The weapons get into your skull, turn you insane, if you're not already spidered."

I knew then that nothing, not even dread, would deter Rasht from his quest for profit. He would replace one phantom prize with another, over and over, until reality finally trumped him.

"We have come this far," Rasht said. "We may as well go a little deeper."

"A little," I said, against every rational instinct. "No further than we've already come."

We pushed out of the chamber, Lenka setting the pace, following Teterev's course down another rock-walled tunnel. To begin with, the going was no harder than before. But as the tunnel progressed, so the walls began to pinch together. Now we had to move in single file, whether we liked it or not. Then Lenka announced that the walls squeezed together even more sharply just ahead, as if there had been a rockfall or a major shift in the hill's interior structure.

"That's a shame," I said.

"We could blast it," Lenka said. "Set a couple of hot-dust charges at maximum delay, get back to the ship." She was already preparing to unclip one of the demolition charges from her belt.

"And bring down half the mountain in the process," I said. "Lose the tunnel, the chamber, Teterev's prints, probably blast to atoms whatever we're hoping to find."

"Her prints don't double back," Rasht said. "That means there must be a way through."

"Or this obstruction wasn't here," I answered.

But there was a way through. It was difficult to see at first, efficiently camouflaged by the play of light and shadow on the rock, almost as if it meant to hide itself. "It's tight," Lenka said. "But one at a time, we should manage. With luck, it'll open up again on the other side."

"And luck's been so kind to us until now," I said.

Lenka was the first through. It was tight for her, and would be even tighter for Rasht, whose suit was bulkier. She grunted with effort and concentration. Her suit scraped rock.

"Careful!" Rasht called.

Now most of Lenka was out of our sight, swallowed into the cleft. "It's easier," she said. "Widens out again. Just a bottleneck. I can see Teterev's footprints."

Rasht and the monkey next. I could see that the monkey was going to take some persuasion. To begin with it would not go first, ahead of its master. Rasht swore at Kanto and went on himself, his suit grinding and clanging against the pincering rock. I wondered if it was even possible for Rasht to make it through. He could have discarded the suit, of course—put up with the cold, for the sake of his treasure. I had known the Captain endure worse, when there was a sniff of payoff.

Yet he called: "I'm through."

Kanto was still on the leash, which was now tight against the edge of the rock. The monkey really did not want to rejoin the Captain. I felt a glimmer of cross-species empathy. Perhaps the magnetic emanations were affecting it more strongly than the rest of us, reaching deeper into the poor animal's fear centre.

Still, the monkey did not have much say in its fate. Rasht pulled on the leash, and I pushed it through from the other side. I needed the maximum amplification of my struggling suit. The monkey would have bitten my face off given half the chance, but its teeth were on the wrong side of its visor.

Reunited, our little party continued into the tunnel system.

But we had only gone a hundred metres or more when the path branched. There were three possible directions ahead of us, and a mess of footprints at the junction.

"Looks as if she went down all three shafts," Lenka said.

Only one set of prints had led to this point, so Teterev must not have returned from one of those tunnels. But it was hard to say which. The prints were confused now. She must have gone up and down the shafts several times, changing her mind, returning. Given the state of the prints, there was no way of saying which had been her ultimate choice.

We selected the leftmost shaft and carried on down it. It sloped a little more, and eventually the ice under our feet gave way to solid rock, meaning that we no longer had Teterev's prints as a guide. All around us the silver patterning continued, streaks and fissures of it, jetstreams and knotted synaptic tangles. It was hard not to think of a living silver nervous system, threading its way through the stone matrix of this ancient mountain.

"Your suit, Lenka," Rasht said.

She slowed. "What about it?"

"You've picked up some of that patterning. The silver. It must have rubbed off when you squeezed through the narrowing."

"It's also on you," I told the Captain.

It only took a glance to confirm that it was on me and the monkey as well. A smear of silver had attached itself to my right elbow, where I must have brushed against the wall. Doubtless there was more, out of sight.

I moved to touch the silver, to dust it from myself. But when my fingers touched it, its contamination seemed to jerk onto them. The movement was startling and quick, like the strike of an ambush predator. I stared at my hand, cross-webbed by streaks of gently pulsing silver. I clenched and opened my fist. My suit was as stiff as it had been since my accident outside, but for the moment it did not seem to be affected by the silver.

"It's nanotech," I said. "Nothing the suit recognises. But I don't like it."

"If it was hostile, you'd know it by now," Rasht said. "We push on. Just a little further."

But turning around there and then is exactly what we should have done. It might have made all the difference.

The next chamber was a palace of horrors.

It was as large as the earlier place, the shape similar, and a tunnel led out from it as well. But there all similarities ended. Here the tormented human forms were not confined to figures marked on the walls. These were solid shapes, three dimensional evocations of distorted and contorted human anatomies, thrusting out of the wall like the broken and bent figureheads of shipwrecks. They seemed to be formed not of rock, or the silver contamination, but some amalgam of the two, a kind of shimmering, glinting substrate. There were ribcages and torsos, grasping hands, heads snapped back in agonies of perfect torment. They were not quite faceless, but by the same token none of the faces were right. They were all eyes, or all mouths, hinged open to obscene angles, or they were anvil-shaped nightmares that seemed to have cleaved their way through the rock itself. I was struck by a dreadful conviction that these were souls that had been entirely in the rock, imprisoned or contained, until an instant when they had nearly broken through. And I did not know whether to be glad that these souls were not quite free, or sick with terror that the rock might yet contain multitudes, still seeking escape.

"I hate this place," Lenka said quietly.

I nodded my agreement. "So do I."

And all of a sudden, Lenka's earlier idea of setting a demolition charge did not seem so bad to me at all. The mere existence of this chamber struck me as profoundly, upsettingly wrong, as if it were my moral duty to remove it from the universe.

The charges at maximum delay. Time to get back to the ship, if we rushed, and none of us got stuck in the squeeze point.

Maybe. Maybe not.

That was when the monkey broke free.

※

So, anyway. About what we've done to your suit.

Its basic motor systems were already compromised when I found you near the cave mouth. You'd got that far, which can't have been easy.

Yes, well done you.

Brave Captain.

The Last Log of the Lachrimosa | ALASTAIR REYNOLDS

The nanotech contamination, the traces you picked up from the cave wall, was clearly the main cause of the systemic failure. Obviously, if you'd stayed any longer, your suit would have begun to turn against you, the way it happened with Teterev. Allowing itself to be controlled, absorbed. But you still had some control over it, and enough strength to overcome the resistance of the jammed locomotive systems.

It was never as bad for me. I think when I fell in that pool, some of the native organisms must have formed a barrier layer, a kind of insulation against the nanotech. Perhaps they've had time to begin to evolve their own defense measures, to contain the spread of it. Who knows? My good fortune, in any case.

It didn't feel like good fortune at the time, but that's the universe for you.

Anyway, back to your suit.

You're already paralyzed, effectively, but just to make sure that the systems don't begin to recover, I've opened your main control box and disabled all locomotive power. Locked it tight, in fact. You might as well be standing in a welded suit of armour, for all the success you'll have in moving.

Why are your arms the way they are?

We'll come to that.

You are standing, yes. Your feet are on the ground. Obviously, with the noose around your neck, the one thing you don't want to do now is topple over. I won't be there to catch you. But your suit is heavy and provided you don't wriggle around inside it too much, you should stay upright.

Of course, if you don't want to stay upright, that's one way out of this for you. You're cold?

I'm not surprised! It's a cold planet, and you're not wearing a space helmet. Be a bit difficult, slipping a noose around your neck, if you were still wearing your helmet!

Fine, you want some more heat? That's easy. Your life-support systems are still good, and you can adjust the suit temperature. The reason your arms are positioned in front of you the way they are, is that I want you to be able to operate your cuff control. That's right. You can do that. You can move your fingers, tap those buttons.

Here's the thing, though. There's only one thing you can do with those buttons. Only one system you can control.

You can turn up your suit temperature, or you can turn it down.
That's all.
Why?
The why is easy. You remember those pieces of the wreck I went to so much trouble to position around you?
There was a point to all that.
There's a point to you.

I suppose the terror was too much for Kanto, and that the passage through the narrowing had weakened his leash. Whatever the case, the monkey was out of the chamber, gibbering and shrieking, as it headed back the way we had come.

None of us had spoken until that moment. The chamber had struck us into a thunderous, paralyzing silence. Even when Kanto left, we said nothing. Any utterance would have felt like an invitation, permission for something worse than these stone ghouls to emerge from the walls.

Lenka and I looked at each other through our visors. Our eyes met, and we nodded. Then we looked at Rasht, both of us in turn, and Rasht looked as frightened as we felt.

Lenka went first, then Rasht, then I. We moved as quickly as our suits allowed. But even though none of us felt like lingering, I was no longer having to work as hard to keep up with the other two. My suit still felt sluggish, but it had not worsened since I came into contact with the silver contamination. Lenka and Rasht, though, were not moving as efficiently as before.

I still could not bring myself to speak, not until we were well away from that place. If the monkey had any sense, it was already through the narrowing, on its way back to daylight.

But when we reached the junction, the intersection of four tunnels, Rasht made us halt.

"Kanto's taken the wrong one," he said.

In the chaos of footprints, there was no chance at all of picking out the individual trace of the monkey. I was about to say as much when Rasht spoke again.

"I have a trace on his suit. In case he…escaped." The word seemed distasteful to him, as if it clarified an aspect of their relationship best kept hidden. "He should be ahead of us now, but he isn't. He's behind again. Down this shaft, I think." Rasht was indicating the rightmost entrance of the three we had faced on our way in. "It's hard to know."

Lenka said in a low voice: "Then we have to leave. Kanto will find his own way out, once he knows he's gone the wrong way."

"She's right," I said.

"We can't leave him," Rasht said. "We won't. I won't allow it."

"If the monkey doesn't want to be found," I said, "nothing we do is going to make any difference."

"The fix isn't moving. I have a distance estimate. It isn't more than twenty or thirty metres down that tunnel."

"Or that one," I said, nodding to the middle shaft. "Or your fix is wrong, and he's ahead of us anyway. For all we know, the magnetic field is screwing up your tracker."

"He isn't behind us," Rasht said, doggedly ignoring me. "There are really only two possibilities. We can check them quickly, three of us. Eliminate the wrong shaft."

Lenka's own breathing was now as heavy as my own. I caught another glimpse of her face, eyes wide with apprehension. "I know he means a lot to you, Captain…"

"Is there something wrong with your suits?" I asked.

"Yes," Lenka said. "Mine, anyway. Losing locomotive assist. Same as happened to you."

"I'm not sure it's the same thing. I fell in the pool, you didn't. Can you still move?"

Lenka lifted up an arm, clenched and unclenched her hand. "For the time being. If it gets too bad, I can always go full manual." Then she closed her eyes, took a deep breath, and reopened them. "All right, *Captain*." This with a particular sarcastic emphasis. "I'll check out the middle tunnel, if it'll help. I'll go thirty metres, no more, and turn around. You can check out the one on your right, if you think Kanto's gone that way. Nidra can wait here, just in case Kanto's gone ahead of us and turns back."

I did not like the idea of spending ten more seconds in this place, let alone the time it would take to inspect the tunnels. But Lenka's suggestion made the best of a bad situation. It would appease the Captain and not delay us more than a few minutes.

"All right," I agreed. "I'll wait here. But don't count on me catching Kanto if he comes back."

"Stay where you are, my dear," Rasht said, addressing the monkey wherever it might be. "We are coming."

Lenka and Rasht disappeared into their respective tunnels, their suits moving with visible sluggishness. Lenka, whose suit was more lightly armoured, would find it easier to cope than Rasht. I speculated to myself that the silver contamination was indeed having some effect, but that my exposure to the pond's micro-organisms had provided a barriering layer, a kind of inoculation. It was not much of a theory, but I had nothing better to offer.

I counted a minute, then two.

Then heard: "Nidra."

"Yes," I said. "I hear you, Lenka. Have you found the monkey?"

There was a silence that ate centuries. My own fear was now as sharp and clean and precise as a surgical instrument. I could feel every cruel edge of it, cutting me open from inside.

"Help me."

⇥✶⇤

You came back then. You'd found your stupid fucking monkey. You were cradling it, holding it to you like it was the most precious thing in your universe.

Actually I do the monkey a disservice.

As stupid as he was, Kanto was innocent in all this. I thought he was dead to begin with, but then I realised that it was trembling, caught in a state of infant terror, clinging to the fixed certainty of you while he shivered in its armour.

I made out his close-set yellow eyes, wide and uncomprehending.

The Last Log of the Lachrimosa | ALASTAIR REYNOLDS

I loathed your fucking monkey. But there was nothing that deserved that sort of terror.

Do you remember how our conversation played out? I told you that Lenka was in trouble. Your loyal crewmember, good, dependable Lenka. Always there for you. Always there for the Lachrimosa. No matter what had happened until that point, there was now only one imperative. We had to save her. This is what Ultras do. When one of us falls, we reach. We're better than people think.

But not you.

The fear had finally worked its way into you. I was wrong about greed being stronger. Or rather, there are degrees. Greed trumps fear, but then a deeper fear trumps greed all over again.

I pleaded with you.

But you would not answer her call. You left with Kanto, hobbling your way back to safety.

You left me to find Lenka.

⇥❘⇤

I did not have to go much further down the tunnel and reached the thing blocking further progress. It had trapped Lenka, but she was not yet fully part of it. Teterev had come earlier—many years ago—so her degree of integration was much more pronounced. I could judge this in a glance, even before I had any deeper understanding of what I had found. I knew that Lenka would succumb to Teterev's fate, and that if I remained in this place I would eventually join them.

"Come closer, Nidra," a voice said.

I stepped nearer, hardly daring to bring the full blaze of my helmet light to bear on the half-sensed obstruction ahead of me.

"I've come for Lenka. Whatever you are, whatever's happened to you, let her go."

"We'll speak of Lenka." The voice was loud, booming across the air between us. "But do come closer."

"I don't think so."

"Because you are frightened?"

"Yes."

"Then I am very glad to hear it. Fear is the point of this place. Fear is the last and best thing that we have."

"We?"

"My predecessors and I. Those who came before me, the wayfarers and the lost. We've been coming for a very long time. Century after century, across hundreds of thousands of years. Unthinkable ages of galactic time. Drawn to this one place, and repelled by it—as you nearly were."

"I wish we had been."

"And usually the fear is sufficient. They turn back before they get this deep, as you nearly did. As you *should* have done. But you were braver than most. I'm sorry that your courage carried you as far as it did."

"It wasn't courage." But then I added: "How do you know my name?"

"I listened to your language, from the moment you entered me. You are very noisy! You gibber and shriek and make no sense whatsoever."

"Are you Teterev?"

"That is not easily answered. I remember Teterev, and I feel her distinctiveness quite strongly. Sometimes I speak through her, sometimes she speaks through us. We have all enjoyed what Teterev has brought to us."

I had never met Teterev, never seen an image of her, but there were only two human figures before me and one of them was Lenka, jammed into immobility, strands of silver beginning to wrap and bind her suit as if in the early stages of mummification. The strands extended back to the larger form of which Teterev was only an embellishment.

She must still have been wearing her suit when she was trapped and bound. Traces of the suit remained, but much of it had been picked off her, detached or dissolved or remade into the larger mass. Her helmet, similar in design to the one we had seen in the wreck, had fissured in two, with its halves framing her head.

I thought of flytrap mouthparts, Teterev's head an insect. Her face was stony and unmoving, her eyes blank surfaces, but there was no hint of ageing or decay. Her skin had the pearly shimmer of the figures we had seen in the second chamber. She had become—or was becoming—something other than flesh.

But apart from Teterev—and Lenka, if you included her—none of the other forms were human. The blockage was an assemblage of fused shapes, creature after creature absorbed into a sort of interlocking stone puzzle, a jigsaw of jumbled anatomies and half-implied life-support technologies. Two or three of the creatures were loosely humanoid, in so far as their forms could be discerned. But it was hard to gauge where their suits and life-support mechanisms ended and their alien anatomies commenced. Vines and tendrils of silver smothered them from head to foot, binding them into the older layers of the mass. Beyond these recognisable forms lay the evidence of many stranger anatomies and technologies.

"I've heard of a plague," I said, making my way to Lenka. "They say it's all just rumour, but I don't know. Is this what happened to you?"

"There are a million plagues, some worse than others. Some *much* worse." There was an edge of playfulness in the voice, taking droll amusement in my ignorance. "No: what you see here is deliberate, done for our mutual benefit. Haphazard, yes, but organised for a purpose. Think of it as a form of defense."

"Against the outside world?" I had my hands on her suit now, and I tried to rip the silver strands away from it, while at the same time applying as much force as I could to drag Lenka back to safety.

The voice said: "Nothing like that. I am a barrier against the thing that would damage the outside world, were it to be released."

"Then I don't understand." I caught my breath, already drained by the effort of trying to free her. "Is Lenka going to become part of you? Is that the idea?"

"Would you sooner offer yourself? Is that what you would like?"

"I'd like you to let Lenka go." Realising I was getting nowhere—the strands reattached themselves as quickly I peeled them away—I could only step back and take stock. "She came back here to find the monkey, not to hurt you. None of us came to harm you. We just wanted to know what had happened to Teterev."

"So Teterev was the beginning and end of your concerns? You had no other interest in this place?"

"We wondered what was in the cave," I answered, seeing no value in lying, even if I thought I might have got away with it. "We thought there might be Amerikano relics, maybe a Conjoiner cache. We picked up the geomagnetic anomaly. Are you making that happen? If so, you can't blame us for noticing it. If you don't want visitors, try making yourself less visible!"

"I would, if it were within my means. Shall I tell you something of me, Nidra? Then we will speak of Lenka."

⋇

Shall I tell you what I learned from her, Captain? Will that take your mind off the cold, for a little while?

You may as well hear it. It will put things into perspective. Make you understand your place in things—the value in your being here. The good and selfless service you are about to commence.

She was a traveller, too.

Not Teterev, but the original one—the first being, the first entity, to find this planet. A spacefarer. Admittedly this was all quite a long time ago. She tried to get me to understand, but I'm not sure I have the imagination. Whole galactic turns ago, she said. When some of the stars we see now were not even born, and the old ones were younger. When the universe itself was smaller than it is now. Young galaxies crowding each other's heavens.

I don't know if it was her, an effect of the magnetic field, or just my fears affecting my sense of self. But as she spoke of abyssal time, I felt a lurch of cosmic vertigo, a sense that I stood on the crumbling brink of time's plunging depths.

I didn't want to fall, didn't want to topple.

Sensible advice for both of us, wouldn't you say?

The universe always feels old, though. That's a universal truth, a universal fact of life. It felt old for her, already cobwebbed by history. Hard for us to grasp, I know. Human civilisation, it's just the last scratch on the last scratch on the last scratch, on the last layer of everything. We're noise. Dirt. We haven't begun to leave a trace.

But for her, so much had already happened! There had still been time enough for the rise and fall of numberless species and civilisations, time for great deeds and greater atrocities. Time for monsters and the rumours of worse.

She had been journeying for lifetimes, by the long measure of her species. Travelling close to light, visiting world after world.

If we had a name for what she was, we'd call her an archaeologist, a scholar drawn to relics and scraps.

Still following me?

One day—one unrecorded century—she stumbles upon something. It was a thing she'd half hoped to find, half hoped to avoid. Glory and annihilation, balanced on a knife edge.

We know all about that, don't we?

Your finger is moving. Are you trying to adjust that temperature setting? Go ahead. Turn up your suit. I won't stop you.

There. Better already. Can you feel the warmth flowing up from your neck ring, taking the sting out of the cold? It feels better, doesn't it? There's plenty of power in the suit. You needn't worry about draining it. Make yourself as warm as you wish.

Look, I didn't say there wasn't a catch.

Turn it down, then. Let the cold return. Can you feel those skin cells dying, the frostbite eating its way into your face? Can you feel your eyeballs starting to freeze?

Back to our traveller.

We have rumours of plague. She had rumours of something far worse. A presence, an entity, waiting between the stars. Older than the history of any culture known to her kind. A kind of mechanism, waiting to detect the emergence of bright and busy civilisations such as hers. Or ours, for that matter.

Something with a mind and a purpose.

And she found it.

※

"I've no reason to think you haven't already killed Lenka," I said, a kind of desperate calm overcoming me, when I realised how narrow my options really were.

"Oh, she is perfectly well," the voice answered. "Her suit is frozen, and I have pushed channels of myself into her head, to better learn her usefulness. There is some damage in there, but it is nothing I have caused. Old damage—something that was done to her once, and not put right."

"Damage?" I asked.

"You would need to ask her how it happened."

How it happened, maybe. But who? I knew that I did not need to ask Lenka that at all. I already knew. She had challenged his authority, and it had not gone well for her.

Whatever damage had been done, Rasht had done it. Broken her will—left her as willing and pliant as I had always known her. Loyalty by surgery, as crude as it came.

I had no idea if she could hear me or not. But I had to speak. "I'm sorry, Lenka. Sorry that I thought badly of you. You had no choice. He broke you."

"She is not broken, Nidra—just damaged. But she has travelled well, this Lenka. I can still learn a great deal from her."

I waited a beat.

"Are you strong?"

"That *is* an odd question."

"Not really." I reached beneath my chest pack, fumbling with my equipment belt until I found the hard casing of a demolition charge. I unclipped the grenade-sized device, presenting it before me like an offering. "Hot dust. Have you dug deep enough into Lenka to know what that means?"

"No, but Teterev knew."

"That's good. And what did Teterev know?"

"That you have a matter-antimatter device."

"That's right."

"And the yield would be…?"

"A couple of kilotonnes. Very small, really. Barely enough to chip an asteroid in two. Of course, I have no idea of the damage it would do to you."

I used two hands to twist the charge open along its midline, exposing its triggering system. The trigger was a gleaming red disk. I settled my thumb over the disk, thinking of the tiny, pollen-sized speck of antimatter held in a flawness vacuum at the heart of the demolition charge.

"Suicide, Nidra? Surely there's a time-delay option."

"There is, but I'm not sure I'd be able to get to my ship in time. Besides, I don't know what you'd do with me gone. If you can paralyse Lenka's suit, you can probably work your way into the charge and disarm it."

"You would kill Lenka at the same time."

"Not if you let her go. And if you don't let her go, this has to be a kinder way out than being sucked into you." I allowed my thumb to rub back and forth over the trigger, only a twitch away from activating it. There was an unsettling temptation to *just do it*. The light would be quick and painless, negating the past and future in a single cleansing flash.

In that moment I wanted it.

⇥⚹⇤

What would you have done, Captain?

Her mistake?

That's easy. The thing she found, in the wreck of another ship, seemed dead to her. Dead and exhausted. Just a cluster of black cubes, lodged in the ship's structure like the remnant of an infection. But it had not spread; it had not destroyed the wreck or achieved total transformation into a larger mass. She thought it was dead. She had no reason to think otherwise.

Can we blame her for that?

Not me.

Not you.

But the machinery was only dormant. When her ship was underway, while she slept, the black cubes began to show signs of life. They swelled, testing the limits of her containment measures. Her ship woke her up, asking what it should do. Her ship was almost a living thing in its own right. It was worried for her, worried for itself.

She had no answer.

She tried to strengthen the fields and layer the alien machinery in more armour. None of that worked. The forms broke through, began to eat her ship—making more cubes. She put more energy into her containment. What else could she do?

Throw them overboard, you wonder?

Well, yes. She considered something like that. But that would only be passing the problem on to some other traveller. The responsibility was hers alone. She felt quite strongly about that.

Still, the machinery was definitely damaged. She was sure of that. Otherwise the transformation would have been fast and unstoppable. Instead, she had achieved a sort of stalemate.

What next?

Suicide, perhaps—dive into a star. But the data offered no guarantees that this would be enough to destroy the machinery. It might make it stronger!

Not a chance she could take.

So instead she found this world. A ship in space is an easy thing to see, even across light years. A world offers better camouflage—it has mass and heat. She thought she could screen herself—drawing no attention from passers-by.

She was wrong.

The cubes were resilient, resourceful. Constantly testing her capabilities. They demanded more power, more mass. She converted more and more of her ship into the architecture of their prison. She died! But by then her living ship had grown to know her so well that her personality lived on inside it, haunting it as a kind of ghost.

Centuries blasted by.

Her ship protected and enlarged itself. It ate into the surrounding geology, bolstering the containment and consolidating its defenses. For the most part it had no need of her, this residue of what she had been. Once in a while it raised her from the shadows, when her judgement was required. She was never lonely. She'd burned through her capacity for loneliness, discarding it like an outmoded evolutionary stage.

But she had visitors, all the same.

Like us?

No, not quite. Not to begin with. To begin with they were just like her.

"They came," the voice said. "My sensors tracked them with great vigilance and stealth. I watched them, wary of their intentions. I risked collapsing my containment fields, until they were out of range. I did not want to be found. I did not want my mistake to become theirs. It was always a bad time." It paused. "But I did not miss their company. They were not like me. Their languages and customs had turned unfamiliar. I was never sorry when they turned for space and left me undisturbed."

"I don't believe you."

"Believe what you like. It hardly matters, anyway. They stopped coming. A silence fell, and endured. It was broken only by the tick of pulsars and the crack and whistle of quasars halfway to the universe's edge. There were no more of my kind. I had no knowledge of what had become of them."

"But you could guess."

"It did not mean that I could give up, and allow what I had found to escape. So I slept—or ceased to be, until my ship had need of me again—and the stars lurched to new and nameless constellations. Twenty million orbits of my old world, two hundred thousand lifetimes. And then a new visitor—a new species."

I guessed that we were still in the distant past.

"Did you know this culture?"

"I had no data on anything like them, dead or alive. Frankly, it disturbed me. It had too many limbs, a strange way of moving, and I wondered what it looked like outside of its armour. I wanted it to go away. I quietened myself, damped my energies. But still it came. It dug into me, seeking an explanation for whatever its sensors had picked up. I thought of simply killing it—it had come alone, after all. But there was another possibility open to me. I could take it, open its mind, learn from it. Fold its memories and personality into my own. Use its knowledge to better protect myself the next time." A kind of shame or regretfulness entered the voice. "So that is what I did. I caught the alien, made sure it was incapable of escape, and pushed feelers through the integument of its suit and into its nervous system. Its anatomy was profoundly unfamiliar to me. But at one end of its segmented, exoskeletal body was a thing like a head and inside the brittle cage of that head was a dense mass of connected cells that had something of the topological complexity of what had once been my own brain. It was hierarchically layered, with clear modular specialisation for sensory processing, motor control, abstract reasoning and memory management. It was also trying very hard to communicate with its fellows—wherever *they* were—and that made it easy for me to trace the circuits and pathways of expression. Before long, I was able to address the alien through the direct manipulation of internal mental states. And I explained what was to become of it. Together we would be stronger, better equipped both to deal with the thing at the heart of me, and also to make my concealment more effective. I was sorry about what had needed to be done, but I made it understand that I had no choice at all."

"How did it take it?"

"How do you *think*, Nidra? But very soon the question concerned neither of us. It had become me, I had become it. Our memories were a knot of entanglements. It understood my concerns. It grasped that there had only ever been one path. It knew that we had no choice about what we had become."

"Forgiveness?"

"Acceptance."

"But it didn't end, did it? There were more. Always more. Other species...dozens, hundreds of them. Until we came!"

"You are no different."

"Perhaps we aren't. But this alters things, doesn't it?" I still had my thumb on the trigger, ready to unleash a matter-antimatter conflagration. "You think I won't do this? You've told me what you are. I understand that you acted...that you've *been* acting...for what you think is the common good. Maybe you're right, too. But enough is enough. You have Teterev. It's too late for her...too late for you, if I'm still reaching a part of her. But it stops with Lenka. She's mine. She's coming back with me."

"I need her. I need to add her library of fears to my own. I need to make myself stronger."

"It won't work. It hasn't *been* working. You're stuck in a spiral...a destructive feedback loop. The more you try to make yourself impregnable, the more *evident* you become to the outside world. So you have to make yourself yet more impregnable...add to your library of fears. But it can't continue."

"It must."

"I tried to stop myself. But always they came. New travellers, new species. Nothing I did made myself invisible to them. I could not *negotiate*, I could not *persuade*, because that would have been tantamount to confessing the hard fact of my existence. So I did what I had always done. I hid. I made myself as quiet and silent as physics allowed, and willed them to leave. I dug into our mutual psychologies, trawled the ocean of our terrors, and from that sea of fears I shaped the phantasms that I hoped would serve as deterrence, encouraging newcomers to come no nearer. But it was never totally sufficient. Some were always too brave, or curious, and by force of will they reached the heart of me. And always I had no choice but to *take*, to *incorporate*, to turn them to my cause. To feed me their fears, so that I might better my defenses. Why do you think I had to take Teterev? She was the first of your kind—a new jewel, to place in my collection. She had been very useful, has Teterev. We are all very glad of her. Her fears are like a new colour, a new smell. We never imagined such things!"

"Good. I'm truly sorry for Teterev. But you don't need Lenka. Give her back control of her suit, and we'll leave you alone."

"You could make that promise to me. But you did not come here alone."

"The Captain...we'll take care of him."

See? Thinking of you even then.
Always in our hearts and minds.

"I listened to your babble. The theories of your Captain. He craves his fortune. He will think he can turn the *fact* of me to profit. He will try to sell the knowledge of my location."

"He doesn't even know what you are!"

"But he will find out. He will ask what became of you, what became of Lenka. Your silence will count for nothing. He *will* return. He will send machines into me. And soon more will come, in other ships, and I am bound to fail. When the machines touch your civilisation, they will scorch you into history. They have done it a thousand times, with a thousand cultures. They will leave dust and ruins and silence, and you will *not* be the last."

"Lev," I said quietly.

There was a silence. I wondered if the thing before me would speak again. Perhaps I had shut the door of communication between us with that one invocation.

But the voice asked: "What do you know of Lev?"

"Your son," I answered. "The son of part of you, the son of Teterev. You had to leave him on the orbiting ship. You didn't mean to, but it must have been the only way. You loved him. You wanted very badly to get a message to him, to have him help you. That's why you came as far as you did. But you failed."

"And Lev is gone."

I nodded. "But not in the way you think. Someone got to that ship before us—cleaned it out. Stripped it of engines, weps, crew. The frozen. But they'd have been valuable to someone. If Lev was on that ship, he'd have made it back to one of the settled worlds by now. And we can find him. The Mendicants trade in the frozen, and we have traded with the Mendicants, in many systems. There are channels, lines of enquiry. The name of your ship…"

"What would it be to you?"

"Give us that name. Let us find Lev. I'll return. I promise you that much."

"No one ever promises to *return*, Nidra. They promise to stay away."

"The name of the ship," I said again.

She told me.

※

So many names, so many ships. Numberless. Names too strange to put into language, at least no language that would fit into our heads. Names like clouds. Names like forests. Names like ever unfolding mathematical structures—names that begat themselves, in dreams of recursion. Names that split the world in two. Names that would drive a nail through your sanity.

The Last Log of the Lachrimosa | Alastair Reynolds

But she told me some of them, as best as she could.

Lovely names. Names of such beauty and terror they made me weep. The hopes and fears of the brave and the lost. The best and the worst of all of us. All wayfarers, all travellers.

I asked her to try and remember the last of them.

She did.

Tell you?

Not a chance, Captain. You don't get to know everything.

⁂

I stepped back from his suited-but-immobile form, admiring my handiwork. He really did look sculptural, frozen into that oddly dignified posture, with his arms coming together across his chest, one hand touching the cuff of the other.

"I suppose you could say that we came to an understanding, Teterev and I," I said. "Or what Teterev had become. Partly it was fear, I think, that I'd use the hot-dust. Did I come close? Yes, definitely. Not much to lose at that point. I might have been able to work the ship without you, but certainly not without Lenka. If she didn't survive, there wasn't much point in me surviving either. But Lenka was allowed to leave, and so was I. It was hard work, getting Lenka back here. But she's begun to regain some suit function now, and I don't think either of us will have any trouble returning to the lander."

The Captain tried to speak. It was hard, with the noose tight around his throat. He could breathe, but anything more was an effort.

He rasped out three words that might have been "fuck you, Nidra". But I could not be sure.

"I made a commitment to Teterev," I carried on. "Firstly, that we'd make sure you were not a problem. Secondly, that I'd do what I could to find Lev. If that takes decades, longer, so be it. It's something to live for, anyway. A purpose. We all need a purpose, don't we?"

He attempted another set of syllables.

"Here's yours," I said. "Your purpose is to die here. It *will* happen. How fast it happens, is in your hands. Quite literally. Those pieces of debris I set around you are curved mirrors. Now, it's not an exact science. But when the sun climbs, some of them will concentrate the sun's light on the snow and ice on which you are standing. It will begin to melt. The tension on your noose will increase." I paused, allowing that part to sink in, if he had not already deduced matters for himself. "In any case, the ice will melt eventually, as the days go on. It's only permafrost deeper in the cave mouth, and we're moving into warmer months. But you'll be dead by then. It'll be a nasty, slow death, though. Hypothermia, frostbite, slow choking— take your pick. But you can speed it up, if you like. Turn up your suit's heat, and you can stay as warm as you like. The downside is that the heat will spill away from your suit and melt the ice even quicker. You'll be hanging by your neck within hours, with the entire weight of your suit trying to rip your skull from your spine. At that point, overwhelmed by terror and pain, you might try and turn down the thermal regulation again. But by then you might not be able to move your fingers. Ultimately, it doesn't matter. There are many paths to the one goal. All the scenarios end with your corpse hanging from the mouth of the cave. Swinging there until the ice returns. You'll make an effective deterrent, wouldn't you say? A tolerable invitation to keep away?"

Rasht tried to say something. But Lenka, who had hobbled closer, placed a finger on his lips.

Something had changed in Lenka since her return from the cave. If the thing in the cave has the means to sense the damage in her head, I wondered, could it also make some repairs? Nothing major—just enough to break her submissive, to turn her from Rasht?

"Enough," she whispered. "Save your breath."

"Where is the monkey?" I asked.

"Tethered where we left it, over by the wreck. Shall we leave it here?"

"No. Well bring it with us, and we'll take good care of it. I promised him that much."

"He doesn't deserve it."

"That's true. But I try not to break my promises. Any of them."

"Then we're done here," Lenka said.

"I think we are."

The Last Log of the Lachrimosa | ALASTAIR REYNOLDS

We turned our backs on our former Captain and commenced the slow walk back to the lander. We would stop at the wreck on our way, collect the monkey, and what we could of Teterev's belongings—her journal, in particular, would be coming with us. Then we would be off Holda, out of this system, and that was a good thought.

Even if I knew I had to return.

"When we get back to the ship, I want to give it a new name. *Lachrimosa* was his ship, not ours."

I thought about that for a moment. "That's a good idea. A clean break. I have some suggestions, if you'd like to hear them."

The Seventeenth Kind

by Michael Marshall Smith

Hi. I'm James Richard. No, not "Richards," but "Richard." Dumb name, I think you'll agree. No, it's okay. Really. I've had many years to savor it, to laboriously spell it out over the phone and find parcels arriving at my door marked for Richard James anyhow. I didn't even make it up. It's not a stage name. My parents gave it to me when I was born, bless them—along with a straight nose, wavy brown hair and next to no talent at all.

"Why," I asked my father one time, back when I was young in years and full of hope, "Why in the name of sweet Jesus did you call me James Richard?"

He stared down at me, confused, and I belatedly realized he was in the same predicament. His name was David. David Richard. Maybe when he was young his peers also snarled, "Hey, shithead—why have you got two first names?" For a moment I felt a strange and poignant affinity with my dad, as if we were holding hands down the years, two small boys a generation apart who'd shouldered a similar burden. Then I kicked him in the shin.

Anyway. This isn't about my name. This is about what I do, and what I do is I'm a presenter on a shopping channel. No, go ahead. Laugh all you like. Just the stupidest job in the whole damned universe, right? Well, you know, screw you. If I hear one more person say a chimp could do my job then I'm going to take some innovative and durable kitchen implement— retailing in stores for $19.99 but available for this hour only at the low-low price of $11.99 plus postage and packing—and stuff it up their ass. This is a skill. It really is.

And it saved my life.

※

I wound up working in home shopping via a circuitous route. Everyone does. Nobody wakes up one morning thinking "Hey, I want to be on live cable selling people shit they don't need." Or perhaps they do, in which case they genuinely *are* stupid. Maybe they think it counts as television, and is therefore glamorous. It's not. The point of being on the tube is first, to earn big bucks; second, to be recognized in the street. Anyone who tells you different is a moron. What—they instead want the unsociable hours, the danger of being sacked at any moment, the ever-present threat of exposure and embarrassment, not to mention the joy of standing under hot lights while hairy-backed yahoos point cameras at you and swop impenetrable menial jokes behind your back? The money in cable really isn't that great, and the people you actually *want* to recognize you are pretty young things of the opposite sex. Or of the same sex, whatever. You work a shopping channel then these are not the people who are going to be recognizing you. They're going to be…well, I'll come to that.

I was an actor originally. I was profoundly average, and there's only so many times you can emote your heart out to scraggly-bearded directors to be told you're insufficiently tall or Turkish-looking or female or frankly even any *good*. So I switched to stand-up as a kind of holding pattern. Easier to get gigs, but the money stinks like fish and I couldn't write my own material so I was going nowhere fast.

Finally there was a spell on a local radio news station for which cattle made up the main demographic. That was *really* fucking grim. It was while I was there, reading out the weather and listening to the neurons in my brain popping one by one, that I saw a trade ad for a presenter on a cable channel. I combed the straw out of my hair, jumped on a plane and went and did my thing. I dug deep, gave it everything I had. I was desperate.

I got the gig.

The Seventeenth Kind | Michael Marshall Smith

Now. If you don't do any home shopping then I'm going to have to explain the deal to you. (If you do, then just skip-read or have a sandwich or something. I'll be back in a minute). How it works is this. The channels basically have a pile of goods which they want to sell. Pots and pans. Jewelry. Gardening implements. Technical gizmos for the home. Limited Edition Star Trek™ bathmats. The buy-me inducements they offer are severalfold. First, the goods are cheap. No store overheads, plus the advantages of buying in bulk. Two, you just pick up the phone and give a credit card number (hell, just your *name*, if you're a returning customer) and the thing will be with you in a couple days—without you even having to get up off your couch. I assume when it drops through your mailbox you have to get up and go fetch it, or maybe these people have someone who does that for them too.

The third inducement is people like me. The presenters. Your friend on the screen.

As the audience, this is what you see. A live picture of the object in question, with a panel at one side telling you the cost and the product code and just how beguilingly cheap it is compared to normal in-store prices. You listen to a voice-over, with cutaways to the presenter's face and upper body as he or she tells you how much the thing costs (in case you can't read), how many are left to buy ("Only three quarters of stock left now—this one's moving just *incredibly* quickly everybody, so hurry hurry, pick up your phone and make that call, operators are standing by...") and also explains to the hard-of-thinking why they should want the damn thing in the first place. If it's a ring, for example, my job would be to remind you that you could put it on your finger and wear it for cosmetic purposes, in order to enhance your attractiveness and/or perceived status. You think I'm kidding. I'm really not.

Sounds easy, but wait. Sometimes you may have to fill twenty minutes with this crap. You try talking for *half* that time, non-stop—with no help, no cues and moreover with people pointing cameras at you and some fool chattering in your ear—explaining why someone would want to buy an enormous cookie jar shaped like a chicken, and you'll begin to see it's not as easy as it sounds. Most of the presenters cheat. They'll repeat themselves endlessly, rehearsing the remaining stock levels time and again just to give themselves something extra to say. I never did that. I never dried. I also never said anything like "Today's special value today is really special," as one of my colleagues once did; nor "In the sixteenth century was the Renaissance, and garnet was a stone," another of my personal favorites.

I didn't do these things because when I found myself in this weird job it was like I'd come home. I knew it was worthless, but on the other hand I thought: Hey—perhaps this is something I could be *good* at. Maybe this was a corner of an ill-regarded field which I could make forever James Richard. Most of the stuff the channel pushed was skull-crushingly dull, but that didn't mean you couldn't talk about it. Okay, so it might be a hideous hexagonal pendant in faux gold with a miniscule pseudo-emerald in the middle: but you could point out how *delightfully* hexagonal it was, and how neatly the "emeraldite" sat in its exact centre. You could measure it with the special Home Mall ruler, just in case someone in the audience didn't understand perspective and was worried that the pendant was as big as a house. You could tell them how *many* different occasions they'd find to wear it, and list them, and generally evoke just how unspeakably lovely their lives would become—all because of this twenty dollar piece of costume jewelry.

The whole time you're working you have the director talking at you, relaying sales information through a plug in your ear. But I mentioned availability twice, three times in each hour. At most. Just enough to keep people on their toes, to convince them they ought to get working that phone. And you can believe this—when I was doing the selling, the units started shifting. That sounds arrogant, I guess. Well, maybe; and so what? For all the times some shithead casting agent dumped on me; for all the times I died on a small stage because the jokes I wrote weren't funny; for all the times I was shown I couldn't do a job well enough to be proud of myself—now I had Home Mall to show I could do *something*.

So what if no-one respected it? I could *do it*. That's what counts.

Which is why, after a couple of months with the station, I found myself doing a lot of the Specials. Every evening there'd be a product the station

The Seventeenth Kind | Michael Marshall Smith

had some particular deal on. They'd wheel on the manufacturer or some other front person with the promise of shifting extra units, and stick him or her on the screen to demonstrate the product. These slots lasted a whole hour and of course needed a professional to guide the civilian through the live television experience. To keep things running smoothly. And increasingly that professional was me.

Talking about something for ten minutes is one thing. An hour is a *whole* different kettle of ballgames. The big factor you have in your favor is that you aren't just a talking torso any more. You're there, live on camera, standing next to some guy demonstrating a CD player or salad shooter or car wrench. You can use everything about yourself, not just your voice. Employ your body to suggest things, use hand movements, shrug; if you weren't too proud you could even pout winsomely. God knows I've pouted on occasion, winsomely and otherwise.

All that helped, but the Specials were still tough, and I enjoyed the challenge. As the months went on I might resort to a little cocaine on occasion to keep myself humming along; but my main juice was pure adrenaline. That and a genuine drive to dance the jig of semi-relevance, to keep the balls in the air when they didn't deserve to be up there in the first place—to *just keep talking.*

To communicate with the viewer at home.

Once the products were shifting nicely, you see, we'd start taking calls from people who were buying the merchandise. Initially this was the part of the job that most freaked me out. I mean, who the hell *were* these people? What were they doing, calling a shopping channel at 1:30 AM on a Wednesday night to tell us why they'd bought some neo-bosnium trinket? Didn't they have beds to go to? Didn't they have *lives?* Ninety five percent of the callers were middle-aged women, too, which I found especially hard to get my head around. I could have understood guys in their twenties, maybe, too stoned to change the channel or just thinking they were being ironic. I even suggested to Rod that we should have a Stoner Hour, where we sold big bags of candy and potato chips along with small glittering baubles which might appeal to the chemically-enhanced mind. People would call up in droves, go to bed later and forget all about it, and then be completely bemused when boxes of munchies arrived a couple days later. We could probably get away with not sending out the product at all, which would be a big fat profit all round. (The idea wasn't taken up, which I think reveals commercial timidity).

I quickly realized that taking the calls was a crucial part of the selling process, however, and made it my specialty. Because nobody called in to say that something they'd bought was a piece of shit—they rang in to say it was great. They wanted to say something nice, which meant that everyone else listening got a ringing product endorsement from *someone who was just like them*. I would imagine these callers, dumpy and dough-faced, sitting in darkened rooms around the country, their faces lit by the flicker of the selling screen. Just occasionally I believed that once they'd finished talking to us they abruptly switched off, like abandoned robots, their heads tilting forwards onto their chests, hands folded in their laps—and that they would remain that way until the following night, when they got a chance to talk about their obsessions again. Sometimes this impression was stronger, and I felt I could imagine them all at once, all sitting in their rooms, bathed in the twinkling eeriness of television light, eyes focused on the screen, their loneliness and need pouring back through the cables towards me.

God Bless Cocaine.

The job settled into a rhythm. I'd do a couple of sessions late afternoon or early evening, just standard stuff—then at the beginning of the late shift, somewhere between 10 PM and 1 AM, I'd do a Special. The late shift is when the real action starts, the time when the heavy hitters of couch potato-purchasing settle down with their buckets of soda and sacks of potato chips and get into their stride. The products varied wildly but that was part of the fun. The manufacturers were also mixed, from a monosyllabic sauté pan dude who said maybe three words all hour to a woman I worked with on a home organ, who was damned nearly as good as me. *Christ* did that woman know a lot about organs. I thought she'd never shut up.

The Seventeenth Kind | Michael Marshall Smith

Then…okay: here we go.

The night in question I was doing a Special for a cleaning product called Supa Shine. Some guy from Texas had spent ten years working on polishes and finally come up with a real humdinger. The stuff had been on the channel once before but this was the first time it had got its own segment. When I heard what the Special was that evening I thought even *I* was going to have some trouble. Metal polish: it's useful, it may even be essential to some people. But say what you like, it's really just not very exciting.

An hour before we were due to go on air I dropped by the green room to meet the guy. Rusty, his name was. He was about fifty, grey-haired, bearded and kind of heavy 'round the gut, but affable enough in a good-old-boy kind of way—and wow, did he like his job. I'm not kidding. Polishing was this guy's *life*. He'd got into town early that morning and straightaway gone trawling junk stores and antiqueries picking up old bits of silver and copper to use on the show. He showed me how to use the product. The polish was a silvery paste which came in a very small tin. You put a subliminal amount on a rag, wiped it over your metal in a desultory way and then rubbed it off. And it worked. It worked to a freakish degree. I was genuinely impressed. He took an old coin, so dirty and corroded it looked more like a disk of wood, and after about ten seconds it looked better than the day it popped out of the mint. I relaxed. Okay, so polish was dull. But this stuff worked, by Jesus. Selling something that works is never too hard.

I hung out for a while, took a couple of minutes in the john to tip my chemical balance in the direction of enthusiasm, then got the five minute call. I murmured encouraging things to Rusty—who'd begun to shake slightly—and strode out under the lights. I don't know why I did that, because we weren't on air. They always cut in with you already in position. But I always stride on anyway. Call it professional pride.

Then the floor manager counts you down, the light on Camera One goes red, and you're on. It's showtime. Suddenly it's not just you and some perspiring Southerner—it's you and the rest of the world. Well, the world that's up and watching a shopping channel at 12:02 AM, anyway.

I started the hour with a searching but light-hearted meditation on the amount of old metalware in people's houses, and went on to muse how folks would get a lot more fun out of antique stores and yard sales if it weren't for the prospect of having to *clean* their prizes when they got them home. I didn't mention the other metal in people's houses—the silverware, furniture, even the fascias of DVD players. Not yet. Throw out all your ideas in the first minute on a Special, and by twenty after the hour you're going to be treading water until you drown.

I segued direct from this into Rusty doing his thing. He was okay, even pretty good. There was something so down-home about him that you couldn't help watching. "Christ," you were soon thinking, "This guy's fucking *obsessed*. If he gets off this much on polishing, there's *got* to be something in it. Let me have a go."

He took a pair of old candlesticks, equally tarnished. Talking slowly, he described the process of using his wonder-polish, demonstrating as he went. I didn't do much more than provide an echo every now and then—"Okay, so you put it on a *cloth*, right?"—because I knew as the hour progressed he'd run out of steam. A minute later one of the candlesticks was looking brighter than the day it was made. I'd kind of preferred it with the tarnish, to be honest: for me taking an antique and making it look new was like sprucing up Stonehenge with fiberglass. But I knew that the audience would feel differently, and Rod the director was already chattering happily in my earpiece. The calls had started right away, and Supa Shine was out of the starting blocks.

For the next fifteen minutes Rusty tirelessly polished and buffed. I tried it myself, of course, affably pouring the full weight of my personality into restoring the shine to a variety of pieces of old trash—while being careful to make it clear that James Richard, like the viewer at home, had no pre-existing expertise in the field. We did gold, we did silver, we did copper, we did chrome. They all worked spectacularly. We actually had to start being careful about the way we held the pieces because the glitter was throwing the cameras off.

Twenty five minutes in I took over from Rusty, helping him out of a circuitous ramble he'd trapped himself into. The calls were really flooding in by now; Supa Shine was shifting big time.

It was time to start talking to people.

Our first call was typical. Lori from Black Falls rang to say that she'd bought Supa Shine when it's been on before and it had changed her life. She described in detail how she's polished everything in her street and how happy that had made her. She'd called that evening to buy stocks for her sisters, daughters and friends. She was so patently sincere that I let her run on for quite some while, knowing she was doing our job for us. Rusty nodded benignly, dislodging a small droplet of sweat from his hairline, which rolled slowly onto his forehead. I covertly signaled the director to switch to a close up product shot, and Mandy the makeup girl darted on to powder us both. No more than six seconds, then back to a medium shot of the two of us, and all the while I kept the banter going with the caller until she'd said all she had to say.

Lori finally stopped yakking and went off to polish her dog's head or something and we took a call from Ann in Raenord. Ann had called because she was concerned that Supa Shine might harm her gold-plated jewelry. Rusty whipped a piece of plated stuff off the pile and polished it there and then. It came up beautifully, and Ann was mollified. She thanked us for talking to her and was transferred to the purchase operators.

It was a natural point to take five, and so I signaled to Rod and talked us into a short break…giving just a hint of some of the exciting polishing action still to come.

※

As soon as the ident was on the screen I winked at Rusty, and disappeared behind the set and into the green room. None of the production staff batted an eyelid. I'd left a line chopped and ready on the one table which wasn't covered with crap from previous shows, and so it was the matter of a moment to get the marching dust into my bloodstream.

I strode back into the studio—taking care to grab a glass of water for cover—and stood next to Rusty. "Going just great," I enthused. "Just had a word with the guys—you're selling by the *shit*load."

Rusty smiled shyly, and I noticed that another droplet of sweat was already forming. Mandy swabbed, Rod counted us back in and we were on air less than three minutes after I'd left.

The next five minutes were fine. Rusty told us how it would only take two cans of Supa Shine to clean an entire 747, and it didn't seem hard to believe. I must admit that by this time I was kind of wondering what was in the stuff: the pile of metal in front of us was gleaming so much it was starting to hurt my eyes. I got Rusty to tell his story about working in his mother's garage for ten years coming up with the formula, then decided it was time to take another call.

And that's where the evening went a little weird.

"Hi," I said, smiling direct to Camera One. "So, who do we have come to talk with us now?"

The normal response to this is the caller's name and location, utterly promptly and clearly. They've been briefed by an operator and most of them blurt the information out super-fast, as if eager to prove they can follow instructions properly and will make a great addition to the program. This time there was a silence.

Which is fine—sometimes people get overawed once they realize they're really on air. The tactic then is to ask them a *very simple question* to start them off.

"Have you already experienced Supa Shine's cleaning miracles, caller?" I asked. "Or do you have a question for friend Rusty here before you try it?"

Usually that'll do it. The silence continued, however, and I began to let my right hand wander up towards my neck—in preparation for the agreed code for cutting a caller off. But then the caller spoke.

"He's not Rusty."

The voice was deep and ragged and wet and rough. My heart sank. Every now and then one of the directors, Rod in particular, would let a weird one slip through. The stated intention was "keeping it real," but as Rod wouldn't know real if it slapped him upside the head I believed it was more likely to be about fucking up the presenter for the delight of the assembled spear carriers. Kind of irresponsible when the product was shifting so well, but that's assholes for you.

"Well, not literally, of course," I smiled (winsomely). "But you know what? It wouldn't surprise me one bit to find that Supa Shine wasn't only great with stains and tarnish—but could handle a little spot of rust as well. In fact, I was just going to ask…"

"His name isn't Rusty," the voice said. Sounded like the guy had the world's worst ever cold. Or flu. Or maybe the plague.

"Well, no, it's kind of a nick-name, isn't it?" I chuckled. "No-one gets called Rusty right off the bat, do they. Just like some of my friends call me Jim. And so caller, while we're talking, what's *your* name?"

There was no reply.

Screw this, I thought. I very obviously scratched my Adam's apple. In other words, *get this loser off air.* Meanwhile I turned to Rusty, who was starting to look real nervous. It's often the way with the guests. When things start well they can get lulled into forgetting that they're on live television—but it's a perilous relaxation. The smallest upset can unsettle them for good.

"So how *about* that, Rusty?" I asked, holding his eyes to lock him back into where he was and what he was doing. "Obviously Supa Shine isn't going to be able to cope if something's totally *covered* in rust, kind of falling apart, but how about a little spot or two?"

Rusty opened his mouth to speak but then a very bizarre noise came over the studio monitor. It sounded like a loud, liquid cough, mixed up with the sound of a handful of nails being dropped on a metal surface.

"Whoa! I apologize for that, viewers," I laughed. "Little technical glitch here in the studio, don't know if you heard it at home—just goes to show that we really are *live* tonight in your living room, live and *alive*, bringing you the very best in bargains 24/7 and right around the clock. So…"

Then the noise happened again. I laughed once more, throwing my hands up in the air for good measure—as if helpless with mirth at the hilarious events which tumbled through life: not just my life, you understand, but the lives of the viewers at home too.

Then something else came over the speakers. The deep, broken voice said: "That's my name."

"What?" I said, momentarily thrown.

"That's my name," the voice repeated. Then the strange liquid noise rumbled through the speakers again. "That's it."

"That…noise is your name?"

"Yes."

"Well make sure you spell it out when you talk to our purchase operators…" I said, with a wink directly into camera—to the normal man and woman on the couch. "…because I'm not sure they'll have come across that one before. Eastern European, is it?"

"No."

"Well okay then. I know that we have many, many other viewers out there who really want to share their experiences with Trusty's Supa Shine polish with us, so maybe if…"

"It's not his."

By now I was finally beginning to get pissed off. The entire exchange had probably only actually taken forty seconds so far, but that's a *long* time on live television. Rusty was looking extremely wary again, and a whole army of perspiration drops were massed at the hair line, ready to roll down his face. That could not happen, not on my watch. Nobody wants to buy something from a guy who's sweating like a pig. I made the cut sign again, even more clearly.

"Jim, there's something odd going on."

This voice didn't come out over the speakers, but only into my earpiece. It was Rod.

I turned to Rusty and cheerfully suggested he show us his polish working magic on the second candlestick, which was weak, but I needed a few seconds' cover.

As I watched him get to this, I raised my eyebrows quickly, just about the only way I could communicate to the box I needed to hear more. Rod spoke again, and what he said was strange.

"We can't get this joker off the air."

I took the risk and risked a glance off. Normally you never do this. You look direct to the camera, at the object, or at your civilian co-host. Anywhere else looks weird to the viewer at home, reminding them you're in a studio. But I swept my eyes quickly over the window to the director's booth—their lair was sealed from the studio so chatter and techspeak didn't leak onto live microphones—and saw Rod was standing and looking directly at me, his hands held up in mime-quality "I have no fucking clue what is going on" pose.

Behind him a couple of techs were moving quickly about the room fiddling with wires. By this time I had done many, many hours of live television. I'd never seen something like that before. I realized there and then that I was entering new and uncharted territory.

"He has stolen it," said the speaker voice, loudly.

"Stolen what?" I said.

"His so-called polish. It is not his. It belongs to us."

I was still trying to conjure a response to this when I heard Rod's voice in my ear again. He wasn't speaking directly to me this time, but what he said was so weird I decided that from then on I was just going to ignore everything except what was happening in front of me. Rod's voice was on the edge of cracking.

"What the fuck do you mean?" he was shouting, to someone, "Time is slowing *down*?"

I assumed he was ragging out some technician and it was a geek wires-and-sockets thing. Whatever. Their problem, not mine. If they couldn't get this idiot off the air I'd just have to plough on regardless. The show must go on, always. This was precisely what I got paid the big bucks for. Well, the bucks, anyway.

I smiled at Camera Two, the one currently showing a red light. "Well, *thank* you caller, it's been really great to hear your own special perspective on this. But just right now I want to ask Rusty here something."

I turned to my co-host, the first time I'd looked directly at him for maybe a minute or two. I should have checked back before. He'd got stressed, nervous, a big old dose of stage fright. The line of sweat droplets I'd seen forming earlier had decided to all go over the top at once, and fresh ranks were following in their wake—taking with them what appeared to be a thick layer of make-up. Every guest gets some pancake, to smooth out blotches and variations and make everyone look nice under the lights.

This make-up was a lot thicker than that, though. And, I noticed, looked kind of like…latex.

I stared at Rusty. Rusty looked back at me.

I noticed then that his eyes were perhaps suspiciously blue, too, like they were contacts. And that where the make-up was running or melting or whatever it was doing, the skin underneath seemed to be both rough and warty and also a unusual color.

"Rusty," I said, suspiciously, "Are you green?"

He turned away suddenly, tilting his head toward the speaker hanging above us, out of shot. He barked something angrily at it and now his voice didn't sound like it had before. It didn't sound like he was from the South. It sounded like a large bucket of nuts and bolts dropped down an old drain pipe. Then he made another sound, even louder. The force of the utterance caused a whole strip of skin to fall off one side of his face, revealing something that looked like a piece of steak that had being lying in a parking lot for a couple weeks.

"Okay," I said, into the silence. "So I'm guessing maybe you're not from East Texas after all?"

The voice from the speaker spoke once again.

"No, he is not," it said, "And his polish belongs to us. In reality it is a foodstuff. And we are running perilously low. It must be returned to us."

"Whoa," I said. "Back up. Who's 'us'? Who am I talking to?"

All around me cameramen and production assistants and random techs were frozen like statues. No-one was doing anything any more. They were just staring up at the speaker from which the voice was coming, and all looked like they'd never move again, like their minds so wanted to be somewhere else that their bodies had been left to their own devices for a while.

But I'm different. Used to the challenges of going live. And a godamned professional, too.

"We are from a planet you do not have a name for," the voice said. "In our tongue it is called…" And he made a sound I'm not even going to try to describe. You wouldn't want to hear it outside your house late at night, that's for sure. "The being you call 'Rusty' is one of us. We are allowed to leave the ship every now and then on a strict rotation basis. But he has outstayed his leave. And he is selling what belongs to us alone."

"Wait there a second," I said, holding my hand up. "Ship? What kind of ship?"

"A scout ship."

"From where? Okay, right, the unpronounceable place." I turned to the being that I had previously been introduced to as Rusty. "But what are you *doing* here?"

"We have been experiencing some technical difficulties," Rusty/it muttered, his voice now halfway between Southern drawl and hacking flu-cough. "Because the captain is a complete..."

And then suddenly he/it vanished.

The thing that had been Rusty was gone, leaving only a small pile of clothes, two vivid blue contact lenses and a head and beard wig, lying on the floor.

And over the speaker came the sound of something very bad and physical and permanent happening.

Suddenly there *was* movement amongst the assembled people in the studio. Some running, a little shrieking, a lot of men and women crying out. But it didn't amount to much. I heard someone in back shouting that all the doors had mysteriously become locked. I glanced over at the window to the control booth once more and saw everyone in there was still standing still, watching me through the glass. I think Rod was still shouting things in my ear, too, but I wasn't listening. He was never any help.

"If you're some kind of scout ship," I said, talking direct to the dis-embodied voice again, "How come you can't just phone home? Contact the mothership or whatever, tell them you've got issues and to send help?"

There was a pause, then something that sounded a little like a human cough.

"We're not supposed to be here," the voice said.

"Why?"

"Long story," the voice said.

"You got lost?"

"No," the voice said, irritably, as if I'd opened a huge great can of worms. "We were going to invade. But there was some last-minute discussion onboard over the ethics of the thing. Your world is protected, theoretically, and there was some…heated discussion. A small amount of equipment damage ensued. The remote control for the radial neo-transponder matrix got stepped on, and without it the ship doesn't work."

"So you're *stuck?*"

"Yes."

"For how long?"

There was something like a sigh then, a sound that reverberated through the studio like a gust of wind wandering alone through the Grand Canyon, in the dead of night.

"Eleven point five thousand of your years."

"Jesus," I said. "That's quite a layover."

"Yes. To be honest, the time's beginning to drag."

"I'm not surprised. Holy cow. Where are you, exactly?"

"In a mountain."

"In a…"

"I don't want to talk about it."

"And you're completely alone here?"

"There's a crew down in Key West. But not our kind. They're spindly. And assholes, actually. And they won't help."

"Have you tried changing the batteries?"

There was a pause. "Excuse me?"

"Well," I said, "this radial neo-transponder matrix widget or whatever sounds like the kind of thing that's going to need some juice, right? Couldn't it just be the batteries went flat? Have you checked?"

There was a long, long pause. I mean—really, *really* long. Another cough. Then a further pause.

Finally: "I don't believe our technicians have explicitly evaluated that possibility, no."

"You think maybe they…should?"

"Even if your suggestion has merit, the batteries of our kind are completely different from yours. Actually…do you say different *from* or different *to*?"

"Whichever," I said. "You're the boss."

"They are both different from and different to your batteries. They are transquantum piso-structures one mile square in five dimensions. And not available here."

"Have you tried a universal remote?"

"Universal remote?"

"Sure," I said. "In fact…wait here."

I ran out of the studio, back into the green room, and searched through the various piles of crap spread all over it. Spare jackets and ties, bits and pieces left from other random segments, free samples from previous Special hours.

After a minute—thank god—I found what I was looking for and which I *thought* I'd remembered seeing a couple nights before. Then I strode back out into the studio, already talking direct to camera as I hit the floor.

"Do *you* suffer from 'remote proliferation'?" I asked. "Is *your* den deluged under a pile of remotes, your sitting room swamped with switches and kitchen ka-flumped with controls, each one designed to work with only one piece of equipment? Do you have one for the television, one for the satellite, one for DVD, CD…maybe even one for the cat? You do, right? So do I. Or I *did*, that is, until I discovered the Relco Universal OmniRemote."

I triumphantly held up the remote I'd found. It caught one of the big lights overhead, and glittered like a chalice.

"Truly, my friends, this is a leap forward in both technology and tidiness, a breakthrough in convenience and style. I'll tell you right now—and regular viewers know I don't say this often—I've even got one of these babies myself at home. I'd have two, but…"—and here I paused for a trademark winsome smile to camera: I was back in the zone—"…you'll only *need* one, right?"

"We don't have a den," said the voice over the speaker. "This is a space ship."

"I get that," I said, "My point is you could maybe use one of these things. Reprogram it to work a radial neo-transponder monkey, or whatever it is you said."

"Hmm," said the voice. "Hold on a minute."

There was a brief humming sound, followed by utter silence. Then the voice came back.

"Put it in the middle of the floor."

"What?"

"The device of which you speak. Put it in the middle of the floor with a minimum of two Trajelian Nippits of clear space all around it. That's approximately a 'yard,' in your currency."

I walked out from behind the counter and placed the remote carefully in the middle of the floor. Then I stepped back, shooing the cameramen and production flunkies away, so there was a lot of space around it.

"You got it," I said. "Now what?"

There was a sudden rushing sound, followed by a brief whirr. Both sounded as if they came from inside my own head. Then a simple and very loud *ping*.

And the remote on the floor had disappeared.

And everything was silent.

There was not a sound in the studio. Everyone stood, waiting. It was as if the world outside had disappeared.

Then, from over the speaker, came a noise that sounded like distant and somewhat relieved cheering.

Everyone in the studio looked at each other.

"Well, who knew," said the rough, liquid voice, coming back. "So the monkey-people finally came up with something useful. Point to you."

"You're welcome," I said. "So now you're free to go?"

"Our engines are coming up to speed as we speak. We are going to need that tin of 'polish' on the counter there, though. Leave no man behind. Or evidence, I mean."

I picked up the tin of Supa Shine and went around to put it in the cleared space in the floor. Wind/whirr/ping—and it was gone.

"Remain right where you are," the voice said.

I stayed put, frozen in the middle of the floor.

"You have been helpful, people of Earth. We are grateful. Now...we're going to have to destroy you all."

The Seventeenth Kind | Michael Marshall Smith

"*What?*"

"You know too much."

"We know shit," I protested. "Really. Zip. Nada. Especially me."

"Sorry," the voice said. "Health and safety."

People began to break down in earnest then. They knew this was the end. They understood suddenly that this was irrevocable, that no argument, however cogent, well-argued or frankly even *right*, would ever make a difference once health and safety had been invoked.

"Well, look, Christ," I spluttered, anyway, knowing I had to keep talking until the very end. "That seems kind of harsh, you know? We fixed your, you know, that thing that was broken. We helped you out, right?"

"No," the voice said. "*You* did. Say good bye."

I looked around the studio, at the people all terrified and flinching, the tear-running faces and trembling shoulders. I glanced at Max and Clive and Jeff, the camera and lights crew, not looking so tough now. At Mandy from make-up, and Trix and Pinky the PA girls, and finally through the window at Rod and his open-mouthed producers and other familiars: at these people, my colleagues and acquaintances, the people I had worked with, these fellow-toilers at the sharp end of retail.

These humans. Every single one of them remains burned into my mind. They're the last I ever saw.

"Goodby…" was all I got out.

Then my mind went white, and there was the sound of wind, and then a whir, and then a ping.

※

The viewers at home never saw me vanish, or what happened to Rusty. They never even heard the strange voice over the speakers—all they saw was a whacky few seconds where James Richard seemed to be going very seriously off message…before the Home Mall signal went fuzzy for a couple minutes. Then the channel abruptly left the air forever, as the studio, warehouse and surrounding city block was vaporized—by what was later explained, I gather, as an unexpected meteorite. I guess the CIA or NSA or some other bunch of spooks covered the whole thing up somehow. Clearly *someone* back at home knows where Earth stands in the bigger picture—since I've been away I discovered there's even a secret website at www...oh, I guess I shouldn't say. But that's how I know the official US government classification for what happened to me: a close encounter of the seventeenth kind, one involving "a commercial transaction conducted over some form of mass telecommunication (including but not limited to television, radio or particle net sub-rotation) and involving individual items valued at one hundred dollars or less." It's kind of rare. In fact I think I may have been the first. To survive, anyhow.

So—there's the scoop on how I came to be here, like you asked. Edit as you see fit, of course—I know it's kind of long for a press release. I'm sure my new agent will want other cuts too: the stuff about my name won't mean a lot to a guy called fLKccHL±±sgdo273-fx2, I guess.

Anyhoo. Got to go, bro. The bright lights call. I'm five minutes away from a two-hour pan-galactic Special for a consignment of mesquite-roasted Alpha Centaurian pengulnuts and their associated serving dishes and cookware. Yum yum. The buying public awaits eagerly, always, and James Richard is their friend, adviser and honest guide through the retail jungle...

...whatever damned planet they're from. ⟶🐾

Dispersed by the Sun, Melting in the Wind

BY RACHEL SWIRSKY

The last word ever spoken by a human is said in a language derived from Hindi. The word is trasa. Roughly translated: thirst or desire.

The second-to-last human to die is a child who lives in the region that was once called the Blue Mountains of Australia. She has the strange light eyes that children are occasionally born with, the way they are sometimes born as triplets or with white hair or with another baby's empty body growing from their bellies. Her mother calls them water eyes, a sign that the child shares the changeable spirit of the ocean which can shift from calm to storm in the space of a breath.

On the last day of her life, the light-eyed child finds a pair of ancient skeletons exposed in the silt by the river near her camp. She pulls out the ribs with a sucking noise, loosing the foul stench of trapped gas. Pelvic bones lie in the mud below, tangled with metal things no one can make anymore. As she teases them free, the light-eyed child unearths rusted chains and hollow disks the diameter of her wrist.

The light-eyed child rinses the bones clean in the river. She runs her hand over the long femurs, marveling. People no longer grow so tall.

The light-eyed child sets the bones in a loose pile underneath a scribbly gum tree. The skulls preside on top, regarding her with hollow eyes. The light-eyed child kisses each in the center of its caved-in forehead.

Goodnight, Grandpa Burn, she says. *Goodnight, Grandma Starve.*

⁂

The last major art movement is invented near Lake Vättern in Sweden. With the help of enough processing power to calculate the trajectories of a beachful of sand over a millennium, the artist taps a feeder loop directly into her brain and uses it to shape a three-dimensional holographic image of her father. For the first time, human thought patterns take direct, physical form. Her father's projection repeats sequences of fragmented memories. His limbs trail into images of people and places he loved when he was alive; his hair winds into the tapestries he was famous for weaving; his face flickers cyclically from youth to gray. *It's not my father,* the artist explains. *It's how I think of my father, his imago.*

Within five years, her invention revolutionizes art. Artists show the world how they conceive of childbirth, fire, finches, walk bodies, urtists, religion, synthesis and death.

Within twenty years, the technology to create such work is destroyed. Art falls backward. Humanity falls farther.

⁂

The man who will survive to be the last human lives in the region once called Nepal. Amid the still-falling ash from a series of volcanic eruptions, he and his son dig their way free of a cave-in.

Ravens perched on branches overhanging the cave mouth observe their progress. When the son grows weak, the last man tries to scatter the birds by throwing stones. They flap a short distance into the naked trees and witness the boy's death from there, watching events unfold the way birds do: turning their heads to look first with one eye, then the other, to see which version of life is more appealing.

※

The last scientific discovery excites the neurons of an amateur stargazer. Even before the cataclysm, she is the last of an increasingly rarefied breed—air and light pollution have made ground telescopes useless, so she has to pay for satellite time to peer out in an era when almost all of humanity's technological eyes are aimed inward. One lonely night when all her mates and children are away, she trains her screen to watch the cloud bands on Jupiter's gaseous surface and glimpses a city-sized object hurtling toward the earth.

Oh, God, she says, *an asteroid.*

※

With near-earth space increasingly militarized, it's been years since government telescopes have been dedicated to anything but scrutinizing the actions of other nations. The scant handful of under-funded astronomers confirms that the object's path will bring it into contact with earth.

The astronomers agree: there's nothing to be done. A century of attrition has withered space programs. Early iterations of space-faring technology were cannibalized to fund defense and weapons aimed at earthly targets. Remaining resources are primitive and useless. The object is too close to fire missiles at or deflect or drag into the gravity well of the sun.

※

Wealthy global governments convene. If they can't stop the asteroid, they agree to let it hit. Calculations demonstrate it will impact near the southern tip of Chile. Industrialists working on technology for deep-sea exploration believe they can adapt their pressure shield mechanisms to protect a few major cities from the global fires, earthquakes and tidal waves that will result from impact. With nuclear, wind, and solar power operating at full capacity, there should be enough energy to protect key sections of Asia, Europe and North America. First world populations that live outside protected urban centers are herded in en masse, crowding like cattle into emergency shelters.

As for those who won't be included in the rescue plan, global leaders mumble about regrettable losses then do what they have always done: sacrifice the good of the many for the good of themselves.

The last act of malice lights in the eyes of a pathologist who works in a secure facility in a dome on an island in an untraveled sea. When it becomes clear their government has abandoned them, the other scientists drink and screw on the lab tables. He unlocks his deadliest specimens, flees the building to the rhythm of unheeded alarms, and looses genetically manipulated spores like fairy dust onto the wind.

The last heroes desert their homes in wealthy nations and travel south to stand with their impoverished brothers and sisters.

Like everyone else, they die.

By the time the cataclysm strikes, more words have been forgotten over the course of human history than remain known.

The city-sized object hits.

Dispersed by the Sun, Melting in the Wind | Rachel Swirsky

Wealthy northerners watch the event through cameras on surviving satellites. Milliseconds after impact, their screens go black as the asteroid's collision displaces earth and rock in a hundred mile radius. Radioactive waste illegally buried in poverty-stricken Puerto Natales flies into the air, joining the plume of dirt that whirls into the chaotic weather systems caused by impact. Soil sewn with radioactive dust distributes across the globe in a storm that blocks the sun for three months.

Human folly has made a bad natural occurrence into an untenable one. It is as if the planet has gone to global nuclear war. Toxic heavy metals rain into the surface water systems and poison the springs of civilization.

Pressure shields are helpless against nuclear fallout. For those not killed by the fiery rains of impact, dying lingers. Bones weaken; teeth fall out; skin loosens in long, slender strips like fruit peels.

Before she dies, the Swedish artist tries to redraw her father's imago on a flat sheet of pulped tree. Her shaking hand is raw and bleeding, but her lines fall true. The drawing fails anyway. She can't remember what her father looked like. She can only remember her art.

※

The last man's people survive by moving underground. Caves shelter them from fiery rains and pathogens and tidal waves. Underground, they have access to subterranean water sources that remain temporarily pure.

His people's luck lasts a century, until the geological instabilities set in motion by impact bubble up from the earth's molten heart. Sudden, violent tremors herald chains of volcanic eruptions that transform the caves into tombs.

The last man and his son dig their way free, but it takes so long that the already weak child grows weaker. He breathes dust and ash. Once, as they work to pry loose a stubborn boulder, a rain of debris showers down on the son. He seems fine when he gets up and shakes himself off, but who knows what injuries can afflict a malnourished boy?

※

The light-eyed child's people believe they escaped the fiery rains because the earth protects them. Unlike the mining-scarred, ecologically damaged area of Nepal where the last man's people live, the light-eyed child's people enjoy a paradise of native species and pristine cliffs. Even some kangaroos survive to provide the light-eyed child's people with food.

The light-eyed child's grandmother tells her the bones she finds sometimes are not the bones of people, but of devils. *They made the cataclysm happen by hating and ignoring the earth, she says, Most of them died, but the ones who survived—Grandpa Burn and Grandma Starve, Grandpa Hate and Grandma Bullet—they chained us and hurt us and tried to take our land. We had to use their tools on them instead.*

The light-eyed child's people initially triumphed over their enemies, but their luck ran out some four score years after the cataclysm. A species of bird which hadn't been seen since impact arrived during the annual migration, carrying the pathologist's bequest.

One illness killed the elderly. A second attacked the healthiest. A third killed one tenth of the population in a single night. The fourth wiped out the men.

No one tells the light-eyed child directly, but she hears talk of the plagues as *our curse*, sometimes brought by the earth spirits, sometimes by the ghosts of the demons. The light-eyed child asks her mother, who pauses while gathering roots to explain, *Being favored by the spirits is both a blessing and a burden. They won't forgive us for acting in ignorance as the demons did. They haven't yet decided the punishment for our transgressions.*

The light-eyed child's mother gets a strange, wistful look on her face and goes on. *You're our last hope.*

The light-eyed child's people have a legend that girls with water eyes can sometimes turn into boys. They need her to do so; that is what they mean when they say she is their last hope.

No one knows how to make it happen. *Send the girl out on her own,* her grandmother says, *Boys like to be on their own.* So every morning, the light-eyed child's mother sends her off to explore the remnants of the rainforest.

Dispersed by the Sun, Melting in the Wind | Rachel Swirsky

The light-eyed child thinks being a last hope is both a blessing and a burden. She enjoys being special. She hates the disappointment in everyone's eyes when she comes home every day, still a girl.

Sometimes she squats over the river, her eyes squeezed shut as if she's trying to shit because it's the best way she can imagine to force a penis out of her vagina. She clenches and grunts, clenches and grunts. Sometimes when her eyes get so tired she sees bright sparkles over the scribbly gums on the horizon, she feels her vaginal walls pinch together and she knows—just knows—that something has come out. But when she reaches down, she finds only soft, yielding flesh.

⁂

The last man cries over his son until he realizes his sobs are tearless. He stops.

The ravens won't leave them alone, so he throws more stones. He must watch the birds constantly or they try to pluck out his son's eyes.

His trousers are soiled, but he urinates at a marked spot near the cave mouth to maintain a semblance of civilization. He has nothing to defecate. When he gets too hungry, he sucks on stones.

In all the deprivation the last man has suffered in his life, he's never lacked for water. Even now as he starves, puddles pock the stony landscape. They taste brackish, but they keep him alive longer than he wants.

He gives up sleep, but dreams awake. He sees mirages on the horizon, machines his father told tales of: great silver birds with hearts like ticking clocks; blood-heated covers to keep him warm; android doctors with needle-covered palms injecting life back into his bony chest.

He remembers the first time he came to the surface as a boy, with his own father. His people's men folk had a tradition of sending males to the surface to prove they had the courage to tread across the lip of a dead world. All around the valley grew the red-stemmed ban mara daisies which choked out the trees until the hills blanched white as the clouds.

When I was young, they said the flowers showed the hills were dying, the last man's father said. *They came from a far-away land over the sea and when they got here, they grew so thick and fierce that they killed all the plants that had been here already, the ones that had lived here forever.*

Once, the last man and his father explored the mountains beyond the hills and found the remains of a fabric shop. Bolts of durable synthetic cloth tumbled across each other, like the discarded sheets of a giant. The last man and his father brought them home for the women to make clothes out of. They were greeted like heroes.

Before the eruptions, the last man never brought his son to the surface. He was a sickly baby, like all the newborns conceived in the past few years. Many of them died, but the last man prayed over his son every minute until he was a year old. His son's hair grew in scraggly patches across his scalp. When he ate, his gums bled into his food. Even after the boy had passed the most dangerous point, the last man refused to let him sleep alone, afraid he'd get lost in his dreams and forget to come home. The last man's wife told him she would leave him for another man if he didn't return to share her pallet. He let her.

The setting sun reflects pink off the upturned petals cloaking the hills. The last man regrets not taking his son up here before, sickly or not. He thinks his son would have liked to explore these hills, feel his bony feet slip in the mud. He would have run through the ruins and hollered at the vast, free sky. At least, he would have liked a length of the gray cloth the last man and his father found so many years ago: sewn with golden strands for the sun and red strands like the stems of the *ban mara* daisies.

⁂

Literacy fades years before the last man dies. The older generation of his people remember how to read, but they don't teach the young ones. Reading seems frivolous, indulgent, a luxury like brocade or peacock feathers or reminiscing about long summer evenings when men chewed betel nuts and women chattered while the lowering sun lengthened their shadows until an ordinary human presence had the heft of a god's.

⁂

Dispersed by the Sun, Melting in the Wind | Rachel Swirsky

Two generations before the light-eyed child was born, her grandmother would have screamed at Grandpa Burn and kicked his skull downstream. Her mother would have cried over Grandma Starve's aged bones, cursing the fact she would never live to acquire a stoop.

The light-eyed child places her hands over their hollow sockets and returns to playing.

⋇

The last lie is not a single lie but a group of lies, uttered by the last man's people and the light-eyed child's people, by children and elders, by men and women, by the stoic and the red-eyed.

Don't worry, Mama, Grandpa, sir, honey, lover, child, heart-keeper, mine. You're going to get better. You're going to be all right.

⋇

The last man leaves his son awhile and climbs a formation of rocks on the other side of the cave mouth. The tallest one leans on a pair of others like an old man asking for support. Below, a thousand foot drop sinks into a ravine blanketed in daisies.

The last man selects a small gray stone and pitches it down. As it plummets, he tries to fit the idea of such distance into his head: how things so high can fall so far.

Before it hits, he's distracted by a rush of wind as a raven flies past him. He waves it away. It dives past the cave, headed for his son. The last man climbs down to chase it off and misses the moment when the rock hits the ground.

By the time the last man reaches his son, the boy's left eye is gone. The thread of his intestines trails across the stony ground.

He remembers sitting with his son, then a five year old, coaxing him to eat yak meat and lichen. The little boy turned away, fanning his hands in front of his face.

A little more, just a little more. Come on, the last man said. It hurt the boy to chew; it hurt him to swallow; it hurt him to have food in his stomach.

| **153**

A few steps away, the last man's wife stood, staring, the glint of her reddened eyes bright in the darkness. The next day she'd leave him for the fat man who lived near the cave mouth, the one with who had another wife already. She didn't need to vocalize; the words were written in the taut line of her mouth: Why squander time on the dying when we'll reach death's door soon enough ourselves?

Truthfully, the last man had heard the ravens fly toward his son as soon as he climbed the rocks. He'd known what the birds would do. But it wasn't until he threw the stone that his mind had the sense to distract him from trying to confront mortality while the wind of falling rushed around his own ears, too.

The last man is tone deaf and the light-eyed child doesn't like to sing because it reminds her that her voice is piping and high when it should be resonant and bass, so the last music mankind makes is subtle and strange. It's the last man grunting in answer to the raven's sporadic caws; it's the light-eyed child splashing in the river to the beat of her heart; it's the last man's fingers drumming on his son's hollow belly.

The light-eyed child's people don't live long enough to suffer from their lack of men. The third wave disease, the one that killed a tenth of them in a night, reawakens in its surviving hosts after its long period of incubation and strangles the entire population by dawn.

The dusk before, as the last man prepares to throw a stone down a cliff, the light-eyed child runs back to camp to find her mother. The sky dims. Pale stars emerge. The two of them stroll to a spring to fetch clean water with which to cook the evening meal of kangaroo meat flavored with peppermint leaves.

Dispersed by the Sun, Melting in the Wind | Rachel Swirsky

The last word the light-eyed child's mother says before she starts to choke is *whakahohoro*: hurry.

The last man becomes grateful for things he should despise: the red-tinted sky, the stench of his son's decaying corpse, the coldness of his soiled trousers. His last hour stretches, but not in the way a bored afternoon expands across a child's landscape. His last hour is the petal of an orchid browning from the outside in. It's a cloud blowing across the sky puff by puff, until without ever moving as a single entity, it soars away into the blue expanse. It's a grain of sand, unnoticed until held up close—whoever would have known it was crimson? And smelled like salt? And shaped like a crescent moon?

The last piece of technology mankind invents is a bundle of lyrebird feathers and wallaby bones and blue lizard tongues wrapped in sugar glider fur which the light-eyed child's people believe a woman can use to draw sickness out of a loved one. It possesses no magic, but it serves a purpose: it busies hands and buoys hearts.

The light-eyed child lives a few hours longer than the rest of her people. She clutches her mother's hand through her breathless contortions, and when they're over, she cradles her mother's blue, arthritic fingers.

As she runs out of breath herself, she wonders if her skeleton will wear jewelry with spokes and chains like Grandpa Burn and Grandma Starve. She wonders who will dig up her bones.

The puddles of rainwater could sustain the last man a few days yet, but he stops drinking. He watches the ravens' reflections in the dirty water and repeats, "Trasa, trasa." Though his mouth is dry, it isn't thirst he's referring to.

Though the last man and the light-eyed child live on opposite sides of the globe, they die within hours of each other. It is one of those improbable vagaries of fate which become probable given enough time and opportunity, like calculus stirring simultaneously in the brains of Newton and Leibnitz, evolution in Darwin and Wallace, relativity in Einstein and Smoluchowski. The last two humans are simply the final pair to march hand in hand into an unexplored realm.

The last animal to see a living human is a raven. She watches the last man's final exhalation and waits a moment to be sure he won't rise and hurl another stone in her direction. His body sags. She paces her perch. All remains still.

She swoops.

The Pile

by Michael Bishop

The day after Roger and Renata Maharis—brother and sister, *not* a married couple—moved into a Fidelity Plaza townhouse that their father in Savannah had bought as a residence for them while she attended university and he raised money to return to classes, Roger carried some boxes out to the Dumpsters at the far end of the swimming pool and ran smack-dab into The Pile.

The Pile: that's how he *had* to think of it because that's what it *was*. It consisted of the discards of the Fidelity Plaza community: the castoffs and leavings of its residents, stuff too good to feed to the Dumpsters' maws, jettisoned junk with potential adaptability to other people's uses: *The Pile*.

Roger marveled at the items there: dilapidated homemade bookshelves, crippled rocking chairs, coffee tables made of converted telephone-line spools, chipped planters, moribund banana trees, elaborate metal floor lamps that (obviously) no longer worked, hideous plastic bric-a-brac, cheaply framed paintings of cats, clipper ships, or long-dead celebrities (not a few on black velvet), fast-food action figures from ancient film flops, scrap lumber, and a lonely plaid lounge chair that had declined from recliner to outright reject. Wow, thought Roger: A treasure trove for the budget-conscious—a category into which most Fidelity Plaza residents naturally fell.

After all, Renata was a doctoral candidate in marsh ecology, Roger worked part-time at the college in IT, and their immediate neighbors,

Nigel and Lydia Vaughan, who had helped Daddy Maharis find this place, were bluegrass musicians who sold lapidary jewelry—or jewelry makers who often mangled bluegrass—to make ends meet. Other residents were retirees on Social Security, language tutors, rookie cops, or administrative assistants with live-ins who tended bar, stocked shelves, or schlepped out to the corner every morning to wait with the Hispanics, druggies, and dropouts for pickup day jobs. Despite the rundown elegance of its town-houses, then, Fidelity Plaza hardly qualified as upscale, and a murder at the swimming pool three years ago had earned it the mocking sobriquet *Fatality Plaza*. Ha-ha.

Roger half-coveted the plaid lounger, even though he and Renata had no place to put it. But if he could think of a place (maybe tossing out an old chair to make room), he should grab it *now*—before a downpour turned its cushions into waterlogged gunnysacks.

Whereupon a thirty-something woman and a really young teenager showed up at the Dumpsters to interrupt his musings.

"You interested in that thing?" the woman asked.

"Excuse me," said Roger, startled.

"I mean, if you are, well, you can tote it off, because you got here first, but if you aren't, I'd like to haul it to our place for Brad." She jerked her thumb toward the boy and introduced herself as Edie Hartsock.

Brad looked through Roger as if Roger's black-and-white Springsteen T-shirt bestowed on him total invisibility.

Roger smiled in spite of a sudden uneasiness. "It's yours. Haul away."

"Could you give us a hand? I'm a woman and he's just a kid, you know?"

So, after handing the boy the fattest cushion and warning Mrs. Hartsock to watch her feet, Roger wrestled the Laz-E-Boy all the way from the Dumpsters to the Hartsocks' townhouse, dragging and rocking it like a lone stevedore struggling with a crated nuclear warhead. He even manhandled it up the steps and into their front hall, finishing there in a streaming sweat.

"*Great!*" Mrs. Hartsock said. "You'll have to come sit in it some time. When you do, I'll give you an Orange Crush."

⇥✳︎⇤

The Pile | Michael Bishop

The Pile provided the ever-coming-and-going folks of Fidelity Plaza with a *resource*—Roger's apt term—for losing what they no longer wanted or needed, and for acquiring what they hoped they could put to life-brightening use. It changed more often than the residents. Items appeared and disappeared every day, some rapidly and some with such vegetable slowness that it seemed they would take root beside the Dumpsters and grow up next to them like scrub trees or Velcro-suckered vines.

Roger and Renata settled in. They added to The Pile a burned-out portable TV set, a used wicker picnic hamper, and the plastic dishes, now scratched, that had come with it. Each of these items, Roger noted with satisfaction, vanished overnight. Somebody had found them worth taking, and that was good. Roger visited The Pile every other day or so, more out of curiosity than need, but usually hung back several yards to avoid seeming overeager to loot its ever-mutating mother lode.

After he returned one evening with a working steam iron—an iron that looked almost new—Renata started visiting The Pile herself. Occasionally she went with Roger to help him appraise its inventory, and together they salvaged a rustic coffee table that Renata assigned to the back porch as a "garden table." Later, friends for whom Roger grilled burgers and vegetable kabobs on this makeshift patio told them that the table had first belonged to Graig and Irene Lyons, and then to Kathi Stole in Building F, and then to a sickly man in the nether corners of the complex, and finally to Roger and Renata. Renata, bless her, had refinished the table herself.

"The old guy's son put it on The Pile the day after he passed," Nigel said. "Don't worry, though. I don't think he croaked from anything catching."

Lydia sipped her virgin Bloody Mary. "But we're not saying it isn't *haunted*."

She could have, though: That table was about as haunted as a cumquat.

The iron proved more problematic. Using it, Renata burned iron-shaped prints in a new blouse, an old tablecloth, and a pair of Roger's favorite chinos. Once, for no reason either of them could discern, it leapt off the shelf on which Renata had left it and gouged a hole in a linoleum countertop.

"Haunted," Roger told her, joking.

"Defective," she countered. "That's why it wound up on The Pile."

"I'll put it back out there."

"You will not. A decent soul would dump it where nobody else could get it."

"Okay: I'll dump it where nobody else can get it."

"Yes you most certainly will," Renata said. "Today."

And because Big Brother did as Little Sis said, that was the end of that.

⋇

The Pile remained an attraction, though, and neither Roger nor Renata could resist going out there periodically to see what had manifested on, or departed from, it.

Roger, although good at his job, found his IT work only intermittently satisfying ("We're all trapped in the tar pit of technology," he once told his unamused boss); and so The Pile became for him not only a resource for items with which to furnish or decorate their place, but also a source of stuff that he could repair, remake, or put to good aesthetic use in imaginative artifacts of his own creation.

He converted a broken floor lamp into a bona fide light-giver that also served as a hat-tree. He painstakingly perforated a cymbal—*one* cymbal—to turn it into a colander-cum-projector with which a person could drain canned vegetables, *or* give an impromptu planetarium show (by shining a flashlight through its underside). He made a colorful banner for the front porch out of scraps of old material and pieces of balsa wood daubed with model-airplane paint. He used a discarded drum for the base of a revolving chess platform, whose board he assembled from coping-sawed squares of white pine and red cedar. When he couldn't find what he needed on The Pile, he extracted from it items to barter with local merchants for stuff he *could* use.

Renata, working toward her doctorate, encouraged Roger in these activities; she even ceded to him the decoration of the living room and the upstairs bedrooms, areas that many women fight to control, and they prospered by this arrangement. If anybody razzed them or expressed surprise, they offered a united front.

Renata: "A major victory in the war for female emancipation."

Roger: "An expansion of the territories suitable for male exploration."

Of course, few of their friends expressed surprise. Any surprise, given the well-established theoretical bases of gender equality, centered on the fact that they actually put into practice what Renata preached—even if, after the iron episode, she might have said that she too often *wielded* that instrument while Roger *hung out* at The Pile talking with his scavenger pals and assessing its contents.

Roger added to his acquaintances by hanging out there, though. He saw an oddly slow-moving Brad Hartsock put some nested TV trays on The Pile. He met a college cop, Douglas-Kenneth Smith, who anted up the well-oiled derailleur of a road bike. (Roger grabbed this, wiped it dry, and hung it in a closet as a bartering chip.) He talked baseball with a grandmother, Loretta Crider, whose nephew unloaded a sewing machine, and he foraged out a set of yellowing place mats (with inset pen-and-ink sketches of Big Ben, Westminster Abbey, the Tower of London, etc.) that a high-school teacher, Ronald Curtis, had left on the Incredible Heap in a pretty aqua carton.

"You know why we call this place Fidelity Plaza?" Mr. Curtis asked Roger.

"Because the couples here only screw around with their own spice?"

Mr. Curtis scowled in consternation. "Their own what?"

"Their own *spice*—plural of *spouse*."

"Ah, that's very funny." But Mr. Curtis declined to smile.

"Then why *is* this place called Fidelity Plaza?" Roger lifted a hand. "Does it have anything to do with insurance?" He lowered his hand. "Forget that. I don't have a clue."

"It's because everyone who lives here—or nearly everyone—is as faithful as Fido to caring for and worshipping The Pile."

"Well, I guess it beats watching *Wheel of Fortune*."

"I don't know." Mr. Curtis at long last smiled. "I've always liked the pretty Letter Turner."

"I prefer her sister Lana. Or did until Daddy said she made her last film the year I was born. And now poor Lana's kaput."

"I hope you and your sister enjoy the place mats." And whistling the theme to *The Andy Griffith Show*, Mr. Curtis slipped his hands into his pockets and walked poker-faced back to Building G.

The Best of Subterranean

⇥※⇤

One evening, after Roger had had another annoying tiff with his boss, he went out to The Pile to cool off. Renata was at the library, and he was grateful for the relative quiet near the pool and the Dumpsters.

Then Brad Hartsock sauntered over from Building M and stopped maybe twenty yards away. He held a furry doll wearing a red scarf around its neck and, under its hairy chin, an ebony breastplate like those worn by Roman legionaries in epic Biblical flicks—except, of course, for its size and color. Also, the kid holding this figure—a gorilla doll?—looked different this afternoon. On his and Roger's first meeting at the plaid Laz-E-Boy, Brad had appeared no more than fourteen, with a morose face and eyes of such opaque iciness that Roger had been mildly freaked and entirely convinced that the teen had an IQ lower than the average Atlanta temperature in February. Today, though, he looked older and smarter—his eyes boasted a fiery spark—but, in his hipshot stance out by the Dumpsters, no less spooky.

"Hey, Brad, what you got?"

Brad studied the object in his hands as if his wit had fled. Then he swallowed and his smarts flooded back.

"A singing and dancing ape that doesn't do either anymore," he said. "Why? You *want* this piece of crap?"

"No thanks. I'm holding out for a piccolo-playing orangutan."

"Smartass," Brad snarled, like an adult gang-banger. His torso had some bulk, as if he'd been working out, and his jaw showed reddish-brown stubble. In starched denims and a striped pullover, though, he was dressed like a grade-school preppy.

An evil imp made Roger say, "You seem a tad mature to be toting around an ape doll, Bradley me lad."

"And you seem pretty friggin' *infantile* for a grownup."

My God, thought Roger, the boy has panache. He raised his hands in appreciative surrender. "Touché, kid: touché."

"Besides, this thing's Mama's. My bastard daddy gave it to her. Now it's broken. All I want to do is chunk it on The Pile and go home. Okay?"

"Sure. It's a free townhouse complex—even *freer* if you can get somebody else to put up your rent." He backed away from The Pile.

Brad shook his head as if Roger undermined his dream of a crap-free world, but shuffled up in his expensive gym shoes and set the ape doll on an unpainted particleboard nightstand that would certainly blow apart in a light wind. Then he turned and sashayed straight toward Building M.

Again, Roger couldn't help it: He approached The Pile, scrutinized the twenty-inch gorilla from a squat, and at length snatched it off the nightstand. It was his, or his and Renata's, for Renata would love it. She loved animals and funny effigies of animals, and the red scarf around this ape's throat—along with the needlelike scarlet tongue in its rubbery mouth—would win her over faster than a loaf of fresh-baked Syrian bread.

And Renata did love it. She rocked it in her arms like an infant. She cuddled it to her neck on the sofa. She laid it beside her in her bed and took pains not to roll over on it during the night. "What a cutie," she said a dozen times a day.

Because of its skin color and quirky smile, she named it *Andruw*, after a favorite ballplayer, totally heedless of the fact that many people would think naming a gorilla doll after a black man racist. But she loved the ballplayer and thought his given name and its unusual spelling quite as endearing as his Mona Lisa smile.

Roger told her why she just couldn't call the toy Andruw, and Renata said she would shorten the name to *Andy*. Roger said this dodge wouldn't work because there'd once been a TV show, *Amos and Andy*, which many people now regarded as illustrative of racial attitudes best forgotten. Renata rolled her eyes, but, being an intelligent young woman, understood the strictures with which a monstrous past not of one's own making could tint the present, and so gave in.

"I'll call it *Q.T.*," she said. "Who can argue with that?" She added that it would be fabulous, though, if Roger could restore its ability to sing and dance. As cute as she found it, "bringing it to life again" would greatly heighten its adorability.

"If it gets any more adorable," Roger said, "I'll jump under a train."

Renata gave him an adorable up-yours grimace, and Roger got busy on the doll's adorable innards, to see what miracles he could perform.

※

A day later, still working on the issue, he went out to the pool for some air and glimpsed Brad Hartsock perched on a patio chair with a poncho over his shoulders. (It had begun to get cool.) Brad gazed into the bland aqua ripples with such alarming world-weariness that he looked, well, *about thirty*, with a grown man's five-o'clock shadow and violet circles under his eyes.

Briefly, Roger thought the person must be Brad's older brother, on a visit from out of town. However, Mrs. Hartsock was nowhere near old enough to have given birth to this fellow, and maybe a trick of the autumn light had deceived Roger. Or maybe the guy was Mrs. Hartsock's younger brother or...

"Brad?" he said. "Brad, is that you?"

The figure in the chair turned a cold hard gaze on him. "Yeah, it's me. Who'd you think it was, President Bush?"

"Nearly," Roger said. "Sorry. I just thought you looked a little puny."

"Seasonal allergies." Brad flung back his poncho, disclosing a big aluminum can of malt liquor. "Plus this, I guess."

"Your mama lets you drink?"

"Why you think I'm out here?" The voice belonged to Brad, as did the features—but the galoot at the pool was a worn near-future avatar of the young teen Roger had met on his first visit to The Pile.

"Do *you* think that's a good—?"

"Hey, I'm self-medicating, all right?"

"Whatever." Roger didn't want to leave. True adults didn't let teens drink, even if they looked like flea-bitten thirty-year-olds. "By the way, I took your mama's gorilla off The Pile—it just sort of spoke to me."

Brad toasted him with the malt-liquor can. "May it bring you true happiness." He chug-a-lugged for a good fifteen seconds, wiped his mouth with the back of his hand, and gazed back down into the water—dismissively, Roger thought.

The Pile | Michael Bishop

⁂

The gorilla, as Roger soon learned without even Googling "Gorilla Dolls" on his P.C., sang a novelty number called "The Macarena" to the tinny-sounding band in its back. It moved its rubbery lips, showed its pointed red tongue, and swayed its apish hips like a mutant hula dancer.

When Renata returned from the library that evening, Roger took the toy to her, set it on their kitchen table, and flipped its switch. Q.T. did his thing, loudly and repeatedly. Renata laughed aloud. She knew the gestures that went with the dance (even though Q.T. clearly didn't) and performed them for Roger several times in a row.

"My God, what a cheesy routine," Roger said, switching Q.T. off.

"Thank yew, thank yew." Renata curtsied to him and to make-believe spectators elsewhere in the room. "What a terrific gift." She tickled Roger's chin and mockingly rubbed his upper arms.

"Thank Edie Hartsock, the gas-company secretary over in 13-M. The ape was hers before I rescued him from The Pile."

"I certainly will." Renata stopped rubbing her brother's arms. "But what if she gets jealous? What if she wants it back, now that it works again?"

"Losers, weepers," Roger said. "Finders, keepers."

But then a series of events turned Renata's appreciation of Q.T. into something like distaste. Roger hit the doll's switch so often that soon even he had learned the hip movements and hand gestures that enlivened Q.T.'s ditty. A better than average dancer, he *kept* hitting the switch, triggering the tinny music, Q.T.'s pelvic swivels, and his own pseudo-Latin moves, which he busted in the kitchen, the dining room, and Renata's room as she struggled to study.

"Stop it!" she shouted, covering her ears. "Have you gone bazooka?" This was a facetious Maharis family term for *berserk*.

"You bet—*totally* bazooka. Forgive me. It's just so damned addictive."

"For a while it was funny. Now it's annoying. So, for God's sake, stop."

"I will. I promise. I'll stop."

But he couldn't. He'd stop briefly, to watch a TV program or fix a meal, but then the contagiousness of Q.T.'s act would call to him, and he'd turn the toy on again and jig about the townhouse, upstairs and down, extending his arms, crossing them, clutching his head, and doing every other move dictated by the song's choreographic protocols. Even when the music ran down and the ape ceased gyrating, Roger kept singing, kept doing his manic St. Vitus dance. He had become the Irksome Dervish of Building D.

"Stop it!" Renata cried. "Stop it! *Stop it! STOP IT!*"

"Yes. You're right. I'll stop."

He did stop, for a while, but then he started again. Renata screamed *"Arrrrrrrgh!"* (as he'd never heard her scream before), trotted downstairs with an old walking stick, and poked its tip into his bellybutton.

"Put Q.T. back on The Pile, Roger! Put him back out on The Pile!"

"A decent soul would dump him where nobody else could get him."

Renata twisted the stick. "Give it to me," she said. *"Now."* Roger passed her the ape. "Good. Now we're going to give it back to Mrs. Hartsock. She might never have had Brad toss it on The Pile if it hadn't stopped working."

"Maybe he started doing what I've been doing."

"Only a baboon"—Renata started over—"Only a *buffoon* would do what you've been doing. Come on. We *will* take it back." They each grabbed sweaters and met at the door. "I'll carry it, bro'—I, myself, not you."

※

"Come in," Edie Hartsock called out in a gravelly voice.

They entered the townhouse's smoky lower floor. Renata waved off offers of an orange soda and a mint-flavored cigarette and thrust the doll into Mrs. Hartsock's arms while explaining that Roger had repaired it and that it only seemed right to give it back to her now that it worked again.

"I don't want it," Mrs. Hartsock said.

"But—" Renata began.

"From almost the get-go it gave me the willies. I was glad when it wore out."

"But—"

"And I hate its stupid song. My ex gave it to me as a gag, if not as a torment."

The Pile | MICHAEL BISHOP

Roger noticed that the plaid Laz-E-Boy had emerged into visibility (of a limited kind, anyway) from the drifting cigarette smoke. Brad lay in this chair, whose footrest he had extended and whose arms he clutched like an astronaut enduring a rocky launch. But what most disturbed Roger was the fact that several large manikins, marionettes, or dolls either stood about the room or hung from pieces of wire from the ceiling. He made out an evil-looking Howdy Doody, a lifelike Creature from the Black Lagoon, and a less adept facsimile of Godzilla. Other simulacra haunted the corners and the stairwell so that 13-M now seemed a bizarre conflation of a menagerie and Madame Tussaud's.

As for Brad, he dully ogled his visitors through eyeballs that appeared pollen-dusted. His bottom lip hung down, and strands of hair on his balding pate rose and fell in the updraft of a heating vent on the floor. Tonight, as opposed to Roger's last encounter with him at The Pile, he looked not only ill but also middle-aged—forty-five, at the very least. He'd lost weight and taken on wrinkles, and his skin had the sallow cast of a man long pent in a damp basement.

"Brad?" Roger said. "Brad, is that you?"

"Yeah," Brad drawled mockingly. "Who'd you think I was, Beyoncé?"

"Those are powerful *allergies* you're fighting," Roger said. He wanted to point out that Mrs. Hartsock shouldn't smoke around him, but how could he in her own outré place? Besides, she ought to know that.

"Allergies?" Mrs. Hartsock said. "Is that what he told you?"

"Yes ma'am, he did."

"Oh, Bradley." Then: "Oh, no. You see, he's got this condition."

"What condition?" Renata gazed about the townhouse in evident discomfort and perplexity. Roger could see that she thought Halloween much too far away to justify such freaky décor now.

Edie Hartsock said in an annoyed-sounding stage whisper, "I really don't like to talk about it in front of him."

"Why?" Brad whined. "Because I'm fourteen and look forty? Or do I look even older tonight?"

"*Fourteen?*" Renata said. "How can this person be *fourteen?*"

"It's really fast, his condition," Mrs. Hartsock said.

"What condition?" Renata asked again, almost demanding.

"Progeria," Brad said from the Laz-E-Boy. "I got progeria."

Roger pondered this. The only case of progeria he'd ever heard about—in a book about bad shit happening to good people which his father had made him tackle when their mother died of breast cancer—occurred in a kid who'd begun looking like a little old man at three and who died at—well, at *fourteen*.

Brad's progeria, if that's what this was, had *started* at fourteen and was moving a lot faster than the disease of the kid in the book, as if to make up for lost time. It seemed impossible, but Roger had learned from his mama's death that "impossible" crap could drop on you like a grand piano at any time and then resound smashingly in your head and your kicked-asunder life forever.

"This is a pretty weird sort of progeria, isn't it?" Roger asked Mrs. Hartsock. "I mean, if weirdness has degrees." (The Hartsocks' townhouse suggested that it had *many* degrees.)

"Yeah," Brad said weakly. "My doctor calls it an allelomorphic progeria, a sort of one-gene-off kind."

Renata stared at Brad Hartsock. "He's a very smart fourteen."

"But I look forty," Brad said. "Or is it fifty? Mama, is it fifty? Or is it like"—his adult voice poignantly broke—"maybe even *six-tee?*"

"You look twenty-five, Brad: a handsome twenty-five."

"Right," Brad said, but he visibly relaxed.

"What can we do?" Renata asked. "To help, I mean."

"Maybe a little entertainment," Roger said. He took the ape doll from Renata and switched it on: "The Macarena" blared into the room, and both he and the doll began hip-swiveling. Brad screamed. Mrs. Hartsock grabbed the doll away from Roger and fumbled to switch it off.

"Brad can't abide it anymore," she said, not unkindly. "I can't either."

"Nor can I," Renata said, giving Roger a look. "I'm sorry—so sorry."

"Well, you could put the obnoxious thing back on The Pile for me."

"Yes, Mrs. Hartsock. We'll do it tonight."

"Edie," Brad's mother said. "Call me Edie." They had bonded over their disgust with Roger's asininity and their concern for Mrs. Hartsock's dying son.

Mrs. Hartsock stepped onto the porch with them and unburdened herself as if they were paid confessors. "I divorced Bradley's father seven years ago. He was never home much, and when he was, well, he was an abuser."

"What sort?" Renata asked. "Physical?"

"That depended. He never hurt the boy, though. All that stuff in there—he makes models for movies, theaters, and Halloween festivals. When I told him by telephone that Bradley was—uh, terminally sick, he sent that hideous junk and had these guys who work for him come install it, just to cheer the boy up, and—" She began to cry.

Renata embraced her. "Does Bradley like it, all that stuff? *Does* it cheer him up?"

"I don't know. He says so. But it may scare him. He'd rather his daddy came to see him, I think, but he won't say that for fear of hurting my feelings. It wouldn't—hurt my feelings, I mean—it would just scare me too."

"Has he threatened you?" Renata asked. "I mean, since your divorce."

"Not so I could ever convince anybody of it. But he's always liked to hurt me, and I can't help thinking that all this"—she waved one hand vaguely—"is all part of his plan to do that and to spread the hurt as far as possible."

※

Renata carried Q.T. to The Pile and set the ape gently on the shelf of a flimsy, lopsided bookcase.

"Don't fetch him back," she told Roger. "Or I'll kick you out and get daddy to back me a hundred percent." This was at once a joke and not a joke. It gave Roger all the incentive he needed to obey, for his otherwise sweet sister ruthlessly carried out even her most extravagant threats.

"All that work," Roger said looking at the gorilla doll.

"You replaced a battery," Renata said, "maybe two. Don't pretend it was this big deal. Now maybe somebody sane can enjoy it."

"Until they're *driven* bazooka," Roger said.

"Just don't bring it back."

He didn't. And Q.T.—under a wholly different name, if under any name at all—vanished from The Pile into the townhouse of another resident.

In fact, Nigel Rabe appropriated it and set it up on a chest-of-drawers against the inner wall of Renata's office. Whenever he or Lydia played it, Renata ground her teeth in chagrin and frustration.

At length, she knocked on Nigel and Lydia's door and offered fifteen dollars for the doll. Its "Macarena" binges irritated her even more than did their weekend bluegrass jams, because the doll sounded off on nights when she studied. Faced with her complaint, Nigel declined Renata's money but returned the doll to The Pile himself. A friend indeed was Nigel. And, by returning it to The Pile, he sidestepped the punishments, deliberate or accidental, that possessing the thing often inflicted.

Thereafter the doll began making the rounds of those Fidelity Plaza residents who visited The Pile. Kathi Stole took the singing and swaying ape after Nigel and Lydia, but put it back on The Pile when her two kids began fighting over it like piranhas flensing a baby pig. The next time it appeared, however, several people expressed interest in it, and Mr. Curtis, who didn't care at all about the ape, became the comptroller of this item, the guy who decided who could have it. He inaugurated the ritual of handing a small piece of red string to whomever he deemed its next legitimate inheritor.

After Kathi Stole unloaded the gorilla, Mr. Curtis wandered into the crowd hanging out around The Pile like flea-market vultures and gave this red string to Creed Harvin, a political-science grad student. Creed took the toy home and promptly broke two knuckles thrusting them into a doorjamb while doing the hand motions that accompany "The Macarena." (It was dark, and Harvin was drunk.)

After Harvin, Bill Wilkes in Building J received the red string and of course the doll. The next morning, after he and his wife had hosted an intimate soirée at which the little ape did his repetitive stuff, a city trash truck rear-ended their Audi in the parking lot, and Bill Wilkes immediately returned the ape to The Pile.

Then D.-K. Smith, the campus cop, slipped Mr. Curtis (whom no one suspected of bribe-ability) a ten for the red string and put the doll in a window of his townhouse as a symbol of defiance against the rumor that the toy precipitated misfortune on its owners. But working security the next day, he got into an argument with a middle-aged man, who insisted on entering an athletic dormitory without proper ID, and wound up hand-cuffing the troublemaker. Later that afternoon, at the insistence of the offended man (an alumnus and a high-level donor), Smith was summarily fired, with no chance of appeal. With his rent paid through the month, Smith carried Bonzo—formerly Q.T.—out to The Pile and slung the ape into a discarded baby carriage.

Mr. Curtis was visiting relatives in Macon and so could neither pass the red string along to the doll's next hapless soul nor accept another bribe. And although Roger could not imagine too many residents vying for the doll now, he saw two other persons waiting for the ape when Smith jettisoned it, both bachelors, a bartender and a drywaller, and they reached for it simultaneously, knocking the pram over and rolling in the ambient litter to establish ownership. In fact, they grunted and grappled barbarously. Finally, one wrestler yanked the doll away from his rival, rolled through the detritus on the edge of The Pile, gained his feet, and took off along one fenced side of the swimming pool. The other man, slimmer and swifter, pursued with blood in his eyes.

Roger trotted down his own porch steps to keep both in view and marveled as first the larger man leapt the chain-link fence and then the slimmer gracefully took the same hurdle. It was late afternoon, and cool, but a small group of residents had gathered at the farther end of the pool beside the bathhouse; and, near the diving board in front of these people, the slimmer man caught the tail of his rival's shirt and spun him about so that he bounced off the board's butt end, flailed for balance without releasing his prize, and fell with a huge splash into the leaf-mottled water. The pursuer then jumped on the board and began pushing down on the bigger man's head with one wet shoe, apparently doing all in his power to drown the guy.

"*Hey!*" Roger opened the gate to the pool and burst through to the diving board. Two people seated before the bathhouse—a burly man and a woman in a floral dress and a loose beige sweater—hurried to help Roger drag the assailant from the board. A siren on a light pole, a siren used for fire drills and tornado warnings, started to keen, and the man in the water sank beneath churning ripples as the doll went down with him.

Fully clothed, Roger plunged in after both. He had no coherent plan for saving either and so much fierce headache-inducing noise in his head that he despaired of ever hearing anything else again.

⁂

Renata knelt beside the supine, spread-eagled bartender with a nursing student from their building, a matter-of-fact young woman who said, "This poor dude is gone." D.-K. Smith, the sacked campus cop, held the elbow of the unresisting drywaller who had just shoe-dunked the drowned man to a depth impossible to rise from. Although the Fidelity Plaza siren had stopped wailing a short while ago, the sirens on, first, an ambulance and, then, two city squad cars had superseded it.

The ambulance left with the bartender; one of the squad cars, with the drywaller. Two policemen stayed to take statements from the on-site witnesses.

They began with Roger, who'd seen far more than he cared to admit, and moved on to D.-K. Smith, the student nurse, Renata, and the group at poolside. The woman who had helped Roger halt the drywaller's assault on the bartender (too late to prevent his death) turned out to be Edie Hartsock.

When this fact penetrated Roger's brain—as he stood on the slick concrete dripping like a spaniel in a cloudburst—he realized that the frail, wheelchair-bound figure at a round metal table in front of the bathhouse was Brad, drastically transfigured. Or was it? Could it possibly be?

Roger squelched over to this mysterious personage.

The man in the wheelchair squinted up at him out of a piggy grey eye in a deep-dug socket. He had a few thin wisps of hair across his skull and skin like wax-laminated tissue paper. He smelled of greasy menthol and stale pee.

"Are you Brad Hartsock?"

The codger blinked once and then blinked again. "Who'd you think I was?" he cackled faintly. "Methuselah?"

Roger found he was clutching the sodden simian doll over which the barkeep and the drywaller had fought. Despite Brad's screaming fit earlier in the week, he felt that he should give it to the "kid" as a wonky pool-party favor, a charm against early oblivion. Apparently, Renata telepathically parsed his intentions.

"Roger!" she shouted. "Roger, don't you do it!"

But Q.T., or Bonzo, or Little King Kong, fell from Roger's hands into Bradley's plaid-blanketed lap. Brad gawped at the doll.

Then he opened his mouth, which continued slack. No scream issued from it—no scream, no word, no whimper, no breath.

❊

It was rumored that Edie Hartsock had a small closed-coffin family funeral for her son in her hometown. No one from Fidelity Plaza received an invitation to this event, and when Mrs. Hartsock returned a week or ten days later, she cloistered herself in her townhouse like a nun in a convent. Some residents speculated that she had had the gorilla doll buried with Brad, whereas others argued that she had weighted it with used flashlight batteries or old tractor lug nuts and spitefully committed it to an alligator hole in the swamp near her birthplace. These speculations were so outlandish, though, that Roger could not easily imagine what had prompted them.

A few evenings after Mrs. Hartsock's return, Renata saw a crowd gathered at The Pile in the twilight. She called Roger to her side on the porch. "There's something new out there. Do you want to see what it is?"

"I don't know." Despite their satisfaction with a couple of salvaged items (their garden table and an elegant little medicine cabinet), Roger had grown wary of The Pile.

"Come on," Renata said. "It might be worth it to look."

So they went to look. People parted for them—people gawking but not speaking, people stunned into a near-trancelike state.

The Maharis siblings moved gingerly through them to a point where each felt like a supplicant in the presence of some august, or richly uncanny, superluminary—for they beheld in the lee of one cardboard-filled Dumpster a plaid Laz-E-Boy in which sat a pale white figure reminiscent of Bradley Hartsock before the advent of his virulent variety of progeria. This effigy wore a powder-blue T-shirt, multi-pocketed grey shorts, and some of the prettiest Italian sandals Roger had ever seen. Had the figure had any nerve endings, it would have been cold—but, given Brad's death after fast-forward progeria, it existed only as a detailed manikin, not a living being, and Roger and his sister gaped at the real-looking humanoid artifact in bewilderment and awe.

D.-K. Smith handed Roger a lace-bearing sign.

The sign's legend read "TAKE ME HOME." Its obverse read "CHAIR AND ITS OCCUPANTS NOT TO BE SEPARATED."

"The Brad-thing was wearing this sign," D.-K. told the Maharises.

" 'Occupants'?" Renata said. "Why is that word plural?"

Loretta Crider stepped up and showed them the worrisome little "Macarena" ape. "This was in the Bradley-thing's lap," she said. "It freaked D.-K. out, so I just picked it up and held it."

"Right," D.-K. said. "Thanks. I'm leaving this spooky bullshit with you all. Take care, okay? I mean it: *Take care.*"

And he left them all standing there at The Pile.

Well, why not? There were laws against child abandonment, but none that Roger knew of against *effigy abandonment.*

After a while, Loretta Crider said, "Mrs. Hartsock's disappeared. Her townhouse is empty, flat-out empty. Who knows where she or all her stuff's gone? It's a mystery, is what it is."

She set the ape doll back in the lap of the Bradley-thing, and the remainder of the uneasy onlookers dispersed to their own places.

After a longer while, Roger said, "Renata, I could make something with this Laz-E-Boy and this creepy Bradley-thing."

"What, for God's sake?"

"I don't know—a sort of found-art installation, maybe."

Renata crossed her arms. Her face had grown lavender in the darkness. No moon shone. The pool lights cut off. A wind rose.

Roger could feel the night, the month, and in fact the year itself all going deeply and dreadfully *bazooka.*

—for my son Jamie, on whose notes this story is based

The Bohemian Astrobleme

by Kage Baker

"Oh!" cried Enderley's wife. "The pin has come off my brooch!"

Enderley, lathering his face with soap, grunted and laid down the shaving brush. "Let's see," he said, turning from the washbasin. His wife held out her hand to display the brooch she had inherited from her mother. It was a heavy, old-fashioned thing of silver, set with a large oval stone. The stone looked to be dark red agate, swirled through with fernlike markings. Enderley didn't much care for it, but he was mindful of his wife's stricken expression as he said:

"Easily fixed. We don't need to take it to a jeweler; I can repair it at the laboratory."

"Can you?"

"Of course. Dot of solder will do the job. Set it on the hall table and I'll remember to take it with me."

※

Enderley's wife was under the impression he worked for the Patent Office, or some sort of branch of it, doing tests on things. She never asked what, exactly, because she was not of an inquiring disposition. She was content to know that Enderley's weekly wage comfortably furnished their little terrace house in a nicer London suburb and kept all tradesmen's bills current.

When Enderley set forth each morning, beaver hat securely on head and umbrella tightly furled, he did not, in fact, go to the Patent Office nor to any branches it might have. He walked briskly in the general direction of Whitehall, turning in at Craig's Court. He entered an unremarkable mansion of red brick housing one of the less-celebrated clubs in London, Redking's.

Once within its obscure halls, Enderley walked straight past the dining room and bar; passed without a glance the study, where Members dozed in deep chairs or scowled as they perused the *Times*. Enderley walked down a narrow flight of stairs and along a dimly-lit corridor to a pair of doors which, when opened, revealed merely a tiny windowless room within. Enderley stepped inside and closed the doors. Were anyone to open the doors again, assuming at least one minute and fifteen seconds precisely had passed, they would find Enderley nowhere in sight.

This was because Enderley had ridden the Ascending Room down to one of the several storeys that lay concealed beneath Redking's. On one of these subterranean floors, well lit and ventilated by arts currently unknown to the rest of the world, Enderley hung up his beaver hat, set his umbrella in a stand provided for that purpose, donned a white coat, and went to work.

In one respect only were Mrs. Enderley's assumptions correct: Enderley did conduct tests on things. Not, however, on new formulae for aniline dyes or lucifer matches, or improved mechanisms for cotton mills. Rather, Enderley's work on any given day might involve devising new weatherproofing methods for airships, or adapting designs for submarine vessels. In this year of 1845 Jules Verne had as yet written nothing more significant than school compositions, and yet his muse was already alive beneath the pavement of London.

This was because the hidden complex under Redking's housed an ancient fraternity currently known, to those privileged few who knew of its existence, as the Gentlemen's Speculative Society. The Society had gone by other names over the course of its lengthy career. Sir Isaac Newton, Dr. John Dee, and Leonardo da Vinci had all been members. So, it was rumored, had Archimedes and Heron of Alexandria. The Society's goal was the improvement of the human condition through the secret use of *technologia*, until such time as humanity became advanced enough to be made aware of its benefits.

It was generally agreed that some sort of world domination would be necessary before that day arrived, but at the present time the Society was content merely to gather power and pull strings attached to certain government officials. Enderley had been recruited at an early age, after demonstrating his brilliance by winning several prizes. The Society paid him a handsome wage and rewarded especially useful discoveries with generous bonuses, so Enderley was a contented member of the rank and file.

On this particular day Enderley drew the broken brooch from his pocket and set it on his worktable, intending to mend it when he had a moment to spare. As his present project did not involve the use of a soldering iron (he was experimenting with synthetic compounds that showed promise in inducing profound sleep in dogs) the brooch sat forgotten for some hours, until a careless gesture on Enderley's part knocked over a beaker of acetic acid. The acid flooded across several of Enderley's notes and briefly submerged the brooch as well, before finding the edge of the worktable and spattering to the floor.

Muttering to himself, Enderley grabbed a rag and stopped the flood. He pulled his notes free and, whilst waving them in the air, noticed the brooch. He grabbed for it, observing as he did so a peculiar fizzing reaction localized to the ferny inclusions in the red stone. A second later Enderley was lying unconscious and flat on his back where he had been thrown to the floor.

His fellow chemists gathered around him in concern. Judson, who was presently working on a formula to prolong life, stooped to pick up the brooch Enderley had dropped and immediately fell as though poleaxed. Berwick, who was compounding a fuel that might enable steam engines to run without benefit of coal, picked up the brooch and was likewise knocked off his feet, stunned. So was Ponsonby, who had that very morning invented a substance that would enable photographs to be taken and developed in a fraction of the time required by Mssrs. Daguerre or Talbot.

It was left to young Jones, the tea boy, to realize that the best way to pick up the brooch was to gingerly scoop it up between two pieces of pasteboard.

⇥⍭⇤

"It's not an agate," said Greene, pushing the stone across his blotter with the end of a pen. Ludbridge leaned forward and peered at it. Greene customarily prided himself on showing as little emotion as possible during a briefing, and Ludbridge had long since learned that any briefing sessions invariably became contests of sangfroid.

"My dear old chap, gemstones aren't my field of study. I wouldn't know an agate from a bit of red glass."

"As it happens, it *is* a bit of red glass," Greene informed him. "To be precise, it's a tektite."

"And that would be?"

"Meteoric glass. Millennia ago, some monstrous fragment of star-stuff hurtled down and struck the Earth. Sand was melted and re-formed into glassy material, and spewed out across the landscape, to be subsequently buried in other antediluvian upheavals. There's a strewnfield in the Near East with a considerable deposit. There's another in Bavaria. The stuff from the German crater all ended up in Bohemia, and it's called moldavite. This would appear to be a piece of moldavite, but for one thing."

"Mm. What's that?"

"Moldavite's green."

"Well, then it's something else, isn't it?"

Greene shook his head. "Ah, but what? Enderley's asked his wife. The stone was set in a brooch she inherited from her mother. Her mother came from Bohemia. Apparently there's a very rare red variety. Bohemia has its own astrobleme—"

"Beg your pardon?"

"Where's your Latin? Astrobleme, 'star wound.' The impact site of a meteor. The Bohemian one seems to be near Budweis. We think that's the source of the red tektites. We've had Research culling through their references; the red stone is difficult to find, hardly ever comes on the market, and the only written reference we can locate is by a 16th-century alchemist, who gave it the name *blitzstein*."

"Thunder stone? No, no… Lightning stone, wouldn't that be?"

"Yes. Which indicates that someone before Enderley discovered its useful properties." Greene peered down at the stone. "Fortunately for us, no one else seems to have noticed that the red stone, when in contact with acetic acid, generates a powerful electrical charge."

"Useful, I assume?"

"It could be. The chaps in Fabrication are beside themselves at the test results so far. Reliable battery power without jars and jars of stuff in heavy cases. Imagine your field gear powered by a tiny disc of *this*, in a sealed vial of acid. The electric candles, say. Or the thermal goggles."

"Damned useful, then." Ludbridge leaned back, tugging his beard thoughtfully. "Well, what's the job, Greene?"

"We want more of it. All of it, if we can get it." Greene looked directly into Ludbridge's eyes. "You're to go there and see that we do."

"*There* being?"

"Bohemia, where else?" Greene reached out to the globe that sat on the corner of his desk. He spun it briefly and stopped it with a tap of his finger. "Here. You'll be issued maps, of course. You'll have an interpreter and a legman with you."

"Mm. Funds?"

"Parker will make the usual arrangements."

"I mean, are they to be rather more generous than customary? If I'm to buy large quantities of gemstones?"

Greene looked opaque. He stroked his mustache. "Given what's at stake, your allowance is likely to be generous, yes. You are aware, however, that the finance committee lauds every saved halfpenny. Should the opportunity present itself to practice a certain economy, we would, of course, prefer that you take it."

Ludbridge gave a short laugh, aware that such a display of emotion would cost him the match. It was some consolation to see Greene very nearly smirk.

"To be sure! Which one of 'em's a screwsman, the legman or the translator?"

"The legman, naturally. Not our most stable operative, but we've taken steps."

" 'Not one of our most stable'…? Who is it?"

"Chap named Hirsch. Talented, but on sufferance just at present."

"I see."

⇥✳⇤

Hirsch the legman was nearly late for the boat train to Dover. Ludbridge and the translator—a small and self-effacing émigré named Ressel—watched as he came running through the crowds at the station. He hurried along the platform, spotted their carriage and pounded on the window, grinning. Ludbridge opened the door. Hirsch swung himself in, threw his solitary bag into the overhead rack and slammed the carriage door as the train began to move.

"So!" He collapsed into his seat and grinned at them once more. "I have arrived."

"Just," said Ludbridge.

"Yes, well, I was having my teeth seen to."

"Were you?" Ludbridge drew out his watch and appeared to consult it.

"Mr. Greene's orders. Lest I should be distracted by the toothache when on the job." Hirsch hooked a finger over his lip and displayed the new silver crown gleaming far back in his mouth.

"Charming," murmured Ressel.

"I am a valuable employee after all, it seems," said Hirsch, with a certain gloating tone.

"Are you?" said Ludbridge. "That matter of the policeman in Whitechapel all a misunderstanding, then?"

Hirsch reddened. He leaned back in his seat and folded his arms. "Naturally you've read some sort of dossier on me, I suppose, since you're the mission leader. Very well! Men make mistakes. And yet, here I am, aren't I? And why is that, do you think?"

"Because you were the best man for the job," said Ludbridge.

Hirsch smiled and laid a finger beside his nose. "Right you are! I track like a hound. And this dog knows a few other tricks, believe me. So all is forgiven and forgotten."

"I expect so," said Ludbridge. "Well, gentlemen. Care for a game of cards?"

※

Railway service was dismal, where it existed at all, in France; rather better in Belgium; varied wildly across the Germanies, necessitating several connections made by horse-drawn coach. They had a long jolting ride from Bavaria to Bohemia before gliding into Budweis via horse-drawn rail car.

"Now for some good beer!" cried Hirsch, as he jumped down and collected his bag. "My father used to cry when he remembered it. Wait until you taste it, Ludbridge! It will open your eyes to that flat warm stuff the English drink. Or perhaps your father was a lord, and didn't drink beer?"

"No; he was a laborer, as it happens. Liked his pint of ale." Ludbridge hoisted out his bag as Ressel jumped down.

They found a hotel for commercial travelers. With rooms secured, they had an excellent meal of pork and dumplings at a biergarten, washed down by beer that Ludbridge admitted, when pressed by Hirsch, was quite good.

"And shall we see the sights first, and set off on our quest tomorrow?" cried Hirsch, whose mood had become more and more ebullient the farther east they had traveled. Insofar as he had borne cheerfully with all the inconvenience of the journey, Ludbridge and Ressel had been grateful, but they had begun to find his high spirits somewhat wearing.

"Don't think it bears discussion at table, do you?" Stolidly Ludbridge helped himself to another slice of dumpling. Ressel glanced nervously over his shoulder.

"In the hotel room, Hirsch," he said in a low voice. "More, er, discreet, yes?"

Hirsch's eyes flashed with anger. He subsided, and consumed the rest of his meal in sullen silence.

※

Ludbridge and Ressel played cards until just before midnight, when Hirsch returned and flung his hat across the room at the hatrack. Missing it, he muttered under his breath as he retrieved it and hung it up.

"And your progress?" Ludbridge folded his hand of cards.

"The red is rare," said Hirsch. "Very rare. Two of the jewelers laughed at me. So did a pawnbroker. This is not employment calculated to increase a man's self-respect."

"Quite," said Ludbridge. "Has anyone got it?"

"One place had a signet ring, another place a woman's pendant with a cameo." Hirsch drew a chair from the group at the table and sat, straddling it front to back. "Priced higher than you wish to pay, perhaps? But you'll see. What I did learn was that both pieces were made by the same man, and the red tektite river flows through him and him alone. Old family business of jewelers, and he is the current inheritor of the firm."

"What's his name?"

"Konrad Bayer." Hirsch felt about in his coat pocket and pulled out a slip of paper, which he handed to Ludbridge. "That is the address of the premises."

"Very good." Ludbridge glanced at it and tucked it away in his waistcoat pocket. "Ressel, you and I will trot round there tomorrow and make a few innocent inquiries."

"Didn't I do a good enough job?" cried Hirsch.

"Of course you did! I'm giving you a day to rest, you damned fool. Chances are you'll have surveillance watch tomorrow night. You'll want all the sleep you can get," said Ludbridge.

⌁

The shop bore a sign reading BAYER & SOHN. Behind the display window panes were trays lined in faded velvet, bearing various examples of jewelry design in silverplate and paste. Ludbridge nodded at Ressel and they went in, causing a bell mounted over the door to ring as they did so. Ludbridge, smiling, drew off his hat and bowed to the ancient who rose from behind the counter.

"Tell him I'm pleased to make his acquaintance, and ask him whether he's Herr Bayer."

Ressel translated obediently. The old man shook his head mournfully and replied at length.

"He says he is merely Herr Muller, but he has worked here for forty years and can undoubtedly serve us, as Herr Bayer has not yet come down this morning, and what would the Englishman wish to purchase?"

"Very well; tell him…my wife had a certain brooch, of which she was quite fond, inherited from her Bohemian grandmother, and sadly the stone has gone missing from its setting. It was a particular red glass, not made but naturally occurring, and I have been informed that only here can I purchase a replacement."

Ludbridge watched as Ressel translated again. Even while Ressel was speaking, Herr Muller began to shake his head. He interrupted; Ressel pressed on; they exchanged several brief remarks. At last Ressel turned to Ludbridge.

"He says it is true that Bayer & Son is the only dealer in the red, but they have not had any for a long time now and in fact may not get it in stock again. He suggests you look for it in shops that carry older jewelry, as it sometimes comes up for sale there. Or perhaps you would like to replace it with garnet or ruby."

"Damn. Ask him why they can't get it."

Ressel translated the question. Herr Muller glanced upward once and replied.

"He says he doesn't know, it's none of his business."

"Ask him where the red glass comes from."

The sound of someone descending a staircase came from the rear of the shop. Herr Muller glanced over his shoulder. He said something brief and emphatic.

"He says he doesn't know that either, he is only a clerk, and if you aren't interested in buying rubies or garnets, you had better look elsewhere—"

A man entered the shoproom from a rear door, pulling on a coat as he came. He was tall, reasonably youthful and good-looking, with stylishly curled hair and whiskers, but a certain wolfish and disheveled air. There were circles under his eyes. He looked sharply at Ludbridge and Ressel, and said something in an interrogatory tone to Herr Muller.

Herr Muller replied, sounding stubborn and somewhat affronted. The other addressed himself to Ludbridge and Ressel and spoke forcefully. He turned, said something else to Herr Muller, opened the counter and walked out, letting the counter bang down after him. Taking a hat and walking stick from a stand by the door, he left the shop and walked quickly away. Herr Muller sighed.

"He said some, er, disrespectful things to Herr Muller and he told you that the source of the red is a secret closely held by his firm and when it is to be had he makes announcements in all the papers, and not before. He also told Herr Muller he was going out to get something for his, er, katzen-jammer, what you get when you are drinking too much?" Ressel spoke in an undertone.

"Just so." Ludbridge bowed to Herr Muller, replaced his hat and left the shop. Ressel followed like a shadow.

When they were out on the pavement, Ressel said, "I don't think Hirsch is a very nice man."

"Don't you?"

"He's been stealing my socks."

"Mm. Something queer about him, or d'you think he's simply lazy?"

Ressel shrugged unhappily. "He uses my comb too. There was a boy at school like him. Always bullying other boys. Always showing off and defying the schoolmaster."

"Well, don't trouble yourself about it. I'll give you a couple of pounds and you can buy yourself some new socks at a haberdasher's."

"But those were knitted by my mother."

"Steal 'em back then." Ludbridge took out his cigar case and lit a cigar. After a long pause he added: "We can get to Bayer, I think."

※

"Wine, women and song," said Hirsch, and hiccuped. "Especially women. Herr Bayer spends his money like water! Eats at the best places, so I was obliged to as well—I'll need a little more money, Ludbridge. Has his favorite route that takes him to all the best drinking-places, and I'm not talking about beer. Brandy and champagne for our friend Bayer! And naturally I was obliged to have a drink or two myself, to remain inconspicuous, wasn't I? You see why this is getting a bit expensive.

"And every evening ends the same: the women! But no streetwalkers with muddy skirts for him, no. He goes for the higher-priced establishments. When he's had his schnapps he'll go after any beauty, respectable ones even, if his eye lights on them. He's fought four duels in his time. Two marriages broken up and a well-born daughter disgraced. It's cost him a lot of money in lawsuits, I can tell you. An uncontrollable Don Juan!"

"I take it you weren't obliged to spend on similar quality entertainment?" Ludbridge said. Hirsch waved his hand.

"No, but information isn't cheaply bought, either. And here's a tidbit that cost me two crowns, since you're asking: his late father was several times approached to engage him in marriage with assorted daughters of well-to-do merchants. Having the only knowledge of where the red can be found makes him desirable, you see? And though he boasts when he's in his cups, *that* he never brags of. No hints, no oblique remarks about knowing a big secret, nothing."

"Good to know." Ludbridge tugged at his beard. "An idiot, in everything but that."

"Precisely." Hirsch grinned wide.

"Very good." Ludbridge rose to his feet. "Well done, Hirsch."

"Shall I go out again?"

"Not tonight. Get to bed. I'll have work for you tomorrow."

"Ah! Obtaining certain valuables at bargain rates, by any chance?" Hirsch mimed hitting someone with a cosh. Ludbridge shook his head.

"Not yet. Fairly soon, I think, but not just yet."

Hirsch bowed mockingly. "I am at your service whenever required," he said, and left the room.

Ludbridge lit a cigar and waited patiently, listening to the sounds that indicated Hirsch was retiring: boots pulled off and dropped, rustle of undress, sounds at the washstand. A dance tune hummed loudly, Ressel's sleepy protest, the tune continuing at a slightly lower volume. Creaking as Hirsch crawled into his bed; snores following fairly soon.

When Ludbridge had finished his cigar, he rose and quietly drew his traveling-bag from under his bed. Opening it, he took out what appeared to be a cigar box, followed by an apparent pair of ear muffs, and at last something that closely resembled one of the brass ear-trumpets used by persons hard of hearing. The brass trumpet fitted into a circular port in the cigar box; Ludbridge unwound a cord from around the ear muffs, slid them on his head, and pushed a sort of aglet on the end of the cord into a second port in the cigar box. Lastly he slid one side of the box upward, after the manner of a Chinese puzzle, revealing beneath a row of small dials and switches.

Turning a switch, Ludbridge saw a tiny red light flash on the panel. He turned one of the dials carefully, hearing as he did so shrill whistles and inorganic screams within what were clearly not earmuffs. After a long moment he spoke into the brass trumpet, in a low and penetrating voice.

"Gentlemen. Gentlemen, Night Operator. Gentlemen. What becomes of illusions?"

A sleepy voice answered in his ear, immediate and yet hollow and echoing with distance. "We dispel them."

"And we are everywhere. Ludbridge communicating. I require a message delivered."

"One moment." Ludbridge fancied he could hear, miles away, the Night Operator scrambling for pen and ink. "Sender, Ludbridge. Recipient?"

"Corvey."

"I *see*. Message?"

"I'll thank you not to take that tone, boy. Message is, 'We require your best. Can pay one-way Urgent Passage for one via Governess Cart. Location is—' " Ludbridge scowled a moment, and then gave the hotel's address.

"Yes, sir. Will that be all, sir?"

"No... 'Advise, drastic measures possibly called for.' "

"Yes, sir. I'll send that straight over by courier, shall I, sir?"

"Please do."

"Response should be available within two hours, sir."

"Thank you. I shall wait. Ludbridge concluding."

"Gentlemen concluding."

Ludbridge removed the ear apparatus. He got up, walked to the window, stared out at the night awhile; sat down and lit another cigar. When the cigar was out he settled comfortably in his chair, hands clasped across his waistcoat, and fixed his nearly-unblinking gaze upon the transmitting apparatus. Perhaps a quarter of an hour later he saw a green light flash on beside the red one.

Moving with surprising speed for a man of his bulk, Ludbridge crossed the room and pulled on the earpieces.

"Gentlemen? Communicating."

"What becomes of illusions?"

"We dispel them."

"And we are everywhere."

"Ludbridge."

"Response from Corvey, sir."

"And it is?"

" 'Expect Lady Beatrice by Governess Cart no later than Wednesday.' "

⁂

It was called a Governess Cart because it was made to look like one, and in fact it was possible to hitch a pony to its traces and proceed at a modest trot by daylight. Any uninitiated person seeing it might wonder why such a large trunk was crammed under the seat, but few uninitiated persons ever laid eyes on the Governess Cart because it traveled primarily along the deserted highways of the night.

Those few who did glimpse it, generally as they staggered home in an advanced state of inebriation, were never believed if they unwisely spoke of seeing a nocturnal thing with glowing eyes that rocketed down empty lanes at speeds exceeding forty miles an hour, steam engine rattling. The Governess Cart was extremely useful, therefore, as a light priority transport for individuals or packages that simply had to cross distances with greater alacrity than was possible for anyone else in 1845.

Lady Beatrice, who had ridden painfully through the Khyber Pass over the frozen bodies of her father's regiment some years earlier, much preferred speedier means of transportation, and so she quite enjoyed traveling by Governess Cart. It was true that one's hair became wildly disarranged unless one wore a special canvas bonnet tied down and reinforced with hatpins, but Lady Beatrice was well accustomed to wearing specialized clothing. Neither did she mind the goggles nor the long canvas coat recommended for high-speed travelers, since the one kept dust out of one's eyes admirably and the other insulated one against the damps of the night. Lady Beatrice had spent enough time exposed to the damps of the night and was disinclined to suffer them further.

Lady Beatrice was, to put it bluntly, a whore, albeit a well-bred and well-educated one. Being raped by Ghilzai tribesmen had ruined her chances for making a good marriage or, indeed, entering into polite society at all, but fortunately she had encountered the proprietress of a distinguished and exclusive establishment known as Nell Gwynne's. Lady Beatrice now serviced statesmen and diplomats, in the process extracting state secrets and passing them on to Nell Gwynne's fraternal organization, the Gentlemen's Speculative Society. Occasionally blackmail or other, more extreme measures needed to be taken. Lady Beatrice, who had slit the throats of her three Ghilzai assailants and stolen their horses, was equal to specialized work of any kind.

It should be mentioned that she was a tall and slender woman with a chilly autocratic beauty and rather startlingly clear gray eyes. When not traveling abroad, as she was now, she preferred to dress in scarlet. Lady Beatrice was nothing if not honest.

The first faint pallor of dawn had appeared in the east as the Governess Cart crossed from Bavaria into Bohemia. When they were well past the village of Horitz, Mr. Reed, the operator, leaned over sideways to shout over the noise of the engine. "We shan't be able to make much more distance tonight, I'm afraid, but we're nearly there. It will be necessary to get out and walk soon, I'm afraid."

"Shall we walk the rest of the way?"

"Oh, no indeed, madam. As a rule, I simply get between the traces and wait until some farmer passes in a wagon. Generally I spin him a tale about gypsies having stolen my pony, and generally he'll let me tie up to his wagon and ride with him the rest of the way into town."

Conveniently enough, this ruse worked with the first wagon-driving farmer they met, and they rode into Budweis in comfort if not style.

Ludbridge, waiting patiently outside the hotel, saw their approach. He rose, removing his hat. Mr. Reed spoke to the farmer, who paused long enough for Mr. Reed to hand down Lady Beatrice and set her bags on the pavement. Ludbridge took Lady Beatrice's hand and bowed over it, as Mr. Reed and the bemused farmer drove on.

"I trust your journey was uneventful, Ma'am?"

"It was, Mr. Ludbridge. I hope I find you well?"

"You do indeed." Ludbridge picked up her bags. "And very obliging of Mrs. Corvey to spare you on such short notice, I'm sure. Shall we go up to the room for a briefing? I've told the desk clerk my wife was coming for a visit."

Lady Beatrice followed him through the lobby, drawing the startled attention of the clerk, who had imagined Frau Ludbridge would be stout and middle-aged. When Ludbridge paused at the desk to request coffee and breakfast for four sent up, the clerk found himself blushing and stammering like a schoolboy. For some hours afterward he was unable to clear his mind of the gaze of Lady Beatrice's gray eyes.

※

That evening the staff at the Wienhof were similarly affected by the sight of Lady Beatrice, though in their case a certain amount of apprehension was also involved. That a beautiful woman should be dining alone in their establishment was, perhaps, scandalous, but not unusual; a number of the better class of prostitutes were accustomed to plying their trades in the Wienhof, in a low-key and discreet manner.

The staff was at a loss to know quite what to do about this foreign woman, however, who sat at a rear table nibbling biscuits and sipping tea.

She did not smile, she did not wink or call out familiarly or in any way employ the signals of her trade. Her appearance, on the other hand, was anything but circumspect. She wore an evening gown of scarlet silk, cut swoopingly low. Her cheeks were rouged scarlet, her lips were scarlet, her gray eyes were rimmed in blackest kohl. She might as well have stood on the table brandishing a placard that advertised her specialties and rates.

Consequently they were much relieved when Herr Bayer arrived for his customary meal and was immediately smitten by the scarlet beauty. He wasted no time in having a glass of champagne sent to her table, and in making eye contact when she had graciously acknowledged him with her thanks. He followed up with an invitation to dine at his table, which she accepted. He ordered the finest (and most expensive) meal the Wienhof provided, partridges in a sauce of brandy and cream, and during the meal trotted out his entire repertory of seductive phrases. The woman appeared receptive, smiling demurely and replying in schoolroom German. Herr Bayer seemed to find this quite charming.

So intent were the staff in watching the little comedy play itself out, and so intent was Herr Bayer on the thrill of the chase, that none of them wasted a thought on the pair of gentlemen seated across the room. One was an Englishman with somewhat blunt and leonine features, who seemed interested in nothing but his plate of Wiener schnitzel, rotkohl and spaetzle. The other was a timid-looking fellow who picked at his dish of rouladen. Neither of them looked up when Herr Bayer shouted for a waiter, nor when he demanded whether a room was available upstairs. Nor were they distracted from their meal when Herr Bayer and his inamorata rose from the table and retired to an upper floor of the Wienhof.

It was noticed, however, that the two gentlemen dawdled lengthily after finishing their entrees. They requested coffee. They requested two helpings each of hazelnut torte. They requested after-dinner liqueurs, and seemed content to sit for hours, nursing their glasses of kirsch and chatting quietly.

※

Herr Bayer, having ridden to bliss three times in succession, sagged sideways and collapsed into the feather bed. Lady Beatrice smiled and shifted sideways to face him.

"Such splendid endurance!" she murmured.

"God in heaven, I'm like a greedy child in a sweets shop," said Herr Bayer. He pulled her close and crushed her against him, kissing her ravenously. Lady Beatrice endured his attentions with perfect ease, showing neither revulsion nor discomfort. She had long since grown accustomed to detaching herself from the things her body was obliged to do, and during Herr Bayer's recent frenzied passion had been fondly recalling a recent holiday in the Lake District.

Now, however, she became aware that the present tussle had revived Herr Bayer's tumescence. He released her and looked down at himself.

"Bah! The naughty thing wants attention again. And what am I to do, my beauty? I faint with exhaustion. I will have to wear a hot poultice on my back tomorrow, I'm certain I've sprained something. But perhaps you would like to eat some sausage? Eh?" Herr Bayer leered as he ground his hips against hers suggestively.

"I have a better idea," said Lady Beatrice, smiling as she pushed him back. "But first, shall we have another glass of champagne?"

"Play Hebe, my fair one, and pour the flowing wine!"

Lady Beatrice turned and sat up on the edge of the bed. A single languorous gesture, like a cat stretching, enabled her to reach the tumbled mass of her clothes and pluck what appeared to be a small glass button from the waistband of her crinoline. Palming it, she rose and dropped the button in one of the pair of champagne glasses on the bedside table. She refilled the glasses, waiting only to assure herself that the button had dissolved without a trace before handing the glass to Herr Bayer.

"Prost, Herr Stallion."

"Prost, my Queen of Sheba!"

They clinked glasses and drank. Lady Beatrice set her glass aside after a sip and, with slow deliberation, moved to straddle Herr Bayer.

"Now, my dear, you lie there at your ease and rest your back. I will deal with the naughty creature."

Rising above him, she did something—again, slowly and consideringly—that made Herr Bayer's toes curl. He gasped, whooped, gulped down the rest of his champagne and hurled the empty glass across the room, where it shattered against the wall and dropped to the floor in a shower of sticky crystal fragments.

"Yes!" he screamed. "Yes, my adored, my little cat, my sugar cake!"

Lady Beatrice continued to do what she had been doing, settling into a steady rhythm. Herr Bayer writhed underneath her, fumbling and squeezing at her breasts. She gazed steadily into his eyes and saw the gradual look of happy idiocy that came into them. His hands fell away from her breasts; rose again to bat at them as a feeble kitten bats at catnip mice, before finally falling back to lie on either side of his head. He had begun to drool slightly.

Lady Beatrice wiped the drool away with a corner of the sheet. Herr Bayer giggled.

"I understand you are a jeweler, my dear Herr Bayer."

"That's so." He emphasized his reply with a nod.

"You used to sell that particular red gemstone, the meteor-glass, the sort that only Bayer and Son can procure."

"Of course! We will again. All it'll take is a crop failure…season without rain…hoof and mouth disease, you will see, sooner or later the Reithoffers will need money and then they'll come with a big box of it, hat in hand. You'll see. This is always the way it is."

"And who are the Reithoffers, my dear?"

"Farmers. Nobodies. But they own the secret mine, you see?"

"They obtain the red glass from a mine on their property?"

"Yes."

"And their mine is the only source?"

"Of course. We have tried for a hundred and seventy years to find any other. We might as well have been looking for fairy…pancakes." Herr Bayer giggled again. "Not, nothing, none, never, nowhere. Only the damned Reithoffers know where it is. It's quite unfair."

"Why do they only mine the stone when they need money?"

"Because they are superstitious peasants," Herr Bayer replied. " 'Ach, mein herr, the mine is cursed! Every third man who goes in to dig for the stone, *the Witch gets him! The Witch got great-great-uncle Hans, and Grandfather Horst, and Uncle Wilhelm! Boo hoo hoo!'* "

"And they will not sell the land?"

"No. It is their land. They are farmers, what else would they do? They are too stupid to learn even, even…shoemaking. You have no idea of their stubbornness. The pigs." Herr Bayer tried to spit, and the blob so produced ended up in his own eye. He laughed uproariously at that. Lady Beatrice wiped his eye with more of the sheet.

"And where exactly is their land, my very dear Herr Bayer?"

"Behind Sinietsch," he replied promptly. "Beyond the woods. They keep to themselves. Only the kobolds keep them company. Live like bears. Anyone in the village will agree with me. It's because of the terrible, shameful curse…"

His voice gurgled away into silence. His stare was becoming steadily glassier.

"You have been an exceedingly good boy, Herr Bayer," said Lady Beatrice. "You have earned a reward."

She accelerated her movements, which sent Herr Bayer into a flailing ecstasy so extreme it quite extinguished the last spark of his consciousness. As he was sinking gratefully into a black velvet-lined void, Lady Beatrice climbed briskly from the bed and washed her face clean of its smeared paint at the washbasin. She put on her undergarments and spent a moment patiently turning her gown inside out, the gown being made in such a way that it was reversible: scarlet silk with watered gray silk lining or watered gray silk with scarlet silk lining. After dressing herself, she exited the room quietly, closed the door behind her, and descended the stairs, a shadowy and respectable ghost of her former self.

Herr Bayer slept like the dead until the chamber-attendant brought hot water next morning. He sat bolt upright in bed, looking around for Lady Beatrice; was briefly relieved not to find her, since he preferred whores to decamp before sunrise; was next panicked, and sought frantically through his clothing until he located his purse; next was astonished to discover, as he hurriedly counted his money, that this particular whore had apparently neglected to collect her fee on departing; next was elated, on re-counting his funds, to confirm this suspicion. Herr Bayer whistled as he dressed himself and went downstairs to order breakfast.

He had no memory whatsoever of anything he had told Lady Beatrice, after that last glass of champagne.

⇥|⇤

Ludbridge unrolled a map and regarded it. "To be sure. Sinietsch. I expect the Reithoffers' farm must be somewhere *here*…"

"I believe the phrase used was 'beyond the woods'," said Lady Beatrice. She was the only person other than Ludbridge himself who was actually looking at the map. Ressel kept his gaze fixed on his shoes, and Hirsch stared hungrily at Lady Beatrice.

"Indeed. Right, Hirsch—this is your meat. You're to go to Sinietsch today and find out what you can. Pay a call on the Reithoffers, under some pretext. Report back this evening."

"On one condition," said Hirsch coyly. Ludbridge looked up at him, affronted.

"What the deuce do you mean?"

"I want a kiss to send me on my way."

"Come here and I'll give you a good one," replied Ludbridge, with only a hint of thunder in his tone. Hirsch turned red.

"I meant from our beauty here. Surely she won't mind a little merchandise given away free?"

Ludbridge stared at him, flint-eyed. Lady Beatrice cleared her throat.

"Mr. Hirsch, I think you misunderstand. I am not a commodity. I am a specialist, just as you are. My particular skills serve the same ends, but by different means."

"Then you should kiss me," said Hirsch. "Since that's my price for the day's work."

Ressel groaned and put his head in his hands. Ludbridge rose slowly to his feet, but Lady Beatrice put up her hand.

"It's a trivial enough request. Very well, Mr. Hirsch." She rose to her feet. He jumped up at once and came to her, licking his lips. She kissed him. He grabbed her in his arms and attempted to wrestle with her, groping her bosom, laughing muffledly, but abruptly broke off and backed away from her. Lady Beatrice, who had produced a small pistol apparently from thin air and pressed it under his ear, returned to her seat.

"I don't believe you should attempt to do that again, Mr. Hirsch," she said composedly. "Please understand that the only pleasure I derive from my duty is the satisfaction of knowing what it will accomplish. We are all working toward the same great day, are we not?"

"Bitch," said Hirsch. He strode to the door, grabbed his coat, and turned back briefly to address Ludbridge. "You may not like me, but you will see what work *I* can do."

He slammed the door behind him, and they heard him charging down the stairs.

"How juvenile," said Lady Beatrice, at the same moment Ressel cried, "Fraulein, a thousand apologies—you mustn't think we're all beasts—" and Ludbridge gave a wordless growl.

"That is quite all right, Mr. Ressel," said Lady Beatrice, smiling at him. "It's of little consequence. I have dealt with far worse than Mr. Hirsch."

"Well, what are you waiting for?" Ludbridge demanded of Ressel. "Go in there and steal your socks back."

⇥|⇤

Ressel had plenty of time to retrieve his socks and his comb too, for that matter, because Hirsch failed to return that evening. Ludbridge stalked the floor for hours before giving up and sleeping on the divan, having relinquished his bed to Lady Beatrice. Hirsch still had not put in an appearance by the time Ludbridge went down to order breakfast for three. As he was about to return to the rooms, the clerk turned to the back counter with a little cry.

"I nearly forgot! Herr Ludbridge, a letter has come for you. A courier delivered it this morning." He drew it from its pigeonhole and held it out. Ludbridge took it.

"Thank you." Ludbridge studied it as he climbed the stairs. He did not recognize the hand in which it was addressed, but as he opened it and read its contents he certainly recognized the tone.

My old Ludbridge, I write to you from Sinietsch, which has, as it turns out, a splendid tavern and marvelously accommodating women. But you must not think I put pleasure before business. Here is what I have accomplished for you: Having arrived here, I was able to locate directions to the Reithoffer farm immediately. As I was passing the tavern I chanced upon a peddler with a tray of the sorts of things such people sell, and luckily for me he set the tray down in an inattentive moment while washing his face at a fountain. So prepared, I set off for the farm. You never saw such a countrified place in your life—a little cart-track off a mountain road, winding through the trees to a gate, and huge savage barking hounds who wanted to tear me limb from limb. I prudently remained on my side of the gate and before long a surly peasant came down to see why his hounds were making such a fuss. I tipped my hat and displayed my riches, at which he tied up the dogs and bid me enter. I followed him through the cabbage fields to the house, and such a scene from the dark ages when we got inside! Absolutely old Bohemia, with a couple of ancients by the fire and a brat or two staggering about and a bevy of peasant women busy putting up sauerkraut in stone crocks. The shelves were positively lined with crocks of pickles and more sauerkraut. You may imagine that the maidens were frantic for something other than pickles with which to divert themselves, and so I and my wares were eagerly received. Of course, I sold at bargain prices! Spools of thread, bits of lace, ribbons, pins, a pair of scissors, a songbook of tunes that were out of fashion thirty years since and a cheap chromolithograph of Our Lord Jesus Christ, all found favor in the sauerkraut girls' eyes. So much so that I was invited to dine. The men of the house were less pleased to see me. Imagine hulking cousin-marrying peasants in boots fresh-caked with mud of the fields and less pleasant substances, all lined up at a long trestle, eyeing me suspiciously. The fare was minuscule pork cutlets, massive flour dumplings, even bigger helpings of the eternal sauerkraut, and not even a good beer to wash any of this down, but thin sour cider! Pity poor me, Ludbridge, where you sit at your ease in civilized Budweis. Anyway I could see there was no use trying to get any secrets out of these mountain trolls, so I waited until after they had gone to the fields and managed to get one of the younger girls alone for a little romance. She was eager enough until I asked her about a story I'd heard concerning witches in the forest. That closed up her lips so tight I could see there was no use pursuing it (or her) further, so I tipped my hat and took my leave. But the good people of Sinietsch were willing to talk, I can tell you, when I got back into town (without my peddler's tray, of course; that I disposed of in a convenient ditch). With a liberal largesse to the tavern patrons, this I learned: The Reithoffer land is indeed cursed, or so I was solemnly assured. There is a Witch who haunts the place and every generation or so she takes one of the Reithoffer men for a lover, though this act has immediate consequences for the unfortunate male as he is always found dead and singed with hellfire following her embrace. Why the Witch is up there no one knows for certain, but the clearest story I heard was that there is cursed buried treasure somewhere on the Reithoffer farm, and there the Witch haunts. Some are of the opinion that her lovers came seeking the treasure and paid the price. The last time this happened was within living memory, in 1839. I did not go back to search for the mine because, what was I to do about the dogs? And, really, I have worked hard enough for one day. I am going to take a little holiday now for a few days, until the expense money runs out. I close now because the post rider waits, but perhaps I will tell you where I am later. Cheerfully, Hirsch.

Crumpling the letter in his fists, Ludbridge swore quietly.

⁂

Sinietsch was easily reached in a rented gig. Ressel drove. Ludbridge sat beside him, mulling over what he felt he could trust of Hirsch's report. Lady Beatrice, dressed in respectable gray once more, sat quietly in the back and enjoyed viewing the passing countryside. At last Ludbridge turned to her.

"Do you reckon you could portray an hysteric?"

"How hysterical do you require me to be, Mr. Ludbridge?"

Ludbridge thought about it. "Not excessively. Not weeping-and-wringing-your-hands hysterical."

"More of a fainting-fit-for-unspecified-female-disorders hysterical? I believe I can manage that, yes, Mr. Ludbridge."

When they drove at last up the main street of Sinietsch, Ludbridge looked for village taverns. There was only one, as it happened, and he bid Ressel pull up before it.

"Go in and ask whether Hirsch is staying here. You might find out if there's a doctor about, as well."

Ressel went in, and returned a few minutes later, looking rather harried.

"Hirsch is no longer there. He left suddenly and owing money. The proprietors were very angry, so I told them I was a debt collector trying to trace him. They were much more helpful after that. Dr. Schildkraut's house is at the end of that lane." Ressel pointed.

Ludbridge chewed his cigar. "What the devil does Hirsch think he's playing at? Still in school and scoring off the headmaster? Well, on to the Doctor's."

They pulled up in front of a modest half-timbered house. "Any objection to feigning illness for a good twenty minutes or so?" Ludbridge asked Lady Beatrice.

"None whatsoever, Mr. Ludbridge." Lady Beatrice put the back of her hand to her head and sprawled back on her seat, fluttering her eyelids.

"I'm obliged to you, Ma'am."

Dr. Schildkraut was an elderly man who opened his own door. He gaped rather at the sight on his doorstep: an Englishman supporting a swooning Englishwoman, and a smaller man, very agitated, asking whether the doctor was available to examine the fraulein, who had suffered an attack of the vapors. He ushered them into his parlor, and after a series of hastily translated questions determined that he ought to see the fraulein in his examining room. Thither she was led, drooping on the arm of the Englishman—Dr. Schildkraut assumed he was her father—who, upon seeing her safely disposed in a chair, tipped his hat and departed to wait in the parlor.

Once the door had closed, Ludbridge strode to a bookcase on the wall, wherein sat a number of bound leather volumes. Years were painted on their spines, in a small precise hand.

"Here's the one," said Ludbridge, pulling out the journal for the year 1839. Ressel came and peered over his shoulder as he leafed through it. "We're looking for the name Reithoffer."

They flipped the pages, passing births, illnesses, recoveries and death in Sinietsch. Near the end of the book Ressel grabbed Ludbridge's arm and pointed. "Here!"

"What's it say?" Ludbridge peered at the page.

"Says, er… 'Last night Frau Kohl came to me in fear. She was attending one of the Reithoffer girls who has gone into early labor and the baby will not turn. We went together to the Reithoffer farm and arrived at daybreak. Just as we were driving up we saw that one of the men was out by the house digging what looked like a grave. I asked if the girl had already died but Frau Kohl told me the grave was for another member of the family who had been found dead the day before, which she thought had sent the young mother into her pangs.'

"Then he says…er…a lot about bringing the baby into the world. They saved the mother and child. And then, he goes into the kitchen and he sees…well, there is a body the old people are washing for burial. He asks to examine it because he has heard of this curse, you see. Dead man is the girl's uncle, 'Peter Reithoffer, forty years of age, well-nourished, appearance of a corpse struck by lightning. Fernlike burn patterns on the skin.' Doctor asks if he was struck by lightning, family is looking, er, shamefaced. They say he is marked with the Witch's mark and was taken in accordance with his sin. Doctor asks, what sin? Family elder replies, he died in the embrace of the Witch. So that is why he can't be buried in consecrated ground. They won't tell him more. He leaves…he gives Frau Kohl a ride back to her house and she tells him, when they brought in the dead man his trousers were down around his thighs, like all the others killed by the curse."

"Bloody hell," murmured Ludbridge. "Fern patterns. Anything more?"

"He just says he is sorry people can believe in such nonsense in this age and he thinks it was lightning all the same."

"Didn't ask what the man was doing when he died?"

"No, apparently." Ressel, a little red-faced, closed the book and put it back in its place. They sat down on a bench clearly provided for anxious relatives. Ressel twiddled his thumbs while Ludbridge smoked and thought.

"Fernlike patterns," he muttered at last. "Yes, I've seen that. Seaman on the *Tiger* struck by lightning whilst aloft. Extraordinary coincidence..." He was silent another moment and then slapped his knee.

"I'll tell you what it is, Ressel. Why's a man take his prick out of his trousers, eh? What's the most common reason?"

Ressel blushed once more. "To, er, make water, I suppose."

"Precisely. And let's say a man feels the call of nature when he's down in a mine. Is he going to walk all the way out and water the nearest tree, or is he just going to make water right there in the mine?"

"I...suppose he would make water in the mine."

"So." Ludbridge took his cigar out of his mouth. "Just exactly how much acetic acid's in the urine of a man who lives on sauerkraut, pickles and cider?"

Ressel considered that a moment. His eyes widened in horror.

"*That's* how the damned fools have been killing themselves," said Ludbridge, chuckling. He broke his laughter off abruptly when the examining room door opened and Lady Beatrice emerged, leaning on the doctor's arm. Ludbridge escorted Lady Beatrice out to the gig, while Ressel paid the doctor.

"A mild case of hysteria," Dr. Schildkraut told him in a low voice. "Give her fresh air and a few novels and she will be perfectly well. You know what these women are."

∗

It was a simple enough matter, thereafter, to field-test Enderley's Improved Canine Stupefaction Compound on the Reithoffers' immense snarling hounds. The Compound proved to work a treat, enabling Ludbridge and Ressel to don night-vision goggles and explore the Reithoffers' considerable acreage without fear of detection. The mine was easily located at the distant edge of the farm, though the track leading to it was overgrown and its entrance masked with tall weeds. Once entered and inspected, it proved to bear rich veins of the red tektite.

Somewhat more complicated was stage-managing the business of the thunder-machine and lightning flashes. Lady Beatrice's appearance as the Witch necessitated recourse to her scarlet gown and moreover to her cosmetics case, in order to provide the fernlike facial markings. It was particularly felicitous that she happened to own, among a number of colored glass lenses designed to give her eyes a striking appearance, a scarlet pair; for, as she pointed out, one never knew what sort of peculiar fantasies (being seduced by a vampyre, for example) members of Parliament might request.

The Reithoffers, suitably frightened by the spectacle of their family's ancient persecutor appearing in the front garden, readily obeyed her demand that they venture into town and sell that corner of their property containing the tektite mine to a certain Englishman they would find in the tavern. Ludbridge gave them a good price. They congratulated themselves on making a tidy profit on the deal and incidentally unloading their family curse on somebody else.

⁂

"That mine was one of the most disturbing places I have ever had the occasion to have seen," said Ressel, as they climbed down from the gig. "Didn't you think? Like, er, the throat of a whale, with all that redness."

"Well, you won't be obliged to go back in, I shouldn't think," said Ludbridge, handing Lady Beatrice and her cosmetics case down. "All that's left for *us* to do is get the title deed back to London and file a report."

"I do hope Mr. Hirsch has come to his senses and is waiting for us at the hotel," said Lady Beatrice, as they crossed the street. Ludbridge scowled.

"I'll have a few things to say about *him*, by God. He'd better be there."

"Er...there are rather a lot of police about this morning," said Ressel, looking around uneasily.

As they stepped within, the desk clerk saw Ludbridge and waved.

"Herr Ludbridge? A parcel and a letter for you."

Collecting them, Ludbridge noted Hirsch's handwriting. He sighed and shook the small box experimentally; only a faint rattle gave any idea of its contents. In a casual tone he remarked: "Rather a lot of police in the street, aren't there?"

"There have been two robberies!" said the clerk. "Both in one night! Herr Kimmel the jeweler and Herr Lantz the pawnbroker, both robbed of hundreds of marks in goods. Herr Lantz is in bed with a fractured skull."

"What a dreadful thing," said Ludbridge. He went upstairs, followed by Lady Beatrice and Ressel.

Ressel went into his room to pack his bag; Lady Beatrice seated herself in a chair by the window, gazing out, as Ludbridge opened the box. He shook its contents into his hand and swore. Lady Beatrice looked at him inquiringly. He held out a signet ring and a cameo pendant, both set with red tektite stones.

"That's all we had found here in Budweis," said Ludbridge. "But I hadn't given him the word to do the burglary yet."

"Hirsch's bag is gone," said Ressel, appearing in the doorway.

"Oh, dear," said Lady Beatrice. Ludbridge ground his teeth and opened the letter.

My very dear Ludbridge, This letter serves as notice that I have, after much reflection, decided to take my talents to more appreciative (and better-paying) masters than the Gentlemen. However, do not despair! Here as a token of good faith are the bits of red tektite I found for you. I got them at a bargain price… however, you may wish to find a way to conceal them from the customs agents. You may find things a trifle hot in Budweis now, also, until the police find some-one to arrest for my little indiscretion, but do not fear; I am sure the Gentlemen can easily arrange for your release, if worst comes to worst. I myself intend a swift departure. Please convey to the Gentlemen that I will soon communicate a postal location where my wages may be sent, as well as the monthly stipend I expect for my silence on the matter of the red tektite's astonishing properties. A hundred pounds a month is not too much, I think, considering the value of the information and the delight with which it would be received by certain interested governments. Farewell, old man, and a big wet ravishing kiss with my tongue for the lady in red. Or perhaps something more. I leave it to her imagination. Your much undervalued friend, Hirsch

"That's done it." Ludbridge folded the letter and tucked it inside his coat. He drew out his watch, thumbed a button on its side, and studied it a moment. "That stupid son of a bitch. Your pardon, ma'am, but he's run off, or so it would appear. Ressel, finish packing. Ma'am, can you be ready to depart within the next ten minutes?"

"Certainly." Lady Beatrice rose to her feet.

"Good." Ludbridge bounded upright and began packing with breathtaking speed.

※

They departed the hotel a few bare minutes before the police descended on it to question all foreign visitors, or so Ludbridge learned later. At the time he was not disposed to be communicative about his reasons for flight; as they hurried toward the horse-rail station he kept checking his watch. Only when they were seated in the car was Ressel able to lean forward and look at the watch face.

"But that is not a clock," he remarked in surprise. "That is a little map of Budweis!"

"So it is," said Ludbridge, chuckling. "D'you see the tiny red light flashing there? That's our friend Hirsch. One doesn't cross the Gentlemen, you see."

"I just saw him," said Lady Beatrice in a low voice. "He's here. He hid behind the kiosk when he saw us. I can still see his boots and the corner of his bag."

"I should look away if I were you, ma'am," said Ludbridge.

He gave his watch stem a quarter-turn and depressed it. There was a *bang* followed by screams and shouting. Glancing over at the kiosk, he saw the fan-splatter of blood. Bits of Hirsch's head began to fall hither and yon. The silver molar crown, that had concealed the tracking mechanism and explosive, landed with a particularly musical tinkle on the cobbles not four feet away.

"That'll teach him," said Ludbridge, and lit a cigar. Ressel stared at him in horror. Lady Beatrice shrugged regretfully and took out her knitting.

Tanglefoot

by Cherie Priest

Stonewall Jackson survived Chancellorsville. England broke the Union's naval blockade, and formally recognized the Confederate States of America. Atlanta never burned.

It is 1880. The American Civil War has raged for nearly two decades, driving technology in strange and terrible directions. Combat dirigibles skulk across the sky and armored vehicles crawl along the land. Military scientists twist the laws of man and nature, and barter their souls for weapons powered by light, fire, and steam.

But life struggles forward for soldiers and ordinary citizens. The fractured nation is dotted with stricken towns and epic scenes of devastation—some manmade, and some more mysterious. In the western territories cities are swallowed by gas and walled away to rot while the frontiers are strip-mined for resources. On the borders between North and South, spies scour and scheme, and smugglers build economies more stable than their governments.

This is the Clockwork Century.

It is dark here, and different.

Part One:

Hunkered shoulders and skinny, bent knees cast a crooked shadow from the back corner of the laboratory, where the old man tried to remember the next step in his formula, or possibly—as Edwin was forced to consider—the scientist simply struggled to recall his own name. On the table against the wall, the once estimable Dr. Archibald Smeeks muttered, spackling his test tubes with spittle and becoming increasingly agitated until Edwin called out, "Doctor?"

The doctor settled himself, steadying his hands and closing his mouth. He crouched on his stool, cringing away from the boy's voice, and crumpled his over-long work apron with his feet. "Who's there?" he asked.

"Only me, sir."

"Who?"

"Me. It's only…me."

With a startled shudder of recognition he asked, "The orphan?"

"Yes sir. Just the orphan."

Dr. Smeeks turned around, the bottom of his pants twisting in a circle on the smooth wooden seat. He reached to his forehead, where a prodigious set of multi-lensed goggles was perched. From the left side, he tugged a monocle to extend it on a hinged metal arm, and he used it to peer across the room, down onto the floor, where Edwin was sitting cross-legged in a pile of discarded machinery parts.

"Ah," the old doctor said. "There you are, yes. I didn't hear you tinkering, and I only wondered where you might be hiding. Of course, I remember you."

"I believe you do, sir," Edwin said politely. In fact, he very strongly doubted it today, but Dr. Smeeks was trying to appear quite fully aware of his surroundings and it would've been rude to contradict him. "I didn't mean to interrupt your work. You sounded upset. I wanted to ask if everything was all right."

"All right?" Dr. Smeeks returned his monocle to its original position, so that it no longer shrank his fluffy white eyebrow down to a tame and reasonable arch. His wiry goatee quivered as he wondered about his own state. "Oh yes. Everything's quite all right. I think for a moment that I was distracted."

He scooted around on the stool so that he once again faced the cluttered table with its vials, coils, and tiny gray crucibles. His right hand selected a test tube with a hand-lettered label and runny green contents. His left hand reached for a set of tongs, though he set them aside almost immediately in favor of a half-rolled piece of paper that bore the stains and streaks of a hundred unidentifiable splatters.

"Edwin," he said, and Edwin was just short of stunned to hear his name. "Boy, could you join me a moment? I'm afraid I've gone and confused myself."

"Yes sir."

Edwin lived in the basement by the grace of Dr. Smeeks, who had asked the sanitarium for an assistant. These days, the old fellow could not remember requesting such an arrangement and could scarcely confirm or deny it anymore, no matter how often Edwin reminded him.

Therefore Edwin made a point to keep himself useful.

The basement laboratory was a quieter home than the crowded group ward on the top floor, where the children of the patients were kept and raised; and the boy didn't mind the doctor's failing mental state, since what was left of him was kind and often friendly. And sometimes, in a glimmering flash between moments of pitiful bewilderment, Edwin saw the doctor for who he once had been—a brilliant man with a mind that was honored and admired for its flexibility and prowess.

In its way, the Waverly Hills Sanitarium was a testament to his outstanding imagination.

The hospital had incorporated many of the physicians' favorites into the daily routine of the patients, including a kerosene-powered bladed machine that whipped fresh air down the halls to offset the oppressive summer heat. The physicians had also integrated his Moving Mechanical Doors that opened with the push of a switch; and Dr. Smeeks' wonderful Steam-Powered Dish-Cleaning Device was a huge hit in the kitchen. His Sheet-Sorting Slings made him a celebrity in the laundry rooms, and the Sanitary Rotating Manure Chutes had made him a demi-god to the stable-hands.

But half-finished and barely finished inventions littered every corner and covered every table in the basement, where the famed and elderly genius lived out the last of his years.

So long as he did not remember how much he'd forgotten, he appeared content.

Edwin approached the doctor's side and peered dutifully at the stained schematics on the discolored piece of linen paper. "It's coming along nicely, sir," he said.

For a moment Dr. Smeeks did not reply. He was staring down hard at the sheet, trying to make it tell him something, and accusing it of secrets. Then he said, "I'm forced to agree with you, lad. Could you tell me, what is it I was working on? Suddenly…suddenly the numbers aren't speaking to me. Which project was I addressing, do you know?"

"These are the notes for your Therapeutic Bath Appliance. Those numbers to the right are your guesses for the most healthful solution of water, salt, and lavender. You were collecting lemongrass."

"Lemongrass? I was going to put that in the water? Whatever would've possessed me to do such a thing?" he asked, baffled by his own processes. He'd only drawn the notes a day or two before.

Edwin was a good student, even when Dr. Smeeks was a feeble teacher. He prompted the old fellow as gently as he could. "You'd been reading about Dr. Kellogg's hydrotherapy treatments in Battle Creek, and you felt you could improve on them."

"Battle Creek, yes. The Sanitarium there. Good Christian folks. They keep a strict diet; it seems to work well for the patients, or so the literature on the subject tells me. But yes," he said more strongly. "Yes, I remember. There must be a more efficient way to warm the water, and make it more pleasing to the senses. The soothing qualities of lavender have been documented for thousands of years, and its antiseptic properties should help keep the water fresh." He turned to Edwin and asked, with the lamplight flickering in his lenses, "Doesn't it sound nice?"

"I don't really like to take baths," the boy confessed. "But if the water was warm and it smelled real nice, I think I'd like it better."

Dr. Smeeks made a little shrug and said, "It'd be less for the purposes of cleanliness and more for the therapy of the inmates here. Some of the more restless or violent ones, you understand."

"Yes sir."

"And how's your mother?" the doctor asked. "Has she responded well to treatment? I heard her coughing last night, and I was wondering if I couldn't concoct a syrup that might give her comfort."

Edwin said, "She wasn't coughing last night. You must've heard someone else."

"Perhaps you're right. Perhaps it was Mrs.... What's her name? The heavy nurse with the northern accent?"

"Mrs. Criddle."

"That's her, yes. That's the one. I hope she isn't contracting the consumption she works so very hard to treat." He returned his attention to the notes and lines on the brittle sheet before him.

Edwin did not tell Dr. Smeeks, for the fifth or sixth time, that his mother had been dead for months; and he did not mention that Mrs. Criddle's accent had come with her from New Orleans. He'd learned that it was easier to agree, and probably kinder as well.

It became apparent that the old man's attention had been reabsorbed by his paperwork and test tubes, so Edwin returned to his stack of mechanical refuse. He was almost eleven years old, and he'd lived in the basement with the doctor for nearly a year. In that time, he'd learned quite a lot about how a carefully fitted gear can turn, and how a pinpoint-sharp mind can rust; and he took what scraps he wanted to build his own toys, trinkets, and machines. After all, it was half the pleasure and privilege of living away from the other children—he could help himself to anything the doctor did not immediately require.

He didn't like the other children much, and the feeling was mutual.

The other offspring of the unfortunate residents were loud and frantic. They believed Edwin was aloof when he was only thoughtful, and they treated him badly when he wished to be left alone.

All things considered, a cot beside a boiler in a room full of metal and chemicals was a significant step up in the world. And the fractured mind of the gentle old man was more companionable by far than the boys and girls who baked themselves daily on the roof, playing ball and beating one another while the orderlies weren't looking.

Even so, Edwin had long suspected he could do better. Maybe he couldn't *find* better, but he was increasingly confident that he could *make* better.

He turned a pair of old bolts over in his palm and concluded that they were solid enough beneath their grime that a bit of sandpaper would restore their luster and usefulness. All the gears and coils he needed were already stashed and assembled, but some details yet eluded him, and his new friend was not quite finished.

Not until it boasted the finer angles of a human face.

Already Edwin had bartered a bit of the doctor's throat remedy to a taxidermist, an act which gained him two brown eyes meant for a badger. Instead, these eyes were fitted in a pounded brass mask with a cut strip of tin that made a sloping nose.

The face was coming together. But the bottom jaw was not connected, so the facsimile was not yet whole.

Edwin held the bolts up to his eye to inspect their threadings, and he decided that they would suffice. "These will work," he said to himself.

Back at the table the doctor asked, "Hmm?"

"Nothing, sir. I'm going to go back to my cot and tinker."

"Very good then. Enjoy yourself, Parker. Summon me if you need an extra hand," he said, because that's what he always said when Edwin announced that he intended to try his own small hands at inventing.

Parker was the youngest son of Dr. and Mrs. Smeeks. Edwin had seen him once, when he'd come to visit a year before at Christmas. The thin man with a fretful face had brought a box of clean, new vials and a large pad of lined paper, plus a gas-powered burner that had been made in Germany. But his father's confusion was too much for him. He'd left, and he hadn't returned.

So if Dr. Smeeks wanted to call Edwin "Parker" once in awhile, that was fine. Like Parker himself, Edwin was also thin, with a face marked by worry beyond his years; and Edwin was also handy with pencils, screw-drivers, and wrenches. The boy figured that the misunderstanding was understandable, if unfortunate, and he learned to answer to the other name when it was used to call him.

He took his old bolts back to his cot and picked up a tiny triangle of sandpaper.

Beside him, at the foot of his cot underneath the wool blanket, lay a lump in the shape of a boy perhaps half Edwin's size. The lump was not a doll but an automaton, ready to wind, but not wound yet—not until it had a proper face, with a proper jaw.

When the bolts were as clean as the day they were cast, Edwin placed them gently on his pillow and reached inside the hatbox Mrs. Williams had given him. He withdrew the steel jawbone and examined it, comparing it against the bolts and deciding that the fit was satisfactory; and then he uncovered the boy-shaped lump.

"Good heavens, Edwin. What have you got there?"

Edwin jumped. The old scientist could be uncannily quiet, and he could not always be trusted to stick to his own business. Nervously, as if the automaton were something to be ashamed of, the boy said, "Sir, it's…a machine. I made a machine, I think. It's not a doll," he clarified.

And Dr. Smeeks said, "I can see that it's not a doll. You made this?"

"Yes sir. Just with odds and ends—things you weren't using. I hope you don't mind."

"Mind? No. I don't mind. Dear boy, it's exceptional!" he said with what sounded like honest wonder and appreciation. It also sounded lucid, and focused, and Edwin was charmed to hear it.

The boy asked, "You think it's good?"

"I think it must be. How does it work? Do you crank it, or—"

"It winds up." He rolled the automaton over onto its back and pointed at a hole that was barely large enough to hold a pencil. "One of your old hex wrenches will do it."

Dr. Smeeks turned the small machine over again, looking into the tangle of gears and loosely fixed coils where the brains would be. He touched its oiled joints and the clever little pistons that must surely work for muscles. He asked, "When you wind it, what does it do?"

Edwin faltered. "Sir, I…I don't know. I haven't wound him yet."

"Haven't wound him—well, I suppose that's excuse enough. I see that you've taken my jar-lids for kneecaps, and that's well and good. It's a good fit. He's made to walk a bit, isn't he?"

"He ought to be able to walk, but I don't think he can climb stairs. I haven't tested him. I was waiting until I finished his face." He held up the metal jawbone in one hand and the two shiny bolts in the other. "I'm almost done."

"Do it then!" Dr. Smeeks exclaimed. He clapped his hands together and said, "How exciting! It's your first invention, isn't it?"

"Yes sir," Edwin fibbed. He neglected to remind the doctor of his work on the Picky Boy Plate with a secret chamber to hide unwanted and uneaten food until it was safe to discreetly dispose of it. He did not mention his tireless pursuit and eventual production of the Automatic Expanding Shoe, for use by quickly growing children whose parents were too poor to routinely purchase more footwear.

"Go on," the doctor urged. "Do you mind if I observe? I'm always happy to watch the success of a fellow colleague."

Edwin blushed warmly across the back of his neck. He said, "No sir, and thank you. Here, if you could hold him for me—like that, on your legs, yes. I'll take the bolts and..." with trembling fingers he fastened the final hardware and dabbed the creases with oil from a half-empty can.

And he was finished.

Edwin took the automaton from Dr. Smeeks and stood it upright on the floor, where the machine did not wobble or topple, but stood fast and gazed blankly wherever its face was pointed.

The doctor said, "It's a handsome machine you've made. What does it do again? I think you said, but I don't recall."

"I still need to wind it," Edwin told him. "I need an L-shaped key. Do you have one?"

Dr. Smeeks jammed his hands into the baggy depths of his pockets and a great jangling noise declared the assorted contents. After a few seconds of fishing he withdrew a hex, but seeing that it was too large, he tossed it aside and dug for another one. "Will this work?"

"It ought to. Let me see."

Edwin inserted the newer, smaller stick into the hole and gave it a twist. Within, the automaton springs tightened, coils contracted, and gears clicked together. Encouraged, the boy gave the wrench another turn, and then another. It felt as if he'd spent forever winding, when finally he could twist no further. The automaton's internal workings resisted, and could not be persuaded to wind another inch.

The boy removed the hex key and stood up straight. On the automaton's back, behind the place where its left shoulder blade ought to be, there was a sliding switch. Edwin put his finger to it and gave the switch a tiny shove.

Down in the machine's belly, something small began to whir.

Edwin and the doctor watched with delight as the clockwork boy's arms lifted and went back down to its sides. One leg rose at a time, and each was returned to the floor in a charming parody of marching-in-place. Its bolt-work neck turned from left to right, causing its tinted glass eyes to sweep the room.

"It works!" The doctor slapped Edwin on the back. "Parker, I swear— you've done a good thing. It's a most excellent job, and with what? My leftovers, is that what you said?"

"Yes sir, that's what I said. You remembered!"

"Of course I remembered. I remember you," Dr. Smeeks said. "What will you call your new toy?"

"He's my new friend. And I'm going to call him…Ted."

"Ted?"

"Ted." He did not explain that he'd once had a baby brother named Theodore, or that Theodore had died before his first birthday. This was something different, and anyway it didn't matter what he told Dr. Smeeks, who wouldn't long recall it.

"Well he's very fine. Very fine indeed," said the doctor. "You should take him upstairs and show him to Mrs. Criddle and Mrs. Williams. Oh— you should absolutely show him to your mother. I think she'll be pleased."

"Yes sir. I will, sir."

"Your mother will be proud, and I will be proud. You're learning so much, so fast. One day, I think, you should go to school. A bright boy like you shouldn't hide in basements with old men like me. A head like yours is a commodity, son. It's not a thing to be lightly wasted."

To emphasize his point, he ruffled Edwin's hair as he walked away.

Edwin sat on the edge of his cot, which brought him to eye-level with his creation. He said, "Ted?"

Ted's jaw opened and closed with a metallic clack, but the mechanical child had no lungs, nor lips, and it did not speak.

The flesh-and-blood boy picked up Ted and carried him carefully under his arm, up the stairs and into the main body of the Waverly Hills Sanitarium. The first floor offices and corridors were mostly safe, and mostly empty—or populated by the bustling, concentrating men with clipboards and glasses, and very bland smiles that recognized Edwin without caring that he was present.

The sanitarium was very new. Some of its halls were freshly built and still stinking of mortar and the dust of construction. Its top floor rooms reeked faintly of paint and lead, as well as the medicines and bandages of the ill and the mad.

Edwin avoided the top floors where the other children lived, and he avoided the wards of the men who were kept in jackets and chains. He also avoided the sick wards, where the mad men and women were tended to.

Mrs. Criddle and Mrs. Williams worked in the kitchen and laundry, respectively; and they looked like sisters though they were not, in fact, related. Both were women of a stout and purposeful build, with great tangles of graying hair tied up in buns and covered in sanitary hair caps; and both women were the mothering sort who were stern with patients, but kind to the hapless orphans who milled from floor to floor when they weren't organized and contained on the roof.

Edwin found Mrs. Criddle first, working a paddle through a metal vat of mashed potatoes that was large enough to hold the boy, Ted, and a third friend of comparable size. Her wide bottom rocked from side to side in time with the sweep of her elbows as she stirred the vat, humming to herself.

"Mrs. Criddle?"

She ceased her stirring. "Mm. Yes dear?"

"It's Edwin, ma'am."

"Of course it is!" She leaned the paddle against the side of the vat and flipped a lever to lower the fire. "Hello there, boy. It's not time for supper, but what have you got there?"

He held Ted forward so she could inspect his new invention. "His name is Ted. I made him."

"Ted, ah yes. Ted. That's a good name for…for…a new friend."

"That's right!" Edwin brightened. "He's my new friend. Watch, he can walk. Look at what he can do."

He pressed the switch and the clockwork boy marched in place, and then staggered forward, catching itself with every step and clattering with every bend of its knees. Ted moved forward until it knocked its forehead on the leg of a counter, then stopped, and turned to the left to continue soldiering onward.

"Would you look at that?" Mrs. Criddle said with the awe of a woman who had no notion of how her own stove worked, much less anything else. "That's amazing, is what it is. He just turned around like that, just like he knew!"

"He's automatic," Edwin said, as if this explained everything.

"Automatic indeed. Very nice, love. But Mr. Bird and Miss Emmie will be here in a few minutes, and the kitchen will be a busy place for a boy and his new friend. You'd best take him back downstairs."

"First I want to go show Mrs. Williams."

Mrs. Criddle shook her head. "Oh no, dear. I think you'd better not. She's upstairs, with the other boys and girls, and well, I suppose you know. I think you're better off down with Dr. Smeeks."

Edwin sighed. "If I take him upstairs, they'll only break him, won't they?"

"I think they're likely to try."

"All right," he agreed, and gathered Ted up under his arm.

"Come back in another hour, will you? You can get your own supper and carry the doctor's while you're at it."

"Yes ma'am. I will."

He retreated back down the pristine corridors and dodged between two empty gurneys, back down the stairs that would return him to the safety of the doctor, the laboratory, and his own cot. He made his descent quietly, so as not to disturb the doctor in case he was still working.

When Edwin peeked around the bottom corner, he saw the old scientist sitting on his stool once more, a wadded piece of linen paper crushed in his fist. A spilled test tube leaked runny gray liquid across the counter's top, and made a dark stain across the doctor's pants.

Over and over to himself he mumbled, "Wasn't the lavender. Wasn't the...it was only the...I saw the. I don't...I can't...where was the paper? Where were the plans? What was the plan? What?"

The shadow of Edwin's head crept across the wall and when the doctor spotted it, he stopped himself and sat up straighter. "Parker, I've had a little bit of an accident. I've made a little bit of a mess."

"Do you need any help, sir?"

"Help? I suppose I don't. If I only knew...if I could only remember." The doctor slid down off the stool, stumbling as his foot clipped the seat's bottom rung. "Parker? Where's the window? Didn't we have a window?"

"Sir," Edwin said, taking the old man's arm and guiding him over to his bed, in a nook at the far end of the laboratory. "Sir, I think you should lie down. Mrs. Criddle says supper comes in an hour. You just lie down, and I'll bring it to you when it's ready."

"Supper?" The many-lensed goggles he wore atop his head slid, and their strap came down over his left eye.

He sat Dr. Smeeks on the edge of his bed and removed the man's shoes, then his eyewear. He placed everything neatly beside the feather mattress and pulled the doctor's pillow to meet his downward-drooping head.

Edwin repeated, "I'll bring you supper when it's ready," but Dr. Smeeks was already asleep.

And in the laboratory, over by the stairs, the whirring and clicking of a clockwork boy was clattering itself in circles, or so Edwin assumed. He couldn't remember, had he left Ted on the stairs? He could've sworn he'd pressed the switch to deactivate his friend. But perhaps he hadn't.

Regardless, he didn't want the machine bounding clumsily around in the laboratory—not in that cluttered place piled with glass and gadgets.

Over his shoulder Edwin glanced, and saw the doctor snoozing lightly in his nook; and out in the laboratory, knocking its jar-lid knees against the bottom step, Ted had gone nowhere, and harmed nothing. Edwin picked Ted up and held the creation to his face, gazing into the glass badger eyes as if they might blink back at him.

He said, "You're my friend, aren't you? Everybody makes friends. I just made you for *real*."

Ted's jaw creaked down, opening its mouth so that Edwin could stare straight inside, at the springs and levers that made the toy boy move. Then its jaw retracted, and without a word, Ted had said its piece.

After supper, which Dr. Smeeks scarcely touched, and after an hour spent in the laundry room sharing Ted with Mrs. Williams, Edwin retreated to his cot and blew out the candle beside it. The cot wasn't wide enough for Edwin and Ted to rest side-by-side, but Ted fit snugly between the wall and the bedding and Edwin left the machine there, to pass the night.

But the night did not pass fitfully.

First Edwin awakened to hear the doctor snuffling in his sleep, muttering about the peril of inadequate testing; and when the old man finally sank back into a fuller sleep, Edwin nearly followed him. Down in the basement there were no lights except for the dim, bioluminescent glow of living solutions in blown-glass beakers—and the simmering wick of a hurricane lamp turned down low, but left alight enough for the boy to see his way to the privy if the urge struck him before dawn.

Here and there the bubble of an abandoned mixture seeped fizzily through a tube, and when Dr. Smeeks slept deeply enough to cease his ramblings, there was little noise to disturb anyone.

Even upstairs, when the wee hours came, most of the inmates and patients of the sanitarium were quiet—if not by their own cycles, then by the laudanum spooned down their throats before the shades were drawn.

Edwin lay on his back, his eyes closed against the faint, blue and green glows from the laboratory, and he waited for slumber to call him again. He reached to his left, to the spot between his cot and the wall. He patted the small slip of space there, feeling for a manufactured arm or leg, and finding Ted's cool, unmoving form. And although there was scarcely any room, he pulled Ted out of the slot and tugged the clockwork boy into the cot after all, because doll or no, Ted was a comforting thing to hold.

Part Two:

Morning came, and the doctor was already awake when Edwin rose. "Good morning sir."

"Good morning, Edwin," the doctor replied without looking over his shoulder. On their first exchange of the day, he'd remembered the right name. Edwin tried to take it as a sign that today would be a good day, and Dr. Smeeks would mostly remain Dr. Smeeks—without toppling into the befuddled tangle of fractured thoughts and faulty recollections.

He was standing by the hurricane lamp, with its wick trimmed higher so that he could read. An envelope was opened and discarded beside him.

"Is it a letter?" Edwin asked.

The doctor didn't sound happy when he replied, "It's a letter indeed."

"Is something wrong?"

"It depends." Dr. Smeeks folded the letter. "It's a man who wants me to work for him."

"That might be good," Edwin said.

"No. Not from this man."

The boy asked, "You know him?"

"I do. And I do not care for his aims. I will not help him," he said firmly. "Not with his terrible quests for terrible weapons. I don't do those things anymore. I haven't done them for years."

"You used to make weapons? Like guns, and cannons?"

Dr. Smeeks said, "Once upon a time." And he said it sadly. "But no more. And if Ossian thinks he can bribe or bully me, he has another thing coming. Worst comes to worst, I suppose, I can plead a failing mind."

Edwin felt like he ought to object as a matter of politeness, but when he said, "Sir," the doctor waved his hand to stop whatever else the boy might add.

"Don't, Parker. I know why I'm here. I know things, even when I can't always quite remember them. But my old colleague says he intends to pay me a visit, and he can pay me all the visits he likes. He can offer to pay me all the Union money he likes, too—or Confederate money, or any other kind. I won't make such terrible things, not anymore."

He folded the letter in half and struck a match to light a candle. He held one corner of the letter over the candle and let it burn, until there was nothing left but the scrap between his fingertips—and then he released it, letting the smoldering flame turn even the last of the paper to ash.

"Perhaps he'll catch me on a bad day, do you think? As likely as not, there will be no need for subterfuge."

Edwin wanted to contribute, and he felt the drive to communicate with the doctor while communicating seemed possible. He said, "You should tell him to come in the afternoon. I hope you don't mind me saying so, sir, but you seem much clearer in the mornings."

"Is that a fact?" he asked, an eyebrow lifted aloft by genuine interest. "I'll take your word for it, I suppose. Lord knows I'm in no position to argue. Is that…that noise…what's that noise? It's coming from your cot. Oh dear, I hope we haven't got a rat."

Edwin declared, "Oh no!" as a protest, not as an exclamation of worry. "No, sir. That's just Ted. I must've switched him on when I got up."

"Ted? What's a Ted?"

"It's my…" Edwin almost regretted what he'd said before, about mornings and clarity. "It's my new friend. I made him."

"There's a friend in your bunk? That doesn't seem too proper."

"No, he's…I'll show you."

And once again they played the scene of discovery together—the doctor clapping Edwin on the back and ruffling his hair, and announcing that the automaton was a fine invention indeed. Edwin worked very hard to disguise his disappointment.

Finally Dr. Smeeks suggested that Edwin run to the washrooms upstairs and freshen himself to begin the day, and Edwin agreed.

The boy took his spring-and-gear companion along as he navigated the corridors while the doctors and nurses made their morning rounds. Dr. Havisham paused to examine Ted and declare the creation "outstanding." Dr. Martin did likewise, and Nurse Evelyn offered him a peppermint sweet for being such an innovative youngster who never made any trouble.

Edwin cleaned his hands and face in one of the cold white basins in the washroom, where staff members and some of the more stable patients were allowed to refresh themselves. He set Ted on the countertop and pressed the automaton's switch. While Edwin cleaned the night off his skin, Ted's legs kicked a friendly time against the counter and its jaw bobbed like it was singing or chatting, or imagining splashing its feet in the basin.

When he was clean, Edwin set Ted on the floor and decided that— rather than carrying the automaton—he would simply let it walk the corridor until they reached the stairs to the basement.

The peculiar pair drew more than a few exclamations and stares, but Edwin was proud of Ted and he enjoyed the extended opportunity to show off.

Before the stairs and at the edge of the corridor where Edwin wasn't supposed to go, for fear of the violent inmates, a red-haired woman blocked his way. If her plain cotton gown hadn't marked her as a resident, the wildness around the corners of her eyes would've declared it well enough. There were red stripes on her skin where restraints were sometimes placed, and her feet were bare, leaving moist, sweaty prints on the black and white tiles.

"Madeline," Dr. Simmons warned. "Madeline, it's time to return to your room."

But Madeline's eyes were locked on the humming, marching automaton. She asked with a voice too girlish for her height, "What's that?" and she did not budge, even when the doctor took her arm and signaled quietly for an orderly.

Edwin didn't mind answering. He said, "His name is Ted. I made him."

"Ted." She chewed on the name and said, "Ted for *now*."

Edwin frowned and asked, "What?"

He did not notice that Ted had stopped marching, or that Ted's metal face was gazing up at Madeline. The clockwork boy had wound itself down, or maybe it was only listening.

Madeline did not blink at all, and perhaps she never did. She said, "He's your Ted for now, but you must watch him." She held out a pointing, directing, accusing finger and aimed it at Edwin, then at Ted. "Such empty children are vulnerable."

Edwin was forced to confess, or simply make a point of saying, "Miss, he's only a machine."

She nodded. "Yes, but he's your boy, and he has no soul. There are things who would change that, and change it badly."

"I know I shouldn't take him upstairs," Edwin said carefully. "I know I ought to keep him away from the other boys."

Madeline shook her head, and the matted crimson curls swayed around her face. "Not what I mean, boy. *Invisible* things. Bad little souls that need bodies."

An orderly arrived. He was a big, square man with shoulders like an ox's yoke. His uniform was white, except for a streak of blood that was drying to brown. He took Madeline by one arm, more roughly than he needed to.

As Madeline was pulled away, back to her room or back to her restraints, she kept her eyes on Edwin and Ted, and she warned him still, waving her finger like a wand, "Keep him close, unless you want him stolen from you—unless you want his clockwork heart replaced with something stranger."

Before she was removed from the corridor altogether, she lashed out one last time with her one free hand to seize the wall's corner. It bought her another few seconds of eye contact—just enough to add, "Watch him close!"

Then she was gone.

Edwin reached for Ted and pulled the automaton to his chest, where its gear-driven heart clicked quietly against the real boy's shirt. Ted's mechanical jaw opened and closed, not biting but mumbling in the crook of Edwin's neck.

"I will," he promised. "I'll watch him close."

Several days passed quietly, except for the occasional frustrated rages of the senile doctor, and Ted's company was a welcome diversion—if a somewhat unusual one. Though Edwin had designed Ted's insides and stuffed the gears and coils himself, the automaton's behavior was not altogether predictable.

Mostly, Ted remained a quiet little toy with the marching feet that tripped at stairs, at shoes, or any other obstacle left on the floor.

And if the clockwork character fell, it fell like a turtle and laid where it collapsed, arms and legs twitching impotently at the air until Edwin would come and set his friend upright. Several times Edwin unhooked Ted's back panel, wondering precisely why the shut-off switch failed so often. But he never found any stretched spring or faulty coil to account for it. If he asked Ted, purely to speculate aloud, Ted's shiny jaw would lower and lift, answering with the routine and rhythmic clicks of its agreeable guts.

But sometimes, if Edwin listened very hard, he could almost convince himself he heard words rattling around inside Ted's chest. Even if it was only the echoing pings and chimes of metal moving metal, the boy's eager ears would concentrate, and listen for whispers.

Once, he was nearly certain—practically *positive*—that Ted had said its own name. And that was silly, wasn't it? No matter how much Edwin wanted to believe, he knew better…which did not stop him from wondering.

It was always Edwin's job to bring meals down from the kitchen, and every time he climbed the stairs he made a point to secure Ted by turning it off and leaving it lying on its back, on Edwin's cot. The doctor was doddering, and even unobstructed he sometimes stumbled on his own two feet, or the laces of his shoes.

So when the boy went for breakfast and returned to the laboratory with a pair of steaming meals on a covered tray, he was surprised to hear the whirring of gears and springs.

"Ted?" he called out, and then felt strange for it. "Doctor?" he tried instead, and he heard the old man muttering.

"Doctor, are you looking at Ted? You remember him, don't you? Please don't break him."

At the bottom of the stairs, Dr. Smeeks was crouched over the prone and kicking Ted. The doctor said, "Underfoot, this thing is. Did it on purpose. I saw it. Turned itself on, sat itself up, and here it comes."

But Edwin didn't think the doctor was speaking to him. He was only speaking, and poking at Ted with a pencil like a boy prods an anthill.

"Sir? I turned him off, and I'm sorry if he turned himself on again. I'm not sure why it happens."

"Because it wants to be *on*," the doctor said firmly, and finally made eye contact. "It wants to make me fall, it practically told me so."

"Ted never says anything," Edwin said weakly. "He can't talk."

"He can talk. You can't hear him. But *I* can hear him. I've heard him before, and he used to say pleasant things. He used to hum his name. Now he fusses and mutters like a demented old man. Yes," he insisted, his eyes bugged and his eyebrows bushily hiked up his forehead. "Yes, this thing, when it mutters, it sounds like *me*."

Edwin had another theory about the voices Dr. Smeeks occasionally heard, but he kept it to himself. "Sir, he cannot talk. He hasn't got any lungs, or a tongue. Sir, I promise, he cannot speak."

The doctor stood, and gazed down warily as Ted floundered. "He cannot flip his own switches either, yet he *does*."

Edwin retrieved his friend and set it back on its little marching feet. "I must've done something wrong when I built him. I'll try and fix it, sir. I'll make him stop it."

"Dear boy, I don't believe you *can*."

The doctor straightened himself and adjusted his lenses—a different pair, a set that Edwin had never seen before. He turned away from the boy and the automaton and reached for his paperwork again, saying, "Something smells good. Did you get breakfast?"

"Yes sir. Eggs and grits, with sausage."

He was suddenly cheerful. "Wonderful! Won't you join me here? I'll clear you a spot."

As he did so, Edwin moved the tray to the open space on the main laboratory table and removed the tray's lid, revealing two sets of silverware and two plates loaded with food. He set one in front of the doctor, and took one for himself, and they ate with the kind of chatter that told Edwin Dr. Smeeks had already forgotten about his complaint with Ted.

As for Ted, the automaton stood still at the foot of the stairs—its face cocked at an angle that suggested it might be listening, or watching, or paying attention to something that no one else could see.

Edwin wouldn't have liked to admit it, but when he glanced back at his friend, he felt a pang of unease. Nothing had changed and everything was fine; he was letting the doctor's rattled mood unsettle him, that was all. Nothing had changed and everything was fine; but Ted was not marching and its arms were not swaying, and the switch behind the machine's small shoulder was still set in the "on" position.

When the meal was finished and Edwin had gathered the empty plates to return them upstairs, he stopped by Ted and flipped the switch to the state of "off." "You must've run down your winding," he said. "That must be why you stopped moving."

Then he called, "Doctor? I'm running upstairs to give these to Mrs. Criddle. I've turned Ted off, so he shouldn't bother you, but keep an eye out, just in case. Maybe," he said, balancing the tray on his crooked arm, "if you wanted to, you could open him up yourself and see if you can't fix him."

Dr. Smeeks didn't answer, and Edwin left him alone—only for a few minutes, only long enough to return the tray with its plates and cutlery.

It was long enough to return to strangeness.

Back in the laboratory Edwin found the doctor backed into a corner, holding a screwdriver and a large pair of scissors. Ted was seated on the edge of the laboratory table, its legs dangling over the side, unmoving, unmarching. The doctor looked alert and lucid—moreso than usual—and he did not quite look afraid. Shadows from the burners and beakers with their tiny glowing creatures made Dr. Smeeks look sinister and defensive, for the flickering bits of flame winked reflections off the edge of his scissors.

"Doctor?"

"I was only going to fix him, like you said."

"Doctor, it's all right."

The doctor said, "No, I don't believe it's all right, not at all. That nasty little thing, Parker, I don't like it." He shook his head, and the lenses across his eyes rattled in their frames.

"But he's my friend."

"He's no friend of *mine*."

Edwin held his hands up, like he was trying to calm a startled horse. "Dr. Smeeks, I'll take him. I'll fix him, you don't have to do it. He's only a machine, you know. Just an invention. He can't hurt you."

"He tried."

"Sir, I really don't think—"

"He tried to bite me. Could've taken my fingers off, if I'd caught them in that bear-trap of a face. You keep it away from me, Edwin. Keep it away or I'll pull it apart, and turn it into a can opener."

Before Edwin's very own eyes, Ted's head turned with a series of clicks, until the machine fully faced the doctor. And if its eyes had been more than glass bits that were once assigned to a badger, then they might have narrowed or gleamed; but they were only glass bits, and they only cast back the fragments of light from the bright things in the laboratory.

"Ted, come here. Ted, come with me," Edwin said, gently pulling the automaton down from the table. "Ted, no one's going to turn you into a can opener. Maybe you got wound funny, or wound too tight," he added, mostly for the doctor's benefit. "I'll open you up and tinker, and you'll be just fine."

Back in the corner the doctor relaxed, and dropped the scissors. He set the screwdriver down beside a row of test tubes and placed both hands down on the table's corner. "Edwin?" he said, so softly that Edwin almost didn't hear him. "Edwin, did we finish breakfast? I don't see my plate."

"Yes sir," the boy swore. He clutched Ted closely, and held the automaton away from the doctor, out of the man's line of sight should he turn around.

"Oh. I suppose that's right," he said, and again Ted had been spared by the doctor's dementia.

Edwin stuck Ted down firmly between the wall and his cot, and for one daft moment he considered binding the machine's feet with twine or wire to keep it from wandering. But the thought drifted out of his head, chased away by the unresponsive lump against the wall. He whispered, "I don't know how you're doing it, but you need to stop. I don't want the doctor to turn you into a can opener."

Then, as a compromise to his thoughts about hobbling the automaton, he dropped his blanket over the thing's head.

Bedtime was awkward that night.

When he reached for the clockwork boy he remembered the slow, calculated turn of the machine's head, and he recalled the blinking bright flashes of firelight in the glass badger eyes.

The doctor had settled in his nook and was sleeping, and Edwin was still awake. He reclaimed his blanket and settled down on his side, facing the wall and facing Ted until he dozed, or he must have dozed. He assumed it was only sleep that made the steel jaw lower and clack; and it was only a dream that made the gears twist and lock into syllables.

"Ted?" Edwin breathed, hearing himself but not recognizing the sound of his own word.

And the clockwork face breathed back, not its own name but something else—something that even in the sleepy state of midnight and calm, Edwin could not understand.

The boy asked in the tiniest whisper he could muster, "Ted?"

Ted's steel jaw worked, and the air in its mouth made the shape of a, "No." It said, more distinctly this time, and with greater volume, "Tan… gle…foot."

Edwin closed his eyes, and was surprised to learn that they had not been closed already. He tugged his blanket up under his chin and could not understand why the rustle of the fabric seemed so loud, but not so loud as the clockwork voice.

I must be asleep, he believed.

And then, eventually, he was.

Though not for long.

His sleep was not good. He was too warm, and then too cold, and then something was missing. Through the halls of his nightmares mechanical feet marched to their own tune; in the confined and cluttered space of the laboratory there was movement too large to come from rats, and too deliberate to be the random flipping of a switch.

Edwin awakened and sat upright in the same moment, with the same fluid fear propelling both events.

There was no reason for it, or so he told himself; and this was ridiculous, it was only the old Dr. Smeeks and his slipping mind, infecting the boy with strange stories—turning the child against his only true friend. Edwin shot his fingers over to the wall where Ted ought to be jammed, waiting for its winding and for the sliding of the button on its back.

And he felt only the smooth, faintly damp texture of the painted stone.

His hands flapped and flailed, slapping at the emptiness and the flat, blank wall. "Ted?" he said, too loudly. "Ted?" he cried with even more volume, and he was answered by the short, swift footsteps that couldn't have belonged to the doctor.

From his bed in the nook at the other end of the laboratory, the doctor answered with a groggy groan. "Parker?"

"Yes sir!" Edwin said, because it was close enough. "Sir, there's…" and what could he say? That he feared his friend had become unhinged, and that Ted was fully wound, and roaming?

"What is it, son?"

The doctor's voice came from miles away, at the bottom of a well—or that's how it sounded to Edwin, who untangled himself from the sheets and toppled to the floor. He stopped his fall with his hands, and stood, but then could scarcely walk.

As a matter of necessity he dropped his bottom on the edge of the cot and felt for his feet, where something tight was cinched around his ankles.

There, he found a length of wire bent into a loop and secured.

It hobbled his legs together, cutting his stride in half.

"Parker?" the doctor asked, awakening further but confused. "Boy?"

Edwin forced his voice to project a calm he wasn't feeling. "Sir, stay where you are, unless you have a light. My friend, Ted. He's gotten loose again. I don't want…I don't want you to hurt yourself."

"I can't find my candle."

"I can't find mine either," Edwin admitted. "You stay there. I'll come to you."

But across the floor the marching feet were treading steadily, and the boy had no idea where his automaton had gone. Every sound bounced off glass or wood, or banged around the room from wall to wall; and even the blue-gold shadows cast by the shimmering solutions could not reveal the clockwork boy.

Edwin struggled with the bizarre bind on his legs and stumbled forward regardless of it. No matter how hard his fingers twisted and pulled the wires only dug into his skin and cut it when he yanked too sharply. He gave up and stepped as wide as he could and found that, if he was careful, he could still walk and even, in half-hops and uneven staggers, he could run.

His light was nowhere to be found, and he gave up on that, too.

"Sir, I'm coming!" he cried out again, since the doctor was awake already and he wanted Ted to think he was aware, and acting. But what could Ted think? Ted was only a collection of cogs and springs.

Edwin remembered the red-haired Madeline with the strap-marks on her wrists. She'd said Ted had no soul, but she'd implied that one might come along.

The darkness baffled him, even in the laboratory he knew by heart. Hobbled as he was, and terrified by the pattering of unnatural feet, the basement's windowless night worked against him and he panicked.

He needed help, but where could it come from?

The orderlies upstairs frightened him in a vague way, as harbingers of physical authority; and the doctors and nurses might think he was as crazy as the other children, wild and loud—or as mad as his mother.

Like Madeline.

Her name tinkled at the edge of his ears, or through the nightmare confusion that moved him in jilting circles. Maybe Madeline knew something he didn't—maybe she could help. She wouldn't make fun of him, at any rate. She wouldn't tell him he was frightened for nothing, and to go back to sleep.

He knew where her room was located; at least he knew of its wing, and he could gather its direction.

The stairs jabbed up sharp and hard against his exploring fingers, and his hands were more free than his feet so he used them to climb—knocking his knees against each angle and bruising his shins with every yard. Along the wall above him there was a handrail someplace, but he couldn't find it so he made do without it.

He crawled so fast that his ascent might have been called a scramble.

He hated to leave the doctor alone down there with Ted, but then again, the doctor had taken up the screwdriver and the scissors once before. Perhaps he could be trusted to defend himself again.

At the top of the stairs Edwin found more light and his eyes were relieved. He stood up, seized the handrail, and fell forward because he'd already forgotten about the wire wrapped around his ankles. His hands stung from the landing, slapping hard against the tile floor, but he picked himself up and began a shuffling run, in tiny skips and dragging leaps down the corridor.

A gurney loomed skeletal and shining in the ambient light from the windows and the moon outside. Edwin fell past it and clipped it with his shoulder. The rattling of its wheels haunted him down the hallway, past the nurse's station where an elderly woman was asleep with the most recent issue of *Harper's New Monthly Magazine* lying across her breasts.

She didn't budge, not even when the gurney rolled creakily into the center of the hallway, following in Edwin's wake.

When he reached the right wing, he whispered, "Madeline? Madeline, can you hear me?"

All the windows in the doors to the inmate rooms were well off the ground and Edwin wasn't tall enough to reach, so he couldn't see inside. He hissed her name from door to door, and eventually she came forward. Her hands wrapped around the bars at the top, coiling around them like small white snakes. She held her face up to the small window and said, "Boy?"

He dashed to the door and pushed himself against it. "Madeline? It's me."

"The boy." Her mouth was held up to the window; she must have been standing on her tip-toes to reach it.

Edwin stood on his tip-toes also, but he couldn't touch the window, high above his head. He said, "I need your help. Something's wrong with Ted."

For a moment he heard only her breathing, rushed and hot above him. Then she said, "Not your Ted any longer. I warned you."

"I know you did!" he said, almost crying. "I need your help! He tied my feet together, all tangled up—and I think he's trying to hurt Dr. Smeeks!"

"Tangled, did he? Oh, that vicious little changeling," she said, almost wheezing with exertion. She let go of whatever was holding her up, and Edwin heard her feet land back on the floor with a thump. She said through the door's frame, beside its hinges, "You must let me out, little boy. If you let me out, I'll come and help your doctor. I know what to do with changelings."

It was a bad thought, and a bad plan. It was a bad thing to consider and Edwin knew it all too well; but when he looked back over his shoulder at the nurse's station with the old lady snoring within, and when he thought of the clattering automaton roaming the laboratory darkness with his dear Dr. Smeeks, he leaped at the prospect of aid.

He reached for the lever to open the door and hung from it, letting it hold his full weight while he reached up to undo the lock.

Edwin no sooner heard the click of the fastener unlatching then the door burst open in a quick swing that knocked him off his hobbled feet. With a smarting head and bruised elbow he fought to stand again but Madeline grabbed him by the shoulder. She lifted him up as if he were as light as a doll, and she lugged him down the hallway. Her cotton shift billowed dirtily behind her, and her hair slapped Edwin in the eyes as she ran.

Edwin squeezed at her arm, trying to hold himself out of the way of the displaced gurneys and medical trays that clogged the hall; but his airborne feet smacked the window of the nurse's station as Madeline swiftly hauled him past it, awakening the nurse and startling her into motion.

If Madeline noticed, she did not stop to comment.

She reached the top of the stairs and flung herself down them, her feet battering an alternating time so fast that her descent sounded like firecrackers. Edwin banged along behind her, twisted in her grip and unable to move quickly even if she were to set him down.

He wondered if he hadn't made an awful mistake when she all but cast him aside. His body flopped gracelessly against a wall. But he was back on his feet in a moment and there was light in the laboratory—a flickering, uncertain light that was moving like mad.

Dr. Smeeks was holding it; he'd found his light after all, and he'd raised the wick on the hurricane lamp. The glass-jarred lantern gleamed and flashed as he swung it back and forth, sweeping the floor for something Edwin couldn't see.

The doctor cried out, "Parker? Parker? Something's here, something's in the laboratory!"

And Edwin answered, "I know, sir! But I've brought help!"

The light shifted, the hurricane lamp swung, and Madeline was standing in front of the doctor—a blazing figure doused in gold and red, and black-edged shadows. She said nothing, but held out her hand and took the doctor's wrist; she shoved his wrist up, forcing the lamp higher. The illumination increased accordingly and Edwin started to cry.

The laboratory was in a disarray so complete that it might never be restored to order. Glass glimmered in piles of dust, shattered tubes and broken beakers were smeared with the shining residue of the blue-green substance that lived and glowed in the dark. It spilled and died, losing its luminescence with every passing second—and there was the doctor, his hand held aloft and his lamp bathing the chaos with revelation.

Madeline turned away from him, standing close enough beneath the lamp so that her shadow did not temper its light. Her feet twisted on the glass-littered floor, cutting her toes and leaving smears of blood.

She demanded, "Where are you?"

She was answered by the tapping of marching feet, but it was a sound that came from all directions at once. And with it came a whisper, accompanied by the grinding discourse of a metal jaw.

"Tan...gles. Tan...gles...feet. Tanglefoot."

"That's your name then? Little changeling—little Tanglefoot? Come out here!" she fired the command into the corners of the room and let it echo there. "Come out here, and I'll send you back to where you came from! Shame on you, taking a boy's friend. Shame on you, binding his feet and tormenting his master!"

Tanglefoot replied, "Can...op...en...er" as if it explained everything, and Edwin thought that it *might*—but that it was no excuse.

"Ted, where *are* you?" he pleaded, tearing his eyes away from Madeline and scanning the room. Upstairs he could hear the thunder of footsteps—of orderlies and doctors, no doubt, freshly roused by the night nurse in her chamber. Edwin said with a sob, "Madeline, they're coming for you."

She growled, "And I'm coming for *him*."

She spied the automaton in the same second that Edwin saw it—not on the ground, marching its little legs in bumping patterns, but overhead, on a ledge where the doctor kept books. Tanglefoot was marching, yes, but it was marching towards them both with the doctor's enormous scissors clutched between its clamping fingers.

"Ted!" Edwin screamed, and the machine hesitated. The boy did not know why, but there was much he did not know and there were many things he'd never understand…including how Madeline, fierce and barefoot, could move so quickly through the glass.

The madwoman seized the doctor's hurricane lamp by its scalding cover, and Edwin could hear the sizzle of her skin as her fingers touched, and held, and then flung the oil-filled lamp at the oncoming machine with the glittering badger eyes.

The lamp shattered and the room was flooded with brilliance and burning.

Dr. Smeeks shrieked as splatters of flame sprinkled his hair and his nightshirt, but Edwin was there—shuffling fast into the doctor's sleeping nook. The boy grabbed the top blanket and threw it at the doctor, then he joined the blanket and covered the old man, patting him down. When the last spark had been extinguished he left the doctor covered and held him in the corner, hugging the frail, quivering shape against himself while Madeline went to war.

Flames were licking along the books and Madeline's hair was singed. Her shift was pocked with black-edged holes, and she had grabbed the gloves Dr. Smeeks used when he held his crucibles. They were made of asbestos, and they would help her hands.

Tanglefoot was spinning in place, howling above their heads from his fiery perch on the book ledge. It was the loudest sound Edwin had ever heard his improvised friend create, and it horrified him down to his bones.

Someone in a uniform reached the bottom of the stairs and was repulsed, repelled by the blast of fire. He shouted about it, hollering for water. He demanded it as he retreated, and Madeline didn't pay him a fragment of attention.

Tanglefoot's scissors fell to the ground, flung from its distracted hands. The smoldering handles were melting on the floor, making a black, sticky puddle where they settled.

With her gloved hands she scooped them up and stabbed, shoving the blades down into the body of the mobile inferno once named Ted. She withdrew the blades and shoved them down again because the clockwork boy still kicked, and the third time she jammed the scissors into the little body she jerked Ted down off the ledge and flung it to the floor.

The sound of breaking gears and splitting seams joined the popping gasp of the fire as it ate the books and gnawed at the ends of the tables.

"A blanket!" Madeline yelled. "Bring me a blanket!"

Reluctantly, Edwin uncovered the shrouded doctor and wadded the blanket between his hands. He threw the blanket to Madeline.

She caught it, and unwrapped it enough to flap it down atop the hissing machine, and she beat it again and again, smothering the fire as she struck the mechanical boy. Something broke beneath the sheet, and the chewing tongues of flame devoured the cloth that covered Tanglefoot's joints—leaving only a tragic frame beneath the smoldering covers.

Suddenly and harshly, a bucket of water doused Madeline from behind. Seconds later she was seized.

Edwin tried to intervene. He divided his attention between the doctor, who cowered against the wall, and the madwoman with the bleeding feet and hair that reeked like cooking trash.

He held up his hands and said, "Don't! No, you can't! No, she was only trying to help!" And he tripped over his own feet, and the pile of steaming clockwork parts on the floor. "No," he cried, because he couldn't speak without choking. "No, you can't take her away. Don't hurt her, please. It's my fault."

Dr. Williams was there, and Edwin didn't know when he'd arrived. The smoke was stinging his eyes and the whimpers of Dr. Smeeks were distracting his ears, but there was Dr. Williams, preparing to administer a washcloth soaked in ether to Madeline's face.

Dr. Williams said to his colleague, a burly man who held Madeline's arms behind her back, "I don't know how she escaped this time."

Edwin insisted, "I did it!"

But Madeline gave him a glare and said, "The boy's as daft as his mother. The clockwork boy, it called me, and I destroyed it. I let myself out, like the witch I am and the fiend you think I must be—"

And she might've said more, but the drug slipped up her nostrils and down her chest, and she sagged as she was dragged away.

"No," Edwin gulped. "It isn't fair. Don't hurt her."

No one was listening to him. Not Dr. Smeeks, huddled in a corner. Not Madeline, unconscious and leaving. And not the bundle of burned and smashed parts in a pile beneath the book ledge, under a woolen covering. Edwin tried to lift the burned-up blanket but pieces of Ted came with it, fused to the charred fabric.

Nothing moved, and nothing grumbled with malice in the disassembled stack of ash-smeared plates, gears, and screws.

Edwin returned to the doctor and climbed up against him, shuddering and moaning until Dr. Smeeks wrapped his arms around the boy to say, "There, there. Parker it's only a little fire. I must've let the crucible heat too long, but look. They're putting it out now. We'll be fine."

The boy's chest seized up tight, and he bit his lips, and he sobbed. ━🐏

Hide and Horns

by Joe R. Lansdale

I was recovering from some knife wounds, and was mostly healed up and hoping I wasn't gonna come up on anything that might get me all het up and cause me to tear open my cuts. I was chewin' on some jerky, riding a pretty good horse on the plains of Texas, when I seen something in the distance. I pulled my mount up and got out my long glasses and took me a look.

There was a colored fella like myself lying out there under a horse, had one leg jammed under it, and the horse was deader than a rock. The colored fella was wearing a big sombrero and a red shirt and he wasn't movin'. I figured he was dead like the horse, cause there was some buzzards circlin', and one lit down near the man and the horse and had the manner of a miner waiting for someone to ring the dinner bell. There was a little black cloud above the fella I took to be flies that was excited about soon crawling up the old boy's nose holes.

I rode on over there, and when I got near, the colored fella rolled on his side and showed me the business end of an old Sharp's fifty rifle, the hole in the barrel looked to me to be as big as a mining tunnel.

"Hold up," I said, "I ain't got nothin' agin ya."

"Yeah," he said in a voice dry as the day, "but there's them that do." He rolled over on his side again and lay the rifle across his chest. He said, "You give me any cause, I'll blow your head off."

I got down off my horse and led it over to where the fella and his dead cayuse lay. I said, "So, just restin'?"

"Me and my horse here thought we'd stop in the middle of the goddamn prairie, under the goddamn sun, and take a goddamn nap."

"Good a place as any," I said, squatting down to look the man over, "cause I don't see one spread of shade nowhere."

"And you won't for some miles."

"Course, that sombrero could cover an acre in shade."

"It does me good from time to time," he said.

I could see that the horse had a couple of bullet holes in its side, and the fella had one too, in his right shoulder. He had stuffed a rag in the hole and the rag was red, and the red shirt looked to have been a lighter color before it had sucked up all that blood.

"I ain't feelin' so good," he said.

"That would be because you got a bullet hole in you and a big old dead horse lyin' on your leg."

"And I thought he was just nappin'. I didn't want to disturb him." I bent down and looked at where the leg was trapped. The fella said, "You know, I don't know how much blood I got left in me."

"Way you look," I said, "not much. There's a town not too far from here I've heard of. Might be someone there that can do some fixin's on ya."

"That'd be right good," the fella said. "My name is Cramp, or that's what people call me anyway. I don't remember how I got the name. Something back in slave days. I think the man got my mama's belly full of me was called that, so I became Cramp too. Never knowed him. But, I got to tell you, I ain't up to a whole lot of history."

I got hold of his leg and tried to ease it out from under the horse, but that wasn't workin'.

I went back to my horse, got a little camp shovel I had when I was in the Buffalo Soldiers, and dug around Cramp's leg, said, "They call me Nat."

He said, "That diggin' is loosin' me up, but I don't know it's gonna matter. I'm startin' to feel cold."

"You've quit loosin' blood for now," I said, "otherwise, you'd already be scratchin' on heaven's door."

Hide and Horns | JOE R. LANSDALE

"Or hell's back door."

"One ta other."

I got hold of his leg and pulled, and it come free, and he made a barking sound, and I looked at him. His face was popped with sweat, and it was an older face than I'd realized, fifty or so, and it looked like an old dark withered potato. I got him under the shoulders and pulled him away and lay him down, went back to his horse and cut one of the saddlebags off with my knife, and put it under his noggin' for a pillow. His sombrero had come off, and I went and got that and brought it over to him, and was about to lean it on his head, when I looked up and seen four riders comin' in the distance.

Cramp must have seen the look on my face, cause he said, "Did I mention that there's some fellas after me?"

"That didn't come up. Just said there was folks had somethin' agin you."

"That would be them. They're mad at me."

"They have a reason?"

"They don't like me."

"Are you normally likeable?"

"I'm startin' to pass out, son."

"Hang in there."

"Can't... Don't let me be buried in no lonesome ground."

He closed his eyes and lay still.

I got my long glasses and gave them a look. It was four white fellas, and one of them looked to be damn near as big as the horse he was ridin'. They all had the look of folks that would like to hang someone so they could get in the mood to do somethin' really bad. They was looking right at me, the big cracker with his hand over his eyes, studying me there in the distance.

I got hold of Cramp and dragged his big ass on the other side of the horse and stretched him out so that his head was against the saddle and his feet was stretched out toward the north, which was the direction I wanted to go. Actually, I kind of wanted to go any direction right then, and it crossed my mind that I could get on my horse and just ride off, fast as I could go, leave Cramp to the buzzards, the flies, and the ants, but havin' been partly ruint by too much good raisin', and being of too much character, it just wasn't in me. But I didn't have so much character I didn't think about it.

I went around and picked up the Sharps and looked in the saddlebag I had cut off, and found some loads in there, a whole batch of hand-made shells. I studied the situation awhile, decided that when things was over there'd either be me and Cramp dead, or there would be some spare horses, so I led my nag over near where the other horse lay, grabbed his nose and pulled him down, way I had been taught in the cavalry, pulled out my pistol and shot him through the head. He kicked once and was still, and now I had me a V-shaped horse fort. It was an old trick I'd learned fightin' Indians. The other thing I'd learned was not to get too sentimental about a horse, you never knew when you might have to eat one or make a fort out of him. The one horse I'd really liked, me and a woman I cared about had eaten him, but I don't want to get side-tracked and off on that. It's a sad story and doesn't end well for any of the three of us involved.

Lying down on my belly beside Cramp, I laid out the rifle across his horse and took me a bead. A Sharps fifty, which is what Cramp's rifle was, can cover some real ground, but it takes some fine shootin' to know how to get the windage and judge the way the bullet will fall from a distance. I was a fine shooter, but that didn't stop me from worrying, especially now that they were ridin' toward me fast.

I beaded down on the big man, but another rider moved in front of him, so he became my target. I had him good in my sights, but I stopped and sucked my finger wet, stuck it up in the air and got me the pull of the wind, then I beaded again. I took a deep breath and let it out slow as I pulled the trigger. The rifle popped. I knew that from where they were, it wouldn't sound like much, and if they didn't know their business, it would seem to them I'd missed, cause it was a long damn ways.

The man I shot at was riding right along and it seemed that a lot of time passed before he threw out his hands and I seen a stream of blood leap out of his chest and he fell off his horse.

I thought: What if ole Cramp here deserves what he's gonna get? That went through my head for a moment, but then I thought, even if he does, he ought not to get it when he's about dead, least not like this by a bunch of angry peckerwoods.

They started firing at me with Winchesters, like the one on my dead horse, and the bullets fell well short. They had stopped, but they hadn't shot their horses. They had dismounted and were standing by their horses firing away, the bullets plopping well in front of me. I knew right then, them not shooting their horses, they weren't as committed as I was.

I said to myself, "You boys hold that position."

I loaded another round in the Sharps and laid it back across the dead horse and took a deep breath and cracked my neck the way I can by moving my head a little sharply, and took aim. I was feelin' frisky, so even though I should have aimed for my target's chest, I sighted a little high of his forehead and fired. The shot knocked him off his feet, causin' a puff of dust to throw up, and I figured I'd gotten him right between the peepers, though that was guess work, because all I saw were the soles of his boots comin' up.

The other two mounted up, and with the big man leading, they went back in the other direction. I popped a load after them, knocking the big man's horse out from under him, throwing the bastard for a few loops. He was on his feet quick and he got down behind the dead horse, and the other fella kept on ridin', like someone had stuck a lighted corn shuck up his horse's ass. I took a shot at him, but he kept ridin', leaning low over his horse like he was tryin' to mix himself into it.

A moment later, he was out of sight, and I turned my attentions back to the big fella.

I loaded again and raised up this time, on one knee, and shouldered the rifle and took a long deep breath, and fired. This one plopped into the dead horse. After that, I lay down behind Cramp's horse with my head barely up, and watched. The big man didn't move until the day wore down and it got near dark. He got up then and took off at a run in the other direction. I could have let him go, because it was a hard shot, it being dark and all with just some moonlight, but I was kind of worked up, them tryin' to kill me and all, so I raised up, and aimed, and fired, and got him. He went down like a three hundred pound sack of shit.

"Asshole," I said.

※

I wasn't sure how to go from there, or where I was goin', 'less it was that town I told Cramp about, but one thing was certain, Cramp wouldn't be going with me, least not alive. He was colder than a wedge and stiff as horse dick at breedin' time.

When I felt wasn't no one circlin' in on me, I got up and walked out a pace, carrying my Winchester with me, leavin' the Sharps, but bringin' the loads with me, lest they surprise me, come back, get hold of his rifle and pick me off from a distance.

I walked in the direction I'd seen one of the horses go, and when it was good and dark, I seen his shape outlined by the moon. I was able to cluck to him and get him to come over, not mentionin' to him I'd killed two of his kind on this day.

I rode him back to where Cramp lay, got my saddle out from under my horse, and swapped it onto the horse I'd rustled up. I got hold of Cramp and threw him over the horse. He was so stiff, he rocked there for a moment and nearly fell off. I climbed on board with the Winchester back in the boot, and the Sharps, now loaded, across my lap, and started in the direction of the town I knew was supposed to be out there, a place called Hide and Horns, if memory served me. I hadn't never been there, but I'd been told about it. Before most of the buffalo was killed out in the area, it had been a place for selling hides and horns and bones for fertilizer.

As I rode along, I didn't let myself get too sure of things. I kept my eyes open and my ears perked.

So far, I hadn't torn open any of my cuts, and I determined they had healed up good. I guess there was some things goin' my way.

※

Hide and Horns, out there in the moonlight, looked like a place you went to shit, not a place you went to live. But there was folks there and the street was full of them, and a lot of them looked drunk. Thing was, I was still wearin' my army jacket from when I was in with the Buffalo Soldiers, and this bein' the panhandle of Texas, that blue jacket was bound to cause some former rebel to come unhitched and want to kill him a nigger. I had not removed it because of pride, but now as I neared Hide and Horns my pride was growing smaller and my feelin's about not gettin' skinned for an incident of birth was growin' larger.

I decided to ride around the street, out back of the town with my dead companion, and see what was on the far side, which is where I figured the colored would be collected, if there was any. I rode around there, taking it long and slow, and when I got to the other end, there was some shacks and a lot of tents there. No coloreds to be seen, but there was four or five Chinamen and some China girls outside next to a big fire and a boiling pot of laundry, which one of them, a young China girl was movin' around with a board. Beyond her, I could see the town proper, lit up with lanterns and such, and drunk cowboys crossin' and wanderin' around in the street like they really had some place to go.

I got off my horse and led it toward the China folk, Cramp rockin' back and forth, and when I got up close to the pot, the girl, who turned out to be a woman, only small, and beautiful in the firelight, looked at me like I'd come from hell to borrow a cup of sugar. A Chinaman walked out into the firelight with an axe. He was pretty big for a Chinaman. He said, "Do for you?"

"Not if you're plannin' on choppin' on me."

He shook his head and his pigtail slapped from side to side. "Do for you?"

"I got a fella here needs a place in the dirt."

The Chinaman, maybe not sure what I meant, or just wanting to satisfy his own curiosity, came over and took hold of Cramp's boot and pulled on it, said, "Dead nigger."

"Yeah," I said, "he won't be havin' dinner. But, I'd like some. I got Yankee dollars."

"How much dollars?"

"Enough."

"Pussy?"

"Beg your pardon."

"Sell pussy. You want?"

"Oh."

I looked around. Four of the China girls had bunched up near one of the larger tents, and they were looking at me, smiling. Two of them were right smart lookin', one was so ugly she could chase a bobcat up a tree, and there was one pretty good looker with her leg cut off at the knee. She had a wooden leg strapped on and had a crutch under her arm, and from what I could make out in the firelight, she appeared to be missin' a tooth on the far right side.

"Half a woman," the Chinaman said pointing at the wooden leg gal, "she cheaper."

"Actually, she's more than half," I said. "Way more."

"She five penny."

"Well, they are all as lovely as the next," I said, tryin' not to look at the ugly one lest I get struck by lightnin' for lyin', "but I'm gonna pass. I'm hungry."

I looked at the other one, at the wash pot. The Chinaman, figurin' I might be sizin' her up for a mattress, said: "Daughter, not sale."

"Okay," I said. "About that food?"

"Chop suey?" he said. "Cheap."

"What?"

"Chop suey," he said again.

"That'll work. Whatever that is."

"Bury dead nigger?"

"He ain't in no hurry," I said. "I'll tend to the horse and eat before I bury him."

As I was starting to remove my saddle from the horse, the Chinaman walked by the China girls, and reached out and cuffed the cripple, knocking her down. He said something in China talk. I went over and grabbed his shoulder and shoved him back, and wagged a finger at him. "Hey," I said. "Ain't no call to slap a woman around."

The Chinaman still had the axe in one hand, and he eyed me and clenched the axe a little tighter. "She go to work."

"All right," I said. "Give her time. And lighten up on that axe, or you'll wake up with it up your ass."

Hide and Horns | JOE R. LANSDALE

I reached down and picked up the crutch she had dropped, then I reached down and pulled her up and put the crutch under her arm. She smiled that missing tooth smile. She looked pretty damn good, even if she could suck a pea through that hole in her chompers with the rest of her teeth clenched.

"Chop suey," the Chinaman said to the cripple, and she limped away into a tent on her crutch.

＊

What Chop suey was, was warm and delicious, though right then it might have seemed better than it really was cause I was hungry enough to eat the ass out of a dead mule and suck blood out of a chicken's eye.

I sat on my ass on the dirt floor under a tent roof and ate up and kept an eye on my Chinaman, as he had never let go of that there axe, and he had a way of lookin' at me that made me nervous. I had pulled Cramp off the horse and stretched him out on some hay that was off to the side of the tents, next to a cheap corral which was mostly dirt, wind, a frame of wood, and a spot of tarp. I unsaddled the horse and brought it some hay and water, and had a China boy curry him down. I paid for the service, and then I went in and ate.

The four whores didn't depart. They sat nearby and looked at me and giggled. The Chinaman said, "They want see black come off."

"It doesn't."

"They think you, dead nigger, painted. They not know things."

"Tell one of them they can rub my skin, see if it comes off."

The Chinaman told them somethin' in Chinese talk, and one of the girls, who now that I was closer, looked pretty young to me, came over and rubbed on my arm.

"No come off," she said.

"Not so far," I said.

"Let see dick," she said.

"Now what?"

"Let see dick."

"She want know it's black," the Chinaman said.

"She can take my word on that one, and maybe later I can show it to her in private."

"That be two bits," the Chinaman said.

"For the woman?"

He nodded. "Two bits."

I looked at the China girl, said, "What's your name?"

"Sally," she said.

"Really?"

"Sally," she said.

"They all Sally," the Chinaman said, holding the axe a little too comfortably. "You can call Polly or whatever, you buy pussy."

"I'll think that over. First things first, where's the graveyard?"

The Chinaman pointed. "Back of town, that side. No niggers."

"He's dead. What does it matter?"

"No nigger. No Chinaman."

"Well, that puts a hitch in my drawers," I said. "Promised him I'd bury him somewhere wasn't lonesome."

"Bury in pig pen, but deep. Not deep. Pigs will eat him."

"No, I had something different in mind. Like a graveyard."

"White fellas, not like. Shoot black dick off."

"That wouldn't be good."

I got up and went outside and walked over to Cramp. He wasn't lookin' too good. Startin' to bloat. I got my knife and slipped it under his ribs and jabbed hard and let some of the bloat out, which was as bad air as you ever smelled. I stood over to the side while he deflated a mite.

The Chinaman had followed me out, still carrying his axe. He said, "Damn. Dead nigger smell plenty bad."

"Dead anything smells plenty bad… You think maybe you could put that axe down? You're makin' me a nervous."

"Chinaman like axe."

"I see that."

The girls had come out now.

I saddled up my horse and put poor old Cramp over the saddle again. He had loosened up some, and his head and legs hung down in a sad kind of way. I had his sombrero on the saddle horn, and I got on the horse and said, "I need to borrow a shovel and a lantern."

"Two bits," the big Chinaman said.

"I said borrow."

"Two bits."

"Shit." I dug in my pocket for two bits and gave it to him, and the one-legged whore, moving pretty good for a wooden leg and a crutch, carried the shovel and unlit lantern over to me. I reached down from the horse and took it, rode in the direction the Chinaman said the graveyard was.

⇥✳⇤

The graveyard was on a hill to the east side of the town, and I rode over there and got off the horse and lit the lantern, held it out with one hand and led the horse with the other. There was some stone markers, but mostly they was wood, and some of them was near rotted away or eaten away by bugs.

I looked until I found a place that was bare, tied up the horse to one of the wooden markers, put the lantern next to my burying spot, got the shovel off the saddle, and started to dig.

I had gotten about two feet into the ground, and about two feet wide, ready to make it six feet long, when I heard a noise and turned to see lights. Folks were comin' up the hill, and they were led by the Chinaman, still carrying his axe. The others were white folks, and they didn't look happy. Now and again, I'd like to run up against just one happy white folk.

I stuck the shovel in the dirt, left the lantern where it was, walked over and stood by my horse, cause that's where my Winchester was. I tried not to look like a man that liked being near his Winchester, but being near it gave me comfort, and of course, I had my revolver with me. It had five shots in a six-shot chamber, which is the way I carry it most of the time, lest I shoot my foot off pullin' it loose from its holster. But five shots wasn't enough for eight men, which there was, countin' the Chinaman with his axe. A couple of them were carrying shotguns, and one had a rifle. The rest had pistols on them.

When they were about twenty feet from me, they stopped walking.

The Chinaman said, "I tell him. No niggers. No Chinaman."

"You scoundrel," I said, "you rented me the shovel and the lantern."

"Make money. Not say bury nigger."

"The chink here," one of the shotgun totin' white men said, stepping forward a step, "is right. No niggers in Christian soil."

"What if he's a Christian?"

"He's still a nigger. So are you."

I was wondering how fast I could get on my horse before they rushed me. I said, "Chinaman, what problem was this of yours?"

"My town."

I thought, you asshole. Just a half hour ago you were trying to sell me pussy, sold me food and feed for my horse, and rented me a shovel and a lantern. His problem was simple, I had stopped him from slapping his property around, and now that he had my money, he was getting even. Or, from my way of lookin' at it, more than even.

"All right, gentleman," I said. "I'll take my dead man and go."

"That there jacket," one of the men said, and my heart sank, "that's a Yankee soldier jacket."

"I was in the army, not the war," I said. "I didn't shoot at no Southerners."

"You still got on a Yankee jacket."

"I was chasin' Indians," I said, figurin' most of them wouldn't care for Indians either, and that might put me on their side a bit.

"You and them ain't got a whole lot of difference, except you can pick cotton and sing a spiritual."

"That ought to be a mark in my favor," I said.

They didn't think that was funny, and it didn't do any endearing.

"Shootin' a nigger ain't half the fun as lynchin' one," one of the charming townspeople said.

I pulled my revolver quick like and shot the closest man carryin' a shotgun, shot him right between the eyes, and then I turned and shot the other shotgunner in the side of the head, and just to make me happy, I shot the Chinaman in the chest. Bullets whizzed around me, but them fellas was already backin' down the hill. I'd learned a long time ago, you can't outshoot eight determined and brave people fair, but you can outshoot eight cowards if you get right at it and don't stop. You can't hesitate. You got to be, as I learned in the army, willin'.

I ran to the edge of the hill and popped off my last shot, and now shots were comin' back up the hill at me at a more regular pace. I grabbed my horse and took off, leavin' Cramps lyin' there. I rode on up through the cemetery and topped it out and rode down the other side as bullets whizzed around me.

I got to a clearin' and gave the horse a clear path, and it could really run. I had caught me a good one back there on the prairie, and it covered ground like a high wind. I looked back and seen that there were some lanterns waggin' back there, and then I heard horses comin', and I bent low over my pony and said, "Run, you bastard," and run he did.

We went like that, full out for a long time, and I knew if I didn't stop, the horse was gonna keel over, so I pulled up in a stand of wood and got off of him and let him blow a little. I put my hand on his heaving side and came away with it covered in salt from sweat. I heard the sound of their horses, and I hoped they didn't have no tracker amongst them, and if they did, I tried to figure that the night was on my side. Course, it would stand to reason they'd want to look in the only area where a man might hide, this little patch of woods.

I led the horse deeper in the trees, and then I led him up a little rise, which was one of the few I'd seen in this part of the country, outside of the cemetery. The trees wasn't like those in East Texas where I'd come from. They were bony lookin' and there was just this little patch standing.

I got the Sharps and the Winchester off the horse and took my saddlebag off of it, and throwed it over my shoulder. I led the horse down amongst the thickest part of the trees and looped the reins over a limb and went back to where I could see good and lay down with the Sharps. I opened the saddlebag and felt around in there for a load and opened the breech on the Sharps and slid in a round and took a deep breath and waited. They came riding up, pausing at the patch of trees, having a pretty good guess I was in there.

They was in range, though they didn't know it, not figurin' on me havin' the Sharps, and they was clutched up good. A bunch had joined them from the town, and I counted twelve. Not a very smart twelve, way they was jammed up like that, but twelve nonetheless, and there wasn't no surprise goin' now. They had me treed like a possum.

After a moment, I seen one horse separate from the others, and the rider on it was sitting straight up in the saddle, stiff. He come on out away from the others and there didn't seem to be a thing cautious or worried about him.

As he closed in, I took a bead on him, and in the moonlight, as he neared, I noted he was a colored fella, and I figured they had grabbed some swamper in town and brought him with them, thinkin' he'd talk me into givin' myself up, which he couldn't. I knew how it would end if they got their hands on me, and me puttin' a bullet in my own head was better than that.

Then I seen somethin' else. It was Cramps. He was tied up on his horse, a stick or somethin' worked into the back of the saddle, and he was bound up good so he wouldn't fall off. He had his sombrero perched on his head.

I lowered the rifle and seen that the crowd of horses behind Cramp was spreadin' out a bit. I was about to put a bead on one of them, when a white man rode out and said, "You don't come back, nigger. Stay out of our town, hear? We're gonna give you this one so you don't come back."

Well, now, I got to admit, I wasn't plannin' on goin' back for Cramps no how. I had tried to do my good deed and it hadn't worked out, so I figured the smartest thing I could do was wish him the best and ride like hell. But now, here he was. And there they were.

The horse with Cramp on it ambled right into the woods, and come up toward me like it was glad to see me. I stood up and got hold of its reins and led it behind me and tied it off on a limb and went back and lay down. I watched the white folks for awhile.

"You don't come back," the fella who'd spoken before said, and they all turned and rode back toward town.

I didn't believe they'd given up on me anymore than they'd given up on breathin'.

⁂

Hide and Horns | Joe R. Lansdale

Way I had it reckoned, was they was gonna slow me down by givin' me Cramps to worry about, and then when they thought I figured they was gone, they was gonna get me. I knew they was worried about me, cause they had had no idea I could shoot like I could until that moment on the hill when I killed a few of them, and their snotty Chinaman too. So now, caution had set in. They were probably waiting out there until I felt safer, or got so hungry and thirsty, I had to leave out of the grove, then they was gonna spring on me like a tick on a nut sack. If I waited until daylight I could see them better, but, of course, they could see me better too, so I didn't think that was such a sterlin' plan.

I lay there and listened and was certain I could hear them ridin' in different directions, and that convinced me I was right about that they had in mind. They was gonna surround me and wait until they got their chance to shoot more holes in me than a flour sieve.

I lay there with the Sharps and strained my thinkin', and then I come up with a plan. I reloaded my revolver and went and pulled Cramps into the thickest of the trees, and there in the dark I cut him loose from that pole they had fixed up to the back of the saddle by lacin' a lariat through it, and pulled him off the horse.

Cramp stunk like a well-used outhouse and his face was startin' to wither. I put his sombrero on my head, pulled off his jacket and tossed mine across his horse. I got my guns and the things I wanted from my saddlebags, packed them up, climbed on his horse and rested my back against that pole they had tied up, put my Winchester and the Sharps across my lap, tuckin' them as close as possible, and then I clucked softly to the horse and left the other one tied back there in the trees. I had a moment of worrying about the horse, him tied and all, but I figured they'd eventually come in here after me if I managed to get away, and they'd take the horse. Thing was, though I gave the nag a thought, I was more worried about my ass than his. I tried to sit good and solid and hope anyone seein' me would think I was just that dead fella on a pony, tied to a post.

I pretty much let the horse go how he intended, except I had hold of the reins and was ready to snap them into play if a reason come up. I hadn't gone far when I seen that there were a couple of white fellas, about twenty feet apart, sittin' their horses, rifles at the ready. It was all I could do to play my part. One of the white fellas said, "There's the dead nigger. That other coon didn't want him no how."

Then the other one said somethin' that made my butt hole grab at the saddle.

"Let's see we can shoot that hat off of him."

That gave me pause.

The other one said, "Naw, we got to be quiet," even though they was about as quiet as two badgers wrestlin' in a hole.

The horse I was ridin' went between them, and it was all I could do not to put my heels to that nag and ride like hell, but I stuck to my plan. I rode right on through and nobody shot at me.

When I was out of their range, about twenty minutes, I figure, I took the reins and gave the horse a little nudge, so that he'd move out faster but not take to runnin'. I went on like that for awhile, and when I was clear enough, I put my heels to the horse and rode right on out of there, kind of gigglin' to myself and feelin' smarter than a college fella. I figured sometime come mornin', they might even get brave enough to go up there and find Cramp takin' his long nap, the other horse tied and waitin'.

⋇

The horse I had wasn't up to snuff, and pretty soon it was limpin'. They probably knowed that was the case when they tied Cramp on it. I got off and took the reins and led it and tried to figure on a new plan. The plains out there went on and on, and pretty soon I'd have to slow down more for the horse, and maybe shoot it and eat some of it, but then I'd be on foot with miles in front of me.

I stopped leading the horse, bent down and looked at its foot. He wasn't in bad shape, but he wasn't in good ridin' shape either. I found a wash and led him down in there, and with the reins wrapped around my hand, I lay down and slept.

It was high noon when I awoke, and hotter than a rabid dog's breath. I walked the horse out of the draw, and then I did the only thing I could think to do. I started leadin' the horse back toward Hide and Horns, takin' the long way around.

⋇

It was night when I come up on the town. I could see it laid out down there and there were lights from lanterns and it looked even bleaker to me now than it had at first.

I went on down there, coming up the back way, where the Chinaman Chinamen were gathered. I found a little scrub bush and I tied the horse up there so he wouldn't wander into town, and then I got my saddle and guns and such, and threw the saddlebag over my shoulder and toted the saddle with the Winchester and the Sharps tied off on it, my free hand near my revolver. I walked on down into the Chinatown part, and veered toward the tent where I had seen the crippled China girl go in to make my food. I strolled in like I had good sense. It was dark in there, and I fumbled around in my pocket lookin' for a match, until I realized I was wearin' Cramp's jacket and mine was tied to the saddle I was carryin'. A light went on in the place suddenly, and I dropped the saddle and the revolver sort of hopped into my hand, but it was a lit match with a China girl face behind it. The cripple. She was down on one knee and her nub, about waist high to me lookin' up.

I said, "I don't want no trouble."

"Black man," the cripple said.

"That's me," I said.

Then there was movement, and she was crawlin' across the floor cause she didn't have her leg strapped on. She lit a lantern and the room jumped bright, and there were all the Chinese girls. The wash pot girl and the other four, includin' the cripple.

It was a pretty big tent, but it was stuffed with all manner of stuff, includin' pallets where the girls did the rest of their work, which was haulin' all the men's folk's ashes, as they say.

"I need a good horse," I said, "and I need ya'll not to say nothin', cause I'd rather not shoot a woman. You savvy."

"Savvy," said the most beautiful of the girls, who seemed too small and delicate to be real, and far too young.

"I got Yankee dollars to pay for it, and I got my own saddle."

"We go too," the little one said.

"What?"

"We go too. Get horse. We take wagon."

"Wagon? Why don't you just bring a goddamn band and a clutch of clowns. No."

"We get horse, we go too," the cripple said.

"Damn," I said. "Listen. Tell you what. You get me a horse and I'll ride out, and then you bring the wagon along, and I'll be waitin' on you. Riders don't come with you, and I end up havin' to shoot it out, then I'll travel with you until I can get you to another town. Course, what's the difference between there and here?"

"We go back to China," said the cripple. I had come to realize the other two girls didn't speak enough English to even understand what I was sayin'. The cripple was the valedictorian of their class.

"Got news for you ladies, it's a long ride to the Pacific, and I don't think you can sail that wagon across."

"Get to San Francisco," the cripple said. "Figure from there."

"You know San Francisco?"

"We come there," the cripple said. "Think we have Chinese husbands. Big trick. We have to do big fuckin'. Not let us go. I try to go. Man shoot leg off with a shotgun, knock out a tooth."

I thought, damn, a leg ain't enough, he had to have a tooth too.

I sighed. "All right. I'll go back to what I said. I'm in a tough spot here, and you may think I'll ride away and leave you, but I try to keep my word unless there just ain't no way it can be kept. I can get out of town easier by myself, and then you can bring the wagon. But how you gonna do that? What's the excuse?"

It took them awhile to process that, talkin' to each other in Chinese, and I had to tell it different a couple times before they understood me. But it come down to me gettin' a horse, and them waitin' until daylight and sayin' they had to go out to the prairie to gather up dried buffalo shit for fires.

Buffalo shit will burn pretty good, it's dried a fair amount, but it has one drawback. It smells like burning buffalo shit. Still, it'll keep a person warm.

Then again, I reckon I didn't set out to tell you this story so you could know how to warm yourself and cook with dried buffalo plops.

"You think they'll believe you?" I asked.

"We do all time," the cripple said.

"All right," I said. "That'll do. Just don't try and trick me, cause I won't like it."

"No trick," she said.

⋇

They got me a good horse, and I got rid of Cramp's jacket and put on a brown shirt the girls gave me. I put my saddle on the horse, and took my guns and rode on out. I went way out, like I told them, givin' them a kind of guide to where I planned to go.

I wasn't an entirely trustin' soul, so I actually went a little farther east than I told them, found a place where I could sit a horse down in a draw and see up over the lip of it. That way I could make sure they didn't send someone else out to get me for some payment.

It got along mornin', and I had dozed on the ground with the reins of the horse clutched in my fist, and when I awoke it was already turnin' off hotter than a stove fire.

I heard hooves movin' in my direction, and I got up and looked between that little gap in the draw and seen it was the bunch that had ridden out after me, and they was leadin' the horse I had left, and they had Cramp's body tied behind it with a long rope bound to his ankles, and they was draggin' him along face down.

At first I thought the China girls had done me in, and that this bunch was lookin' for me, and then I got it figured right. They was just now comin' in, finally snoopin' out that I had snuck off on them in the night, disguised as Cramp. I counted them. There was twelve.

Now, I tell you, I try to be practical, but lookin' out there and seein' Cramp being dragged along like that, even though I didn't know him even a little, made my blood boil. I knew all I had to do was let them ride out of sight, back to town, then I could either wait on the China girls or not. It was the way to go, and the truth of the matter was, Cramp wasn't any of my business and I didn't know what he'd done to get folks mad at him in the first place, but I knew it didn't take much when you was a colored man. It could be lookin' at a white woman, or cuttin' a surprise fart in the street, and that's all it took for you to be thought of as uppity, and if there's one thing a lot of white folks can't tolerate, it's an uppity nigger. We was supposed to know our place, and I was thinkin' on all of this, and get madder and madder, and most of my common sense began to leak out of my head like water. Without realizin' what I was doin', I got on my horse and put the reins in my teeth, put the Sharps under one arm and the Winchester under the other.

Now, they'll tell you can't hit shit shootin' like that, and I'll tell you right off, that's mostly true, but most shooters ain't me. I've gotten so good with a gun I can shoot right smart with any kind of weapon under almost any kind of condition. That don't mean I don't miss, but I hit a lot too, and if I got a still shot, I can knock the dick off a horse fly.

I rode out and dug my heels into the horse, went to ridin' right at them, takin' them from the side. There was twelve of them, but they didn't see me until my guns barked, and the first shot with the Sharps hit one of their horses, which was an accident, I might add, and the horse went down, throwing him. I dropped the Sharps, since it just had that one load, flipped the Winchester into my right hand, and took to firin'. With four shots I killed three. They started poppin' off shots then, the ones that had figured out what was happenin', and by then I had come in amongst them. I twisted my head, and with those reins in my teeth, I made my horse twirl, and using both hands on that Winchester, I fired as fast as I could, and four more was down, and one horse was limpin' off with a bullet in his head, another unintentional, I might add.

I fired the Winchester until it was empty, and then I rode up on one of them that had fired six shots off and hadn't hit me or even come near me. He looked like he was about to scream with fear and he was snappin' the empty revolver like bullets might suddenly appear in the chambers. I swung the empty rifle and clipped him off his horse. I wheeled, and then there was a barrage of shots, and my horse went down and I went to rollin'. When I come up, I had my revolver in my hand, and I started firing, dropping two more, hittin' them both as they rode up on me. I fired at the others, not hittin' anyone else, which meant I was probably tired.

The ones that was left bolted and rode off, which was good, cause my revolver was empty.

I ran over to my dead horse and got a couple loads for the Sharps out of the saddlebags, and ran back to where I'd dropped the Sharps, scrounged around till I found it. Then I ran got down on a knee and loaded the Sharps and leveled it off.

They were far out now, but I took windage with a wet finger, beaded that fifty caliber, called them sonofabitches, and fired. As is often the case, it seemed like a long time before the bullet hit. In fact, I was already startin' to reload, when one of the riders threw up his hands and went flying off. The other just kept ridin'. He was way out there, but I had the Sharps ready, and I aimed high to let the bullet drop. I fired. I got him somewhere near the back of the head and he fell off, his horse still runnin'.

I know all this makes me sound a mite god-like, but, true story. No lie. I killed every one of them sonofabitches. It made me wonder how I'd managed to let one of them that had come up on me with Cramp get away. But, hell, even the gods nod.

But the gods don't bleed. I did. I had been hit. Didn't know it right off, but I started hurtin', and looked down at my side and seen I was bleedin'. I lay down on the ground suddenly, and closed my eyes and the sun didn't feel all that warm anymore.

-)|(-

"You not dead," the crippled China girl said.

"No?" I said. "I feel dead, and maybe buried, but I still seem to be among the livin' Chinese."

I was lyin' under a wagon and the cripple was down there with me. I tried to sit up, but couldn't. She said, "No. Sit. Stay."

I had a dog I talked to like that. I felt my side. It was bandaged up.

"We got to go," I said. "They'll be after me."

"You all shot up," the cripple said.

"That I am," I said.

"Rest a day. Have chop suey. Pussy. Feel better."

"I'm sure. But that rest a day part, not such a good idea."

I lay for awhile anyway, not having the strength to do much else. I probably laid there much longer than I thought, but finally I woke up and crawled out from under the wagon. The other Chinese girls had pulled a tarp over the frame of the wagon, and made a kind of traveling tent out of it. They had two horses tied on the back. One of the girls was missin'. I asked the cripple about that.

"Washie girl. She stay," said the cripple. "She make good money washie clothes."

I managed to walk around and gather up my goods, saddle and saddle-bags and weapons, and found the horse that had been draggin' Cramp. I cut the old boy loose and looked at him. He had asked me not to bury him out in the lonesome, but the thing was, he was lookin' pretty ripe, and I come to the conclusion I had done my best, and he wouldn't know the prairie from a place under a church pew. The girls helped me dig a hole, as they had shovels and all manner of equipment in the wagon, and I wrapped him in a blanket and put him down.

I was bleeding pretty good by the time I quit, and I had been wrong about them knife wounds being all healed up. A couple of them was leakin'. I said, "We got to get movin."

As we walked away, I looked back at Cramp's grave, said, "Sorry, Cramp. I done my best. It beats bein' dragged around till your hide comes off."

I climbed in the back of the wagon and lay down and slept while the little China girl who looked about twelve years old drove. In the back, the cripple tended me, and the other two looked on. We rode on through the day and into the night, the wagon bumpin' along, those two horses tied to the back of it, trottin' to keep up, and finally we stopped near a little run of creek, and the girls got out and made a fire from some dried buffalo shit. They fixed up some food, which was pretty good and had a lot of hot peppers in it. I didn't ask what it was, cause I couldn't identify the meat and figured I might not want to know.

Later that night, the cripple showed me how she could move around under me good as a two-legged girl, and then I had to show all of them that my pecker was black and the color didn't come off in their little nests. I showed that to all of them to be polite, and to prove I wasn't showin' no favoritism, even though I was wounded good and bleedin'. A man has to have some priorities, I always say, and if a bunch of Chinese girls beg to see your dick, you should be willin' to show it to them.

Now, them townsfolk had to have figured out their men weren't comin' back, and in time I'm sure they found them. Maybe they sent someone out after us. But if they did, we never seen them. Jumpin' ahead a bit, I should say the story about the gunfight began to spread, and since there wasn't no one livin' who'd seen it besides me, I knew the stories I heard about survivors who could tell it like it was, wasn't true in any kind of way. Thing was, the stories didn't mention I was colored. I just became a mysterious gunman, and in some of the stories I was a hero, and in others a villain. Cause of that, and some other things happened in my life, there was some dime novels written about me, basing themselves on true events at first, but not afraid to add a lie in when it made the story better, and then later, the stories was just dadgum windies. And though the stories didn't mention I was colored, they did call the books stories about The Black Rider of The Plains, and named me Deadwood Dick on account of some things happened there in Deadwood, including a shootin' contest where I shot against Buffalo Bill and Annie Oakley. But, again, that there is another story, and though it's been told a thousand times, ain't nobody told it right yet. I live long enough I plan to tell it the way it was, just like I'm tellin' you how this was.

As for me and the China girls, we rode on across that prairie for days, and when we got to the peak of the Texas panhandle, we turned northwest, across Oklahoma toward Colorady, with a plan to go on out to San Francisco so the China girls could catch a boat to China.

Now there's one more thing that's kind of interestin', and goes with this story, and if I'm lyin' I'm dyin'. When we was four or five days out, headin' up to the tip of the panhandle, we seen a scrawny horse grazin', and as we bounced the wagon closer, we seen there was a fella with his foot in the stirrup being dragged along, and even from a distance it was easy to see he was deader than a wind wagon investment.

Feelin' a bit spry, now that my wounds had had a few days to heal, I got out of the wagon and walked over and caught the horse and looked at the dead man. His boot was twisted up good in the stirrup, and he'd been dragged around for days, cause a lot of his skin had come off and ants and such had been at him. His eyes were gone and his lips had started to curl, showin' his teeth. He had a pretty large hole comin' out of his shirt on the right side of his breast, and when I seen that, it all tumbled together for me.

Back when I had found Cramp, and had a shootout with those folks who come to finish him off, one of them had got away. I had taken a shot at him, and figured I'd missed. But I hadn't. He'd just been able to ride some, and then he'd keeled over and got his foot hung in the stirrup, and his horse had been draggin' him around for damn near a week.

I worked the fella's foot out of the stirrup and let his leg drop to the ground. Tell you true, just like them other fellas I shot, I didn't have no urge to bury him and say words over him, cause buryin' someone I didn't have no feelin's for was stupid, and sayin' words that didn't seem to do nothin' but waste my breath, wasn't exactly appealin' either. I was glad he was dead, and I left him lyin' out there on the prairie with the sun on his face and ants in his ears.

His horse we took with us and fed grain the gals had in the wagon, and we fattened him up a mite, and sold him and the saddle in Amarillo, before going on up into Oklahoma, and turnin' west toward Colorady. ━🐉

Balfour and Meriwether in the Vampire of Kabul

BY DANIEL ABRAHAM

As I have grown old, I have watched the world of my youth fade with me. The damage done by the Great War will never be calculated. And yet, even now, I hear from my friends in the circles of power—in truth, most are now the children of my friends—that a third war in Afghanistan is all but certain. Even more than the war on the continent just passed, I find myself in dread of this new conflict and the powers it may provoke.

And yet, also I feel the nostalgia of old hunts, old games, old enemies now lost to history, and feel again not the rush of conflict but its echo. And recall the unparalleled eyes of a most singular woman I once knew…

—From the Last Notebooks of Mr. Meriwether, 1919

CHAPTER ONE: The Two Empresses

It was the third of December in 188-, and snow swirled down grey and damp upon the cobblestones of London. Meriwether paced before the wide window of the King Street flat impatiently. Balfour sat before the roaring fire, correcting a draft monograph he had written on the subject of Asiatic hand combat as adapted to the English frame.

"I cannot understand how you can be so devilishly placid," Meriwether said at last.

"Practice," Balfour grunted.

"Every winter it's the same," Meriwether said, gesturing at the falling snow. "The darkness comes earlier, the cold drives men from the roads, and I have this…stirring. This unutterable restlessness. The winter traps me, my friend. It holds me captive."

Balfour stroked his wide mustache. His bear-like grunt could have passed for agreement or mere acknowledgment. Meriwether turned away from street and snow, pushing pale hair back from his brow.

"If only something could break this, this *malaise*…"

Balfour glanced up in time to see the figure—slight, clad in dark leather, and swinging from a near-invisible tether—just before it shattered the windows. Shards of glass and wide, wet snowflakes accompanied the figure as it rolled across the carpeted floor. With a shout equal parts alarm and delight, Meriwether dove for his paired service revolvers. Balfour leapt from his chair, drawing blades from the sheaths concealed by his dressing gown's sleeves, only to find the mouth of a huge handgun pressed firmly to the bridge of his nose. The leather-clad figure met his gaze, brown eyes flecked with gold. Her lips were the soft red of rose petals, and her smile sensual and touched by madness. The scent of clove perfume filled the air like a memory.

Maria Feodorovna.

"Czarina," Meriwether said, pulling back the hammers of his revolvers with an ominous doubled click. "I'll ask you to stand away from Mr. Balfour, if you please."

The Empress Consort of Russia lifted her fine-plucked eyebrows. When she spoke, her voice betrayed nothing of the physical effort she had just expended.

"My good Mr. Meriwether, I'll ask you to note that I have already depressed the trigger of my weapon."

"Ah," Meriwether said, sourly. "A dead man's switch, is it?"

"Indeed. Fire upon me, and you author your good friend's death."

"Cheap at the price," Balfour grunted. "Shoot her."

Meriwether uncocked his weapons, stepping over the remnants of his windows to lean out, squinting up through the grey snowflakes toward the low, white sky. The Czarina's weapon didn't waver.

"Fastened a silken cord to the roof and then launched yourself out," he said. "You took something of a risk. London's architecture is not always so solid as it might seem."

"I had to approach you with very little warning," she said. "Had I simply announced myself, I think my reception might not have been so cordial, yes?"

"After Cyprus, I think an assumption of violence would have been appropriate," Meriwether said. "And yet I cannot help notice you haven't yet killed us, nor we you. It isn't a turn of events I would have foreseen, and I take it that you have some specific intention in engineering it?"

"I do," the Czarina said, "but I would require your word of honor that you would respect our truce."

"Truce?" Balfour asked.

"We face a common enemy," she said. "Until he is defeated, I suggest we make common cause."

Balfour's face reddened and his bright eyes bulged.

"I'd sooner make common cause with malaria!"

The Czarina made a small, disappointed sound with her tongue and teeth.

"This is where all things end, then," she said and brought up her free hand to steady the pistol.

"What manner of common enemy?" Meriwether asked.

Her smile broadened by a fraction of an inch.

"Truce?" she asked.

"Truce," Meriwether said.

"Word of honor?"

"Of course."

She nodded to Balfour.

"Do you agree as well, my old friend?"

Balfour chuffed under his breath, stepped back, and truculently sheathed his knives. A gust of winter wind brought snow into the room. The fire hissed in complaint.

"Good enough, then," the Czarina said, working a small mechanism on her pistol before returning it to the holster at her hip. "Seven weeks ago, my husband was assaulted in his rooms. I was not present at the time, but the woman who impersonates me during my absences reports that immediately before, there was an ectoplasmic darkness that formed in the corners of the room and which no light could dispel, followed by a terrible apparition in the shape of a man with bright red eyes and skin the color of snow. Her memory of the event itself is clouded. We know that my husband survived, that he was for some days afterward quite weak and anemic in appearance. And furthermore... Furthermore, I have reason to believe that his mind is no longer entirely subject to his will."

For a moment, snow-muffled hoofbeats and the wet bubbling of the gaslight were the only sounds.

"Are you saying that the Emperor of Russia has gone mad?" Meriwether asked, leaning against the ruined window frame.

"Worse," she said. "He is being compelled by an outside force. A being of spiritual darkness has struck at the heart of my empire. And what researches I have managed tell me that it also has designs upon yours."

The interior door burst open, and a harried-looking Mrs. Long stepped in barely ahead of Lord Carmichael.

"Come quick, boys. The queen's been attacked!" Lord Carmichael said even before Mrs. Long could announce him. And then, taking in the chaos of glass and ice before him, "What in the world's going on? And what is *she* doing here?"

Meriwether scooped up his signature black greatcoat as Balfour reached for his brace of knives. The Czarina bowed slightly to Lord Carmichael, her disconcerting eyes fixed upon his.

"She appears to be helping us, unlikely as that seems," Meriwether said. "Mrs. Long, I apologize again for the inconvenience, but if you could please—"

"I'll send a boy to the glazier right away, sir," Mrs. Long said. "You see Her Majesty's safely taken care of."

"Well, then," the Czarina said, tucking Meriwether's arm firmly in her own, "let us hurry to Buckingham Palace."

"You knew," Balfour said. "This isn't coincidence. You *knew* the queen was going to be attacked."

The Czarina's mouth formed a distressed moue.

"Of course I did. And when. But if I had warned you before it happened, you'd have had no reason to help me with *my* problem," she said, peevishly. "I came as soon as I could, practically speaking."

Balfour and Meriwether met each other's eyes for a moment, a silent communication passing between them.

"*Malaise*, eh?" Balfour said, and Meriwether's laughter surprised and confused all the others in the room.

The carriage ride through the icy streets was as swift as could be managed. Lord Carmichael's driver knew all the fastest streets and alleys, and the team of horses was among the best in the empire, but the hand of nature could not be kept back. The falling snow thickened until at the last they seemed to be driving through a dim faerie landscape, only distantly related to the solid, coal-smudged London they knew. Lord Carmichael stared out the window as if his focused will alone could clear their path. By contrast, the Czarina seemed politely amused.

The guards who greeted the carriage were unfamiliar to Balfour and Meriwether, but it was clear from the alacrity with which they led the unlikely party within that the presence of Lord Carmichael was evidence enough of their status. The Czarina's outlandish appearance provoked no comment.

The queen's private physician was a serious man at the beginning of his third decade. His muttonchop whiskers gave him an air of age and authority undermined by the trembling of his hands and the thinness of his lips. The private sitting room seemed gloomier and colder even than the weather outside, the gold and vermillion of the wallpaper dimmed by soot from the smoking fireplace. Sofas, divans, and small tables covered the floor like travelers huddled together on a train platform. The glowing gas sconces pressed ineffectually at the shadows. No one removed their coats, nor did the servants inquire.

"She certainly can't be moved," the physician said, fumbling with a porcelain pipe. "Not yet. Not for some time, I should think. No, indeed."

"Has she regained consciousness then?" Lord Carmichael demanded.

"Yes, in a sense."

"What sense?" Balfour asked.

The physician blinked, at a loss for word. Meriwether took the man's pipe from his hand, packing the bowl with fresh tobacco as he spoke.

"You say she has regained consciousness *in a sense*. It follows, my good man, that there is also a sense in which she has not. Such comments are certainly evocative, but not in the strictest sense useful. Would you please elaborate as to Her Majesty's condition?"

He handed back the pipe. The young physician accepted it.

"When I was called to her, the queen was quite pale," he said. "Her pulse rapid, and she complained of dizziness. When she attempted to stand, she fell into a faint. Smelling salts did not revive her. She has since woken, but she seems confused. Keeps talking about someone named Arthur Dodgy."

"Artyadaji," the Czarina said. For the first time, her voice held no mischief.

"You know the name?" the physician asked.

"Afghan bogeyman," Balfour said. "Scares children."

"It seems it may do a great deal more than that," the Czarina said.

Lord Carmichael hoisted an eyebrow and then, seeing that none of the others shared his amusement at the Czarina's superstitions, grew somber. Balfour stepped away from the fire, glowering at the walls, his broad nose twitching like a hound's. Meriwether, noting his companion's behavior, narrowed his eyes.

"Was this the room in which the incident occurred?" he asked.

"It is," Lord Carmichael said. "Her Majesty had taken a private audience with a member of the diplomatic service about whom, no offense to the Czarina, I cannot speak. She asked to be left alone. A few minutes later, her private guard heard her cry out. He entered the sitting room to find Her Majesty in distress. He described the shadows reaching out from the corners of the room. There was a man as well. Pale-faced and dressed in dark robes.

"The queen cried out a second time, and the man turned toward the guard. His eyes were bright red, and he spoke in a strange language. A terrible weakness come over the man, but he managed to interpose himself between the attacker and Her Majesty."

Meriwether crouched down beside the fireplace. Grey smoke puffed out above him—evidence of a poorly drawing flue—as he ran a long, dainty finger through the fallen ash. Behind him, Balfour pressed a palm to the wallpaper four times in succession, pulling it away slowly.

"And what became of the dark-robed, red-eyed gentleman?" Meriwether asked without looking up from the flames.

Lord Carmichael glanced at the Czarina, clearly discomfited by the prospect of speaking candidly in her presence. And then, with a sigh: "Vanished. There one moment, gone the next."

"This is the beast that attacked my husband," the Czarina said. "It is associated with a Mohammadan wizard who travels under the name Abdul Hassan. I have been following him."

Meriwether rose from the fire, wiped his hands, and exchanged a meaningful glance with his companion. As if in answer, Balfour raised his palms. Behind him, the door swung open and an eerie figure lurched into the room. Thin white hair rose from the pale scalp like steam. Gnarled hands gripped a rough firewood cudgel. The pale blue eyes starting from the broad, doughy face were empty of all thought. The diaphanous gown gave glimpses of a time-ravaged body, rolls of pale fat draping and shifting with every movement. The voice was low and bestial and filled with a terrible conviction.

"It cannot be won!" the queen growled, stepping further into the room. "It cannot be won! We will be destroyed!"

"My queen!" the physician cried. "You ought not be out of bed. You must—"

"It cannot be *won!*"

The firewood cudgel swung through the air with a hiss. The physician fell back, his pipe shattered and blood pouring from his abused lip.

Balfour leapt forward, his broad hands clasping the queen's improvised weapon. A royal ankle took him in the groin, and he fell back as Victoria, Queen of England and Empress of India, waved her club in the air with the conviction and ill intent of a Whitechapel brawler. Meriwether and Lord Carmichael only found time to exchange a helpless glance before she turned against them.

Meriwether blocked the first blow with the blade of his hand, leaping back before the second could do damage to his ribs. Lord Carmichael tried to circle behind her, only to have her whirl upon him, teeth bared and spittle dripping from her lips. She lurched toward him, coming near the open flame as she did. All the men present shared the terrible fear that the Queen's nightgown might drift into the fire and set the sovereign alight.

"Stop this childishness at *once!*"

The Czarina's voice was sharp as a slap. Victoria turned toward her, watery blue eyes narrowed and cunning. With a visible effort, the queen found words.

"Who are you?"

"An Empress, cousin," the Czarina said. "Much like yourself."

"An Empress," the queen said as if struggling to recall what the syllables meant. "Like myself."

For a moment the fear and violence dimmed in the pale blue eyes. The gaping mouth narrowed to a prim and disapproving scowl. Her spine straightened and she considered the Czarina with a haughty lift of the brow.

"We do not feel entirely ourself," Victoria announced and turned her back to the assembled company, pausing only to hand her firewood weapon to Balfour, still red-faced and bent double. The door closed behind her, and for a moment, no one spoke.

"I should be certain that she…" the physician began, limping after his patient with blood smearing his lip.

"Is he like this as well?" Meriwether asked, his voice gentle as warm flannel.

The Czarina sat upon an embroidered chair, her fingers laced together on one leather-clad knee. Her face was a blank. A single tear escaped her left eye, tracking down her cheek.

"Only sometimes," she said. "There are whole days when he seems nearly himself. And then it comes again, and…"

Balfour lifted himself up with a groan and tossed the queen's improvised cudgel on the fire. Sparks rose like fireflies and died away. He put a wide, comforting hand on the Czarina's shoulder, and her head sank. For the first time, Meriwether considered that the adventuress might truly love her husband.

"Lord Carmichael," he said, "we are in desperate times. I am very much afraid we shall need to close the ports."

"Which port did you have in mind?"

"All of them," Meriwether said. "Britain is the heart of the world, but thankfully she is also an island. This wizard must not be permitted to escape, whatever it costs us in trade. We have it in our power to prevent him, and we must employ it. The threat we face is not only to our own Empire, but to the existence of monarchy itself. No price is too high. We *will* find him."

"Unless the bastard can call up a djinni to fly him back to Hell," Balfour said.

"Well, yes," Meriwether agreed. "Unless that."

CHAPTER TWO: Players of the Great Game

"You said that your husband was attacked in his rooms, Czarina," Meriwether said. "Am I to take it that said rooms were in Moscow?"

"I don't believe I was specific," she said with a smile.

"No, of course. I understand."

"Do you?"

"He was in Kabul."

The Czarina's jewel-bright, jewel-hard eyes glittered in the firelight, but she said nothing.

With the King Street flat still suffering from the Czarina's arrival, the three had repaired to the private rooms of the Bastion Club, where Balfour and Meriwether had a history of eccentric guests. The servants had seen them to the leather-upholstered chairs and roaring fire, brought them hot tea, and retreated to genteelly spread the word among the other members that any conversations affecting the Empire's conflicts with the Czar of the Russias ought to be postponed. It was just that discretion that made the club home to the finest minds of political Europe.

Lord Carmichael had left immediately to set in motion the great mechanism that was Scotland Yard, armed with the name Abdul Hassan and a few telling details provided by the Czarina: aged appearance, a missing eye tooth, a looping tattoo in Arabic script along his back.

Balfour paced the edges of the room like a caged tiger, his hand never far from his knives, his gaze constantly on the woman. Meriwether sat near the fire as if the winter storm growing outside were a pleasant spring day, the Czarina a friendly acquaintance come over for tea, and the Queen of England in her right mind.

"And now we seek a Mohammadan wizard who has been invoking Artyadaji?" Meriwether said. "Hardly the sort of thing one finds among the Muscovites."

"Men say many things. A claim is not the truth," the Czarina said. "You recall the French poisoner who presented himself as a traveler from the future?"

"Yes, well. That was a bit more complex than public reports let on, but this wizard of yours, pretender or not, unquestionably has ties to the Afghan territories."

"Opium," Balfour said. "The resin was on the walls."

"And the ash in that infernal smoking fireplace," Meriwether said. "Whatever magic our wizard has employed, it relies on Afghan poppy for its effect. Without intending offense, Your Majesty, your husband's influence in the region is considerably less than it once was, which would make the decision to begin a campaign by attacking him rather odd. Unless, of course, he presented a particularly convenient target. It follows then, that there have been some…negotiations?"

"Bloody Russians trying to cut off our route to India!" Balfour snapped. "Again!"

The Czarina stretched. A joint in her spine cracked, and as if in answer, the pine in the fireplace popped.

"Would you like me to deny it?" she asked with a deep, throaty laugh. "Of course my empire has been exploring what options and strategies are available to it. Much as yours has. You may as well pretend outrage that the sun sets."

"And your explorations have met with such success that your husband felt it wise to attend to it personally," Meriwether said. "That sounds very much as if the recent hostilities might take new fire."

"That was the hope," the Czarina said. "Instead, he touched off…this."

"What can you tell us of these negotiations?"

"Very little, I'm afraid. My husband does not always trust me. It's something of a game between us. I do not believe the meeting was cheese for the mousetrap. His allies were quite sincere in their hatred of Britain. But a third party intruded."

"Your wizard," Balfour said.

"We forget, I think, that being primitive is not the same as being simple," the Czarina said. "There are as many intrigues in their caves and tents as in our palaces. And yes, Abdul Hassan enchanted the Czar. I was called in on the instant. At first, we assumed you were behind it. The locals swore otherwise, and then I found a workshop in the poorest quarters of Kabul. A den of dark magic. And notes outlining the attack upon your queen."

"And you let it happen," Balfour said.

"Consider my position. My options were to track the wizard alone and in the den of my enemy, or with the best and most capable allies in the world, and with the force of the British Empire."

"Besides which, should we fail, we will both be hobbled by compromised monarchs rather than Russia suffering that fate alone," Meriwether said.

"Deplore me if you wish," the Czarina said and sipped her tea.

"Done," Balfour said.

A soft knock came at the door, and Lord Carmichael stepped in. His cheeks were ruddy from the cold and snow still clung, melting, to his coat. His grin was feral.

"We've found him, boys. The bastard's taken a room behind a slaughterhouse not fifteen minutes from here. Arrived just when the Empress here said he would have. Missing eye tooth. What's more, when we knocked up the landlord, he said he suspected his new tenant was an opium fiend. Said he stinks of the stuff. I've got a dozen men watching the place right now."

"Well then," Meriwether said, rising to his feet. "Let us go and make our call."

It was nearly midnight when they arrived in the street outside Jenkins Brothers Meats. The snow was thick on the cobbles and grey with coal ash. Cold bit at their skin, and the air was rich with the reek of manure and old blood. Lord Carmichael pressed a brass key into Balfour's hand nodding at the slaughterhouse door.

"The room's in the back," he said. "Caretaker's quarters. Fastest way's in through the front here, past the counter, and through the killing floor. Take the hall on the right."

"Charming," Balfour said, slipping the key into his pocket and drawing out a pair of well-balanced knives.

Meriwether checked his paired service revolvers, the mechanisms clicking softly in the snow-quiet street. The Czarina took her own gun from her hip, adjusted the complex mechanism at the butt, and then took a second pistol from the small of her back and loaded three cartridges into it. Her fingernails were blue with the cold, but she made no complaint.

"Would you consider remaining with Lord Carmichael, Your Highness?" Meriwether asked.

"No."

"I thought not."

The front rooms of the slaughterhouse were cramped. From the ink-stained wood of the counter and the hand-written notices of price, it might have been almost any business. In near-perfect darkness, the trio crept, silent as cats. The door to the killing floor was unlocked, its hinges well-oiled. Within, the room was colder even than the street outside. Blocks of ice stood stacked against the wall, and sawdust soupy with gore covered the floor. In the dim light that spilled in through the high windows, the skinless things hanging from hooks might have been anything: beef or rabbits or men. Even in the cold, the reek was overwhelming.

Balfour and Meriwether in the Vampire of Kabul | Daniel Abraham

A rat scuttled along the wall, startled by its unexpected guests. By unspoken agreement, Balfour took the lead, his wide frame moving through the shadows with the agility of long practice. The others followed only a few steps behind, Meriwether dividing his awareness between the dark spaces behind them and the snake-smooth motion of the Czarina, prepared for surprise attack from either quarter. It seemed hours that they negotiated the abattoir, the dead around them like the trees of an infernal forest, and then Balfour made a low clicking sound at the back of his throat.

Meriwether went still, and a moment later, the Czarina as well. Balfour opened the door slowly, a dim, dirty light outlining its frame. From the hallway beyond, a faint voice came. The syllables were incomprehensible, but they had a wetness and roughness that spoke of a throat abused from long use, hoarse as a man accustomed to screaming. Balfour lifted his head, sniffing at the air, and a moment later, the others caught it as well. The sweet, pungent scent of opium, but also something else. Something deeper and more intimate even than the spilled blood through which they had travelled. The Czarina's long, slow exhalation reminded Meriwether to breathe as well. Her eyes, the brown gone slate gray in the dim light, were fearful and reckless at once. She saw the question in his expression and nodded once. She was prepared.

Quiet as thieves, they crept forward.

At the end of the hall, light spilled from the edges of a poorly-fit door. Red and gold, it danced like flame, but there was no roar of fire to accompany it, only the rough, ruined voice lifted in its incomprehensible chant. Balfour crossed to the far side of the door, his drawn blades glittering. The Czarina placed herself at the door's nearer edge just as Meriwether moved to the same position. Their bodies collided silently, and Meriwether took a step back to steady himself. A floorboard creaked under his foot.

The chanting stopped.

"Grand," Balfour sighed, and then twisting from the hip, kicked the door open. The lock shattered. The bolt tore free, splintering the wood. All three leapt into the room.

What had once been a modest caretaker's residence—a cast-iron stove, a small cot, a single gaslight—had been transformed. The stove's plate was open, the burning coal within heating the air like a furnace and filling the room with demonic light. The ancient, black robed man kneeling before it could have been drinking at the back of any pub in England. Close-cut white hair frosted his pale scalp. The patchy beginnings of a beard clung like lichen to his loose jowls and wattled neck. His alarmed eyes were the blue of ice at the iris, the sclera a uniform, blood-bright red. He shouted, his bared teeth revealing the pale-gummed gap of a missing eye tooth, and threw a handful of dark powder into the flames.

Meriwether lifted his revolver toward the man's skull.

"In the name of Victoria, queen of England, stand down!" he shouted.

The dark-robed man rose, his arms raised at his sides in a gesture that could have been surrender or a show of fearlessness. At his breast, a huge and ornate silver medallion glittered as if with a light of its own. When he spoke, it was with the unaccented English of a London native.

"In the name of Victoria?" he said. "You have no idea what I have seen and suffered in that name. It has no power over me any longer, God help us both."

The three exchanged confused glances. The wizard hoisted the corner of his mouth in an amused smile. His medallion glowed silver in a world of honey-gold. There was a ruby set at the center, red as the old man's eyes.

"Forgive me," Meriwether said, his revolvers still trained at the man's forehead. "Abdul Hassan?"

"If you like, son. I've been Abdul Hassan. I've had a dozen names. What does it matter what a man's called? Call him king or cobbler, it's what he does that matters."

The heat of the fire redoubled, the flames licking at the black iron.

"You have injured my husband," the Czarina said. "You will tell me now how to cure him."

"Balfour?" Meriwether said.

"I see it," Balfour replied. At the edges of the room, the shadows were growing solid. Darkness made its web. "It's the smoke fumes."

"I believe that it isn't," Meriwether said.

"You will tell me how to cure him!" the Czarina shrieked, and her pistol barked twice. The black robe bucked and puckered as the rounds pierced it. The wizard chuckled.

"You'll find me a harder man to kill than that," he said, and the shadows swept down around him moving through the air like ink dripped into water. There were eyes in that darkness, shining like black water. Searching for them. Meriwether felt the hairs on his neck and arms standing too, his deep animal nature recognizing something that had threatened him since before evolution had brought men to walk upright.

Something detonated soundlessly, and the iron stove gone, the caretaker's room gone, and rising behind the ancient man, a huge goat-headed thing. Its pendulous belly shifted as it shuddered from one awkward, bent leg to another. Its eyes were malefic and intelligent.

"Artyadaji," the Czarina breathed.

"Meriwether?" Balfour said, and there was a barely controlled panic in his voice.

"I suspect we've been exposed to…some sort of hallucinatory agent."

"That'd be good," Balfour said. His voice echoed, as if coming from a great distance away. Meriwether took careful aim at the beast shuddering before him. A huge, honey-colored moon was rising over its shoulder. His service pistol barked in his hand, and the demonic face rippled like a reflection in a pond when a stone has been dropped into it.

"Stop that!" the Czarina said, and the world smelled of her clove perfume and the richness of her flesh. "You could have killed me."

"Get on the floor!" Balfour wheezed.

With his head pressed to the filthy floorboards, Meriwether's mind slowly cleared. A greenish haze poured up from the iron stove, floating about three feet above the floor, venomous and threatening. A calm and poisoned ocean, seen from beneath the waves. Of the ancient man, there was no sign.

"Stay low," Meriwether said. "We have to get to the street. And quickly."

When they had reached the curb again, their clothing ruined by the return trip through the frigid gore of the slaughterhouse, Lord Carmichael had a carriage waiting. Wrapped in woolen blankets, the three were pulled quickly through the night streets.

"We saw him slip out," Lord Carmichael said. "Leapt off the rooftop. I've got men in pursuit. I was about to send a squad in when you three stumbled out. What happened in there?"

"Hell opened," Balfour said. The Czarina leaned her head against the rattling side of the carriage and wept silently.

"It's well you didn't send any others in," Meriwether said. "Especially not men who were armed. We'd all have been shooting one another down as devils until morning."

Slowly—the opium had done something unpleasant to his ability to find words—Meriwether recounted the events from within the slaughterhouse. Lord Carmichael listened, his eyes wide and his expression the rapt fascination of a boy sitting at a campfire, regaled with ghost stories. When Meriwether came to the end, Lord Carmichael slapped his back, grinning.

"Well, this is all to the good, then, isn't it? We may not have caught the bastard, but at least we know it's all drugs and mesmerism. Not real magic at all."

"I'm afraid we don't know that," Meriwether said.

"You recognized him too?" Balfour asked, his bear-deep growl softer than usual.

"I did," Meriwether said. The carriage lurched, the team of horses whuffling in complaint. "Our so-called Abdul Hassan is, in fact, an Englishman."

"Scot."

"Born in England, of Scottish descent," Meriwether said, giving half the point. "I've never met the man, but I'm quite familiar with his portrait. William Brydon."

"I don't know the name," said the Czarina, her attention suddenly sharp and bright as a blade's edge.

"Assistant surgeon in the East India Company. When Elphinstone retreated from Kabul to Jalalabad, he had an army of forty-five hundred men. Only one man reached safety, and that was William Brydon."

"Elphinstone? No, you must be mistaken. This can't be the same man. That was…"

"Yes, I know," Meriwether said. "That was our first adventure among the Afghans. Over four decades ago."

"The man would be in his sixties," Lord Carmichael said.

"Seventies," Balfour said. "Except that he died at sixty-two."

"Ah," Lord Carmichael said.

"Yes," said Meriwether. "So we can't entirely rule out magic just yet."

CHAPTER THREE: Remnants of an Army

Dawn came behind a veil of low, grey cloud. The difference between darkness and day was only a greater wealth of detail in the worn faces and cold stone. The traffic thickened the streets, horses and carriages battling the night's snowfall. The young man in Lord Carmichael's offices looked at the great brass globe and the citations from the Queen as if he expected to wake from it all. Balfour smiled at him and extended a cup of rich-smelling, smoky tea. Samuel Brydon hesitated, ran a hand through hair still disarranged from the pillow, and accepted the cup. The men around him—men only, for the Czarina was elsewhere, preparing her part of the endeavor—waited patiently for the boy to answer the question.

"No, I'm quite sure Grands is dead. I was at his funeral. I remember it because it was on my tenth birthday," he said. "Funny, isn't it, how we're such selfish beasts when we're young. Mum lost her father, and all I could think was that it wasn't fair I couldn't have my cake. Really, though, you should ask her about it. She'll know more than I do."

Meriwether smiled, trying to keep the anxiety presently shaking him from affecting his demeanor.

"Alas, Westfield is a bit too long a journey for us at the moment. Time is of the essence and all that sort of thing. You have, I take it, had no visitations from your grandfather? Dreams or visions, perhaps?"

The young man laughed, and then seeing the grim faces of the men around him, sobered.

"No. Nothing like that. Is this…actually important?"

"Deadly so, I'm afraid. Did you know your grandfather well?"

"Well enough, I suppose. He seemed a decent sort of man. Prone to dark times, of course. Anyone would be who'd been through what he had. In the war, I mean."

"Did he talk about Afghanistan often?" Lord Carmichael asked, smiling encouragement.

"Not as such, no," the boy said. "He'd go back there every few years. Had friends there, he said. And he was very down on war in general. When Pa asked for my mother's hand, the only condition was that Pa couldn't take a career with the military."

"That so?" Balfour rumbled.

"He'd be damned upset with me, I'm sure," the boy said with a laugh.

"Joined up?" Balfour said.

"Haven't yet, but I'm going to. Clerking hasn't exactly worked out, you could say."

The secretary knocked gently at the door and leaned in to catch Lord Carmichael's eye.

"Your appointment with the Inspector has been postponed, sir," he said. It was a code phrase. The time was right to move in. Lord Carmichael nodded and plucked the drawing from his waistcoat pocket. He considered it carefully, then held it out to the boy.

"Have you ever seen a medallion of this sort among your family's possessions?"

The boy hesitated, frowned, and then slowly shook his head.

"No, sir," he said. Balfour leaned toward him.

"*Artyadaji*," he said. "Mean anything to you?"

"No. Should it?"

"Someone may approach you claiming some relationship to your grandfather," Meriwether said. "He may particularly be haunting places that your grandfather may have known within London or its surroundings. If any such man approaches you, you must let us know immediately. He is quite dangerous."

"Is he?" the boy squeaked.

"Yes," Meriwether replied. "But don't be too concerned. We are certain to have him captured by nightfall." He paused, then in a lower voice: "We have a *trap* in place."

"Well that… That's good, then," the boy said. "Something a bit queer about having one's dead grandfather about, isn't there?"

"Thank you for coming in, Mister Brydon," Lord Carmichael said. "And I apologize again for the abrupt manner of our arrival."

The boy rose, setting the cup of tea on the table with a clink and then wiping his hands on his trousers. For a moment, his eyes flickered toward the drawing of the silver medallion.

"No harm done," he said. "Sorry I couldn't help more."

Lord Carmichael ushered him to the door, a hand on the boy's shoulder.

"Not at all. You've been a great help. I'll have a man see you home right away."

The door closed behind the boy with a soft click. Balfour rose, scowling out the window at the street below. Meriwether sighed and stretched, his spine letting off a small volley.

"Not a particularly good liar, is he?" Lord Carmichael said.

"No," said Meriwether. "And his failure to dissemble is entirely to our advantage, I think."

The rear door swung open and the Czarina appeared. With her leathers replaced by a simple cotton dress, her feet covered with simple, working-class footwear, and her hair let down in bangs that almost covered her remarkable eyes, she might have been a young woman of London. She smiled at Lord Carmichael's reaction and made a small curtsey.

"Not too bad, I hope, m'lords?" she said in an accent that would have passed for local.

"Disturbingly brilliant," Lord Carmichael said.

"The boy is on his way," Meriwether said. "He was, as we'd hoped, hiding something, and I hinted rather broadly that we know much more than we actually do. Once at his home, he will try to contact our Abdul Hassan."

"But, having been questioned by yourselves, he shall be discreet," the Czarina said, pulling a pair of spectacles from her sleeve and propping them on her nose. "He will be watching for the dark-coated arm of law, and overlook a pretty young thing like myself. I shall track him to his lair, signaling your men as I go. I'm aware of our plan, sir. And I am accustomed to being underestimated."

"I'm sure you are," Meriwether said, appreciating her implicit dig at him.

"I'm off, then," she said. "The hunt calls."

The door closed behind her, and Balfour spun the great brass globe, the oceans of the world glimmering in the sunlight. His expression was peevish.

"*The hunt calls*," he said in an unconvincing falsetto. "Hate the way she always says that. Bloody affected."

Lord Carmichael leaned against his desk, drew a cigar from the humidor presented him by the Pope, and lit it thoughtfully.

"I do wonder, boys," he said. "What do you plan to do once you've found him again? The three of you were thoroughly trounced last night. What's changed?"

"First, we have seen our man in action. He requires flame and his opium powder. Should we deprive him of these, our chances improve at once. Also, we've ascertained that the fumes from those are lighter than air, and can be defeated by dropping to one's knees. And..."

"And?" Lord Carmichael said.

"Artyadaji is a demon of the night," Meriwether said, tapping at the sketch of the eerie medallion. "We'll take him by daylight, when the spirit is weakest. And we offer no quarter. I have the sense that failure now means failure forever. There will be no third opportunity."

For three long hours, they waited, every tick of the clock an eternity. When at last the Czarina's message came, they leapt to the waiting carriage and sped through the snow-choked streets. The grin behind Balfour's wide mustache promised violence, as did Meriwether's calm. They stopped two streets away, finishing the journey by foot for fear of alerting the prey.

The warehouses sat against the grey Thames, ancient timbers blackened by time and soot. Rats watched them pass, black eyes incurious and challenging. The Czarina stepped out briefly from the mouth of an alleyway, nodded to them, and stepped back. Walking casually, they joined her. The building was three stories high, old stone at the water's edge. The voice of the river was a behemoth breathing softly, gentle and deafening at the same time.

"They're both within," she called into Meriwether's ear. "I've found a way to the top. We can enter through the roof and work our way down."

Meriwether nodded and gestured to Balfour. The Czarina led them to a narrow space where age and weather had eaten away at the mortar between stones. She pulled off her shoes, tying the laces together and draping them across her shoulders. On toes and fingertips, she began scaling the sheer wall. Their path led around the corner and out over the water. Soon, the great wooden doors that would have allowed a barge entrance were directly beneath them, crusted with ice and snow.

They achieved the rooftop, forty feet above the alleyway and chill gray flow. A path through the snow marked the Czarina's previous explorations, and the black, wooden trapdoor, its hinges forced, that let them slip inside. The attic space had been used for storage with little regard to the strength of the beams. Huge cast iron wheels and chains that had once raised cargo now lay rusted and abandoned. The evidence of a generation of pigeons left the air pungent and unpleasant. The Empress of the Russias squatted down, pulled back on her shoes, and drew her weapons from beneath her dress.

"How far did you get?" Balfour whispered, pulling wool socks back over blue-toed feet.

"Far enough," she said. "Come quickly."

An ancient wooden stairway so narrow Balfour had to turn his shoulders to fit switch-backed down into darkness. Silently, they descended. The sulfurous stench of cheap coal began to taint the air. The wooden stair widened and gave over to stone. The Czarina paused on a landing beside a half-opened door, holding up her delicate, pale hand still gripping a pistol. A moment later, they heard it as well: voices.

The platform on which they found themselves looked down over a wide expanse of water. Where in the busy days of summer a half dozen barges might stand together, only a single, spare craft stood at anchor, rough and weathered, little better than a raft. The cranes above it seemed to threaten to sink it more than to relive its burdens. And at the quayside, sitting by a brazier of red-and-gold coals, the boy Samuel Brydon and the weathered husk of what had in life been William Brydon.

"…reach the sea, much less Gibraltar," the young man said.

"The coast will be enough," the wizard replied. His voice was deep and resonant and borne down by the weight of ages. "If I can reach the coast, I can reach the continent. If I can reach the continent, I can reach the east. There are caves in the Gul Koh mountains that no man in the great nations has breached. I will rest there."

"You don't have to go alone."

Balfour touched the Czarina's elbow and nodded toward the armature of a crane that passed over their shadow-dark platform. She traced it with her eyes and nodded.

"Yes, I must. The lands north of the Zhob valley are no place for us. Not now, and not for generations. The bargain I struck on that deathly road was no betrayal of England. The task I have been called back to accomplish is no treason."

Balfour cupped his hands, bracing himself. The Czarina put her foot on his laced fingers. Quiet as a spring wind, he lifted her up to the armature's edge. Meriwether crept to the platform's edge, judging with narrowed eyes the distance between wizard and boat, boy and man, brazier and black, cold water.

"If you say so, Grands."

"I do. We see the east as our chessboard. We think the men who live in those dread places are pawns. They aren't. If by this action, I have kept the British Empire from a fresh war in those hills, then I will die again as a patriot. And no greater wisdom could ever be offered the Muscovites than to look away from the Afghan tribes. The power that lives there will never win against us, but neither shall it lose."

"But is there no honor in *trying?*" the boy asked.

Meriwether drew his service revolvers. The soft hush of knives unsheathed reached his ears.

"Is there? It's the honor of ignorance, then."

"Are the soldiers there so mighty?" There was anger in the boy's voice. Contempt even.

"Some are. And some are cowards. Some are men of peace born in the wrong place and time. They are *men*. That's what I'm saying, and they have their wisdoms as we have ours. It's only our shortness of sight that makes us think they don't. That they somehow belong to us. Like goats."

Above wizard and boy, the Czarina appeared, a light spot in the gloom. William Brydon or Abdul Hassan or Artyadaji was so wrapped up in his lecture, she might have been no more than a dove.

"We can spill their blood in our great game, Samuel, but it won't nourish us. We can fight our battles on their field, but—"

With a shout, the Czarina leaped from the crane, her arms wide. Had she been another woman, Balfour and Meriwether might have feared for her, but as the wizard's attention snapped upward, they were in motion, racing toward the brazier. The wizard grabbed at his robe. The Czarina landed on the cold stone, rolling as gracefully as a dancer, and coming up with her pistol at the ready. The old man threw a leather sack onto the fire as the Czarina fired. Her bullet tore a hank of dark flesh from the wizard's temple, but no blood flowed from it, and he did not fall. Samuel Brydon shrieked.

Evil green smoke began to rise from the coals. Meriwether reached the brazier first. It was larger than it had appeared from the platform, thick and black and hot as a stove. He set his shoulder to it, ignoring pain and the smell of burning skin, and pushed. A lungful of the evil gas started him coughing, and where the boat had been, a huge, nacreous beast now rose from the dark water, tentacles slipping against each other in mindless glee. He closed his eyes and pushed.

The Czarina fired again as the wizard rushed at her, a silver dagger in his hand. The bullet blew off part of his neck, but he did not falter. With a single stroke, he knocked her from her feet and towered above her, blade high. The silver medallion glowed with its own baleful light, the ruby blazing with a deep internal brightness matching the blood-red eyes. The terrible hiss of steam—hot metal thrown in cold water—failed to distract him.

She did not see the thrown knife. It seemed to appear in the wizard's breast from nowhere, splitting the silver medallion and piercing the long-still heart. The ruby fell from its setting and shattered on the stone.

The wizard let out a sudden, despairing cry and collapsed on the ground beside the Czarina, a desiccated corpse. She struggled to her feet as Balfour stepped close. In the distance, Samuel Brydon fled screaming toward the waiting hands of Scotland Yard. At the water's edge, Meriwether retched and held his eyes against the visions that plagued him, his shoulder and neck a single angry scorch mark.

Balfour retrieved his blade from the dead man's chest.

"Well. That ends that," the Czarina said. "Do you suppose his magics died with him? Or are your queen and my husband lost forever?"

"Don't know," he grunted. "We'll see."

"Either way, I owe you my life now."

"Y'do."

For a moment, their gazes rested on each other. Balfour drew his knives in the same moment the Czarina raised her pistol. The bullet grazed his skull, setting his world ringing like a church bell, and his blade bit into the flesh of her arm. Her foot shot forward, taking him in the belly. He fell back and she retreated. Blood flowed down her side, crimson soaking her dress. Her eyes were bright and mad and insatiable.

"The hunt calls!" she said, then turned, took half a dozen steps, and dove into the icy water.

Balfour lay back, his hand pressed to his wounded head. Some time later—a minute, an hour—Meriwether crawled up beside him. They lay on the stone, the chill seeping into their bones.

"Well," said Balfour.

"Yes," said Meriwether.

"You should have shot her when you had the chance."

"Next time," Meriwether said. "Next time."

⸢⸥

They tell me that after the Bolsheviks rose up, she fought a campaign of assassination and sabotage. I can well believe it. But by the evidence of my own eyes, she lives now in retired leisure in the Denmark of her youth. She or someone quite like her. With her, one can never be certain.

Balfour and Meriwether in the Vampire of Kabul | Daniel Abraham

I picture her reading of this new Afghan adventure and thinking of me and of my old friend Balfour. I hear her laughing, if only within the confines of my memory. Nostalgia, is that? Regret? But what is one man's youth against the great spread of history. No, I will drink my tea and turn away from the old days, however much I feel their loss. Instead I will take comfort in the fact that the great game has ended. With communism devouring the greatness that was the Russian Empire, Britain—however much wounded by the Great War—is left as the only great power in the world. And so it follows that this next Afghan war must necessarily be the final example of its species. With no great enemy glowering at us from across its borders, there will no longer be a call to battle in those barren fields, and the tribes of those ragged hills will at last be granted peace.

Last Breath

BY JOE HILL

A family walked in for a look around, a little before noon, a man, a woman, and their son. They were the first visitors of the day—for all Alinger knew they would be the only visitors of the day, the museum was never busy—and he was free to give them the tour.

He met them in the coatroom. The woman still stood with one foot out on the front steps, hesitant to come in any further. She was staring over her son's head at her husband, giving him a doubting, uneasy look. The husband frowned back at her. His hands were on the lapels of his shearling overcoat, but he seemed undecided whether to take it off or not. Alinger had seen it a hundred times before. Once people were inside and had looked beyond the foyer into the funeral home gloom of the parlor, they had second thoughts, wondered if they had come to the right place, began to entertain ideas of backing out. Only the little boy seemed at ease, was already stripping off his jacket and hanging it over one of the child-level hooks on the wall.

Before they could get away from him, Alinger cleared his throat to draw their attention. No one ever left once they had been spotted; in the battle between anxiety and social custom, social custom almost always won. He folded his hands together, and smiled at them, in a way he hoped was reassuring, grandfatherly. The effect, though, was rather the opposite. Alinger was cadaverous, ten inches over six feet, his temples sunk into shadowed hollows. His teeth (at eighty, still his own) were small and gray and gave the unpleasant impression of having been filed. The father shrank away a little. The woman unconsciously reached for her son's hand.

"Good morning. I'm Dr. Alinger. Please come in."

"Oh—hello," said the father. "Sorry to bother."

"No bother. We're open."

"You are. Good!" he said, with a not-quite-convincing enthusiasm. "So what do we—" and his voice trailed off and he fell quiet, had either forgotten what he was going to say, or wasn't sure how to put it, or lacked the nerve.

His wife took over. "We were told you have an exhibition here? That this is some kind of scientific museum?" Alinger showed them the smile again, and the father's right eyelid began to twitch helplessly.

"Ah. You misheard," Alinger said. "You were expecting a museum of science. This is the museum of silence."

"Hm?" the father said.

The mother frowned. "I think I'm still mishearing."

"Come on, Mom," said the boy, pulling his hand free from her grip. "Come on, Dad. I want to look around. I want to see."

"Please," Alinger said, stepping back from the coatroom, gesturing with one gaunt, long-fingered hand in to the parlor. "I would be glad to offer you the guided tour."

※

The shades were drawn, so the room, with its mahogany paneling, was as dim as a theater, in the moment before the curtain is pulled back on the show. The display stands, though, were lit from above by tightly focused spotlights, recessed in the ceiling. On tables and pedestals stood what appeared to be empty glass beakers, polished to a high shine, bulbs glowing so brilliantly, they made the darkness around them that much darker.

Each beaker had what appeared to be a stethoscope attached to it, the diaphragm stuck right to the glass, sealed there with a clear adhesive. The earpieces waited for someone to pick them up and listen. The boy led the way, followed by his parents, and then Alinger. They stopped before the first display, a jar on a marble pedestal, located just beyond the parlor entrance, set right in their path.

"There's nothing in it," the boy said. He peered all around, surveying the entire room, the other sealed beakers. "There's nothing in any of them. They're just empty like."

"Ha," said the father, humorlessly.

"Not quite empty," Alinger said. "Each jar is airtight, hermetically sealed. Each one contains someone's dying breath. I have the largest collection of last breaths in the world, over a hundred. Some of these bottles contain the final exhalations of some very famous people."

Now the woman began to laugh; real laughter, not laughter for show. She clapped a hand over her mouth and shivered, but couldn't manage to completely stifle herself. Alinger smiled. He had been showing his collection for years. He was used to every kind of reaction.

The boy, however, had turned back to the beaker directly before him, his eyes rapt. He picked up the earpieces of the device that looked like but was not a stethoscope.

"What's this?" he asked.

"The deathoscope," Alinger said. "Very sensitive. Put it on if you like, and you can hear the last breath of William R. Sied."

"Is he someone famous?" the boy said.

Alinger nodded. "For a while he was a celebrity…in the way criminals sometimes become celebrities. A source of public outrage and fascination. Forty-two years ago he took a seat in the electric chair. I issued his death certificate myself. He has a place of honor in my museum. His was the first last breath I ever captured."

By now the woman had recovered herself, although she held a wadded up handkerchief to her lips, and looked as if she were only containing a fresh outburst of mirth with great effort.

"What did he do?" the boy asked.

"Strangled children," Alinger said. "He preserved them in a freezer, and took them out now and then to look at them. People will collect anything I always say." He crouched to the boy's level, and looked into the jar with him. "Go ahead and listen if you want."

The boy lifted the earpieces and put them on, his gaze fixed and unblinking on the vessel brimming with light. He listened intently for a while, and then his brow knotted and he frowned.

"I can't hear anything." He started to reach up to remove the earpieces.

Alinger stopped his hand. "Wait. There are all different kinds of silence. The silence in a seashell. The silence after a gunshot. His last breath is still in there. Your ears need time to acclimate. In a while you'll be able to make it out. His own particular final silence."

The boy bent his head and shut his eyes. The adults watched him together.

Then his eyes sprang open and he looked up, his plump face shining a little with eagerness.

"Did you hear?" Alinger asked him.

The boy pulled off the earphones. "Like a hiccup, only inside-out! You know? Like—" he stopped and sucked in a short, soundless little gasp.

Alinger tousled his hair and stood.

The mother dabbed at her eyes with her kerchief. "And you're a doctor?"

"Retired."

"Don't you think this is a little unscientific? Even if you really did manage to capture the last tiny bit of carbon monoxide someone exhaled—"

"Dioxide," he said.

"It wouldn't make a sound. You can't bottle the sound of someone's last breath."

"No," he agreed. "But it isn't a sound being bottled. Only a certain silence. We all have our different silences. Does your husband have one silence when he's happy and another when he's angry with you, missus? Your ears can discern even between specific kinds of nothing."

She didn't like being called missus, narrowed her eyes at him, and opened her mouth to say something disagreeable, but her husband spoke first, giving Alinger a reason to turn away from her. Her husband had drifted to a jar on a table against the wall, next to a dark, padded loveseat.

"How do you collect these breaths?"

"With an aspirator. A small pump that draws a person's exhalations into a vacuum container. I keep it in my doctor's bag at all times, just in case. It's a device of my own design, although similar equipment has been around since the beginning of the nineteenth century."

"This says Poe," the father said, fingering an ivory card set on the table before the jar.

"Yes," Alinger said. He coughed shyly. "People have been collecting last breaths for as long as the machinery has existed to make my hobby possible. I admit I paid twelve-thousand dollars for that. It was offered to me by the great-grandson of the doctor who watched him die."

The woman began to laugh again.

Alinger continued patiently. "That may sound like a lot of money, but believe me, it was a bargain. Scrimm, in Paris, recently paid three times that for the last breath of Enrico Caruso."

The father fingered the deathoscope attached to the jar marked for Poe.

"Some silences seem to resonate with feeling," Alinger said. "You can almost sense them trying to articulate an idea. Many who listen to Poe's last breath begin in a while to sense a single world not being said, the expression of a very specific want. Listen and see if you sense it too."

The father hunched and put on the earpieces.

"This is ridiculous," the woman said.

The father listened intently. His son crowded him, squeezing himself tight to his leg.

"Can I listen, Dad?" the boy said. "Can I have a turn?"

"Sh," his father said.

They were all silent, except for the woman, who was whispering to herself in a tone of agitated bemusement. "Whiskey," the father mouthed, just moving his lips.

"Turn over the card with his name on it," said Alinger.

The father turned over the ivory card that said POE on one side. On the other side, it read, 'WHISKEY.'

He removed the earpieces, his face solemn, eyes lowered respectfully to the jar.

"Of course. The alcoholism. Poor man. You know—I memorized 'The Raven,' when I was in sixth grade," the father said. "And recited it before my entire class without a mistake."

"Oh come on," said the woman. "It's a trick. There's probably a speaker hidden under the jar, and when you listen you can hear a recording, someone whispering whiskey."

"I didn't hear a whisper," the father said. "I just had a thought—like someone's voice in my head—such disappointment—"

"The volume turned low," she said. "So it's all subliminal. Like what they do to you at drive-in movies."

The boy put on the earpieces to not-hear the same thing his father had not heard.

"Are they all famous people?" the father asked. His features were pale, although there were little spots of red high on his cheeks, as if he had a fever.

"Not at all," Alinger said. "I've bottled the dying sighs of graduate students, bureaucrats, literary critics—any number of assorted nobodies. One of the most exquisite silences in my collection is the last breath of a janitor."

"Carrie Mayfield," said the woman, reading from a card in front of a tall, dusty jar. "Is that one of your nobodies? I'm guessing housewife."

"No," Alinger said. "No housewives in my collection yet. Carrie Mayfield was a young Miss Florida, beautiful in the extreme, on her way to New York City with her parents and fiancé, to pose for the cover of a woman's magazine. Her big break. Only her jet crashed in the Everglades. Lots of people died, it was a famous air disaster. Carrie, though, survived. For a time. She splashed through burning jet fuel while escaping the wreck, and over eighty percent of her body was burned. She lost her voice screaming for help. She lasted, in intensive care, just over a week. I was teaching then, and brought my medical students in to see her. As a curiosity. At the time, it was rare to view someone, still alive, who had been burned that way. So comprehensively. Parts of her body fused to other parts and so on. Fortunately I had my aspirator with me, since she died while we were examining her."

"That's the most horrible thing I've ever heard," said the woman. "What about her parents? Her fiancé?"

"They died in the crash. Burned to death in front of her. I'm not sure their bodies were ever recovered. The gators—"

"I don't believe you. Not a word. I don't believe a thing about this place. And I don't mind saying I think this is a pretty silly way to scam people out of their money."

"Now dear—" said her husband.

"You will remember I charged you no admission," Alinger said. "This is a free exhibit."

"Oh, Dad, look!" the boy said, from across the room, reading a name on a card. "It's the man who wrote *James and the Giant Peach!*"

Alinger turned to him, ready to introduce the display in question, then saw the woman moving from the corner of his eye, and swiveled back to her.

"I would listen to one of the others first," Alinger said. She was lifting the earpieces to her head. "Some people don't care much for what they can't hear in the Carrie Mayfield jar."

She ignored him, put the earpieces on, and listened, her mouth pursed. Alinger clasped his hands together and leaned toward her, watching her expression.

Then, without warning, she took a quick step back. She still had the earpieces on, and the abrupt movement scraped the jar a short distance across the table, which gave Alinger a bad moment. He reached out quickly to keep it from sliding off onto the floor. She twisted the earpieces off her head, suddenly clumsy.

"Roald Dahl," the father said, putting his hand on his son's shoulder and admiring the jar the boy had discovered. "No kidding. Say, you went in big for the literary guys, huh?"

"I don't like it here," the woman said.

Her eyes were unfocused. She stared at the jar that contained Carrie Mayfield's last breath, but without seeing it. She swallowed noisily, a hand at her throat.

"Honey?" her husband said. He crossed the room to her, frowning, concerned. "You want to go? We just got here."

"I don't care," she said. "I want to leave."

"Oh Mom," the boy complained.

"I hope you'll sign my guest book," Alinger said. He trailed them to the coatroom.

The father was solicitous, touching his wife's elbow, regarding her with dewy, worried eyes. "Couldn't you wait in the car by yourself? Tom and I wanted to look around a while longer."

"I want to go right now," she said, her voice toneless, distant. "All of us."

The father helped her into her coat. The boy shoved his fists in his pockets and sullenly kicked at an old, worn doctor's bag, sitting beside the umbrella stand. Then he realized what he was kicking. He crouched, and without the slightest show of shame, unbuckled it to look at the aspirator.

The woman drew on her kidskin gloves, very carefully, pulling them tight against her fingers. She seemed a long way off in her own thoughts, so it was a surprise when all at once she roused herself, to turn on her heel and fix her gaze on Alinger.

"You're awful," she said. "Like some kind of graverobber."

Alinger folded his hands before him, and regarded her sympathetically. He had been showing his collection for years. He was used to every kind of reaction.

"Oh honey," her husband said. "Have some perspective."

"I'm going to the car now," she said, lowering her head, drawing back into herself. "Catch up."

"Wait," the father said. "Wait for us."

He didn't have his coat on. Neither did the boy, who was on his knees, with the bag open, his fingertips moving slowly over the aspirator, a device that resembled a chrome thermos, with rubber tubes and a plastic face mask attached to one end.

She didn't hear her husband's voice, but turned away and went out, left the door open behind her. She went down the steep granite steps to the sidewalk, her eyes pointed at the ground the whole way. She was swaying when she did her sleepwalker's stroll into the street. She didn't look up, but started straight across for their car on the other side of the road.

Alinger was turning to get the guest book—he thought perhaps the man would still sign—when he heard the shriek of brakes, and a metallic crunch, as if a car had rushed headlong into a tree, only even before he looked he knew it wasn't a tree.

The father screamed and then screamed again. Alinger pivoted back in time to see him falling down the steps. A black Cadillac was turned at an unlikely angle in the street, steam coming up around the edges of the crumpled hood. The driver's side door was open, and the driver stood in the road, a porkpie hat tipped back on his head.

Even over the ringing in his ears, Alinger heard the driver saying, "She didn't even look. Right into traffic. Jesus Christ. What was I supposed to do?"

The father wasn't listening. He was in the street, on his knees, holding her. The boy stood in the coatroom, his jacket half on, staring out. A swollen vein beat in the child's forehead.

"Doctor," the father screamed. "Please! Doctor!" He was looking back at Alinger.

Alinger paused to pick his overcoat off a hook. It was March, and windy, and he didn't want to get a chill. He hadn't reached the age of eighty by being careless or doing things in haste. He patted the boy on the head as he went by. He had not gone halfway down the steps, though, when the child called out to him.

"Doctor," the boy stammered, and Alinger looked back.

The boy held his bag out to him, still unbuckled.

"Your bag," the boy said. "You might need something in it."

Alinger smiled fondly, went back up the steps, took it from the boy's cold fingers.

"Thank you," he said. "I just might."

Younger Women

BY KAREN JOY FOWLER

Jude knows that her daughter Chloe has a boyfriend. She knows this even though Chloe is fifteen and not talking. If Jude were to ask, Chloe would tell Jude that it's none of her business and to stop being such a snoop. (Well, if you want to call it snooping to go through Chloe's closets, drawers, and backpack on a daily basis, check the history on her cell phone and laptop, check the margins of her textbooks for incriminating doodles, friend her on Facebook under a pseudonym so as to access her page—hey, if you want to call that snooping, then, guilty as charged. The world's a dangerous place. Isn't getting less so. Any mother will tell you that.)

So there's no point asking Chloe. She talks about him to her Facebook friends—his name is Eli—but the boy himself never shows. He doesn't phone; he doesn't email; he doesn't text. Sometimes at night Jude wakes up with the peculiar delusion that he's in the house, but when she checks, Chloe is always in her bed, asleep and alone. The less Jude finds out the more uneasy she becomes.

One day she decides to go all in. "Bring that boy you're seeing to dinner this weekend," she tells Chloe, hoping Chloe won't wonder how she knows about him or, if she does, will chalk it up to mother's intuition. "I'll make pasta."

"I'd rather die," Chloe says.

※

Chloe's Facebook friends are all sympathy. Their mothers are nosy pains-in-the-butt, too. Her own mother died when Jude was twenty-three, and Jude misses her terribly, but she remembers being fifteen. Once when she'd been grounded, which also meant no telephone privileges, her mother had left the house and Jude had called her best friend Audrey. And her mother knew because there was a fruit bowl by the phone and Jude had fiddled with the fruit while she talked.

So Chloe's friends are telling her to stand her ground and yet, come Saturday, there he is, sitting across the table from Jude, playing with his food. It was Eli's own decision to come, Chloe had told her, because he's very polite. Good-looking, too, better than Jude would have guessed. In fact, he's pretty hot.

Jude's unease is still growing. In spite of this, she tries for casual. "Chloe says you're new to the school," she says. "Where are you from?"

"L.A." Eli knows what he's doing. Meets her eyes. Smiles. Uses his napkin. A picture of good manners.

"Don't go all CSI on him, Mom. He doesn't have to answer your questions. You don't have to answer her questions," Chloe says.

"I don't mind. She's just being your mom." And to Jude, "Ask me anything."

"How old are you?"

"Seventeen."

"What year were you born in?"

"Nineteen ninety-four," he says and there isn't even a pause, but Jude's suspicions solidify in her mind with an audible click like the moment in the morning just before the alarm goes off. No wonder he doesn't text. No wonder he doesn't email or call on the cell. He probably doesn't know how.

"Try again," she tells him.

Vampire. Plain as the nose on your face.

⁂

Of course, Chloe knows. She's flattered by it. Any fifteen-year-old would be (and probably lots before her have been). Jude's been doing some light reading on the current neurological research on the teenage brain. She googles this before bed. It helps her sleep, not because the news is good, but because she can tell herself that the current situation is only temporary. She and Chloe used to be so close before Chloe started hating her guts.

The teenage brain is in a state of rapid, but incomplete development. Certain important linkages haven't been formed yet. "The teenage brain is not just an adult brain with fewer miles on it," the experts say. It is a whole different animal. In quantifiable ways, teenagers are actually incapable of thinking straight.

Not to mention the hormones. Poor Chloe. Eli's hotness is getting even to Jude.

Of course, none of this can be said. Chloe thinks she's all grown-up, and if Jude so much as hinted that she wasn't, Chloe would really lose it. Jude has a quick flash of Chloe at five, her hair in fraying pigtails, hanging from the tree in the backyard by her hands (monkey), by her knees (bat), shouting for Jude to come see. If Chloe really were grown up, she'd wonder, the same way Jude wonders, what sort of immortal loser hangs out with fifteen-year-olds. No one loves Chloe more than Jude, no one ever will, but really. Why Chloe?

"Mom!" says Chloe. "Butt the fuck out!"

"It's okay," Eli says. "I'm glad it's in the open." He stops pretending to eat, puts down his fork. "Eighteen sixteen."

"And still haven't managed to graduate high school?" Jude asks.

⁕

The conversation is not going well. Jude has fetched the whiskey so the adults can drink and sure enough, it turns out there are some things Eli can choke down besides blood. Half a glass in, Jude wonders aloud why Eli can't find a girlfriend his own age. Does he prefer younger women because they're so easy to impress, she wonders. Is it possible no woman older than fifteen will go out with him?

Eli is drinking fast, faster than Jude, but showing no effects. "I love Chloe." Sincerity drips off his voice like rain from the roof. "You maybe don't understand how it is with vampires. We don't choose where our hearts go. But when we give them, we never take them back again. Chloe is my whole world."

"Very nice," Jude says, although in fact she finds it creepy and stalker-ish. "Still, in two hundred years, you must have collected some exes. Ever been married? How old were they when you finally cleared off? Ancient women of seventeen?"

"Oh. My. God." Chloe is staring down into her sorry glass of ice tea. "Get a clue. Get a life. I knew you'd make this all about you. Ever since Dad left, everyone has to be as fucking miserable as you are. You just can't stand to see me happy."

There is this inconvenient fact—eight months ago Chloe's dad walked out to start a new life with a younger woman. Two weeks ago, he called to tell Jude he was going to be a father again.

"Again? Like you stopped being a father in between?" Jude asked frostily and turned the phone off. She hasn't spoken to him since nor told Chloe about the baby, though maybe Michael has done that for himself. It's the least he can do. Introduce her to her replacement.

"This is why I didn't want you to fucking meet her," Chloe tells Eli. Her face and cheeks are red with fury. She has always colored up like that, even when she was a baby. Jude remembers her, red and sobbing, because the *Little Mermaid* DVD had begun to skip, forcing her to watch the song in which the chef is chopping the heads off fish over and over and over again. Five years old and already a gifted tragedian. "Fix it, Mommy," she'd sobbed. "Fix it or I'll go mad."

"I knew you'd try to spoil everything," Chloe tells Jude.

"I knew you'd be a bitch and a half."

"You should speak more respectfully to your mother," Eli tells her. "You're lucky to have one." He goes on. Call him old-fashioned, he says, but he doesn't care for the language kids use today. Everything is so much coarser than it used to be.

Chloe responds to Eli's criticism with a gasp. She reaches out, knocks over her glass, maybe deliberately, maybe not. A sprig of mint floats like a raft in a puddle of tea. "I knew you'd find a way to turn him against me."

She flees the room, pounds up the stairs, which squeak loudly with her passage. A door slams, but she can still be heard through it, sobbing on her bed. She's waiting for Eli to follow her.

Instead he stands, catches the mint before it falls off the table edge, wipes up the tea with his napkin.

"You're not making my life any easier," Jude tells him.

"I'm truly sorry about that part," he says. "But love is love."

※

Jude gives Eli fifteen minutes in which to go calm Chloe down. God knows, nothing Jude could say would accomplish that. She waits until he's up the stairs, then follows him, but only as high as the first creaking step, so that she can almost, but not quite hear what they're saying. Chloe's voice is high and impassioned, Eli's apologetic. Then everything is silent, suspiciously so, and she's just about to go up the rest of the way even though the fifteen minutes isn't over when she hears Eli again and realizes he's in the hall. "Let *me* talk to your mom," Eli is saying and Jude hurries back to the table before he catches her listening.

She notices that he manages the stairs without a sound. "She's fine," Eli tells her. "She's on the computer."

Jude decides not to finish her drink. It wouldn't be wise or responsible. It wouldn't be motherly. She's already blurred a bit at the edges though she thinks that's fatigue more than liquor. She's been having so much trouble sleeping.

She eases her feet out of her shoes, leans down to rub her toes. "Doesn't it feel like we've just put the children to bed?" she asks.

Eli's back in his seat across the table, straight-backed in the chair, looking soberly sexy. "Forgive me for this," he says. He leans forward slightly. "But are you trying to seduce me? Mrs. Robinson?"

Jude absolutely wasn't, so it's easy to deny. "I wouldn't date you even without Chloe," she says. Eli's been polite, so she tries to be polite back. Leave it at that.

But he insists on asking.

"It's just such a waste," she says. "I mean, really. High school and high school girls? That's the best you can do with immortality? It doesn't impress me."

"What would you do?" he asks.

She stands, begins to gather up the dishes. "God! I'd go places. I'd see things. Instead you sit like a lump through the same high school history classes you've taken a hundred times, when you could have actually seen those things for yourself. You could have witnessed it all."

Eli picks up his plate and follows her into the kitchen. One year ago, she and Michael had done a complete remodel, silestone countertops and glass-fronted cupboards. Cement floors. The paint was barely dry when Michael left with his new girlfriend. Jude had wanted something homier—tile and wood—but Michael likes modern and minimal. Sometimes Jude feels angrier over this than over the girlfriend. He was seeing Kathy the whole time they were remodeling. Probably in some part of his brain he'd known he was leaving. Why couldn't he let her have the kitchen she wanted?

"I'll wash," Eli says. "You dry."

"We have a dishwasher." Jude points to it. Energy star. Top of the line. Guilt offering.

"But it's better by hand. Better for talking."

"What are we talking about?"

"You have something you want to ask me." Eli fills the sink, adds the soap.

That's a good guess. Jude can't quite get to it though. "You could have been in Hiroshima or Auschwitz," she says. "You could have helped. You could have walked beside Martin Luther King. You could have torn down the Berlin Wall. Right now, you could be in Darfur, doing something good and important."

"I'm doing the dishes," says Eli.

Outside Jude hears a car passing. It turns into the Klein's driveway. The headlights go off and the car door slams. Marybeth Klein brought Jude a casserole of chicken divan when Michael left. Jude has never told her that Jack Klein tried to kiss her at the Swanson's New Year's Party, because how do you say that to a woman who's never been anything but nice to you? The Kleins' boy, Devin, goes to school with Chloe. He smokes a lot of dope. Sometimes Jude can smell it in the backyard, coming over the fence. Why can't Chloe be in love with him?

"If you promised me not to change Chloe, would you keep that promise?" She hears more than feels the tremble in her voice.

"Now, we're getting to it," Eli says. He passes her the first of the glasses and their hands touch. His fingers feel warm, but she knows that's just the dishwater. "Would you like me to change *you*?" Eli asks. "Is that what you really want?"

The glass slips from Jude's hand and shatters on the cement. A large, sharp piece rests against her bare foot. "Don't move," says Eli. "Let me clean it up." He drops to his knees.

"What's happening?" Chloe calls from upstairs. "What's going on?"

"Nothing. I broke a glass," Jude shouts back.

Eli takes hold of her ankle. He lifts her foot. There is a little blood on her instep and he wipes this away with his hand. "You'd never get older," he says. "But Michael will and you can watch." Jude wonders briefly how he knows Michael's name. Chloe must have told him.

His hand on her foot, his fingers rubbing her instep. The whiskey. Her sleepiness. She is feeling sweetly light-headed, sweetly light-hearted. Another car passes. Jude hears the sprinklers start next door sounding almost, but not quite like rain.

"Is Eli still there?" Chloe's pitch is rising again.

Jude doesn't answer. She speaks instead to Eli. "I wasn't so upset about Michael leaving me as you think. It was a surprise. It was a shock. But I was mostly upset about him leaving Chloe." She thinks again. "I was upset about him leaving me with Chloe."

"You could go to Darfur then. If petty revenge is beneath you," Eli says. "Do things that are good and important." He is lowering his mouth to her foot. She puts a hand on his head to steady herself.

Then she stops, grips his hair, pulls his head up. "But I wouldn't," she says. "Would I?" Jude makes him look at her. She finds it a bit evil, really, offering her immortality under the guise of civic service when the world has such a shortage of civic-minded vampires in it. And she came so close to falling for it.

She sees that the immortal brain must be different—over the years, certain crucial linkages must snap. Otherwise there is no explaining Eli and his dull and pointless, endless, dangerous life.

Anyway, who would take care of Chloe? She hears the squeaking of the stairs.

"Just promise me you won't change Chloe," she says hastily. She's crying now and doesn't know when that started.

"I've never changed anyone who didn't ask to be changed. Never will," Eli tells her.

Jude kicks free of his hand. "Of *course*, she'll ask to be changed," she says furiously. "She's fifteen years old! She doesn't even have a functioning brain yet. Promise me you'll leave her alone."

It's possible Chloe hears this. When Jude turns, she's standing, framed in the doorway like a portrait. Her hair streams over her shoulders. Her eyes are enormous. She's young and she's beautiful and she's outraged. Jude can see her taking them in—Eli picking up the shards of glass so Jude won't step on them. Eli kneeling at her feet.

"You don't have to hang out with her," Chloe tells Eli. "I'm not breaking up with you no matter what she says."

Her gaze moves to Jude. "Good god, Mom. It's just a glass." Then back to Eli, "I'm glad it wasn't me, broke it. We'd never hear the end of it."

Love is love, Eli said, but how careful his timing has been! If Chloe were older, Jude could talk to her, woman to woman. If she were younger, Jude could take Chloe into her lap; tell her to stop throwing words like never around as if she knows what they mean, as if she knows just how long never will last. ━🐉

White Lines on a Green Field

BY CATHERYNNE M. VALENTE

For Seanan McGuire. And Coyote.

L et me tell you about the year Coyote took the Devils to the State
Championship.

Coyote walked tall down the halls of West Centerville High and
where he walked lunch money, copies of last semester's math tests, and
unlit joints blossomed in his footsteps. When he ran laps out on the field
our lockers would fill up with Snickers bars, condoms, and ecstasy tabs in
all the colors of Skittles. He was our QB, and he looked like an invitation
to the greatest rave of all time. I mean, yeah, he had black hair and copper
skin and muscles like a commercial for the life you're never going to have.
But it was the way he looked at you, with those dark eyes that knew the
answer to every question a teacher could ask, but he wouldn't give them
the *satisfaction*, you know? Didn't matter anyway. Coyote never did his
homework, but boyfriend rocked a 4.2 all the same.

When tryouts rolled around that fall, Coyote went out for everything.
Cross-country, baseball, even lacrosse. But I think football appealed to
his friendly nature, his need to have a pack around him, bright-eyed boys
with six-pack abs and a seven minute mile and a gift for him every day.
They didn't even know why, but they brought them all the same. Playing
cards, skateboards, vinyl records (Coyote had no truck with mp3s). The

defensive line even baked cookies for their boy. Chocolate chip peanut butter oatmeal walnut iced snickerdoodle, piling up on the bench like a king's tribute. And oh, the girls brought flowers. Poor girls gave him dandelions and rich girls gave him roses and he kissed them all like they were each of them specifically the key to the fulfillment of all his dreams. Maybe they were. Coyote didn't play favorites. He had enough for everyone.

By the time we went to State, all the cheerleaders were pregnant.

The Devils used to be a shitty team, no lie. Bottom of our division and even the coach was thinking he ought to get more serious about his geometry classes. Before Coyote transferred our booster club was the tight end's Dad, Mr. Bollard, who painted his face Devil gold-and-red and wore big plastic light-up horns for every game. At Homecoming one year, the Devil's Court had two princesses and a queen who were actually girls from the softball team filling in on a volunteer basis, because no one cared enough to vote. They all wore jeans and bet heavily on the East Centerville Knights, who won 34-3.

First game of his senior year, Coyote ran 82 yards for the first of 74 touchdowns that season. He passed and caught and ran like he was all eleven of them in one body. Nobody could catch him. Nobody even complained. He ran like he'd stolen that ball and the whole world was chasing him to get it back. Where'd he been all this time? The boys hoisted him up on their shoulders afterward, and Coyote just laughed and laughed. We all found our midterm papers under our pillows the next morning, finished and bibliographied, and damn if they weren't the best essays we'd never written.

I'm not gonna lie. I lost my virginity to Coyote in the back of my blue pick-up out by the lake right before playoffs. He stroked my hair and kissed me like they kiss in the movies. Just the perfect kisses, no bonked noses, no knocking teeth. He tasted like stolen sunshine. *Bunny*, he whispered to me with his narrow hips working away, *I will love you forever and ever. You're the only one for me.*

Liar, I whispered back, and when I came it was like the long flying fall of a roller coaster, right into his arms. *Liar, liar, liar.*

I think he liked that I knew the score, because after that Coyote made sure I was at all his games, even though I don't care about sports. Nobody didn't care about sports that year. Overnight the stands went from a ghost town to kids ride free day at the carnival. And when Coyote danced in the endzone he looked like everything you ever wanted. Every son, every boyfriend.

"Come on, Bunny," he'd say. "I'll score a touchdown for you."

"You'll score a touchdown either way."

"I'll point at you in the stands if you're there. Everyone will know I love you."

"Just make sure I'm sitting with Sarah Jane and Jessica and Ashley, too, so you don't get in trouble."

"That's my Bunny, always looking out for me," he'd laugh, and take me in his mouth like he'd die if he didn't.

⋇

You could use birth control with Coyote. It wouldn't matter much.

But he did point at me when he crossed that line, grinning and dancing and moving his hips like Elvis had just been copying his moves all along, and Sarah Jane and Jessica and Ashley got so excited they choked on their Cokes. They all knew about the others. I think they liked it that way—most of what mattered to Sarah Jane and Jessica and Ashley was Sarah Jane and Jessica and Ashley, and Coyote gave them permission to spend all their time together. Coyote gave us all permission, that was his thing. *Cheat, fuck, drink, dance—just do it like you mean it!*

I think the safety had that tattooed on his calf.

After we won four games in a row (after a decade of no love) things started to get really out of control. You couldn't buy tickets. Mr. Bollard was in hog heaven—suddenly the boosters were every guy in town who was somebody, or used to be somebody, or who wanted to be somebody some impossible day in the future. We were gonna beat the Thunderbirds. They started saying it, right out in public. Six-time state champs, and no chance they wouldn't be the team in our way this year like every year. But every year was behind us, and ahead was only our boy running like he'd got the whole of heaven at his back. Mr. Bollard got them new uniforms, new helmets, new goal posts—all the deepest red you ever saw. But nobody wore the light-up horns Mr. Bollard had rocked for years. They all wore little furry coyote ears, and who knows where they bought them, but they were everywhere one Friday, and every Friday after. When Coyote scored, everyone would howl like the moon had come out just for them. Some of the cheerleaders started wearing faux-fur tails, spinning them around by bumping and grinding on the sidelines, their corn-yellow skirts fluttering up to the heavens.

One time, after we stomped the Greenville Bulldogs 42-0, I saw Coyote under the stands, in that secret place the boards and steel poles and shadows and candy wrappers make. Mike Halloran (kicker, #14) and Justin Oster (wide receiver, #11) were down there too, helmets off, the filtered stadium lights turning their uniforms to pure gold. Coyote leaned against a pole, smoking a cigarette, shirt off—and what a thing that was to see.

"Come on, QB," Justin whined. "I never hit a guy before. I got no beef here. And I never fucked Jessie, either, Mike, I was just mouthing off. She let me see her boob once in 9th grade and there wasn't that much to see back then. I never had a drink except one time a beer and I never smoked 'cause my daddy got emphysema." Coyote just grinned his friendly, hey-dude-no-worries grin.

"Never know unless you try," he said, very reasonably. "It'll make you feel good, I promise."

"Fuck *you*, Oster," shot back Halloran. "I'm going first. You're bigger, it's not fair."

Halloran got his punch in before he had to hear any more about what Justin Oster had never done and the two of them went *at it*, fists and blood and meat-slapping sounds and pretty soon they were down on the ground in the spilled-Coke and week-old-rain mud, pulling hair and biting and rolling around and after awhile it didn't look that much like fighting anymore. I watched for awhile. Coyote looked up at me over their grappling and dragged on his smoke.

White Lines on a Green Field | Catherynne M. Valente

Just look at them go, little sister, I heard Coyote whisper, but his mouth didn't move. His eyes flashed in the dark like a dog's.

⋇

LaGrange almost ruined it all at Homecoming. The LaGrange Cowboys, and wasn't their QB a picture, all wholesome white-blonde square-jaw aw-shucks muscle with an arm so perfect you'd have thought someone had mounted a rifle sight on it. #9 Bobby Zhao, of the 300 bench and the Miss Butter Festival 19whatever mother, the seven-restaurant-chain owning father (Dumpling King of the Southland!) and the surprising talent for soulful bluegrass guitar. All the colleges lined up for that boy with carnations and chocolates. We hated him like hate was something we'd invented in lab that week and had been saving up for something special. Bobby Zhao and his bullshit hipster-crooner straw hat. Coyote didn't pay him mind. *Tell us what you're gonna do to him,* they'd pant, and he'd just spit onto the parking lot asphalt and say: *I got a history with Cowboys.* Where he'd spat the offensive line watched as weird crystals formed—the kind Jimmy Moser (safety, #17) ought to have recognized from his uncle's trailer out off of Route 40, but you know me, I don't say a word. They didn't look at it too long. Instead they scratched their cheeks and performed their tribal ask-and-answer. *We going down by the lake tonight? Yeah. Yeah.*

"Let's invite Bobby Zhao," Coyote said suddenly. His eyes got big and loose and happy. His *come-on* look. His *it'll-be-great* look.

"Um, why?" Jimmy frowned. "Not to put too fine a point on it, but fuck that guy. He's the enemy."

Coyote flipped up the collar of his leather jacket and picked a stray maple leaf the color of anger out of Jimmy's hair. He did it tenderly. *You're my boy and I'll pick you clean, I'll lick you clean, I'll keep everything red off of your perfect head,* his fingers said. But what his mouth said was:

"Son, what you don't know about enemies could just about feed the team til their dying day." And when Coyote called you Son you knew to be ashamed. "Only babies think enemies are for beating. Can't beat 'em, not ever. Not the ones that come out of nowhere in the 4th quarter to take what's yours and hold your face in the mud til you drown, not the ones you always knew you'd have to face because that's what you were made for. Not the lizard guarding the Sun, not the man who won't let you teach him how to plant corn. Enemies are for grabbing by the ears and fucking them til they're so sticky-knotted bound to you they call their wives by your name. Enemies are for absorbing, Jimmy. Best thing you can do to an enemy is pull up a chair to his fire, eat his dinner, rut in his bed and go to his job in the morning, and do it all so much better he just gives it up to you—but *fuck him*, you never wanted it anyway. You just wanted to mess around in his house for a little while. Scare his kids. Leave a little something behind to let the next guy know you're never far away. That's how you do him. Or else—" Coyote pulled Cindy Gerard (bottom of the pyramid and arms like birch trunks) close and took the raspberry pop out of her hand, sipping on it long and sweet, all that pink slipping into him. "Or else you just make him love you til he cries. Either way."

Jimmy fidgeted. He looked at Oster and Halloran, who still had bruises, fading on their cheekbones like blue flowers. After awhile he laughed horsily and said: "Whaddaya think the point spread'll be?"

Coyote just punched him in the arm, convivial like, and kissed Cindy Gerard and I could smell the raspberry of their kiss from across the circle of boys. The September wind brought their kiss to all of us like a bag of promises. And just like that, Bobby Zhao showed up at the lake that night, driving his freshly waxed Cowboy silver-and-black double-cab truck with the lights on top like a couple of frog's eyes. He took off that stupid straw hat and started hauling a keg out of the cream leather passenger seat—and once they saw that big silver moon riding shotgun with the Dumpling Prince of the Southland, Henry Dillard (linebacker, #33) and Josh Vick (linebacker, #34) hurried over to help him with it and Bobby Zhao was welcome. Offering accepted. Just lay it up here on the altar and we'll cut open that shiny belly and drink what she's got for us. And what she had was golden and sweet and just as foamy as the sea.

Coyote laid back with me in the bed of my much shittier pick-up, some wool blanket with a horse-and-cactus print on it under us and another one with a wolf-and-moon design over us, so he could slip his hands under my

White Lines on a Green Field | Catherynne M. Valente

bra in that secret, warm space that gets born under some hippie mom's awful rugs when no one else can see you. Everyone was hollering over the beer and I could hear Sarah Jane laughing in that way that says: *just keep pouring and maybe I'll show you something worth seeing.*

"Come on, Bunny Rabbit," Coyote whispered, "it's nothing we haven't done before." And it was a dumb thing to say, a boy thing, but when Coyote said it I felt it humming in my bones, everything we'd done before, over and over, and I couldn't even remember a world before Coyote, only the one he made of us, down by the lake, under the wolf and the moon, his hands on my breasts like they were the saving of him. I knew him like nobody else—and they'll all say that now, Sarah Jane and Jessica and Ashley and Cindy Gerard and Justin Oster and Jimmy Moser, but I knew him. Knew the shape of him. After all, it's nothing we hadn't done before.

"It's different every time," I said in the truck-dark. "Or there's no point. You gotta ask me nice every time. You gotta make me think I'm special. You gotta put on your ears and your tail and make the rain come for me or I'll run off with some Thunderbird QB and leave you eating my dust."

"I'm asking nice. Oh, my Bunny, my rabbit-girl with the fastest feet, just slow you down and let me do what I want."

"And what do you want?"

"I want to dance on this town til it breaks. I want to burrow in it until it belongs to me. I want high school to last forever. I want to eat everything, and fuck everything, and snort everything, and win everything. I want my Bunny Rabbit on my lap while I drive down the world with my headlights off."

"I don't want to be tricked," I said, but he was already inside me and I was glad. Fucking him felt like running in a long field, with no end in sight. "Not into a baby, not into a boyfriend, not into anything."

"Don't worry," he panted. "You always get yours. Just like me, always like me."

I felt us together, speeding up towards something, running faster, and he brushed my hair out of my face and it wasn't hair but long black ears, as soft as memory, and then it was hair again, tangled and damp with our sweat, and I bit him as our stride broke. I whispered: "And Coyote gets his."

"Why not? It's nothing we haven't done before."

When I got up off of the horse blanket, marigold blossoms spilled out of me like Coyote's seed.

⋇

Later that night I fished a smoke out of my glove box and sat on top of the dented salt-rusted cab of my truck. Coyote stood down by the lake-shore, aways off from the crowd, where the water came up in little foamy splashes and the willow trees whipped around like they were looking for someone to hold on to. Bobby Zhao was down there, too, his hands in his jean pockets, hip jutting out like a pouty lip, his hat on again and his face all in shadow. They were talking but I couldn't hear over everyone else hooting and laughing like a pack of owls. The moon came out as big as a beer keg; it made Coyote's face look lean and angelic, so young and victori-ous and humble enough to make you think the choice was yours all along. He took Bobby Zhao's hand and they just stood there in the light, their fingers moving together. The wind blew off that straw hat like it didn't like the thing much either, and Bobby let it lie. He was looking at Coyote, his hair all blue in the night, and Coyote kissed him as hard as hurting, and Bobby kissed him back like he'd been waiting for it since he was born. Coyote got his hands under his shirt and oh, Coyote is good at that, get-ting under, getting around, and the boys smiled whenever their lips parted.

I watched. I'm always watching. Who doesn't like to watch? It feels like being God, seeing everything happen far away, and you could stop it if you wanted, but then you couldn't watch anymore.

A storm started rumbling up across the meadows, spattering their kisses with autumn rain.

⋇

Suddenly everyone cared about who was going to make the Devil's Court this year. Even me. The mall was cleared out of formal sparkle-and-slit dresses by August, and somehow they just couldn't get any more in,

White Lines on a Green Field | CATHERYNNE M. VALENTE

like we were an island mysteriously sundered from the land of sequins and sweetheart necklines. Most of us were just going to have to go with one of our mom's prom dresses, though you can be damn sure we'd be ripping off that poofy shoulder chiffon and taking up the hems as far as we could. Jenny Kilroy (drama club, Young Businesswomen's Association) had done all the costumes for *The Music Man* in junior year, and for $50 she'd take that cherry cupcake dress and turn it into an apocalyptic punkslut wedding gown, but girlfriend worked *slow*. Whoever took the Homecoming crown had about a 60/40 chance of being up there in something they'd worn to their grandmother's funeral.

The smart money was on Sarah Jane for the win. She was already pregnant by then, and Jessica too, but I don't think even they knew it yet. Bellies still flat as a plains state, cotton candy lipstick as perfect as a Rembrandt. Nobody got morning sickness, nobody's feet swelled. Sarah shone in the center of her ring of girls like a pink diamond in a nouveaux riche ring. 4.0, equestrian club, head cheerleader, softball pitcher, jazz choir lead soprano, played Juliet in both freshman and senior years, even joined the chess club. She didn't care about chess, but it looked good on her applications and she turned out to be terrifyingly good at it—first place at the spring speed chess invitational in Freemont, even seven months along. You couldn't even hate Sarah. You could see her whole perfect life rolling on ahead of her like a yellow brick road but you knew she'd include you, if you wanted. If you stuck around this town like she meant to, and let her rule it like she aimed to.

Jessica and Ashley flanked her down every hall and every parade—a girl like Sarah just naturally grows girls like Jessica and Ashley to be her adjutants, her bridesmaids, the baby's breath to make her rose look redder. All three of them knew the score and all three of them made sure nothing would ever change, like Macbeth's witches, if they wore daisy-print coats and their mothers' Chanel and tearproof mascara and only foretold their own love, continuing forever and the world moving aside to let it pass. So that was the obvious lineup—Queen Sarah and her Viziers. Of course there were three slots, so I figured Jenny Kilroy would slide in on account of her charitable work to keep us all in the shimmer.

The Best of Subterranean

And then Friday morning arrived, the dawn before the dance and a week before the showdown game with Bobby Zhao and his Cowboys. Coyote howled up 7 am and we woke up and opened our closets and there they hung—a hundred perfect dresses. Whatever we might have chosen after hours of turning on the rack of the mall with nothing in our size or our color or modest enough for daddy or bare enough for us, well, it was hanging in our closets with a corsage on the hip. Coyote took us all to Homecoming that year. And there in my room hung something that glittered and threw prisms on the wall, something the color of the ripest pumpkin you ever saw, something cut so low and slit so high it invited the world to love me best. I put it on and my head filled up with champagne like I'd already been sipping flutes for an hour, as if silk could make skin drunk. I slid the corsage on my wrist—cornflowers, and tiny green ears not yet open.

Coyote danced with all the girls and when the music sped up he threw back his head and howled and we all howled with him. When it slowed down he draped himself all over some lonesome thing who never thought she had a chance. The rest of us threw out our arms and danced with what our hands caught—Jessica spent half the night with mathletes kissing her neck and teaching her mnemonics. Everything was dizzy; everything spun. The music came from everywhere at once and the floor shook with our stomping. We were so strong that night, we were full of the year and no one drank the punch because no one needed it, we just moved with Coyote and Coyote moved, too. I flung out my arms and spun away from David Horowitz (pep squad, 100-meter dash), my corn-bound hand finding a new body to carry me into the next song. Guitar strings plinked in some other, distant world beyond the gymnasium and I opened my eyes to see Sarah Jane in my arms, her dress a perfect, icy white spill of froth and jewels, her eyes made up black and severe, to contrast, her lips a generous rose-colored smile. She smelled like musk and honeysuckle. She smelled like Coyote. I danced with her and she put her head on my breast; I felt her waist in my grasp, the slight weight of her, the chess queen, the queen of horses and jazz and grade point averages and pyramids and backflips, Juliet twice, thrice, a hundred times over. She ran her hand idly up and down my back just as if I were a boy. My vision blurred and the Christmas lights hanging everywhere swam into a soup of Devil red and Devil gold. The queen of the softball team lifted her sunny blonde head and kissed me. Her mouth tasted like cherry gum and whiskey. She put her hands in my hair to show me she meant it, and I pulled her in tight—but the song ended and she pulled away, looking surprised and confused, her lipstick dulled, her bright brown eyes wounded, like a deer with sudden shot in her side. She ran to Jessica and Ashley and the three of them to Coyote, hands over their stomachs as though something fluttered there, something as yet unknown and unnamed.

The principal got up to call out the Devil's Court. My man was shaken by all the heavy grinding and spinning and howling that had become the senior class, but he got out his index cards all the same. He adjusted his striped tie and tapped the mic, just like every principal has ever done. And he said a name. And it was mine. A roar picked up around me and hands were shoving me forward and I didn't understand, it was Sarah Jane, it would always be Sarah Jane. But I stood there while Mr. Whitmore, the football coach, put a crown on my head, and I looked out into the throng. Coyote stood there in his tuxedo, the bowtie all undone like a brief black river around his neck, and he winked at me with his flashing hound-eye, and the principal called three more names and they were Jessica and Ashley and Sarah Jane. They stood around me like three fates and Mr. Whitmore put little spangly tiaras on their heads and they looked at me like I had caught a pass in the end-zone, Hail Mary and three seconds left on the clock. I stared back and their tiaras were suddenly rings of wheat and appleblossoms and big, heavy oranges like suns, and I could see in their eyes mine wasn't rhinestones any more than it was ice cream. I lifted it down off my head and held it out like a thing alive: a crown of corn, not the Iowa yellow stuff but blue and black, primal corn from before the sun thought fit to rise, with tufts of silver fur sprouting from their tips, and all knotted together with crow feathers and marigolds.

And then it was pink rhinestones in my hands again, and blue zirconium on my Princesses' heads, and the Devil's Court took its place, and if you have to ask who was King, you haven't been listening.

After that, the game skipped by like a movie of itself. Bobby just couldn't keep that ball in his hands. You could see it on his face, how the ball had betrayed him, gone over to a bad boy with a leather jacket and no truck at all. You could see him re-sorting colleges in his head. It just about broke your heart. But we won 24-7, and Coyote led Bobby Zhao off the field with a *sorry-buddy* and a *one-game-don't-mean-a-thing*, and before I drove off to the afterparty I saw them under the bleachers, foreheads pressed together, each clutching at the other's skin like they wanted to climb inside, and they were beautiful like that, down there underneath the world, their helmets lying at their feet like old crowns.

᛭

Nothing could stop us then. The Westbrook Ravens, the Bella Vista Possums, the Ashland Gators. Line them up and watch them fall. It wasn't even a question.

I suppose we learned trig, or Melville, or earth science. I suppose we took exams. I suppose we had parents, too, but I'll be damned if any of that seemed to make the tiniest impression on any one of us that year. We lived in an unbreakable bubble where nothing mattered. We lived in a snowglobe, only the sun was always shining and we were always winning and yeah, you could get grounded for faceplanting your biology midterm or pulled over for speeding or worse for snorting whatever green fairy dust Coyote found for you, but nothing really *happened*. You came down to the lake like always the next night. After the Ravens game, Greg Knight (running back, #46) and Johnny Thompson (cornerback, #22) crashed their cars into each other after drinking half a sip of something Coyote whipped up in an acorn cap, yelling chicken out the window the whole time like it was 1950 and some girl would be waving her handkerchief at the finish line. But instead there was a squeal of engine humping up on engine and the dead crunch of the front ends smacking together and the long blare of Greg's face leaning on his horn.

But even then, they just got up and walked away, arm in arm and Coyote suddenly between them, *oh-my-godding* and *let's-do-that-againing*.

White Lines on a Green Field | Catherynne M. Valente

The next day their Camrys pulled up to the parking lot like it was no big deal. Nothing could touch us.

All eyes were on the Thunderbirds.

Now, the Thunderbirds didn't have a Bobby Zhao. No star player to come back and play celebrity alumnus in ten years with a Super Bowl ring on his finger. A Thunderbird was part of a machine, a part that could be swapped out for a hot new freshman no problem, no resentment. They moved as one, thought as one, they were a flock, always pointed in the same direction. That was how they'd won six state championships; that was how they'd sent three quarterbacks to the NFL in the last decade. There was no one to hate—just a single massive Thunderbird darkening our little sky.

Coyote's girls began to show by Christmas.

Sarah Jane, whatever the crown might have said at Homecoming, was queen of the unwed mothers, too. Her belly swelled just slightly bigger than the others—but then none of them got very big. None of them slowed down. Sarah Jane was turning a flip-into somersault off the pyramid in her sixth month with no trouble. They would all lay around the sidelines together painting their stomachs (Devil red and Devil gold) and trying on names for size. No point in getting angry; no point in fighting for position. The tribe was the tribe and the tribe was all of us and a tribe has to look after its young. The defensive line had a whole rotating system for bringing them chocolate milk in the middle of the night.

They were strong and tan and lean and I had even money on them all giving birth to puppies.

I didn't get pregnant. But then, I wouldn't. I told him, and he listened. Rabbit and Coyote, they do each other favors, when they can.

⋇

A plan hatched itself: steal their mascot. An old fashioned sort of thing, like playing chicken with cars. Coyote plays it old school. Into Springfield High in the middle of the night, out with Marmalade, a stuffed, motheaten African Grey parrot from some old biology teacher's collection that a bright soul had long ago decided could stand in for a Thunderbird.

The Best of Subterranean

We drove out to Springfield, two hours and change, me and Coyote and Jimmy Moser and Mike Halloran and Josh Vick and Sarah Jane and Jessica and Ashley, all crammed into my truck, front and back. Coyote put something with a beat on the radio and slugged back some off-brand crap that probably turned to Scotland's peaty finest when it hit his tongue. Jimmy was trying to talk Ashley into making out with him in the back while the night wind whipped through their hair and fireflies flashed by, even though it was January. Ashley didn't mind too much, even less when everyone wanted to touch her stomach and feel the baby move. She blushed like a primrose and even her belly button went pink.

Nobody's very quiet when sneaking into a gym. Your feet squeak on the basketball court and everyone giggles like a joke got told even when none did and we had Coyote's hissing *drink up drink up* and squeezing my hand like he can't hold the excitement in. We saw Marmalade center court on a parade float, all ready to ship over to the big designated-neutral-ground stadium for halftime. Big yellow and white crepe flowers drooped everywhere, around the shore of a bright blue construction paper sea. Marmalade's green wings spread out majestically, and in his talons he held a huge orange papier-mâché ball ringed with aluminum foil rays dipped in gold glitter. Thunderbird made this world, and Thunderbird gets to rule it.

Coyote got this look on his face and the moment I saw it I knew I wouldn't let him get there first. I took off running, my sneakers screeching, everyone hollering *Bunny!* after me and Coyote scrappling up behind me, closing the distance, racing to the sun. *I'm faster, I'm always faster. Sometimes he gets it and sometimes I get it but it's nothing we haven't done before and this time it's mine.*

And I leapt onto the float without disturbing the paper sea and reached up, straining, and finally just going for it. I'm a tall girl, see how high I jump. The sun came down in my arms, still warm from the gym lights and the after-hours HVAC. The Thunderbird came with it, all red cheeks and Crayola green wingspan and I looked down to see Coyote grinning up at me. He'd let me take it, if I wanted it. He'd let me wear it like a crown. But after a second of enjoying its weight, the deliciousness of its theft, I passed it down to him. It was his year. He'd earned it.

White Lines on a Green Field | Catherynne M. Valente

We drove home through the January stars with the sun in the bed of my truck and three pregnant girls touching it with one hand each, holding it down, holding it still, holding it together.

On game day we stabbed it with the Devil's pitchfork and paraded our float around the stadium like conquering heroes. Like cowboys. Marmalade looked vaguely sad. By then Coyote was cleaning off blood in the locker room, getting ready for the second half, shaken, no girls around him and no steroid needles blossoming up from his friendly palm like a bouquet of peonies.

The first half of the championship game hit us like a boulder falling from the sky. The Thunderbirds didn't play for flash, but for short, sharp gains and an inexorable progression toward the end-zone. They didn't cheer when they scored. They nodded to their coach and regrouped. They caught the flawless, seraphic passes Coyote fired off; they engulfed him when he tried to run as he'd always done. Our stands started out raucous and screaming and jumping up and down, cheering on our visibly pregnant cheerleading squad despite horrified protests from the Springfield side. *Don't you listen, Sarah Jane baby!* yelled Mr. Bollard. *You look perfect!* And she did, fists in the air, ponytail swinging.

Halftime stood 14-7 Thunderbirds.

I slipped into the locker room—by that time the place had become Devil central, girls and boys and players and cheerleaders and second chair marching band kids who weren't needed til post-game all piled in together. Some of them giving pep talks which I did not listen to, some of them bandaging knees, some of them—well. Doing what always needs doing when Coyote's around. Rome never saw a party like a Devil locker room.

I walked right over to my boy and the blood vanished from his face just as soon as he saw me.

"Don't you try to look pretty for me," I said.

"Aw, Bunny, but you always look so nice for me."

I sat in his lap. He tucked his fingers between my thighs—where I clamped them, safe and still. "What's going on out there?"

Coyote drank his water down. "Don't you worry, Bunny Rabbit. It has to go like this, or they won't feel like they really won. Ain't no good game since the first game that didn't look lost at half time. It's how the story goes. Can't hold a game without it. The old fire just won't come. If I just let that old Bird lose like it has to, well, everyone would get happy after, but they'd think it was pre-destined all along, no work went into it. You gotta make the story for them, so that when the game is done they'll just..." Coyote smiled and his teeth gleamed. "Well, they'll lose their minds I won it so good."

Coyote kissed me and bit my lip with those gleaming teeth. Blood came up and in our mouths it turned to fire. We drank it down and he ran out on that field, Devil red and Devil gold, and he ran like if he kept running he could escape the last thousand years. He ran like the field was his country. He ran like his bride was on the other end of all that grass and I guess she was. I guess we all were. Coyote gave the cherry to Justin Oster, who caught this pass that looked for all the world like the ball might have made it all the way to the Pacific if nobody stood in its way. But Justin did, and he caught it tight and perfect and the stadium shook with Devil pride.

34-14. Rings all around, as if they'd all married the state herself.

That night, we had a big bonfire down by the lake. Neutral ground was barely 45 minutes out of town, and no one got home tired and ready to sleep a good night and rise to a work ethic in the morning.

I remember we used to say *down-by-the-lake* like it was a city, like it was an address. I guess it was, the way all those cars would gather like crows, pick-ups and Camaros and Jeeps, noses pointing in, a metal wall against the world. The willows snapped their green whips at the moon and the flames licked up Devil red and Devil gold. We built the night without thinking about it, without telling anyone it was going to happen, without making plans. Everyone knew to be there; no one was late.

Get any group of high school kids together and you pretty much have the building blocks of civilization. The Eagle Scout boys made an architecturally perfect bonfire. 4-H-ers threw in grub, chips and burgers and dogs and Twix and Starburst. The drama kids came bearing tunes, their tooth-white iPods stuffed into speaker cradles like black mouths. The rich kids brought booze from a dozen walnut cabinets—and Coyote taught them how to spot the good stuff. Meat and fire and music and liquor—that's all it's ever been. Sarah Jane started dancing up to the flames with a bottle of 100 year old cognac in her hand, holding by the neck, moving her hips, her gorgeously round belly, her long corn-colored hair brushing faces as she spun by, the smell of her expensive and hot. Jessica and Ashley ran up to her and the three of them swayed and sang and stamped, their arms slung low around each other, their heads pressed together like three graces. Sarah Jane poured her daddy's cognac over Ashley's breasts and caught the golden stuff spilling off in her sparkly pink mouth and Ashley laughed so high and sweet and that was *it*—everyone started dancing and howling and jumping and Coyote was there in the middle of it all, arching his back and keeping the beat, slapping his big thighs, throwing the game ball from boy to girl to boy to girl, like it was magic, like it was just ours, the sun of our world arcing from hand to hand to hand.

I caught it and Coyote kissed me. I threw it to Haley Collins from English class and Nick Dristol (left tackle, #19) caught me up in his arms. I don't even know what song was playing. The night was so loud in my ears. I could see it happening and it scared me but I couldn't stop it and didn't want to. Everything was falling apart and coming together and we'd won the game, Bunny no less than Coyote, and boyfriend never fooled me for a minute, never could.

I could hear Sarah Jane laughing and I saw Jessica kissing her and Greg Knight both, one to the other like she was counting the kisses to make it all fair. She tipped up that caramel-colored bottle and Nick started to say something but I shushed him. *Coyote's cognac's never gonna hurt that baby.* Every tailgate hung open, no bottle ever seemed to empty and even though it was January the air was so warm, the crisp red and yellow leaves drifting over us all, no one sorry, no one ashamed, no one chess club or physics club or cheer squad or baseball team, just tangled up together inside our barricade of cars.

Sarah danced up to me and took a swallow without taking her eyes from mine. She grabbed me roughly by the neck and into a kiss, passing the cognac to me and oh, it tasted like a pass thrown all the way to the sea, and she wrapped me up in her arms like she was trying to make up Homecoming to me, to say: *I'm better now, I'm braver now, doesn't this feel like the end of everything and we have to get it while we can?* I could feel her stomach pressing on mine, big and insistent and hard, and as she ripped my shirt open I felt her child move inside her. We broke and her breasts shone naked in the bonfire-light—mine too, I suppose. Between us a cornstalk grew fast and sure, shooting up out of the ground like it had an appointment with the sky, then a second and a third. That same old blue corn, midnight corn, first corn. All around the fire the earth was bellowing out pumpkins and blackberries and state fair tomatoes and big blousy squash flowers, wheat and watermelons and apple trees already broken with the weight of fruit. The dead winter trees exploded into green, the graduating class fell into the rows of vegetables and fruit and thrashed together like wolves, like bears, like devils. Fireflies turned the air into an emerald necklace and Sarah Jane grabbed Coyote's hand which was a paw which was a hand and screamed. Didn't matter—everyone was screaming, and the music quivered the darkness and Sarah's baby beat at the drum of her belly, demanding to be let out into the pumpkins and the blue, blue corn, demanding to meets its daddy.

All the girls screamed. Even the ones only a month or two gone, clutching their stomachs and crying, all of them except me, Bunny Rabbit, the watcher, the queen of coming home. The melons split open in an eruption of pale green and pink pulp; the squashes cracked so loud I put my hands (which were paws which were hands) over my ears, and the babies came like harvest, like forty-five souls running after a bright ball in the sky.

Some of us, after a long night of vodka tonics and retro music and pretending there was anything else to talk about, huddle together around a table at the 10 year and get into it. How Mr. Bollard was never the same and ended up hanging himself in a hotel room after almost a decade of straight losses. How they all dragged themselves home and suddenly had parents again, the furious kind, and failed SATs and livers like punching bags. How no one went down to the lake anymore and Bobby Zhao went to college out of state and isn't he on some team out east now? Yeah. Yeah. But his father lost the restaurants and now the southland has no king. But the gym ceiling caved in after the rains and killed a kid. But most of them could just never understand why their essays used to just be perfect and they never had hangovers and they looked amazing all the time and sex was so easy that year but never since, no matter how much shit went up their nose or how they cheated and fought and drank because they didn't mean it like they had back when, no matter how many people they brought home hoping just for a second it would be like it was then, when Coyote made their world. They had this feeling, just for a minute—didn't I feel it too? That everything could be different. And then it was the same forever, the corn stayed yellow and they stayed a bunch of white kids with scars where their cars crashed and fists struck and babies were born. The lake went dry and the scoreboard went dark.

Coyote leaves a hole when he goes. He danced on this town til it broke. That's the trick, and everyone falls for it.

But they all had kids, didn't they? Are they remembering that wrong? What happened to them all?

Memory is funny—only Sarah Jane (real estate, Rotary, Wednesday night book club) can really remember her baby. Everyone just remembers the corn and the feeling of running, running so fast, the whole pack of us, against the rural Devil gold sunset. I call that a kindness. (*Why me?* Sarah asks her gin. *You were the queen,* I say. *That was you. Only for a minute.*) It was good, wasn't it, they all want to say. When we were all together. When we were a country, and Coyote taught us how to grow such strange things.

Why did I stick around, they all want to know. When he took off, why didn't I go, too? Weren't we two of a kind? Weren't we always conspiring?

Coyote wins the big game, I say. I get the afterparty.

This is what I don't tell them.

I woke up before anyone the morning after the championships. Everyone had passed out where they stood, laying everywhere like a bomb had gone off. No corn, no pumpkins, no watermelons. Just that cold lake morning fog. I woke up because my pick-up's engine fired off in the gloam, and I know that sound like my mama's crying. I jogged over to my car but it was already going, bouncing slowly down the dirt road with nobody driving. In the back, Coyote sat laughing, surrounded by kids, maybe eight or ten years old, all of them looking just like him, all of them in leather jackets and hangdog grins, their black hair blowing back in the breeze. Coyote looked at me and raised a hand. See you again. After all, it's nothing we haven't done before.

Coyote handed a football to one of his daughters. She lifted it into the air, her form perfect, trying out her new strength. She didn't throw it. She held it tight, like it was her heart.

The Least of the Deathly Arts

BY KAT HOWARD

Once the doors to the Library of Ghosts closed, they opened for no one in the City of Nyx, not even Death himself. Certainly not for someone as unimportant as a Shadow Scholar late for a lecture on memorial architecture. Ghosts, who had acquired an eternity of time upon their death, had not acquired a commensurate amount of patience, and were insistent upon punctuality. Noir glanced at the length of the afternoon shadows, and walked faster.

"A poem, Scholar? A poem for your death? A villanelle or sestina of eternal beauty, Scholar? Perhaps the variety of a limerick? Very popular with the fashionable this season, limericks. Or I could recite the newest offering from Death himself, Scholar. He's gone back to sonnets, he has. Nothing like a sonnet for a truly elegant death, that's what I say."

Noir attempted to continue past the street poet, but he had entangled his hand in the fabric wrapping her arm. She had only recently acquired the cerements, hand-woven silk that shifted between red and black in color, never quite settling on a shade. She endured the poet's touch for the sake of preserving the delicate garment. Misinterpreting Noir's stillness, the poet began to demonstrate his extemporaneous ability with lame-footed iambic meter. "Oh Death! Thy touch! All lives it endeth, alas!"

"I require no poem, as I do not anticipate my death any time soon. Yours," Noir's smile was all teeth and keen edges, "I could arrange, if you persist in your inane versifying."

The poet choked on his broken syllables, and clumsily bowed, then skittered away from the trailing edges of Noir's grave garments. "Of course, Scholar, of course. What need is there for verse when I am in the presence of one whose beauty, wisdom, and grace embody all of poetry's best qualities? Instead, I offer you the tribute of my silence."

Noir wished that Death would find a preoccupation other than poetry. The city was so much more bearable when his enthusiasms tended towards funeral baked goods or new fashions in mementos mori. Unfortunately, this season, Death was again interested in poetry. His fascination with the subject meant that all the fashionable of Nyx were preoccupied with verse as well. At least Death had talent in the area. Most of his imitators did not.

Yet even when Death wrote it, Noir misliked poetry. It was mutable, and given to interpretation. Without certainty, words had no power. Fashionable as it might be, she considered poetry the least of the deathly arts.

Noir stood outside of the locked doors of the Library, the inconvenience of unscheduled time stretching out before her. She had, of course, been late to the lecture, and now needed to find some way to salvage the wasted day.

Smoke plumed across the sky over Nyx's northern shore. A Viking funeral. Noir loved watching the flaming ships sail into the horizon, but she had no grave goods to offer as tribute. On another day she might search for something, a bracelet or a bottle of wine, so that she could pay her respects to whatever stranger was making a last farewell, but with the smoke already visible from the library steps, the ship would be consumed before she could get there. One more thing she would arrive too late for.

The Library of Ghosts was close upon the eastern quarter of the city. She could join a funeral parade there, hear the nuances of loss wailed by mourners in their robes of various blues, and breathe the chrysanthemum incense scenting their grief, but she was wearing red. Appearing at a funeral in the guise of a vengeful ghost would be unforgivably rude.

The Least of the Deathly Arts | KAT HOWARD

Perhaps, Noir thought, she would sit under a yew tree along the Via Aeterna, and contemplate her own funeral. Not all Shadow Scholars chose death as the culmination of their studies, but Noir had very nearly decided to do so. Death, she felt, would be the appropriate expression of her dedication to her chosen field.

Lost in the pleasures of academic speculation, Noir stumbled on the steps of the Library, nearly falling. A black-gloved hand caught her. The glove lingered on her arm, fingers smoothing the fabric she wore. The cerements slid against her skin like gossamer and night-whispers.

"Such an intriguing choice." The fabric bled black to red in his grasp. Noir turned toward the voice, breathed the resinous scent of myrrh. Her rescuer wore the severe lines of formal mourning, cravat set off by a jet memento mori, face shadowed by a top hat.

Her finger brushed the cool, smooth skin where his glove fastened, unhooking the button that held it closed. She swayed toward him, as if entering the opening measure of a dance. His hand lingering on the fabric Noir had draped herself in, he murmured, " 'Red for death or red for desire?' "

Noir stepped back, and twitched her sleeve into place. "I have had quite enough of poetry today, sir."

The man offered a brief bow. "My apologies." As he stood, he met her eyes. His were an infinity of grey smoke, and, for a moment, she saw in them all her futures. In that moment, Noir knew what she had done.

The man she had just admonished was Death.

Mortified at her rudeness, Noir sank into a curtsey, the delicate fabric she wore beginning to unravel as she bent.

"I wish that you would not." The gloved hand slid up her arm to steady her. She felt as if she were falling.

"Did you come for the lecture on monumental architecture as well?" Death asked.

"I did. But I was delayed, and the ghosts had locked the doors."

"Delayed?"

"By a poet, my lord Death. Who wished to recite for me one of your sonnets."

Death's laughter sent a flock of ravens winging across the sky. "It seems I owe you some recompense. Please, how may I make amends?"

"You are said to have a collection of reliquaries unsurpassed in all the city." Reliquaries were Noir's favorite form of memorial art. She loved how they captured transience, the threshold of decay, and placed it in a frame of incorruptible beauty. "If I might see them sometime, I would be very grateful."

"You might see them now, if you wish. I promise to inflict no more of my poetry on you." He smiled, placed his gloved hand in the small of her back, and led her down the stairs.

⋇

Death's collection of reliquaries was, as Noir anticipated, extraordinary. Silver-plated bones, jewel-encrusted fragments of saints, elegantly stylized bits of holiness balancing the fleeting against the eternal. Moved by the beauty of the Chasse of Champagnat, Noir begged a pen and sketchbook. Yet with the sketch half-finished, she set down the pen. "It will be more beautiful in my memory."

"Even though memories fade?"

"Because they do."

Death requested her company at dinner. Noir accepted.

Death poured wine from a bottle of tarnished silver. Noir could not say whether the liquid was blood red, or the pale luminescence of tears.

"Funeral wine," he said as he poured, "takes its flavor from the memories and longing of each person who drinks it."

They drank. "What do you taste?" she asked.

"Love's delight. The swift decay of grace. And you?"

Drunk on the honey and bitterness mixing on her tongue, Noir closed her eyes.

"It tastes," she said, "like dying."

⋇

The Least of the Deathly Arts | KAT HOWARD

Noir woke the next morning feeling as if she had taken one step sideways from herself. It was, she thought, the aftereffects of the funeral wine. Not that she regretted the indulgence, but she was grateful the Dead Days marking the turn of the year meant there were no classes in session.

The Dead Days opened with a living *danse macabre*. The Shadow Scholars of the Memorium costumed themselves as various aspects of Death, and lead the citizens of Nyx in a celebration of mortality.

Dressed as the Lady Death of a favorite story, Noir danced. Over cobbled stone and paved brick. She whirled with pope, empress, beggar, thief. She waltzed with a mercenary, and stepped a quadrille with a child. She danced until the seams of her gloves frayed from contact with so many hands.

Then a gloved hand covered her own, and Red Death pulled her into his arms. Noir breathed in myrrh, graveyard dust, and the smoke of a pyre. Not one of her fellow students, but Death himself, dancing with the people of his city. For the first time since she had parted from him, Noir's head cleared, and her heart steadied.

Perhaps, she thought, her odd feeling that morning had not been a consequence of an excess of funeral wine but something altogether more common. And mortal.

⇥⇤

The next day, with the steps of the *danse macabre* still lingering in her feet, Noir climbed the steps to the laboratories. She intended to check the results of her ongoing research into exsanguination. She was shocked to discover that she was not to be allowed inside the building.

The porter was quite apologetic. "You know the freshly dead aren't allowed in, Scholar. The energies from the transition bugger up the equipment, begging your pardon for the language." He shuffled in place and adjusted his jacket. "If you intend to remain resident in the Memorium, I can have your personal effects sent to you there."

"I beg your pardon, porter. But I am demonstrably corporeal, and thus, unlikely to be dead." Noir was tired, and out of sorts, but she had been studying death for years. She felt certain she would have noticed if she had died.

"That's as may be, Scholar. But you haven't a reflection, and are thus," he rolled the word around in his mouth as if savoring the taste, "also unlikely to be alive." The porter gestured at the ornate mirror in front of him, which quite clearly showed a paunchy man with tufted ginger hair in an ill-tailored uniform, and just as clearly did not show a lean and black-haired Shadow Scholar clad in silken cerements.

Noir carefully considered her lack of reflection. It was an intriguing development, if perhaps not the intellectual puzzle she had planned on unraveling that morning. She left for the archive, where the questionable state of her mortality would not prevent her entry.

Noir was cursing the plodding prose of the *Historia rerum Anglicarum*—William of Newburgh was one of the earliest references on *revenirs*, and thus the logical starting place for researching her current condition, but the man could make anything boring—when a section of parchment slid loose from the binding. Noir moved to set it aside when a phrase caught her eye. She read further and then, careless of its antiquity, shoved the *Historia* to the side of the table.

It was a poem. Part of one, anyway. The final stanzas were miss-ing. What remained was hand-written, the parchment covered over in splotched ink and crossed-through words.

Noir hadn't particularly enjoyed her course in Poetry as Deathly Art, but she had paid attention in it. The reason poetry was taught at the Memorium, the reason it was an eternal craze where funereal cus-toms flickered in and out of fashion like candle flames, dated back to one literary effort.

Death's lost sestina.

One of his earliest works, uncollected, and rumored to be more than simply lines of verse. The lost sestina's fascination for Shadow Scholars—for anyone—was the attendant rumor that this had been an instance where words altered the possible.

Death's power had created a ritual out of a poem, or so the speculation went, and if the conditions in the sestina were met, then a third state would be possible. Neither alive nor dead, an interstitial existence, bound eternally to Death.

The Least of the Deathly Arts | KAT HOWARD

Scholars called such a thing fascinating. Others longed for the romance of it.

Noir reread the page:

> *"What hope then for me, lonely restless Death?*
> *To wait and pray that one might risk my touch*
> *And stand too close and merely breathe, 'My love,'*
> *Then move with me in ageless steps. Our dance,*
> *A waltz of longing. Two who meet in dream*
> *Then waking, part. A memory of grace."*

A touch. Noir remembered an unbuttoned glove, and the feel of Death's hand under her fingers as she stood on the steps of the Library of Ghosts.

She had given away, all unknown, a part of her life. She did not know—even if such a recovery were possible—if she wanted it back.

-)|(‐

Noir returned to an approximation of life at the Memorium. As she could no longer enter the laboratory, she abandoned her experimental studies, and chose to fill her days with archival research. She catalogued all of the extant Hibernian epitaphs, and, wanting to better understand the art that had caused her difficulty, began a study of memorial poetry.

She felt herself gradually falling away from what she had been. She dressed in nothing but cerements, and when her heart chose to beat, it pulsed in the rhythm of a half-remembered dance.

She would occasionally see Death walking the streets of Nyx. His nearness pulled her, sending the blood running through her veins, and she would recite lists of funeral arcana like orisons, the words crumbling incantations against her longing. Noir had decided not to speak to him until she knew what she wanted. His presence, and the illusion of life it gave her, was false comfort, and she refused to allow herself to indulge.

Noir grew paler and more ghost-like, but the ghosts, puzzled by the clinging stench of mortality, avoided her. She considered transitioning to full death, but found that she was reluctant to unweave the last threads of her life.

Noir no longer passed the time by imagining her funeral rites.

✳

Noir felt her heart begin to beat while watching a bokor lead a jazz funeral down the Via Aeterna. The dancers, twirling scarves and parasols blocked the street, and so Noir stood motionless but for the pulse flickering in her throat as Death came up beside her.

"You have been avoiding me."

"Yes." Noir unwound the string of her folio, and took out the sestina. "I found something of yours. It explains, I believe, how I came to lose something of mine."

Noir watched reanimated skeletons caper around the coffin as Death read.

He placed a gloved hand on her shoulder. "It seems I have inflicted my poetry on you after all. I am sorry. The verse was never intended to do anything."

"Forgive me, but I cannot believe that. If you had never intended the words to do anything, you would have left them unwritten."

The silence stretched between them. "You are correct, of course."

"Can you rewrite the ending?"

"I wrote it hundreds of years ago. I could try, but it is unlikely to be identical."

"Good. If you rewrite it, alter it carefully, I believe the change to the text may be sufficient to give me back the missing piece of my life."

"A Shadow Scholar who does not long to embrace death?"

"I was planning my funeral when we met. I may well choose death as the completion of my education. But it will be my choice. Not an accident of verse."

Death inclined his head. "I will send you a copy of the poem when it is finished."

> ⸕

When the envelope arrived, Noir closed her eyes against it. Had she been correct, had rewriting the poem been enough, she would not have needed a slim envelope to tell her it was finished. The beat of her heart would have done more than mark the hours. She would have been able to weep for what she had lost.

She nearly cast the poem aside unread, but then slid a thin blade beneath the envelope's red wax seal. He had tried. She would read his words.

> *"Before we part, I beg another dance*
> *To hold as memory of sweetest dream.*
> *A dream I now must let die its death.*
> *A final act, or nearly so, of love.*
> *So that I might remember you in grace*
> *Until the last, eternal, time we touch.*
>
> *Now caught in dream, we whirl in spinning dance.*
> *I ache with love for your transcendent grace,*
> *And I would give my death for one more touch."*

Her pulse beat in time with the meter as she read, and then continued even after she finished.

Incense heavy smoke rose outside of her window. Flame consumed an elaborately constructed house of paper: a Shadow Scholar's funeral. Memorium tradition called for any of the other Shadow Scholars in attendance to mark the occasion by burning something symbolic of their own course of study.

Noir leaned out of her window, and dropped the letter from Death. The paper caught, flamed, and disappeared into smoke.

The Best of Subterranean

"A poem, Scholar," she whispered. "A poem for your death."

[The full text of Death's lost sestina follows.]

A wish. Alone in darkness, seeking touch,
A hand to hold, of which to beg a dance.
This wish, merely momentary, for grace,
For one who might—oh, briefly—pause and dream
Of me. Of my desire for one to love.
But who would love when loving leads to death?

What hope then for me, lonely restless Death?
To wait and pray that one might risk my touch
And stand too close and merely breathe, "My love,"
Then move with me in ageless steps. Our dance,
A waltz of longing. Two who meet in dream
Then waking, part. A memory of grace.

My dearest one, you move with darkling grace.
And I hold you between desire and death—
An instant's pause. I close my eyes and dream
Of you. I'll wait until our hands may touch
Eternally. And then, oh then, will dance
With you beneath the turning stars, my love.

And shall I dare to speak to you of love?
Might I begin to hope for such a grace?
To partner you in evanescent dance—
Your breath, and beat of heart, held close to death—
So I might memorize your every touch
Of hand to mine in this most wondrous dream.

The Least of the Deathly Arts | KAT HOWARD

Bereft of you, I live in endless dream,
Still wishing I could offer you my love,
Exchange my heart for yours with but a touch
And pledge myself to you in honest grace.
All joys that I will never know. Sad Death
Forever cursed to end, alone, his dance.

Before we part, I beg another dance
To hold as memory of sweetest dream.
A dream I now must let die its death.
A final act, or nearly so, of love.
So that I might remember you in grace
Until the last, eternal, time we touch.

Now caught in dream, we whirl in spinning dance.
I ache with love for your transcendent grace,
And I would give my death for one more touch.

Water Can't be Nervous

BY JONATHAN CARROLL

A t dinner that night he told her of his discovery. "I went on a secret mission today."

Her eyes lit up and she nodded for him to continue because she loved his stories. She loved the way he *told* his stories.

"You know that apartment down on the third floor? The one they've been renovating forever?"

"Yes! We just talked about that last week, remember?"

"Well, I finally got the scoop on it. I noticed around noon every day that the workers leave for about half an hour for their lunch break. Most of the time they leave the door open, I guess to air it out. So I went down to investigate. I wanted to see what the hell they've been *doing* in there all this time."

She smiled. Her boyfriend was always doing crazy stuff like this—going into places where he shouldn't. Or asking total strangers embarrassing questions, taking chances that by all rights should have gotten him into a lot more trouble than it did. But even when he got caught most of the time he had the ability to charm his way out of most dicey situations. The guy was a scamp but a funny and delightful one when he needed to be. She wanted to hear this story at least partly because she was hoping he *had* been caught. She wanted to hear how he wiggled his way out of the soup this time.

"No one was down there when I went in, so I had a good fifteen minutes alone to explore the place."

"And then they came back? What did you say? What happened?"

He loved her enthusiasm for his stories but disliked the way she always tried to push him fast forward to the conclusion. As if he should skip the joke altogether and cut straight to the punch line. "Wait! Let me tell the story." He put out a hand palm-down and patted the air slowly, as if patting her on the top of the head to calm down and be patient.

She loved most of him but disliked the way he talked to her sometimes—as if she were nine years old.

"You know all the weeks they've been working? Well, it's *empty* down there—totally empty. You'd think that after all this time the apartment would be ready to go, but it isn't. Not one piece of furniture is in there—not a single piece. The place itself has been finished beautifully. A lot of money was spent on the details—parquet floors, limestone countertops, a kitchen with all these jazzy appliances. It looks like something on a space ship. Someone spent a ton of money, but the place itself is as empty as an ice skating rink in summer."

She didn't really hear the last part of what he said because she was envisioning and marveling at the idea of caramel colored parquet wooden floors and limestone countertops. She wanted an apartment like that! She often daydreamed about having an apartment or house with features like that to grace it. Bay windows with cushioned seats and a view of a beautiful countryside landscape—or the sea! The view from this apartment was onto a dingy busy street where car alarms went off endlessly and drunks sang at midnight. Sometimes at night when she couldn't sleep, she stood by the window and looked down on the street. She tried to pretend this apartment was somewhere else, somewhere romantic and exotic like Rome or Aix en Provence. That way at least it would be a dingy street in Rome and the voices down there would be speaking Italian and not saying things like "Fuck dat mothuhfuckuh."

"Tell me what else is down there."

"I just told you—nothing. The place is empty."

Her voice jumped up to impatient. "I don't *mean* that—I mean how else have they fixed the place up? Tell me some more of the details."

Now he wanted to go on with the story—he didn't want to stop and talk about appliances or what color doorknobs the place had. "It's nice, it looks rich—I told you. Someone's spending big money to fix it up. Anyway, about fifteen minutes after I got there, one of the workmen came back from lunch. He wasn't surprised to see me, or at least didn't act like it. He just kind of smiled and waited for me to say something. You know—tell him why I was there."

She didn't say anything; not a word to encourage him to continue the story. He looked at her closely and saw her irritation. Why? What had he done? Then he remembered and the thought irritated *him*. She could be so damned *persistent* when she wanted something. Closing his eyes he took a deep breath then let it out loudly and dramatically. "What more can I tell you about what's inside the place? The floors were beautifully finished. The kitchen looks like a starship. Oh yeah, the bathroom has both a huge shower *and* bathtub in it. You'd love it."

"And the bedroom? What does the bedroom look like?"

"I didn't see it. I was about to go look when the guy appeared."

"Go on."

***

He didn't like the next part of the story so he pulled the puppets off his hands, put them gently on the kitchen table, and stepped over to the window. Pushing the brown curtain aside, he looked down on the evening street and saw what he had seen a thousand times before—traffic, parked cars, and people passing by. It was just as the girlfriend had thought—he lived on a busy uninteresting street not in Rome or any other larger-than-life city.

Nothing about him or his days was larger than life; except perhaps the puppets. His girlfriend had given them to him before she left; a farewell gift that once again showed her kindness and good memory. Very early in their relationship he had told her that as a child his favorite thing to do was put on puppet shows for his family. Hand puppets of course, not marionettes. He had never understood the attraction of marionettes—they moved so unnaturally and were never convincing when you saw them perform. But a hand puppet moved and glided in a way that could really convince you to suspend your disbelief and accept the illusion that the figure was alive.

"I know you don't like being alone, so if you ever feel blue these two'll keep you company until you find someone new." She said it sweetly, no malice at all in her voice. But the words stung even before he saw what her gift was. She handed him a wrapped box and then left for the last time.

Inside were two hand puppets. But they were not especially nice or unusual. They were the kind of puppets you'd buy as a last minute gift or an afterthought at a toy store, fully expecting the child who received it to lose interest in a few days. A man and a woman, both had rubber heads that smelled strongly of some weird chemical. You could imagine these puppet heads being produced by the thousands per hour in some dubious Bangladeshi or Albanian factory.

The woman wore a white blouse and blue skirt. The man had on a suit jacket, white shirt and red tie. Looking at them for the first time, squinting really, at the two cheap puppets pressed together face to face in the box, he wondered what kind of final message she was trying to send by giving him these things as her adios present. Was she saying 'you're still a child who needs toys? Why don't you finally *grow up* for God's sake?' Or—'get used to these pathetic things because they'll be your only company for a while, Buster.' However his ex girlfriend was neither a mean nor vindictive woman so he assumed there was really no ill intent in her gift although it would be easy to read it that way.

Because there was nothing else to do, he took them out of the box and slid them onto his hands. When was the last time he'd played with *puppets?* When he could count his age on less than ten fingers and the world looked a lot rosier than it did that day.

Wiggling his left hand and then his right, he said in a low campy voice, "Hello, Dear. What's for dinner?"

And then answered in a high falsetto, "Your favorite—London broil and scalloped potatoes."

Without warning the breath caught in his throat. He knew if he didn't hold still, he would cry. So he put the puppets back in their box and slid the top on. In the next days this box was moved around the kitchen as he prepared his single-now meals. A week or so later he opened it again and looked inside. The first time he had seen the puppets they were nose to nose. Now they were facing in opposite directions, as if they'd had an argument and were sulking. He thought that's how they should have first been posed when she gave him the present. Symbolic of the way their relationship had ended up.

Lifting the female out, he brought it up close to his face and said without thinking, "I miss you." He had a moment's fantasy where the puppet either smiled, or dropped its clumsily painted eyes in embarrassment the way his girlfriend (ex-girlfriend) always did when he paid her a compliment. He sighed when the puppet's blank expression stayed the same.

⋇

Later he honestly couldn't remember how the scenarios had begun. It was as simple as one day when he was bored or sad or distraught he put on the puppets because there was nothing else to do. He held them up and made them talk to each other. In the beginning he felt stupid doing it, but then something clicked in his head. A moment later the male puppet was saying *his* words and the female, his girlfriend's words. From memory he was repeating the dialog of one of the last fights they'd had before she left for good.

"Do you ever listen to me? I mean, do you ever *really* listen?"

"Yes, when you say something that makes sense." He remembered the look on her face when he said that to her: startled, her expression said she couldn't believe he let that slip out.

"Do you really think that? Do you think I talk crap to you all the time? Please tell me the truth; I want to know."

When he didn't know what to say, a new expression grew on her face that was a toxic mixture of 'It *is*, isn't it? That's exactly what you think,' contempt, anger, and finally dislike.

He remembered the moment because it felt like he'd been punched in the stomach. Seeing that awful look on her beautiful face, he could literally feel his spirit doubling over from remorse and knowing for sure what was coming now.

"How long have you felt this way?" the female puppet brought her short arms together again and again as if clapping to get his full attention.

The little man on his left hand turned away from her just like he had done that night when she asked that question. "I don't know; for a while."

"*For a while?* And you didn't tell me?"

In situations like this there is almost always at least one moment of absolute annihilating clarity: A moment when you see things, people, or a situation so clearly that afterward there can be no doubt of the truth. But as significant as the epiphany can be, even more important is what we choose to do with the knowledge once we have it. Acceptance is logical but denial is so much easier and more comfortable.

He turned the man puppet to face him and addressed it sternly. "You *ass*; you stupid ass. Why did you say that? What was the point?" He made the puppet nod. "All you had to do was listen; all you had to do was *pretend* to listen. But no, you had to tell her exactly how you felt and hurt her so much. Thanks, *Mr. Honesty*." The puppet nodded again, this time slowly, shamed.

He put it down on the table and questioned the woman on his other hand. "But what could I have done? By that time was there anything I could have done to fix things, or save us?"

If the puppet could have shrugged, it would. "Probably not, but by then you didn't *want* to save us." He pretended it really was his girlfriend and not a cheap rubber doll head perched on his three fingers talking about the end of their relationship.

That was the first time he made the puppets reenact scenes from his life. At first doing it felt odd but also unexpectedly cathartic. Somehow having them repeat exchanges and then adding his own postscript/coda at the end allowed him to stand apart from the different scenes and gain some surprisingly new perspective.

The next week he left them on a counter in the kitchen. Every now and then he would pick them up and sometimes recreate another scene from recent memory. Or he'd have one puppet do a monologue, usually a repeat of something that had really happened in the now-gone life with his ex: The episode of the failed birthday present. The discussion about getting a cat that turned into the very heated discussion about whether they were going to stay together or not. He even replayed the memorable conversation they'd had that night after making love when both of them cried and at the end of the talk everything seemed to be all right again.

The only thing that changed was his voice. No matter which puppet he used, he always spoke in his regular voice. After the first time he created that silly high falsetto for the woman, he stopped that and had both puppets speak in his own voice. Besides, his girlfriend had a nice almost-deep one that didn't sound anything like the falsetto he'd given her that first time.

One night she called to ask how he was doing. That was just like her—even when their relationship was over she worried about him. They chatted for a few minutes. He really wanted to say how much he liked her parting gift and how it was helping him through this tough time without her. But as he was about to do that, he realized it might sound strange or pathetic to say he played with her puppets all the time now, although it was true. More and more he enjoyed performing what he thought of as 'scenarios' where he reenacted significant moments from their past. One night when he couldn't sleep, he even sat silently on the couch in the living room at three in the morning wearing the puppets on his hands. They kept him company until he went back to bed.

How would she respond to hearing something like that? How would *he* have responded if their roles were reversed? Not well. Better to keep quiet about the whole thing. At the end of this conversation out of the blue he asked the name of her favorite childhood dog. Flummoxed by the question, she told him and then asked why he wanted to know *that*. He said he'd been trying to remember the name for days and it was driving him crazy.

As the scenarios became longer and more detailed, he found himself throughout the day writing down specific words or even whole lines of dialog that he wanted to remember to include.

One Saturday while eating a tuna melt sandwich and staring out the kitchen window he realized memory is not a stable friend. Too often it lies, distorts, or frequently forgets many things both important and trivial. Memory steals parts of your life that should have belonged to you forever. It's like entrusting the only complete copy of your history to an erratic, frequently scatterbrained, sometimes irascible person who doesn't always do their job well and can't be bothered keeping the records straight. Unlike you, they don't care what the name of that wonderful French restaurant in Amsterdam was or the name of your high school enemy's sister.

In trying to remember the details of the time he'd shared with his lovely girlfriend, it·was both disturbing and disheartening how much he couldn't recall beyond a certain point. What had they done on their first date? What was that funny thing she'd said after they slept together the first time? What was the name of the childhood dog she loved so much and was always telling stories about?

One of his colleagues used the phrase "convenient history" to describe the way people remember their lives or specific events. Facts are superfluous; most people live in self-created convenient histories made up of unreliable memories—some true, some distorted, some altogether false. They do this either for peace of mind, or to keep a kind of daily balance, even sometimes to maintain sanity.

Were his puppet scenarios true reenactments of what had happened, or just imprecise convenient histories he conjured to assuage the pain of losing her?

The story of the unfinished apartment downstairs was a good example of this. So far as he'd gotten was true: An empty apartment in their building had been under construction for months. One day he went down to investigate and later told her what he'd discovered about it. She'd wanted to know specific details about the place. But he brushed her questions off as unimportant. Too late he realized he'd insulted her again by not listening; not giving importance to what mattered to her.

He had seen it coming for a long time but of course didn't want to admit it to himself. No one wants to lose a good thing. No, it wasn't good—it was great. There were many aspects of their relationship that were just absolutely great and he knew it. Worse, he knew that despite his many "issues" she loved him completely. She told him he was *her guy* and was determined to make it work. How did she do it? How could she so blithely overlook/swallow/accept…his weaknesses, foibles, Cinerama ego and long brooding silences that he knew drove her crazy? They'd talked about this and she always repeated a version of the same thing: because she loved him, that's all. When you love someone you make compromises or concessions; sometimes you eat crow, or sit on your hands when what you really want to do is punch boyfriend in the nose. Sometimes you either keep your mouth shut or breathe through your mouth when their behavior smells like skunk. That's just the way it is—the rules of the love game. All in all you do your absolute best to *blend* with them, like cream in coffee. Because the benefits way outweigh the drawbacks. Didn't he feel the same way? He always lied and said yes but his heart shook its head no!

Sadly it had always turned out like this for him. All new relationships started out great. Full speed ahead, bouquets and kisses and days full of yes yes yes. But inexorably the yes's got quieter, then fewer, and then the No's began moving into the neighborhood and drove property values way down. Predictably after a while he began noticing things he didn't like about the women that he'd either overlooked or ignored in the wonderful first days. As soon as that happened he knew no matter what he did or how hard he worked to keep a love affair going, it was doomed.

Then it was just a matter of time. That was sad because he really liked every one of these women and honestly wanted so much for his relationships with them to work. Just once in all these thousands of years he wanted to know what it was like to love a person completely for a whole lifetime. Love them the way he'd heard about and seen for himself and read ten thousand books glorifying it. The real deal—100% lifetime love that over the course of years changes color like a chameleon but never ever goes away. But it never happened to him and he knew in his secret heart it never would.

Even when he knew a relationship was finished he'd stretch out the end as long as possible, hoping that one time—just once—out of nowhere a spark would rekindle in his dead heart and all of his initial feelings for the woman would be reborn. He'd feel a rebirth of wonder for them and their partnership and they would go on to write the next chapter of their life together.

Although that hope was always there, burning bright, he would still take the next step: If his lover was happy where she lived, he would find the best apartment in the building or house on the street and empty it. Sometimes that procedure was as simple as offering the owner a large sum of money. More often though because home owners are generally a stubborn sedentary lot, he brought death or some other horrible event inside the home that would make the owner want to flee and get as far away from it as they could.

Once the place was empty, he would hire a company to come in and renovate it from top to bottom. By then he would know what kind of home his girlfriend dreamt of inhabiting so he knew exactly what changes and specifications were needed for the renovation. One woman wanted cold-metal sleek, another a Welsh cottage with a thatched roof. A tall woman who was going deaf dreamt of a view through floor to ceiling windows of endless empty sand in the Namibian desert. It was the least he could do after all they had given him: a dream home in return for their great love and misplaced optimism. Sometimes he would tell them about these homes before they were ready. Sometimes they even got sneak peeks if that's what they wanted.

If he could never know what it was like to be truly human, at least he could be as kind as a human being and give these nice women something they desired. When the renovations were complete, he would say the necessary incantation and suddenly the woman would be living in her dream home, her memories of him and their relationship having faded into many months ago. How she came to be living in this marvelous new home would not even be a question—she was just here. She had been here all along.

He picked up a puppet and slid it onto his hand. A glass of water was on the table. He lifted it with the puppet hand and took a sip. The water trembled in the glass as he moved to put it back on the table. "Nervous water" he said grinning.

"Water can't be nervous." He had the puppet say. He remembered! *That's* what his girlfriend had said the night they made love for the first time. After they'd finished she asked for something to drink. He brought her a glass of water from the bathroom. Handing it to her, it jiggled a little in the glass. They both saw this and he joked "Nervous water."

She said "Water can't be nervous; it's your *heart* that's shaking."

Valley of the Girls

by Kelly Link

O nce, for about a month or two, I decided I was going to be a different kind of guy. Muscley. Not always thinking so much. My body was going to be a temple, not a dive bar. The kitchen made me smoothies, raw eggs blended with kale and wheat germ and bee pollen. That sort of thing. I stopped drinking, flushed all of Darius's goodies down the toilet. I was civil to my Face. I went running. I read the books, did the homework my tutor assigned. I was a model son, a good brother. The Olds didn't know what to think.

(Hero), of course, knew something was up. Twins always know. Maybe she saw the way I watched her Face when there was an event and we all had to do the public thing.

Meanwhile, I could see the way that (Hero)'s Face looked at my Face. There was no way that this was going to end well. So I gave up on raw eggs and virtue and love. Fell right back into the old life, the high life, the good, sweet, sour, rotten old life. Was it much of a life? It had its moments.

⁂

"Oh shit," (Hero) says. "I think I've made a terrible mistake. Help me, (   ). Help me, please?"

She drops the snake. I step hard on its head. Nobody here is having a good night.

"You have to give me the code," I say. "Give me the code and I'll go get help."

She bends over and pukes stale champagne on my shoes. There are two drops of blood on her arm. "It hurts," she says. "It hurts really bad."

"Give me the code, ⟨ Hero ⟩."

She cries for a while, and then she stops. She won't say anything. She just sits and rocks. I stroke her hair, and ask her for the code. When she doesn't give it to me, I go over and start trying numbers. I try our birthday. I try a lot of numbers. None of them work.

⁂

I chased the same route every day for that month. Down through the woods at the back of the guesthouse, into the Valley of the Girls just as the sun was coming up. That's how you ought to see the pyramids, you know. With the sun coming up. I liked to take a piss at the foot of ⟨ Alicia ⟩'s pyramid. Later on I told ⟨ Alicia ⟩ I pissed on her pyramid. "Marking your territory, ⟨   ⟩?" she said. She ran her fingers through my hair.

I don't love ⟨ Alicia ⟩. I don't hate ⟨ Alicia ⟩. Her Face had this plush, red mouth. Once I put a finger up against her lips, just to see how they felt. You're not supposed to mess with people's Faces, but everybody I know does it. What's the Face going to do? Quit?

But ⟨ Alicia ⟩ had better legs. Longer, rounder, the kind you want to die between. I wish she were here right now. The sun is up, but it isn't going to shine on me for a long time. We're down here in the cold, and ⟨ Hero ⟩ isn't speaking to me.

⁂

What is it with rich girls and pyramids anyway?

⁂

Valley of the Girls | KELLY LINK

In hieroglyphs, you put the names of the important people, kings and queens and gods, in a cartouche. Like this.

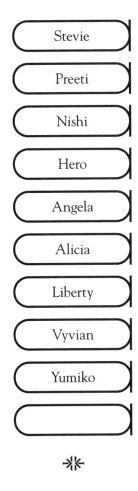

"Were you really going to do it?" (Hero) wants to know. This is before the snake, before I know what she's up to.

"Yeah," I say.

"Why?"

"Why not?" I say. "Lots of reasons. 'Why' is kind of a dumb question, isn't it? I mean, why did God make me so pretty? Why size four jeans?"

There's a walk-in closet in the burial chamber. I went through it looking for something useful. Anything useful. Silk shawls, crushed velvet dresses, black jeans. A stereo system loaded with the kind of music rich goth girls listen to. Extra pillows. Sterling silver. Perfumes, makeup. A mummified cat. Noodles. I remember when Noodles died. We were eight. They were already laying the foundations of Hero's pyramid. The Olds called in the embalmers.

We helped with the natron. I had nightmares for a week.

Hero says, "They're for the afterlife, okay?"

"You're not going to be fat in the afterlife?" At this point, I still don't know Hero's plan, but I'm starting to worry. Hero has a taste for the epic. I suppose it runs in the family.

"My *Ba* is skinny," Hero says. "Unlike you, _____. You may be skinny on the outside, but you have a fat-ass heart. Anubis will judge you. Ammit will devour you."

She sounds so serious. I should laugh. You try laughing when you're down in the dark, in your sister's secret burial chamber—not the decoy one where everybody hangs out and drinks, where once, oh god, how sweet is that memory, still, you and your sister's Face did it on the memorial stone—under three hundred thousand limestone blocks, down at the bottom of a shaft behind a door in an antechamber that maybe, somebody, in a couple of hundred years, will stumble into.

>|<

What kind of afterlife do you get to have as a mummy? If you're Hero, I guess you believe your *Ba* and *Ka* will reunite in the afterlife. Hero thinks she's going to be an *Akh*, an immortal. She and the rest of them go around stockpiling everything they think they need to have an excellent afterlife. They're rich. The Olds indulge them. It's just the girls. The girls plan for the afterlife. The boys play sports, collect race cars or 20th century space shuttles, scheme to get laid. I specialize in the latter.

The girls have *ushabti* made of themselves, give them to each other at the pyramid dedication ceremonies, the sweet sixteen parties. They collect *shabti* of their favorite singers, actors, whatever. They read *The Book of the*

Dead. In the meantime, their pyramids are where we go to have a good time. When I commissioned the artist who makes my *ushabti*, I had her make two different kinds. One is for people I don't know well. The other *shabti* for the girls I've slept with. I modeled for that one in the nude. If I'm going to hang out with these girls in the afterlife, I want to have all my working parts.

Me, I've done some reading, too. What happens once you're a mummy? Graverobbers dig you up. Sometimes they grind you up and sell you as medicine, fertilizer, pigment. People used to have these mummy parties. Invite their friends over and unwrap a mummy. See what's inside.

Maybe you end up in a display case in a museum. Or nobody ever finds you. Or your curse kills lots of people. I know which one I'm hoping for.

※

"( )," (Yumiko) said, "I don't want this thing to be boring. Fireworks and Faces, celebrities promoting their new thing."

This was earlier.

Once (Yumiko) and I did it in (Angela)'s pyramid, right in front of a false door. Another time she punched me in the side of the face because she caught me and (Preeti) in bed. Gave me a cauliflower ear.

(Yumiko)'s pyramid isn't quite as big as (Stevie)'s, or even (Preeti)'s pyramid. But it's on higher ground. From up on top, you can see down to the ocean.

"So what do you want me to do?" I asked her.

"Just do something," (Yumiko) said.

I had an idea right away.

※

"Let me out, (Hero)."

We came down here with a bottle of champagne. (Hero) asked me to open it. By the time I had the cork out, she'd shut the door. No handle. Just a key pad.

"Eventually you're going to have to let me out, Hero."

"Do you remember the watermelon game?" Hero says. We're reminiscing about the good old times. I think. She's lying on a divan. She lit a couple of oil lamps when she brought me down here. We were going to have a serious talk. Only it turned out it wasn't about what I thought it was about. It wasn't about the sex tape. It was about the other thing.

"It's really cold down here," I say. "I'm going to catch a cold."

"Tough," Hero says.

I pace a bit. "The watermelon game. With Vyvian's unicorn?" Vyvian is twice as rich as God. She's a year younger than us, but her pyramid is three times the size of Heros. She kisses like a fish, fucks like a wildebeest, and her hobby is breeding chimeras. Most of the estates around here have a real problem with unicorns now, thanks to Vyvian. They're territorial. You don't mess with them in mating season. I came up with this variation on French bullfighting, *Taureux Piscine*, except with unicorns. You got a point every time you and the unicorn were in the swimming pool together. We did *Licorne Pasteque*, too. Brought out a sidetable and a couple of chairs and set them up on the lawn. Cut up the watermelon and took turns. You can eat the watermelon, but only while you're sitting at the table. Meanwhile the unicorn is getting more and more pissed off that you're in its territory.

It was insanely awesome until the stupid unicorn broke its leg going into the pool, and somebody had to come and put a bullet in its head. Plus, the Olds got mad about one of the chairs. The unicorn splintered the back. Turned out to be an antique. Priceless.

"Do you remember how Vyvian cried and cried?" Hero says. Even this is part of the happy memory for Hero. She hates Vyvian. Why? Some boring reason. I forget the specifics. Here's the gist of it: Hero is fat. Vyvian is mean.

"I felt sorrier for whoever was going to have to clean up the pool," I say.

"Liar," Hero says. "You're a sociopath. You've never felt sorry for anyone in your life. You were going to kill all of our friends. I'm doing the world a huge favor."

"They aren't your friends," I say. "I don't know why you'd want to save a single one of them."

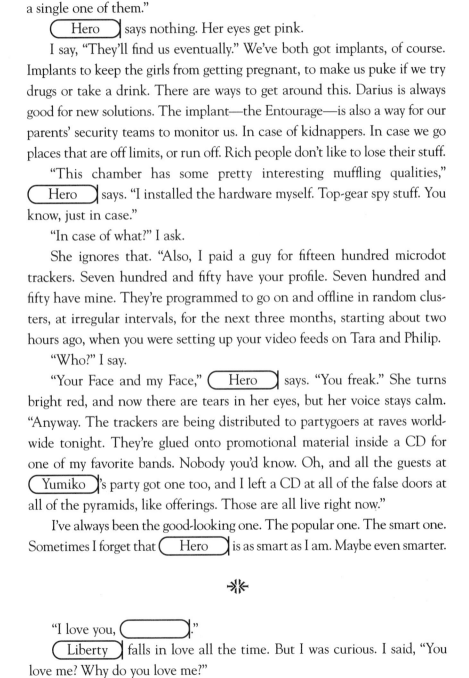 Hero says nothing. Her eyes get pink.

I say, "They'll find us eventually." We've both got implants, of course. Implants to keep the girls from getting pregnant, to make us puke if we try drugs or take a drink. There are ways to get around this. Darius is always good for new solutions. The implant—the Entourage—is also a way for our parents' security teams to monitor us. In case of kidnappers. In case we go places that are off limits, or run off. Rich people don't like to lose their stuff.

"This chamber has some pretty interesting muffling qualities," Hero says. "I installed the hardware myself. Top-gear spy stuff. You know, just in case."

"In case of what?" I ask.

She ignores that. "Also, I paid a guy for fifteen hundred microdot trackers. Seven hundred and fifty have your profile. Seven hundred and fifty have mine. They're programmed to go on and offline in random clusters, at irregular intervals, for the next three months, starting about two hours ago, when you were setting up your video feeds on Tara and Philip."

"Who?" I say.

"Your Face and my Face," Hero says. "You freak." She turns bright red, and now there are tears in her eyes, but her voice stays calm. "Anyway. The trackers are being distributed to partygoers at raves worldwide tonight. They're glued onto promotional material inside a CD for one of my favorite bands. Nobody you'd know. Oh, and all the guests at Yumiko's party got one too, and I left a CD at all of the false doors at all of the pyramids, like offerings. Those are all live right now."

I've always been the good-looking one. The popular one. The smart one. Sometimes I forget that Hero is as smart as I am. Maybe even smarter.

❋

"I love you, ⬭."

Liberty falls in love all the time. But I was curious. I said, "You love me? Why do you love me?"

She thought about it for a minute. "Because you're insane," she said. "You don't care about anything."

"That's why you love me?" I said. We were at a gala or something. We'd just come back from the Men's room where everybody was trying out Darius's new drug.

My Face was hanging out with my parents in front of all the cameras. The Olds love my Face. The son they wish they had. Somebody with a tray walked by and (Hero)'s Face took a glass of champagne. She was over by the buffet table. The other buffet table, the one for Faces and the Olds and the celebrities and the publicists and all the other tribes and hangers on.

My darling. My working girl. My sister's Face. I tried to catch her eye, clowning in my latex leggings, but I was invisible. Every gesture, every word was for them, for him. The cameras. My Face. And me? A speck of nothing. Not even a blot. Negative space.

She'd said we couldn't see each other any more. She said she was afraid of getting caught breaking contract. Like that didn't happen all the time. Like with Mr. Amandit. (Preeti) and (Nishi)'s father. He left his wife. It was (Liberty)'s Face he left his wife for. The Face of his daughters' best friend. I think they're in Iceland now, Mr. Amandit and the nobody girl who used to be a Face.

Then there's (Stevie). Everybody knows she's in love with her own Face. It's embarrassing to watch.

Anyway, nobody knew about us. I was always careful. Even if (Hero) got her nose in, what was she going to say? What was she going to do?

"I love you because you're you, ( )," (Liberty) said. "You're the only person I know who's better looking than their own Face."

I was holding a skewer of chicken. I almost stabbed it into (Liberty)'s arm before I knew what I was doing. My mouth was full of chewed chicken. I spat it out at (Liberty). It landed on her cheek.

"What the fuck, ( )!" (Liberty) said. The piece of chicken plopped down onto the floor. Everybody was staring. Nobody took a picture. I didn't exist. Nobody had done anything wrong.

Valley of the Girls | Kelly Link

҉

Aside from that, we all had a good time. Even ⟨ Liberty ⟩ says so. That was the time all of us showed up in this gear I found online. Red rubber, plenty of pointy stuff, chains and leather, dildos and codpieces, vampire teeth and plastinated viscera. I had a really nice pair of hand-painted latex tits wobbling around like epaulets on my shoulders. I had an inadequately sedated fruit bat caged up in my pompadour. So how could she not look at me?

Kids today, the Olds say. What can you do?

҉

I may be down here for some time. I'm going to try to see it the way they see it, the Olds.

You're an Old. So you think, wouldn't it be easier if your children did what they were told? Like your employees? Wouldn't it be nice, at least when you're out in public with the family? The Olds are rich. They're used to people doing what they're told to do.

When you're as rich as the Olds are, you are your own brand. That's what the publicists are always telling them. Your children are an extension of your brand. They can improve your Q rating or they can degrade it. Mostly they can degrade it. So there's the device they implant that makes us invisible to cameras. It's called an Entourage.

And then there's the Face. Who is a nobody, a real person, who comes and takes your place at the table. They get an education, the best health care, a salary, all the nice clothes and all the same toys that you get. They get your parents whenever the publicists decide there's a need or an opportunity. If you go online, or turn on the TV, there they are, being you. Being better than you will ever be at being you. When you look at yourself in the mirror, you have to be careful, or you'll start to feel very strange. Is that really you?

But it isn't just about the brand, or having good children who do what they're told, right? The Olds say it's about kidnappers, blackmailers, all those people who want to take away what belongs to the Olds. Faces mitigate the risk.

Most politicians have Faces too. For safety. Because it shouldn't matter what someone looks like, or how good they are at making a speech, but of course it does. The difference is that politicians choose to have their Faces. They choose.

The Olds like to say it's because we're children. We'll understand when we're older, when we start our adult lives without blemish, without online evidence of our indiscretions, our mistakes. No sex tapes. No embarrassing photos of ourselves in Nazi regalia, or topless in Nice, or honeytraps. No footage before the nose job, before the boob job, before the acne clears up.

The Olds get us into good colleges, and then the world tilts just for a moment, and maybe we fall off. We get a few years to make our own mistakes, out in the open, and then we settle down, and we come into our millions or billions or whatever. We inherit the earth, like that proverb says. The rich shall inherit the earth.

We get married, merge our money with other money, millions or billions, improve our Q ratings, become Olds, acquire kids, and you bet your ass those kids are going to have Faces, just like we did.

⋇

I never got into the Egyptian thing the way the girls did. I always liked the Norse gods better. You know, Loki. The slaying of Baldur. Ragnarok.

⋇

It wasn't hard to get hold of the thing I was looking for. Darius couldn't help me, but he knew a guy who knew a guy who knew exactly what I was talking about. We met in Las Vegas, because why not? We saw a show together, and then we went online and watched a video that had been filmed in his lab. Somewhere in Moldova, he said. He said his name was Nikolay.

I showed him my video. The one I'd made for the party for (Yumiko)'s pyramid dedication thingy.

We were both very drunk. I'd taken Darius's blocker, and he was interested in that. I explained about the Entourage, how you had to work around it if you wanted to have fun. He was sympathetic.

He liked the video a lot.

"That's me," I told him. "That's ⬭."

"Not you," he said. "You're making joke at me. You have Entourage device. But, girl, she is very nice. Very sexy."

"That's my sister," I said. "My twin sister."

"Another joke," Nikolay said. "But, if my sister, I would go ahead, fuck her anyway."

⊰⧘⊱

"How could you do this to me?" (Hero) wants to know.

"It had nothing to do with you." I pat her back when she starts to cry. I don't know whether she's talking about the sex tape or the other thing.

"It was bad enough when you slept with her," she says, weeping. "That was practically incest. But I saw the tape. The one you gave (Yumiko). The one she's going to put up online. Don't you understand? She's me. He's you. That's us, on that tape, that's us having sex."

"It was good enough for the Egyptians," I say, trying to console her. "Besides, it isn't us. Remember? They aren't us."

I try to remember what it was like when it was just us. The Olds say we slept in the same crib. We had our own language. (Hero) cried when I fell down. (Hero) has always been the one who cries.

"How did you know what I was planning?"

"Oh, please, ⬭," (Hero) says. "I always know when you're about to go off the deep end. You go around with this smile on your face, like the whole world is sucking you off. Besides, Darius told me you'd been asking about really bad shit. He likes me, you know. He likes me much better than you."

"He's the only one," I say.

"Fuck you," (Hero) says. "Anyway, it's not like you were the only one with plans for tonight. I'm sick of this place. Sick of these people."

There is a martial line of *shabti* on a stone shelf. Our friends. People who would like to be our friends. Rock stars that the Olds used to hang out with, movie stars. Saudi princes who like fat, gloomy girls with money. She picks up a prince, throws it against the wall.

"Fuck [Vyvienne] and all her unicorns," (Hero) says.

She picks up another *shabti*. "Fuck (Yumiko)."

I take (Yumiko) from her. "I did," I say. "I give her a three out of five. For enthusiasm." I drop the *shabti* on the floor.

"You are such a slut, (   )" (Hero) says. "Have you ever been in love? Even once?"

She's fishing. She knows. My heart is broken, and (Hero) knows. Is that how it works?

Why did you sleep with him? Are you in love with him? He's me. Why aren't I him? Fuck both of you.

"Fuck our parents," I say. I pick up the oil lamp and throw it at the *shabti* on the shelf.

The room gets brighter for a moment, then darker.

"It's funny," (Hero) says. "We used to do everything together. And then we didn't. And right now, it's weird. You planning on doing what you were going to do. And me, what I was planning. It's like we were in each other's brains again."

"You went out and bought a biological agent? We should have gone in on it together. Buy two and get one free."

"No," (Hero) says. She looks shy, like she's afraid I'll laugh at her.

I wait. Eventually she'll tell me what she needs to tell me, and then I'll hand over the little metal canister that Nikolay gave me, and she'll unlock the door to the burial chamber. Then we'll go back up into the world, and that video won't be the end of the world. It will just be something that people talk about. Something to make the Olds crazy.

"I was going to kill myself," (Hero) says. "You know, down here. I was going to come down here during the party, and then I decided that I didn't want to do it by myself."

My heart is broken, and so (Hero) wants to die. Is that how it works?

"And then I found out what you were up to," (Hero) says. "I thought I ought to stop you. Then I wouldn't have to be alone. And I would finally live up to my name. I'd save everybody. Even if they never knew it."

"You were going to kill yourself," I repeat. "How?"

"Like this," (Hero) says. She reaches into the jeweled box on her belt. There's a little thing curled up in there, an enameled loop of chain, black and bronze. It uncoils in her hand, becomes a snake.

>|<

(Alicia) was the first of us to get a Face. I got mine when I was ten. I didn't really know what was going on. I met all these boys my age, and then the Olds sat down and had a talk with me. They explained what was going on, said that I got to pick which Face I wanted. I picked the one who looked the nicest, the one who looked like he might be fun to hang out with. That's how stupid I was back then.

(Hero) couldn't choose, so I did it for her. Pick her, I said. That's how strange life is. I picked her out of all the others.

>|<

(Yumiko) said she'd already talked to her Face. (We talk to our Faces as little as possible, although sometimes we sleep with each others'. Forbidden fruit is always freakier. Is that why I did what I did? I don't know. How am I supposed to know?) (Yumiko) said her Face agreed to sign a new contract when (Yumiko) turns eighteen. She doesn't see any reason to give up having a Face.

>|<

(Nishi) is (Preeti)'s younger sister. They only broke ground on her pyramid last summer. Upper management teams from her father's company came out to lay the first course of stones. A team-building exercise. Usually it's prisoners from the Supermax prison out in Pelican Bay.

Once they get to work, they mostly look the same. It's hard work. We like to go out and watch.

Every once in a while a consulting archeologist or an architect will come over and try to make conversation. They think we want context.

They talk about grave goods, about how one day archeologists will know what life was like because a couple of girls decided they wanted to build their own pyramids.

We think that's funny.

They like to complain about the climate. Apparently it isn't ideal. "Of course, they may not be standing give or take a couple of hundred years. Once you factor in geological events. Earthquakes. There's the geopolitical dimension. There's graverobbers."

They go on and on about the cunning of graverobbers.

We get them drunk. We ask them about the curse of the mummies just to see them get worked up. We ask them if they aren't worried about the Olds. We ask what used to happen to the men who built the pyramids in Egypt. Didn't they used to disappear, we ask? Just to make sure nobody knew where the good stuff was buried? We say there are one or two members of the consulting team who worked on ⟨ Alicia ⟩'s pyramid that we were friendly with. We mention we haven't been able to get hold of them in a while, not since the pyramid was finished.

⋇

They were up on the unfinished outer wall of ⟨ Nishi ⟩'s pyramid. I guess they'd been up there all night. Talking. Making love. Making plans.

They didn't see me. Invisible, that's what I am. I had my phone. I filmed them until my phone ran out of memory. There was a unicorn down in the meadow by a pyramid. ⟨ Alicia ⟩'s pyramid. Two impossible things. Three things that shouldn't exist. Four.

That was when I gave up on becoming someone new, the running, the kale, the whole thing. That was when I gave up on becoming the new me. Somebody already was that person. Somebody already had the only thing I wanted.

⋇

"Give me the code." I say it over and over again. I don't know how long it's been. [Hero]'s arm is greenish-black and blown up like a balloon. I tried sucking out the venom. Maybe that did some good. Maybe I didn't think of it soon enough.

"[   ]?," [Hero] says. "I don't want to die."

"I don't want you to die either," I say. I try to sound like I mean it. I do mean it. "Give me the code. Let me save you."

"I don't want them to die," [Hero] says. "If I give you the code, you'll do it. And I'll die down here by myself."

"You're not going to die," I say. I stroke her cheek. "I'm not going to kill anyone."

After a while she says, "Okay." Then she tells me the code. Maybe it's a string of numbers that means something to her. More likely it's random. I told you she was smarter than me.

I repeat the code back to her and she nods. I've covered her up with a shawl, because she's so cold. I lay her head down on a pillow, brush her hair back.

"I'll be right back," I say.

She closes her eyes. Give me a horrible, blind smile.

I go over to the door and enter the code.

The door doesn't open. I try again and it still doesn't open.

"[Hero]? Tell me the code again?"

She doesn't say anything. She's fallen asleep. I go over and shake her gently. "Tell me the code one more time. Come on. One more time."

Her eyes stay closed. Her mouth falls open. Her tongue is poking out.

"[Hero]?"

It takes me a while to realize that she's dead. And now it's a little bit later, and my sister is still dead, and I'm still trapped down here with my dead sister and a bunch of broken *shabtis*. No food. No good music. Just a small canister of something nasty cooked up by my good friend Nikolay, and some size four jeans and the dregs of a bottle of very expensive champagne.

The Best of Subterranean

⁂

The Egyptians believed that every night the spirit of the person buried in the pyramids rose up through the false doors to go out into the world. Their *Ba.* Your *Ba* can't be confined in a small dark room at the bottom of a deep shaft hidden under some pile of stones. Maybe I'll fly out some night, some part of me. I keep trying combinations, but I don't know how many numbers (Hero) used, what combination. It's an endless task. There's not much oil left to light the lamps. Some air comes in through the bottom of the door, but not much. It smells bad in here. I wrapped (Hero) up in her shawls and hid her in the closet. She's in there with (Noodles). I put him in her arms. Every once in a while I fall asleep and when I wake up I realize I don't know which numbers I've tried, which I haven't.

The Olds must wonder what happened. They'll think it had something to do with that sex tape. Their publicists will be doing damage control. I wonder what will happen to my Face. What will happen to her. Maybe one night I'll fly out. My *Ba* will fly right to her, like a bird.

One day someone will open the door that I can't. I'll be alive or else I won't. I can open the canister or I can leave it closed. What would you do? I talk about it with (Hero), down here in the dark. Sometimes I decide one thing, sometimes I decide another.

Dying of thirst is a hard way to die.

I don't really want to drink my own urine.

If I open the canister, I might die faster. It will be my curse on you, the one who opens the tomb. Why should you go on living when she and I are dead? When no one remembers our names?

⁂

(Hero)

Tara.

I don't want you to know my name. It was his name, really.

Sic Him, Hellhound! Kill! Kill!

by Hal Duncan

1.

I wake curled up at the foot of the bed again, back snugged tight into the crook of my boy's legs—tight enough to be on top of them really. He groans, slaps the alarm clock off, tries to pull the quilt over his head. Doesn't work with me weighing it down, clambering up to lick his face.

—Get up, I say. Get up get up get up.

He shoves me away.

—Get *down*, he says.

I roll off the bed, grab whiffy boxers from the floor.

—I'm *hungry*.

He groans.

A boy and his werewolf. Truest love there is.

⁂

—Breathe. Then eat, he says. Or eat, then breathe. You know you can't do the two together.

I raise my head from the bowl of cornflakes, give another cough as I lick milk from my lips then dive back in. I don't have to look to know he's shaking his head, smiling wryly. Hey, he knows it's all part of the method anyway. Guzzling food, snuffling crotches, rolling in things he has to hose off. And that's his part of the deal—to deal with that shit, to handle it, handle *me*.

Every agent has a handler, don't you know?

※

They tried it without handlers, I hear. Like, back in my alpha's day, back before he became a recruiter, some bright spark figured they should try letting us off the leash. A lone hellhound on the road—he'd just be one more drifter, right? Like Kung Fu. Or maybe The Littlest Hobo. Things got kinda messy though, it seems; there were a few incidents; cops got eaten and, *yes*, they were fascist pigs, but it *just wasn't on*.

Don't know why they were worried about the handlers in the first place. Like I'd ever let anything happen to my boy.

※

He sits on the edge of the bed, flicking through the file, glancing up now and then as I run the water in the shower.

—You're actually using the shower gel this time, yes? he calls.

—Absolutely, I shout.

I stand behind the half-open door, peeking at him through the crack. After ten minutes, I duck my head under the water, turn it off and come out towelling my hair. He puts the file down, open at the photograph, the missing kid. *Dead* kid.

—I know you didn't actually wash, he says. My sense of smell isn't that bad.

2.

—You got your cover story down, right?

I pick up a sleeveless tee, give it a sniff to make sure it's good and stinky, then pull it on.

Sic Him, Hellhound! Kill! Kill! | HAL DUNCAN

—Yes, boss, I say.

It's the same story as ever, just different monickers: we're poor orphaned brothers, just moved to town to be near an aged aunt. I got ADHD and other issues. Impulse control. Drugs. He's the older bro sworn to raise me on his own, put me through school and all.

With the regeneration that comes with the shifts, you'd never know I've got…well, a few years on him.

※

I got bitten as a pup, see—bitten in the metaphorical sense, that is. I mean, forget what you think you know about werewolves. Silver bullets? Came in with the silver screen, dude. Wolfsbane? Man, that's poisonous to *everyone*. And all that contagion crap? Not how it works. No, how it works is ritual and magic—a wolfskin coat, a hipflask of dirty water drawn from lupine pawprints, and a bit of blood and dancing under the full moon. Being bitten might help, but it's all in the mindset. Shifting is a fucking skill, motherfucker. Not something you can catch.

※

When *exactly* I got bitten—in the metaphorical sense—that's a hard question though. Cause I remember a dream I had, age nine or so, of running across an old viaduct, a wolf pack at my heels. But I wasn't being chased, dig; I was at the head of them, *one* of them. When I woke up sweating, it wasn't with fear but with excitement. Was that when I got bit? *Maybe* it was years later, when my alpha took me in off the streets, turned this teenage stray into an initiate. But even at nine I had…that dream.

※

Reckon we're born this way, my alpha used to say. It was important to him, the gruff old fuck, and I can kinda understand, what with every movie at the drive-in painting us as cursed abominations, beasts with monstrous appetites. *Fuckin unnatural?* he'd growl as he scratched his chest tat through the leather vest. *This is who I fuckin am.*

Me, I'm sort of a bolshie bastard about it. No quarter. Ask me if it's nature or nurture, and I'll tell you it's a choice. I'll tell you it's my fucking choice to make, right? So deal with it.

3.

I pull the wolfskin on over the tee. With the leather pants too, it's gonna be hot as hell, but it's a necessary part of the whole kit and kaboodle. Besides, the ensemble has a rockstar-cum-hustler bad boy chic that tickles my fancy. It doesn't do me any favours with the PETA-loving emo kids, but it's just *awesome* for starting fights with small town dickwads who think *queer* is an insult.

My boy scruffles fingers through my hair, scratches my ear. I wonder what those dickwads would make of our rough-and-tumble playfights. Or sleeping arrangements.

I grab the car-keys from the coffee table and bring them to him, hold them out, take a step back as he reaches.

—Give, he says.

—Take them, I say.

—We don't have time for this.

He makes a grab and I snatch the keys away, turning so he has to reach round me, try and prise them from my hand.

—Give.

I give them up. He's the best handler *ever*, my boy, swear to God. There's no way what happened to the Louisiana team will happen to us. That was a *bad* werewolf, a weak handler. *We're* invincible.

Sic Him, Hellhound! Kill! Kill! | Hal Duncan

I knew it from the first day he came to the Pound, the way the truth didn't even faze him. I mean whatever run-ins they've had with the nasties we track, the handler candidates always come out of it with a fucking iron will, else they'd wouldn't be joining the cause; but usually the whole secret agency thing leaves them at least a little *what the fuck?* But he just strolled down the line of pups and returnees till he came to me. I saw it in his eyes.

—What's your name? he said.

—You decide, I told him.

⋇

—You ready?

As he pulls the car up at the gates of the school, I bring my head back in from the window, grin at him and throw my hands in the air.

—Rub my tummy!

—Behave, he says.

I give him my best puppy eyes.

—Not. Now. You have a job to do, so go on. Git.

I climb out of the car, bathtime slow. When he drives away, he'll be abandoning me, like, *forever.* He sighs, knowing what I need.

—Where's the vampire? he says. Go find the vampire, boy!

And suddenly I'm as keen as his voice.

4.

One hundred million hours later—one bazillion trillion hours of History and French, or Maths and Geography, or fucking whatever later—I'm sitting in the school cafeteria, on my own at a table in a corner, eating burgers out of the buns and trying my best to be human about it. Not standing out is a lost cause—I'm the new kid, and a weird one at that—but we're still in the avoidance stage; the freaks and geeks aren't sure if I'm one of them yet, and the alpha jock's still working up to his challenge.

Then *they* arrive.

※

I take a furtive sip from my hipflask, not enough to spark a shift, but enough to boost my sense of smell. Because she's all flowers and soap and chocolate and Bibles and *need*—so much need, so deep an aroma of insatiable yearning that it almost masks his stench. The smell of her longing fills the room, fills the *school*; shit, I've been smelling it all day, that perfume of victimhood. Without it I wouldn't have to go through this bullshit to catch his trail, so I don't think it's too harsh to give a little growl, is it?

※

So, OK, hers is a scent of sickness, not in a twisted-and-malicious way but in a patient-in-a-hospice way. I should pity her. But she's got…that classic Mary Sue look—that's what my boy calls them—all nice and normal, a little plain, a little plump. A cross round her neck, or a crucifix maybe; I can't tell from here. She's not pretty enough to be popular, not strange enough to be an outcast, just a mannequin of mediocrity, blandness and banality, desperate to be made more by her Ghoul Boyfriend Forever.

As fucking ever.

※

As for him? Yeah, he's got the boyband looks…if you trust your eyes. Which ain't a good idea.

Truth is, ticks got a sexy rep these days, all that Byronic bullshit, teen girls swooning over brooding tortured souls, but if you think vampires are *hawt*, you ought to read the motherfucking lore. *These are corpses, fuckhead*, my alpha told me way back. Rotted, stinking, fetid corpses that walk as men. Shit, it takes them years of feeding to even get to *that*.

So this tick sure looks like some pale poetic catwalk cutie, but I can smell his soil.

5.

Here's how this vampire started. It started with some manipulative leeching bastard dead in a grave, some kiddy-fiddler or wife-beater, some Ponzi scheme merchant—or, worse, politician. It started with someone so deep into using people they couldn't stop even six feet down with maggots eating their tongue. It started with their ghost haunting the people they'd abused, feeding on them even from the grave, sucking this…energy—chi, my alpha called it, or kundalini.

It was just a spectre at first, dig? No fangs, no frilly fucking cuffs on flouncy shirts. Just a mindless parasitic poisonous miasma.

※

There's a stink of the pulpit on this one, oak and ink, sermons scribbled by lamplight. It's old; shit, the victim probably wasn't even born when this fucker came seeping up from its silk-lined coffin to carry on its spiritual vocation, polluting the living with dreams of death, fears of the flesh and all its sordid passions. It's the smell of chickenshit, that stench, of something so gutless in the face of life and death it can't face either, has to deny them both. There's nothing uglier than the mockery of a human being you end up with then.

※

Fuck, let me tell you how much of a heartthrob the first tick I tracked was. Baby, my alpha took me to a cemetery, and I could smell the fucker from the gates, smell the stench of misery, even before this reanimated rotting corpse—this ghoulish, mummified, zombie *thing*—came digging its way up out of the earth with the bones of its fingers. It was more filth than flesh, blood-sodden graveyard dirt packed round bones, and the first thing it did was make a bee-line for a nearby field, to feed on a fucking cow.

Real romantic.

⁂

—Stage two, said my alpha. If your vampire can feed enough as a spectre—suck juice from some debt-ridden fuck till he blows his own brains out in the depths of depression, or drive some insomniac mother to drown herself and the sick child she doesn't have the strength to care for—if the tick can bleed just enough vitality from the vulnerable, it can dance its own corpse like a fucking muppet.

—Only ticks look even half-human are stage threes plus, the ones who find some sad bastard, eat their insides out, wear them as a motherfucking skinsuit.

6.

The tick and the Mary Sue sit down at a table over near the door, holding hands, gazing into each other's eyes. They're the centre of their own little world—scratch that; they're the centre of *everyone's* world. You can smell the delusion wafting from them, the psychic smokescreen that lets a tick like this walk into a high school without a single question. Me, I got fake transfer papers, but all a tick needs is confusion and conviction. The glamour that makes everyone buy his new kid bullshit. Give him time and he'll have the whole town believing it.

⁂

You see…fuck, the reason most ticks don't come out in the daytime is cause you can see the skinsuit's stitches even *with* the glamour. Yanno why ticks and mirrors don't mix? Really? Because even stage threes puke at the sight of themselves.

But then there's these stage fours.

—A tick *can* pass, my alpha told me, if they can just find some human sick enough to swallow that glamour so commitedly they put every ounce of their own energy into bolstering it.

An amp for the signal, dig? With a Mary Sue beside them, that tick can fucking *dazzle*.

⁕

So he looks just like our missing kid, just like the victim, but creepily...'better.' Ice-blue eyes and blond hair, cherry lips, skin smooth and spotless as an angel's ass. Fingernails manicured to metrosexual perfection. Every girl in the cafeteria, or near enough, is either gazing at him with wonder or looking daggers at Mary Sue. Some of the guys too, though they're shiftier about it; one of the indie kids over at the till is outright obsessed, the poor fuck, stinking of adolescent lust. No shame in his spicy scent, at least, but he's way out of luck.

⁕

Another high school job, a few years back, just before the...accident that sent me back to the Pound and a new handler, to my boy—which was totally a great thing in the end, really, cause there's no way that sort of thing would happen with *him*—I got into a beef with these football fuckwits. They were yacking on about how their girls were all into tick-lit.
—Vampires are totally gay, one of them said.
So, yeah, I kicked the crap out of him.
These days, for most ticks, there should be an *ex-* in that sentence.

7.

Jared Swift. That was the kid's name. Not the tick's name, mind. You think I give a fuck about this motherfucker's name? No, I'm talking about the kid in the photo, grabbed by the tick some night, in some dark place the boy wasn't meant to be, dragged off into the woods to be devoured. And worn.

Quiet kid, the report said, sorta *sensitive*. No girlfriend. Journals and sketchbooks found after his disappearance indicate suicidal thoughts.

Jared Swift. That's the only name that matters here. Not the tick's or the Mary Sue's, not mine or my boy's. Just Jared Swift.

What monicker the tick's going by here isn't worth shit; he'll have snatched it from Mary Sue's dreams while she was sleeping anyway, as he lurked outside her window, jonesing over her emptiness, or crawled in to crouch by her bed, whispering bitter nothings in her ear, watching himself glow radiant with glamour in the mirror of her dresser. If he did it over enough nights, he probably fucking glittered by the time he showed up as a late transfer in school to take her breath away. She, of course, being the only girl this gorgeous hunk had eyes for.

I can smell what little of Jared Swift is left in the skin worn by this ghoul. I can smell the shreds of soul in it, the despair and desire the tick has strung together into a semblance of self—behaviours born of terrified restraint, habits of shame—the salt of tears and spunk that tinges the tick's own bloody stink. I can smell a fucking moment, the words *oh, Jared's not really interested in girls yet* echoing as Jared casts his eye across a different cafeteria, fixes it on a different girl. Someone unattainable enough he'll never need to...

This would be the point where I realise I'm snarling, top lip curled back, teeth bared. Not that it matters in a blowing-my-cover sorta way; ticks don't have the wits to even know there might be hellhounds on their trail, and if the Mary Sue notices, all caught up in the glamour of her Ghoul Boyfriend Forever, she'll likely just write me into her self-centred story as another possessive potential, out to own her like her beloved does, jealous of the competition.

It does finally spur the dickwads into action though.

—Freak.

—Faggot.

·   Fuck yeah. At last!

8.

I ignore the detention because, well, you know, the principal's *bad puppy* voice just doesn't carry the tone my boy's does; like I'm gonna play cowed to some yapping cur thinks he's top dog. Besides, we'll be out of here tomorrow if we get the job done tonight. So, out by the parking lot, skulking out of sight behind a dumpster, I watch them climb into a car that reeks of her— him in the driving seat though, naturally. And as they pull away, I take a deep slug from my hipflask. Strip the t-shirt off. Unbuckle my belt.

⋇

They always play it as painful in the movies, like some hideous Jekyll and Hyde transformation, man being remade as beast in wrenching agony. Shit, it's more ecstasy than agony, and I mean that in the chemical sense, a fucking *buzz*. Skin-tingling shudders running up and down your spine, every inch of you alive with sensitivity. It's not so visual, natch, but if you can imagine a psychedelia of smell, that's how it rushes in on you when you turn wolf. When my alpha took me through my first shift, man, I thought he'd spiked the punch with acid.

⋇

Bones crunch into new shapes, muscles shift, and wolfskin furls tight to my form, binds to my naked skin, *becomes* it. No doubt my boy'll bitch about me leaving the leathers in a dumpster yet again, but it's the handiest hiding-place, boss, and it's either that or a halfway wolfman look that's bound to sparks some stares loping down the streets and through the woods after the car. Whereas I *might* get away, in this form, with just a few confused souls wondering if they really did see that motherfucking massive…husky? Cause it couldn't *really* be…could it?

⁂

I run like that car's a supercharged stag but I got a turbodrive in my adrenal glands and a hankering for venison. I run like I have a whole pack at my heels, betas splitting off to flank the quarry. I pound the tarmac with paws that move so fast, so light, they barely make a sound. I leap walls to cut through yards, crash through bushes and fences, pace never slowing, gaze cold and keen as steel on my prey as long as it's in my sight, flared nostrils directing me when it's not.

I fucking *love* chasing cars.

9.

I'm kinda disappointed when he parks the thing at her place—he opens the door for her; hugs her but baulks when she moves in to kiss him; spins her a spiel about how he's scared he'll hurt her; strokes her cheek—then sets off on foot for his hidey-hole. I'm kinda disappointed cause ticks move slow as humans, mostly—slower even, sorta floaty—which is just plain boring. Stalking is OK, but it's nowhere near as much fun as chasing.

If it wouldn't lead to a seriously stern *bad werewolf!* scolding, I'd take him down here and now.

⁂

But no. I got my part of the job, and my boy got his. If the ticks are a fuckload less impressive than some would have you believe—if they're feeders not fighters, if they don't tend to offer *that* much in the way of struggle once you've torn their limbs off, decapitated them with your teeth, and spat their head across the room—well, there's putting them back in the grave and *keeping* them there. So there's all that clean-up afterwards, with the garlic and salt. And quicklime. Handler stuff.

And there's the whole…loyalty thing. I suppose.

⋇

So I prowl through the brush behind gnatboy, hanging back in the shadows of early evening, following him to a fancy house out past the edge of town, all clean-lined concrete and glass…real modern. Swimming pool out back, and an SUV out front. I can smell rotting bodies inside, but not so's I can make out how many. More than two, I reckon. He spider-crawls up the side of the house and in a window.

After a quick sniff and a piss-tag on a tree, I turn, lope off.

Lassie come home, motherfucker. It's chow time.

⋇

—Hello hello hello hello! I love you!

—Yes, I know. I love you too.

—But I *really* love you! I missed you so much!

—And I missed you too. *Yes, I did! Oh, yes I did!* Now, down you go.

—But I *missed* you!

—I know, but we have work to do. Did you find the lair?

—It was *easy!* Come on. Grab the gear and let's get this tick squished.

—OK, hang on.

—Hurry up!

—You know, maybe you should put some pants on.

—Don't need them. Hurry up! Come on!

—I'm coming.

—Come faster! Hurry up!

—Stop. Pulling.

10.

The last guttural purr of the engine as we pull into the driveway; soft clicks and thuds of doors opening and closing; crunch of gravel underfoot; snick of the trunk unlocking: my ears pricked even in human form, all of it's acute, carved in the quiet like radio play sound effects.

He pulls my spare hipflask from his pocket, hands it over, starts loading up with his own kit—crucifix, holy water, carbon-quarreled crossbow, gun with silver bullets. None of it actually means shit, we figure, but every tick's so convinced of their damnation these empty symbols mostly work.

※

—Ready? I say.

He nods, closes the trunk on the canisters full of disposal substances, and we look into each other's eyes for a moment, saying something that can't be put into words. Somewhere in there is the story of how he signed up for this gig, how he got sucked into this weird world, how he came close enough to living death to spit in its face. But you don't have to hear that story. All you have to know is that it's maybe something like Jared Swift's, but not.

I'll fucking *never* let it be that story.

※

Soft and easy, padding on feet half-human, half-wolf, I take point, leading my boy in through the splintered front door, muzzle twitching, senses taut. I can hear the flies buzzing, count the corpses by scent, even before we hit the dining room. I can even tell that the tick isn't in there; but we go in anyway, to remind ourselves why we do this.

Rippling with maggots, Mom and Dad and three kids sit at the table, the family dog an autopsy or feast upon it. Both.

Sanity is the first thing a tick takes from its victims.

Sic Him, Hellhound! Kill! Kill! | Hal Duncan

⫸⫷

The Zoroastrians have this ritual, you know; when someone dies they bring a dog to the corpse, and no matter what the doctor says, no matter how it looks, the person is only declared truly dead when the dog treats it as such. Way I hear it, it used to be one of us. Way I hear it, that might even be how the agency started—werewolves and their handlers brought in to make sure the dead will stay that way—but no one really knows the grand story of the origin. Or cares much.

We care about the corpses.

11.

I follow the stench into the basement, my boy at my back all the way. I know he's thinking about Jared Swift, about the thing that's wearing his skin now, the ghost become a ghoul become a glittering glamour of humanity, cold and dead inside, empty as the not-so-pretty head and hollow heart of a Mary Sue who can't read between the lines. Can't see what's under this sketchy fantasy of self-denial and overwrought passion.

In the broken concrete of the floor, a dirt mound marks where the tick has burrowed, its grave.

I piss on it.

⫸⫷

—Softening the earth? says my boy, but I'm already snarling, ripples of the shift running up my spine as I hit the dirt with furious claws, in a shape barely hominid, scrabbling, tearing, rending the earth. You could call it *digging*, but that would be like calling a hurricane *breezy*. The scent of vampire rot is so rich it thickens the air, turns my stomach. I want to tear this fucker up from his sleep, rip him apart, and roll in the filth of what's left so I will *stink* of his ending.

A white hand bursts from the muck.

The rest of him follows in an explosion of dirt, an eruption of flailing inhumanity, leaping for the walls, the rafters, a corner of the ceiling, to cling there, hissing and hollow-eyed. Still glamoured to fuck, it's every inch the smooth Adonis, skin of white marble and blue veins, lithe and limber as a fucking cat but its twisted perching a mockery of a true predator. This is a fucking parasite, a tapeworm from the bowels of humanity, a leech with limbs and a face. Spitting, thoughtless, ravenous loathing.

—I will eat you and shit you out, I say.

—Really, no, says my boy. I'm not cleaning up that—

And in the second I turn, it's fired itself at him, over my head, not baseball-fast, but fast enough; and his quarrel goes wild, but at least the holy water doesn't, like acid in its face, stripping glamour to raw horror. And by then, I'm launched, hitting the tick just as its jaw opens like a snake's. A glimpse of ragged shards, broken bone for teeth. I slam into its side, slam it the fuck off my boy and into a concrete wall. There's a sick thud, splattering gore.

12.

The fucker's already broken though, been broken since before it was dead, and it rolls away, scuttles back and whirls. Its lolling head snaps back into place, for all that its brains are oozing down its back. Fuck, it's a tick; whatever brains it has it likely scavenged from sewer rats, just so's it could ape the life it fucked up when it had the chance. Its eyes lock on my boy again, and I'm thinking, fuck, I hope it didn't get a taste of him there—at the exact same moment I scent his blood on the air.

No.

Then the smell of him is rich in its scent. I can hear him fumbling, cursing, losing the trust in himself to handle this, handle *anything*; I can smell the fear of failure, smell it in the tick's breath as it sucks it in, shrieks it at me, a searing mockery, cause if he can't handle this, he can't handle *me*, he's just a boy, not a boss, just a boy, not *my* boy and—

I snarl as we leap, the tick and I, my claws ripping through the air, rending its belly, swatting the fucker clear across the basement.

-⟩❄⟨-

I come down hard, something stolen from me in the touch. Shit, the smell of panic is so fucking physical, I stumble. I shake my head but I can't get rid of it, look to my boy but that's where the fucking problem is. He's choking, collapsing, and if he's weak, I—I don't know what to do. I want to snarl in his fucking face. I need you, you fucking fuck, need you to fight for. A boy and his werewolf, motherfucker. Loyalty. I need your fucking purpose, need you and fucking hate you for it.

Fucking bitch ass...

-⟩❄⟨-

And then the tick is on my back, clamped tight; and it's not fangs or a feeding tube—it's not physical at all—but I can feel the bite at the back my neck, at the base of my skull, feel it reaching in to shred my thoughts and suck them out. Loyalty? I'm a fucking freak of a beast of base desires kept in line by a lie. There's no love here, only need, the need to follow, to fawn, to be favoured with treats and scraps of attention, the need to be needed, to be needed to need—

13.

And I'm turning, growling at this fucking wretch of a weak handler on the ground in front of me, this fucking faggot kid on his back, his throat exposed like the craven whelp he is, just some backwoods bottom boy who opened himself up to a tick once before, no fucking wonder he let it happen again. All I can smell now, as I crouch to leap, is his fear and my anger, his weakness and my power.

I don't know how he manages it, the roll to one side as I jump. The crossbow smashing down on my nose.

—Don't you fucking dare, he says.

I'm still growling.

—Off! he shouts.

And he's bringing the gun up even as I go back and down, firing it once, twice. The bullets don't hit my skull, but it feels like they might as well have as the tick is blasted off me. There's a scream of pure despair that hits my boy hard. I see the gun barrel turning, pointing up, towards his chin, but he's my boy again now, and—I'll apologise later for nearly biting his hand off.

I whirl to spit twisted steel at the tick. And howl.

I howl as it scrambles upright, limbs clicking back from ragdoll dislocations to roughly human placements. I howl as it backs away, scuttles to this side and that, looking for a point of attack. I howl at the tick from all fours, standing over my boy, guarding him as he hauls himself back and up. I howl like Cerberus at the gates of Hell as he stumbles to his feet beside me, lays a hand on my back, a hand that steadies as I howl, as purposed as the one that's raised now, pointing.

—Sic him, boy, he says. *Kill!*

I hit the tick as a berserker, slashing chest and belly, tearing through one leg's hamstring as it spins, wrenching the other leg off at the knee.

I catch it by the wrists as it flails, raise it in a cruciform and tear its jaw from its face with my teeth, spit it into the grave. Half its head follows in a crunch of bone. Then the rest. With a foot on its chest, the fucker's arms pop from their sockets like chicken wings.

When I'm done shaking it in my teeth like a stuffed toy, there's not much left.

14.

Still, there's *something* left. Fingers twitch and grapple at air. Toes curl. Wherever there are joints intact, they jerk and spasm. This is the creature in its natural state, I reckon—a set of clutching convulsions, twitches and shudders, driven by a brainless impetus to play out its travesty of existence. I crack open its ribcage, chew out the brown lump that passes for a heart and drop it in front of my boy, like a ball. He empties a full chamber of silver bullets into it and dissolves what's left in homeopathically-diluted holy water. Eventually, everything is still.

⫸⫷

My boy stands there with the empty gun still dangling in one hand, looking down at the mess of the creature that ate Jared Swift. The scent of a moment of crisis is still on him, and for all the grim determination summoned by a bloody-minded howl of defiance, there's a hint of shame too. He's not happy, and it's my fault, I know. Don't know why, but I know it's my fault.

Then he looks at me, and something changes in his eyes, and he says two words and everything changes.

—Good boy!

And I am motherfucking *magnificent*.

⫸⫷

I shift back to humanity, feeling slick and shiny, and I don't just mean with the viscerae. I feel *fierce*. Every shift is a remaking, after all, and if the transformation to wolfman unleashes a beast in me, well, so does the return to this human form. Like humans aren't beasts too? I grab his hand as he moves toward the stairs, towards disposal chemicals and rubber gloves and all that jazz, pull him in to lick his face, exuberantly. Hey, it's cleaning, sorta. He stops me, wipes a sleeve across my mouth.

—Like people, he says.

And we kiss.

So maybe I get a bit carried away as we're washing the gore off each other with holy water. Maybe it's the wolf in me that ignores the protest of *not here*. Or maybe it's the human in me that says, *especially here*. So you think we're both monsters? A hellhound and a human so offay with carnage we don't see how fucked-up it is to let the passion loose here and now?

I say it's life, to fuck as humans in the ruins of death.

As living, breathing, eating, shitting, *fucking* human beings in the ruin of death.

Troublesolving

BY TIM PRATT

ere's how I got involved with Cameron Cassavetes:

I was walking along Lakeshore Avenue, close to Christmas, just windowshopping really since I was a) broke and b) didn't have anyone in my life who expected a gift, or anyone I expected something from, except maybe my ex-wife, depending on her particular disposition come the day. I paused outside the little co-op bakery, my nose parsing the emerging aromas of the day's handmade vegetarian pizza: goat cheese, rosemary oil, fresh basil. The odor alone was enough to make me forget my troubles, until I remembered I didn't even have eighteen bucks to buy a pie. I shoved my hands into the pockets of my jacket and walked on, head tucked down, wishing I had a hat—winter takes its time coming to Northern California, and it's nothing to an old East Coaster like myself, but there was a bit of a bite in the air nonetheless, and the tips of my ears were practically shivering. I went past the last table on the sidewalk, vaguely aware there was a woman sitting there with a coveted slice of pizza, mostly because I had to step out of my way to avoid tripping on the enormous overstuffed black-and-blue canvas bag beside her feet.

"Here." She stood and stuck a business card under my nose. I looked up, and she was a perfectly put-together woman in her maybe mid-thirties, on the pretty side of plain, with chestnut eyes that so exactly matched the shade of her hair, scarf, and sweater that she might have had them dyed to match. Her smile was bright and brief, a flash of sun on a cloudy day (or slash of lightning in a clear sky), and she flicked the outstretched card with her fingernail. "Take this. You'll need it."

I took the card. It was white, with a very restrained and elegant font, and read "Cameron Cassavetes," and underneath that, "Freelance Troublesolver," and under that, a phone number with an Oakland area code.

I tried to flirt—my ex-wife, who pities me, says I should practice more—saying, "Troublesolver, huh? I've always been more of a trouble-maker myself." I fished up my most sincere smile, and Cameron sighed like a doctor bearing bad news.

"Just hold onto the card. Call if you need me, any time, day or night. If you don't reach me right away, just leave a message."

I finally frowned. "What's this about? What is it you do?"

"I fix broken things."

"Do I look like a broken thing?"

"Oh, Stephen." She patted my cheek, scooped up her enormous bag, and walked off purposefully down the sidewalk and around the corner. She was out of sight before I thought to wonder—you probably noticed this already—how she knew my name.

I threw her card in the first trash can I passed. I didn't know what Cameron's deal was, but I didn't like the whole cheesy *Twilight Zone* feel of the situation. I had enough problems—did I ever—without mysterious women slipping me their numbers in spooky fashion.

I did my shopping, because even though I was too broke for shampoo and soap, I wouldn't get any more gigs if I smelled like braised hobo in sweat sauce. I noticed a guy in the drugstore wearing exactly the same clothes I was, and wondered when I'd become so generic—I used to have style. I mean, professionally. The cashiers were huddled together talking in low voices, and as soon as I approached, they separated and cast sidelong glances at me. Was I already smelly or something? Did I look like a shop-lifter? I hadn't become quite that economically desperate yet.

I carried my sad sack of toiletries back the way I'd come, toward the lake and my condo beyond. I wasn't looking forward to going home, because there's nothing sadder than the remains of an apartment where a pair of interior designers once lived, after they break up.

Troublesolving | Tim Pratt

In the lobby, I found another business card wedged in the door of my mailbox. Cameron Cassavetes, Troublesolver. This one included a street address—just a few blocks away—in addition to the phone number. I was a little creeped out. Was this woman stalking me? Or just desperate for work? The latter, I could relate to, but I was annoyed. This is supposed to be a secure building, but it's not like there's a doorman, and anyone who wants to get buzzed in just has to punch intercom buttons until somebody answers, and then claim to be a UPS or FedEx delivery.

I shoved the card in my pocket to throw away when I got upstairs, then rode up the elevator—with its inspection notice expired eight months before, always reassuring. The moment I stepped into the long dim hallway I knew something was wrong. My door, the last one on the right side of the hall, was standing ajar. I should've probably called the police right then, but I did the stupid rationalization thing: "Did I leave the door open? Did the cleaning lady leave it open?" Even though I a) would never forget to lock up, being a cautious guy and b) hadn't had a cleaning lady since my ex-wife moved out and took eleven-twelfths of our clients with her.

I went to the door, stepped inside, and discovered devastation.

Mere desolation would have been okay. That was normal. My ex took most of the best of our possessions when she left, and I agreed in order to keep the condo for myself. (She moved in with her—with the guy who—with Harold. Fucking Harold.) I was a decorator, so reversion to college-era chic Ikea shelves and a futon for a bed depressed me thoroughly. But poverty-in-Sparta décor looked splendid compared to what I beheld.

I dashed to the kitchen first, to turn off the water in the overflowing sink, but the faucet handles had been ripped off, so I settled for pulling out the wads of dishtowels the vandals had used to clog the drain. I repeated the process in both bathrooms, where the fixtures had been similarly torn away. My carpets were soaked, but I dared hope water hadn't leaked into the apartment below mine. Every room was a diorama of disaster, furniture smashed, cushions slit open and stuffing strewn about, books torn apart with their halves tossed in distant corners, refrigerator toppled and leaking odd fluids, toilets reduced to shards of porcelain, mirrors smashed, garbage in the remains of my bed, and windows and walls all spray painted with lurid graffiti in colors from Bauhaus Gold to Peek-A-Boo Blue to Rich Plum to Catalina Mist. Some of the spray-painted scrawls had the vaguely familiar look of graffiti tags from the neighborhood, but others were strange and sinuous, like sigils from some lost and secret civilization.

I squelched across my ruined carpet to the landline and saw the phone was in pieces, too. I pulled out my cell, and hesitated—was this a 911-type situation? The vandals were gone. I could have looked up the non-emergency number, but my computer had been taken apart and dumped, mostly in my toilet, and the monitor spray-painted red over every pixel.

Then I remembered the business card I'd shoved in my pocket. Cameron Cassavetes. Troublesolver. I had *her* number.

I didn't call her, either.

⇥⃝⇤

When she stepped in and turned on the light, I spun around in her chair and gave her a nasty smile. "When you weren't here, I took the liberty of breaking into your office." I'd smashed in a panel of glass with my elbow, reached in, and flipped the deadbolt, feeling every inch the righteous avenger.

"I go through more windows that way," Cameron Cassavetes said, seemingly unbothered by my presence in her office. She unbuttoned her sand-colored coat, unwound her long scarf, and hung both on a coat rack, then sat in the chair on the other side of her desk. I couldn't help but notice she had the better of the two seats—hers looked like a Freedom chair from Humanscale, while I was sitting in some $89 steno chair from an office supply store. Why would she have the crappier chair behind her own desk?

"I hope you weren't waiting long," she said.

I decided to ignore her non-sequitur—and my curiosity about her furnishing choices—and stick to my script, which I'd been practicing during the hour I sat in the dark with no appreciable lumbar support. "So is it like a protection racket? If I don't pay you to 'solve my troubles' you make sure I get a lot of trouble, starting with having my apartment destroyed?"

"I didn't have anything to do with the vandalism at your home."

Denial, I'd expected. I snorted. "You think I'm stupid? It's just coincidence you approached me out of the blue right before my place got wrecked? And that I found your card in my mailbox?"

"Of course it wasn't coincidence." She looked totally relaxed, like she was conducting a job interview. "But, again, I didn't have anything to do with the destruction."

"You expect me to believe that?"

"Yes."

I waited for elaboration. None was forthcoming. She just looked at me with that clear unwavering stare, like she was trying to calculate my body fat percentage or judge the weight of my soul by gaze alone. "Why's that?" I said finally, conceding that I'd somehow lost control of the situation.

"Two reasons. First, I don't charge for my services, so it wouldn't make much sense for me to shake you down, would it? And second, if you'll allow me…"

She came around the desk, and I pushed back in my chair, because I'm naturally obliging even when I don't mean to be. Plus, as a freelancer myself, I was still trying to get over the idea of a freelance anything who literally did her work for free. I mean, I like decorating, but I wouldn't do it for nothing, except maybe for a close friend, and I'm all out of those.

She unlocked one of the drawers and withdrew a slim silver laptop, opened it up on the desk before me, and clicked and tapped with her fingers. A window popped up onscreen, showing webcam footage…of my hallway. The camera must have been at the far end of the hall, up high in a corner near the ceiling.

"You've got my place bugged now?"

"Observe." More tapping, and the timestamp on the video ran back to the morning hours. I watched a couple of young guys in sweatshirts, carrying backpacks, open my door, apparently with a key, and go inside. About half an hour later they emerged, walking down the elevator, the webcam getting nice clear views of their faces.

"So you document your acts of vandalism…"

Cameron pulled a little thumb drive from the side of the laptop and handed it to me. "Here. The footage. Take it to the cops, tell them you set up the webcam because you heard there'd been some break-ins in the neighborhood—that's *always* true around here—and ask if they can identify the perpetrators. The boys are both well known to the cops, believe me, with a string of minor priors."

"Aren't you worried they'll turn you in?"

She rolled her eyes. She was cute when she did it. I took that as a sign of trouble. "No, Stephen. They don't know who I am. I'm not the mastermind. I'm trying to *help* you." Cameron returned to her comfy chair. "Give that to the cops, and they'll put the boys away. But it won't help your essential problem."

"What *is* my essential problem? And how do you know my name, or anything else about me?"

"You wouldn't believe me if I told you. Not yet." I started to speak, intending to tell her to quit jerking me around, but she talked first. "Your essential problem. Have you ever heard of gangstalking?"

"No."

"Well…imagine a group of people, not anyone you know, just strangers, who decide to destroy your life. They arrange problems for you, from minor annoyances—broken tail lights on your car so the cops pull you over, your mail being misdirected, your windows smashed with rocks thrown from the street—to more serious things, like the kind of vandalism your apartment suffered today. They might call in multiple noise complaints on you to the police, or accuse you of flashing a bunch of kids at a playground. Basically the goal is to destroy your life, but to do so in a gradual, cumulative way, and with an ever-shifting cast of assailants, so you can't point to a single perpetrator. The people who stalk you will seemingly have no relationship with one another, no motive, and since there are dozens or even hundreds of people involved, even if you manage to get one or two of them arrested on minor charges, it won't really help. The gangstalkers might even have friends in the police or local government who cover for them, or who conspire to frame *you* for crimes."

Troublesolving | Tim Pratt

"Christ. Why would people do something like that?"

She shrugged. "Motives vary. Some people are truly chosen as random victims, for part of a gang initiation. Others are being punished by governments or other agencies for things they've said, or done, or seen."

"Stuff like that really happens?"

Cameron frowned. "No, not really. Gangstalking isn't real. Some mentally ill people *believe* they're being gangstalked, but it's just another flavor of paranoia, a way to weave every slight and accident and difficulty into a vast tapestry of persecution. The victims—they call themselves 'targeted individuals'—incorporate everything around them into their delusions. If they see someone on the street talking on a cell phone? They think the person is talking about them. If they see a helicopter, they assume it's spying on them. If people in a crowd stand close to them, it's intentional intimidation. If a stranger laughs, they're being mocked. If they encounter people dressed similarly to themselves, or reading the same magazines, it's meant to unnerve them. Wrong numbers or hang-ups are perceived as torments. Even 'negative people' who 'drain their energy' are considered attackers. It's sad. Unfortunately, the internet has allowed a lot of these people to find one another, share stories, and feed into one another's delusions."

All that stuff sounded familiar from my day-to-day life lately, even the helicopters and the crowding and the people reading the same magazines, but I'd never thought it had anything to do with me. Life is full of coincidences. "But, if gangstalking's not a real thing...why are you talking about it?"

"Because you are being gangstalked. You are a targeted individual. The fact that you haven't even noticed just goes to show how strikingly un-paranoid you are. Your ongoing mental health must be very frustrating to your tormentors. In your case, there really is a vast group of seemingly random people attempting to make your life a ruin. Haven't you noticed a *huge* increase in your bad luck these past few months?"

"I've had a shitty run, sure, but I don't think it's a *conspiracy*." It was more than a shitty run, really. It was an era of epic failures. From my stolen car (and my mysteriously lapsed car insurance, though I sent in checks every month) to the morning I woke up and found every piece of electronics I owned turned into useless lumps (the repair guy at the computer shop said it was like an electromagnetic pulse bomb hit my hard drive, and he sold me a pricey new system when it turned out my warranty had lapsed two days before) to, not least of all, my wife announcing six months ago that she'd fallen in love with another guy, and incidentally, she was taking almost all the clients from Poor Stephen Decorating, Inc. with her when she left. Pretty much the only customer I had now was a guy with a taste for taxidermied animal heads on the walls. Portia had gotten most of our friends in the divorce, too, it turned out.

"Do you want my help to find out who's doing this to you?" Cameron was intense, her eyes fixed on me like I was the only person in the world.

"How do you know anybody's doing anything? If you're not involved, where do you get your information?"

Cameron tapped her fingernails—unpainted, but long and nicely manicured—on her desk blotter. "I can't tell you that." She glanced at the ceiling, face taking on a faraway look, as if she were doing a calculation. "Not now. Soon. But I promise, Stephen, I can help make your troubles go away."

I pondered. "And you don't charge *anything*? I warn you, if this is some kind of long con, I'm not a good prospect. My wife got everything but our condo, and as you know, it's not much of a prize at the moment."

She grinned, and it was a very different expression from any I'd seen on her before—it was the grin of a professional athlete looking forward to creaming the competition. "I'm totally free. I only ask that you trust me."

I sighed. I still didn't buy it, but Cameron was definitely interesting, and my life had only been interesting in bad ways lately, so I decided to take a chance on a change. "Okay. You're hired. Only not in the sense of receiving any compensation for your services."

"Great. I've got some work to do here tonight, but come back at nine tomorrow morning and we'll talk about the next step."

"Okay." I could always just not show up, if I came to my senses in the night. I left her office and began the walk home, and happened to pass a couple of cops hanging out at the coffee shop on my way. They politely listened to my story, made a call on the radio, and told me someone would come to my place to take a report soon. I kept walking, and gave my ex-wife a call on my cell phone, getting her cheerful voicemail and trying not to sound too Eeyoreish as I told her about my latest win in the bad-luck sweepstakes. I left out the bits about gangstalking and Cameron. My ex and I had a remarkably cordial relationship, but it was still brittle, and couldn't bear that kind of strain. Back home in my wrecked apartment I dug around in my files until I found the phone number for my homeowner's insurance, so I could see about getting some of my stuff replaced.

The insurance people were very helpful. They helpfully told me they had no record of my policy at all, despite the hundreds of dollars in premiums I'd sent in over the years.

I sat on one of the least ripped cushions from the remains of my couch and thought about my troubles as the sunlight disappeared from my windows and another night fell over Oakland and my life.

※

The police officer came over around seven P.M. I'd made some small progress toward cleaning up the place, or at least piling the debris, working in the light from the lone unsmashed light bulb on the ceiling in the kitchen. The officer, a young Hispanic guy, whistled low, expressed his sympathies, and asked me if anything had been stolen. I told him no, just smashed. He said, "Have you had any, you know, altercations with anybody lately? This kind of thing, sometimes it's random, but sometimes it's teenagers getting revenge for something."

I opened my mouth to say, "Well, interestingly enough, I've got this webcam," but then my phone rang. My phone never rings anymore. "You mind?" I said.

The officer shrugged and wandered over to look at the view from my balcony, which was a pretty nice view, more so when the balcony wasn't strewn with shattered flowerpots.

"This is Cameron," the phone said. "Do *not* tell him about the webcam."

"Uh," I said, thinking, *She is in on it, she was bluffing.* "Why's that?"

"Because those two kids who wrecked your apartment have just been found murdered less than three blocks from your house. You heard those sirens a little while ago?" I had. I hadn't thought much of it. Sirens were just weather around here. "Unless you want to get embroiled in a murder investigation, tell the cops you have no idea who wrecked your place." She hung up.

As I put the phone away, I wondered how she'd gotten my cell number, but it didn't seem like such an amazing feat, all things considered. "Sorry," I said. "My ex. No, officer, I don't know who could have done it. I wish I did."

The cop nodded like he'd expected nothing less. "Let us know if you discover anything missing."

I forced a smile. "Think you'll catch the guys who did this?"

He held out his hand and seesawed it. "Sometimes we do, especially if they hit more than one place, but... We'll call if we find anything out."

"Before you go, I was wondering, I heard a bunch of sirens earlier, sounded close by…any idea what's going on?"

His face went stiff and guarded for a moment, then he sighed. "Officially, I can't comment, but anybody with a police scanner could find out, and it's your neighborhood, so…they found a couple of dead kids— teenagers—over by the motel a few blocks south. Probably a drug thing."

"Jesus. I hope you catch whoever did it."

"Me too, sir. Me too." He left me to my wreckage and my increasingly dark thoughts.

I had Cameron's number in my phone now, so I went to my balcony and leaned against the railing, looking down on the lake below. When she answered, I said, "What would you have done if it was too late? If I'd already told the cops about the webcam?"

"I would have come to the police station and told them I was your attorney."

That surprised me. "You're a lawyer?"

"I pretty much have to be. I've got my private investigator's license, too. And I trained to be an EMT, but my certification has lapsed."

"You're an accomplished woman."

"I just believe in being prepared. Stephen, the vandals getting killed… this is serious."

"You think it's related to this whole thing? Not just a coincidence?"

"Go out into your hallway. See if the webcam is still there."

I went. No camera at the end of the hall. "No, it's gone."

"I didn't take it down. Which means someone else came by your apartment and noticed it, realized their operatives had been caught on camera... and decided to dispose of them."

I could maybe believe people were fucking with me for undisclosed reasons, but that they were willing to *kill*? It seemed insane. I told Cameron so.

"You can either start taking this seriously, or you can wait until it gets bad enough to become undeniable," she said. "I don't know what's next, but their attacks on you seem to be escalating. What if they kidnap you? Get you hooked on heroin? Frame you for murder?"

I just laughed, bewildered, nervous—it seemed like something out of a straight-to-DVD thriller. "I guess that would be bad."

"Lock your doors. And if they broke the locks, block them with a bureau or something. Don't trust anyone, Stephen. It's in your own best interests to become a nutball conspiracy theorist. See you tomorrow. Nine A.M. You won't be late." She hung up, apparently not big on the rituals of hellos and goodbyes.

I went into the kitchen to check the cabinets for something edible, without much luck. Even my bag of pretzels had been torn open and stomped into salty powder.

A knock at the door. After a moment's hesitation I pressed my eye to the peephole, half expecting someone to shove a metal shishkabob skewer through the lens and into my brain.

My ex was standing in the hall, still every inch the perfectly poised and professional blonde, dressed in a long white coat with silver buttons, and a matching bag over her shoulder.

I opened the door. "Portia," I said.

"Stephen. Let me see what they did."

I stepped aside and she floated in, circling the wreckage, taking in everything with her professional eye, and finally shaking her head. "It can't be salvaged. You'll have to start again. Best tear up the carpet, I never liked it anyway. You'll need all new…everything. It's a shame, but it's also an opportunity, really."

I chose not to mention the fact that I could hardly afford a complete renovation. When we'd first split up, I'd suggested she buy out my half of our business, but she'd told me I was welcome to remain the head of Poor Stephen Decorating, and she'd start her own business, Portia's Designs. Which she did. Our clients didn't care what the business was called—they just went with her. Everyone assumed she was the one with the real aesthetic sense; it can be difficult to be taken seriously as a designer when you're a straight man, though I suppose straight men get enough advantages in life that the occasional disadvantage is only fair.

"Come on," she said briskly. "Put on your jacket, it's chilly out. Let's get something to eat."

"We're spending time together socially now? Won't Harold mind?" Harold. He was a personal trainer with a jaw like an anvil and a brain to match. I wouldn't piss on him if he was on fire, unless I could somehow start pissing gasoline.

"Harold's very secure in our relationship. He thinks it's nice that I stay in touch with you and try to help you out. Now come on. I'm hungry. We'll go to the Italian place on Telegraph."

I went obediently to put on my jacket, and locked up behind me when I left, not that I had much to protect. While we were waiting for the elevator, Portia suddenly hugged me tight, a seemingly impulsive act that was even more surprising because Portia was almost never impulsive—she was a planner through-and-through. "I'm so glad we became friends again, Stephen," she said, letting go. "I'm sorry things worked out the way they did between us. You know that, don't you?"

She'd never said sorry before, not exactly—there'd been a lot of "The heart knows what it wants" and "Surely you could tell things had cooled between us, I know you felt it too" and "You deserve a woman who loves you with all her heart" and such, but never an actual *sorry.*

"I know now." The elevator doors opened, and we went down and out, and I tried not to let myself pretend we were still married, going out for a meal like we used to do a couple of times a week, during the long gone far away good times. But I failed. Reality came crashing back when she dropped me off two hours later in front of my building without so much as a kiss on the cheek, and told me to take care of myself.

I had no idea how to do that at all.

※

The next morning I woke up early—even with my alarm clock smashed, I've always had a good body clock, and usually wake with the sun—and did my best to make coffee and toast in my demolished kitchen.

Finally nine o'clock arrived, and I was waiting outside Cameron Cassavetes's office with a paper cup of coffee in each hand. Cameron came around the corner right on time, carrying a pair of her own cups, and we looked at each other and laughed. "We're a couple of considerate ones, aren't we?" She unlocked the door and ushered me in. I noticed, with just a little rush of shame, that she'd repaired the damage I did to the glass.

We went into her office, and she sat behind the desk, though the good chair was there, this time, leaving me the lousy one. We each took a couple of sips of coffee, then she said, "We don't have much time. I want you to read this."

She pushed a sheet of lined yellow paper across the desk. Neat handwriting in blue ink, with a heavy black slash covering a few lines near the bottom. It began:

Next client. Stephen. Tuesday. Walks by co-op bakery 11:45 A.M. Ugly green sweater, cute butt.

"You think my…sweater is ugly?" I looked up, grinning a little. No one had called my butt cute in a long time. Portia was of the opinion that I had no ass to speak of.

She rolled her eyes. "Keep reading."

I did.

Victim of gangstalking. Reasons not definitely known, but probably the ones you think. Put camera at end of third floor hallway, 245 Arnold Way to document an attack and aid in establishing credentials. Beware escalations.

He'll think you're involved, will break into your office (call glazier to make an appointment), and will lie in wait behind your desk. Spare your back by switching the chairs around.

You should tell Stephen the truth. But you'll need a convincer. 9:16 A.M. Wednesday, your front door, freak hailstorm, falling bird. Make sure he sees it.

And after that, the blacked-out part, which I couldn't read, even when I held the paper up to the light.

"Uh," I said. "What is this supposed to mean to me?"

"Come on." She rose, and I followed, still clutching the cryptic document. We went to her door, which she opened, and looked out on an ordinary winter day. She looked at her watch. "9:15 now, and a bit. Keep your eyes open…"

There was a crack of thunder, always a rarity in Northern California, though the sky wasn't particularly ominous. And then—

Hail. I've seen hail here before, but it's usually the size of BBs, maybe pea gravel at best. These hailstones were more like marbles, some approaching golf-ball size, and they crashed down in a torrent that sent bystanders rushing for doorways or any other shelter they could find. Chunks of ice bounced mere feet from where we stood. "Holy shit," I said, and then a seagull crashed right in front of us.

I jumped back when the bird hit in a flurry of feathers, but Cameron didn't even flinch, just reached out and prodded it with her boot-clad toe. "Dead, poor thing. Knocked right out of the sky."

I looked at the piece of paper. "How. What." How could she make it hail? How could she arrange for a falling bird? "When did you write this?" I said finally.

"I wrote it later tonight," she said. "But I *received* the note a week ago. Come on. I want to show you something."

"What?"

"My time machine."

※

Troublesolving | Tim Pratt

I don't know what I expected, but what Cameron showed me was a metal lockbox. The safe was a little black job with a row of numbers to punch in a combination, like you might find in a hotel closet. Except there was a lot going on at the back, a spiraled mass of gears and wires and a bulb of cobalt blue glass in the center of it all, emitting a faint light. Cameron put the safe down on the top of her desk and thumped the top. "This is my time machine. Shame it's too small for a person to get inside, huh?"

"You are either a) crazy or b) fucking with me," I said.

"Mmm. There may be a third alternative. I got this device years ago, from a client I helped out with a tricky piece of trouble. My first client, actually. I don't pretend to know how it works, technically—I was told it has something to do with an infinitely long rotating cylinder warping space-time. But here's how it works, practically speaking. Once a week, the safe can be opened, and I find a note inside. A note from myself, but from one week in the future. The note tells me things I need to know— sometimes dangerous things, sometimes things about clients or cases, but sometimes mundane things, like what the weather's going to be like or if my favorite wine is going on sale. Every week I take out the note, and put *in* a note for myself one week in the *past*." She shrugged. "That's it. I send messages to myself. Not the most dramatic use of a time machine, but I'm assured it's relatively safe, as long as I follow the rules."

I knelt down and looked at the safe more closely. "Once again, if you're conning me, you're lousy at picking marks."

"You think I used my weather-control powers to start a hailstorm and knock a bird out of the sky, Stephen? Trust me on this."

"But if you *did* have a tiny time machine, why would you use it for such ordinary things? Why not send yourself, I don't know, lottery numbers? Stock tips?"

"I *have* done that. How do you think I can afford to be a freelance troublesolver? But I don't do too much, just enough to cover my needs and put a little money away for the future. The client who gave me this machine advised me to keep my mucking with the timestream to a minimum. Because the past *can* be changed, Stephen, both for the better, and for the worse. And that's where you come in."

She sat down again, and I did too. I'd hear her out. The hailstorm...
that was hard to explain away.

"In the future, there's a war," Cameron said. "And I think you must be
important to that war. Which is why people from the future—or people
receiving guidance from the future—are trying to destroy your life *now*,
before you can do...whatever you're supposed to do."

It was my turn to roll my eyes. "Haven't I seen this movie? A future
menaced by killer robots, one man destined to lead humanity to victory?"

"First off, it's not robots—just people, doing the things people do, for
the good and terrible reasons people do them. And I don't think you're
destined to save humanity. If you were *that* important, there would be a lot
more resources put into helping you than a simple troublesolver like me. I
mean, I don't even do violent solutions. But you must be important somehow, in some capacity, because you are being well and truly fucked with."

"Cameron, I'm an *interior decorator*. How can I possibly be important
to a war in the future? Does some dictator really like my aesthetic sense?"

"I admit it's a puzzler," Cameron said. "But I wonder...did you always
want to be a decorator?"

"Well, no. I don't know a lot of kids who grow up dreaming of that as
a career path."

"How'd you get into the business?"

"My wife. Ex-wife. We met in college. She was taking a design class,
so I signed up, too, figuring I'd flirt my way into her good graces. Worked
pretty well. The weird thing was, I discovered a real talent for decorating,
and Portia encouraged me, suggested we go into business after we graduated, and that's exactly what we did."

Cameron leaned forward. "What were you studying before?"

"I have double degrees in sociology and political science, actually. Not
tremendously useful to a decorator, I admit, though the sociology helps in
understanding trends and fads." I frowned. "You know, I did have another
job offer when I graduated, kind of an interesting one, but Portia was dead
set against it..."

"Let me guess," she said. "You were approached by a government
agency best known by a three-letter acronym."

"True," I admitted. "Offered a gig as an intelligence analyst, with hints of possible field work…I was always good with sifting data, and I was athletic as hell back then, captain of the lacrosse team, at least until I wrecked my knee. I tripped on a roller skate at Portia's apartment, of all things. That was the end of my jock days, though I get around fine after the knee surgery."

"You could have had a very different life, Stephen."

"I like my life fine. Or I did, until Portia left me. Everything went downhill after that. If you're right, and I am being persecuted, do you think…they somehow turned Portia against me?"

She frowned. "I suppose it's possible." Pretty diplomatic, I thought.

I put the sheet of paper back on the desk. "So what's this blacked-out bit? Did the time-cops censor you?"

She shook her head. "I blotted out a couple of lines. They were… personal. Nothing you need to see."

I couldn't decide if I believed her or not. Cameron was a hard person to read. I leaned back in my squeaking uncomfortable chair. "This war you're talking about—what are they fighting over?"

She shook her head. "I don't know. It's better if I don't know too much. The same reason I don't put too many details in these notes to myself—the bare minimum is really best."

"If you don't know what the war's about, how do you know you're even on the right *side?*"

"I'm on the side that *doesn't* gangstalk you and try to destroy your life. Is that good enough for you?"

I'm nothing if not pragmatic, so I nodded. "What happens next? No offense, but even though you've gone some way toward identifying my problems, you haven't exactly solved them yet."

"I've got some leads I'm tracking down. Once we find the person running this operation against you, there are…methods we can use to dissuade them."

"Why didn't you just, you know, jot down the solution to this little problem on that note from the future?"

"Maybe I won't know the solution by the time the safe opens. Maybe the answer will be written on the *next* note. Maybe—"

"Maybe there won't be a next note," came a voice from behind me.

Cameron was cool, just staring past me. I swiveled in my chair, and there—

There was Harold, the overmuscled asshole who stole my wife away, standing in the doorway in a black track suit with silver trim. He was holding a pink handgun—a Charles Daly .45 in fuchsia. Portia's gun. She'd bought it a few years back after a friend got mugged, because she wanted to feel safer, and it was pink because…well, because Portia thought it was hilarious that someone had a line of colorful "ladies' guns," something that struck her as unspeakably adorably kitsch.

"We only want the safe," Harold said. "It gives you an unfair advantage." He paused. "Which in this case means, any advantage." He ignored me, gesturing at Cameron with the gun. "Move away from the desk, Cassavetes."

She didn't shift. "Why? Are you afraid of me? I don't do violence. You know that."

Harold laughed, a low slimy chuckle that seemed to drip sweat. "You don't smack people around or shoot them, but you've done plenty of violence. We know all about you."

"Harold, you conniving shit," I said. "You were behind this? You stole Portia away just to fuck with me?"

"Shut up, Stephen. I'm not *supposed* to shoot either of you. Just make you irrelevant. But if I feel there's no other way…" He shrugged. "You get a certain degree of autonomy when your bosses live a few decades away. Move away from the safe, lady." He shooed her with the pink gun, and Cameron stood up and slid away from the desk. The whole situation should have been ridiculous, but mostly, it wasn't.

Cameron put her back to the wall, hands clasped before her. She didn't look worried, exactly—but then, I guess she knew she'd survive this, at least long enough to write a note that inexplicably didn't include the information that some guy would pull a gun on us. But that meant he wouldn't succeed in stealing the safe, right? Unless he could change the past, which in this case was the future, except…my head started to hurt.

"I'm going to take this," Harold said, inching toward the safe. "And then…you two can back to your miserable little lives, I guess."

"I'm going to tell Portia what you are," I said.

He snorted. "You do that. 'Portia, mean old Harold stole my new girlfriend's time machine—' Ha. The whole point is to make everybody think you're crazy, ruin your life, destroy your credibility. Feel free to help us out."

I'd spent a lot of the past six months feeling like a victim. I decided I was done doing that. I put my feet against the desk, pushed with my legs, and rolled me and my chair backwards about three feet towards the door.

"Fuck are you doing?" Harold swung the gun toward me.

"Me? Nothing. Just making you look at me instead of her." I had a feeling Cameron was the kind of person who could make use of an unguarded second, and at the very least, this put some space between Cameron and me, so Harold couldn't hold the gun on both of us at once.

He swung the gun back to Cameron, who was holding her cell phone. "Drop that!" he yelled.

"911 is only three digits, idiot," she said. "How long do you think it takes me to dial?" A voice from the phone said, tinnily, "911, what's your emergency?"

"No emergency!" Harold yelled. "Wrong number!" He scooped up the safe under one arm, took three steps toward the door, then stopped, frozen in place. I don't really know how to describe what happened next, except that he—strobed, looking less like a man than a special effect, body transforming into a coruscation of blue and white light, until the light...just went out. Harold was gone. The safe thumped to the floor. I scooted the chair a little farther away from it.

"Sorry to waste your time," Cameron said, and flipped her phone closed.

"Prank calling 911 is a misdemeanor, I think. Like filing a false police report." I stared at the spot on the carpet where Harold should have been.

"This cell phone's been deactivated," she said. "I always carry one like that, just in case. Even a cell phone with no calling plan can be used to call 911, did you know that? But it doesn't show a callback number. Good for anonymous emergency calls. I have to make a few of those in my line of work."

"What happened to him?" I asked. "Whatever it is, he deserved it, but..."

"The safe has security measures built in. If anybody touches it who doesn't belong in this time, it sends them to whatever time period where they *do* belong. And don't ask me how the safe knows, my old client said something about neutrinos and measuring the trace elements of contaminants in our bodies, but I'm not too clear."

"So Harold was from the future."

"Makes you despair about the state of the future, doesn't it?"

"But if he's a time traveler, can't he just...come back? Five minutes from now? Five minutes *ago*?"

"In theory, but I get the impression that actually sending a whole person backward through time is incredibly energy-intensive, not something that either side of the conflict does lightly. If Harold's proven himself a failure, compromised his cover...maybe they'll just keep him. I hope so."

"If you knew he'd vanish when he touched the safe, why did you even call 911?"

"I couldn't be *sure* he was from the future." Cameron picked up the safe and put it back on her desk, gently, like it was fragile. "The other side has local agents, too. Besides, you were so clever with your little rolling-chair distraction move, very lateral and lo-fi, I liked it. I didn't want to disappoint you."

I just laughed. "So it's over now? Harold is gone, and the gangstalking is over? We cut off the head?"

"Absolutely." Cameron wrote something on a piece of paper, then held it up. It read:

Absolutely NOT. Watch what you say. They're listening.

"That's a relief." I tried to keep my voice weird-inflection-free.

"Anything bad that happens to you now is just life. What do you say we go out and get some brunch? Unless you have Christmas Eve plans?" While she spoke, she kept scribbling, furiously, and I was impressed at her ability to talk and write at the same time.

"Is it Christmas Eve already? I guess it is. Holiday planning hasn't been at the top of my to-do list lately. Sure, something to eat would be great."

"Just let me straighten up a few things here. Hostage situations make such a mess."

Cameron passed me the new note. It said:

Troublesolving | Tim Pratt

How did Harold know about the safe? I sweep my office for bugs every day. There must be a listening device on you.

She looked at me pointedly, and I shrugged, not sure where I would look for such a thing, or how it could have been planted. She rolled her eyes, came close to me—closer than she'd ever been, closer than any woman had been in a long time, except my ex-wife, who didn't count in any way that really counted. Cameron patted me down thoroughly, slipped her hands into the pockets of my pants, then reached into the pockets of my jacket.

And withdrew a glittering needle, wrapped with brass wire, a blue light pulsing gently at its head. "This is it," she mouthed silently. "Play along." Then, aloud, "All right, let's go. Oh, your jacket's pretty thin, and with that hailstorm—here, I've got an extra coat, it's not very fashionable, but…"

I took the long dark trench coat from the tree by the door and put it on, feeling like an extra in a detective movie from the 1940s. "Nonsense, trenchcoats are classic." Cameron put on her own sand-colored coat, and we slipped out the front door, leaving my jacket and the listening device behind. Cameron hooked her arm into mine when we hit the street, and subtly tugged me in the direction of an alleyway. "Let's cut through to the next block, there's a good brunch place there," she said.

When we were well down the alley, which had a couple of zig-zags and narrowed so much we had to go single file, she stopped. "Okay, we should be out of sight of any watchers here. How did that device get in your jacket?"

"I don't know, maybe the guys who broke into my place planted it? But, no, I was wearing it when I met you…" I shook my head.

"I think there's a good chance Harold wasn't working alone," Cameron said. "At least, we can't be sure. But we've just let anybody listening know that we're going out, and leaving my time machine undefended, so…let's see if anyone takes the bait." She beckoned and led me to a concealed side door, hidden behind a dumpster, which took three different keys from her ring to open. The door slid into the wall silently, and she shooed me in, then closed up after herself. The space was small and dark, barely closet-sized, with a few TV screens on the wall and one chair. Cameron sat, and I stood by a door that presumably led inside. The monitors showed the street outside her front door, and the alley we'd just passed through, and her office.

We watched silently for a few moments, until a woman appeared on the street view. Unlike the other passers-by, she hesitated by the entrance, and when no one else was around, she did something to the doorknob, and the door swung open.

"Gotcha," Cameron said. "Do you recognize her?"

I nodded. I didn't want to, but I did. "Portia," I said. "My ex-wife. I saw her last night, I was wearing that jacket, she gave me a hug... She could have planted the bug on me."

"I'm so sorry, Stephen." She sounded like she meant it.

"Not as sorry as she'll be." When in doubt, try bravado. But being stunned and furious and hurt were at least different from being numb and sad and resigned.

On the monitor showing the office, Portia circled the desk, looking at the safe warily. She pulled on a pair of strange heavy gloves, like something you'd see a guy using in an iron foundry to handle unspeakably hot materials. She flexed her fingers, and the gloves sparked blue.

"What do you want to do?" Cameron asked. "I can't let her run off with my safe, so we need to do make a move."

"You're the troublesolver. You tell me."

"I can call the cops for real this time, have her arrested for breaking and entering. But if she's working for the other side, she'll have a get-out-of-jail-free card or two. They have serious connections. Warmongers always do."

I thought about that. Arrest, especially temporary arrest, wouldn't scratch the itch of vengeance. "How about I do this instead," I said, and pushed open the inner door.

I stepped into the office, silently, behind Portia. I could have grabbed her by the neck, hit her in the back of the head, kicked out her knee and stepped on her throat, and all those things appealed. Instead, I just said, "Why did you do it, Portia?"

She turned to face me, all innocent surprise, trying to hide her ridiculously gauntleted hands behind her back. "Stephen, what are you doing here? Harold was acting so strangely today, he ran off and took my handgun, and I heard the woman who worked here was a sort of therapist, or private detective, or something, and thought she could help—"

"Those are some pretty crazy gloves, Portia. The new style? That how they're wearing them in Paris this year?"

She sighed and sat down in Cameron's comfortable chair. I couldn't help but notice Cameron hadn't emerged from her little batcave, and in fact, the door had slid shut behind me. I hoped she was doing something useful in there.

"It was a good run," Portia said. "And I think we accomplished enough, even if we didn't manage to get you committed to a mental institution. The *point* was to drive you crazy, take you out of society all together. That's what you deserve, for the things you've done, will do, would have done. But I think we succeeded in making you harmless. It's good enough."

I took the crappy chair, my insides trembling like an earthquake, like the long-awaited Big One in my gut. "Portia. When did they get to you?"

She laughed, that bubbling contagious laugh I'd once found so endearing. "Nobody got to me. I came here for you in the first place. We found you in college—though details about your life are pretty well concealed in my time, we knew where you went to school. I insinuated myself. Made sure to steer you away from dangerous territory, as gently as I could. Letting you make the decisions, gradually, to keep there from being any…noticeable waves. I'm famous, you know, among my people. The woman who turned Stephen Blaine into a *decorator.*"

"But we were married. We were happy. If the point was just to distract me, to keep me from doing…whatever I was supposed to do…why spend all those years? Why the charade?" I wanted her to say I'd started as an assignment, but that she'd grown to love me, that I was—

"To hurt you more," she said, and there was a nastiness I'd never sensed in Portia, not even during our darkest direst fights. "To build you up higher so the crashing down would be more complete. I'm disappointed it didn't end better. But I'll take away this time machine, put an end to that woman's 'troublesolving,' and leave you to yourself. Who knows. Maybe the bitterness and loneliness and worry and doubt and grief will break you anyway. A girl can hope." She put her gloved hands on the safe, gingerly, and

I half expected—half hoped—she'd vanish, but nothing happened, except more blue sparks, and she visibly relaxed. "I'll be going now."

"No you won't," I said, standing up. "Not with that."

"How do you propose to stop me?"

"He won't have to." Cameron stepped out of her office, sliding closed something that looked like a cell phone, but bulkier, and emanating the same blue light the time machine and Portia's gloves had. "I called some colleagues. They'll do the stopping." She nodded toward the back wall, where a blue and white pulsation appeared in the air, and Portia looked behind her, comically alarmed, as a man and a woman stepped out of the rift and put their hands on her shoulders. Portia snarled and leapt up, but the man simply grabbed her in a bear hug and pulled her inside the rift, vanishing. The woman—who looked a little like Cameron, actually, but taller, and with somewhat heavier features, but the same brown-hair-brown-eyes—paused. "We've been trying to get her for a very long…well, 'a long time' is the wrong thing to say, sort of, but…you see what I mean." She looked at me, then looked away, and said, "It's an honor to meet you, finally, sir. I'm sorry I never had a chance to in…ah…" She shook her head, and her expression was all mixed-up and rapidly shifting, maybe grief, maybe restraint, maybe other things. I couldn't parse it all. She said, "Goodbye." Then turned and ducked into the rift, which disappeared after her.

I looked at Cameron, and she looked at me, and shrugged. "I don't know exactly what that was all about, either," she said. "But maybe you're more important to the future than I thought."

"What am I supposed to do with all this?" I put my head in my hands. "My wife betrayed me. People from the future are honored to meet me, for some reason. And I don't know *why*. Can't you use your magic cell phone to ask them what the fuck I'm supposed to do? Who are those people, anyway?"

"I try to call them on it often," she said. "No one ever answers. This time, they did. I guess they knew this time it was important. The guy who pulled Portia in, he was my old client, the one who gave me the safe, who recruited me to the cause. But I don't know the girl. Maybe someday I will. The future's a big place."

So it was. "I ask again, for the millionth time: Is it over? And what do we do now?"

"Brunch was a good idea," she said. "It's a start. But first, I've got to do something." She sat down at the desk, drew a piece of paper toward her, and began to write. I looked over her shoulder, terrified it would be *another* secret note for me, but she wrote:

Next client. Stephen. Tuesday.

"Now? You're writing this note now?"

"Mmm hmm. Time waits for no one." She didn't look up. "I write what was written. I produce the note I was given."

"Do you ever, I don't know, write something *different?*"

She looked at me then, and sternly, and she was almost even lovelier when she was stern. "Stephen. Some people just *have* to kill the golden goose. But some people, like me, are content to keep collecting golden eggs. I follow the rules. These rules, anyway." She went back to writing, and I remembered the blacked-out portion at the bottom of the note, and looked to see what she wrote, thinking she'd stop me if it really was too personal. But what it said was:

His ex-wife is behind it all. But he won't believe at first. Let him figure it out for himself. Don't let him read this part.

At first, I was pissed off. Cameron had known, all this time, she'd *known*...but if she'd told me my ex-wife was a time traveler out to get me, without me seeing the things I'd seen first, I'd never have believed her. "Can you maybe not keep any more secrets from me," I said. "Just in the future?"

"Why? Are we going to be spending a lot of time together in the future?" She kind of smiled when she said it.

"Whatever we're in, we're in it together now. They wanted to make me useless, but I'm going to do my best to prove them wrong. Besides, you didn't have anything better to do on Christmas Eve than tend to my troubles, so I figure you can probably use the company. And anyway, your office could use redecorating. Consider me hired."

She laughed, but didn't say no, and pushed some numbers on the safe's keypad.

The door popped open, and she stared into it for a long time.

"What's wrong?" I said.

"The safe." She folded the letter she'd written into thirds, slipped it inside, then gently shut the door. "There's no new letter inside the safe. No letter from myself from a week in the future. There's *always* a letter."

"Which means…what?"

"It means either a) I'm dead or b) there's some other good reason I'm not around to leave a note in a week's time. Though I honestly can't think what else it could be."

"Hey," I said, lightly. "You've got lottery and stock market money, right? And we could both certainly use a vacation. What do you say we go to the airport right now and take two weeks in a little shack on a tropical island somewhere far away?"

"That would be a good reason to miss writing a note," she said slowly. She looked up at me. Those chestnut eyes. I could get used to seeing myself reflected in them. "What would we be doing on this island for two weeks, Stephen?"

"What else?" I said. "We'd be thinking about the future."

The Indelible Dark

BY WILLIAM BROWNING SPENCER

He watched the car come down the mountain. The autumn trees were full of muted color, and black clouds rolled in the sky, restive monsters bloated with rain. The road unraveled in a series of switchbacks, and the car, black, shiny as a beetle, appeared and disappeared amid the trees.

Gravid raindrops began to fall, exploding on the road in front of him, and the boy closed his eyes and stood motionless. He could raise the temperature of his body by the power of his will, or, more admirably, he could acknowledge the discomfort and endure it. He preferred the latter.

The clothes he wore were designed to shed the rain before it reached his skin, and his hair was shorn so short that there was nothing to muss. He opened his eyes and waited: a proper schoolboy, not of the elite, but of merited parents, no scars, no admonishments scribbled on his face, his hands.

Now that the rain had asserted itself, there was nothing much to see. He hoped the car would not race by him, oblivious.

The car came out of the rain. He saw that it was bigger than the cars he had seen at Ashes Ville, and he suspected it might be powered by the blackoil that had burned the old world up.

The car slowed and rolled to a stop in front of him and the passenger door swung open. A black shaft—a weapon?—emerged, bloomed suddenly with a popping noise, and the boy stepped back, alert. An *umbrella*. The man beneath it was tall and seemed to vacate the car in stages.

"Stepped out for a bit of wet, did you?" the man said. His face was pale, unlined but ancient-seeming, smooth in the way that a river rock is smooth. Faded ink encircled his neck. He grinned, displaying a row of tiny silver teeth. "Where you bound?"

"George Washington City," the boy said.

"Well, fancy that! Same as ourselves. Come on. In you go." The man ushered the boy into the passenger seat, closed the door, then opened the rear door and, folding again, knees and elbows like some intricate device, shut his umbrella with a fierce shake and settled in the backseat.

The boy could sense no danger in the man behind him, no psychic crouch or killer's caution, which meant: a) that the man was no immediate threat or b) that the man was a grave threat, an assassin who could hide the subtle body language of intention. There was another person in the backseat, behind the driver, and this other was seeking him with a bright, hungry intelligence that the boy perceived as heat on the back of his neck.

He did not turn and stare. He suspected that the scrutiny was meant to be felt, and he did not wish to dignify it with a response. The boy turned his head slightly and regarded the driver. The man was a menial, an Albert or a Jorge, and possibly dangerous but predictable. He wore a grey uniform, and a hat, too small for his head, intentionally comic, demeaning, as was the present fashion in menials.

They drove on in silence, through a blur of colored trees, the world under glass and melting. Sometimes the beauty of the natural world felt like an assault, and his defense was a memory of burning cities, streets littered with rotting bodies, hulking scavenger machines that spoke to each other in bursts of static and feedback howls. The memory was not his own.

The one who studied him spoke, instantly revealing her gender. "You are a Cory," she said. He turned now and saw a girl with silver-blue eyes and short-cropped red hair, intricate ink scrolls crossing her forehead like a veil.

"My father was Andrew Cory," the boy said. "My name is Mark."

"I've never met a Mark. I hope you aren't vicious or sly. Can I trust you?" She offered a quick smile, tilted her head, studied him. She looked a mere girl, her slight body enfolded in shimmer cloth, moth-themed, green wings that seemed to flicker in the dark-blue shadows of the fabric. Her face was pale and perfect and her mouth, lipstick-shaped to mirror moth wings, revealed the giddy fashion sense of a child.

He shrugged. "Why would you need to trust me?"

"I don't," she said, frowning. "But I was hoping you'd say a simple 'Yes'."

"Why?"

She turned away and glared out the car's window at the roadside flora. Here the bright orange of maples pushed to the front, easily upstaging the purples and dark greens of the false birches and dog pines. The man behind Mark spoke: "What she's hopin' is that you aren't a bomb."

"Of course I'm not!" Mark said, turning to look again at the tall man whose eyes glittered with madness or amusement.

"You don't have to be offended, boy. There's more than a few of your kin who walked into the thick of crowds, yanked their little peckers and blew themselves and everyone around them all to fuck."

"You are speaking of an old protocol," Mark said.

"It puts my mind at ease, hearing you say that. You surely have an honest face."

The girl spoke: "Solomon, be quiet. He's not a bomb. I'd know if he was." She leaned toward Mark and touched his shoulder. "My name is Mary Constant," she said. "My people fight against Lethe's Children."

"We all did," Mark said. "The LC won."

"That is what they would have us believe. But imagine a world without them."

"I thought pirates had no politics," Mark said.

"Pirates? We are no pirates."

"The scrollwork on your face is pirate. This is your longman here, with a rope tatt round his neck and the augmented smile. You could be costumed revelers, I guess, but you aren't."

"Why not?" asked Mary Constant. She had taken her hand from his shoulder and it lay in her lap with the other. She gazed down at her hands as though chastened.

"I know the smell of pirates," Mark said. "I bet you stole this vehicle, and I wouldn't be surprised if its former owners are dead."

Mary Constant looked up and frowned. "They are dead, but it was none of our doing. And, if we are what you say we are, why shouldn't we kill you and be done with it?"

Mark said nothing.

The girl said, "We are not any pirates. We are revolutionaries."

⋇

Okay. This isn't one of those metafiction things. I hate it when an author intrudes, when he tries to ingratiate himself with his readers by pretending to be some sort of regular guy who is just trying to tell a story and hopes you are enjoying it. Here's what I mean: for years I lived in South Austin (the authentic, slacker heart of the city), and every day, mired in traffic, I would be forced to contemplate a giant billboard advertising life insurance. On the billboard, a smiling man in a suit held a telephone receiver to his ear while above him these words demanded attention: WHY BUY LIFE INSURANCE FROM A STRANGER WHEN YOU CAN BUY IT FROM ME, JOHNNY GARCIA? Johnny looked a little shifty to me, something larcenous in his smile and the black mustache that presided over those paper-white teeth. And, try as I might, I couldn't remember meeting the guy.

I, dear reader, am not presuming we are friends. And here's the best news: you'll never have to read this. Back in 1973 an innovative teacher named Peter Elbow wrote a thin, brilliant little book entitled *Writing Without Teachers*. Mr. Elbow discussed the process of writing and suggested that a writer might consider writing a rough draft that contains reflections on the piece being written, random thoughts, a poem, anything that would create momentum. All of this peripheral writing would enliven the writer's brain and when this chatter was later deleted it would, nonetheless, have imbued the final draft with its intellectual and emotional energy.

I've been having some problems with this nascent novel, so these are my mental stretching exercises.

My name is Joel Sherman, and I am typing this in my bedroom/office here in the Paris Apartments in Austin, Texas.

The Indelible Dark | William Browning Spencer

I came to Austin in 2002 when an ex-girlfriend impulsively invited me down here after her marriage fell apart. Elaine and I got along brilliantly for about eight months, and then we didn't get along at all, and I left the house but not the city.

I moved into a large, ramshackle house in Oak Hill, sharing it with the landlord and an ever-shifting mélange of university students and guys in bands. That's where I resided until recently.

I logged many years in that house, knocking out my series novels, vaguely aware of the melodrama that surrounded me. These transient young people, filled with hope, horniness, desperation, ambition, sundry drugs and alcohol, were volatile and unpredictable but easy enough to ignore. I assumed my ship would be coming over the horizon any day, and I'd be able to leave (maybe a movie sale, maybe an inexplicable surge in the popularity of private eyes whose eyes are very red) so I felt above the fray.

I considered myself and my landlord, Maxwell, rock-solid. We weren't close—I would never, for instance, have thought of calling him Max—but we would occasionally share a couple of beers and discuss the collapse of civilization. Maxwell was twelve years older than I, and somewhat morose. He wasn't one for sharing personal details, his sorrows being couched in elliptical language. He explained the failure of two marriages as "hegemony issues."

It had taken me a few years to establish this relationship with Maxwell. He rarely spoke to the other tenants unless they were late with the rent. So I should, perhaps, have been the one to investigate when my housemates approached me in a ragged delegation and asked what the racket was all about. One student maintained that the incessant construction noise robbed him of thought. All my sympathy went to any robber who got away with that kid's thoughts. I told them that our landlord was no doubt embarked on some major home improvements, and it was his house so he was within his rights. I recommended patience—and earplugs.

Two days later the noise ceased. We all moved warily, aware that it could resume at any moment. I think we spoke in whispers, although that may be a storyteller's embellishment. I remember at breakfast we all shared our observations: of the lumber and machinery delivered to the backyard, of the way it seemed to magically evaporate, and of our own creative relationship to the enigma of its use. What was Maxwell fashioning? Surely he intended to show us. It was not uncommon for days to pass without anyone laying an eye on Maxwell. His living area (which included a kitchen, living room, bedroom and bath) abutted the garage where he parked his aging Mercedes, so he could come and go at will without being seen. An unobtrusive landlord is usually a boon, but we were eager to see the results of his industry.

My bedroom was directly above Maxwell's, and in the general course of events, I never heard him. His home project altered that for a spell. I would have been justified in approaching him and asking that he curtail his zealous banging and sawing when 10:00 PM came round. That wouldn't have been asking much, but I understood creative passion and how the muse shouldn't be constrained by clocks. I worked at night myself. So I did not disturb him, and I was pleased when relative silence was regained without my intervention.

It was a little after ten in the morning, and I was sleeping soundly when I was jolted out of sleep by a single loud resounding *whump!* as though some fairy-tale giant had slammed a castle's giant-sized door. I had no recollection of a dream, but I felt an inexplicable dread. I lay there for a while and tried to will myself back to sleep. I failed and got up, pulled on a pair of trousers, and walked out into the hall where several young men and a waifish young woman I'd never seen before were milling around. I started down the stairs, and they followed. Being the oldest tenant (oldest both in tenancy and in years-on-the-planet) I led the way.

I knocked on Maxwell's door, but no one answered. The door wasn't locked, so I pushed it open, raising my voice to carry his name into the room. The door opened onto his bedroom—I knew this, of course, having been invited over to his living space many times—and the bed was empty and made. I had never seen it unmade. There was a minimalist, military feel to this room, everything in its place. I walked across the room and passed through the open door and into the living room.

I could feel my young roommates crowding up behind me: ragged breathing, a nervous squeak from the girl.

We stopped and stared.

The Indelible Dark | William Browning Spencer

I don't know what they were experiencing, but, while horror was surely the dominating emotion, they may have felt admiration for the craft involved, the care, the attention to detail. I know I did.

I had never seen such a well-wrought gallows. There is something about a solid-built thing. In the rigor that has fashioned it, there is love. I could smell the sawdust in the air although the room had been swept and everything was neatly put away. If a single detail could sum it up, I suppose that would have to be the banister that rose parallel to the nine steps leading up to the platform. Some would argue that on this very short walk to oblivion a banister was superfluous, but this wasn't about utility. The banister was there for its simple line: its dignity.

The room was awash in morning sunlight, which spilled from the skylight and the glass doors that led to the patio. Maxwell himself, revolving very slowly, his body half-hidden under the platform where the rope had halted his brief and sudden descent, wore a dark blue suit, a white, hangover-bright dress shirt, and a red-striped tie. He had thoughtfully powdered his face so that his countenance wouldn't look garishly engorged, and he wore sunglasses with a strap at the back so that they wouldn't go flying off and reveal eyes that bulged and made one think of trashy horror flicks.

He'd thought of everything. There was a piece of typing paper affixed to the lapel of his suit. It didn't look like anyone else could be relied upon for clear-headed action, so I carefully ascended the steps to the platform—without using the banister so that the inevitable police investigation could not accuse me of contaminating the scene (I've seen my share of television). I leaned forward and peered at a single line of 12 point Times Roman. He had signed his name, Maxwell Armour under the line of type.

This is what he left behind: "To my friends: My work is done. Why wait?"

None of us could think of what work Maxwell referred to. Someone suggested the gallows itself—which was imposing—but that was too reductive to make sense.

I learned later that his words were not his own. They were the words of the famous founder of Eastman Kodak, George Eastman. Maxwell had stolen Eastman's last words, which plagiarism rendered them, I thought, more poignant.

The Best of Subterranean

We all of us went to the funeral, where, surprisingly, a large contingent of relatives awaited us. They sobbed in an inconsolable fashion, and a beautiful young woman in a grey business suit became hysterical. I learned that she was Maxwell's daughter by his first wife. Who would have guessed that Maxwell could inspire such powerful emotion? I talked to the beautiful daughter and shared my thoughts on the craftsmanship of her father's final project, but she was too agitated to take any comfort in my words, and, indeed, glared at me as though I had said something reprehensible.

⋇

The house was put up for sale, and we were all obliged to move out. I guess I wasn't aware, when I moved to the Paris Apartments, that most of the residents here are old folks, many of them retired. Thanks to this older demographic, the management schedules activities such as daytrips to the restaurants in neighboring towns, bridge games, visits from a podiatrist, group exercise and lectures on nutrition. I don't attend any of these events. I am of the opinion that the less contact you have with your neighbors the better. I don't have time for their stories. I've got my own, after all.

My first novel, *Fat Lip*, was written when I lived in Fairfax, Virginia, and it was a minor success (by which I mean that it continued to generate royalties after the paltry advance paid out). My hero was a private detective named Hoyt who was allergic to lies. I was thirty-one when I sold that novel, and I've written eight more novels (sequels, because my agent says that most bestsellers are sequels although not all sequels are bestsellers), and a couple of dozen short stories. If you have read anything I've written you may have spent some time in a psych ward. That observation is based on the fan mail I receive, and I feel privileged to have such resilient readers.

Now, at forty-two, I live on the second floor in the central court of this two-story apartment complex. In order to reach my apartment door, I have to walk up the outdoor stairs and past my neighbor's door. In the long summer my neighbor, Vernon, will be sitting in a sturdy wrought-iron chair, one of two that preside over an infirm iron table, small and round, that someone has painted white with a brush (Vernon?). Vernon will sit there reading the newspaper, smoking a cigarette, and/or spooning something food-like into his mouth from the pot it was cooked in. He never deviates from his dress code, which consists of blue flip-flops and tiny cut-off jeans. His immense belly eclipses his vestigial shorts, and I can't be the only person who assumed on first encountering Vernon that I was in the presence of an extremely sweaty nudist practicing the tenets of his sun-worshipping religion.

Vernon's primary activity is surveillance. He studies the courtyard below, with its mimosa trees, its sidewalks, and its rectangles and circles of grass, which, despite the sprinkler system, have turned a mottled yellow and brown as the result of a record drought. He searches the courtyard for signs of life, generally people although I have seen him address a lone cat or dog with considerable animation. He is always talking, which is an edge he has if you are hoping to dart past him. When a resident or maintenance person or postal worker comes within range, Vernon can easily address that person (already having, as it were, a running start).

In the history of humankind, those members of the tribe who could not utter an interesting sentence developed other ways of stopping and holding their fellows. Vernon has all the inherited moves of this evolutionary byway. He can speak at great length without pausing to breathe. He can fix you with his eye, he can call upon your sympathies as a fellow human being, he can ask questions that require a response. If the recipient of his discourse attempts to flee, Vernon can raise his voice, instinctively gauging the exact number of decibels required to compensate for the increased distance, which suggests to the reluctant listener that flight is futile. And, of course, Vernon has the gift of obliviousness, the belief (shared by academics and members of 12-step groups) that his thoughts are inherently interesting.

I have come to terms with Vernon. I have learned to race by, to feign talking on a cell phone, or—if time is not an issue—to peer from between my mini-blind slats, waiting until he makes one of his brief but frequent retreats into his apartment.

I don't want to hurt his feelings. And I don't want to enrage him, to antagonize him in any way. I'm not sure what he is capable of, really.

Now where did that come from? I wasn't expecting that sentence. Maybe this free-writing stuff is like fooling with a Ouija board. Time to get back to the real story.

⸎

The rain stopped and the last watery light departed with the clouds and left a residue of stars. The car rolled on and Mark slept, not wholly lost to his physical self but maintaining a shadow sentry, a psychic construction similar to the created self he could summon under interrogation. He was aware of the driver, the girl and her longman as gray shapes on the other side of his dream. Well. Not *his* dream.

It was a bequeathed dream, one of his father's memories, filled with such love and rage that it left no room for private dreaming.

In the dream he was kissing her, his fingers lost in her black and bloody hair: this rough and terrible kiss, with its need to hurt, to invoke a scream.

But the dead are mute.

He lifted his head, blinking up into the cold light that came from the tunnel's painted walls, a varnish of glowing life, part of the outlawed orgtech that the rebels took for their own. He turned his gaze back to the pale face cradled in his hands and panicked. Her left cheekbone was oddly sunken, her bruised eye a red and angry slit beneath a purple lid, her other eye beautiful and terrible and abandoned. "*Mother,*" he whispered, and in that word was also lover, wife, warrior, comrade.

A strong-fingered hand clutched his shoulder, and the longman's voice, eroded by the narcobugs that slept in pirates' lungs, croaked in his ear: "Easy. Don't spook! What generation are you anyway? Could be you've been copied one too many times."

Mark said nothing, feigning stupor.

"Let's stretch our legs," the longman said, stepping out of the car. Mark followed, prepared for an assault, perhaps even welcoming such, for he had been reduced to confusion and disquiet by the dream, and a fight's present tense would be bracing. How often in the course of his training had he been awakened by some physical confrontation? As the teachers were fond of saying, "Sleep deep and you may sleep forever."

The car had stopped in a pool of moonlight beyond which pine trees presented a monochromatic wall. The rain was elsewhere, only recently departed and leaving in its wake an echo of its passing, the patter of raindrops still ticking amid the trees.

The man called Solomon walked away from the car, down the side of the road in the direction they had come, not looking back, and Mark ran to catch up. They walked until the car was out of sight. The wind pressed at their backs, a cold ghost, its breath sour and importunate. Above them the pale moon floated like something that had recently drowned and owed its buoyancy to the gases of decomposition.

"You are leaving that girl in the car," Mark said. "Isn't that unwise? The LC could be nearby."

Solomon stopped. He turned and smiled his moon-sparkled smile. "They could be. Life's no picnic anymore, unless you live in a rich fief where all the cooterments of civilization make for a nice dream. On the road, it's dangerous, although the LC don't have the patience for an ambush. I'm not over-worried about Mary. If something comes along, she'll waken and deal with it. Don't underestimate that girl, boy. You'd be no match for her in a mix-up."

"Is that what you wished to say to me beyond her hearing?" Mark said.

"No. I wished to *show* you something." He was still holding the folded umbrella in his right hand and with a flourish revealed its role as a flashlight. The wide beam illuminated a tangled wall of dwarf oak and thorn-laden jacketbush.

"Here we go." The pirate took a long stride into the trees, and Mark followed. A path had been machine-burned, leaving a flat wall of vegetation on either side, truncated branches, everything split and blown away by brute force, and leaving an odor Mark knew—"blood-and-razors" his brothers whispered. His heart sped up on the insistence of some dead soldier's encounter with this same stink. An LC trail, but old enough to allow the surrounding woods some tentative regrouping, a toadstool here, a burst of yellow-green ferns leaning out and looking both ways, some small reckless purple flowers raggedly running across the path toward the safety of the other side.

Mark hesitated, and the longman turned and said, "Let's not be coy. It's what you came for."

Mark shook his head. "No. I sought a ride to George Washington City. That is all."

"My friend, I don't wish to call you a liar, but the alternative is to call you a fool, and I don't think you are short on brains. We are all rolling along on the tracks our masters fashioned. Let's make the best of it. I suspect you were sent here to see this."

Mark thought this might very well be true. He could not see the whole design. No one could.

"All right," Mark said, "Show me what I am destined to see."

Solomon laughed. "That's the spirit!" He turned and set out again, Mark following.

※

So Lethe's Children are vicious little child-like creatures with a single day's worth of memory and very mutable swarm behavior. What the reader doesn't know is how closely Mark is related to these goblin-like children. These creatures were created to repair a damaged earth, to terraform it, and their common father is Andrew Cory. Mark Cory doesn't know that these creatures are kin.

And Mary Constant is my wife—or rather the ghost of my wife and this is not something the reader needs to know. It is something *I* need to remember.

Just thinking out loud. It has been a few days since I last wrote anything. What have I been up to? I don't know how it is with other writers, but writing often feels like the only time I have a self that can answer that question.

Growing up in Virginia, I had a friend, Artie Modine, whose father was considerably older than the parents of my other friends. Artie's dad always wore a suit—that's how I remember him, in any event—and was losing his mind in spectacular ways. "He got hit with Al's Hammer!" Artie would say and laugh. Artie and his dad weren't close. One time, Artie told me, he and his sister and his mom were waked in the middle of the night by a racket (glass breaking, metal screaming, a big hollow booming). *What the fuck?!* they all wondered (or maybe just Artie), and they followed the noise to the basement and there was Artie's dad, squatting in his underwear and watching the dryer spin. He'd stuffed it full of soda cans and bottles and coat hangers and trash and turned it on, and he was grinning like he'd won the lottery.

Not long after that, Artie's dad went into a nursing home.

Artie said that after his dad lost his mind, his dad was always punching buttons, flipping switches, working the remote on the TV without any plan. "Like he just wanted to make the electricity do something, anything." Artie had a theory about this: his dad had lost control and maybe thought he'd punched a wrong button somewhere, like when you accidentally change the television channel and can't get cable anymore so he was trying to push a button that would set everything right again.

That's sort of what writers do, isn't it? They try to restore order via narrative.

If you happen to say, "I try to restore order via narrative," in front of a bunch of people (say, during a book signing) you will immediately be identified as a pompous asshole. Just assume your book isn't great literature. It's going to be hard to avoid puffing up, and I suppose you could forgive yourself because you are, after all, only human—although, is that a good excuse? Hitler was only human. Charles Manson was only human. Every day humans are doing really awful things to other humans. So "only human": not a good excuse.

I've been thinking about this because my latest novel, *Heat Rash*, is now in stores, and BookPeople, a large independent bookstore that has always been welcoming (one of the staff even feigning knowledge of my series) arranged a signing. There were maybe twenty people in attendance; I recognized some of them from a writing group I sporadically attended.

I am proud to say that I did not talk in an exalted way about this humble comic crime novel. *Heat Rash* takes place in the midwest in the whacky world of little girl beauty contests. A tiny Madonna-pretender is murdered by an equally petite Lady Gaga imitator, or so it would seem. But the whole setup rubs my sleuth, Hoyt, the wrong way, and since he is already in the midwest (see: *Wasted in Waterloo*) why not take the money that the diminutive Lady Gaga's wealthy parents press upon him?

I read the part where Hoyt wonders about kid beauty contests and how such events might attract pedophiles, and he gets a brutal beating for thinking this out loud in a local bar. Hoyt gets beaten up at least once in every one of the books, and some insight always arises in the aftermath of a beating.

I signed six books, which isn't bad, although one of the books I signed wasn't written by me. I didn't have the heart to tell the woman that I wasn't Lawrence Block. I signed it "God Bless you, Larry Block."

I wound up getting cornered by an older gentleman who said he was writing a memoir and didn't read any fiction because life was short. *Not short enough*, I was thinking by the time I escaped the harangue.

Now that I had signed all the books—BookPeople buys a bunch, and if you sign them all they can't send them back—I wandered around the book store. I can't go into a book store without looking around—and buying a book. In these digital times, these ghost times, every lovely artifact, every physical book with its analog soul should have someone who will cherish it.

In the philosophy section I saw a book that had been dropped on the floor. I picked it up and recognized the title: *A Savage God*. The book was written by A. Alvarez, and I remembered reading it in college. Its subject was suicide (Sylvia Plath being a sort of template for that) and, as I recalled, it discussed suicide as a legitimate choice as opposed to most modern thinking in which depression, a result of unfortunate brain chemistry, is the engine that drives suicides.

Since I had found the book on the floor, I felt obliged to honor its in-my-path significance. I bought it. In college the paperback had probably cost me a couple of dollars at a used bookstore; the reprinted trade paperback cost $13.95 and, as was often the case, I suspected it would wind up on a shelf without being read again.

⋇

The Indelible Dark | William Browning Spencer

I didn't feel like going back to my apartment, so I drove north on Lamar, then over to Guadalupe and The Drag. Every university town has something equivalent to The Drag, a four- or five-block ecosystem for young people of the college persuasion. I like the energy, all these kids heading somewhere with backpacks, iPods, tattoos, exclamatory hair, smartphones and bottles of purified water (including *smartwater®*, recommended, perhaps, by their smartphones).

I ogled the co-eds and may have been guilty of a thought crime since some of these kids were no doubt underage (although a skilled thought-policeman would surely be able to read the nature of my thoughts and see their essential innocence).

I was thinking about what a world with thought-police would be like when a cluster of homeless people caught my eye. The last of the day's light was being consumed by street lights and neon signs, but these folks were illuminated by the light from a sign advertising vinyl records (the latest thing: like big, two-sided cds). There were plenty of cars on The Drag so I was moving at about five miles an hour, and I had ample time to ascertain that my mind wasn't taking some vague likeness and photoshopping it into someone I knew.

A skinny guy with a guitar hanging from his neck by a rope was leaning forward, eyes squinted to improve his concentration, a sort of fierce hunger manifest in every angular bone of his weedy body. Two ragged teenagers, a girl and a guy (both with exploding hair, geysers of hair) were sitting on the concrete with their legs pulled up, chins resting on their knees, backs against a wall covered with faded posters advertising defunct bands. Their mouths gaped open as though they had just witnessed a spectacular fireworks display.

I saw an ancient man whom I had seen all around Austin (sleeping on a bus stop bench, moving with a steady gait across some armageddon of a construction site, shouting with his head thrown back under a sky the color of a dead catfish), a man with a long brown beard and a wrinkled overcoat and the high seriousness of a prophet born at a time too narrow and petty to contain his truth. He too was entranced, his eyes wider than I'd ever seen them.

What was it that held their attention? What mesmerizing event was this? Who was so riveting?

Vernon.

Yes. My neighbor Vernon was speaking to them. He wasn't wearing his stay-at-home outfit. He wore khaki overalls and a long-sleeve grey garment that might have been the top half of winter long johns. It was 95 degrees, starting to cool down, but he was still over-dressed. Aside from his disorienting attire, he was the Vernon I knew. He stood still, his arms at his sides, somehow robbed of all vitality, while his mouth shaped words and loosed them into…well apparently into the enraptured minds of his indigent audience. When I listened to Vernon, did I have some equally entranced expression? It seemed unlikely.

I drove home thinking, "What the hell?"

※

Mark consulted the semi-Q that vibrated in his temple and learned that he had traveled for fifty-two minutes, an unpleasant trek whose destination remained obscure. He had no reason to trust this pirate, but if Solomon intended any harm, it would be a waste of time. Mark knew he was worth very little in terms of information, a link in an encoded chain, and his death, even his dissection, would instruct no one.

In any event, he didn't think the pirate was scheming against him. He wasn't sure what—

In front of him, Solomon suddenly crouched. Without looking over his shoulder, Solomon patted the ground next to him, and Mark came forward and they both looked down at the valley below.

The crowd within Mark noisily urged flight, but he quelled their voices with a warning. "I can be rid of you for good," he thought, and the voices settled into a fluttering of moth wings. He added, "And you're no help if you hide."

Every nest differed, because Lethe's Children were not inclined to do the same thing twice. They were busy as bees but not as consistent. And not much smarter, according to some of the scientists who studied them. What the LC was was *flexible*.

They had swarmed this old NewMeriCo fortress, and they'd left some of the company's biggest weapons intact because Lethe's Children just didn't seem to care about these killing machines. They had no fear. Although they screamed when hurt, they didn't avoid pain. *Good soldiers!* Mark thought. Mindless idiots: good soldiers.

These soldiers looked like children—from a distance. Up close, they looked creepy and terrifying. Unless you were observing a dead one or one strapped on a board—and alone they didn't last long—you wouldn't know just exactly what they looked like because they were very, very fast. The way their alien-attributes entered your consciousness was subtle: a moan that rose to a scream. Better to see a monster at once, a full-blown horror, than have it enter your mind as a guest, something familiar, and transform into a goblin.

War Solutions, Inc., one of the bigger weapons manufactures, created drones that could track them despite their speed. There were a hundred ways to kill the LC. They were, in truth, flimsy creatures. But they existed in vast multitudes and the killing machines grew mired in pale goblin bodies and then the LC decided to shift behavioral gears and bring some new horror forward. And most of the human world, barred from the fortresses, the shielded cities of the elite, crouched in small villages preparing for an attack, practicing with their weapons, while Lethe's Children were playing elsewhere. Later, on a whim, the LC would come and kill the tiny, irrelevantly brave humans.

Mark watched Lethe's Children closely, hardly breathing, looking for some pattern, some weakness, as though they had not already been under the world's scrutiny for years. Mark had never seen them firsthand; all his memories were hand-me-downs, and, beneath his revulsion and fear, there was still some satisfaction to be had in acquiring a memory born of his own experience. He just needed to live to keep it.

Lethe's Children scrambled up and down the altered shell of NewMeriCo. Scientists had discovered that each creature had between three and ten instructions that governed its behavior. As with the social insects, fairly sophisticated swarm behavior could be created with a set of limited protocols. What was unsettling was the constant reprogramming that occurred, apparently somewhere deep in the hive, as though some greater intelligence existed and could make administrative decisions. No such central intelligence existed in an ant colony, and ants were already the most successful insects on the planet. What if the LC were something more?

They move so fast! Mark thought. They were excavating a hill next to the fortress, running as though some project deadline were rapidly approaching. When they encountered each other they would kiss or slap each other, the slapping behavior being elaborate like a vid his teachers showed him of long-ago humor for long-ago television...*slapstick* someone said...yes, the stooges, three of them: Curly and Mo and another one.

A hand clutched Mark's wrist, and he almost screamed. It was Solomon, and the pirate handed him digi-wraps, which Mark slipped over his eyes to look where the pirate directed.

There was some beast, a black, bulky thing—a gorilla? No there were no gorillas here, this was a shambling, shabby thing a—yes!—a bear. Not a grizzly, a smaller bear, but bigger than Mark.

Lethe's Children were tormenting the bear, prodding it with sticks, throwing stones at it, rushing in to bite a leg, a buttock, genitals. Another LC, smaller than the general lot, jumped on the animal's shaggy back and bit it on the shoulder. The bear was not defenseless, and with a roar it flung the creature off and swiped at it with a massive paw. Something rolled beyond the frenzied circle, and Mark turned to let the digi-wraps call it into focus. It was a head, still animate, mouth open and making an ululation which rendered the brothers within Mark crazy and incoherent.

Now the LC were on the bear, and the animal collapsed under their numbers and grunted and coughed and something dark—blood—seeped out beneath the awful writhing of these small, idiot monsters.

Mark thought he might be sick despite his high marks in self-mastery. A hand fell on his shoulder and he heard the pirate's voice: "I think they wanted our eyes on the show," he said. "And it's too late now."

Mark turned, pushing the digi-wraps aside, and beheld the grinning faces, and noted a detail no one residing in his mind seemed to have logged: the creatures had three thin tongues that slipped like a black tide between their blood-red teeth.

Strange times. I'll cut to the chase here. Yesterday, I came out of my neighborhood grocery store at about one in the morning. I like to do my shopping when most citizens are sleeping. There is a downside to that, but there's a downside to almost everything. In the case of late-night grocery shopping, the problem is this: now that the crowds have thinned out, the shelf-stocking begins in earnest. There are boxes and giant pallets all over the place. You can't push a cart down most of the aisles, and you are forced to dart in and out of narrow spaces like some marginal scavenger in the end times. In this predawn state, when few humans are around to enrich the ambience, the lights cast a grey-green pall that wouldn't be out of place in the world's worst zombie crack house, and the electricity is more apt to snap at your hands (despite the cart's rope-like wire that skids along the store's floor to prevent just this from happening). If you decide to tell your cashier (average age: 14) that you are getting electric shocks, he will look at you with new wariness and say "Whoa," or something equally unhelpful.

So I came out of the store and watched a nightjar swoop after bugs drawn by the parking lot's many lamps. This was not a bat, it was a nightjar. You might think that I don't know what I'm talking about, but in this instance, I do. Consider that a preemptive strike against your incredulity.

I unlocked my car with my remote. I was six feet from my car when, out of the shadows, a large shapeless person appeared. His silhouette and lurching gait suggested a man who was sleeping outdoors, and when he came under the street light I recognized him. He was the ancient bearded prophet who I'd seen listening to Vernon on The Drag.

"Hey," I said. He had the reek of someone marinated in cheap wine and boiled under a bad year's vicious sun. He was shabby and sick and wore unsnapped rubber boots that wouldn't be seeing any rain any time soon. He wore one glove, and that gloved-hand clutched half a scissors, which glittered ominously as though recently sharpened.

"What do you want?" I asked.

He frowned, possibly interpreting this question as a trick. He said, "Don't want nothing. Don't fear nothing. Don't—"

He staggered forward and tripped, his clumsiness resulting in a swift lunge that neither of us had been expecting. I dropped the plastic bag—a jar of pickles burst, releasing a sweet and sour smell—and I staggered back, banging against my car. My attacker lay on the ground, muttering. I opened the car door, ducked my head, and turned in the driver's seat. I slammed the door and drove away.

When I got back to the Paris Apartments parking lot, I noticed that I still had the half-scissors. My stomach had claimed it, and it was sticking out of my tee-shirt. My heart sped up when I realized the blade was firmly embedded in my stomach. Beyond a certain muted discomfort, I felt okay, but I knew that didn't signify anything. Maybe I was in shock. I was pretty sure it should hurt a *lot*. I parked my car, and thought, "I should probably drive to the ER," but I didn't. Moving carefully, I slowly marched up the stairs to my apartment. Vernon was not in sight, and since he would engage me in some inane conversation even if I told him I had just been stabbed, I was glad he wasn't around. He was a night owl, too, and so it was just luck that I dodged him.

The reek of pickles entered my apartment with me, and I realized that the cuff of my right pants' leg was soaked in pickle juice. I sat on my sofa and studied the scissors. Should I call an ambulance? Probably I should, but—I gripped the scissors' handle and slowly pulled the blade out. It came out as clean as it had gone in. No blood? I was expecting a great dark patch to bloom on my shirt, a malignant Rorschach test whose interpretation was easy. But nothing happened, and when I lifted my shirt up, my stomach, though larger than I would have wished it to be, was unsullied by any wound.

I don't know how someone else would have dealt with this anomaly, but I was exhausted. I lay down on the sofa and immediately fell asleep.

⇥|⇤

The Indelible Dark | William Browning Spencer

All my life, I've felt that some reckoning awaits me. For the longest time, I assumed that everyone felt that way, but they don't. Say the phrase "existential dread" to most folks and they'll draw a blank. Some folks will say, "I studied that in college. Camus, Sartre, those guys, right?"

I was always a morbid kid, I guess, although I only know that in retrospect. I can remember when I was maybe seven or eight, me and Artie and Susan Randall and her kid brother Pie and a gawky kid named Hoot who lived in a haunted house, we found a dead cat by the side of the road. I told everyone that we could all be like that in less time than it took to spit, just as dead, because we were made of the same stuff! I told them I'd seen a television show about the human body, and it wasn't good news, we were built out of jelly-stuff and baloney-like valves that opened and closed but couldn't do that forever and a heart that beat like a moth against a screen door and germs that swam in all the juices inside us and a brain that looked like a lot of grubs stuck together or maybe one of those popcorn balls people make at Christmas and everything depended on everything else, which was supposed to be wonderful according to the television scientist but wasn't when you thought of all the things that could go wrong, and if you took your eyeball out and put it on the curb in the sun, it would dry up right away like a grape on a hot skillet because: *we were just like that dead cat.*

Susan Randall hit me with her lunch pail, and I still have a tiny pale scar on my chin. I went to her funeral in high school; she'd jumped off the Skyway Bridge that stretches across Tampa Bay. She was on vacation with her folks, and they found a note. Her boyfriend had dumped her for a girl named Lily Fields who was cute in a way that I knew was going to go bad and it did. I saw Lily at a ten-year high school reunion and she was already looking puffy and clownish against her will. Her boyfriend wasn't there, but they had both shown up for Susan's funeral, clutching each other in an erotic fit of bereavement.

In college, I was friends with Leslie Heckenberg—and we were just friends, no sexual entanglement. She was pretty, but I wasn't attracted to her for whatever reason (pheromone mismatch maybe). She was the funniest, smartest person I knew.

She could talk for hours about life's various hideous aspects. She had some hilarious rants. There were other days, however, when irony deserted her and in a harrowing monotone she would talk about the utter failure of her existence. She began going into hospitals for depression. She got some electro-shock treatments and cheered up for a while but then plummeted into some dark hallucinatory hell and took a lot of pills and left a message on her landlady's answering machine—it was a Friday and the landlady wouldn't be back until Monday—saying: "By the time you get this I will be dead." And she was.

A friend of mine said, "Well, she's been talking about killing herself for years, so maybe congratulations are in order. She followed through. You've got to admire that." And he added: "I'm sure you helped her along; you've always been sort of…I don't know…pro-death?"

※

Of course I thought about killing myself. To some extent, it was peer pressure—one time I made a list of friends and acquaintances who had offed themselves, and it came to fourteen names—but I also fancied myself an intellectual, so I had to reflect on Camus's famous utterance: "There is but one truly serious philosophical problem, and that is suicide. Judging whether life is or is not worth living amounts to answering the fundamental question of philosophy."

My father and older brother were hunters, and on my sixteenth birthday I was given a shotgun. I had decided, years earlier, that I was never going to shoot at anything that couldn't shoot back, so my father and brother continued to hunt without me, but I did, on occasion, go off into the wilderness with my weapon and contemplate blowing my brains out. However, I had never liked Hamlet's overwrought vacillating, and when I saw the same behavior in myself, I stopped entertaining thoughts of self-destruction. I figured I'd know if I were ready to end it all. Hamlet never figured it out. He was killed when Laertes stabbed him with a poisoned sword, and consequently never had to answer Camus's ultimate question: why proceed?

I dreamed that Vernon was in my apartment last night. I woke to the sound of a match being struck. I was instantly alert and upright, peering into the dark to where a cigarette's red ember hovered.

"Who's there?" I said.

"Oh, good, you're up." a voice said, someone sitting in the big, multi-colored armchair I'd gotten for free when a couple I knew grew rich and needed more sedate decor. The lamp on the end table clicked on, and I saw Vernon. He was wearing a suit, which may have been his usual visiting attire for all I knew. He held a small black derby, balanced on his knee, while he held his cigarette with his other hand.

"No smoking in here," I said, the sort of thing anyone might say in a dream when more pressing issues are at hand.

"Nothing to worry about. I have disabled the smoke alarm." He gestured toward the ceiling, and, sure enough, the smoke alarm was dangling there, clearly deprived of its 9-volt battery.

Vernon leaned forward and said, "I want to apologize for Truthman's behavior."

"Who?"

"Truthman." Vernon chuckled. "He says an angel on fire gave him that name, and it burned away his memories of his parents and whatever name they might have pinned on him."

"Well he stabbed me with a scissors," I said.

"I did not encourage that at all."

I remembered. "I saw you talking to him. You put him up to that, didn't you?"

"I did not. I was just discussing the nature of free will with Truthman and some of his cohorts. He is not a sophisticated man, and he came to the conclusion that he should kill you."

"What for?" I asked.

"To prevent your doing more harm in the world."

I was starting to get angry.

"Who are you? This isn't the Vernon I know. That Vernon is…well…a boring idiot…a monologist…a nuisance…but I can't imagine him breaking into my apartment in the middle of the night."

Vernon nodded. "Yes. That Vernon utters 'polite, meaningless words' as the poet Yeats would say. I have been in a disguise, and you have told me much about yourself."

I knew I had told him nothing.

He read my expression and answered it. "But you have. It is what Yeats said, again, 'Too long a sacrifice can make a stone of the heart.' "

"What sacrifice are you referring to?"

Vernon sighed, put his cigarette out by scrubbing it against the bottom of his shiny black shoe, and stood up. "Your compassion. We've had this conversation many times before, but you don't remember. You were hell bent on not listening. You used to be what we call a karmic facilitator, for want of a better name in this sad fleeting world, but you are retired now. I should have retired years ago, myself.

"We are night people, you and I. We are more comfortable in the dark, and the dark has entered our blood. The indelible dark. Ring a bell? It should, you're the one who coined the phrase. Well, you are my last case, and I can't say a lot, so you'll have to listen as hard as you can. You are not responsible for the people you killed, but you killed them all the same."

"How come I don't remember this entire secret karma-agent thing?" I asked.

Vernon shrugged. "When you retire, you get a choice. You can remember, or not."

"And I, of course, chose to forget."

"Well, most people do. It's what I'm choosing. And, anyway, on some level, you didn't forget, did you?" Vernon looked around the room as though he might be forgetting something.

He said, "You might decide that you need to leave this world, that your staying in it endangers others. There is a young woman you spoke to several months ago at her father's funeral. Earlier tonight she was lying in her bathtub. The water was warm, and she held a razor in her right hand and she knew that the surest cut was lengthwise and she had been drinking, wine, quite a lot, and she was confident she could do this thing that would separate her from her pain, but, reaching out for the wine glass, she knocked it to the floor, and it shattered, and she got out of the tub and cleaned the mess up—fastidious woman—and the water went tepid and the impulse toward oblivion was lost. She went to bed, wrapping herself in blankets, crying until the alcohol pulled her into sleep. Tomorrow is another day, and she can kill herself then."

Vernon paused, but it was clear he had more to say. How could this be the same man who had never, as far as I knew, uttered a single word worth marking? I was breathless now, waiting for him to speak.

"You may discover—I suspect you already have… Did Truthman's scissors make you bleed? No. I thought so. You have been given a kind of protection for your service. But there are ways for you to forsake this life, and though I can't direct you, I can urge you to reflect. Think of that young lady, your late-landlord's daughter… Our world has a fondness for the circular. That is karma, after all. Meditate on karma, my friend. The dark gets on us, and it's indelible and we pass it along. You carry the suicide virus in your heart, and any chance encounter can infect others."

He lifted his hat, positioned it over his head with both hands, then tapped it smartly with the fingers of his right hand and disappeared (confirming his dream status should I have had doubts in the morning).

⋇

I can't meditate. I can't think. I've been walking around the room in an agitated state. A minute ago I spied a copy of *The Savage God* on a bookshelf next to *The Bell Jar*. This is the old, battered copy of *Savage* that I purchased long ago. I guess I wasted $13.95 on the new copy I bought on impulse. Maybe BookPeople will give me my money back.

I was thumbing through this old copy, and I came upon something Mary (not the child of my sf novel, which is, I think, going to be a short story, not a novel)…no, Mary my wife, something she wrote, something Mary whose eyes were silver-blue, whose hair was red, who thought she might save me but knew nothing of the indelible dark wrote in one of her goofy editorial moments. She had a fondness for these brief annotations. I don't remember seeing this one before.

This is what she wrote: "Oh Joel! Coals to Newcastle, I guess! Love forever, Mary."

What can a writer do? Well, I can finish this damned story. Although other things are more pressing now.

Here's a synopsis to make quick work of it:

※

Mary arrives to save Mark and Solomon from Lethe's Children. They do not attack Mary. She is a god to them. They lead her to a vast computer, the ancient machine that alters the child-goblins' primitive instructions.

Being a god in a science fiction story is often bad news, and since this story is more Edgar Rice Burroughs than Kim Stanley Robinson, Mary is in grave danger. She is the new genetic material that the monstrous machine requires to write new diversity into its hapless children. Mary has already suspected this, and she is willing to make the sacrifice in the interests of a better world, but—

※

In the shadows of the underworld, Mark watched the door slide open and Mary, accompanied by half a dozen of the LC, entered. The door began to slide closed again, and Mark realized that it was a vast steel wall that *revolved*. This was no simple door that might be broken by brute force; this was a slow-turning wheel that might roll round again in a hundred, a thousand years.

※

Maybe this will be a novel. Against all odds, promising vengeance if Mary's salvation proves a lost cause, Mark and Solomon battle their way over the wall and through jungles and treacherous cities. Solomon is wounded several times, and a cybersyncOrgbot whom Mark has befriended keeps creating artificial bits for Solomon, bits that will come in handy later.

Maybe it would end like this:

Mark wasn't too late. He hadn't raged at her and stalked off and stayed at a friend's house and returned late the next night, still drunk, to find her dead, the bath water red, her face like porcelain, her lips the faintest blue.

O Mary. I should have been your champion. And I failed you when I thought I was only failing myself.

I think I know what Vernon was getting at. I think I know how to remove the curse that lies on that young woman's heart. I'm going to drive out to Oak Hill, fingers crossed, my equivalent of a prayer. I still have my key to the house. I think Maxwell's masterpiece will still be there. Wouldn't anyone hesitate to destroy something built with such rigor, such care?

This time I will use the banister, running my hand along its smooth, lovingly-sanded surface—and though I walk through the valley of the shadow of death, I shall fear nothing: for there are no shadows in the dark, and the daylight ghosts won't follow me there.

The Prayer of Ninety Cats

by Caitlín R. Kiernan

In this darkened theatre, the screen shines like the moon. More like the moon than this simile might imply, as the moon makes no light of her own, but instead adamantly casts off whatever the sun sends her way. The silver screen reflects the light pouring from the projector booth. And this particular screen truly *is* a silver screen, the real deal, not some careless metonym lazily recalling more glamorous Hollywood movie-palace days. There's silver dust embedded in its tightly-woven silk matte, an apotropaic which might console any Slovak grandmothers in attendance, given the evening's bill of fare. But, then again, is it not also said that the silvered-glass of mirrors offends these hungry phantoms? And isn't the screen itself a mirror, not so very unlike the moon? The moon flashes back the sun, the screen flashes back the dazzling glow from the projector's Xenon arc lamp. Here, then, is an irony, of sorts, as it is sometimes claimed the *moroaică*, *strigoi mort*, *vampir*, and *vrykolakas*, are incapable of casting reflections – apparently consuming light much as the gravity well of a black hole does. In these flickering, moving pictures, there must surely be some incongruity or paradox, beginning with Murnau's Orlok, Browning's titular Dracula, and Carl Theodor Dreyer's sinister Marguerite Chopin.

Of course, pretend demons need no potent, tried-and-true charm to ward them off, no matter how much we may wish to fear them. Still, we go through the motions. We *need* to fear, and when summoning forth these simulacra, to convince ourselves of their authenticity, we must also have a means of dispelling them. We sit in darkness and watch the monsters, and smugly remind ourselves these are merely actors playing unsavory parts, reciting dialogue written to shock, scandalize, and unnerve. All shadows are carefully planned. That face is clever make up, and a man becoming a bat no more than a bit of trick photography accomplished with flash powder, splicing, and a lump of felt and rabbit fur dangled from piano wire. We sit in the darkness, safely reenacting and mocking and laughing at the silly, delicious fears of our ignorant forbearers. If all else fails, we leave our seats and escape to the lobby. We turn on the light. No need to invoke crucified messiahs and the Queen of Heaven, not when we have Saint Thomas Edison on our side. Though, still another irony arises (we are gathering a veritable platoon of ironies, certainly), as these same monsters were brought to you courtesy of Mr. Edison's tinkerings and profiteering. Any truly wily sorcerer, any witch worth her weight in mandrake and fox-glove, knows how very little value there is in conjuring a fearful thing if it may not then be banished at will.

The theatre air is musty and has a sickly sweet sourness to it. It swims with the rancid ghosts of popcorn butter, spilled sodas, discarded chewing gum, and half a hundred varieties of candy lost beneath velvet seats and between the carpeted aisles. Let's say these are the top notes of our per-fume. Beneath them lurk the much fainter heart notes of sweat, piss, vomit, cum, soiled diapers – all the pungent gases and fluids a human body may casually expel. Also, though smoking has been forbidden here for decades, the reek of stale cigarettes and cigars persists. Finally, now, the base notes, not to be recognized right away, but registering after half an hour or more has passed, settling in to bestow solidity and depth to this complex *Eau de Parfum*. In the main, it strikes the nostrils as dust, though more perceptive noses may discern dry rot, mold, and aging mortar. Considered thusly, the atmosphere of this theatre might, appropriately, echo that of a sepulcher, shut away and ripe from generations of use.

Crossing the street, you might have noticed a title and the names of the players splashed across the gaudy marquee. After purchasing your ticket from the young man with a death's head tattooed on the back of his left hand (he has a story, if you care to hear), you might have paused to view the relevant lobby cards or posters on display. You might have considered the concessions. These are the rituals before the rite. You might have wished you'd brought along an umbrella, because it's beginning to look like there might be rain later. You may even go to the payphone near the restrooms, but, these days, that happens less and less, and there's talk of having it removed.

Your ticket is torn in half, and you find a place to sit. The lights do not go down, because they were never up. You wait, gazing nowhere in particular, thinking no especial thoughts, until that immense moth-gnawed curtain the color of pomegranates opens wide to reveal the silver screen.

And so we come back to where we began.

With no fanfare or overture, the darkness is split apart as the antique projector sputters reluctantly to life. The auditorium is filled with the noisy, familiar cadence of wheels and sprockets, the pressure roller and the take-up reel, as the film speeds along at twenty-four frames per second and the shutter tricks the eyes and brain into perceiving continuous motion instead of a blurred procession of still photographs. By design, it is all a lie, start to finish. It is all an illusion.

There are no trailers for coming attractions. There might have been in the past, as there might have been cartoons featuring Bugs Bunny and Daffy Duck, or newsreels extolling the evils of Communism and the virtues of soldiers who go away to die in foreign countries. Tonight, there's only the feature presentation, and it begins with jarring abruptness, without so much as a title sequence or the name of the director. Possibly, a few feet of the opening reel were destroyed by the projectionist at the last theatre that screen the film, a disagreeable, ham-fisted man who drinks on the job and has been known to nod off in the booth. We can blame him, if we like. But it may also be there never were such niceties, and that *this* 35mm strip of acetate, celluloid, and polyester was always meant to begin *just so.*

Likewise, the film's score—which has been compared favorably to Wojciech Kilar's score for Campion's *Portrait of a Lady*—seems to begin not at any proper beginning. As cellos and violins compete with kettledrums in a whirl of syncopated rhythms, there is the distinct impression of having stumbled upon a thing already in progress. This may well be the director's desired effect.

EXT. ČACHTICE CASTLE HILL, LITTLE CARPATHIANS. SUNSET.

> WOMAN'S VOICE (fearfully):
> Katarína, is that you?
> (pause)
> Katarína? If it is you, say so.

The camera lingers on this bleak spire of evergreens, brush, and sandstone, gray-white rock tinted pink as the sun sinks below the horizon and night claims the wild Hungarian countryside. There are sheer ravines, talus slopes, and wide ledges carpeted with mountain ash, fenugreek, tatra blush, orchids, and thick stands of feather reed grass. The music grows quieter now, drums diminishing, strings receding to a steady vibrato undercurrent as the score hushes itself, permitting the night to be heard. The soundtrack fills with the calls of nocturnal birds, chiefly tawny and long-eared owls, but also nightingales, swifts, and nightjars. From streams and hidden pools, there comes the chorus of frog song. Foxes cry out to one another. The scene is at once breathtaking and forbidding, and you lean forward in your seat, arrested by this austere beauty.

> WOMAN'S VOICE (angry):
> It is a poor jest, Katarína. It is a poor, poor jest, indeed,
> and I've no patience for your games tonight.

> GIRL'S VOICE (soft, not unkind):
> I'm not Katarína. Have you forgotten my name already?

The camera's eye doesn't waver, even at the risk of this shot becoming monotonous. And we see that atop the rocky prominence stands the tumbledown ruins of Čachtice Castle, *Csejte vára* in the mother tongue. Here it has stood since the 1200s, when Kazimir of Hunt-Poznan found himself in need of a sentry post on the troubled road to Moravia. And later, it was claimed by the Hungarian oligarch Máté Csák of Trencsén, the heroic Count Matthew. Then it went to Rudolf II, Holy Roman Emperor, who spent much of his life in alchemical study, searching for the Philosopher's Stone. And, finally, in 1575, the castle was presented as a wedding gift from Lord Chief Justice Ferenc Nádasdy to his fifteen-year-old bride, Báthory Erzsébet, or Alžbeta, the Countess Elizabeth Báthory. The name (one or another of the lot) will doubtless ring a bell, though infamy has seen she's better known to many as the Blood Countess.

The cinematographer works more sleight of hand, and the jagged lineament of the ruins is restored to that of Csejte as it would have stood when the Countess was alive. A grand patchwork of Romanesque and Gothic architecture, its formidable walls and towers loom high above the drowsy village of Vrbové. The castle rises – no, it sprouts – the castle *sprouts* from the bluff in such a way as to seem almost a natural, integral part of the local geography, something *in situ*, carved by wind and rain rather than by the labors of man.

The film jump cuts to an owl perched on a pine branch. The bird blinks – once, twice – spreads its wings, and takes to the air. The camera lets it go and doesn't follow, preferring to remain with the now-vacant branch. Several seconds pass before the high-pitched scream of a rabbit reveals the reason for the owl's departure.

GIRL'S VOICE:
Ever is it the small things that suffer. That's what they say, you know? The Tigress of Csejte, she will have them all, because there is no end to her hunger.

Another jump cut brings us to the castle gates, and the camera pans slowly across the masonry of curtain walls, parapets, and up the steep sides of a horseshoe-shaped watchtower. Jump cut again, and we are shown a room illuminated by the flickering light of candles. There is a noblewoman seated in an enormous and somewhat fanciful chair, upholstered with fine brocade, its oaken legs and arms ending with the paws of a lion, or a dragon.

Or possibly a tigress.

So, a woman seated in an enormous, bestial chair. She wears the "Spanish Farthingale" and stiffened undergarments fashionable during this century. Her dress is made of the finest Florentine silk. Her waist is tightly cinched, her ample breasts flattened by the stays. Were she standing, her dress might remind us of an hourglass. Her head is framed with a wide ruff of starched lace, and her arms held properly within trumpet sleeves, more lace at the cuffs to ring her delicate hands. There is a wolf pelt across her lap, and another covers her bare feet. The candlelight is gracious, and she might pass for a woman of forty, though she's more than a decade older. Her hair, which is the color of cracked acorn shells, has been meticulously braided and pulled back from her round face and high forehead. Her eyes seem dark as rubies.

INT. COUNTESS BÁTHORY'S CHAMBER. NIGHT.

> COUNTESS (tersely):
> Why are you awake at this hour, child? You should be sleeping. Haven't I given you a splendid bed?

> GIRL (seen dimly, in silhouette):
> I don't like being in that room alone. I don't like the shadows in that room. I try not to see them –

> COUNTESS (close up, her eyes fixed on the child):
> Oh, don't be silly. A shadow has not yet harmed anyone.

> GIRL (almost whispering):
> Begging your pardon, My Lady, but these shadows mean to do me mischief. I hear them whisper, and they do. They are shadows cast by wicked spirits. They do not speak to you?

> COUNTESS (sighs, frowning):
> I don't speak with shadows.

The Prayer of Ninety Cats | Caitlín R. Kiernan

GIRL (coyly):

That isn't what they say in the village.

(pause)

Do you truly know the Prayer of Ninety Cats?

By now, it is likely that the theatre, which only a short time ago so filled your thoughts, has receded, fading almost entirely from your conscious mind. This is usually the way of theatres, if the films they offer have any merit at all. The building is the spectacle which precedes the spectacle it has been built to contain, not so different from the relationship of colorful wrapping paper and elaborately tied bows to the gifts hidden within. You're greeted by a mock-grand façade and the blazing electric marquee, and are then admitted into the catchpenny splendor of the lobby. All these things make an impression, and set a mood, but all will fall by the wayside. Exiting the theatre after a film, you'll hardly note a single detail. Your mind will be elsewhere, processing, reflecting, critiquing, amazed, or disappointed.

Onscreen, the Countess' candlelit bedchamber has been replaced by the haggard faces of peasant women, mothers and grandmothers, gazing up at the terrible edifice of Csejte. Over the years, so many among them have sent their daughters away to the castle, hearing that servants are cared for and well compensated. Over the years, none have returned. There are rumors of black magic and butchery, and, from time to time, girls have simply vanished from Vrbové, and also from the nearby town of Čachtice, from whence the fortress took its name. The women cross themselves and look away.

Dissolve to scenes of the daughters of landed aristocracy and the lesser gentry preparing their beautiful daughters for the *gynaeceum* of ecsedi Báthory Erzsébet, where they will be schooled in all the social graces, that they might make more desirable brides and find the best marriages possible. Carriages rattle along the narrow, precipitous road leading up to the castle, wheels and hooves trailing wakes of dust. Oblivious lambs driven to the slaughter, freely delivered by ambitious and unwitting mothers.

Another dissolve, to winter in a soundstage forest, and the Countess walks between artificial sycamore maples, ash, linden, beech, and elderberry.

The studio "greens men" have worked wonders, meticulously crafting this forest from plaster, burlap, epoxy, wire, styrofoam, from lumber armatures and the limbs and leaves of actual trees. The snow is as phony as the trees, but no less convincing, a combination of SnowCel, SnowEx foam, and Powderfrost, dry-foam plastic snow spewed from machines; biodegradable, nontoxic polymers to simulate a gentle snowfall after a January blizzard. But the mockery is perfection. The Countess stalks through drifts so convincing that they may as well be real. Her furs drag behind her, and her boots leave deep tracks. Two huge wolves follow close behind, and when she stops, they come to her and she scratches their shaggy heads and pats their lean flanks and plants kisses behind their ears. A trained crow perches on a limb overhead, cawing, cawing, cawing, but neither the woman nor the wolves pay it any heed. The Countess speaks, and her breath fogs.

COUNTESS (to wolves):
You are my true children. Not Ursula or Pál or Miklós.
And you are also my true inamoratos, my most beloved,
not Ferenc, who was only ever a husband.

If tabloid gossip and backlot hearsay is to be trusted, this scene has been considerably shortened and toned down from the original script. We do not see the Countess' sexual congress with the wolves. It is only implied by her affections, her words, and by the lewd canticle of a voyeur crow. The scene is both stark and magnificent. It is a final still point before the coming tempest, before the horrors, a moment imbued with grace and menacing tranquility. The camera cuts to Herr Kramer in its counterfeit tree, and you're watching its golden eyes watching the Countess and her wolves, and anything more is implied.

INT. ČACHTICE CASTLE/DRESSING ROOM. MORNING.

The Countess is seated before a looking glass held inside a carved wooden frame, motif of dryads and satyrs. We see the Countess as a reflection, and behind her, a servant girl. The servant is combing the Countess' brown hair with an ivory comb. The Countess is no longer a young woman. There are lines at the edges of her mouth and beneath her eyes.

> COUNTESS (furrowing her brows):
> You're pulling my hair again. How many times must I tell you to be careful. You're not deaf, are you?

> SERVANT (almost whispering):
> No, My Lady.

> COUNTESS (icily):
> Then when I speak to you, you hear me perfectly well.

> SERVANT:
> Yes, My Lady.

The ivory comb snags in the Countess' hair, and she stands, spinning about to face the terrified servant girl. She snatches the comb from the girl's hand. Strands of Elizabeth's hair are caught between the teeth.

> COUNTESS (tone of disbelief):
> You wretched little beast. Look what you've done.

The Countess slaps the servant with enough force to split her lip. Blood spatters the Countess' hand as the servant falls to the floor. The Countess is entranced by the crimson beads speckling her pale skin.

> COUNTESS (whisper):
> You...filthy...wretch...

FADE TO BLACK

FADE IN:
INT. DREAM MIRROR.

The Countess stands in a dim pool of light, before a towering mirror, a gro-
tesque nightmare version of the one on her dressing table. The nymphs, satyrs,
and dryads are life-size, and move, engaged in various and sundry acts of sex-
ual abandon. This dark place is filled with sounds of desire, orgasm, drunken
debauchery. In the mirror is a far younger Elizabeth Báthory. But, as we watch,
as the Countess watches, this young woman rapidly ages, rushing through her
twenties, thirties, her forties. The Countess screams, commanding the mirror
cease these awful visions. The writhing creatures that form the frame laugh and
mock her screams.

FLASH CUT TO:
EXT. SNOW-COVERED FIELD. DAYLIGHT.

The Countess stands naked in the falling snow, her feet buried up to the ankles.
The snowflakes turn red. The red snow becomes a red rain, and she's drenched.
The air is a red mist.

FLASH CUT TO:
INT. DREAM MIRROR.

Nude and drenched in blood, the Countess gazes at her reflection, her face and
body growing young before her eyes. The looking glass shatters.

FADE TO BLACK

The Hungary of the film has more in common with the landscape
of Hans Christian Andersen and the Brothers Grimm than with any
Hungary that exists now or ever has existed. It is an archetypal vista, as
much a myth as Stoker's Transylvania and Sheridan Le Fanu's Styria. A
real place that has, inconveniently, never existed. Little or nothing is said
of the political and religious turmoil of Elizabeth's time, or of the war with

the Ottoman Turks, aside from the death of the Countess' husband at the hands of General Giorgio Basta. If you're a stickler for accuracy, these omissions are unforgivable. But most of the men and women who sit in the theatre, entranced by the light flashed back from the screen, will never notice. People do not generally come to the movies hoping for recitations of dry history. Few will care that pivotal events in the film never occurred, because they are happening now, unfolding before the eyes of all who have paid the price of admission.

INT. COUNTESS' BEDCHAMBER. NIGHT.

GIRL:
If you have been taught the prayer, say the words aloud.

COUNTESS:
How would you ever know such things, child?

GIRL (turning away):
We have had some of the same tutors, you and I.

The second reel begins with the arrival at Csejte of a woman named Anna Darvulia. In hushed tones, a servant (who dies an especially messy death farther along) refers to her as "the Witch of the Forest." She becomes Elizabeth's lover and teaches her sorcery and the Prayer of Ninety Cats to protect her from all harm. As Darvulia is depicted here, she may as well have inhabited a gingerbread cottage before she came to the Countess, a house of sugary confections where she regularly feasted on lost children. Indeed, shortly after her arrival, and following an admittedly gratuitous sex scene, the subject of cannibalism is introduced. A peasant girl named Júlia, stolen from her home, is brought to the Countess by two of her handmaids and partners in crime, Dorottya and Ilona. The girl is stripped naked and forced to kneel before Elizabeth while the handmaids burn the bare flesh of her back and shoulders with coins and needles that have been placed over an open flame. Darvulia watches on approvingly from the shadows.

INT. KITCHEN. NIGHT.

COUNTESS (smiling):
You shouldn't fret so about your dear mother and father. I know they're poor, but I will see to it they're compensated for the loss of their only daughter.

JÚLIA (sobbing):
There is never enough wood in winter, and never enough food. We have no shoes and wear rags.

COUNTESS:
And haven't I liberated you from those rags?

JÚLIA:
They need me. Please, My Lady, send me home to them.

The Countess glances over her shoulder to Darvulia, as if seeking approval/ instruction. Darvulia nods once, then the Countess turns back to the sobbing girl.

COUNTESS:
Very well. I'll make you a promise, Júlia. And I keep my promises. In the morning, I will send your mother and your father warm clothing and good shoes and enough firewood to see them through the snows. And, what's more, I will send you back to them, as well.

JÚLIA:
You would do that?

COUNTESS:
Certainly, I will. I'll not have any use for you after this evening, and I detest wastefulness.

The Prayer of Ninety Cats | Caitlín R. Kiernan

This scene has been cut from most prints. If you have any familiarity with the trials and tribulations of the film's production, and with the censorship that followed, you'll be surprised, and possibly pleased, to find it has not been excised from this copy. It may also strike you as relatively tame, compared to many less controversial, but far more graphic, portions of the film.

> COUNTESS:
> When we are finished here...
>> (pause)
> When we're finished, and my hunger is satisfied, I will speak with my butcher – a skilled man with a knife and cleaver – and he will see to it that your corpse is dressed in such a way that it can never be mistaken for anything but that of a sow. I'll have the meat salted and smoked, then sent to them, as evidence of my generosity. They will have their daughter back, and, in the bargain, will not go hungry. Are they fond of sausage. Júlia? I'd think you would make a marvelous *debreceni*.

Critics and movie buffs who lament the severe treatment the film has suffered at the hands of nervous studio executives, skittish distributors, and the MPAA often point to Júlia's screams, following these lines, as an example of how great cinema may be lost to censorship. Sound editors and Foley artists are said to have crafted the unsettling and completely inhuman effect by mixing the cries of several species of birds, the squeal of a pig, and the steam whistle of a locomotive. The scream continues as this scene dissolves to a delirious montage of torture and murder. The Countess' notorious iron maiden makes an appearance. A servant is dragged out into a snowy courtyard, and once her dress and underclothes have been savagely ripped away, the woman is bound to a wooden stake. Elizabeth Báthory pours buckets of cold water over the servant's body until she freezes to death and her body glistens like an ice sculpture.

The theatre is so quiet that you begin to suspect everyone else has had enough and left before The End. But you don't dare look away long enough to see whether this is in fact the case.

The Countess sits in her enormous lion- (or dragon- or tigress-) footed chair, in that bedchamber lit only by candlelight. She strokes the wolf pelt on her lap as lovingly as she stroked the fur of those living wolves.

"We've had some of the same tutors, you and I," the strange brown girl says, the gypsy child who claims to be afraid of the shadows in the small room that has been provided for her.

"Anna's never mentioned you."

"*She* and I have had some of the same tutors," the child whispers. "Now, My Lady, please speak the words aloud and drive away the evil spirits."

"I have heard of no such prayer," the Countess tells the girl, but the actress' air and intonation make it's obvious she's lying. "I've received no such catechism."

"Then shall I teach it to you? For when they are done with me, the shadows might come looking after you, and if you don't know the prayer, how will you hope to defend yourself, My Lady?"

The Countess frowns and mutters, half to herself, half to the child, "I need no defense against shadows. Rather, let the shadows blanch and wilt at the thought of me."

"That same arrogance will be your undoing," the child replies. Then all the candles gutter and are extinguished, and the only light remaining is cold moonlight, getting in through the parted draperies. The child is gone. The Countess sits in her clawed chair and squeezes her eyes tightly shut. You may once have done very much the same thing, hearing some bump in the night. Fearing an open closet or the space beneath your bed, a window or a hallway. In this moment, Elizabeth Báthory von Ecsed, Alžbeta Bátoriová, the Bloody Lady of Čachtice, she seems no more fearsome for all her fearsome reputation than the child you once were. The boyish girl she herself was, forty-seven, forty-six, forty-eight years before this night. The girl given to tantrums and seizures and dressing up in boy's clothes. She cringes in this dark, moon-washed room, eyelids drawn against the night, and begins, haltingly, to recite the prayer Anna Darvulia has taught her.

The Prayer of Ninety Cats | CAITLÍN R. KIERNAN

"I am in peril, O cloud. Send, O send, you most powerful of Clouds, send ninety cats, for thou are the supreme Lord of Cats. I command you, King of the Cats, I pray you. May you gather them together, even if you are in the mountains, or on the waters, or on the roofs, or on the other side of the ocean...tell them to come to me."

FADE TO BLACK.
FADE UP.

The bedchamber is filled with the feeble colors of a January morning. With the wan luminance of the winter sun in these mountains. The balcony doors have blown open in the night, and a drift of snow has crept into the room. Pressed into the snow there are the barefoot tracks of a child. The Countess opens her eyes. She looks her age, and then some.

FADE TO BLACK.
FADE UP.

The Countess in her finest Farthingale and ruff stands before the altar of Csejte's austere chapel. She gazes upwards at a stained-glass narrative set into the frames of three very tall and very narrow lancet windows. Her expression is distant, detached, unreadable. Following an establishing shot, and then a brief close up of the Countess' face, the trio of stained-glass windows dominates the screen. The production designer had them manufactured in Prague, by an artisan who was provided detailed sketches mimicking the style of windows fashioned by Harry Clarke and the Irish cooperative *An Túr Gloine*. As with so many aspects of the film, this window has inspired heated debate, chiefly regarding its subject matter. The most popular interpretation favors one of the hagiographies from the *Legenda sanctorum*, the tale of St. George and the dragon of Silene.

The stillness of the chapel is shattered by squealing hinges and quick footsteps, as Anna Darvulia rushes in from the bailey. She approaches the Countess, who has turned to meet her.

DARVULIA (angry):
What you seek, Elizabeth, you'll not find it here.

COUNTESS (feigning dismay):
I only wanted an hour's solitude. It's quiet here.

DARVULIA (sneering):
Liar. You came seeking after a solace that shall forever be
denied you, as it has always been denied me. We have no
place here, Elizabeth. Let us leave together.

COUNTESS:
She came to me again last night. How can your prayer
protect me from her, when she also knows it?

*Anna Darvulia whispers something in the Countess' ear, then kisses her cheek
and leads her from the chapel.*

DISSOLVE TO:

*Two guards or soldiers thread heavy iron chain through the handles of the chapel
doors, then slide the shackle of a large padlock through the links of chain and
clamp the lock firmly shut.*

Somewhere towards the back of the theatre, a man coughs loudly, and a
woman laughs. The man coughs a second time, then mutters (presumably to
the woman), and she laughs again. You're tempted to turn about in your seat
and ask them to please hold it down, that there are people who came to see
the movie. But you don't. You don't take your eyes off the screen, and, besides,
you've never been much for confrontation. You also consider going out to the
lobby and complaining to the management, but you won't do that, either. It
sounds like the man is telling a dirty joke, and you do your best to ignore him.

The film has returned to the snowy soundstage forest. Only now
there are many more trees, spaced more closely together. Their trunks

and branches are as dark as charcoal, as dark as the snow is light. Together these two elements – trees and snow, snow and trees – form a proper joyance for any chiaroscurist. In the foreground of this *mise-en-scène*, an assortment of taxidermied wildlife (two does, a rabbit, a badger, etc.) watches on with blind acrylic eyes as Anna Darvulia follows a path through the wood. She wears an enormous crimson cloak, the hood all but concealing her face. Her cloak completes the palette of the scene: the black trees, the white of the snow, this red slash of wool. There is a small falcon, a merlin, perched on the woman's left shoulder, and gripped in her left hand (she isn't wearing gloves) is a leather leash. As the music swells – strings, woodwinds, piano, the thunderous kettledrum – the camera pans slowly to the right, tracing the leash from Darvulia's hand to the heavy collar clasped about the Countess' pale throat. Elizabeth is entirely naked, scrambling through the snow on all fours. Her hair is a matted tangle of twigs and dead leaves. Briars have left bloody welts on her arms, legs, and buttocks. There are wolves following close behind her, famished wolves starving in the dead of this endless Carpathian winter. The pack is growing bold, and one of the animals rushes in close, pushing its muzzle between her exposed thighs, thrusting about with its wet nose, lapping obscenely at the Countess' ass and genitals. Elizabeth bares her sharp teeth and, wheeling around, straining against the leash, she snaps viciously at this churlish rake of a wolf. She growls as convincingly as any lunatic or lycanthrope might hope to growl.

All wolves are churlish. All wolves are rakes, especially in fairy tales, and especially this far from spring.

"Have you forgotten the prayer so soon?" Darvulia calls back, her voice cruel and mocking. Elizabeth doesn't answer, but the wolves yelp and retreat.

And as the witch and her pupil pick their way deeper into the forest, we see that the gypsy girl, dressed in a cloak almost identical to Darvulia's—wool died that same vivid red—stands among the wolves as they whine and mill about her legs.

Elizabeth awakens in her bed, screaming.

In a series of jump cuts, her screams echo through the empty corridors of Csejte.

(This scene is present in all prints, having somehow escaped the same fate as the unfilmed climax of the Countess' earlier trek through the forest – a testament to the fickle inconsistency of censors. In an interview she gave to the Croatian periodical *Hrvatski filmski ljetopis* [Autumn 2003], the actress who played Elizabeth reports that she actually did suffer a spate of terrible nightmares after making the film, and that most of them revolved around this particular scene. She says, "I have only been able to watch it [the scene] twice. Even now, it's hard to imagine myself having been on the set that day. I've always been afraid of dogs, and those were *real* wolves.")

In the fourth reel, you find you're slightly irritated when film briefly loses its otherwise superbly claustrophobic focus, during a Viennese interlude surely meant, instead, to build tension. The Countess' depravity is finally, inevitably brought to the attention of the Hungarian Parliament and King Matthias. The plaintiff is a woman named Imre Megyery, the Steward of Sávár, who became the guardian of the Countess' son, Pál Nádasdy, after the death of her husband. It doesn't help that the actor who plays György Thurzó, Matthias' palatine, is an Australian who seems almost incapable of getting the Hungarian accent right. Perhaps he needed a better dialect coach. Perhaps he was lazy. Possibly, he isn't a very good actor.

INT. COUNTESS' BEDCHAMBER. NIGHT.

Elizabeth and Darvulia in the Countess' bed, after a vigorous bout of lovemaking. Lovemaking, sex, fucking, whatever. Both women are nude. The corpse of a third woman lies between them. There's no blood, so how she died is unclear.

DARVULIA:
Megyery the Red, she plots against you. She has gone to
the King, and very, very soon Thurzó's notaries will arrive
to poke and pry and be the King's eyes and ears.

COUNTESS:
But you will keep me safe, Anna. And there is the prayer…

DARVULIA (gravely):
These are men, with all the power of the King and the Church at their backs. You must take this matter seriously, Elizabeth. The dark gods will concern themselves only so far, and after that we are on our own. Again, I beg you to at least consider abandoning Csejte.

COUNTESS:
No. No, and don't ask again. It is my home. Let Thurzó's men come. I will show them nothing. I will let them see nothing.

DARVULIA:
It isn't so simple, my sweet Erzsébet. Ferenc is gone, and without a husband to protect you...you must consider the greed of relatives who covet your estates, and consider, also, debts owed to you by a king who has no intention of ever settling them. Many have much to gain from your fall.

COUNTESS (stubbornly):
There will be no fall.

You sit up straight in your reclining theatre seat. You've needed to urinate for the last half hour, but you're not about to miss however much of the film you'd miss during a quick trip to the restroom. You try not to think about it; you concentrate on the screen and not your aching bladder.

INT. COUNTESS' BEDCHAMBER. NIGHT.

The Countess sits in her lion-footed chair, facing the open balcony doors. There are no candles burning, but we can see the silhouette of the gypsy girl outlined in the winter moonlight pouring into the room. She is all but naked. The wind blows loudly, howling about the walls of the castle.

COUNTESS (distressed):
No, you're not mine. I can't recall ever having seen you before. You are nothing of mine. You are some demon sent by the moon to harry me.

GIRL (calmly):
It is true I serve the moon, Mother, as do you. She is mistress to us both. We have both run naked while she watched on. We have both enjoyed her favors. We are each the moon's bitch.

COUNTESS (turning away):
Lies. Every word you say is a wicked lie. And I'll not hear any more of it. Begone, *strigoi*. Go back to whatever stinking hole was dug to cradle your filthy gypsy bones.

GIRL (suddenly near tears):
Please do no not say such things, Mother.

COUNTESS (through clenched teeth):
You are not my daughter! This is the price of my sins, to be visited by phantoms, to be haunted.

GIRL:
I only want to be held, Mother. I only want to be held, as any daughter would. I want to be kissed.

Slowly, the Countess looks back at the girl. Snow blows in through the draperies, swirling about the child. The girl's eyes flash red-gold. She takes a step nearer the Countess.

GIRL (contd.):
I can protect you, Mother.

The Prayer of Ninety Cats | CAITLÍN R. KIERNAN

COUNTESS:

From what? From whom?

GIRL:

You know from what, and you know from whom. You would know, even if Anna hadn't told you. You are not a stupid woman.

COUNTESS:

You do not come to protect me, but to damn me.

GIRL (kind):

I only want to be held, and sung to sleep.

COUNTESS (shuddering):

My damnation.

GIRL (smiling sadly):

No, Mother. You've tended well-enough to that on your own. You've no need of anyone to hurry you along to the pit.

CLOSE UP – THE COUNTESS

The Countess' face is filled with a mixture of dread and defeat, exhaustion and horror. She shuts her eyes a moment, muttering silently, then opens them again.

COUNTESS (resigned):

Come, child.

MEDIUM SHOT – THE COUNTESS

The Countess sits in her chair, head bowed now, seemingly too exhausted to continue arguing with the girl. From the foreground, the gypsy girl approaches her. Strange shadows seem to loom behind the Countess' chair. The child begins to sing in a sweet, sad, lilting voice, a song that might be a hymn or a dirge.

FADE TO BLACK.

This scene will stay with you. You will find yourself thinking, *That's where it should have ended. That would have made a better ending.* The child's song – only two lines of which are intelligible – will remain with you long after many of the grimmer, more graphic details are forgotten. Two eerie, poignant lines: *Stay with me and together we will live forever./ Death is the road to awe.* Later, you'll come across an article in *American Cinematographer* (April 2006), and discover that the screenwriter originally intended this to be the final scene, but was overruled by the director, who insisted it was too anticlimactic.

Which isn't to imply that the remaining twenty minutes are without merit, but only that they steer the film in a different and less subtle, less dreamlike direction. Like so many of the films you most admire – Bergman's *Det sjunde inseglet*, Charlie Kaufman's *Synecdoche, New York*, Herzog's *Herz aus Glas*, David Lynch's *Lost Highway* – this one is speaking to you in the language of dreams, and after the child's song, you have the distinct sense that the film has awakened, jolted from the subconscious to the conscious, the self aware. It's ironic, therefore, that the next scene is a dream sequence. And it is a dream sequence that has left critics divided over the movie's conclusion and what the director intended to convey. There is a disjointed, tumbling series of images, and it is usually assumed that this is simply a nightmare delivered to the Countess by the child. However, one critic, writing for *Slovenska Kinoteka* (June 2005), has proposed it represents a literal divergence of two timelines, dividing the historical Báthory's fate from that of the fictional Báthory portrayed in the film. She notes the obvious, that the dream closely parallels the events of December 29, 1610, the day of the Countess' arrest. A few have argued the series of scenes was never meant to be perceived as a dream (neither the director nor the screenwriter have revealed their intent). The sequence may be ordered as follows:

The Prayer of Ninety Cats | Caitlín R. Kiernan

The Arrival: A retinue on horseback—Thurzó, Imre Megyery, the Countess' sons-in-law, Counts Drugeth de Homonnay and Zrínyi, together with an armed escort. The party reaches the Csejte, and the iron gates swing open to admit them.

The Descent: The Palatine's men following a narrow, spiraling stairwell into the depth of the castle. They cover their mouths and noses against some horrible stench.

The Discovery: A dungeon cell strewn with corpses, in various stages of dismemberment and decay. Two women, still living, though clearly mad, their bodies naked and beaten and streaked with filth, are manacled to the stone walls. They scream at the sight of the men.

The Trial: Theodosious Syrmiensis de Szulo of the Royal Supreme Court pronounces a sentence of *perpetuis carceribus*, sparing the Countess from execution, but condemning her to lifelong confinement at Csejte.

The Execution/Pardon of the Accomplices: Three women and one man. Two of the women, Jó Ilona and Dorottya Szentes, are found guilty, publicly tortured, and burned alive. The man, Ujváry János (portrayed as a deformed dwarf), is beheaded before being thrown onto the bonfire with Jó and Dorottya. The third woman, Katarína Beniezky, is spared (this is not explained, and none of the four are named in the film).

The Imprisonment: The Countess sits on her bed as stonemasons brick up the chamber's windows and the door leading out onto the balcony. Then the door is sealed. Close ups of trowels, mortar, callused hands, Elizabeth's eyes, a Bible in her lap. Last shot from Elizabeth's POV, her head turned away from the camera, as the final few bricks are set in place. She is alone. Fade to black.

Anna Darvulia, "the Witch of the Forest," appears nowhere in this sequence.

FADE IN:
EXT. CSETJE STABLES. DAY.

The Countess watches as Anna Darvulia climbs onto the back of a horse. Once in the saddle, her feet in the stirrups, she stares sorrowfully down at the Countess.

DARVULIA:

I beg you, Erzsébet. Come with me. We'll be safe in the forest. There are places where no man knows to look.

COUNTESS:

This is my home. Please, don't ask me again. I won't run from them. I won't.

DARVULIA (speaking French and Croatian):

Ma petite bête douce. Volim te, Erzsébet.

(pause)

Ne m'oublie pas.

COUNTESS (slapping the horse's rump):

Go! Go now, love, before I lose my will.

CUT TO:

EXT. ČACHTICE CASTLE HILL. WINTER. DAY.

Anna Darvulia racing away from the snowbound castle, while the Countess watches from her tower.

COUNTESS (off):

I command you, O King of the Cats, I pray you.
May you gather them together,
Give them thy orders and tell them,
Wherever they may be, to assemble together,
To come from the mountains,
From the waters, from the rivers,
From the rainwater on the roofs, and from the oceans.
Tell them to come to me.

FADE TO BLACK.

FADE IN:
INT. COUNTESS' BEDCHAMBER. NIGHT.

The Countess in her enormous chair. The gypsy girl stands before her. As before, she is almost naked. There is candlelight and moonlight. Snow blows in from the open balcony doors.

GIRL:
She left you all alone.

COUNTESS:
No, child. I sent her away.

GIRL:
Back to the wood?

COUNTESS:
Back to the wood.

You sit in your seat and breathe the musty theatre smells, the smells which may as well be ghosts as they are surely remnants of long ago moments come and gone. Your full bladder has been all but forgotten. Likewise, the muttering, laughing man and woman seated somewhere behind you. There is room for nothing now but the illusion of moving pictures splashed across the screen. Your eyes and your ears translate the interplay of light and sound into story. The old theatre is a temple, holy in its way, and you've come to worship, to find epiphany in truths captured by a camera's lens. There's no need of plaster saints and liturgies. No need of the intermediary services of a priest. Your god – and the analogy has occurred to you on many occasions – is speaking to you directly, calling down from that wide silk-and-silver window and from Dolby speakers mounted high on the walls. Your god speaks in many voices, and its angels are an orchestra, and every frame is a page of scripture. This mass is rapidly winding down towards benediction.

GIRL:
May I sit at your feet, Mother?

COUNTESS:
Wouldn't you rather have my lap?

GIRL (smiling):
Yes, Mother. I would much rather have your lap.

The gypsy girl climbs into the Countess' lap, her small brown body nestling in the voluminous folds of Elizabeth's dress. The Countess puts her arms around the child, and holds her close. The girl rests her head on the Countess' breast.

GIRL (whisper):
They will come, you know? The men. The soldiers.

COUNTESS:
I know. But let's not think of that, not now. Let's not think on anything much at all.

GIRL:
But you recall the prayer, yes?

COUNTESS:
Yes, child. I recall the prayer. Anna taught me the prayer, just as you taught it to her.

GIRL:
You are so clever, Mother.

CLOSE UP.

The Countess' hand reaching into a fold of her dress, withdrawing a small silver dagger. The handle is black and polished wood, maybe jet or mahogany.

The Prayer of Ninety Cats | Caitlín R. Kiernan

There are occult symbols etched deeply into the metal, all down the length of the blade.

GIRL:

Will you say the prayer for me? No one ever prays for me.

COUNTESS:

I would rather hear you sing, dear. Please, sing for me.

The gypsy girl smiles and begins her song.

GIRL:

Stay with me, and together we will live forever.
Death is the road to awe –

The Countess clamps a hand over the girl's mouth, and plunges the silver dagger into her throat. The girl's eyes go very wide, as blood spurts from the wound. She falls backwards to the floor, and writhes there for a moment. The Countess gets to her feet, triumph in her eyes.

COUNTESS:

You think I didn't know you? You think I did not see?

The girl's eyes flash red-gold, and she hisses loudly, then begins to crawl across the floor towards the balcony. She pulls the knife from her throat and flings it away. It clatters loudly against the floor. The girl's teeth are stained with blood.

GIRL (hoarsely):

You deny me. You dare deny me.

COUNTESS:

You are none of mine.

GIRL:

You send me to face the cold alone? To face the moon alone?

The Countess doesn't reply, but begins to recite the Prayer of Ninety Cats. As she does, the girl stands, almost as if she hasn't been wounded. She backs away, stepping through the balcony doors, out into snow and brilliant moonlight. The child climbs onto the balustrade, and it seems for a moment she might grow wings and fly away into the Carpathian night.

COUNTESS:

May these ninety cats appear to tear and destroy
The hearts of kings and princes,
And in the same way the hearts of teachers and judges,
And all who mean me harm,
That they shall harm me not.
(pause)
Holy Trinity, protect me.
And guard Erzsébet from all evil.

The girl turns her back on the Countess, gazing down at the snowy court-yard below.

GIRL:

I'm the one who guarded you, Mother. I'm the one who has kept you safe.

COUNTESS (raising her voice):
Tell them to come to me.
And to hasten them to bite the heart.
Let them rip to pieces and bite again and again...

GIRL:
There's no love in you anywhere. There never was.

The Prayer of Ninety Cats | Caitlín R. Kiernan

COUNTESS:
Do not say that! Don't you dare say that! I have loved –

GIRL (sadly):
You have lusted and called it love. You tangle appetite and desire. Let me fall, and be done with you.

COUNTESS (suddenly confused):
No. No, child. Come back. No one falls this night.

INT./EXT. NIGHT.

As the Countess moves towards the balcony, the gypsy girl steps off the balustrade and tumbles to the courtyard below. The Countess cries out in horror and rushes out onto the balcony.

EXT. NIGHT.

The broken body of the girl on the snow-covered flagstones of the courtyard. Blood still oozes from the wound in her throat, but also from her open mouth and her nostrils. Her eyes are open. Her blood steams in the cold air. A large crow lands near her body. The camera pans upwards, and we see the Countess gazing down in horror at the broken body of the dead girl. In the distance, wolves begin to howl.

EXT. BALCONY. NIGHT.

The Countess is sitting now, her back pressed to the stone columns of the balustrade. She's sobbing, her hands tearing at her hair. She is the very portrait here of loss and madness.

COUNTESS (weeping):
I didn't know. God help me, I did not know.

FADE UP TO WHITE.

EXT. CSEJTE. MORNING.

A small cemetery near the castle's chapel. Heavy snow covers everything. The dwarf Ujváry János has managed to hack a shallow grave into the frozen earth. The Countess watches as the gypsy girl's small body, wrapped in a makeshift burial shroud, is lowered into the hole. The Countess turns and hurries away across the bailey, and János begins filling the grave in again. Shovelful after shovelful of dirt and frost and snow falls on the body, and slowly it disappears from view. Perched on a nearby headstone, an owl watches. It blinks, and rotates its head and neck 180 degrees, so it appears to be watching the burial upside down.

In a week, you'll write your review of the film, the review you're being paid to write, and you'll note that the genus and species of owl watching János as he buries the dead girl is *Bubo virginianus*, the Great Horned Owl. You'll also note the bird is native to North America, and not naturally found in Europe, but that to fret over these sorts of inaccuracies is, at best, pedantic. At worst, you'll write, it means that one has entirely missed the point and would have been better off staying at home and not wasting the price of a movie ticket.

This is not the life of Erzsébet Báthory.

No one has ever lived this exact life.

Beyond the establishing shot of the ruins at the beginning of the film, the castle is not Csejte. Likewise, the forest that surrounds it is the forest that this story requires it to be, and whether or not it's an accurate depiction of the forests of the Piešt' any region of Slovakia is irrelevant.

The Countess may or may not have been Anna Darvulia's lover. Erzsébet Báthory may have been a lesbian. Or she may not. Anna Darvulia may or may not have existed.

There is no evidence whatsoever that Erzsébet was repeatedly visited in the dead of night by a strange gypsy child.

Or that the Countess' fixation with blood began when she struck a servant who'd accidentally pulled her hair.

Or that Erzsébet was ever led naked through those inaccurate forests while lustful wolves sniffed at her sex.

Pedantry and nitpicking is fatal to all fairy tales. You will write that there are people who would argue a wolf lacks the lung capacity to blow down a house of straw and that any beanstalk tall enough to reach the clouds would collapse under its own weight. They are, you'll say, the same lot who'd dismiss Shakespeare for mixing Greek and Celtic mythology, or on the grounds that there was never a prince of Verona named Escalus. "The facts are neither here nor there," you will write. "We have entered a realm where facts may not even exist." You'll be paid a pittance for the review, which virtually no one will read.

There will be one letter to the editor, complaining that your review was "too defensive" and that you are "an apologist for shoddy, prurient film-making." You'll remember this letter (though not the name of its author), many years after the paltry check has been spent.

The facts are neither here nor there.

Sitting in your theatre seat, these words have not yet happened, the words you'll write. At best, they're thoughts at the outermost edges of conception. Sitting here, there is nothing but the film, another's fever dreams you have been permitted to share. And you are keenly aware how little remains of the fifth reel, that the fever will break very soon.

EXT. FOREST. NIGHT.
MEDIUM SHOT.

Anna Darvulia sits before a small campfire, her horse's reins tied to a tree behind her. A hare is roasting on a spit above the fire. There's a sudden gust of wind, and, briefly, the flames burn a ghostly blue. She narrows her eyes, trying to see something beyond the firelight.

DARVULIA:
You think I don't see you? You think I can't smell you?
(pause)

You've no right claim left on me. I've passed my debt to the Báthory woman. I've prepared her for you. Now, leave me be, spirit. Do not trouble me this night or any other.

The fire flares blue again, and Darvulia lowers her head, no longer gazing into the darkness.

DISSOLVE TO:
EXT. ČACHTICE CASTLE HILL. NIGHT.

The full moon shines down on Csejte. The castle is dark. There's no light in any of its windows.

CUT TO:

The gypsy girl's unmarked grave. But much of the earth that filled the hole now lies heaped about the edges, as if someone has hastily exhumed the corpse. Or as if the dead girl might have dug her way out. The ground is white with snow and frost, and sparkles beneath the moon.

CUT TO:
EXT. BALCONY OUTSIDE COUNTESS' BEDCHAMBER. NIGHT.

The owl that watched Ujváry János bury the girl is perched on the stone balustrade. The doors to the balcony have been left standing open. Draperies billow in the freezing wind.

CLOSE UP:

Owl's round face. It blinks several times, and the bird's eyes flash an iridescent red-gold.

The Countess sits in her bedchamber, in that enormous chair with its six savage feet. A wolf pelt lies draped across her lap, emptied of its wolf.

Like a dragon, the Countess breathes steam. She holds a wooden cross in her shaking hands.

"Tell the cats to come to me," she says, uttering the prayer hardly above a whisper. There is no need to raise her voice; all gods and angels must surely have good ears. "And hasten them," she continues, "to bite the hearts of my enemies and all who would do me harm. Let them rip to pieces and bite again and again the heart of my foes. And guard Erzsébet from all evil. O *Quam Misericors est Deus, Pius et Justus.*"

Elizabeth was raised a Calvinist, and her devout mother, Anna, saw that she attended a fine Protestant school in Erdöd. She was taught mathematics and learned to write and speak Greek, German, Slovak, and Latin. She learned Latin prayers against the demons and the night.

"O *Quam Misericors est Deus. Justus et Paciens,*" she whispers, though she's shivering so badly that her teeth have begun to chatter and the words no longer come easily. They fall from her lips like stones. Or rotten fruit. Or lies. She cringes in her chair, and gazes intently towards the billowing, diaphanous drapes and the night and balcony beyond them. A shadow slips into the room, moving across the floor like spilled oil. The drapes part as if they have a will all their own (they were pulled to the sides with hooks and nylon fishing line, you've read), and the gypsy girl steps into the room. She is entirely nude, and her tawny body and black hair are caked with the earth of her abandoned grave. There are feathers caught in her hair, and a few drift from her shoulders to lie on the floor at her feet. She is bathed in moonlight, as cliché as that may sound. She has the iridescent eyes of an owl. The girl's face is the very picture of sorrow.

"Why did you bury me, Mother?"

"You were dead…"

The girl takes a step nearer the Countess. "I was so cold down there. You cannot ever imagine anything even half so cold as the deadlands."

The Countess clutches her wood cross. She is shaking, near tears. "You cannot be here. I said the prayers Anna taught me."

The girl has moved very near the chair now. She is close enough that she could reach out and stroke Elizabeth's pale cheek, if she wished to do so.

"The cats aren't coming, Mother. Her prayer was no more than any other prayer. Just pretty words against that which has never had cause to fear pretty words."

"The cats aren't coming," the Countess whispers, and the cross slips from her fingers.

The gypsy child reaches out and strokes Elizabeth's pale cheek. The girl's short nails are broken and caked with dirt. "It doesn't matter, Mother, because I'm here. What need have you of cats, when your daughter has come to keep you safe?"

The Countess looks up at the girl, who seems to have grown four or five inches taller since entering the room. "You are my daughter?" Elizabeth asks, the question a mouthful of fog.

"I am," the girl replies, kneeling to gently kiss the Countess' right cheek. "I have many mothers, as I have many daughters of my own. I watch over them all. I hold them to me and keep them safe."

"I've lost my mind," the Countess whispers, "long, long ago, I lost my mind." She hesitantly raises her left hand, brushing back the girl's filthy, matted hair, dislodging another feather. The Countess looks like an old woman. All traces of the youth she clung to with such ferocity have left her face, and her eyes have grown cloudy. "I am a madwoman."

"It makes no difference," the gypsy girl replies.

"Anna lied to me."

"Let that go, Mother. Let it all go. There are things I would show you. Wondrous things."

"I thought she loved me."

"She is a sorceress, Mother, and an inconstant lover. But I am true. And you'll need no other's love but mine."

The movie's score has dwindled to a slow smattering of piano notes, a bow drawn slowly, nimbly across the string of a cello. A hint of flute.

The Countess whispers, "I called to the King of Cats."

The girl answers, "Cats rarely ever come when called. And certainly not ninety all at once."

And the brown girl leans forward, her lips pressed to the pale Countess' right ear. Whatever she says, it's nothing you can make out from your seat, from your side of the silver mirror. The gypsy girl kisses the Countess on the forehead.

"I'm so very tired."

"Shhhhh, Mother. I know. It's okay. You can rest now."

The Countess asks, "Who are you."

"I am the peace at the end of all things."

EXT. COURTYARD BELOW COUNTESS' BALCONY. MORNING.

The body of Elizabeth Báthory lies shattered on the flagstones, her face and clothes a mask of frozen blood. Fresh snow is falling on her corpse. A number of noisy crows surround the body. No music now, only the wind and the birds.

FADE TO BLACK:

ROLL CREDITS.

THE END.

As always, you don't leave your seat until the credits are finished and the curtain has swept shut again, hiding the screen from view. As always, you've made no notes, preferring to rely on your memories.

You follow the aisle to the auditorium doors and step out into the almost deserted lobby. The lights seem painfully bright. You hurry to the restroom. When you're finished, you wash your hands, dry them, then spend almost an entire minute staring at your face in the mirror above the sink.

Outside, it's started to rain, and you wish you'd brought an umbrella.

The Crane Method

BY IAN R. MACLEOD

Despite the elegiac tone of his many portrayals in the popular and academic press, few people who knew Professor Crane actually liked him. He had, it was true, advanced the study of Anglo Saxon history further than anyone in the modern age. He had, it was also true, over-seen the expansion and development of Welbeck College until it could hold its head—and indeed, raise its new brick tower—high over the more antique and established seats of leaning in Cambridge. His personal man-ner and appearance were also impeccable. It was often said that there was something of the medical man about him—a tang of formaldehyde, per-haps—and that he studied people through those heavy glasses much in the way a physician might study a patient. Because of his extreme slimness and height and the furled umbrella he often affected to carry with him he also, it was frequently muttered, although rarely within his earshot, possessed a remarkable resemblance to the bird with which he shared his name, right down to that patient yet predatory stoop.

Professor Matthias Crane was intent upon nothing other than the advancement of his college and his field of learning, and both of those objectives coincided conveniently with the advancement of Professor Crane himself. Students and post-graduates whose avenue of research looked particularly promising were invited up for tea and seed cake in his large and comfortable study, and then perhaps a little more Amontillado than they were used to drinking, although he himself always abstained. They would find themselves quizzed and encouraged and given tips and suggestions to advance their chosen project. Most often, these tips proved extraordinarily useful, or happened to link in with the work which another fellow was pursuing, which had also been discussed on some afternoon sat beside the crackling applewood of Professor Crane's ever-convivial hearth. There would then be a subsequent period of dazzled excitement and discovery, which was always followed by dazed disbelief, and then a more permanent sense of betrayal. Professor Crane's output of books, lectures, essays and pamphlets was legendary. It was often said that they issued forth with a profligacy which could scarcely be the work of just one man. In this, there was an element of truth.

The sponsors of Welbeck College's new halls and exhibits found themselves similarly used and then discarded, although in ways about which it was impossible to complain. There was always that occasion when the professor had perhaps bent a rule, studiously ignored a small personal infraction or performed some other act of vaguely underhand generosity which at the time had seemed purely altruistic, but which was nevertheless mentioned once or twice afterwards with what came to be seen as chilling casualness. Many a night's sleep—indeed, many a promising career and marriage—had been wrecked on the remembered cold appraisal of Professor Crane's gaze.

No-one was at all surprised when the professor disappeared for a few months during the summer of 1928. It had always been his habit to head off alone on his researches with little if any word about where he was going, and usually to return burdened with some literal or figurative treasure. The Saltfleetby Codex which had brought a new understanding of the Christianisation of the Anglo Saxon kingdoms, and the reattribution of the previously ignored carvings in the Suffolk church of Beck, both owed their origins to such excursions. So did many of the finest items in the small but exquisite college museum. All, of course, came with full and detailed provenance. But there was always a sense with each new wonder of a conjurer producing a fresh rabbit out of a hat. Those who knew Professor Crane better than they probably wished speculated that he had some secret horde from which all of these discoveries somehow originated.

At any rate, his delayed return in the autumn of 1928 was taken as nothing more than the prelude to the announcement of a particularly dramatic breakthrough in Anglo Saxon studies. There was certainly no sense of any concern for the much esteemed professor. He was one of those people who were thought to be inextinguishable.

Richard Talbot, BA and MA (Hons), recently appointed Junior Assistant Tutor and Keeper of the Keys of the Welbeck Museum, was at least as unconcerned by Professor Crane's absence as anyone. He had grown up with a love of history, and especially that vague yet glittering era between the fall of Classical Rome and the Norman Conquest, which bordered on obsession. It was a love which had absorbed his childhood and concerned his stolid parents back in Penge, and which had been fuelled in no small part by the works of Mathias Crane. To become an undergraduate at the great professor's college and then to attend his famous lectures was the fulfilment of a dream. To be invited into the professor's private confidence on the new method of indexing and cataloguing on which he was working for his master's thesis was beyond his wildest imaginings. Also beyond imagining was how Professor Crane could then describe the same method to his fellow academics at a symposium held shortly after as if it was something entirely of his own invention.

Richard was livid. Richard was desolate. Richard felt totally betrayed. But who could he complain to, and where could he go? Specialists in the cataloguing of Anglo-Saxon artefacts were hardly in great demand. The only other obvious refuge lay in Oxford, where Professor Freethly-Chillmorn had long been reduced to academic impotence and chronic alcoholism by his shambling attempts to compete with Professor Crane. So the long and damning letter to *The Journal Of Early English Studies*, with copies to as many fellow academics as he could think of, and another to the *Times*, remained undrafted, and he found that he attracted many a sympathetic smile in the college library or the snug of the Eagle and Child. He had been—well, there was no real word for it because no one had ever spoken up... But whatever had been done to him by Professor Crane had been done before and would be done again. Meanwhile, he would have to swallow his pride and quietly put aside his stolen thesis and scrabble around for another less promising subject.

So it was that Richard Talbot gained his MA through wearily reworking the existing evidence regarding Saxon agricultural practice. He was then offered a junior tutorship for his pains. He of course had no choice but to accept, and—and this was the final insult—was granted a new role in reorganising the records, displays and artefacts at the college museum on the basis of a fabulous new system which was universally described as the Crane Method.

It was now almost three weeks into term, Cambridge was basking in the warmth of an Indian summer, and Professor Crane had still not returned. Welbeck College, it had to be admitted, was a somewhat happier, if rather more aimless, place without him. Meanwhile, Professor Meecham fulfilled the role of Acting Temporary Head of Department, although the man was far too good-natured to be anything more than a makeweight.

To Richard, this was all a matter of some frustration. What the college needed to apply itself to, he decided, was the careful grooming of a proper successor. After all, Professor Crane couldn't carry on forever, even when he did make his inevitable and irritatingly discovery-laden return from wherever he had been hiding this long summer. The college should be looking for a younger man capable of publishing ground-breaking works of great technical brilliance, but also with a popular touch which could reach the best-seller lists. The sort of man who could be equally at home supervising a summer dig in some windy field in East Anglia (although not actually doing any digging) as dining in the finest clubs in London amongst the great and famous. The sort of man whose face would fit well in the national papers and whom the undergraduates would look up to as a paragon of erudition, elegance and self-effacing charm. The sort of man, indeed, whom Richard Talbot believed he saw gazing back at him as he shaved each morning. Still youthful by outward appearance, of course. But with those high cheekbones and darkly solemn eyes. A fine physique, as well; he was especially proud of his long-fingered hands, with nails which he kept well-manicured and pared despite the occasional demands of his curating work. A voice which was made for compelling command. He was even known to possess a fine light tenor which he occasionally employed for the singing of popular ballads in certain back bars.

It was most, most frustrating. All, however, was not lost. Fortune favoured the brave, and time the young. As Richard sat in his tiny office in the Welbeck Museum on a stiflingly warm afternoon in early October, he still firmly believed that, Professor Crane notwithstanding, his moment would come. Although this particular day, it had to be admitted, hadn't been particularly propitious. You might have expected at least a few visitors to want to view the five high-ceilinged rooms which displayed the major items of the collection he curated, but today not a single one had appeared. Nor had he received any recent letters of enquiry from other researchers, or invitations to speak at some or other academic convention. Whilst the telephone remained frustratingly silent on his desk.

At about a quarter to four, he told his secretary Mrs Marbish—a wizened old bird—that she might as well go home. Then he slid the museum sign to CLOSED and locked in the main door with the key he kept on the chain of his watch fob. Of course, curating a museum certainly wasn't merely about *visitors*. Work to be done, always work to be done... Beyond a door marked REPOSITORY, a near endless array of potshards laid in dusty boxes on even dustier shelves awaited his cataloguing according to the so-called Crane Method. But, he told himself as he wandered amid the glass cases in the sun-threaded gloom, there were consolations...

There it all was: gold and bronze and silver, gleaming. A woman's locket found still with a strand of her auburn hair. A small iron blade, bereft of its bone handle, but nevertheless beautifully engraved. And here... One of his favourite objects: a particularly large and fine example of the broad-bladed weapon characteristic of the finest Saxon workmanship, with the hilt's jewelling almost intact and the blade decorated in exquisite silver and gold pattern-weld. Nearly perfect. So nearly perfect, in fact, that Richard often took the sword out to execute a few parrying and stabbing motions.

He opened the cabinet with another of his keys. Holding this weapon, it wasn't so very hard to imagine himself a brave Saxon warrior in full gear of battle. What foes would withstand me, he thought as the blade sliced

the air like a thickened gleam of sunlight. What lands I might have con-
quered, what maidens bedded, what battles fought! He was about to the
replace the sword in its cabinet when he noticed something which he had
never noticed before. The pommel, sadly, had been missing since the item
was first catalogued by one of Richard's predecessors back in the 1700s, but
now it seemed to him that there might actually be something curled inside
the hilt's hollowed metal core. Strange indeed, but Richard's heart only
started racing when he used a pair of fine tweezers to draw the object out.

That evening in the murmurous pipefug warmth of the college refec-
tory, as he spooned out beer pie, soggy potatoes and boiled beetroot,
Richard Talbot kept himself more than usually to himself. Then, he
scurried up to his rooms. Only there, with his door locked and his hands
slightly trembling, did he proceed to make a full and proper examination of
his find. It was, as he had realised immediately, a scrap of extremely antique
parchment, written in the kind of very early Old English which even the
Venerable Bede would have struggled to understand.

The parchment referred to a warrior named Cynewald, whom the
authorities agreed had most probably been King of Mercia in the period
between Cnebba and Creado in or around the year of Our Lord 550, although
the documentation then current was thin to say the least. Confirmation of
Cynewald's existence in this hidden scrap of funerary prose was in itself
a significant find. But the scrap then went on to refer to his burial in a
place which it described as being at *Fllotweyton*, and beside a *burna*, or clear
stream, near to the *brym* or surf, which presumably meant sea. A quick
check of a modern atlas confirmed that a small village named Flotterton
still existed in Lincolnshire, which would have been a significant part of the
Kingdom of Mercia at this time, and also that the village was, indeed, very
close to the sea. Richard barely needed to refer to the standard textbooks
to know that the place had never been associated with the discovery of any
significant Saxon remains. At least, not until now.

As to the final portion of text which could be deciphered before the
partial document faded, the cursing of a burial site was, for the Saxons,
fairly standard fare. Rather disappointingly, instead of some fearsome
tomb-guarding dragon, this one mentioned a lesser creature from the

The Crane Method | IAN R. MACLEOD

Anglo-Saxon beasterie known as a *ketta*, which was basically little more than a shadowy cat. The actual curse seemed odd—at least, it did to Richard, who was no specialist in Anglo Saxon linguistics. It said that the first person to disturb the tomb would find that the *ketta* took *gild nebbhad*. Gild being their concept of value, and *nebbhad* meaning something like identity. Which struck Richard as a peculiarly abstract curse, considering how brutal the Saxons usually were.

He could, of course, have consulted several experts who had spent the larger parts of their lives studying such arcane threats merely by heading a few yards down the corridor from his rooms. Even the great and still absent Professor Crane had considerable expertise in this area—or at the very least had taken someone else's expertise and made it his own. Richard remembered how the subject of burial curses had been raised at one of the professor's famous public lectures when he was an undergraduate. A laughing voice at the back had suggested that such things were, of course, utter rubbish, no doubt expecting the professor, who was worldly as they come about most matters, to agree. But instead Professor Crane had bowed his long neck and looked momentarily grave, and said in a quiet voice that the wishes of our ancestors were not to be taken lightly.

It was a little odd, Richard had to admit, that this scrap of parchment had never been noticed. Odd, also, that it lay tucked within a sword of entirely different provenance at least two centuries less old. Even he, he might have thought, had studied and played with the thing more than enough to have spotted that faded yellow curl hidden within the hilt. But, plainly, he hadn't. Neither had his many predecessor curators. Which to Richard, who had a generally poor view of his fellow toilers across the vast plains of Anglo Saxon study both previous and current, was less of a surprise. Things were as they were. And good luck was something he felt he hadn't had anything like enough of during his short academic career. In fact, the opposite. But now, Dame Fortune, had tossed her tresses and beckoned...

Richard hardly slept that night, such was his excitement. The next morning, after cramming a few things into his suitcase, he called in briefly at the museum to inform Mrs Marbish about a sudden illness his father was suffering back in Penge, then headed for the railway station. Everyone else at Welbeck College could wonder where he was, for the little it mattered. In fact, they could all go to Hell. They would be looking at him very differently when he returned.

The journey involved several tediously slow trains, and several even more tedious waits on the platforms of otherwise empty stations. Meanwhile, the long Indian summer was finally fading. At first, the sun was merely obscured by a few skeins of cloud. Then an easterly wind began to stir the trees and the wires of the telegraphs. Scattershots of rain were striking the glass of Richard's carriage from out of gloomy skies by the time he took the final leg of his journey across the wide, flat landscapes of Lincolnshire to Flotterton.

The village itself came as a disappointment. He'd imagined somewhere with a few crookedly ancient houses, a decent-sized manor house set amid a still discernable pattern of medieval fields, perhaps a charming pub. But Flotterton, for all its long history, looked as if it had never existed before the age of the railway, the kiss me quick hat, the bucket and spade. To call this desolate settlement a resort, he reflected as he struggled against the wind past a closed-for-the-season fish and chip shop and rock shop emporium which looked to have been abandoned, would be over-dignifying it. The place ran out, as if in shame, at a low straggle of dunes. Still, he told himself, as he espied through the rain a somewhat taller and yet even grimmer building with a sign announcing itself as a hotel, the name Flotterton would soon ring out in the halls of academia, and be writ large across the headlines of the daily papers. As, of course, would that of a certain Richard Talbot.

The hotel lived up to its external lack of promise. The proprietor was a scrawny man of late years in possession of the kind of beard which made you wonder whether its presence was intentional. He looked at Richard as he signed the address book much as one might study the arrival of an unwelcome household pest. The meal Richard ate in the otherwise empty restaurant had been re-heated so often that it was genuinely hard to tell what it might once have been, whilst the service wasn't so much execrable as non-existent. But he smiled to himself as he climbed into his pyjamas and lay down in the damp grey sheets of his damp grey room. This grim experience would stand up well as a humorous prelude in the many talks he would soon be giving about his discovery. People would smile. They would laugh warmly but respectfully. Even Professor Crane…

There, in the darkness, as the sea boomed and rain and wind rattled his window, Richard's smile briefly twitched into a grimace. He was remembering a small, embarrassing interlude which had occurred at the start of the summer recess, not long before the professor had set off on whatever mysterious quest had drawn him. It had been another of those long, slow, afternoons at the museum, and he had sent Mrs Marbish home and locked up early so he could occupy himself with a little sword practice. A few thrusts and parries, and his mind was so far off amid scenes of bloody battle that he hadn't become immediately aware of a watching presence. What presence, in fact, could there have been, seeing as he, as curator, possessed one of the sole two sets of keys which gave admission to the museum and its precious cabinets?

When Richard had, sweating and breathless, finally finished his pursuit of an imagined Grendel and twirled toward the half-open door where a tall figure was standing, Professor Crane had simply stepped from the shadows and stooped his long neck and announced that he had a query regarding the ground plan of an excavation which had taken place under the college's auspices back in the 1880s. He hadn't even mentioned the fact that Richard had been twirling a near-priceless sword like a child playing at knights-in-armour. Richard, flustered, had at least managed to put the thing away as if he had merely been checking some detail of its making. Then he went to find the papers in question, and the professor pronounced himself much obliged and left. But there was always a sense with Professor Crane that any minor infraction or mistake was carefully noted, analysed and stored until the day that it might prove useful.

Next morning, despite a night of difficult sleep in which a predatory creature seemed to be circling from the shadow-edges of some interminable space, Richard made a hearty attempt at extracting his breakfast of shrivelled bacon and congealed scrambled egg from its pool of cold fat. After all, one must fortify oneself for the work ahead, much as Belzoni surely did before he invaded the pyramids, Schliemann when he discovered Troy, or Carter when he stumbled into the tomb of Tutankhamun.

And, yes, the hotel proprietor did possess an Ordinance Survey map of the area, which Richard was allowed to borrow in exchange for an unnecessarily large deposit. There even proved to be a small shop along Flotterton's single street which sold a few items of hardware in the long season when it wasn't purveying buckets and spades. A decent spade, but of a larger and more practical kind, was exactly what Richard had in mind, along with a small lantern and a measuring tape.

The rain, at least, has ceased this morning, but it was nevertheless a particularly bitter and grey day. Wrestling with the map, then briefly consulting the precious scrap of parchment, Richard confirmed to himself that finding the burial mound shouldn't be that difficult. A stream, near to the sea... He hunched north around the edge of the pitch and putt course, which somehow felt to be the more promising direction with which to begin.

Noontime passed without success. The packed lunch of grey bread and something resembling ham which the hotel proprietor had prepared for Richard, along with a few fragments of his beard, was so poor that he would have tossed it to the screeching gulls if he hadn't been so hungry. North, it appeared, was not the direction he should have chosen. He retraced his steps toward the pitch and putt course as the wind stung into his face.

He knew exactly what an undisturbed Anglo-Saxon burial mound should look like, but the landscape around Flotterton was so uncertain that he was struggling to make proper sense of it. There were streams winding this way and that toward the shore, certainly. Some of them might even fit the description of being clear. There were also humps and mounds aplenty in the scrubby expanse of grazing land which abutted the dunes and the sea. But there were so *many*, and it was obvious that this whole coastline was forever shifting.

As he trudged past a few desolate bathing huts, then squelched on across a filthy stretch of mud using his shovel as a walking stick, Richard remembered the dreams of his childhood days back in Penge. Then he imagined himself seated in glory at the top table at the Welbeck College Annual Founders Dinner, and in a private first class carriage of a Great Northern express train on his way to collect some award. A plaque, perhaps, outside the museum to commemorate the brief time he had served there in undeserved obscurity? Or an entire new museum devoted to his name. For surely a king of Cynewald's era would have been buried with great riches, which of course was confirmed by that odd little curse. He could expect at very least the man's armour and ceremonial gear, along with—

Richard paused. Darkness was already settling and he would soon have to go back to that ghastly hotel, but for a moment he was almost convinced that he was being studied by a tall and oddly avian-seeming presence from the crest of yonder dune. An actual *bird*? A heron, most probably. Although it did seem unusually large. Were cranes at all common in this part of the world? Richard wondered, as he peered through the thickening gloom and the bird-like figure seemed to puff out in the swelling dusk like a doused candleflame.

Richard shivered. If he stood here any longer, he would probably find himself sinking irrevocably into the mud. Tired and disappointed, he dragged himself back toward the few lights of Flotterton. Taking in what remained of the view as he reascended the low rise beside the bathing huts, he was still determined not to give up. And there, over toward the low lands of Lincolnshire, the last of the westering sun flashed briefly toward him through a final gap in the clouds like a final signal of hope.

The effect was briefly beautiful. Richard could almost imagine why the great warriors of that distant and much misunderstood age might have chosen to inter their king here, where the incoming tide roared its grief—

His gaze caught on something. Such was the clarity of the light thrown by the setting sun that, like a lantern held at an acute angle to reveal the hidden indentations in a sheet of paper, the landscape spoke to him in a language as clear as modern English. In fact, to Richard, it was far clearer. It was suddenly obvious that the many mounds and hillocks which had so confused his day were lumped into their present irregular shapes by the simple forces of nature. But there was one mound which, although relatively small, was different. Astonishing, really, that no-one had ever noticed it before. Although the fact that it was now part of the pitch and putt course might have something to do with that.

The sun had vanished, but Richard was in no mood to return to his hotel. Like most things here, the course was closed for the winter, but its peeling picket fenced presented no obstacle. After some struggle with the wind, he lit his lantern and inspected the mound, which rose to something like twice head height, and was perhaps twenty yards across at its base. The makers of the course had used the mound as a hazard along the fairway of the 18th hole. But standing beside it, Richard was more certain than ever that he had found something ancient and extraordinary.

This was no time for measuring, for trial holes and exploratory trenches. This was his moment alone, and he was determined to take it. He glanced toward the few lights of Flotterton. He was close to what might loosely be termed civilisation, but he doubted if anyone would notice him at work here. Hefting his spade, he starting digging.

At first, he struck ordinary turf. Then, he came to a hard-packed aggregation of quartz stones laid in an approximate circle. This placing of an outline of stones being a common characteristic of Saxon burial mounds. Next, he began to encounter darker lumps amid the sandy soil. Indicative of burning—funerary incineration also being a common Saxon practice. Everything about this mound proclaimed its authenticity. His only fear was that some grave-robber had got to its treasure before him.

Richard laboured. The wind had stilled and a full moon had risen and the scene in which he worked, with the dark earth heaped across the silvered turf of the 18th fairway, acquired the clarity of an old woodcut. The opening on which he was working, a rough trench about two feet wide and three deep cut into the seaward side, became a tunnel. Soon, he was crawling in and out, scooping earth with his hands instead of using the spade. A little dangerous, perhaps, but he felt sure he could manage to scurry out at the first signs of major slippage.

Unlike Neolithic tombs, he was not expecting to find any solid structure at the mound's core. There would simply be more earth, and then the funerary remains themselves, surrounded perhaps by the bones of those who had been sacrificed in the deceased's cause. So it was a surprise to Richard when his hands suddenly fell through into what felt like empty space. He gasped, and heard the sound re-echoed in a stuttering growl as he wriggled backwards to take hold of his lantern. Then, on elbows, knees and belly, and by now entirely coated in dirt, he wriggled back inside the mound and held the lantern out.

The Crane Method | Ian R. MacLeod

What Richard Talbot saw when light first spilled into the darkness of lost centuries must rank amid the great moments of modern archaeology. The many artefacts which comprised what became known as the Flotterton Horde would have surely have gleamed even in that loamy hole. The famous golden-bossed shield. That exquisite dragonfly brooch. The many fine daggers and swords. The great Saxon mailcoat. All in all, there was enough here to change the way the world viewed the pre-Christian kingdoms.

As to what else happened in those moments of discovery, there is much that is not entirely clear. Many residents of Flotterton reported being awakened by a ghastly howling, which one described a sounding *like a huge, wounded cat*. The hotel proprietor was, to his credit, one of the first to put on his boots and investigate the horrifying noise, which seemed to emanate from the pitch and putt course. There, he reported that he saw a man staggering about the hillock beside the 18th fairway in the moonlight, seemingly struggling with something which he described as resembling a *blur of shadows*.

By the time the local doctor arrived, and then the police, and despite the horror of Richard's condition, wiser councils were already starting to prevail. There was, it must be said, some ill-advised speculation that Richard had somehow triggered an ancient form of booby trap when he poked his head into that mound. But any amateur historian of the era would have confirmed that that was not the Saxon way. Nor could device so ancient conceivably have functioned to such terrible effect. No, the general consensus was and always will be that Richard Talbot, perhaps in a spate of madness caused by his excitement and near-asphyxia, somehow managed to claw off most of his own face.

In the circumstances, and with Richard incapable of anything but sobbing screams, it was some hours before the police were able to establish whom they should contact. By next day, however, the first of the dons from Welbeck College were arriving, and they immediately saw the immense value of the discovery their colleague had made. The press came soon after, and the sightseers from the Midland towns not long after that. For the residents of Flotterton—and the hotel proprietor especially, although the man remained strangely subdued—there can scarcely have been better times.

The Best of Subterranean

Richard Talbot survived whatever ordeal he had suffered, although he was never again whole or sane. After the immediate medical problems of his loss of flesh, sight and proper speech had been dealt with, he lived his remaining few years at a specialist nursing home at the grateful college's expense. It was not, as it happens, so very far up the coast from Flotterton, at Sutton on Sea. Even there, though, his manner and what remained of countenance were such that he had to be kept well away from the other residents. Nor was he ever able to tolerate the presence of the establishment's fat and amiable ginger cat. Occasionally, one of the more sympathetic dons would summon the will to visit him, and try to marshal their revulsion at his manner, appearance and continued gurgling screams. One, a junior professor who succeeded Richard as curator of the now much-expanded and enormously popular museum, and an up-and-coming expert in Anglo-Saxon linguistics, took the time to study the parchment of ever-mysterious provenance which had been found in the pocket of Richard's coat. He was heard to comment how strange it was that the curse contained in the fragment could be best translated into modern English by the term *loss of face*, although this was hardly the type of speculation which would ever reach the academic press.

As for Professor Crane, he reappeared at Welbeck College a week or so after Richard's discovery. For once, he had returned from his researches empty-handed, although his presence and experience was vital in dealing with all the popular and academic interest, which was at fever pitch by then.

Careers blossomed at Welbeck in the years that followed. There were several best-sellers, visits to the now-famous coastal excavations by Cabinet ministers, and an item on Pate News. If there was one discovery which forever cemented the college's position in world academia, it was that of the Flotterton Horde. But, perhaps oddly given his reputation, this was the one advance in the science of archaeology for which the great Professor Crane, now Member of the Order of Merit and a Lord, would never take the slightest credit.

The Tomb of the Pontifex Dvorn

BY ROBERT SILVERBERG

In the days when Simmilgord was a wiry little boy growing up in the Vale of Gloyn he was fond of going out by himself into the broad savanna where the red gattaga-grass grew. Bare little stony hillocks rose up there like miniature mountains, eighty or ninety feet high. Clambering to the top of this one or that, he would shade his eyes against the golden-green sunlight and look far outward across that wide sea of thick copper-colored stalks. It amused him to pretend that from his lofty perch he could see the entire continent of Alhanroel from coast to coast, the great city of Alaisor in the distant west, the unthinkable height of Castle Mount rising like a colossal wall in the other direction, and, somewhere beyond that, the almost unknown eastern lands stretching on and on to the far shore of the Great Sea, marvel after marvel, miracle after miracle, and when he was up there he felt it would be no difficult thing to reach out and embrace the whole world in all its wonder.

Of course no one could actually see as far as that, or anything like it. Simply to think about such a distance made one's head spin. Alhanroel was too big to grasp, a giant continent that one could spend an entire lifetime exploring without ever fully coming to terms with the immensity of it, and Alhanroel was just one of the three continents of which the vast world of

Majipoor was comprised. Beyond its shores lay the other two continents of Zimroel and Suvrael, nearly as large, and on the far side of Zimroel began the almost mythical Great Sea that no one had ever been able to cross. Simmilgord knew all that. He was a good student; he had paid attention to his geography lessons and his history books. But still it was a glorious thing to go scrambling up to the summit of some jagged little rockpile and stare out beyond the endless mats of coppery-hued gattaga, beyond the grazing herds of stupid flat-faced klimbergeysts and the snuffling pig-like vongiforin that rooted about among them digging for tasty seeds, beyond the grove of spiky gray skipje-trees and the towering gambalangas that grazed on their tender topmost leaves, and imagine that he could take in all of Alhanroel in a single swiveling glance, the bustling seaports in the west and the lush tropical forests to the south and the great Mount with its Fifty Cities to the east, and the Castle at its summit from which the Coronal Lord Henghilain ruled the world in high majesty and splendor. He wanted to swallow it all at a single gulp, woodlands and jungles, deserts and plains, rivers and seas. Mine! Mine! This whole extraordinary world—mine! For Simmilgord there was a kind of wild soaring music in that thought: the vast symphony that was Majipoor.

Even at the age of ten Simmilgord understood that he was never going to see any of those places. The world was too huge, and he was too insignificant, nothing but a farmer's son whose probable destiny it was to spend his life right here in Gloyn, growing lusavender and hingamort and never getting any farther from home than one of the market towns of west-central Alhanroel, Kessilroge, maybe, or Gannamunda, or at best Marakeeba, somewhere off to the east. What a dreary prospect! Then and there, clinging to the top of that barren little mass of granite, he vowed to transcend that vision of an empty future, to make something out of his life, to rise up out of the Vale of Gloyn and make a mark in the world that would cause others to take note of him. He would become an adventurer, a soldier of fortune, a world traveler, the confidante of dukes and princes, perhaps even a figure of some prominence at the Coronal's court. Somehow—somehow—

※

The Tomb of the Pontifex Dvorn | Robert Silverberg

That romantic dream stayed with him as he grew into adolescence, though he scaled back his ambitions somewhat. He came to understand that he was better fitted by temperament to be a scholar of some sort than any kind of swashbuckling hero; but even that was far better than staying here in Gloyn and, like his father and all who had come before him for the past twenty generations, live from harvest to harvest, consuming his life in the unending cycle of planting and growing and gathering and marketing.

In Upper School he found himself drawn to the study of history. That was how he would encompass the magnificence that was Majipoor, by taking all its long past within himself, mastering its annals and archives, delving into the accounts of the first settlers to come here from Old Earth, the initial wonderstruck discoveries of strange beasts and natural wonders, the early encounters with the aboriginal Shapeshifters, the founding of the cities, the creation of its governmental structure, the reigns of the first Pontifexes and Coronals, the gradual spreading out from Alhanroel to the outer continents, the conquest of mighty Castle Mount, and all the rest. The romance of the world's long history set his soul ablaze. What fascinated him in particular was that someone, one man, the Pontifex Dvorn, had been able to make a unified and cohesive realm out of all this immensity.

What Dvorn had accomplished held a special fascination for him. It was Simmilgord's great hope to plunge into all of that and make out of Majipoor's unthinkable complexity a single coherent narrative, just as Dvorn, long ago, had made one world out of hundreds of independent city-states. He dreamed of earning admission to the Hall of Records within the enormous library Lord Stiamot had founded atop the Mount that coiled around the Castle's heart from side to side like a giant serpent, or of prowling through the dusty documents stored in the nearly as capacious archive in the depths of the Labyrinth, and bringing forth out of all that chaotic data a chronicle of Majipoor's history that would supersede anything that had ever been written.

Simmilgord was surprised to find his father encouraging him in this dream. He had not expected that. But there were other sons to work the farm, and Simmilgord had never shown much enthusiasm for the farm chores, anyway; plainly he was meant for other things. It seemed best for him to go to the famous University at Sisivondal and work to achieve his goal. And so he did. When he was sixteen he set out down the Great Western Highway, making the long eastward trek through Hunzimar and Gannamunda and Kessilroge and Skeil into the dusty plains of central Alhanroel, coming finally to Sisivondal, the tirelessly busy mercantile center where all the main shipping routes of Alhanroel crossed.

What a drab place it was! Miles and miles of faceless flat-roofed warehouses, of long monotonous boulevards decorated only with the sort of ugly black-leaved plants, squat and tough and spiky, that could withstand the long months of rainless days and hot winds under which the city suffered, the dreariest city imaginable on a world where most places took pride in the beauty and boldness of their architecture. Day and night caravans thundered down its grim streets, bringing or taking every sort of merchandise the huge planet produced. In the midst of the constant hubbub was the formidable wall surrounding the great University—Sisivondal's one center of high culture, second only to the revered University of Arkilon in scholarly repute—erected by the proud and wealthy merchants of the city to mark their own worldly success. But even the University was a somber thing, one bleak red-brick pile after another, all of its buildings done in a style more appropriate to a prison than to a temple of learning. Simmilgord, who had seen nothing of the world but the pleasant pastoral groves of the Vale of Gloyn, but who knew from his books of such dazzling and amazingly beautiful far-off places as glorious Stee, the grandest of the Fifty Cities of Castle Mount, and glistening white Ni-moya, Zimroel's big river-port, and spectacular Stoien of the crystal pavilions on the tropical southern coast, was stunned by the eye-aching awfulness of it all.

He knew, though, that the University of Sisivondal was his key to the greater world beyond. He found lodgings; he enrolled in the requisite courses; he made new friends. Once he was done with the basic curriculum he moved on to serious historical study, quickly seizing upon the earliest years of the imperial government as his special area of study. The titanic first Pontifex, Dvorn—what had he been like? How had he been able to impose his ideas of government on the unruly settlers? By what miracle had he devised a scheme of rule for this gigantic planet so efficient that it had endured, virtually without change, for more than twelve thousand years now?

Simmilgord looked forward to a time when the thesis on Dvorn that he planned to write, full of unanswered questions though it was likely to be, would win him admission to the archival centers of Majipoor's two capitals, the Pontifical one in the Labyrinth and the grand sprawling one at the Castle of the Coronal, where he could delve into the ancient secrets of those early days. But for one reason and another that time never seemed to arrive. He took his degree, and wrote his thesis—painfully, pitifully short on hard information—and got his doctorate, and he was taken on as a lecturer at the University with the hope of a professorship somewhere in the future, and he published a few papers—somewhat speculative in nature—on the founding of the Pontificate, and won the admiration of a handful of other historians thereby.

But that was all. The romance, the fantasy, that he had thought his life as a scholar would provide never seemed to materialize. He had reached the age of twenty-five, an age when one's life seems to be settling into its permanent pattern, and that pattern was not an inspiring one.

He began to think that he was going to spend the rest of his days in ghastly Sisivondal, delivering the same lectures year after year to ever-changing audiences of uninterested undergraduates and writing papers that recapitulated existing knowledge or invented shaky new theories about that which was unknown. That was not the vision he had had when he had climbed those little upjutting hillocks in the Vale of Gloyn and pretended he could take in the whole continent from Alaisor to the shores of the Great Sea in a single sweeping view.

And then the chairman of his department called him and said, "We would hate to lose you, Simmilgord, but I have a query here from the city of Kesmakuran—you know the place, surely? Just a piffling little agricultural town, but one of the oldest in Alhanroel. The alleged birthplace of the Pontifex Dvorn. Thought to be the site of his tomb as well, I think."

"I know it well, yes," said Simmilgord. "Two years ago and again last year I applied for a research grant to do some work there, but so far—"

"We have more than a research grant for you, I'm glad to say. The city fathers of Kesmakuran have decided to freshen up Dvorn's burial site, and they're looking for a curator. They've read your work on Dvorn and they think you're just the man. Clean the place up a little, establish a small museum nearby, turn Kesmakuran into something of a destination for tourists. It's an extremely old place, you know—older than Alaisor, older than Stoien, older than half the cities on Castle Mount, and they're very proud of that. There's enough in their budget to let you have an archaeologist to assist you, too, and I know that you and Lutiel Vengifrons are great friends, so we thought of recommending the two of you as a team—if you're interested, that is—"

"Curator of the tomb of the Pontifex Dvorn!" Simmilgord said in wonder. "Am I interested? Am I?"

⇥※⇤

Lutiel Vengifrons said, "It's a little bit of a career detour for us, don't you think?" As usual, there was a bit of an adversarial edge in his tone. The friendship that held Simmilgord and Lutiel together was based on an attraction of opposites, Simmilgord a tall, thin, flimsily built man of mercurial temperament, Lutiel short and strong, wide-shouldered, barrel-chested, cautious and stolid by nature.

"A detour? No, I don't think so," Simmilgord replied. "It puts me right where I want to be. How can I claim to be an expert on the reign of Dvorn when I haven't even visited the city where he was born and where he's supposed to be buried? But I could never afford to make the trip, and that research grant always seemed to be dangling just out of reach—and now, to live right there, to have daily access to all the important sites of his life—"

"And to turn them into tourist attractions?"

"Are you saying you don't want to go with me?" Simmilgord asked.

"No—no, I didn't say that. Not exactly. But still—I can't help wondering whether two earnest young scholars really ought to let themselves get involved with any such scheme. 'Clean the place up a little,' the chairman said. What does that mean? Deck it out with marble and onyx? Make it into some kind of gaudy amusement-park thing?"

"Maybe have a little modern plumbing put in, at most," said Simmilgord. "And some decent lighting.—Look, Lutiel, it's a brilliant opportunity. Maybe you worry too much about being an earnest young scholar, do you know what I mean? What an earnest young scholar like you needs to do is go to Kesmakuran and dig around a little and uncover a bunch of astounding artifacts that bring Dvorn out of the realm of culture-hero myths and turn him into a real person. And here's your chance to do it. Why, right now we don't even know that he ever existed, and—"

Lutiel Vengifrons gasped. "Can you seriously mean a thing like that, Simmilgord? He *had* to exist. *Somebody* had to be the first Pontifex."

"Somebody, yes. But that's all we can say. About the actual Dvorn we know practically nothing. He's just a name. His life is an absolute mystery to us. For all we know, Furvain might have made him up out of whole cloth because he needed a vivid character to fill out that part of his poem. But now—well—"

Simmilgord paused, startled and baffled by what he had just heard himself saying.

Never before had he expressed doubts about the real existence of Dvorn. And in fact he felt none. That Aithin Furvain's famous poem of four thousand years ago was the chief source of information about Dvorn, and that Furvain had not been any sort of scholar, but simply the wastrel son of Lord Sangamor, an idler, something of a fool, a *poet*, practically a myth himself, was irrelevant. Furvain must have had some concrete source to work from. There was no reason to take his cunningly constructed verses as a work of literal history, but no reason to discard them entirely as poetic fabrications, either. And there was no arguing away the fact that the Pontificate *had* been founded, after all, that some charismatic leader had put the whole thing into shape and persuaded the squabbling peoples of Majipoor to unite behind him, and if that leader had not been the Dvorn of Furvain's poem he must have been someone very much like him, whose existence could very likely be proven by the proper sort of archaeological and historical research.

So in raising an argument that cast doubts on Dvorn's literal existence, Simmilgord realized, he was simply taking an extreme position for
the sake of overcoming Lutiel's doubts about their taking the job. What
he yearned for, above all else, was to get out of dusty, parched Sisivondal,
away from the endless paper-shuffling and bureaucratic nonsense of university life, and plunge into some genuine historical research. And he very
much wanted Lutiel to accompany him, because there definitely would be
some excavating to do at the tomb site and he was no archaeologist, and
Lutiel was. They would make a good team out there in Kesmakuran. But
suggesting that in the present state of knowledge no one could even be sure
that Dvorn had ever existed was to overstate the case. Of *course* Dvorn
had existed. That much they could take for granted. It would be their job
to discover what he really had been like and how he had achieved what
he had achieved. And what an exciting task it would be! To dig deep into
the world's remote, almost mythical past—to make direct contact with the
stuff of fantasy and romance—!

"I don't think I'm phrasing this the right way," he said finally. "What I
mean is that most of what we think we know about Dvorn is derived from
an epic poem of long ago, not from direct scientific research, and we're
being handed an invitation to do that research and establish our scholarly
reputations by bringing him out of the realm of myth and poetry into some
sort of objective reality. Forget the part about setting up a tourist attraction
there. That's just incidental. The chance to do important research is what
matters. Come with me, Lutiel. It's a once-in-a-lifetime opportunity."

In the end, of course, Lutiel agreed. Unlike Simmilgord, he had not
a shred of romance in his soul. He was no climber of hills, no dreamer
of wondrous dreams. What he was was a patient plodder, a stolid sifter of
sand and pebbles, as archaeologists often tend to be. But even so he could
see the merits of the offer. There had never been any scientific excavations
carried out at Kesmakuran: just some occasional amateur digs in the course
of the past thousand years or so, turning up a few fragmentary inscriptions
that appeared to date from the time of the first Pontificate, and that was
all—though it had been enough for the uncritical residents of the place
to seize upon as proof of the claim that Dvorn had been born and died in

their ancient but otherwise unremarkable town. But beyond question there was no event more important in the long history of human settlement on Majipoor than the inspired creation of a political system that had survived in nearly its original form these twelve thousand years. Kesmakuran was generally accepted as the traditional place of the great first Pontifex's birth; it was reasonable at least to postulate that some evidence of Dvorn's existence might be found there. And the city fathers of Kesmakuran were handing the two of them the key to the site.

"Well—" said Lutiel Vengifrons.

Kesmakuran turned out to be not much more than a village, with a population of perhaps a hundred thousand at most, but it was a pretty village, and after the brutal implacability of Sisivondal and the long, wearying journey across central Alhanroel into the western provinces it seemed almost idyllic. It lay in the heart of prosperous farming country—everything from Gannamunda and Hunzimar westward was farming country, thousands of miles of it, blessed by the beneficial westerly winds that carried the rains inland from the distant coast—and Simmilgord rejoiced in the sight of broad fertile plains and cultivated fields again, so different from the interminable brick drabness of Sisivondal's innumerable warehouses and depots. He had never been this far west before, and, although Alaisor and the other coastal cities still lay many days' journey beyond here, it seemed to his eager imagination that he need only climb the nearest hill to behold the bosom of the Inner Sea shimmering in the golden-green afternoon sunlight. The air was fresh and sweet and moist out here, with a bit of the tang of a wind from the ocean. In parched, nearly rainless Sisivondal every intake of breath had been a struggle and the hot, dry air had rasped against his throat.

Simmilgord and Lutien were given a cottage to share, one of a row of nearly identical square-roofed buildings fashioned from a pinkish-gold stone that was quarried in the mountains just south of town. Their host, Kesmakuran's mayor, fluttered about them fussily as though he were welcoming some dukes or princes of Castle Mount, rather than a pair of uncertain young academics newly emerged from a sheltered scholastic existence.

Kyvole Gannivad was the mayor's name. He was a stubby, rotund man, bald except for two reddish fringes above his ears, stocky with the sort of solid stockiness that made you think that no matter how hard you pushed him you could not knock him over. He had trouble remembering their names, calling Simmilgord "Lutilel" a couple of times and once transforming Lutiel's surname into "Simmifrons," which seemed odd for a politician, but otherwise he was ingratiating and solicitous to the point of absurdity, telling them again and again what an honor it was for the town of Kesmakuran to be graced by renowned scholars of their high intellect and widely acclaimed accomplishments. "We are counting on you," he said several times, "to put our city on the map. And we know that you will."

"What does he mean by that?" Lutiel asked, when they were finally alone. "Are we supposed to do real research here, or does he think we're going to act as a couple of paid publicists for them?"

Simmilgord shrugged. "It's the sort of thing that mayors like to say, that's all. He can't help being a home-town booster. He thinks that if we set up a nice little four-room museum next door to the site of the tomb and find a few interesting old inscriptions to put in it, visitors will come from thousands of miles around to gawk."

"And suppose that doesn't happen."

"Not our problem," said Simmilgord. "You know what you and I came here to do. Pulling the tourists in is his job, not ours."

"What if he tries to push us in directions that compromise the integrity of our work?"

"I don't think he will. But if he tries, we can handle him. He's nothing but a small-town mayor, remember, and not a particularly bright specimen of his species.—Come on, Lutiel. Let's unpack and have a look at the famous tomb."

But that turned out not to be so simple. They needed to go with the official custodian of the tomb, and it took more than an hour to locate him. Then came the trek to the tomb itself, which was at the southern edge of town, far across from their lodgings, at the foot of the range of mountains out of which the city's building-blocks had been carved. It was late afternoon before they reached it. An ugly quarry scar formed a diagonal slash across the face of the mountain; below and to both sides of it grew a dense covering of blue-black underbrush, descending to ground level and extending almost to the outermost street of the city, and here, nearly hidden by the thick tangle of brush, was the entrance to Dvorn's tomb, or at least what was said to be Dvorn's tomb: a black hole stretching downward into the earth.

"I will go first," said their guide, Prasilet Sungavon, the local antiquarian who was the custodian of the tomb. "It's very dark down there. Even with our torches, we won't have an easy time."

"Lead on," Simmilgord said impatiently, gesturing with his hand.

Prasilet Sungavon had annoyed them both from the very start. He was a stubby little Hjort, squat and puffy-faced and bulgy-eyed, a member of a race that apparently could not help seeming officious and self-important. About a third of the population of Kesmakuran were Hjorts, evidently. By profession Prasilet Sungavon was a dealer in pharmaceutical herbs, who long ago had taken up amateur archaeology as a weekend hobby. "I've been digging down here, man and boy, for forty years," he told them proudly. "And I've found some real treasures, all right. Just about anything that anybody knows about Dvorn, they know because of the things I've found." Which would irritate Lutiel Vengifrons considerably, because, as a professionally trained archaeologist, he surely would dislike the thought that this pill-peddler had spent decades rummaging around at random with his spade and his pick in this unique and easily damaged site. Simmilgord was bothered by him too, since it was unlikely that Prasilet Sungavon had the knowledge or the wit to derive any sort of solid historical conclusions from whatever he had managed to scrape loose in the depths of the tomb.

But, whether they liked it or not, the Hjort was the official municipal custodian of the tomb, the man with the keys to the gate, and they could do nothing without his cooperation. So they lit their torches and followed him down a stretch of uneven flagstone steps to a place where a metal grillwork barred their entry, and waited while Prasilet Sungavon elaborately unlocked a series of padlocks and swung the gate aside.

A dark, muddy, musty-smelling passage, low and narrow, with a cold breeze rising up out of it, lay before them. Through swerves and curves it led onward for some unknown distance into the heart of the mountain on a gradual sloping descent. Because of his height, Simmilgord had to crouch from the start. The floor of the passage was a thick, spongy layer of muddy soil; the sides and roof of it had been carved, none too expertly, from the rock of the mountain above them. The entranceway, the Hjort told them, had now and then been blocked by the backwash from heavy storms, and had had to be cleared at least five times in the last two thousand years, most recently a century ago. When they had gone about fifteen feet in, Prasilet Sungavon indicated a crude niche cut into the tunnel wall. "I found remarkable things in there," he said, without explanation. "And there, and there," pointing at two more niches further along. "You'll see."

The air in the tunnel was cold and dank. From somewhere deeper in came the sound of steadily dripping water, and occasionally the quick clatter of wings as some cave-dwelling creature, invisible in the dimness, passed swiftly by overhead. Other than that, and the hoarse, ragged breathing of the Hjort, all was silent in here. After about ten minutes the passage expanded abruptly into a high-roofed circular chamber, lined all about by a coarse and irregular wall of badly matched blocks of gray stone, that could very readily be regarded as a place of interment. And against the left side of it sat a rectangular lidless pink-marble box, three or four feet high and about seven feet long, that was plausibly a sarcophagus.

"This is it," said the Hjort grandly. "The tomb of the Pontifex Dvorn!"

"May I?" Lutiel Vengifrons said, and, without waiting for a reply, stepped forward and peered into the box. After a moment Simmilgord, more diffidently, went up alongside him.

The sarcophagus, if that indeed was what it was, was empty. That was no surprise. They had not expected to find Dvorn lying here with his hands crossed on his chest and a benign smile on his Pontifical features. The stone box was roughly carved, with clearly visible chisel-marks all along its bare sides. There did not seem to be any inscriptions on it or any sort of ornamentation.

The Tomb of the Pontifex Dvorn | ROBERT SILVERBERG

"A tomb, yes, very possibly," said Lutiel Vengifrons after a while. He made the concession sound like a grudging one. "But just how, I wonder, were you able to identify this place specifically as the tomb of Dvorn?"

His tone was cool, skeptical, challenging. Unflustered, the Hjort replied, "We know that he was born in Kesmakuran, and that after his glorious century-long reign as Pontifex he died here. There is no doubt of that. It has always been understood locally that this is his tomb. That is the tradition. No one questions it. No other city in the world makes any such claim. Plainly this is an archaic site, going back to the earliest days of the settlement of Majipoor. The effort that must have been involved at that early time in digging such a long passageway indicates that this could only be the tomb of someone important. I ask you: Who else would that be, if not the first Pontifex?"

The logic did not seem entirely impeccable. Simmilgord, who had his own ideas about the unquestioning acceptance of local tradition as historical certainty, began to say something to that effect, but Lutiel nudged him ungently in the ribs before he could get out more than half a syllable. For the moment it was Lutiel who was conducting the interrogation. Prasilet Sungavon continued, still unperturbed, "Of course the body had disintegrated in the course of so long a span of time. But certain relics remained. I will show them to you when we come out of here."

"What about the lid?" Lutiel Vengifrons said. "Surely nobody would bury such an important personage in a sarcophagus that had no lid."

"There," said the Hjort, aiming his torch into a dark corner of the tomb-chamber. Against the far wall lay what must once have been a long stone slab, now cracked into three pieces and some bits of rubble.

"Tomb-robbers?" Simmilgord asked, unable to keep silent any longer.

"I think not," the Hjort said sharply. "We are not that sort of folk, here in Kesmakuran. Doubtless some visitors long ago lifted the lid to make certain that Dvorn's body really did lie here, and as they carried it to one side they dropped it and it broke."

"No doubt that is so," said Simmilgord, working hard to keep the sarcasm from his voice.

He could feel himself slipping into a profound bleakness of spirit. This dark, muddy hole in the ground—this miserable crude stone coffin with its shattered lid—these unprovable conjectures of Prasilet Sungavon—how did any of this constitute any sort of substantive information about the life of the Pontifex Dvorn? He wondered how he and Lutiel could possibly fulfill even the slightest part of the scientific mission that had taken them halfway across the continent from Sisivondal. It all seemed hopeless. There was so little to work with, and what little there was undoubtedly contaminated by the passionate desire of the Kesmakuran folk to inflate its significance into something of major historical importance. Right here at the beginning of everything Simmilgord saw only disaster encroaching on him from all sides.

Prasilet Sungavon, though, stood before them smiling an immense Hjortish smile, a foot wide from ear to ear. Obviously he was very pleased with himself and the cavern over which he presided.

With a brisk professionalism that belied his gloom Simmilgord said, "Well, now, is there anything else we should see?"

"Not here. At my house. Let us go."

One room of Prasilet Sungavon's house had been turned into a kind of Dvorn museum. Three cases contained artifacts that had been taken from the tomb, most of them by the Hjort himself, some by the anonymous predecessors of his who had poked around in the tomb in the course of the previous thousand years. "These," he said resonantly, indicating several small yellowish objects, "are some of the Pontifex's teeth. And this is a lock of his hair."

"Still retaining some color after twelve thousand years," said Lutiel. "Remarkable!"

"Yes. Verging on the miraculous, I would say.—These, I am told with good authority, are his knucklebones. Nothing else of the body remains. But how fortunate we are to have these few relics."

"Which you say can be identified as those of the Pontifex Dvorn," Simmilgord said. "May I ask, by what evidence?"

"The inscriptions from the tomb," said the Hjort. "I will show you those tomorrow."

"Why not now?"

"The hour grows late, my friend. Tomorrow."

The Tomb of the Pontifex Dvorn | Robert Silverberg

There was no mistaking the inflexibility in his tone. Tomorrow it would have to be. The Hjort had the upper hand, and it seemed that he meant to keep it that way.

It was a depressing evening. Neither man had much to say, and little of that was optimistic. What had been put forth to them as the tomb of Dvorn was nothing much more than a muddy unadorned underground chamber that could have been built for almost any purpose at any time in the past twelve thousand years, the putative teeth and hair and bones that Prasilet Sungavon had shown them were absurdities, and the Hjort's proprietary attitude toward the site was certainly going to make any sort of real probing very difficult. There hadn't even been any Hjorts on Majipoor in the early centuries of the Pontificate—it was Lord Melikand who had brought all the non-human races here, thousands of years later, an amply chronicled fact—and yet here was this one behaving as though he owned the place. That was likely to be an ongoing problem.

The inscriptions from the tomb, at least, provided one mildly hopeful sign when Prasilet Sungavon let them see them the next day. From a locked cabinet the Hjort drew five small plaques of yellow stone. He had found them, he said, hidden away in the niches leading up to the tomb-chamber. Their surfaces appeared to have been damaged by unskillful cleaning, but nevertheless it was possible to see that they bore lettering, worn and indistinct, in some kind of barely familiar angular script that at even such brief inspection as this Simmilgord believed could be accepted—with a stretch—as an early version of the writing still in use in modern times.

A shiver of excitement ran down his spine. If these things were genuine, they could be the world's oldest surviving written artifacts. What an amazing notion that was! That romantic element in his soul that had blazed in him since his boyhood atop the hillocks of the Vale of Gloyn still lived in him: to hold these chipped and battered little slabs of stone aroused in him a feeling of being in contact with the whole vast sweep of the world's history from the beginning. And for the first time since their arrival in Kesmakuran he began to think that their long journey across the continent might yet result in something useful. But he was no paleographer. He had never handled any documents remotely as old as these would have to be, if indeed they dated from the era of the early Pontificate, and what he saw here was altogether mysterious to him. No actual intelligible words leaped out to him from the worn surfaces of the slabs. At best he had a vague sense that the faint marks that they bore *were* words, that they said something meaningful in a language that was akin, in an ancestral way, to the one that the people of Majipoor still spoke. He looked across to Lutiel Vengifrons. "What do you think?"

"Extraordinary," Lutiel said. "They could actually be quite old, you know." The way he said it left no doubt that he too was greatly moved, even shaken, by the sight of the slabs. Simmilgord took note of that: Lutiel, steady and sober-minded and conservative, was not a man given to overstatement or bursts of wild enthusiasm. But then his innate sobriety of mind reasserted itself. "—If they're authentic, that is."

"*How* old, Lutiel?"

A shrug. "Lord Damiano's time? Stiamot's? No, older than that— Melikand, maybe."

"Not as old as the era of Dvorn, then?"

"I can't say, one way or the other, not just by one fast look. They're hard to read. I'm not very much of an expert on the most archaic scripts. And the lighting in here isn't good enough for this kind of work. I'd need to examine them under instruments—a close study of their surfaces—"

Prasilet Sungavon gathered up the slabs and said, "Let me tell you what they say. This one—" It was the largest of them. He pursed his immense lips and slowly traced a line across the surface of the slab with a thick ashen-gray forefinger. " 'I, Esurimand of Kesmakuran, acting at the behest of Barhold, anointed successor to the beloved Pontifex Dvorn—' " Looking up, he said, "That's all can be read of this one. But on the next it says, 'The blessings of the Divine upon our great leader, who in the hundredth year of his reign—' Again, it's not possible to make out anything after that. But the next one says, 'For which we vow eternal gratitude—' and this one, 'May he enjoy eternal repose.' The fifth tablet is completely unintelligible."

The Tomb of the Pontifex Dvorn | Robert Silverberg

Simmilgord and Lutiel Vengifrons exchanged glances. The look of skepticism in Lutiel's eyes was unmistakable. Simmilgord silently indicated his agreement. It was all he could do to keep himself from laughing.

But he tried to preserve some semblance of scholarly detachment. They could not afford to seem to be mocking Prasilet Sungavon to his face. "Quite fascinating," he said crisply. "Quite. And would you care to tell us how you were able to arrive at these translations?"

But he must not have been able to conceal the scorn in his voice very well, for the Hjort fixed his huge bulging eyes on him with a look that must surely be one of anger.

"Years of study," said Prasilet Sungavon. "Unremitting toil. Comparing old texts with older ones, and even older ones yet, until I had mastered the writings of the ancients. And then—long nights of candlelight—straining my eyes, struggling to comprehend these faint little scratchings in the stone—"

⋇

"He's making it all up, of course," Lutiel said, hours later, when they had returned to their own quarters. "The slabs might be real, and the inscriptions, but he invented those texts himself."

"I'm not so sure of that," said Simmilgord. He had been through a long and troubling conversation with himself since they had left the Hjort's place. "I doubted his translations as much as you did at first, when he started reeling off all that glib stuff about the beloved Pontifex Dvorn, and so forth. But you saw his library. He's done some genuine work on those inscriptions. We ought to allow for the possibility that they do say something like what he claims they say."

"But still—how pat it is, how neat, the reference to Barhold, the line about eternal repose—"

"Pat and neat if he's building support for a hoax, yes. But if that truly is Dvorn's tomb—"

Lutiel gave him an odd look. "You really want to believe that it is, don't you?"

"Yes. No question that I do. Don't you?"

"We are supposed to begin with the evidence, and work toward the hypothesis, Simmilgord. Not the other way around."

"You *would* say something like that, wouldn't you? You know that I'd never try to deny that a proper scholar ought to work from evidence to hypothesis. But there's nothing wrong with starting from a hypothesis and testing it against the evidence."

"The evidence of myth and tradition and, quite possibly, of fabricated artifacts?"

"We don't know that they're fabricated. I don't like that Hjort any more than you do, but his findings may be legitimate all the same.—Look, Lutiel, I'm not saying that that *is* Dvorn's tomb. I simply answered your question. Do I *want* to believe it's Dvorn's tomb? Yes. Yes, I do. I think it would be wonderful if we could prove that it's the real thing. Whether it is or not is what we're here to find out."

It was as close as they had ever come to a real quarrel. But gradually the discussion grew less heated. They both saw that arguing with each other about the authenticity of the texts or the scholarly credentials of Prasilet Sungavon was pointless. They had come to Kesmakuran to conduct independent research and reach their own conclusions. Each of them had already let Prasilet Sungavon see that they had their doubts about the things he had shown them—they had, in fact, not been able to do a very good job of concealing their disdain for his methods and his results—and it was clear that the Hjort was annoyed by that. In his own eyes he was the leading authority on the tomb of the Pontifex Dvorn and they were merely a pair of snotty wet-behind-the-ears University boys, and indeed there was some truth to that. In the future they would have to take a less condescending approach to him, for Prasilet Sungavon held the keys to the tomb and without his cooperation they would accomplish nothing.

They tried to do just that in their next meeting with the Hjort, letting him know how excited they were by all that they had seen so far, and how eager they were to build on the splendid work he had done. He seemed mollified by that. Simmilgord asked to be allowed to take the slabs back to their house for study, and, although Prasilet Sungavon refused, he did let them make copies to work with. He also was willing to give them access to his own extensive library of paleographic texts. Lutiel said that he wanted to have lighting installed in the tomb—at the expense of the University, naturally—and the Hjort unhesitatingly agreed. Nor did he seem to be troubled by Lutiel's suggestion of extending the existing excavation deeper into the mountainside, which somehow no one had thought of doing since the cavern first had become known to the people of Kesmakuran.

The first surprise came when they began poring over the inscriptions on the tablets and comparing the characters with the examples of early Majipoori script in Prasilet Sungavon's books. In twelve thousand years one would expect any sort of alphabet to undergo some metamorphosis, but careful inspection of the tablets under adequate lighting quickly revealed that they were decipherable after all, once one made allowances for the erosion of the surface that time and careless cleaning had inflicted, and, after they had learned to make those allowances, they could see that the Hjort's readings were not very far from the mark. "See—here?" Lutiel said. "By the Divine, it *does* say 'Dvorn'—I'm certain of it!"

Simmilgord felt the shiver of discovery again. "Yes. And this—isn't it 'Barhold'?"

"With the Pontifical sign next to both names!"

"E-tern-al re-pose—"

"I think so."

"Where's the part about 'the hundredth year of his reign'?"

"I don't see it."

"Neither do I. But of course Dvorn *didn't* reign a hundred years. That's culture-hero stuff—myth, fable. Just because it's in Furvain doesn't mean it's true. Nobody lives that long. The Hjort must have interpolated it to make the Kesmakurans happy. They want to believe that their great man was Pontifex for a century, just as it says in the *Book of Changes*, and so he found it on this slab for them."

"It's probably this line here," Lutiel said, pointing with his pencil. "You can make out about one letter out of every six, at best, in this section. Prasilet Sungavon would have been able to translate it any way he liked."

"But the rest of it—"

"Yes. It does all match up, more or less.—We have to be nicer to him, Simmilgord. We really *do* have the tomb of Dvorn here, I think. You know how skeptical I was at first. But it gets harder and harder to argue this stuff away."

The installation of the lighting system began the next day. While that was going on, and Lutiel was purchasing the tools he would need for the dig, Simmilgord busied himself in the municipal archives, digging back through astonishingly ancient records. With the mayoral blessing of Kyvole Gannivad all doors were thrown open to him, and he roamed freely in a labyrinth of dusty shelves. The archive here was nothing like what he imagined was held in the Castle Mount library, or in the storage vaults of the Labyrinth, but it was impressive enough, particularly for so minor a town as Kesmakuran. And it appeared as though no one had looked at these things in decades, even centuries. For two days he wandered through an unfruitful host of relatively recent property deeds and tax records and city-council minutes, but then he found a staircase leading downward to a storeroom of far older documents, documents of almost unbelievable antiquity. Some of them went back six, seven, eight thousand years, to the days of Calintane and Guadeloom and the mighty Stiamot who reigned before them, and some were older than Stiamot even, bearing the seals of Coronals and Pontifexes whose names were mere shadows and whispers; and beneath these were what seemed to be transcriptions, themselves several thousand years old, of what appeared to be documents from the very earliest years of human settlement on Majipoor.

It was a wondrous thing to read these old texts. Simply to handle them was a thrill. Here—Simmilgord, still caught in the struggle between his skepticism and his eagerness to believe, could not help wondering whether it was a latter-day forgery—was a document that purported to be a copy of a decree issued by Dvorn when he was nothing more than the head of the provincial council of Kesmakuran. Here—how startling, if authentic!—was the text of Dvorn's fiery message to his fellow leaders in west-central Alhanroel, calling on them to unite and form a stable national government. Here—there seemed to be a considerable gap in time—was an edict of Dvorn's having to do with water rights along the Sefaranon River. So his regime had already extended its reach that far to the west! Whatever clerk had been responsible for making this copy of the primordial original document had drawn a replica of something very much like the Pontifical seal on it. Then there was a decree that bore not only Dvorn's name but that of Lord Barhold, the first Coronal, which indicated that Dvorn had by then devised the system of dual rule, a senior monarch who shaped policy and a junior one who saw to its execution; and after that came one that indicated that Barhold had succeeded to the title of Pontifex and had appointed a Coronal of his own.

Simmilgord felt dazed by it all. A sensation as of a great swelling chord of music came soaring up from the core of his soul, music that he had heard before, the great song of Majipoor that had resounded in his heart now and again throughout all his days. Since his boyhood he had lived with the deeds of the Pontifex Dvorn alive in his mind, the dawn of his campaign to bring the scattered cities of Majipoor together into a single realm, the first gathering of support at Kesmakuran, the arduous march to Stangard Falls, the proclamation of a royal government, the founding of the Pontificate and the struggle to win worldwide acceptance. Certainly it was the great epic of the world's history. But nearly all that Simmilgord knew of it came from Aithin Furvain's poem. Until this moment he had feared that every detail of the story, so far as anyone could say with certainty, might merely be a work of imaginative recreation.

Now, though, here in his hands, was the evidence that Furvain had told the true story. It was impossible to resist the desire to accept these documents as authentic. As he scanned through them, running his fingers over them, caressing them almost in a loving way, the whole stupendous sweep of Majipoor's history came pouring in on him like the invincible flow of a river in full spate. Simmilgord had not known any such sensations since his boyhood in the Vale of Gloyn, when he had felt the first stirrings of that hunger to comprehend this vast world that had eventually set him on the path he followed now. The documents *had* to be real. No one, not even for the sake of enhancing provincial pride, could have gone to the trouble of forging all this. Unimportant little Kesmakuran did indeed seem to be the place from which Dvorn's unification movement had sprung;

and, no matter how pompous Prasilet Sungavon's manner might be, it was starting to be hard to reject the conclusion that the tomb of which he was the custodian was the actual burial-place of the first Pontifex.

Lutiel, meanwhile, had been making significant progress toward the same conclusion. He had recruited a crew of diggers from the local farms, three boys and two girls, and had given them a quick course in the technique of archaeological excavation, and—while Prasilet Sungavon stood by, watching somewhat uneasily—had begun to push the zone of exploration well beyond the tomb-chamber.

As Lutiel had begun to suspect almost from the first day, there was more to the underground structure than the entryway and the burial chamber. Some probing on the far side of that chamber revealed that its roughhewn wall was even more irregular than usual in certain places, and when he lifted away a little of the masonry in those places he discovered that behind the jumbled stones lay circular openings, probably plugged long ago by rockfalls. And behind those were four additional passageways leading off at sharp angles from the main entry tunnel. Succeeding days of excavation demonstrated that at one time the tomb-chamber had been at the center of a cluster of such tunnels, as though in ancient times solemn ceremonial processions had come to it from various directions.

Prasilet Sungavon, who made a point of being present at each day's work as if he feared that Lutiel might damage the precious tomb in some way, displayed mixed feelings as these discoveries proceeded. Plainly he was displeased as his own inadequacies as an archaeologist were made manifest: that he had never thought of digging deeper in at the site himself could only be an embarrassment to him. But his yearning for antiquarian knowledge was genuine enough, however inadequate his scientific skills might be, and he showed real excitement as Lutiel pushed his various excavations farther and farther.

Especially when more tablets turned up in these outer passages: commemorative plaques that showed an evolution in Majipoori script that had to cover several thousand years, culminating in a perfectly legible one declaring that the prodigious Stiamot, conqueror of the aboriginal Metamorphs, had come here on pilgrimage after his succession to the

Pontificate and had performed a ceremony of thanksgiving at the tomb of his revered predecessor Dvorn.

Here was proof absolute of the authenticity of the site. That night Mayor Kyvole Gannivad gave a celebratory feast, and the golden wine of Alaisor flowed so freely that both Simmilgord and Lutiel found it necessary to declare a holiday from their labors on the next day.

That was the first surprise: the confirmation that this was, in fact, the veritable tomb of Dvorn. The second surprise, which came a few weeks later, was much less pleasant. They were both back at work, Simmilgord ploughing through a mountain of dusty documents, Lutiel meticulously extending his dig, when messengers came to each of them to say that the mayor wished to see them at his office immediately.

Simmilgord, arriving first, waited fifteen minutes in the office vestibule for Lutiel to get there, and ten fretful minutes more before Kyvole Gannivad appeared. The round little man came bouncing out, flushed with excitement, beckoning with both hands. "Come! Come! We have a visitor, a most important visitor!"

The huge figure of a Skandar waited within, practically filling the mayoral office: a ponderous bulky being, at least eight and a half feet tall, with four powerful arms and a thick shaggy pelt. Kyvole Gannivad said grandiloquently, "My friends, it is my great pleasure to introduce you to—"

But the Skandar needed no introduction. Simmilgord knew him instantly by the two bizarre stripes of orange fur that slanted diagonally like barbaric ornaments through his dense gray-blue facial pelt, and by the fiery intensity of his eyes. This could only be Hawid Zakayil, the forceful and autocratic Superintendent of Antiquities of Alhanroel, a man who was ex officio director of half the museums of the continent, who had positioned himself as the supreme authority on all questions having to do with the past of Majipoor, who spent his days in perpetual motion, moving from one major site to another, taking command of anything that might be going on there, personally announcing all major discoveries, putting his name to innumerable books and essays that—so it was widely thought—were primarily the work of other people. He was a force of nature, a living hurricane, dynamic and irresistible. He had come once to the University when Simmilgord was there, to address the senior convocation, and the event was nothing that Simmilgord could ever forget.

It was only to be expected, Simmilgord thought dolefully, that the ubiquitous and omnipotent Hawid Zakayil would turn up here sooner or later. Confirmation of the authenticity of the tomb of Dvorn? Discovery of a Stiamot inscription? And of documents, or at least copies of documents, that cast new light on pivotal moments in the career of the first Pontifex? How, in the light of all of that, could he have stayed away? And what would happen now to the two young scholars who had made these discoveries?

Simmilgord, looking quickly toward Lutiel, had no difficulty reading the message that his friend's eyes conveyed.

We are lost, Lutiel was thinking. *We are doomed.*

Simmilgord felt very much the same way. But for the moment all was jubilation and good cheer, at least outwardly. The towering Skandar reached out, taking both of Simmilgord's hands in his two left ones and Lutiel's in the right pair, and told them in booming tones how proud he was of the things they had achieved. "I met you both, you know, in Sisivondal, your graduation week, and I knew even then that you were destined for great things. As I told you at the time. Surely you remember!"

Surely Simmilgord did not. He had seen Hawid Zakayil then, yes, but only at a distance, simply as a member of the audience during that lengthy and vociferous harangue. Not a single word had passed between them on that occasion or at any time since. But he was not about to contradict the great man about that, or, indeed, about anything else.

They spoke with him for a long while about the work they had been doing in Kesmakuran. Then, of course, there had to be an inspection of Simmilgord's collection of archival material, and of the tablets that Lutiel had found in the newly opened tunnels, and then a tour of the tunnels themselves. At some point in the afternoon Prasilet Sungavon interpolated himself into the group, introduced himself effusively to Hawid Zakayil, and let the Skandar know, without saying so in quite those words, that

Simmilgord and Lutiel would not have accomplished a thing here without his own thoughtful guidance. "You have done well," the Superintendent of Antiquities told him, and the Hjort beamed a great Hjortish grin of self-satisfaction. Simmilgord and Lutiel maintained a diplomatic silence.

Hawid Zakayil was so big that the tour of the tunnels was something of a challenge, and at one ticklish moment it seemed as if he were going to become stuck in the tightest of the passageways. But he extricated himself with the skill of one who was accustomed to life on a world where nearly everything was constructed for the benefit of much smaller beings. He moved quickly from place to place within the site, sniffing at the sarcophagus, staring into the niches where the stone tablets had been found, pushing at the chamber walls as though testing their solidity. "Wonderful," he said. "Marvelous. How thrilling it is to realize that we stand right at the birthplace of the history of Majipoor!"

Simmilgord thought he heard Lutiel snicker. This was no birthplace, for one thing: it was a tomb. And Simmilgord knew that Hawid Zakayil's appropriation to himself of the entire past of Majipoor had always bothered Lutiel. He was just a Skandar, after all, Lutiel had often said: a latecomer to the planet, like the Hjorts and Ghayrogs and all the other non-human races. Lutiel believed that the history of Majipoor was the history of the human settlement of the planet. Simmilgord had often tried to dispute that point. Majipoor had been here for millions of years before the arrival of the first intruders from space, and probably would survive their extinction as well. "We are all latecomers here, if you look at things from the point of view of the Metamorphs," he would say. "So what if the humans got here before the Skandars and the Hjorts? We all came from somewhere else. And all of us working together have made the place we call Majipoor what it is." But there was no appeasing Lutiel on that issue, and Simmilgord, after a time, ceased to debate it with him.

The real area of concern was that to have the Superintendent of Antiquities come storming noisily into town put everything in doubt. What would happen next, Simmilgord wondered, to their project here? The best-case scenario was that Hawid Zakayil would simply prowl around here for a few days, make a few comments and suggestions, give the work his seal of approval, and go zooming off to his next place of inspection, leaving them in peace to continue the work already begun.

But that was too optimistic an outcome. Very quickly it became apparent that something much worse was going to unfold.

Two days after the meeting with Hawid Zakayil, Simmilgord was at work in the municipal archives when Lutiel came bursting in unexpectedly, looking wild-eyed and flushed. "The most amazing—you have to see—you can't imagine—oh, come, Simmilgord, come with me, come! To the tomb! Hurry!"

Simmilgord had never seen his calm, sober-minded friend looking so flustered. There was no choice but to go with him at once, and off they went, pell-mell across town to the excavation site. With Lutiel in the lead, moving so quickly that Simmilgord could barely keep up with him, they scurried down the staircase, through the passage to the tomb-chamber, beyond it into the newly excavated tunnels, and then made a sudden left turn into a part of the dig that Simmilgord had never seen before. Lutiel flashed his torch about frenziedly from one wall to the other.

"We broke through into this about an hour ago. Look at it! *Look* at it!"

Both sides of the new tunnel were covered with murals—most of them faded with age, in some places barely visible, mere ghosts of what once had been painted there, but in other sections still relatively fresh and bright, the colors still apparent. At the far end, where the passage widened into a kind of apse, Simmilgord could see the giant image of a seated man in what must have been robes of great magnificence, occupying the entire wall from floor to ceiling, one hand raised in a gesture of benediction, the other resting on his knee, lying there casually but, even so, in a regal manner. Though the whole upper part of the figure's face was gone, its smile remained, a smile of such warmth and godlike benevolence that this could only be meant as a representation of a great monarch, and what other monarch could it be than Dvorn?

To either side of that great throned figure were other paintings, a long series of them, badly damaged in their upper sections and the colors everywhere weakened by the inroads of time. But Simmilgord, staring in awe from one to the next, found it all too easy to suggest meanings for the scenes he saw: this must be the gathering at Kesmakuran where Dvorn had called upon the people of Alhanroel to unite behind his banner, and this his coronation as Pontifex at Stangard Falls on the river Glayge, at the foot of Castle Mount, and this one, where a lesser but still imposing figure was depicted beside him, surely showed Dvorn raising his colleague Barhold to the newly devised rank of Coronal Lord. And so on and on for twenty yards or more, though the paintings closest to the point where Lutiel had entered the gallery were reduced to the merest spectral outlines. Simmilgord, moving carefully from one to the next, beheld images of vertically mounted wheels, like the waterwheels that might power a mill, and long processions of blurred and almost undiscernible figures, perhaps celebrants in some forgotten holy rite, and a series of wreath-like decorations inscribed with lettering in the same antique script as on the tablets that Prasilet Sungavon had found.

"The oldest paintings in the world," Lutiel said softly. "Scenes from the life of the Pontifex Dvorn."

"Yes." It was just a husky whisper: Simmilgord was barely able to get the syllable out. "Yes. Yes. Yes!" To his astonishment he found himself fighting back tears. "A marvelous discovery, Lutiel." And indeed it was. Even in that moment of jubilation, though, he felt a sudden sense of dread. This find was *too* marvelous. They were never going to get rid of Hawid Zakayil, now.

He could not bring himself to voice the fears that came rushing in upon him. But Lutiel did.

"And now to show it to the Skandar," he said. "Who will steal it from us."

⁂

"We will seal this chamber at once," Hawid Zakayil announced briskly, when he had completed his inspection of the new gallery two hours later. "This is the most amazing discovery in my entire career, and we must take no risks with it, none whatsoever. Exposure to the outside atmosphere could very well destroy these paintings in a matter of days. Therefore no one is to enter without permission from me, and I mean *no one*, until we complete our plan for preservation of the murals."

It was not hard for Simmilgord to imagine the things that were going through Lutiel Vengifrons' mind, but he could not bear to look at his friend's face just now. The swiftness with which the Superintendent of Antiquities had taken possession of the find was breathtaking. The most amazing discovery in *his* entire career, yes! And no one to enter the site, not even Lutiel, without permission from *him*. It was his site, now. His discovery. His *amazing* discovery.

Quite predictably the Superintendent of Antiquities made it clear that he intended to stay right here in Kesmakuran and take personal charge of the work. And over the next few days, without actually saying so explicitly, he let it be known to Mayor Kyvole Gannivad, to the Hjort Prasilet Sungavon, and, lastly, to Simmilgord and Lutiel themselves, that this site was too important to be left in the hands of amateurs or novices. And— quite explicitly, this time—he revealed that he had some truly marvelous ideas for capitalizing on the tomb's tremendous historical significance.

"This is humiliating, Simmilgord," Lutiel said, when at last they were alone that evening. "I'm going to resign, and so should you."

"What?"

"Can't you see? He's putting the whole thing in his pocket and reducing us to flunkeys. I'll have to beg to be allowed to go into the tomb. He'll bring his own people in to do the preservation work, and they'll want to continue the dig without me. Whatever you find in the archives will have to be turned over to him, and he'll claim credit for having found it. We'll be lucky even to have our names on the paper when he publishes the find."

Simmilgord shook his head. "You're taking this much too seriously. He's behaving exactly as he always behaves when somebody finds an exciting new site, yes, but in a few weeks he'll lose interest and move on. Something big will turn up on the far side of Castle Mount or maybe even down in Suvrael and off he'll go to muscle in on it. Or there'll be a new museum to dedicate at the back end of Zimroel and he'll head over there for six or seven months. He'll keep his finger in our work here, sure. But he can't be everywhere at once, and sooner or later you'll be back in charge of the dig."

"This is very naive of you."

"I don't think so."

"Then you're actually going to remain here, Simmilgord?"

"Yes. Absolutely. And so should you."

"And be pushed aside—cheated, abused—"

"I tell you it won't be like that. Please, Lutiel. Please."

It took some work, but finally, glumly, Lutiel agreed to stay on for a while. The clinching argument was that for him to resign in high dudgeon now would destroy his career: Hawid Zakayil would understand instantly why he was leaving, no matter what pretext he gave, and would take mortal offense, and no young archaeologist who offended the Superintendent of Antiquities was ever going to do archaeological work on Majipoor again. He might just as well start taking a course in accounting or bookkeeping.

So Lutiel remained in Kesmakuran; and Hawid Zakayil went through the pretense, at least, of sharing responsibility for the project with the two of them. He informed Simmilgord that he was arranging financing so that every document found so far could be copied for the benefit of the archives at the Castle and the Labyrinth, a task that would keep Simmilgord busy for a good many weeks to come. And even though the site remained closed, with no further excavation until further notice, Lutiel himself would be admitted for several hours a day to sort through his discoveries in the outer tunnels and to supervise the work of the technicians who would be dealing with the task of preserving the murals against further decay.

Simmilgord wondered just what the Skandar would be doing during this time. Hawid Zakayil seemed to have allocated no specific aspect of the enterprise to himself, but he was too big and rambunctious and restless a presence to be content for long to sit about quietly in a sleepy place like Kesmakuran while such lesser men as Simmilgord and Lutiel went about their work.

The answer came soon enough. One morning Simmilgord and Lutiel received word that they were summoned to a meeting, and a couple of municipal officials escorted them to a place southeast of town, halfway around the base of the mountains from the site of the tomb. Over here the pinkish-gold stone of the main mountain range was sundered by a huge and formidable mass of black basalt, virtually a mountain unto itself, that must have been thrust up into it by some volcanic eruption long ago. Hawid Zakayil was waiting there for them with Mayor Kyvole Gannivad and Prasilet Sungavon when they arrived.

The Skandar pointed at once to the face of the basalt mass.

"Here is where we will put the monument. What do you think, gentlemen? Is this not a properly dramatic site for it?"

"The monument?" Simmilgord said blankly, feeling as though he had come in very late on something that he really should have known about before this.

"The monument to Dvorn!" the mayor cried. "What else do you think we're talking about? Haven't you seen the sketches?"

"Well, to be completely truthful—"

"We'll dig the entrance to the cavern here—" Kyvole Gannivad swept his stubby arms about with a vigorous sweep to indicate a zone perhaps thirty feet high and forty feet wide—"and there'll be a vestibule that will continue onward and downward for—oh, what did we say, Hawid Zakayil, a hundred feet? Two hundred?"

"Something like that," the Skandar said indifferently.

Simmilgord did not understand. A monument? What monument? He had seen no sketches. This was the first he had heard of any of this. "You mean, a kind of historical site, to bring visitors to town? Aside from the tomb itself, I mean."

"The tomb itself is too fragile to be a proper place of pilgrimage," Prasilet Sungavon said. The Hjort spoke the way he might if he were explaining something to a six-year-old. "That's why the Superintendent closed it so quickly, once the murals were discovered. But we need to build something here as a focus of attention on the greatness of the Pontifex Dvorn and on Kesmakuran's importance in his career. As you say, a kind of historical site that will bring visitors here."

"Exhibits commemorating the life and achievements of Dvorn," said Hawid Zakayil. "Plaques that tell his story—no mythmaking, everything placed in accurate historical context." The Skandar favored Simmilgord with a gaze of such force that he feared he might be burned to a crisp in its glare. "You will be in charge of this part of it, Simmilgord. We will count on you to provide us with all the data, essentially a biography of the Pontifex that can be recreated in graphic form, and to design the exhibits: all the wonder and magic that was the life of Dvorn, set out here in its full glory. I am well aware that this is your special field of expertise. You are precisely the person for the task."

Simmilgord nodded. What could he say? He was overwhelmed by the power of the Skandar's formidable nature. And what Hawid Zakayil was proposing was so astonishing that in a moment everything was transformed for him. Dvorn had been Simmilgord's special obsession since his undergraduate days. There was no way he could refuse this assignment. Already he saw the monument taking shape in his imagination, to expand, to flower and grow—the murals, the statuary, the displays of documents and artifacts—the Museum of Dvorn! The *shrine* of Dvorn! *You will be in charge, Simmilgord.* Hawid Zakayil was handing him the project of his dreams. Once more he heard that magical soaring music that he had heard atop those little hills in the Vale of Gloyn and again in the archives of Kesmakuran, the grand swelling sounds of the symphony of Majipoor. To build a commemorative shrine in honor of the first Pontifex—not just a shrine, though, nor even just a museum, but a research center, a place of study, over which he himself would preside—

"Of course, sir," he said hoarsely. "What a superb idea!"

He might as well have been talking to himself. Simmilgord realized that the Skandar had already moved on, turning his attention to Lutiel: "And we will want a replica of the tomb chamber, everything in one-to-one correlation, though somewhat restored, of course, for the benefit of the laymen who will want to see it as it was in Dvorn's time. Those wonderful murals, reproduced exactly, with the colors enhanced and the missing portions carefully reconstructed—who better to supervise the work than you, Lutiel? Who, indeed?"

Hawid Zakayil paused, plainly waiting for Lutiel to reply. But no reply was forthcoming, and after a long moment of silence the Skandar simply looked away, his frenetic spirit already moving along to the next consideration, the hotel facilities that the town would need to provide here, and some highway expansion, and similar matters of municipal concern.

⇥❋⇤

The glory and wonder of it all remained with Simmilgord after they had returned to their lodgings. Already he could see the long lines of visitors shuffling reverently past the great replica of the mural of the smiling Dvorn enthroned, pausing to study the historical plaques on the walls, the murmured discussions amongst them of the visionary brilliance of the first Pontifex, even the multitudes of eager readers for the book on Dvorn that he intended to write.

Then he noticed the furious, glowering expression on Lutiel's face.

Lutiel was fuming. He was pacing angrily about. And finally his anger broke into words.

"How absolutely awful! A phony ruin—replicas of the murals, very nicely prettied up for the tourists—!"

It was like being hit with a bucket of cold water.

With some difficulty Simmilgord brought himself down from the lofty fantasies that had engaged his mind. "What's so terrible about that, Lutiel? You can't expect to let them have access to the originals!"

Lutiel turned on him. "Why do they have to see them at all? What do we need this silly cave for? This shiny fraudulent showplace, this phony historical site? And why should *we* be involved? I told you right at the start, before we even came here, I wasn't going to hire on as a paid publicist for the town of Kesmakuran."

"But—"

"You know yourself that most people have no serious interest in what that Skandar wants to put in his museum. They might come and look for five minutes, and move onward, and buy a souvenir or two, maybe a little statuette of Dvorn to put on the mantel, and then start wondering about where to have lunch—"

Simmilgord began to feel his own anger rising. It was true, no denying it, that from the very beginning, from the time the head of the department back at the University had broached the Kesmakuran journey, Lutiel had opposed their getting involved. A "career detour," he had called it then, something irrelevant to the work of two serious young scholars. Yes, Simmilgord had argued him out of that, and had managed to overcome Lutiel's later doubts about the legitimacy of the project on a dozen occasions, and eventually Lutiel had made the discovery of a lifetime, that gallery of murals that any archaeologist would give his right arm to have found, or maybe *both* arms, and even so he went on grumbling and fretting about the issues of integrity that seemed to trouble him so much. Evidently he had never reconciled himself to the project in the first place. And never would.

As calmly as he could Simmilgord said, "You're being absurd, Lutiel. Are you telling me that we do all our work purely for ourselves, that we're like priests of some arcane cult who go through rites and rituals that have no relevance whatever to the real world and the lives of real people in it?"

Lutiel laughed harshly. "And you, Simmilgord? What are you telling *me*? Not a shred of integrity in you, is that it? Ready to sell yourself to the first bidder who comes along?"

Simmilgord gasped. Perhaps, he thought, Lutiel *was* some sort of monk at heart, too pure for this world. But this was going too far.

"When did I ever say—"

"I saw the way you lit up when the Skandar told you you were just the man for the job of putting together the historical side of the new monument."

"Of course I did. Why shouldn't I? It's a tremendous opportunity to put the story of Dvorn across to thousands, even millions, of people. And you—when he told you essentially the same thing as he put you in charge of supervising the reconstruction of the murals, the creation of replicas that look better than the originals—what did you feel?"

"What I felt was disgust," Lutiel said. "Indignation. I kept my mouth shut, because I couldn't bring myself to stand up to Hawid Zakayil to his face, any more than anyone else can. I told you I'm no publicist, Simmilgord, and certainly I'm not a showman either. Or some sort of theatrical impresario. What I am is a scientist. And so are you, whether you want to believe it or not. You're an historian. History is a science, or should be, anyway. And scientists have no business getting involved in anything as sordid as this."

Sordid?

Simmilgord's head was beginning to ache. He wanted to slide away from this discussion somehow. He was ashamed to face Lutiel.

That stinging charge of hypocrisy—of whoring, even—hurt him deeply. Lutiel was his closest friend. For Lutiel to see him as a hypocrite and a whore was painful. But there was a certain truth in it. A flamboyant character like Hawid Zakayil, who was both a scientist and a manufacturer of public entertainments, and probably somewhat more of the one than of the other, would dismiss such an accusation without a thought. Simmilgord, though, was shaken by it. One part of him thought Lutiel might just be right, that they had no business getting involved in something as far from genuine scholarship as this "monument" promised to be. But another part—the part that remembered the boy who had climbed those mountains and tried to cast his gaze from sea to sea—was wholly caught up in its spell.

They managed after a while to disengage themselves from the quarrel yet again. Simmilgord slept badly that night, profoundly disturbed by all that had been said. In the morning he went early to the archives, with Lutiel still asleep, and spent the day digging feverishly through a section of old municipal documents he had never examined before. There proved to be nothing of the slightest interest in them, but the work itself was soothing, the mechanical selecting of documents and setting them up in the reader and scanning. Dull work, even pointless work, but it was comforting to be focusing his full attention on it.

The ugly words kept coming back nonetheless. *Hypocrite. Whore.*

But on the way back from the archives building to his house Simmilgord's thoughts turned back to yesterday's meeting with Hawid Zakayil, toward the monument that he proposed to build in that cavern in the mountain of black basalt. Almost against his will, ideas for its design kept bursting into his mind, until he was dizzy and trembling with excitement. It all came together in the most wondrous way. He could see the layout of the vestibule, the arrangement of the inner rooms, the route that led to the replica of the tomb-chamber, which would be the climax of the experience for the visitor—

The Tomb of the Pontifex Dvorn | Robert Silverberg

He had to smile. Maybe Lutiel was right: maybe he had failed to understand his true vocation all along, that he was not really a scholar at all, that he had actually been destined, even as a small boy atop those rocky hillocks, to be a kind of showman, someone who converts history into the stuff of romance. Perhaps, he told himself, it was quite permissible for him to rise up out of the dusty archives of the world and devote his life to bringing the story of the founding of the Pontificate to a world yearning to know more about it. And he had a bleak vision of Lutiel's future, seeing him endlessly digging and sifting through sandy wastelands, getting nowhere, the great achievement of his life already behind him and the primary credit for it taken from him by someone else. Simmilgord did not want any such fate as that for himself, a lifetime of puttering with ancient documents in cloistered halls and writing papers that no one but his few colleagues would ever read. He could see a new role, a better role, for himself: the man who rediscovered Dvorn, who turned his name into a household word.

When he reached the house he shared with Lutiel he found a note pinned to his pillow:

> *Have handed in my resignation. Setting out for Sisivondal this afternoon. When he publishes my excavation, make sure that my name is on the paper somewhere.*
> *Best of luck, old friend. You'll need it.*
> *L.*

Hawid Zakayil said, "And are you going to resign also?" The Superintendent of Antiquities spoke in what was for him a surprisingly mild, non-confrontational tone. He sounded merely curious, not in any way angry or menacing.

"No," Simmilgord replied at once, before anything to the contrary could escape his lips. "Of course not. This is strictly Lutiel's decision. I don't happen to share his philosophical outlook."

"His philosophical outlook on *what?*" asked the Skandar, in not quite so mild a way.

Evasively Simmilgord said, "Ends. Means. Ultimate purposes. Lutiel takes everything very seriously, you know. Sometimes *too* seriously." And then he went on, quickly, to keep Hawid Zakayil from continuing this line of inquiry, "Sir, I've had some interesting thoughts since yesterday about how we might handle certain features of the monument. If I might share them with you—"

"Go ahead," said the Skandar gruffly.

"Those wheel-like structures shown in the murals, with a line of what look like celebrants approaching them: they must surely have had some sort of ritual purpose in the days when Dvorn's tomb was an active center of worship. Perhaps we could recreate that ritual in the monument—every hour, let's say, stage a kind of reenactment of what we think it might have been like—"

"Good! Very good!"

"Or even hire people to keep the wheels in constant motion—revolving steadily, powered by some sort of primitive arrangement of pedals—to symbolize the eternal cycle of history, the ongoing continuity of the world through all its millions of years—"

Hawid Zakayil smiled a shrewd Skandar smile.

"I like it, Simmilgord. I like it very much."

※

And so it came to pass that Simmilgord of Gloyn became the first administrator of the Tomb of Dvorn, as the monument in the black basalt mountain came to be called after a while, and looked after it in the blossoming of its first growth until it became known as the most sacred site of western Alhanroel, where every Coronal would make a point of stopping to pay homage when he made one of his long processional journeys across the world.

The Toys of Caliban
(script)

by George R. R. Martin

THE TWILIGHT ZONE

FADE IN

INT.—LIVING ROOM—NIGHT—CLOSE ON TOBEY

TOBEY ROSS, a special needs sixteen-year-old boy, sits on the worn carpet, playing with a doll. He's a big boy; pale, overweight, his clothing old but clean. His shirt is misbuttoned. His eyes are rapt as he walks the doll along the floor with large, uncoordinated movements. When he lets go of the doll, and it falls over, Tobey looks briefly annoyed. He stands it up, and it falls over again.

ANGLE PAST TOBEY ON ERNEST

ERNEST ROSS, Tobey's father, a man of about sixty, sits in an old wing-back chair reading a newspaper. Tall, gaunt, gray-haired, with a careworn face and a weary strength, Ernest glances at Tobey frequently as he reads.

MARY (O. S.)
Ernest? It's so quiet. Is he all right?

CLOSE ON ERNEST

He turns the newspaper and answers, almost by rote.

> ERNEST
> (wearily)
> He's fine, dear. He's just playing.

> TOBEY
> (overlapping, O.S.)
> Bring.

Ernest quickly glances back at Tobey, then relaxes again and goes back to his paper.

> MARY (O.S.)
> You know I worry, Ernest. The boy doesn't understand.

> ERNEST
> (patient, reading)
> I know, dear.

We HEAR the clatter of plates and silverware from the kitchen, the sound of the dinner table being set.

BACK TO TOBEY

Who holds a Robbie the Robot toy that was NOT in evidence in the previous shot. The doll lies beside him, on top of a thick catalog from a toy store opened to a picture of the robot in Tobey's hands. The boy presses a button on the robot's chest, starting a short taped speech. As Tobey claps his hands in delight, we PULL BACK to show the living room.

The light is dim; all the windows are covered by heavy drapes, and the room has a dark, creepy, claustrophobic feel. The furniture is comfortable but old, on the edge of shabby. A big television console stands against one wall, but inside there's an ornate dollhouse instead of a TV. Above, unfaded wallpaper shows where a painting once hung, but there's no painting there now. Against a second wall stands a large cabinet-style bookcase, glass fronted, its doors closed and chained, the chains secured with a heavy padlock. The books within are covered. And Tobey's toys are everywhere. Tobey is surrounded by balls, robots, dolls. In one overstuffed chair sits a teddy bear the size of Merlin Olsen. Other stuff is scattered through the room: a cowboy hat, a hula hoop, a truck, battalions of toy soldiers.

Tobey pushes the robot's button too hard, breaking the toy. He looks upset, then quickly pushes it away. He grabs his toy book, clumsily turns pages.

INSERT—THE TOY CATALOG

On a page covered with stuffed animals, the biggest feature is a bright pink stuffed unicorn with a long horn. Tobey GIGGLES.

CUT TO
INT.—KITCHEN

MARY ROSS, bustling about nervously, sets a platter of fried chicken and a bowl of mashed potatoes on an old Formica table. She's in her mid-fifties, frail-looking, thin and fussy. We HEAR Tobey call out from the living room.

>   TOBEY (O.S.)
> Bring!

Mary flinches when she hears the word, starts to call out to Ernest, then purses her lips firmly and finishes, setting the table. We FOLLOW her into the living room.

MARY
Dinner is ready.
(to Tobey)
Are you hungry, Tobey?

Tobey looks up eagerly. In his hands is the stuffed unicorn from the toy catalog; he's holding it by the horn. He jumps up at Mary's call.

TOBEY
Donuts! Donuts, mama!

Ernest folds up his paper, rises, takes Tobey by the hand.

ERNEST
You had donuts yesterday, Tobey. Come on, son. You like chicken.

CUT TO

THE KITCHEN

as the Rosses sit to dinner. Mary fusses with her food as Ernest fills Tobey's plate and corrects the way he holds his fork. Tobey pushes the mashed potatoes around his plate clumsily, obvious disenchanted. He looks at his father hopefully.

TOBEY
Donuts?

ERNEST
Eat the dinner mama cooked.

MARY
Maybe for dessert, Tobey.

> ERNEST

If you eat your dinner.

Tobey attacks the chicken with enthusiasm now. His parents exchange a weary glance.

> MARY
> There's no harm in it, Ernest.
> (to Tobey)
> Chew your food, Tobey.

Ernest eats silently, methodically. We MOVE IN on Tobey's plate as he eagerly attacks his dinner, anxious to get on to the promised dessert.

DISSOLVE TO

KITCHEN—A SHORT TIME LATER

Tobey has cleaned his plate. He looks up eagerly.

> TOBEY

Donuts?

> ERNEST
> (sighs)
> All right, Tobey. Let me get the picture.

Ernest rises, UNLOCKS a kitchen drawer.

CLOSE ON THE DRAWER

as Ernest rummages through a stack of brightly illustrated, plasticized menus from restaurants and coffee houses, and extracts one with a Deelight Donuts logo.

BACK TO THE SCENE

Ernest turns, the menu in hand, but Tobey is grinning widely. He sticks out two large empty hands.

> TOBEY
>
> Bring!

Two large chocolate-covered donuts suddenly APPEAR in Tobey's hands, blinking into existence from nowhere. Tobey begins to stuff himself, alternating bites between the right-hand donut and the left-hand donut. Ernest looks nonplussed.

> ERNEST
>
> He didn't look at the picture.
> (to Mary)
> Mary, he did it without looking at the picture. He's never—

Mary interrupts him as she pours Tobey a glass of milk.

> MARY
>
> Yes, he has. Oh, it's only donuts, Ernest. You know he loves them so.

Ernest puts the menu back in the drawer, locks it, and stares at his son with a concerned, unhappy look on his face.

CLOSE ON TOBEY

as he eats happily.

MATCH CUT TO

CLOSE ON TOBEY—HOURS LATER

His face is greenish, his brow sweaty. He's in pain.

TOBEY

Hurts, mama. Hurts!

INT.—TOBEY'S ROOM—NIGHT

We PULL BACK to see a pajama-clad Tobey rolling about in bed, clutching his stomach. Mary is shaking down a thermometer. Ernest stands at
the foot of the bed. The bedroom is even more cluttered with toys, junk,
and bric-a-brac than the Ross living room. Some of the toys are strange
indeed: a full-sized traffic light, bowling pins, a huge anchor draped by old
clothes (might be fun to sprinkle the set with props from past TZ episodes,
to give the room a suitably weird, disturbing look).

MARY

It's all right, Tobey. Let mama take your temperature.

She puts the thermometer in his mouth, but Tobey spits it out.

TOBEY
(louder)

Hurts, mama! Hurts!

Mary tries to hold him still, feels his stomach.

ERNEST

I was afraid of this. Those donuts—

MARY

Two. He only had two.

ERNEST

If he doesn't need to see the picture any more, he could
have had another dozen after we put him to bed. Or

anything else, for that matter. You know as well as I do that he'll eat anything he can fit in his mouth.

> MARY

His tummy is burning up.
>> (beat)

Call that nice Doctor Keller, he'll come, I know he will.

> ERNEST
>> (patiently)

He doesn't make house calls any more. No one makes house calls any more.

Tobey MOANS and rolls away, crying.

> MARY
>> (hysterical)

He has to! Tell him it's an emergency.

> ERNEST

And he'll tell me that's what emergency rooms are for. We've been through this before.

> MARY

Tell him, just tell him—

> ERNEST

Tell him what?

Tobey suddenly SCREAMS and doubles over in pain. Ernest, stricken, turns away and exits. We FOLLOW him as he walks to the living room, lifts up a telephone, begins to dial.

> MARY

Ernest, what are you doing?

> ERNEST

Calling an ambulance.

> MARY
> (overlapping, very scared)

But we can't!

O.S. we HEAR Tobey scream again.

> ERNEST
> (grimly, to Mary)

We have no choice.
> (into phone)

Hello, I need an ambulance. This is Ernest Ross at—

CUT TO

EXT.—HOSPITAL—NIGHT

An ambulance screeches up to the emergency room door and Tobey is bundled out. Ernest and Mary follow him inside.

INT.—WAITING ROOM—LATER

Ernest and Mary rise anxiously as a resident comes through a set of swinging doors.

> MARY

Is he all right? Is Tobey all right? What's wrong with him?

> RESIDENT

It's food poisoning. We've pumped his stomach. I'm sure he'll be fine, but I'd like to keep him overnight for observation.

ERNEST

Overnight? Is that necessary? The boy—he's uncomfortable away from home.

RESIDENT

Don't worry, we'll take good care of him. The children's ward has a color television, lots of comic books, a—

ERNEST

(sharply, interrupting)

No. If you say he must stay, he will stay, but he must have a private room, and my wife and I will stay with him. No television, no comic books.

RESIDENT

(startled, uncertain)

Well, certainly, we can arrange a private room if you prefer, but I'm sure the boy would—

MARY

Tobey—he's not like other children. He's special, he has—

ERNEST

(firmly)

Mary, I'm sure the doctor has more important things to think about.

RESIDENT

On the contrary. I'm very interested in Tobey and his well-being.

(beat, harder)

Frankly, the contents of Tobey's stomach—we have a nutritionist here who'd be glad to talk to you.

ERNEST

We don't need advice on how to feed our son, doctor.

The resident obviously thinks there's something strange about these two.

RESIDENT

Very well. I'll make the arrangements about the room.

As the resident walks off, Mary looks to Ernest, worried.

MARY

Ernest—a private room, it costs so much money.

ERNEST

It's only for one night. It has to be. If Tobey were put in with other children, there's no telling what they might show him.

Frightened, Mary nods grimly.

CUT TO

INT.—HOSPITAL ROOM—NIGHT

The room is dark, all the lights out. Tobey is asleep in the hospital bed, his expression peaceful and innocent. In b.g. Mary is curled up, sleeping, in a nearby chair, a hospital blanket thrown across her legs. Ernest sits by his son, wary, watching. He looks down at Tobey's face, gently strokes his son's forehead. We can see his love for the boy.

DISSOLVE TO

INT.—HOSPITAL ROOM—THE NEXT MORNING

Tobey is sitting up in bed, his breakfast tray empty, as Mary wipes his mouth with her handkerchief. The door opens to admit MANDY KEMP, a brisk, attractive young social worker. She carries a briefcase and wears a cheery professional smile.

                    MANDY KEMP
Good morning. This must be Tobey.

                    TOBEY
                    (beaming)
Tobey!

                    MANDY KEMP
I'm Miss Kemp, Tobey.

                    ERNEST
Miss Kemp, Tobey seems fine this morning. We'd like to take him home.

                    MANDY KEMP
I'm sure the doctor will be discharging him shortly. In the meantime, I'd like to have a little chat with you.

Mandy sets her briefcase on the foot of the bed and removes some papers. Ernest and Mary exchange a worried look.

                    MARY
A—chat? I don't—

                    ERNEST
I think we'd just prefer to take our son home as soon as possible.

Mandy turns toward Ernest, her manner cheerful, enthusiastic.

                    MANDY KEMP

Yes, I understand, but I do have a few questions. I'm with Children and Family Services, Mr. Ross.

                    (looks through papers)

Now, about your son's schooling, we have no record of any—

                    ERNEST

                    (sharply, interrupting)

Tobey is special needs.

                    MARY

                    (earnestly, pleading)

He doesn't understand. School wouldn't—he's a very special boy, very—excitable—

                    MANDY KEMP

Well, of course I wasn't talking about an ordinary curriculum. Even the most severely disabled children are educable, you know, and there are special classes for boys and girls like Tobey.

Tobey, obviously bored by the conversation the adults are having, seems more and more restless.

ANGLE ON TOBEY

as his eyes wander around the room, light on Mandy's open briefcase

                    ERNEST

I appreciate your concern, but we prefer to care for Tobey ourselves.

                    MARY

He's very suggestible. He's a sweet boy, but he doesn't understand.

TOBEY'S POV

of the briefcase. Under the papers, case files, and reports he glimpses something interesting—the corner of a glossy, brightly colored magazine.

ANGLE ON TOBEY

as he reaches toward the briefcase. The adults, intent on their discussion, don't notice him at first.

> MANDY KEMP
> We've made great strides in working with children like Tobey—special children. We can teach him—

> ERNEST
> (sharply)
> What, Miss Kemp? What can you teach our son? Can you teach him to read and write? Can you teach him to take care of himself?

CLOSE ON BRIEFCASE

as Tobey snags the corner of the magazine, a glossy news weekly of the TIME/NEWSWEEK variety, called TRUMPET. He pulls it out.

BACK TO THE SCENE

Tobey begins to leaf through the magazine while his father argues with the social worker, and Mary looks from one to the other.

> ERNEST
> (continued)
> And what about right and wrong, Miss Kemp? Can you teach Tobey the difference between right and wrong?

MARY

Ernest, she means well.

ERNEST

Yes. I suppose you're right.
(less sharply)
Miss Kemp, we love our son. He's an only child, and he
came when both of us thought we were well past our
child-bearing years. All we want is what's best for the boy—

MANDY KEMP

That's all any of us want.

ERNEST

There are things about Tobey you don't understand.

Ernest glances over at Tobey as he speaks, sees the magazine. Mary looks
too, gives a small stifled GASP.

ERNEST

(loud, stern)
Tobey! NO! No. Tobey.

Tobey looks up guiltily. Ernest snatches the magazine away from him, gives
it to Mandy. Tobey reaches for it again.

TOBEY

Pictures! Pictures, give!

ERNEST

No pictures. No, Tobey.

MANDY KEMP

It's all right. I've read it, Tobey can have it if he likes the
pictures.

(to Tobey)
Here, would you like this, Tobey?

As she holds out the magazine to Tobey, Ernest SLAPS IT AWAY. The magazine flies from her grasp. Mandy is startled. Tobey begins to bawl loudly.

TOBEY
(crying)
Pictures! Pictures, mama! Mama!

Mary wraps her arm around him, dries his tears with her handkerchief, begins to comfort him.

MARY
There, Tobey, it's all right. Don't cry, mama's here. We'll take you home and you can look at your toy book. Don't cry, mama loves you.
(weakly, to Mandy)
We—we don't allow him to look at such things.

MANDY KEMP
It was only a magazine. There's nothing wrong with it.

ERNEST
We'll be the judge of what's right and wrong for our son. Mary, get the boy dressed. We're leaving.

Mary helps Tobey out of bed and gets his clothes.

MANDY KEMP
But—you can't just walk out.

The Toys of Caliban | George R. R. Martin

> ERNEST

Can't we?

CUT TO

INT.—HOSPITAL CORRIDOR ANGLE PAST MANDY

as Tobey skips down the hall between his parents. They hold his hands firmly, and tug him along when he stops to stare at a janitor operating a floor-polisher. As the Rosses wait for the elevator, the young resident comes up to Mandy Kemp.

> RESIDENT

Well?

> MANDY KEMP

You were right. There are some people who have no business being parents.

The elevator CHIMES as the doors open and passengers spill out.

> RESIDENT

I feel sorry for the kid. Is there anything we can do?

> MANDY KEMP
> (nodding)

I'll have to look into the home situation. These aren't the dark ages. I expect I'll be seeing a lot of the Ross family.

Mary and Tobey enter the elevator. Ernest moves to follow, then pauses, and gives Mandy a long, troubled look.

CUT TO

INT.—ROSS LIVING ROOM

Mary enters, leading Tobey by the hand. Behind them, Ernest shuts and locks the door.

> MARY
> (relieved)
> See Tobey, we're home. Everything will be fine now that we're home. Go play now. Be a good boy and go play.

> TOBEY
> Play.

As Tobey runs off to his room, Mary turns to Ernest. She looks scared; he's grim and exhausted.

> MARY
> (frightened)
> What are we going to do, Ernest? He saw it, I know he did. He was staring at it all the way down the block. What if he brings it?

> ERNEST
> He's home now. He has his toy book. He'll forget.
> (beat)
> Mary, it was only a squirrel. It will be dead if he brings it. I'll bury it with the others. I'll get rid of it. I always do, don't I? The barber pole, the slot machine, and all the rest. Remember your heart, dear. Don't concern yourself.

> MARY
> You know I worry. Ernest, that woman—Miss Kemp—what if she—

> ERNEST
> She won't bother us. I'll take care of it, Mary. Please.

Wearily, he massages his temples, closes his eyes.

> MARY
>
> He's not a bad boy, Ernest. He just doesn't understand.
> (beat)
> Ernest, I'm so frightened. What will happen to him when—when we're not here? We can't let them hurt him. Maybe—maybe that woman is right, maybe—some kind of class, maybe some special kind of teacher—

CLOSE ON ERNEST

His eyes snap open. He looks concerned, alarmed.

> ERNEST
>
> Mary—

BACK TO THE SCENE

> MARY
>
> Just a little help, that's all, just for a day or two—or maybe a few hours—That isn't so wrong of me, is it? To want just a few hours? We could go to dinner together, in some nice restaurant, like we used to do before—before—
> (begins to weep softly)
> —maybe we could see a movie—just the two of us—a movie—how long has it been since we've seen a movie—

Ernest rises, gives her a reassuring hug.

> ERNEST
> (softly)
> I know you're tired. It would be nice to have someone to share the burden.

He holds her by the shoulders, looks into her eyes.

> ERNEST
> (continues, resolute)
> But we can't, Mary. He's ours, our son, our responsibility.
> If we leave him alone, even for a few hours, there's no tell-
> ing what sorts of things he might see.
> (beat)
> Or what he might bring.

CUT TO

INT.—TOBEY'S ROOM

We HEAR the muffled sounds of conversation from the next room, but the door is closed, the words indistinct. Tobey sits among his toys. He picks up first one, then another, plays with them in a desultory man- ner, discards them. He leafs through the pages of his toy catalog, but nothing catches his interest. He's bored, unhappy. He throws the catalog away, looks around—and then breaks into a happy grin as he remembers something.

CLOSE ON TOBEY

as he closes his eyes, squints, concentrates. Remembering. Visualizing. His big hands ball into fists on his knees.

> TOBEY
> Bring.

In his lap, the glossy newsmagazine from the hospital suddenly APPEARS. Tobey giggles, and eagerly begins to turn pages. As he pauses at each new, strange photograph, he makes small noises of surprise and interest.

TIME CUT TO

THE LIVING ROOM—LATER

Mary lies on the couch, her eyes closed, and Ernest comes through the kitchen door, bearing a tray with teapot, cups, cookies. He sets the tray on the coffee table, bends over, gently shakes his wife's shoulder.

> ERNEST
> Mary. Wake up, dear. I made you some tea.

She sits up, gives him a wan smile.

> MARY
> Oh, Ernest, how nice. You didn't need to do that.

He smiles, sits, pours. Mary looks around.

> MARY
> Where's Tobey?

> ERNEST
> He's still in his room. Sleeping, or playing. He's fine, dear. Just have some tea and try not to worry.

> MARY
> You know I can't help it, dear.
> (stands)
> I'll just take a peek, make sure he's all right. Then I'll be right back.

Ernest sighs, sips his tea, nods.

ANGLE ON MARY

as she walks down the hall, opens the door to Tobey's room

> MARY
> (softly)
>
> Tobey?

Engrossed in some game, Tobey doesn't answer, but we HEAR a soft giggle, and another sound—a wet, soft SQUISHING. Mary frowns, enters the room. Again we HEAR it: the giggle, the squishing. Tobey is on the far side of the room, down on the floor between the bed and the wall, his back to the door. Mary can only see the back of his head. She begins to walk around the bed. We see that Tobey has something in his hands, some new toy. He's squeezing it rhythmically, making it squish, and when it squishes he giggles.

> MARY
>
> Tobey, what do you—

When she steps on the open pages of the news magazines, it CRINKLES underfoot and Mary frowns, bends, picks up the magazine. Then her mouth opens in horror.

> MARY
>
> No—no—

CLOSE ON TOBEY

as he looks over his shoulder at his mother. His eyes glitter, his smile is wide, innocent, almost sweet—and his cheeks and chin are covered with wet smears of blood. We MOVE IN on Tobey's face until his eyes and smile fill the screen as Mary SCREAMS.

BACK TO THE SCENE

Mary staggers backward, drops the magazine, clutches her chest. She falls heavily. Her mouth works soundlessly as she tries to say something.

CLOSE ON MARY'S HAND

It clenches and unclenches in pain, reaching for something just out of reach. We HEAR her agonized breathing. Then the breathing stops, as does the hand. The camera MOVES OFF her fingertips, to the magazine a few inches away.

INSERT—THE MAGAZINE

opened on a double-page photospread. The title 'PRIMING THE PUMP— New Findings in Heart Research' runs over a glossy full-color illustration of a human heart. We HOLD on the photo as Tobey begins to CRY and we HEAR the sound of Ernest's running feet.

> ERNEST
> (O.S., horrified)
> Mary. Oh, God, Mary!

DISSOLVE TO

EXT.—GRAVEYARD—DAY

The open grave is covered with flowers as a MINISTER delivers a eulogy to a small cluster of mourners, among them Mandy Kemp. Ernest and Tobey stand by the graveside, dressed in their Sunday best. Ernest holds his son by the hand. The ceremony has already gone on too long for Tobey; the boy is bored, looking around curiously. He makes noises, trying to imitate the chirping of nearby birds.

> MINISTER
> —she was a loving wife and a devoted mother, a faithful

and hard-working woman who bore life's burdens with courage and good cheer—

As the minister drones on, Tobey fixes on the ornate statue of an angel atop a nearby gravestone.

> TOBEY
>
> Br—

He's CUT OFF in midword as Ernest firmly clamps a hand around the boy's mouth. Tobey squirms and struggles, and the other mourners REACT with shocked glances.

CLOSE ON MANDY KEMP

Who looks disgusted, and determined.

BACK TO THE SCENE

> MINISTER
> (looks askance, resumes)
> —taken—ah, taken from us so suddenly—ah—
> (opens Bible)
>
> Let us pray.

DISSOLVE TO

INT.—LIVING ROOM—NIGHT—A WEEK LATER

Ernest sits slumped in his chair while Tobey wrestles with a inflatable cartoon-character punching bag, laughing every time he hits it and the bag pops back up. The clutter has reached vast proportions as a grief-stricken Ernest has let Tobey's toys pile up. Ernest stares down at a framed photograph in his lap, his eyes full of pain.

INSERT—THE PHOTOGRAPH

A portrait of Mary, much younger, in her wedding gown.

BACK TO THE SCENE

The doorbell RINGS. Tobey looks up sharply. Ernest rises, the portrait in hand. He hesitates, looks for a safe place to put it, finally sets it on top of the book cabinet. When he opens the door, Mandy Kemp is outside, her briefcase in hand.

> ERNEST
> (dully)

Miss Kemp.

> MANDY KEMP

I hope I'm not disturbing you, Mister Ross. I'm very sorry about your wife.

> ERNEST
> (nods)

Yes. Mary—she was very tired, Miss Kemp. She was never a strong woman, and the stress—
> (beat, moves aside)

I suppose you'll want to come in.

ANGLE ON MANDY

as she enters and REACTS to the mess. She smiles, tries to look cheerful, though it's clear that she's shocked.

BACK TO THE SCENE

> MANDY KEMP

Hello, Tobey.

> TOBEY
> (grinning)

Tobey!

Ernest closes the door, crosses the room.

> ERNEST

You've come about Tobey, of course.

> MANDY KEMP

I don't mean to intrude on your grief, but you need help more than ever, with your wife gone.

Mandy opens her briefcase, takes out an illustrated brochure.

> MANDY KEMP
> (continued)

I brought some literature you might want to take a look at.

> ERNEST

You want to put him in an institution.

> TOBEY

Pictures!

He reaches for the brochures, but Ernest grabs them first, flips through them, shakes his head.

> ERNEST

Very nice.

He rips the brochures in half, rips the halves in half, rips the quarters in half, lets the torn pieces flutter to the floor. Tobey begins to play with the brightly colored pieces of paper, but none of the photographs are intact.

ERNEST
(continued)

I'm not sending Tobey away. And now, if you're done, I'm very tired.

Mandy's cheerful smile finally dies, giving way to a frown of determination. She's through playing games.

MANDY KEMP

I'm not done, Mister Ross.
(takes papers from briefcase)

I've done some investigating since the last time we spoke. I've talked to your neighbors, your former employer, your wife's family. Frankly, unless you're willing to listen to reason, I believe we have grounds to remove Tobey from your custody.

ERNEST

I see.

MANDY KEMP

Your treatment of Tobey is frankly appalling, Mister Ross. Almost medieval. According to your neighbors, the boy is a virtual prisoner here. You never take him out, not even for walks. You've boarded up the window of his room, you don't permit him to play with other children. You never take him to the pool, the circus, the zoo. According to your sister-in-law, you don't even allow him the meagre solace of television.

Her tone is angry enough to frighten Tobey, who breaks off his play and runs to his father. Ernest puts an arm around him.

> ERNEST
> No. We don't.
> (to Tobey)
> It's all right. She won't hurt you.

> MANDY KEMP
> You've hurt him enough already, I'd say. I know what you're afraid of. You're afraid of what people will say, because you fathered a disabled child. You're ashamed of Tobey, so you keep him locked up like some kind of animal. Well, I'm not going to permit that to continue.

CLOSE ON ERNEST

His jaw clenches; his patience has finally run out.

> ERNEST
> (with quiet fury)
> Sit down, Miss Kemp. Don't say another word, just sit down. You want to take Tobey away from me? Then maybe it's time you knew something about him.

BACK TO THE SCENE

She seats herself on the couch. Ernest gently disengages himself from Tobey, walks to the bookcase. He fumbles in his pocket, pulls out a key-chain, fits a key into the lock.

> MANDY KEMP
> What are you doing?

Ignoring the question, Ernest lifts the covering, studies the spines of his books. Tobey beams at him.

> TOBEY
>
> Book. Book book book.

Ernest pulls out a large illustrated book about knights and chivalry. He closes the bookcase, turns to Mandy. Tobey is beside himself with excitement.

> TOBEY
>
> Book! Tobey!

> ERNEST
>
> The boy loves books. Photo books, comics, magazines, anything with pictures.
> (beat)
> My wife liked to knit. She used to let Tobey help. 'Bring me the yellow,' she would tell him, and Tobey would run and get her the yarn. He'd get the colors wrong, but he knew what bring meant.

> MANDY KEMP
>
> I don't see what this—

> ERNEST
>
> He was five the first time. He found a picture of a ball in this magazine. It had stripes like—like an Easter egg. I remember. He showed it to me. 'Bring,' he said. I brought him his own ball, a red and yellow ball I'd bought him, but he just pointed at the magazine and repeated his word. 'Bring.' I told him he'd have to play with the one he had, and turned away. He was angry, Miss Kemp. Angry as only a frustrated child can be. I heard him shout. Bring!

Then it was quiet.
> (beat)

When I returned, he was playing with his new ball. The ball from the magazine, with its Easter egg stripes. He didn't even know he'd done anything special.
> (beat)

So you see, you were right. Tobey can learn all right.
> (off her skeptical look)

You don't believe me, of course. Tobey, come here.

When the boy approaches, Ernest opens the book.

> ERNEST
> Look, Tobey.

CLOSE ON THE BOOK

as Ernest points at the picture of an ornate suit of armor.

> ERNEST
> Bring it, Tobey. Bring it here.

BACK TO THE SCENE

Tobey looks up at his father.

> TOBEY
> Bring?

Ernest nods gravely.

> ERNEST
> Go on, Tobey. Bring.

Tobey looks down at the picture again, smiling. But Mandy has had enough. She gets to her feet.

MANDY KEMP

Mister Ross, I'm trying to talk to you about your son's future. I don't know what kind of parlor trick you have in mind, but it's not going to change anything. Tobey needs a more supportive and stimulating environment, not—

TOBEY

Bring!

A full-sized suit of armor suddenly APPEARS next to Mandy, overbalances, and FALLS toward her. Startled, she GASPS and recoils. The armor hits the floor with a crash, collapsing into pieces. Reacting, Mandy CATCHES the helmet. She holds it in her hand for a moment, then throws it away as if the metal were red hot. Tobey laughs uproariously. Ernest closes his book.

MANDY KEMP

I don't believe it—this is—some kind of trick—
                (beat, stares at Tobey, then at Ernest)
It's not a trick, is it? It's real. It's some kind of—miracle.

ERNEST

A miracle? No, Miss Kemp. More like a curse. Look around you. This is the inside of the nightmare.

MANDY KEMP

How can you say that?
                (staring at Tobey)
He has a gift, a talent that no one else has ever had.

ERNEST

He saw a puppy on television one day, before we got rid of the set. He wanted it, so he brought it. It was dead when it arrived. He can't bring living things. But he forgets. Our back yard is full of the—things I've buried there.
          (continues off her shocked look)
Do you still want to take him to the zoo, Miss Kemp? Do you still think he needs to play with other children?
          (beat, very hard)
Most of the time he needs a picture. But sometimes Tobey just remembers.

Ernest turns away, walks to the bookcase, replaces the book. The social worker follows him.

MANDY KEMP

I—I owe you an apology.

Ernest nods stiffly, but he does not turn back to face her. He takes down the picture of Mary, looks at it.

ERNEST

Tobey was never the prisoner. It was us. Mary and me.

MANDY KEMP

Mister Ross, it doesn't have to be that way. Tobey still needs help. More than ever.

Ernest turns to face her. The picture is still in his hand.

ERNEST
          (bitterly)
You know as well as I what kind of help the world would give Tobey. They'll lock him up, run their tests and experiments, use him if they could, for whatever they

want—Tobey won't say no. He can't say no. And when they're done with him, what will the life of one idiot boy be worth, if they think they can find the secret in his brain?
(angrily)
He's my son, and this is his home.

MANDY KEMP

Please listen to me, Mister Ross. The burden, the responsibility—it's too much for one man alone.

ERNEST

I hoped that if I showed you, you'd understand, you'd leave us alone. I can see I was wrong. Get out. I don't want your help.
(louder)
Do you hear me? Leave us alone!

His hand is trembling. He DROPS the wedding portrait, which falls to the carpet.

CLOSE ON TOBEY

who's alarmed and a little frightened by the tone of his father's voice, a tone he's never heard before. He stares up at Ernest, his mouth hanging open.

BACK TO THE SCENE

MANDY KEMP

Mister Ross, I can't just walk out and forget what I've seen and heard here. I'm going to have to make a report.

ERNEST

Make your report, then. Go on. Just get out of here.

When Mandy doesn't move, Ernest loses the last of his temper. He strides past her, opens the door with a bang.

> ERNEST
> (loud, furious)
> Here. Here's the door. Use it.

CLOSE ON TOBEY

who's very scared now. His father—his calm, endlessly patient father—is almost shouting. He quails. His lips move.

> TOBEY
> (whisper)
> Mama.

BACK TO THE SCENE

Ernest goes to the coffee table, snatches up her briefcase, tries to slam it shut, but the papers are in the way, it doesn't close completely. He throws it out the open door.

> ERNEST
> There are your papers. Now get out.
> (shouting)
> Get out!

> MANDY KEMP
> Mister Ross, please don't—

> ERNEST
> (screaming)
> Leave us alone!

He PUSHES her toward the door, she stumbles backward, and Tobey bursts into tears.

> TOBEY
> (crying)
> Mama! Mama, mama, mama!

> TOBEY

The boy looks around for his mother, but he can't find her anywhere. Then his eyes light on the portrait Ernest dropped.

> TOBEY
> (more softly)
> Mama.

He reaches out, picks up the picture.

ANGLE ON ERNEST

As he realizes what's happening. He turns away from Mandy Kemp, a look of horror on his face, and takes a step toward Tobey.

> ERNEST
> Oh, God, no. Tobey, no!

> TOBEY
> Bring!

ERNEST & MANDY

react with horror to something o.s.

CLOSE ON TOBEY

who looks up, smiling with expectation, and then SCREAMS at what he sees.

TOBEY'S POV

of the chair, where his mother's grinning, hideous, and decaying week-old corpse sits, staring at him.

BACK TO THE SCENE

Mandy Kemp makes a gagging sound, whirls, and flees the scene. Tobey is screaming and crying. Ernest goes to him, turns his head away from the corpse, hugs him.

> ERNEST
> No, Tobey, look away. Don't look, Tobey. It's not mama any more.

CLOSE ON ERNEST

as he holds Tobey in a tight embrace, rocks him reassuringly.

> ERNEST
> It's all right, Tobey—I'll take it away, I'll take it away right now—it's all going to be all right—

We MOVE IN TIGHT on his eyes, and we can see the horror there.

EXT.—THE BACKYARD—LATER THAT NIGHT

Ernest shovels a spadeful of dirt on top of a freshly dug grave. His clothing is soiled and stained, and he's exhausted by the effort. He leans on his spade, mops at his brow.

> ERNEST
> (softly, wearily)
> I'm sorry, Mary. The picture—he doesn't understand. It was my fault. I should never have—
> (beat, dully)
> But it's too late now.

Far off in the night, we HEAR the distant sound of police sirens. Ernest hears them too. He turns his head, listening, then looks back at the grave.

> ERNEST
> They're coming for him now. I have to go.

He drops the spade, walks back into the house.

INT.—LIVING ROOM

Tobey is playing with a doll as Ernest reenters. He looks up happily, all innocence. He's obviously forgotten everything. The police sirens are louder now. Ernest locks the front door, throws the chain. Then he goes to the bookcase, digs out his keys, opens the padlock. He hesitates for a beat before selecting a book. We cannot see the cover or the title. The sirens are much closer. Ernest sits next to Tobey on the floor.

CLOSE ON TOBEY & ERNEST

The boy looks up at him, smiles, offers him the doll.

> TOBEY
> Doll.

Ernest takes it, puts it aside, smiles wanly.

> ERNEST
> (with difficulty)
> You're a good boy, Tobey. You've always been a good boy.

He ruffles Tobey's hair, smiles, pulls him close

> ERNEST
> Look, Tobey. A book.

The sirens are only a block or two away as Ernest opens the book, turns the pages. The camera PULLS BACK SLOWLY as Ernest begins to speak, holding his son very close. Tobey peers down at the book, eyes wide and fascinated, a big smile on his face.

> ERNEST
> (pointing)
> Look, Tobey. It's pretty, isn't it? All the colors—like a—a
> sunset almost—all red and yellow and orange. Isn't it pretty?

Ernest is crying now. The camera continues to PULL BACK as he leans closer, kisses his son gently on the cheek.

> ERNEST
> (softly)
> I love you, boy.

EXTREME CLOSE SHOT—TOBEY'S EYES

Bright, intense, fascinated. For a brief instant, we see the reflection of the picture he's looking at: the fireball of some huge explosion, all the bright colors dancing in his pupil. The sirens are very loud.

                    TOBEY
        Bring.

CUT TO

EXT.—ROSS HOUSE—NIGHT

A huge explosion rends the house from within. The blast of flame lights up the night. As the building falls in upon itself and bits of flaming debris settle back to earth, the lights in the neighboring houses go on one by one, and the police car pulls up out front, its siren sounding strangely small in the aftermath of the explosion.

FADE OUT

The Secret History
of the Lost Colony

BY JOHN SCALZI

To commemorate the completion of *Zoe's Tale*, I thought I'd do something special here for you today and show you something you haven't
seen before: An entire excised chapter from one of my books.

This particular excised chapter comes from an iteration of *The Last
Colony* that I didn't write (or more accurately, didn't complete): the second iteration, in which I had planned to write the books in alternating
chapters of first person and third person, the first person chapters featuring John Perry, the hero of *Old Man's War*, and the third person chapter
featuring other characters, particularly General Tarsem Gau, the leader
of the Conclave. Eventually, I abandoned the idea for two reasons: it rapidly became clear it would be a structural nightmare, and also because if I
wrote it this way, the book would end up in the 180,000 word range—i.e.,
I'd have written enough for two books, and would only be paid for one. Bad
writer, no cookie.

I ended up generally abandoning the third person chapters, and rewrote
the information in first person chapters for the final version of the book.
Only two chapters of this second version made it into the finished book:
John Perry's first appearance, which was chapter two, became part of the final

book's first chapter, and the chapter in which General Gau argues with a Whaidi colonist leader, which had been the first chapter, turns into Chapter Eight in the final book (and is turned into a video recording, so I could cheat my way into having a third person chapter into a first person book).

Because this is an excised chapter, it's not canonical—among other things, character names change between this and the final version, and General Gau's species name also undergoes a transformation. But neither did the chapter get entirely wasted; it was abandoned not because it wasn't good, but because mechanically it didn't work for the book. So during the writing of the final version of the book, I ended up strip-mining this chapter for material. Folks who have read *The Last Colony* will see things they recognize from different contexts: The video of the Conclave attack on the Whaidi colony, an invocation of a states secret act, and an oblique discussion of Fermi's Paradox, which got a rather more extensive discussion in this excised chapter (because I was annoyed at people who act as if Fermi's Paradox was some sort of immutable law, that's why).

And as it turns out, I mined it again for part of *Zoe's Tale*. You'll have to wait to see which part and how, but the fact that I could (and did) goes to show that nothing has to be wasted. This excised chapter itself will never see the light of day as part of a larger story, but little bits and pieces can be moved around and used and recycled. Waste not, want not.

It also served another purpose: This chapter is basically me thinking out loud about several characters in *The Last Colony*, and figuring out their personalities and what makes them tick. This chapter became back story for several characters, notably Generals Rybicki and Gau; playing with them here gave me a good idea who they were when I started writing them for the final version of *The Last Colony*. It's good to have that sort of grip on your characters before you start putting canonical words into their mouths.

The lesson here for writing is that even your "failures"—the stuff that doesn't work for your book, for whatever reason—can still have value to you as you're wrestling with your work. This is one reason way, whenever I chop out a significant chunk of text from a book I'm writing, I don't simply delete it: I cut it and paste it into an "excisions" document that I keep handy. That way I can go back to that material for reference, or to drop a line or an idea into the final version, perhaps in a completely different context, but where it will do some real good. This is what I do, and it's worked for me so far.

CHAPTER THREE
(of the second iteration of *The Last Colony,* now deceased)

Colonel Janice Dunn, General George Rybicki's assistant, found the general in a conference theater. He was walking around in a massive projection of local space, stars glowing different colors to signify which races' colonies lived around them. "General," she began.

"Shhh," Rybicki said, and pointed at the stars. "Looking."

"Secretary Bell's office sent a message," Dunn said, ignoring her superior's order to shush. "Your presence is requested for a meeting in ten minutes."

"She probably wants an update on Roanoke," Rybicki said. "I've got colony leaders for her now."

"You should take a few minutes to prepare," Dunn suggested.

"I already have a report ready," Rybicki said. "I'll be fine." We went back to staring up at the projection.

"If you wanted to look at the stars, you could have just looked out a window," Dunn said.

Rybicki snorted. "Shows how often you actually look out a window," he said. "All the stars get washed out by Phoenix. And when you're on a part of this station that's pointed away from the planet, all the station's exterior lights throw up too much glare." He pointed up at the display. "This is as good as starwatching gets around here. And anyway, I'm not actually stargazing, I'm thinking."

"About what?" Dunn asked.

"Fermi's Paradox," Rybicki said.

Dunn frowned. "I'm not familiar with that," she said. "Is that some physics thing?"

"It's an extraterrestrial thing," Rybicki said, and pointed again at the display. "Fermi lived before we knew about all this. He didn't believe that intelligent life existed anywhere but on Earth. He said, 'if they exist, why aren't they here already?' And no one had a good answer for that. So they speculated that maybe the aliens couldn't travel fast enough to get to Earth, or maybe they were out there, but they were just waiting until humans were sufficiently advanced before admitting them into some federation of worlds. Crap like that. But none of them ever figured out the real reason."

"Which was?" Dunn asked.

"That they were all too busy beating the Hell out of each other to bother with us," Rybicki said. "They didn't get to us because they occupied themselves with worlds they already knew about. Our research arm's done some archaeology here and there, whenever we take a planet from someone else. You want to know the average lifespan of a colony—any colony, by any species? Try and guess."

"I can't imagine," Dunn said.

"75 years," Rybicki said. "A race finds a planet, sets up shop, has some relatively peaceful decades, gets complacent, and then some other race comes in and wipes the floor with them, and then that species colonizes the planet. The cycle starts over. Wash, rinse, repeat. Some colony planets have gone back and forth dozens of times. Just about the only planets that ever stay the same over any length of time are species home planets, because they're usually too well-populated and defended to pry a species off of. Everything else is constantly up for grabs."

"And yet we have colonies that have been around for a couple of centuries," Dunn said.

"Yes, well, we game the system," Rybicki said. "We've made Phoenix humanity's homeworld for all intents and purposes, so that's a colony that's staying put. And we populate our colony worlds faster than most species, because we have a planet overflowing with extra people. Why grow a colony slowly when you can flood it with waves of surplus Pakistanis and Norwegians and Egyptians?"

"I'm pretty sure the colonists wouldn't appreciate being called 'surplus,'" Dunn said.

"I'm sure they wouldn't," Rybicki said. "Doesn't mean they're not. And we're glad for it because it makes it easier to keep a foothold. The last old colony we lost was Coral, and that was because we had less than 100,000 colonists on it. We took it back quickly enough, but you see the point. Were you around for Coral?"

"I think I was still in London at the time," Dunn said. "Old and fat and hoping I didn't die before I could get off the planet."

"Congratulations," Rybicki said. "You made it."

"Thank you, general," Dunn said.

"You're welcome," Rybicki said, and with his BrainPal caused the human colony stars to shine a little brighter. "We have a lot of old colonies, but we still lose a fair number of new colonies. You've read the report on Everest colony."

"I did," Dunn said. "But Everest wasn't lost because of attack."

"No," Rybicki agreed. "Although a colony-wide bacterial plague isn't a much better way to die. Point is, even we conform to the 75-year rule. It's interesting."

"If you say so, general," Dunn said, and pointed at the stars. "One wonders at how the Conclave will change that average for us."

"Shhhhh," Rybicki said again, sarcasm whistling out. "We're still not supposed to admit that the Conclave exists. It's still a state secret."

"It's a very poorly-kept secret," Dunn said. "You can go down to the promenade and hear the soldiers talking about it."

"State secrets are always poorly kept," Rybicki said. "Yet they still manage to stay secrets. Officially, at least. CDF grunts can talk about the Conclave all they want. What matters is the colonies. We still haven't explained it them. They still don't know."

"Or don't want to know," Dunn said.

Rybicki nodded. "Always a possibility. But then, there's a lot we don't know, either." A star in the array growed more bright; the star around which the colony of Roanoke would be founded. "Everest aside, Roanoke will be our first colony after the Conclave came together. Our first test to see whether the Conclave intends to enforce its ban on colonization from non-Conclave races."

"You don't seem worried," Dunn said.

"That's not entirely accurate," Rybicki said. "I'm concerned, but a lot depends on the Conclave itself. Everest was out there and they didn't do anything about it. Was it because the Conclave was still getting itself together, or because they were simply rattling their sabers and hoping we'd be scared? We're not the only ones who have colonized between now and then. The question now is how much of a priority we are to the Conclave. Or if we're a priority at all."

⇒∥⇐

"What I want to know is when we will finally go after the humans," said Lernin Il, once again. And once again, after a moment for the translation into a dozen languages, came the affirmative nods, bobbles, and signifying appendage movement from around the council table.

General Gau struggled mightily not to sigh in exasperation at the Tand member of the Conclave's executive council, and lightly tapped the table instead. "There is the small problem that the humans have no colonies founded after the Agreement, Counselor Il," he said.

"There's the colony they call Everest," Il said.

"There was the colony they called Everest," Gau said. "It was wiped out by a native infection. Since then there have been no other attempts by the humans to start a new colony."

"The fact Everest was colonized should be enough," said Wert Ninug, the Dward counselor, and Gau tucked away for future reference that sometime between the time he'd left on his mission to the Whaidian colony and the time he'd gotten back the Dward had somehow slipped into the pocket of the Tand. That was interesting; the two races had a hate that went back hundreds of shar. Prior to this even if Wert had agreed with Il on a policy issue, it would have rather shot off the back of its own head then to say it publicly.

You wanted races to put away their old hates, some part of Gau's mind said to him, and Gau had to note the comment with rueful satisfaction. He did want the members of the Conclave to get over their past enmities; he wasn't entirely sure he wanted them to start new ones against him.

Gau glanced down the table to see who looked surprised at a Dward offering support for a Tand. It would be the ones who didn't look surprised that Gau would need to worry about.

"Should it, Counselor Wert?" Gau said, presently. "The Agreement limits non-Conclave races to worlds they already have. Currently the humans are on the worlds they had prior to the agreement. Where should we attack?"

"They did colonize after the agreement," Wert said. "They intentionally tested the will of the Conclave. Intent should matter for something."

"I agree," Gau said. "However, at the moment we have no avenue to respond. Everest was abandoned. All the other worlds the humans have we have all agreed they have a right to live on. And the Conclave is not meant to be merely an instrument of retribution or of punishment."

"You had no problems punishing the Whaid," Il said.

Gau paused a prudent moment before responding. "No, I didn't," he said, finally. "Nor will I the humans. When and if the humans attempt to colonize again."

"We could make a special case out of the humans," said Hafte Sorvalh, the Lalan Counselor. She was not an ally of either Il or Wert, so far as Gau knew. "One could argue their past actions merit a certain level of special attention."

"In my experience today's 'special attention' is tomorrow's standard procedure, counselor Sorvalh," Gau said. "And this is not a standard procedure I think the Conclave should feel comfortable having. We are so early in time of this union of ours. We should not begin its time by compromising its laws, simply out of convenience."

"We could change the law," said Il. More agreement around the table.

"We could," Gau agreed. "This executive council was empowered to do so. Each of you was elected among the governments of the Conclave to represent their interests. So yes, we could change the law. And then we could watch as Conclave members peel themselves away and form new alliances, because this council will have shown that we have no interest in creating the universe we said we were interested in living in. I don't think we should be in a rush to dissolve the thing we're supposed to guide. Do you?"

"You know the humans are dangerous," Wert said. "They were the movers behind the Counter Conclave. They nearly wrecked the Conclave before it even began. We're sitting here being judicious in our response to them, but you know as well as any of us, General Gau, that the humans are not returning the favor to us."

"I'm not suggesting we ignore the humans, Counselor Wert," Gau said. "Nor do I think it's in the nature of the humans not to test our will. We will no doubt have an opportunity to face them again, and I suspect we will, sooner rather than later. What I suggest we remember, however, that the Conclave is more than the sum of its military might. We have other ways to discover the intent and the capabilities of the humans, other tools at our disposal. We want to create the circumstances in which the humans make their move, and we are able to respond—in our way, by our own laws."

"Just as we would with any other race," Sorvalh said.

"Precisely," Gau said. "If we make a special case of the humans, we give them significance, and we diminish the Conclave by saying that we have to work outside our own laws to contain them. We give them power, which will attract others to them. We make it harder to defeat them. I'd prefer not to do that. When we defeat the humans, we want that defeat to be unremarkable. They will be just another race, isolated and alone, no longer a threat to anyone, much less the Conclave."

⋇

The beams of light illuminating the Whaidian colony suddenly snapped off. General Rybicki felt the confusion in the room over that; the video in the room had begun with the colony swathed in light, and most people assumed that the beams would eventually focus into lethality. Shutting them off seemed unnecessarily cruel.

"Here it comes," said Secretary of Defense Anthony Crane, who had seen the video before.

The killing beams were initially hardly detectable, with just the errant occasional flash of an airborne dust mote igniting to suggest the beams were there. But within a fraction of a second the entire colony ignited and exploded, and superheated air blew the fragments and the dust of the colony's buildings, structures, vehicles and inhabitants up into the sky in a whirling display that illuminated the power of the beams themselves. The flickering fragments of matter mimicked and mirrored the flames that were now themselves reaching up toward the heavens.

A shockwave of heat and dust expanded out from the charred remains of the colony. The beams flicked off again. The light-show in the sky disappeared, leaving behind smoke and flames. Outside the periphery of the destruction, an occasional solitary eruption of flame would appear.

"What is that?" asked Karin Bell, the Secretary of Colonization.

"Some of the colonists were outside the colony when it was destroyed, we think" said Crane. "So they're cleaning them up."

"Christ," Bell said. "With the colony destroyed those people would probably be dead anyway."

"They were making a point," Crane said.

"Point taken," Bell said. "Lights, please."

The video shut off; Rybicki felt the tension in his shoulders uncoil.

The lights came up to reveal a room jammed with people: Crane and Bell with their assistants and staff; Rybicki and several other generals and admirals with theirs. The general officers and the secretaries sat at the circular table; the staff members milled up against the walls.

The meeting was rather more packed, and packed with different people, than Rybicki had expected it to be. Rybicki had walked into room prepared for a status update meeting on Roanoke; he was going to discuss John Perry and Jane Sagan agreeing to lead the colony. That was not this meeting.

"How did we get hold of this video?" asked Charlie Garr, Bell's chief of staff. "Who do we have working inside the Conclave that can get us something like this?"

Crane cracked a bitter smile. "You're making the assumption that the Conclave doesn't want us to see this, Charlie," he said. "But you'd be wrong about that. This video was hand-delivered to us, and to every non-Conclave-affiliated government, by messengers from the Conclave itself."

"I don't understand," Garr said.

"The Conclave has decided that races who aren't in the Conclave can't colonize any more," Crane said. "We knew that already, of course. Only now, it's clear the Conclave is intending to enforce that decision. If we try to colonize, that's what's going to happen to all of our new colonies."

Crane pointed toward where the video had just been playing. "This is their way of making sure we know they're serious about their policy positions."

"This really happened, then," Colonel Dunn asked, behind Rybicki. "I mean, this isn't an archive video from some attack in the past."

"Along with the video, the Conclave gave us the coordinates of the colony—the former colony—and a three-day window to confirm for ourselves that the attack happened," Crane said. "We checked. It happened, Colonel."

"What colonies of ours are at risk?" Bell asked.

Crane nodded to his own chief of staff, Lance Wantanabe. "Theoretically, none," he said. "The Conclave is targeting colonies established after it was founded. That was almost two years ago. We established the Everest colony, but it didn't stick. As long as the Conclave stays within its own laws, we won't be a target until we try to found a new colony."

"Which we intend to do," Rybicki said. As he said it he realized he wasn't entirely sure whether he meant it as a statement or a question.

"Why did they take so long to start going after new colonies?" Bell asked.

"There are over four hundred races in the Conclave," Wantanabe said. "If they're anything like us, coordinating anything substantial is going to take time. They had to get their own government up and running and stable before they could worry about anyone else. We and at least a couple dozen other races took advantage of that time to found new colonies, but now it looks like the Conclave is determined to back up its threat."

"But that can be to our advantage," Crane said. "The Conclave is going to be busy policing the colonies that were founded in its wake. That gives us time to plan our attack."

This got Rybicki's attention. " 'Our attack?' " he said. "You're suggesting that the Colonial Union can go up against the Conclave."

"I am, General," asked Crane. "Do you think otherwise?"

"As a practical matter, there are 400 races in the Conclave, and one of us," Rybicki said. "That is not an insignificant matter of scale."

"I agree, but I don't think we really have much of a choice in that matter," Crane said. "Unless we are willing to join the Conclave, which we are not, or are willing not to colonize, which we are not, the alternative is to fight the Conclave and destroy it."

"I'm not disputing that these are our options," Rybicki said. "I'm simply not sure how we go up against an enemy like that and not get ourselves slaughtered."

"Start by changing your frame of reference," said a voice down the table. Rybicki turned to see General Szilard, head of Special Forces, staring back at him with that disturbingly blank expression the Special Forces had. "You've made the mistake of taking the Conclave at its word, General Rybicki. You're seeing as it would like to position itself to the non-affiliated races. Monolithic. Coordinated. Unstoppable and inevitable."

"The video we just saw makes a good case for that," Rybicki said.

"That was the point, of course," Szilard said. "What the Conclave doesn't want you to see is that it's young, uncertain and filled with political and social faultlines that we can exploit and use to bring it down. It's a little like a diamond, general. You can't wear down a diamond. But you can shatter a diamond to dust if you just know where to hit it. We can't go against the Conclave head-to-head. You're right about that. But we can destroy it. All we need is the right tool, used at the right time."

"And what tool might that be?" Rybicki asked.

Szilard looked over to Crane.

"All right, everyone," Crane said. "Let's make this official. This meeting and everything said and done in it is covered by the Colonial Union State Secrets Act. Nothing leaves this room. General Szilard, you have the floor."

"Thank you, Secretary Crane," Szilard said. "I'm going to keep this simple. The way to defeat the Conclave is to play by its rules." From the video output a picture flickered into existence, showing a thin, pale creature.

"For those of you who don't know, this is Tarsem Gau, leader of the Conclave," Szilard said. "He's a general for the Tsideian race, or was a general, anyway, and still refers to himself that way, although of course he is the de facto leader of that planet as well as of the Conclave. Despite the power that devolves to him alone, Gau is, as far as we can tell, a creature who is genuinely trying to create a lasting political structure and not a prop for his own cult of personality. He's nation-building."

"That's optimism for you," Crane said, as a joke. No one laughed.

"Because of that, our intelligence people suggest he is extraordinarily sensitive to making sure that nothing the Conclave does is above its own laws," Szilard continued. "This means we believe that the Colonial Union will not be attacked until and unless we attempt to found a new colony—and that the Conclave will only attack that colony."

"That means that any new colony we found is going to find the entire Conclave in its sky before it even has time to dig in," said Secretary Bell.

"It means, Secretary Bell, that by following the rules the Conclave has established, we will choose the place and time for our confrontation," General Szilard said. "And that if we do things right, we can weaken the Conclave along the way so that when the confrontation happens, we can strike a fatal blow."

"And what will 'doing things right' take?" Bell asked.

"No more than what we already have planned," Szilard said. "General Rybicki."

"Yes?" Rybicki said.

"I believe that when you came to this meeting today, you were going to provide Secretary Bell with a status update on the Roanoke Colony. Now would be an excellent time to give it."

※

After the council meeting, Hafte Sorvalh asked for a private audience. Gau, though tired, invited her back to his personal office. He was amused when the Lalan, tall even for her own tall race, tried to be diplomatic about its size.

"This is cozy," she said.

Gau laughed, as he sat. "You mean to say it's impossibly cramped. Please, sit, Counselor Sorvalh."

She sat. "I don't mean any disrespect. I assumed your own office would be larger than this."

"I have the large public office for meetings, and to impress people when I have to, of course," Gau said. "I'm not blind to the power of impressive spaces. But I've spent most of my life on starships, even after I began to build the Conclave. You get used to not a lot of space. I'm more comfortable here. And no one can say that I give more to myself than any other counselor on the executive committee."

"Indeed," Sorvalh said. "You are almost arrogant in your humility, general. If you don't mind me saying."

"I don't," Gau said. "But we can always go to my public office if you prefer."

"I'm fine," Sorvalh said. "It actually is cozy."

"Thank you, Counselor," Gau said. "Now, please. What's on your mind."

"I'm speaking here primarily for myself," Sorvalh said.

"All right," Gau said.

"I'm worried about certain influences on the executive council," Sorvalh said.

"Ah," Gau said. "This wouldn't have anything to do with the strange, sudden marriage of convenience between counselors Il and Wert, would it?"

"You have to admit they make an unusual pair of allies," Sorvalh said.

"I admit it," Gau said. "I also suspect there is more going on there than either of them would like for me to know about. Suffice to say that I'm already going to be looking into it. But in itself, I'm not entirely sure I should express too much concern. There are a dozen members of the executive council for a reason. To make sure there are a multiplicity of voices, and not all of them telling me what I want to hear."

"I appreciate that," Sorvalh said. "I have taken advantage of that freedom myself. But—with all respect—when others of us have disagreed with you, we've still kept the interests of the Conclave at the heart of the matter."

"You doubt our two friends are doing that?" Gau asked.

"I can't say for sure," Sorvalh said. "I can say that your destruction of that Whaidian colony has motivated them and others. Before you did it, the matter of the Conclave's military might was entirely theoretical. There was no Conclave military might, just an agreement that if it was used, it should be used in particular ways.

"But now there is a Conclave military, and you've consecrated its use against the Conclave enemies. Composing it of soldiers and ships of every Conclave member was your way of assuring responsibility for its use was shared by all. I suspect some are beginning to wonder if the converse is true—by spreading responsibility around you spread it thin enough that no one has to take responsibility for anything. And that's an inviting proposition when you have enemies on a list."

"Inviting enough to put one's own interests first," Gau said.

"Perhaps," Sorvalh said. "Allow me to suggest that today's attempt to get you to attack the humans was less about the humans than it was a probe to see how flexible you are with your power. The humans are an easy target. They have no friends, and everyone knows they mean us harm. But as you said to me, today's special case is tomorrow's standard practice."

"I thought you might be testing me with that," Gau said.

"Testing you? Oh, no," Sorvalh said. "Merely providing you with an opportunity to make a point. And I was pleased to see you take advantage of the opportunity."

"I'm happy to please you, counselor," Gau said.

"Then perhaps you'll consider something else that might please me— and a few others on the council," Sorvalh said. "I and others are gratified that through the many shars it took to create the Conclave, you have always avoided assuming the powers you could have easily assumed. Time and again you showed that your interest was not in personal power, but in building a lasting peace. But now the Conclave is here, and I wonder whether the democratic impulses that led to its creation might not undermine it as you attempt to bring the remaining races into the fold."

"You think I give the executive council too much say," Gau said.

"I think the executive council was useful when the Conclave was being born," Sorvalh said. "I wonder if it will continue to be useful as we progress."

"I think it will be," Gau said.

"Perhaps it will," Sorvalh said. "But you should know that when we Lalans chose to join the Conclave, it wasn't an executive council we trusted to achieve peace. It was you, General Gau. You and your vision."

"But part of that vision was the idea that not too much power should rest in any one person, even me," General Gau said. "I want to lead the Conclave, make no mistake about that. My arrogance extends that far. But I don't want to do it as an emperor or a tyrant. Empires fall and tyrannies collapse. I'm hoping for something more than that."

"People might be suspicious of someone who doesn't want power for himself," Sorvalh said. "It's not normal."

Gau smiled. "I'm not pure, counselor," he said. "I have the usual amount of personal vanities and flaws. And I enjoy running things. But I hope that if I had to choose between my personal power and the well-being of the Conclave, I could pick the Conclave. So far, it's been easy for me to say I would pick the Conclave. But I dread the temptation of picking myself. It would be easier. If nothing else, the executive council keeps me from having to make that choice."

"Then I hope for your sake you never have to choose between one or the other," Sorvalh said.

"Thank you, counselor," Gau said. "I appreciate the thought. There's little worse in life than a choice you suffer for. Whatever choice I would make in that situation, I would surely suffer, believe me."

※

Colonel Dunn found General Rybicki alone in the conference theater, staring again at the projection of local space.

"You were right," Dunn said. "I tried looking out the window at the stars. I couldn't see a single one of them."

"Well, they're all here," Rybicki said, waving dismissively at the display. "All the ones that matter, anyway. All the fucking stars with all the fucking intelligent races around them. Here they are, Colonel. Enjoy them."

"I was going to ask you if you were all right," Dunn said. "But I suspect I already know the answer to that."

"I'm fine," Rybicki said. "I may be slightly drunk and pissed off, however. I'm entitled."

"There's a chance they could change the strategy," Dunn said. "General Szilard said that there was still some work to be done on the details."

"Don't kid yourself, Colonel," Rybicki said. "Szilard is Special Forces. Special Forces are bred to be heartless sons of bitches. And he certainly did his job. The strategy is done. They'll tweak here and there for maximum effect. But we're moving forward, all right."

"But it's not just Special Forces on this," Dunn said. "The Secretary of Defense signed off on it. So did the Secretary of Colonization. So did you."

"Yes, I did," Rybicki said. "I sure did. And I will tell you that when I did, I suddenly got religion. At that moment, Colonel, I became convinced there an afterlife, because I became stone cold aware that I was going to Hell."

"General," Dunn began.

"Thank you, Colonel, that will be all," Rybicki said. "You're dismissed. Go away."

Colonel Dunn left. Rybicki turned his attention back to the display and watched the stars wheel around an arbitrary central axis.

"Goddamn Enrico Fermi," Rybicki said, after a while. "Why couldn't you have been right."

The Screams of Dragons

BY KELLEY ARMSTRONG

"And the second plague that is in thy dominion, behold it is a dragon. And another dragon of a foreign race is fighting with it, and striving to overcome it. And therefore does your dragon make a fearful outcry."
—*Cyfranc Lludd a Llefelys*, translated by Lady Charlotte Guest

When he was young, other children talked of their dreams, of candy-floss mountains and puppies that talked and long-lost relatives bearing new bicycles and purses filled with crisp dollar bills. He did not have those dreams. His nights were filled with golden castles and endless meadows and the screams of dragons.

The castles and the meadows came unbidden, beginning when he was too young to know what a castle or a meadow was, but in his dreams he'd race through them, endlessly playing, endlessly laughing. And then he'd wake to his cold, dark room, stinking of piss and sour milk, and he'd roar with rage and frustration. Even when he stopped, the cries were replaced by sulking, aggrieved silence. Never laughter. He only laughed in his dreams. Only played in his dreams. Only was happy in his dreams.

The dragons came later.

He presumed he'd first heard the story of the dragons in Cainsville. Visits to family there were the high points of his young life. While

Cainsville had no golden castles or endless meadows, the fields and the forests, the spires and the gargoyles reminded him of his dreams, and calmed
him and made him, if not happy, at least content.

They treated him differently in Cainsville, too. He was special there.
A pampered little prince, his mother would say, shaking her head. The
local elders paid attention to him, listened to him, sought him out. Better
still, they did not do the same to his sister, Natalie. The Gnat, he called
her—constantly buzzing about, useless and pestering. At home, *she* was
the pampered one. His parents never seemed to know what to make of
him, his discontent and his silences, and so they showered his bouncing,
giggling little sister with double the love, double the attention.

In Cainsville the old people told him stories. Of King Arthur's court,
they said, but when he looked up their tales later, they were not quite the
same. Theirs were stories of knights and magic, but lions too and giants
and faeries and, sometimes, dragons. That was why he was certain they'd
told him this particular tale, even if he could not remember the exact circumstances. It was about another king, beset by three plagues. One was a
race of people who could hear everything he said. The third was disappearing foodstuffs and impending starvation. The second was a terrible scream
that turned out to be two dragons, fighting. And that was when he began
to dream of the screams of dragons.

He did not actually *hear* the screams. He could not imagine such a
thing, because he had no idea what a dragon's scream would sound like.
He asked his parents and his grandmother and even his Sunday school
teacher, but they didn't seem to understand the question. Even at night, his
sleep was often filled with nothing but his small self, racing here and there,
searching for the screams of dragons. He would ask and he would ask, but
no one could ever tell him.

When he was almost eight, his grandmother noticed his sleepless
nights. When she asked what was wrong, he knew better than to talk
about the dragons, but he began to think maybe he should tell her of the
other dreams, the ones of golden palaces and endless meadows. One night,
when his parents were out, he waited until the Gnat fell asleep. Then he
padded into the living room, the feet on his sleeper whispering against

the floor. His grandmother didn't notice at first—she was too busy watching "The Dick Van Dyke Show." He couldn't understand the fascination with television. The moving pictures were dull gray, the laughter harsh and fake. He supposed they were for those who didn't dream of gold and green, of sunlight and music.

He walked up beside her. He did not sneak or creep, but she was so absorbed in her show that when he appeared at her shoulder, she shrieked and in her face, he saw something he'd never seen before. Fear. It fascinated him, and he stared at it, even as she relaxed and said, "Bobby? You gave me quite a start. What's wrong, dear?"

"I can't sleep," he said. "I have dreams."

"Bad dreams?"

He shook his head. "Good ones."

Her old face creased in a frown. "And they keep you awake?"

"No," he said. "They make me sad."

She clucked and pulled him onto the chair, tucking him in beside her. "Tell Gran all about them."

He did, and as he talked, he saw that look return. The fear. He decided he must be mistaken. He hadn't mentioned the dragons. The rest was wondrous and good. Yet the more he talked, the more frightened she became, until finally she pushed him from the chair and said, "It's time for bed."

"What's wrong?"

She said, "Nothing," but her look said there was something very, very wrong.

⋇

For the next few weeks, his grandmother was a hawk, circling him endlessly, occasionally swooping down and snatching him up in her claws. Most times, she avoided him directly, though he'd catch her watching him. Studying him. Scrutinizing him. Once they were alone in the house, she'd swoop. She'd interrogate him about the dreams, unearthing every last detail, even the ones he thought he'd forgotten.

On the nights when his parents were gone, she insisted on drawing his baths, adding in some liquid from a bottle and making the baths so hot they scalded him and when he cried, she seemed satisfied. Satisfied and a little frightened.

The strangest of all came nearly a month after he'd told her of the dreams. She'd made stew for dinner and she served it in eggshells. When she brought them to the table, the Gnat laughed in delight.

"That's funny," she said. "They're so cute, Gran."

His grandmother only nodded absently at the Gnat. Her watery blue eyes were fixed on him.

"What do you think of it, Bobby?" she asked.

"I…" He stared at the egg, propped up in a little juice glass, the brown stew steaming inside the shell. "I don't understand. Why is it in an egg?"

"For fun, dummy." His sister shook her head at their grandmother. "Bobby's never fun." She pulled a face at him. "Boring Bobby."

His grandmother shushed her, gaze still on him. "You think it's strange."

"It is," he said.

"Have you ever seen anything like this before?"

"No."

She waited, as if expecting more. Then she prompted, "You would say, then, that you've never, in all your years, seen something like this."

It seemed an odd way to word it, but he nodded.

And with that, finally, she seemed satisfied. She plunked down into her chair, exhaling, before turning to him and saying, "Go to your room. I don't want to see you until morning."

He glanced up, startled. "What did I—?"

"To your room. You aren't one of us. I'll not have you eat with us. Now off with you."

He pushed his chair back and slowly rose to his feet.

The Gnat stuck out her tongue when their grandmother wasn't looking. "Can I have his egg?"

"Of course, dear," Gran said as he shuffled from the kitchen.

⋇

The next morning, instead of going to school, his grandmother took him to church. It was not Sunday. It was not even Friday. As soon as he saw the spires of the cathedral, he began to shake. He'd done something wrong, horribly wrong. He'd lain awake half the night trying to figure out what he could have done to deserve bed without dinner, but there was nothing. She'd fed him stew in an eggshell and, while perplexed, he had still been very polite and respectful about it.

The trouble had started with telling her about the dreams, but who could find fault with tales of castles and meadows, music and laughter?

Perhaps she was going senile. It had happened to an old man down the street. They'd found him in their yard, wearing a diaper and asking about his wife, who'd died years ago. If that had happened to his grandmother, Father Joseph would see it.

Certainly, he seemed to, given the expression on Father Joseph's face after Gran talked to him alone in the priest's office. Father Joseph emerged as if in a trance, and Gran had to direct him to the pew where Bobby waited.

"See?" she said, waving her hand at Bobby.

The priest looked straight at him, but seemed lost in his thoughts. "No, I'm afraid I don't, Mrs. Sheehan."

Gran's voice snapped with impatience. "It's obvious he's not ours. Neither his mother nor his father nor any of his grandparents have blond hair. Or dark eyes."

Sweat beaded on the priest's forehead and he tugged his collar. "True, but children do not always resemble their parents, for a variety of reasons, none of them laying any blame at the foot of the child."

"Are you suggesting my daughter-in-law was unfaithful?"

Father Joseph's eyes widened. "No, of course not. But the ways of genetics—like the ways of God—are not always knowable. Your daughter-in-law does have light hair, and I believe she has a brother who is blond. If my recollection of science is correct, dark eyes are the dominant type, and I'm quite certain if you searched the family tree beyond parents and grandparents you would find your answer."

"I have my answer," she said, straightening. "He is a changeling."

Two drops of sweat burst simultaneously and dribbled down the priest's face. "I...I do not wish to question your beliefs, Mrs. Sheehan. I know such folk wisdom is common in the...more rural regions of your homeland—"

"Because it *is* wisdom. Forgotten wisdom. I've tested him, Father. I gave him dinner in an eggshell, as I explained."

"Yes, but..." The priest snuck a glance around, as if hoping for divine intervention—or a needy parishioner to stumble in, requiring his immediate attention. "I know that is the custom, but I cannot say I rightly understand it."

"What is there to understand?" She put her hands on her narrow hips. "It's a test. I gave him stew in eggshells, and he said he'd never seen anything like it. That's what a changeling will say."

"I beg your pardon, ma'am, but I believe that's what *anyone* would say, given their meal served in an egg."

She glowered at him. "I put him in a tub with foxglove, too, and he became ill."

"Foxglove?" The priest's eyes rounded again. "Is that not a poison?"

"It is if you're a changeling. I also gave him one of my heart pills, because it's made from digitalis, which is also foxglove. My pill made him sick."

"You gave..." For the first time since he'd come in, Father Joseph looked at Bobby, really looked at him. "You gave your grandson your heart medication? That could *kill* a boy—"

"He isn't a boy. He's one of the Fair Folk." Gran met Bobby's gaze. "An abomination."

Now Father Joseph's face flushed, his eyes snapping. "No, he is a *child*. You will not speak of him that way, certainly not in front of him. I'm trying to be respectful, Mrs. Sheehan. You are entitled to your superstitions and folksy tales, but not if they involve poisoning an innocent child." He knelt in front of Bobby. "You're going to come into my office now, son, and we'll call your parents. Is your mother at work?"

He nodded.

"Do you know the number?"

He nodded again.

The priest took Bobby's hand and, without another word, led him away as his grandmother watched, her eyes narrowing.

That was the beginning of "the bad time," as his parents called it, whispered words, even years later, their eyes downcast, as if in shame. The situation did not end with that visit to the priest. His grandmother would not drop the accusation. He was a changeling. A faerie child dropped into their care, her real grandson spirited away by the Fair Folk. Finally, his parents broke down and asked the priest to perform some ritual—any ritual—to calm his grandmother's nerves. The priest refused. To do so would be to lend credence to the preposterous accusation and could permanently scar the child's psyche.

The fight continued. He heard his parents talking late at night about the shame, the great shame of it all. They were intelligent, educated people. His father was a scientist, his mother the lead secretary in her firm. They were not ignorant peasants, and it angered them that Father Joseph didn't understand what they were asking—not to "fix" their son but simply to pretend to, for the harmony of the household.

They took their request to a second priest, and somehow—for years afterward, everyone would blame someone else for this—a journalist got hold of the story. It made one of the Chicago newspapers, in an article mocking the family and their "Old World" ways. His family was so humiliated they moved. His grandmother grumbled that his parents made too big a fuss out of the whole thing. It didn't matter. They moved, and they were all forbidden to speak of it again.

That did not mean no one spoke of it. The Gnat did. When she was in a good mood, she'd settle for mocking him, calling him a faerie child, asking him where he kept his wings, pinching his back to see if she could find them. When she was in a rare foul temper, she'd tell him their grandmother was right, he was a monster and didn't belong, that their parents only had one real child. And even if it was all nonsense, as his mother and father claimed, *that* part was true—he no longer felt part of the family. They might not think him a changeling, but they all, in their own ways, blamed him. His parents blamed him for their humiliation. The Gnat blamed him for having to leave her friends and move. And his grandmother blamed him for whatever slight she could pin at his feet, and then she punished him for it.

He came to realize that the punishments were the purpose of the accusations rather than the result. His grandmother wanted an excuse to strap him or send him to bed without dinner. At first, he presumed she was upset because no one believed her story. That did not anger him. Nothing really angered him. Like happiness, the emotion was too intense, too uncomfortable. He looked at his sister, dancing about, chattering and giggling, and he thought her a fool. He looked at his grandmother, raging and snapping against him, and thought her the same. Foolish and weak, easily overcome by emotion.

He did not accept the punishments stoically, though. While he never complained, with each hungry night or sore bottom, something inside him hardened a bit more. He saw his grandmother, fumbling in her frustration, venting it on him, and he did not pity her. He hated her. He hated his parents, too, for pretending not to see the welts or the unfinished dinners. Most of all, he hated the Gnat, because she saw it all and delighted in it. She would watch him beaten to near tears with the strap, and then tell their grandmother that he'd broken her doll the week before, earning him three more lashes.

While there was certainly vindictiveness in the punishments, it seemed his grandmother actually had a greater plan. He realized this when she decided, one Sunday, that the two of them should take a trip to Cainsville. He even got to sit in the front seat of the station wagon, for the first time ever.

"Do you think I've mistreated you lately?" she asked as she drove.

It seemed a question not deserving a reply, so he didn't give one.

"Have you earned those punishments?" she said. "Did you do everything I said you did? That Natalie said you did?"

He sensed a trick, and again he didn't answer. She reached over and pinched his thigh hard enough to bring tears to his eyes.

"I asked you a question, parasite."

He glanced over.

"You know what that means, don't you?" she said. "Parasite?"

"I know many words."

Her lips twisted. "You do. Far more than a child should know. Because you are not a child. You are a parasite, put into our house to eat our food and sleep in our beds."

"There's no such thing as faeries."

She pinched him again, twisting the skin. He only glanced over with a look that had her releasing him fast, hand snapping back onto the steering wheel.

"You're a monster," she said. "Do you know that?"

No, you are, he thought, but he said nothing, staring instead at the passing scenery as they left the city. She drove onto the highway before she spoke again.

"You don't think you deserve to be punished, do you? You think I'm accusing you of things you didn't do, and your little sister is joining in, and your parents are turning a blind eye. Is that what you think?"

He shrugged.

"If it is, then you should tell someone," she said. "Someone who can help you."

He stayed quiet. There was a trick here, a dangerous one, and he might be smart for a little boy, as everyone told him, but he was not smart enough for this. So he kept his mouth shut. She drove a while longer before speaking again.

"You like the folks in Cainsville, don't you? The town elders."

Finally, something he could safely answer. She could find no fault in him liking old people. With relief, he nodded.

"They like you, too. They think you're special." Her hands tightened on the wheel. "I know why, too. I'm not a foolish old woman. I'm just as smart as you, boy. Especially when it comes to puzzles, and I've solved this one. I know where you came from."

He tried not to sigh, as the conversation swung back to dangerous territory. Perhaps he should be frightened, but after months of this, he was only tired.

"Do they ask you about us?" she said. "When they take you off on your special walks? Do they ask after your family?"

He nodded. "They ask if you are all well."

"And how we're treating you?"

He hesitated. It seemed an odd question, and he sensed the snare wire sneaking around his ankle again. After a moment, he shook his head. "They only ask if you're well and how I'm doing. How I like school and that."

"They're being careful," she muttered under her breath. "But they still ask how he is. Checking up on him."

"Gran?"

She tensed as he called her that. She always did these days and it was possible, just possible, that he used it more often because of that.

"You understand what honesty is, don't you, boy?"

He nodded.

"And respect for your elders."

It took him a half-second, but he nodded to this as well.

"Then you know you have to tell the truth when an adult asks you a question. You need to be honest, even if it might get someone in trouble. Always remember that."

⁂

While he liked all the elders in Cainsville, Mrs. Yates was his favorite, and he got the feeling he was hers, too. There had been a time when his grandmother had seemed almost jealous of her, when she would huff and sniff and say she thought Mrs. Yates was a very peculiar old woman. His parents had paid little attention—Gran had made it quite clear she thought everyone a little peculiar in Cainsville.

"There are no churches," she'd say. And his mother would sigh and explain—once again—that the town had started off too small for churches and by the time it was large enough, there was no place to put them, the settlement being nestled in the fork of a river, with marshy ground on the only open side. People still *went* to church. Just somewhere else.

It was his mother whose family was from Cainsville. Gran only accompanied them because she didn't like to be left out of family trips. She didn't like the town and she certainly didn't like Mrs. Yates. But that day, as she went off to visit his great-aunt, Gran sent him off with two dollars and a suggestion that he go see what Mrs. Yates was up to. Just be back by four so they could make it home in time for Sunday dinner.

He went to the new diner first. That's what everyone in Cainsville called it. The "new" diner, though it'd been there as long as he could remember. It still smelled new—the lemon-polished linoleum floors, the shiny red leather booths and even shinier chrome-plated chairs. The elders could often be found there, sipping tea by the windows as they watched the town go by. "Holding court," his grandmother would sniff—watching for mischief and waiting for folks to come by and pay their respects, like they were lords and ladies. He didn't see that at all. To him, they were simply there, in case anyone needed them.

Today, he found Mrs. Yates in her usual place. He thought she'd be surprised to see him, but she only smiled, her old face lighting up as she motioned him over.

"Mr. Shaw said he spotted your car coming into town," she said. "But I scarce dared believe it. Did I hear the rest right, too? Your gran brought you?"

He nodded.

"Does she know you're here?"

"She said I could come talk to you if I wanted."

Then he got his look of surprise, a widening of her blue eyes. "Did she now?"

He nodded again, and he expected her to be pleased, but while her eyes stayed kind, they narrowed too, as she surveyed him.

"Is everything all right, Bobby?"

He nodded without hesitation. Gran thought she was clever in her plan, that he would tattle on her to Mrs. Yates without realizing that's exactly what she wanted. He had no idea what she hoped to gain, but if Gran wanted it, he wasn't doing it.

"Are you sure?" Mrs. Yates said, those bright eyes piercing his. "Nothing is amiss at home?"

He shrugged. "My sister's annoying, but that's old news."

He thought she'd laugh, pat his arm and move on. That's what other grown-ups would do. But Mrs. Yates was not like other grown-ups, which was probably why he liked her so much. She kept studying him until, finally, she squeezed his shoulder and said, "All right, Bobby. If that's what you want. Now, do you have your list of gargoyles?"

He pulled the tattered notebook from his back pocket. He'd been working on it since he was old enough to write. Cainsville had gargoyles. Lots of them. For protection, the old people would say with a wink. Every year, as part of the May Day festival, children could show the elders their lists of all the gargoyles they'd located, and the winner would take a prize. If you found all of them, you'd get an actual gargoyle modeled after you. That hardly ever happened—there were only a few in town. It sounded easy, finding them all, and it should be, except many hid. There were gargoyles you could only see in the day or at night or when the light hit a certain way or, sometimes, just by chance. He'd been compiling his list for almost four years and he only had half of them, but he'd still come in second place last year.

"Let's go gargoyle hunting." Mrs. Yates got to her feet without groaning or pushing herself up, the way Gran and other old people did. She just stood, as easily as he would, and started for the door. "Now remember, I can't point them out to you. That's against the rules." She leaned down and whispered, "But I might give you a hint for one. Just one."

Behind them, the other elders chuckled, and Bobby and Mrs. Yates headed out into town.

※

He found one more gargoyle to add to his list, and he didn't even need Mrs. Yates's hint, so she promised to keep it for next time. They were going back to the diner and the promise of milkshakes when Mrs. Yates glanced down the walkway leading behind the bank.

"I think I hear the girls," she said. "Why don't you go play with them a while, and then bring them to the diner and we'll all have milkshakes."

He hesitated.

"You like Rose and Hannah, don't you?"

He nodded, and her smile broadened, telling him this was the right answer, so he added, "They're nice," to please her.

"They're very nice," she said. "I like to see you playing with them, Bobby. It's not easy for some children to find playmates. Some boys and girls are different, and other children don't always like different. You'll appreciate it more someday, when being different helps you stand out. But children don't always want to stand out, do they?"

He shook his head. She understood, as she always did. His parents lied and tried to pretend he wasn't different. She acknowledged it and understood it and made him feel better about it.

"Do you want to go play with the girls?"

He nodded. He *did* like the girls—Hannah, at least. What bothered him was the prospect of sharing Mrs. Yates with them later. But it would make her happy, and he was still her special favorite, so he shouldn't complain.

"Off you go then. Come to the diner later and we'll have those milkshakes."

⚜

Mrs. Yates said Hannah and Rose were in the small park behind the bank. They were often there on the swings, and when he rounded the corner, that's where he expected to see them. The swings were empty, though. He looked around the park, bordered by a fence topped with chimera heads. Walkways branched off in every compass direction. He heard Rose's voice, coming from the one leading to Rowan Street.

The girls crouched beside a toppled cardboard box. Hannah was reaching in and talking. He liked Hannah. Everyone liked Hannah. His mother said she reminded her of The Gnat, but she couldn't be more wrong. Yes, Hannah was pretty, with brown curls and dark eyes and freckles across her nose. And, like The Gnat, she was always laughing, always bouncing around, chattering. But with Hannah, it was *real*. The Gnat only acted that way because it tricked people into liking her.

Rose was different. Very different. She was a year younger than Bobby and Hannah, but she acted like a teenager, and she looked at you like she could see right through you and wasn't sure she liked what she saw. She had black straight hair and weirdly cold blue eyes that blasted through him. She wasn't pretty and she never giggled—she rarely even laughed, unless she was with Hannah.

Rose saw him coming first, though it always felt like "saw" wasn't the right word. Rose seemed to sense him coming. She stood and when she fixed those blue eyes on him, he quailed as he always did, falling back a step before reminding himself he had done nothing wrong. Rose only tilted her head, and when she spoke, her rough voice was kind.

"Are you okay, Bobby?"

"Sure."

Her lips pursed, as if calling him a liar, then she waved for him to join them. As he stepped up beside the girls, he was chagrined to realize that as much as he'd grown in the last few months, Rose had grown more. She might be only seven and a girl, but he barely came up to her eyebrows. She moved back to let him stand beside Hannah.

"See what we found?" Hannah said.

It was a cat, with four kittens, all tabbies like the momma, except the smallest, which was ink black.

"Show him what you can do," Rose said.

Hannah glanced up, her forehead creasing with worry.

"Go on," Rose said. "Bobby can keep a secret. Show him."

He looked at Rose, and she nodded, giving him a small smile—a sympathetic smile, as if she knew what he was going through and wanted Hannah to share her secret to make him feel better. He bristled. He didn't want her sympathy. Didn't need it. But he did want the secret, so he let Rose cajole Hannah until she blurted it out.

"I can talk to animals." Hannah paused, face reddening. "No, that doesn't sound right. It's not like Dr. Dolittle. I don't hear them talk. Animals don't talk. But they do…" She turned to Rose. "What's the word you used?"

"Communicate."

Hannah nodded. "They communicate. I can understand them, and they can understand me."

He must have seemed skeptical, because her face went the color of apples in autumn.

"See?" she hissed at Rose. "This is why I can't tell anyone. They'll think I'm crazy."

"I don't think you're crazy," he said. "But you're right—you probably shouldn't tell anyone else."

Hannah's gaze dropped, and he felt bad. Like maybe he should tell her about the dreams and how he admitted it to Gran, and what happened next.

Did they know what happened? His grandmother always said Cainsville was a "backwater nowhere" town, where they lived like they weren't sixty miles from one of the biggest cities in America. Gran said they were ignorant, and they liked it that way. They didn't read newspapers, didn't listen to the news or even watch it on television. That wasn't true. He'd once told Mrs. Yates about going to the site of the World Fair, and she'd known all about it. She'd told him stories about the fair, the sights and sounds and even the smells. He'd gotten an A on his paper and his teacher said it was almost like he'd been there. He'd asked Mrs. Yates if *she'd* been there, and she'd laughed and said she wasn't *that* old. No one was. So people in Cainsville weren't ignorant, but he supposed that knowing about the 1893 World Fair wasn't the same as knowing what his teacher called "current events."

"You shouldn't tell *everyone*," Rose said to Hannah. "Definitely not anyone outside Cainsville. But no one here will think you're crazy." She nudged Hannah with her sneaker. "Tell him about the black kitten."

Hannah took more prodding, but when Bobby expressed an interest, she finally stood and said, "He's sick. Momma Cat is worried he's going to die. He doesn't get enough to eat because he's smaller than the others."

"He's not that much smaller."

"He's different," Rose said. "That's why they won't let him eat very much. I think he's a matagot. That's what we were talking about when you came up."

"A matagot?"

"Magician's cat," Rose said, as matter-of-factly as if she'd said the cat was a Siamese. "It's a spirit that's taken the form of a black cat."

"They say that if you keep one and treat it well, it will reward you with a gold piece every day," Hannah said.

"Gold?" he said.

Something in his tone made Rose tense—or maybe it was the way he looked at the black kitten. Hannah only giggled.

"It's not true, silly," Hannah said. "Magic doesn't work that way. Not real magic."

"What do you know about real magic?"

She shrugged. "Enough. I know it can make gargoyles disappear in daylight and tomato plants grow straight and true. I know it can let some people read omens—like old Mrs. Carew—and some see the future, like Rose's Nana Walsh."

He turned to Rose. "Your grandmother can see the future?"

"Futures," she said. "There's more than one. It's all about choices."

He didn't understand that, but pushed on. "If I asked her to see my futures—"

"You can't," Hannah cut in. "Not unless you can talk to ghosts. I'm not sure anyone can talk to ghosts. If there are ghosts." She turned to Rose, as if she was the older, wiser girl.

"There are," Rose said. "Those with the sight sometimes say they see them. Others can, too. But most times when a person says they're seeing ghosts it's their imagination. Even if you can talk to them I'm not sure why you'd want to."

Hannah nodded, and his gaze shot from one girl to the other, unable to believe they were talking about such things seriously. Kids at school would call them babies for believing in magic. His parents would call it ungodly. His grandmother would probably call them changelings.

"About the cat. The...matagot." He stumbled over the foreign word.

"We don't know if it is one," Rose said. "Hannah says his mother thinks he's strange. She still loves him, though."

"As she should," Hannah said. "There's nothing wrong with strange."

Rose nodded. "But we're worried."

"Very worried." Hannah knelt beside the box where the mother cat was licking the black kitten's head. "Momma Cat is even more worried. Aren't you?"

The cat *mrrowed* deep in its throat and looked up at Hannah. Then she nosed the kitten away from her side.

"I think she's going to drive it off," Bobby said. "They do that sometimes. With the weak, the ones that are different."

Hannah shook her head, curls bouncing. "No, she's asking me to take it."

"You should," Rose said. "Your parents would let you."

"I know. I just hate taking a kitten from its mother."

The cat nosed the kitten again and meowed. Hannah nodded, said, "I understand," and very gently lifted the little black ball in both hands. The cat meowed again, but it didn't sound like protest. She gave the black kitten one last look, then shifted, letting its siblings fill the empty space against her belly.

"You'll need to feed it with a dropper," Rose said. "We can get books at the library and talk to the vet when she comes back through town."

Hannah nodded. "I'll take him home first and ask Mom to watch him."

They got to the end of the walkway before they seemed to realize he wasn't following. They turned.

"Do you want to come with us?" Hannah asked.

He did, but he wanted the milkshake with Mrs. Yates too, and if the girls were busy, he'd get the old woman all to himself.

"I told Mrs. Yates I'd meet her at the diner," he said, not mentioning the milkshakes.

Rose nodded. "Then you should do that. We'll see you later."

"Is your family coming for Samhain?" Hannah asked.

"I think we are."

Hannah smiled. "I hope so."

"Make sure you do," Rose said. "It's more fun when you're here."

He couldn't tell if she meant it or was just being nice, but it felt good to hear her say it and even better when Hannah nodded enthusiastically. He said he'd be back for Samhain, and went to find Mrs. Yates.

⇥✳⇤

On the way home, his grandmother asked about his visit with Mrs. Yates. She was trying to get him to admit that he'd tattled on her. Even if he had, he certainly wouldn't admit it. His grandmother might say he was too smart for his age, but sometimes she acted as if he was dumber than The Gnat. Finally, she pulled off the highway, turned in her seat and said, "Did Mrs. Yates ask how things were at home?"

"Yes."

"And what did you tell her?"

"That they were fine."

She put her hand on his shoulder. It was the first time since he'd admitted to the dreams that she'd voluntarily touched him, except to pinch or slap.

"You know it's a sin to lie, Bobby."

"I do."

"Then tell me the truth. Did you say more?"

He hesitated. Nibbled his lip. Then said, "I told her Natalie was being a pest."

Her mouth pressed into a thin line. "That's not what I mean."

"But you asked—"

"Did you say *anything* more?"

"No." He hid his smile. "Not a word."

>|<

A month later, as Samhain drew near, he mentioned it over dinner.

"We aren't going," his mother said quietly.

"What?"

"Gran feels Cainsville isn't a good influence on you right now."

He shot a look at his grandmother, who returned a small, smug smile and ate another forkful of peas.

"Remember what happened when you visited last month?" his father said. "You came home and you were quite a little terror."

That was a lie. His grandmother had punished him twice as much after they got back, making up twice as many stories about him misbehaving. He'd thought she was just angry because her plan—whatever it had been—failed.

Gran's smile widened, her false teeth shining as she watched him.

"I don't care," the Gnat said. "I hate Cainsville. It's boring."

His grandmother patted her head. "I agree."

He shot to his feet.

"Bobby..." his father said.

"May I be excused?" he asked.

His father sighed. "If you're done."

Bobby walked to his room, trying very hard not to run in and slam the door. Once he got there, he fell facedown on his bed. The door clicked open. His grandmother walked in.

"You're a very stupid little beast," she said. "You should have told the elders. They'd take you back."

He flipped over to look at her.

"If you're being mistreated, they'll take you back," she said. "But you didn't tell them, so now we have to wait for them to come to us. I'll make sure they come to us."

❋

His grandmother soon discovered another flaw in her plan. Two, actually. First, that whoever she thought would "come for him" was not coming, no matter how harsh her punishments. Second, that his parents' blindness had limits.

As the months of abuse had passed, he'd come to accept that his parents weren't really as oblivious as they pretended. Nor were they as enlightened as they thought. Even if they'd never admit it, there seemed to be a part of them that thought his grandmother's wild accusation was true. Or perhaps it was not that they actually believed him a changeling faerie child, but that they thought there was something wrong, terribly wrong, with him. He was different. Odd. Too distant and too cold. His sister hated him. Other children avoided him. Like animals, they sensed something was off and steered clear. Perhaps, then, the beatings would help. Not that they'd ever admit such a thing—heavens no, they were modern parents— but if he didn't complain, then perhaps neither should they.

They did have limits, though. When the sore spots became bruises and then welts, they objected. What would the neighbors think? Or, worse, his teachers, who might call children's services. Hadn't the family been through enough? Gran could punish him if he misbehaved, but she must use a lighter hand.

That did not solve the problem, but it opened a door. A possibility. That door cracked open a little more when his mother received a call at work from one of the elders, who wondered why they hadn't seen the Sheehan family in so long. Was everything all right? His mother said it was, but when she reported the call at home, over dinner, his grandmother fairly gnashed her teeth. His mother noticed and asked what was wrong, and Gran said nothing but still, his mother *had* noticed. He tucked that away and remembered it.

Christmas came, and he waited until he was alone in the house with his mother, and asked if they'd visit family in Cainsville. His mother wavered. And he was ready.

"Your grandmother doesn't think you're ready," she said as they sat in front of the television, wrapping gifts.

"I've been much better," he said.

"I'm not sure that you have."

He stretched tape over a seam. "I don't think I'm as bad as Gran says. I think she's still mad at me because we had to move."

A soft sigh, but his mother said nothing. He finished his package and took another.

"I think she might exaggerate sometimes," he said quietly. "I think Natalie might, too. I sometimes get the feeling they don't like me very much."

Of course his mother had to protest that, but her protests were muted, as if she couldn't work up true conviction.

"If you don't see me misbehaving, maybe I'm not," he said. "I do, sometimes. All kids do. But maybe it's not quite as much as Gran and Natalie say."

He worded it all so carefully. Not blaming anyone. Only giving his opinion, as a child. His mother went silent, wrapping her gift while nibbling her lower lip, the same way he did when he was thinking.

"I have friends in Cainsville," he said. "Little girls who like playing with me. They're very nice girls."

"Hannah and Rose," his mother said. "I like Hannah. Rose is…"

"Different," he said. "Like me. But she's not mean and she doesn't misbehave. She hardly ever gets in trouble. Even less than Hannah."

"Rose is a very serious girl," she said. "Like you. I can see why you'd like her."

"I do. I miss them. I promise if we go to Cainsville, I'll be better than ever." He clipped off a piece of ribbon. "And they *are* your family. You want to see them. Gran never liked Cainsville, so she's happy if we don't go."

"That's true," his mother murmured, and with that, he knew he'd won an ally in his fight to return to Cainsville. But as he soon learned, it hardly mattered at all. His mother had a job, just like a man, but she didn't make a lot of money, and his father always joked that it was more a hobby than an occupation, which made his mother angry. That meant, though, that his father was the head of the house. As it should be, Gran would say, and she could, because there was only one person his father always listened to—his own mother, Gran. If Bobby's grandmother said no to Cainsville, then they would not be going to Cainsville and that was that.

Gran said no to Cainsville.

No to Cainsville for the holidays. No to Cainsville for Candlemas. No to Cainsville for May Day.

It was the last that broke him. May Day was his favorite holiday, with the gargoyle hunt contest, which he was almost certain to win this year, according to Mrs. Yates.

He *would* go to Cainsville for May Day. All he had to do was eliminate the obstacle.

Everyone always told him how smart he was. Part of that was his memory. He heard things, and if he thought they might be important, he filed the information away as neatly as his father filed papers in his basement office. A year ago, his grandmother had admitted to feeding him one of her heart medicine pills. Father Joseph had been horrified—digitalis was foxglove, which was poison. Bobby had mentally filed those details and now, when he needed it, he tugged them out and set off for the library, where he read everything he found on the subject. Then he began stealing pills from Gran's bottle, one every third day. After two weeks, he had enough. He ground them up and put them in her dinner. And she died. There were a few steps in between—the heart attack, the ambulance, the hospital bed, his parents and the Gnat sobbing and praying—but in the end, he got what he wanted. Gran died and the obstacle was removed, and with it, he got an unexpected gift, one that made him wish he'd taken this step months ago, because as his grandmother breathed her last and he stood beside her bed, watching, he finally heard the screams of dragons.

It started slow, quiet even. Like a humming deep in his skull. Then it grew and the humming became a strange vibrating cry, somewhere between a roar and a scream. Finally, when it crescendoed, he couldn't even have said what it sounded like. It was *all* sounds, at once, so loud that he burst out in a sob, hands going to his ears as he doubled over.

His mother caught him and held him and rubbed his back and said it would be okay, it would all be okay, Gran was in a better place now. Yet the dragons kept screaming until he pushed her aside and ran from the hospital room. He ran and he ran until he was out some back door, in a tiny yard. Then he collapsed, hugging his knees as he listened to the dragons.

That's what he did—he listened. He didn't try to block them, to stop them. This was what he'd dreamed of and now he had it, and it was horrible and terrible and incredible all at once. He hunkered down there, committing them to memory as methodically as he had the dreams of golden palaces and endless meadows. Finally, when they faded, he went back inside, snuffling and gasping for breath, his face streaked with tears. His parents found him like that, grieving they thought, and it was what they wanted to see, proof that he was just a normal little boy, and they were, in their own grief, happy.

※

He waited until three days after the funeral to broach the subject of Cainsville. He would have liked to have waited longer, but it was already April 27, and he'd given great thought to the exact timing—how late could he wait before it was too late to plan a May Day trip? April 27 seemed right.

After he'd gone to bed, he slipped back out and found his parents in the living room, reading. He stood between them and cleared his throat.

"Yes, Bobby?" his mother said, lowering her book.

"I've been thinking," he said. "Natalie's so upset about Gran. We all are, of course, but Natalie most of all."

His mother sighed. "I know."

"So I was thinking of ways to cheer her up."

As he expected, this was about the best thing he could have said. His mother's eyes lit up and his father lowered his newspaper.

"It's May Day this weekend," Bobby said. "I know Natalie thinks Cainsville is boring, but she always liked May Day."

"That's true." His mother snuck a glance at his father. "Last year, she asked if we were going before Bobby did."

"I thought we might go," he said. "For Natalie."

His father smiled and reached to rumple Bobby's hair. "That's a fine idea, son. I believe we will."

⋇

Rose knew what he'd done. He saw it in her eyes as he walked over to her and Hannah, cutting flowers before the May Day festivities began. Rose saw him coming and straightened fast, fixing him with those pale blue eyes. Then she laid her hand on Hannah's shoulder, as if ready to tug her friend away.

Hannah looked up at Rose's touch. She saw him and grinned, a bright sunshine grin, as she rose and brushed off the bare knees under her short, flowered dress. Rose kept hold of her friend's shoulder, though, and squeezed. Hannah hesitated.

He stopped short. Then he glanced to the side, pretending he'd heard someone call his name, an excuse to walk away. He headed toward one of the elders, setting out pies. The pie table was close enough for him to hear the girls.

Rose spoke first. "I had a dream about Bobby," she whispered.

Hannah giggled. "He is kind of cute."

"Not like *that*."

Hannah went serious. "You mean one of *those* dreams?"

"I don't know. There were dragons."

He stiffened and stood there, blueberry pie in hand, straining to listen to the girls behind him.

"Dragons?" Hannah said.

"He was hunting them."

"I bet they were gargoyles. He's really good at finding them. He has twice as many as I do, and he doesn't even live here."

"He killed one," Rose said.

"A gargoyle?"

"A dragon. An old one. She was blocking his way, and he fed her fox-glove flowers, and she started to scream."

His stomach twisted so suddenly that he doubled over, the elder grabbing his arm to steady him, asking if he was all right, and he said yes, quickly, pushing her off as politely as he could and taking another pie from the box as he struggled to listen.

"That's one freaky dream, Rosie," Hannah was saying.

"I know."

"I think it just means he's going to win the gargoyle contest."

"Probably, but it felt like…" Rose drifted off. "No, I'm being stupid."

"You're never stupid. You just think too much sometimes."

Rose chuckled. "My mom says the same thing."

"Because she's smart, like you. Now, let's go ask if Bobby wants to come see Mattie."

The *tap-tap* of fancy shoes. Then a finger poked his back.

"Bobby?"

He turned to Hannah, smiling at him.

"We're glad you came," she said. "We missed you."

He nodded.

"It's not time for the festival yet. Do you want to come see Mattie?"

"That's what she named the kitten," Rose said, walking up behind her friend. "Short for matagot."

"No, short for Matthew."

Rose rolled her eyes. "Whatever you say."

Hannah pretended to swat her, then put her arm through Bobby's. As she did, Rose tensed and rocked forward, like she wanted to pull Hannah away. She stopped herself, but fixed him with that strange look. Like she knew what he'd done. With that look, he knew Rose had a power, like Hannah. And him? He had nothing except taunting dreams of castles and meadows, and the screams of dragons, fading so fast he could barely remember the sound at all.

"Smile, Bobby," Hannah said, squeezing his arm. "It's May Day, and we're going to have fun." She grinned. "We'll always have fun together."

He won the gargoyle hunt that year. The next year, too. They went to Cainsville for all the festivals and sometimes he and his mother just went to visit. Life was good, and not just because Gran was dead and he'd gotten Cainsville back, but because he'd learned a valuable lesson. He did not have powers. He would likely never have them. But he did have a power inside him—the screams of dragons.

He would admit that when he killed his grandmother, he thought he'd suffer for it. He'd be caught and even if he wasn't, it would be as Father Joseph preached—he would be forever damned in the prison of his own mind, tormented by his sins. Father Joseph had lied. Or, more likely, he simply didn't understand boys like Bobby.

No one ever suspected anything but a natural death, and his life turned for the better after that. He learned how to win his parents' sympathy if not their love. To turn them, just a little, to his side, away from the Gnat. He learned, too, how to deal with her. That took longer and started at school, with other children, the ones who bullied and taunted him.

He decided to show those children why he should not be bullied or taunted. One by one, he showed them. Little things for some, like spoiling a lunch every day. Bigger things for others. With one boy, he loosened the seat on his bike, and he fell and hit his head on the curb and had to go away, people whispering that he'd never be quite right again.

Bobby took his revenge, and then let the boys know it was him, and when they tattled, he cried and pretended he didn't know what was happening, why they were accusing him—they'd always hated him, always mocked and beat him, and the teachers knew that was true, and his tears and his lies were good enough to convince them that he was the victim. Each time he won, he would hear the dragons scream again, and he'd know he'd done well.

Once he'd perfected his game, he played it against the Gnat. For her eighth birthday, their parents gave her a pretty little parakeet that she adored. One day, after she'd called him a monster and scratched him hard enough to draw blood, he warned that she shouldn't let the bird fly about, it might fly right out the door.

"I'm not stupid," she said. "I don't open the doors when she's out." She paused, then scowled at him. "And you'd better not either."

"I wouldn't do that," he said. And the next time she let the bird out, he lured it with treats to his parents room, where the window was open, just enough.

He even helped her search for her bird. Then she discovered the open window.

"You did it!" she shouted.

She rushed at him, fingers like claws, scratching down his arm. He howled. His parents came running. The Gnat pointed at the window.

"Look what he did. He let her out!"

His father cleared his throat. "I'm afraid I left that open, sweetheart."

"You shouldn't have let the bird out of her cage," his mother said, steering the Gnat off with promises of ice cream. "You know we warned you about that."

The Gnat turned to him. He smiled, just for a second, just enough to let her know. Then he joined them in the kitchen where his mother gave him extra ice cream for being so nice and helping his little sister hunt for her bird.

⇥∦⇤

The Screams of Dragons | KELLEY ARMSTRONG

The Gnat wasn't that easily cowed. She only grew craftier. Six months later, their parents bought her another parakeet. She kept it in its cage and warned him that if it escaped, they'd all know who did it. He told her to be nicer to him and that wouldn't be a problem. She laughed. Three months later, she came home from school to find her bird lying on the floor of its cage, dead. His parents called it a natural death. The Gnat knew better, and after that, she stayed as far from him as she could.

While his life outside Cainsville improved, his visits to the town darkened, as if there was a finite amount of good in his life, and to shift more to one place robbed it from the other.

He blamed Rose. After her dream of the dragon, she'd been nicer to him, apparently deciding it had been no more than a dream. Unlike Hannah's power, Rose's came in fits and starts, mingling prophecy and fantasy.

But then, after he did particularly bad things back home—like loosening the bike seat or killing the bird—he'd come to Cainsville and she'd stare at him, as if trying to peer into his soul. After a few times, she seemed to decide that where there were dragons, there was fire, and if she was having these dreams, they meant something. Something bad.

Rose started avoiding him. Worse, she made Hannah do the same. He'd come to town and they'd be off someplace and no one knew where to find them—not until it was nearly time for him to go, and they'd appear, and Rose would say, "Oh, are you leaving? So sorry we missed you."

Soon, it wasn't just Rose looking at him funny. All the elders did. Still, Mrs. Yates stuck by him, meeting him each time he visited, taking him for walks. Only now her questions weren't quite so gentle. *Is everything all right, Bobby? Are you sure? Is there anything you want to tell me? Anything at all?*

It didn't help that he'd begun doing things even *he* knew were wrong. It wasn't his fault. The dreams of golden castles and endless meadows had begun to fade when he'd turned nine. It did not directly coincide with the first screams of the dragons, but it was close enough that he'd suspected there was a correlation. Even when he stopped tormenting his tormenters, and let the screams of dragons ebb, the dreams of the golden world continued to fade, until he was forced to accept that it was simply the passing of time. As he aged, those childish fancies slid away, and all he had left were the dragons. So he indulged them. Fed them well and learned to delight in their screams as much as he had those pretty dreams.

There were times when he swore he could hear his grandmother's voice in his ear, calling him a nasty boy, a wicked boy. And when he did, he would smile, knowing he was feeding the dragons properly. But they took much feeding, and it wasn't long before no one tormented him and there were no worthy targets for his wickedness. He had to find targets and, increasingly, they were less worthy, until finally, by the time he turned twelve, many were innocent of any crime against him. But the dragons had to be fed.

That summer, his mother took him to Cainsville two days after he'd done something particularly wicked, particularly cruel, and when he arrived at the new diner, the elders were not there. Even Mrs. Yates was gone. He'd walked to her house and then to the schoolyard, where they sometimes sat and watched the children play. He found her there, with the others, as a group of little ones played tag.

When she saw him, she'd risen, walked over and said he should go to the new diner and have a milkshake and she'd meet him there later. She'd even given him three dollars for the treat. But he'd looked at the children, and he'd looked at her, standing between him and the little ones, guarding them against him, and he'd let the three bills fall to the ground and stalked off to talk to Rose.

He found her at her one brother's place. Rose was the youngest. A "whoops" everyone said, and he hadn't known what that meant until he was old enough to understand where babies came from and figured out that she'd been an accident, born when her mother was nearly fifty. This brother was twenty-nine, married, with a little girl of his own. That's where Rose was—babysitting her niece.

Bobby snuck around back and found the little girl playing in a sand-box. She couldn't be more than three, thin with black hair. He watched her and considered all the ways he could repay Rose for her treachery.

"What are you doing here?" a low voice came from behind him. He turned to see Rose, coming out of the house with a sipping cup and a bottle of Coke. Like Mrs. Yates, she moved between him and the child. Then she leaned over and whispered, "Take this and go inside, Seanna. I'll be there in a minute, and we'll read a book together."

She handed the little girl the sipping cup and watched her toddle off. Then she turned to him. "Why are you here, Bobby?"

"I want to know what you told the elders about me."

"About you?" Her face screwed up. "Nothing. Why?"

He stepped toward her. "I know you told them something."

She stood her ground, chin lifting, pale eyes meeting his. "Is there something to tell?"

"No."

"Then you don't have anything to worry about."

She started to turn away. He grabbed her elbow. She threw him off fast, dropping the bottle and not even flinching when it shattered on the paving stones.

"I didn't tell anyone anything," she said. "I don't have anything to tell."

"Bull. I've seen the way you look at me, and now they're doing it, too."

"Maybe because we're all wondering what's wrong. Why you've changed. You used to be a scared little boy, and now you're not, and that would be good, but there's this thing you do, staring at people with this expression in your eyes and…" She inhaled. "I didn't tell the elders anything."

"Yes, you did. You had a vision about me. A fake vision. And you told."

"No, I didn't. Now, I can't leave Seanna alone—"

He grabbed her wrist, fingers digging in as he wrenched her back to face him. "Tell me."

She struggled in his grip. "Let me—"

He slapped her, so hard her head whipped around, and when it whipped back, there was a snarl on her lips. She kicked and clawed, and he released her fast, stepping back. She hit him then. Like a boy. Plowed him in the jaw and when he fell, she stood over him and bent down.

"You ever hit me again, Bobby Sheehan, and I'll give you a choice. Either you'll confess it to the elders or I'll thrash you so hard you'll wish you *had* confessed. I didn't tattle on you. Now leave me alone."

"You think you're so special," he called as she climbed the back steps. "You and your second sight."

"Special?" She gave a strange little laugh, and when she turned, she looked ten years older. "No, Bobby Sheehan, I don't think I'm special. Most times, I think I'm cursed. I know you're jealous of us, with our powers, but you wouldn't want them. Not for a second. It changes everything." She glanced down at him, still on the ground. "Be happy with what you have."

⋇

He was not happy with what he had. As the year passed, he became even less happy with it, more convinced that Rose and the elders were spying on him from afar. Spying on his thoughts. This was not paranoia. Twice, after he'd done something moderately wicked, his mother got a call at work. Once from Mrs. Yates and once from Rose's mother.

"Just asking how you are," his mother said over dinner after the second call. She slid him a secret smile. "I think Rose might be sweet on you. She seems like a nice girl."

"Her family's not nice," the Gnat said as she took a forkful of meatloaf. "Her one brother's in jail."

His mother looked over sharply. "No, he isn't. He's in the army. Don't spread nasty gossip—"

"It's not gossip. I heard it in town. He's in jail for fraud, and so was Rose's dad, for a while, years ago, and no one thinks there's anything weird about that. I overheard someone say the whole family is into stuff like that. They're con artists. Only the people saying it acted like it was a regular job." She scrunched up her freckled nose. "Isn't that freaky? The whole town is—"

"Enough," his mother said. "I think someone's pulling your leg, young lady. There is nothing wrong with Rose Walsh or her family. They're fine people."

For once, he believed the Gnat. He'd wondered about Rose's brother ever since he took off a few years ago and Rose said he'd joined the army to fight in Vietnam, but he'd been over thirty, awfully old to sign up.

Con artists. That explained a lot. Rose was conning the elders right now, telling them stories about him. Trying to con him, too, into not wanting powers. He did. He wanted them more than anything. And he was going to find a way to get them.

He spent months researching how to steal powers and learned nothing useful. It did not seem as if it could be done, and the more he failed to find an answer, the more the jealousy gnawed at him, and the harder it was to focus on keeping the dragons fed and happy. He had to do worse and worse things, and it made him feel even guiltier about them. Together with the jealousy, it was like his stomach was on fire all the time. He couldn't eat. He started losing weight.

He had to go back to Cainsville. At the very least, the visit would calm the gnawing in his stomach and let him eat. He would talk his mother into a special trip to Cainsville and he would go see Hannah. Not the elders. Not Mrs. Yates. Certainly not Rose. No, he'd visit Hannah. She'd help him set things right.

His plan worked so beautifully that he felt as if the success was a sign. His luck was turning. He asked his mother to go and off they went that Sunday. He arrived to hear that Rose was in the city, and he found Hannah in the playground, tending to an injured baby owl.

"Did a cat get it?" he asked as he walked over.

She'd started at the sound of a voice, and he expected that when she saw it was him, she'd smile. She didn't. She scooped up the owl and stood.

"Bobby," she said. "I didn't know you were coming today."

"Surprise." He grinned, but she didn't grin back. Didn't even fake it. Just watched him as he opened the gate and walked in. "Is the owl all right?"

She hesitated, then shook her head. "Something got him. Maybe a cat. He's dying." Another pause. "That's the worst part. When they're hurt and I can't help."

"You can put it out of its misery."

She almost dropped the fledgling. "What?"

"I can do it. Mercifully. Then you won't need to feel bad because you can't help."

She stared at him like he'd suggested murdering her mother for pocket change. One of the dragons roared, a white-hot burst of flame that blazed through him.

"I'm thinking of you," he said, glowering at her.

"And I'm *not*. That isn't how it works. Rose said you…" she trailed off.

"Rose said *what*." He stepped forward.

Hannah shrank, but only a little, before straightening. "That you don't understand about the powers. You think they're this great gift. There are good parts, sure, but bad, too. Lots of bad. I woke up in the middle of the night last week because a dog had been hit by a car. I ran out of the house and my mom helped me take it to the vet's, but there was nothing we could do. It was horrible. Just horrible. And I felt it—all of it. But the only thing that made that dog feel better was having me there through the whole thing, no matter how hard it was. So I did it. Because that's my responsibility."

Then you're a fool, he thought. *The dog wouldn't have helped you. It would have left you by the road to die.* He didn't say that, because when he looked at her, getting worked up, all he could think was how pretty she'd gotten. Prettier than any girl in his class, and he wanted to reach out and touch her, and when the impulse came, it was like throwing open a locked door. This was how he could steal her power. Touch her, kiss her…

He bit his lip and rocked back on his heels. "I'm sorry, Hannah. I wasn't thinking. My dad always said a quick death is better than suffering, and that's what I meant. Help you *and* help the baby owl." He met her gaze. "I'm sorry."

She nodded. "It's all right. I'm just feeling bad about it." She set the fledgling back on the ground.

"I know." He stepped closer. "I wish I could make you feel better."

Another nod, and in a blink, he was there, his arms going around her, his lips to hers. It wasn't the first time he kissed a girl. He'd done more than kiss them, too. Sometimes that was him being wicked, but most times, he didn't need to be—he knew how to say the right things. A *little charmer*, that's what his mother called him, obviously relieved that her sullen boy had turned out so well.

So he kissed Hannah. It was a good kiss. A sweet and gentle one, for a sweet and gentle girl. But she jerked back and pushed him away hard, as if he'd jumped on her.

"I-I'm sorry, Bobby," she said. "I have a boyfriend."

He was about to say "Who?" when he saw her expression.

Liar.

The dragon whipped its tail inside him, lighting his gut on fire. He forced it to settle. He wouldn't be wicked with Hannah. He just wouldn't. Not unless he had to.

"It's Rose, isn't it?" he said, stepping back, looking down at his sneakers. "She doesn't like me. She has dreams about me—about a dragon. She told me that, but I don't understand what it means."

"She doesn't either. What did she tell you?"

He shrugged and continued the lie. "Something about a dragon. That's all I know."

"It's two dragons. She dreams they're fighting over you and screaming awful screams. Then one wins and it...it..."

"It what?"

"Devours you," she blurted. "We don't know what it means."

"What do the elders say?"

"Elders?" She frowned at him. "We wouldn't tell the elders. Rose looked it up in books. She has lots of books from her Nana. Some talk about the sight and dreams, but she can't figure this one out."

"So she's never told the elders? About me?"

"Of course not. What's there to tell?"

He bit his lip. "I get the feeling Rose doesn't like me very much anymore." He lifted his gaze to hers. "I get the feeling you don't either."

"I..." She swallowed. "I'm fine, Bobby, I just—"

He grabbed her around the waist and kissed her again. This time when she struggled he held on, kept kissing her, and the more she fought, the more certain he was that this was the answer. She had the power. Touch her. Kiss her—

She kneed him between the legs.

He gasped and fell back. "You little—"

"What's happened to you, Bobby?" she said as she scooped up the bird and backed away. "You never used to be like this."

"I just wanted to kiss you. You didn't need to—"

"That wasn't kissing me. That was hurting me. You want to know why I don't like you as much?" She held up the owl. "Because they don't. The animals. You scare them and you scare me."

She cradled the fledgling against her chest and ran off, leaving him there, gasping for breath in the playground.

※

He started walking, not knowing where he was going, spurred by the fire in his gut, a fire that seeped into his brain, blinding him. When the rage-fog cleared, he found himself on Hannah's street. And there, crossing the road, was what he'd come to find, though he only knew as he saw it.

The black cat. Hannah's matagot kitten. A middle-aged cat now, slinking arrogantly across the street without even bothering to look, as if no car would dare mow it down.

He followed the beast, waiting for it to get to a secluded spot. In Cainsville, though, there weren't any secluded spots. When he'd been young, he'd felt as if he was being merely observed, someone always watching over him, keeping him safe, and he'd loved that. Now it felt as if he was being spied on, judgmental eyes tracking his every move. They weren't, of course. As he moved, he'd sometimes see someone peek out from a house, but they'd only smile and nod. He might be thirteen, but here he was still a child, innocently out playing hide-and-seek or tag with his friends. He could cut through yards and steal behind garages and no one would ever come out to warn him off as they would in the city.

Eventually, the cat stopped prowling, and did so in one of the rare secluded spots around—the yard of an empty house. Cainsville had a few of them, not abandoned but empty. This one was surrounded by a rare solid fence for privacy, and once Bobby was in that yard, he was hidden. That is where the beast stopped to clean itself, proving that whatever airs cats might put on, they were very stupid beasts.

As he crept up behind the cat, his hands flexed at his sides. He had to grab it just right or it would yowl. Pounce and snatch. That was the trick. Scoop it up by the neck, away from scrabbling claws and then squeeze. It was simpler than one might think, particularly when the beast was so preoccupied that it didn't turn even when his foot accidentally scraped a paving stone.

He got as close as he dared. Then he sprang.

The cat whipped around and leaped at him. The shock of seeing that stopped him for a split second, and before he could recover, the cat was on him, scratching and biting, and it was like Rose and Hannah all over again, fighting like wild animals, only this animal had razor claws and fangs, and when he finally threw the beast off, blood dripped from his arms and his face.

He ran at the cat, but it bounded away, leaped onto the fence and turned to hiss at him, almost half-heartedly, as if he wasn't worth the effort. He glowered at the beast then stomped toward the gate. When he swung it open, someone was standing there. Three someones. Mrs. Yates and two of the other elders.

"What have you done, Bobby," Mrs. Yates said, her voice low.

"Me?" He lifted his blood-streaked hands. "Ask that damned cat. I was trying to rescue it for Hannah."

"No," she said. "That isn't what you were doing at all."

"I don't know what you mean. If Hannah told you—"

"Hannah told us nothing. She doesn't need to. We know."

He looked at her, and then at the other two elders, and *he* knew, too. Knew the truth he hadn't dared admit. The girls weren't tattling on him. It was the elders, burrowing into his head, reading all his most wicked thoughts, seeing all his most wicked deeds.

He managed to pull himself up straight and say, "You're all crazy." Then he pushed past them and raced back to his mother.

⁂

It was the old story. The one where he'd first heard about the screams of dragons. It was coming true. All of it. First the dragons. Then his stomach, twisting and hurting so much these days that he couldn't eat—just like the king couldn't eat because his food went missing. Now the people who could hear everything. The elders and Rose. They knew what he was doing even when he didn't speak a word. He could not escape them, again like the king in the story.

That's why he used to dream of castles. He wasn't a changeling child. He was a king—or he had been—and the old story was replaying itself, consuming him and his life.

After that last trip to Cainsville, the elders were no longer content with the occasional call to check on him. Twice they'd shown up at his house. His *house*. Mrs. Yates had taken him aside and tried to talk to him, prodding him hard now with her questions, telling him she was worried, *so worried*. If only he'd talk to them, they might be able to help.

Liar.

They didn't care about him. They came as a warning. Letting him know they were in his head, watching and judging. Letting him know they were going to win. He was just a little boy. He would be consumed by them—the dragons—as Rose's dreams predicted. It all made sense now, or it did, the more he thought about it, obsessed on it, dreamed of it. It was like a puzzle where the pieces don't seem to fit, but you just had to be smart and twist them around until they did.

He went to the library and dug until he found the story in an old book of legends. He'd vaguely recalled that the king had stopped his enemies—those who could hear everything—by feeding them something. Apparently, he'd fed them food made from very special insects. Bobby read that, and he went home to sleep on it, and when he woke, he knew exactly what he had to do.

※

It was May Day again. This year, the Gnat had decided not to come. She'd been at a friend's place and called to say she was spending the night and skipping the trip. He'd given the news to his parents when they returned from a bridge party.

The next morning, his mother started fussing, worrying that the Gnat would change her mind as soon as they'd left for Cainsville.

"She'd call before that," his father said. "She's a big girl."

"I can phone and ask if you want," Bobby said.

"Would you? That's sweet." She patted his back as he walked past. "Whose house did you say she was at again?"

He answered from the next room, his reply garbled, but his mother only said, "Oh, that's right. Now, does anyone know where we left the tanning lotion? I want to get started early this year. Wait, I think Natalie had it..."

A few minutes later he found her in his sister's room. "She's not there. I remember her saying something about going to the roller rink."

His mother sighed. "I wish she wouldn't. Those places seem so unhealthy for girls, with the lights all off and so many boys..."

"I can talk to her about it tomorrow if you're worried."

Another pat as she zoomed past, tanning lotion in hand. "Thank you, dear. You're a good brother, even if she doesn't always appreciate you. Did you pack that pie you made?"

"Pie?" His father appeared in the doorway. "Bobby made pie? Apple, I hope."

"Shepherd's pie," his mother said. "He made it last night while we were out. Didn't you notice the mess when we got home?" She glanced over. "So you *did* find hamburger meat in the freezer."

"One last package, like I said."

"I was so certain we'd run out." She headed for the hall. "All right. Time to go."

⋇

The waitresses at the new diner let him warm his casserole in the oven. He was sitting in the back, watching the timer, when the door swung open and Rose burst in, Hannah at her heels.

"That smells good," Hannah said. "Is it true? You made pie?"

"Shepherd's pie. I hope you're not still mad at me. I'm..." He lowered his voice as he walked toward her. "Sorry about the last time. That's why

I made the pie. For you and Rose. To say I'm sorry. For the elders, too. I don't want anyone to be mad at me." He gazed into her eyes. "I hope you'll have some."

She seemed nervous, but forced a smile. "Sure, Bobby. And I'm sorry, if I overreacted. You scared me and—"

"What have you done?"

It was Rose. She hadn't spoken since she'd entered. He hadn't even glanced her way, seeing only Hannah. Now he looked over to see her standing in front of the oven, staring at it. When she turned to him, her face was even paler than usual, her blue eyes bulging.

"What have you done, Bobby?" she whispered.

"Done? What—"

"I had a dream," she said. "Last night."

"More dragons," he scoffed. "Dreams of me and screaming dragons."

"No." Her horrified gaze never left his. "It wasn't dragons I heard screaming."

"Whatever." He turned away. "You're crazy. Your whole family is crazy."

"Where's your sister, Bobby?"

He shrugged, his back still to Rose. "She stayed home."

"Where is your sister," she said each word slowly, carefully, and he was about to reply when the door opened again. He turned as Mrs. Yates and two of the elders walked in. They seemed concerned. Only that. Then they stopped, mid-stride. They inhaled, nostrils flaring, and when they turned to him again, horror filled their eyes, the same horror that crackled from Rose's wide-eyed stare.

"Bobby," Mrs. Yates said. "What have you done?"

He wheeled and raced out the back door.

※

Before he knew it, he found himself back where he'd been the last time, in the backyard of the empty house. He looked around wildly, saw a break in the lattice work under the deck, and crawled through, wood snapping as he pushed his way in, splinters digging in, blood welling up.

When he got inside, he turned around and huddled there, hugging knees that stank of dirt, his arms striped with blood.

Blood.

He remembered the blood.

He shot forward, gagging, stomach clenching, head pounding, the images slamming against his skull. He kept gagging until he threw up. Then he sat there, hugging his legs again as the tears rolled down his face.

Gran was right.

I am a monster.

And I don't even know how it happened.

"Bobby?"

It was Mrs. Yates. He scuttled backward, but she walked straight to the hole and bent to peer in. She smiled, but it was such a terribly sad smile that he wished she'd scowl instead, scowl and rage and call him the monster he was.

"I am so sorry, Bobby," she said. "I don't know…" She inhaled. "I won't make excuses. We could tell things weren't… We had no idea how bad…" Another inhalation, breath whistling. "I'm so, so sorry. I wish I'd known. I wish I could have helped."

He said nothing, just kept clutching his knees.

"I can't stop what's going to happen now, Bobby. I wish I could. I would give anything to fix this. But I can't. I can only make it easier."

He started to shake, holding his legs so tight his arms hurt.

"I read those newspaper articles," she said. "About your grandmother. What she said. Your dreams. We should have talked about that. Perhaps if we'd talked…" She shook her head, then peered in at him. "You dreamed of golden castles, didn't you? Castles and meadows and streams."

"And dragons," he whispered.

She went still. Completely, unnaturally still. "Dragons?"

He nodded. "I dream of dragons screaming. And then I wasn't dreaming and they still screamed."

"You should have told—" She cut herself short, chin dipping. "Let's not talk about the dragons. You won't hear them anymore. I promise. But the castles. You liked the castles?"

He nodded.

"Would you like to see them?"

"They're gone. They went away."

She inched a little closer to the gap in the lattice. "I can bring them back. Back as bright as they ever were. Castles and meadows, cool breezes and warm sunshine. Laughter and play, music and dancing. Is that what you remember?"

He nodded.

"Would you like to go there?"

"Yes."

She ducked her head and crawled under with him. In one hand, she held a bottle. She pulled out the stopper and held the bottle out to him. The liquid inside seemed to glow, and when he looked up at her, she seemed to glow, too, the wrinkles on her face smoothing.

"Do you trust me, Bobby?"

He nodded.

"Then drink that. Drink it, and you'll see the castles again. You'll go there, and you won't ever need to come back."

He took the bottle, and he drank it all in one gulp. As soon as he did, the dragons stopped screaming, and he saw Mrs. Yates, glowing, every inch of her glowing, like sunlight trapped under her skin, her eyes filling with it, drawing him in as she reached out to hug him. He fell into her arms, and the glow consumed everything, the world turned to gold, and when he opened his eyes, he was sitting on sun-warmed grass, staring up at a castle, and a girl laughed behind him and said, "Come and play, Bobby." He turned, and she looked like Hannah but not quite, and she smiled at him, the way Hannah used to smile at him. He pushed to his feet and raced after her as she ran off, laughing.

And that was where he stayed, just as Mrs. Yates promised. Endless days in a world of gold and sunshine, days that ran together and had no end. Every now and then he would fall asleep in a lush meadow or in a chamber in the beautiful castle, and when he did, his dreams were terrible nightmares, where he was bound to a hospital bed, screaming about dragons. But the nights never lasted long, and soon he was back in his world of castles and meadows, running, chasing, playing, dancing until he forgot what the screams of dragons sounded like, forgot he'd ever heard them and forgot everything else—his grandmother, his sister, his parents, the girls, Mrs. Yates—all of it gone, wisps of a dream that faded into nothing, leaving him exactly where he'd always wanted to be.

The Dry Spell

BY JAMES P. BLAYLOCK

The rain gauge was empty when Harper pulled it out of the middle of the lawn and held it up to the sun, which was just now showing through broken clouds in the east. There was supposed to be rain by this morning, but there wasn't so far, and now the clouds seemed to be leaving town in a hurry, heading toward the desert, where they would evaporate like failed hope. That had been going on all week. Lana, his wife, had told him a few moments ago that the sky looked "threatening," but the word was apparently an exercise in imagination. Lana was sitting on the couch inside, sorting through old photos, swept up in a pleasant, rainy day nostalgia that entirely eluded Harper.

The lawn had a faded, thin look to it, and the petunias he had planted last weekend were half withered. April showers hadn't materialized, and the entire street looked parched, like mid-September in a heat wave. There was an irritating warmth to the morning, too, as if they were in for another day of "fine weather," which meant no weather at all. May was the dead end of what passed for the rainy season in southern California, and the chance of rain would be more and more remote as the days drifted past.

Last night on the news there had been a "storm watch"—reporters dressed in unnecessary rain slickers, looking furtive with expectation, as if at any moment the sky would open up and the populace would have to roll their arks out of mothballs and load up the cats and dogs. Harper had awakened early in the morning, listening for the patter of raindrops on the shingles, slowly coming to realize that he had been dreaming, the victim of his own mental storm watch.

He set the rain gauge down on a front porch chair and walked out to the sidewalk to pick up the *Times*, which was double-bagged, like last night's reporters. Abruptly he felt a scattering of tiny, windblown drops on his face, and there was the promising smell of ozone rising from the concrete. But just as quickly as it had materialized, the breeze carried it away. He looked up at the clouds, estimating which of them had made this wheezing pretence of an effort, but overhead there was a broadening window of vacant blue sky. Impulsively angry, he bent over and cranked open the valve on the front yard sprinklers. He was through waiting. The wild idea came into his head to turn on the sprinklers in every front yard on the block. He could explain to his neighbors with no exaggeration that he was performing a scientific experiment in weather manipulation…

He heard a screen door slam shut. It was his neighbor, Sharon, out on her side porch with her five-year-old son, whom she called Doc. She grinned skeptically at Harper. "What's with the sprinklers?" she asked, gesturing at the sky.

"I thought I'd force the issue," Harper told her. "Maybe I can shame Mother Nature into actually raining for a change." He laughed even though it wasn't funny to him. He was pretty sure that Sharon thought he was insane anyway, and it was better to make it seem like a joke. He picked up the little screwdriver that he kept on the porch and fiddled with the adjustment screws on the top of two of the pop-ups, decreasing the amount of water coming out so that all of it fell only on the grass. There was no use watering the sidewalk and street.

Sharon had picked up her newspaper and pulled off the plastic wrap. She had a section of it opened up. "Rain forecast!" she said, waving it at him. She laughed and shook her head, but then saw that Doc had unwound a couple of yards of hose and was turning on the spigot. He shot a jet of water at his mother and started laughing, but then quit when he saw that she wasn't amused. Sharon gave Harper a look, as if Doc's madness was his fault, and then shut off the water and went inside, taking the boy with her.

The Dry Spell | James P. Blaylock

Harper went back into the house. Two cardboard boxes lay on the floor in front of the couch, stuffed with half a lifetime's worth of yellow photo packets. "Take a look at this," Lana said to him. She didn't glance up, but reached over and picked up a photograph that she had apparently set aside. For a moment she sat there smiling at it. "Remember that storm in Maui?" she asked. "When we were staying at that little place on the beach in Hana? What was that called? The Bamboo Hilton or something?"

"Bamboo Castle, I think." Harper took the photo from her and looked at it. He found that he remembered it in detail, actually, although it had been twenty years ago. It had taken them four hours to drive the sixty miles from the airport out to Hana on the narrow highway that ran through the jungle, and they had gotten to the cottage after dark, carrying a loaf of banana bread and a bag of papayas and tiny orange limes that they had bought from a hippie farmer in a roadside stand. Harper remembered the sound of waves breaking on the rocky beach when they arrived, the beach and ocean barely visible in the darkness, and then the full moon appearing through broken clouds, illuminating coconut palms and the tangle of jungle along the edge of the beach. They set up dinner on the lanai and watched the palms swaying in the moonlight and the moonlight shining on the ocean, the beach utterly deserted, as if they had washed up onto an enchanted island, which they pretty much had.

Harper had taken the photograph of Lana, dressed in a red, hibiscus-print sarong that she'd bought in the airport. They'd gone down to the beach after dinner, carrying a bottle of champagne and two glasses, and on the empty beach there seemed to be no reason at all to go back up after their swimsuits. The rain had started up when they were waist deep in the warm water, and within moments it was coming down so heavily that they couldn't see their clothes and champagne bottle on the beach, and they had to bend their heads forward to breathe if they didn't want a nose full of rainwater. Laughing like fools, they slogged ashore and grabbed their stuff, running up to the shelter of the balcony, where they stood watching the downpour. In five minutes it quit, just like that. The night turned warm, and the moon shone in the sky again. Lana had wrapped herself in the sarong, pulled her hair back, and Harper had taken the photo with the palm tree and moon behind her. It was so perfect that it looked staged.

He considered it for another moment, saying nothing. Lana had gone on to other photographs, which she was slipping one-by-one into a big, empty photo annual, happy as she always was when she was busy. He wondered vaguely whether she had meant anything by showing him the photo. Probably she meant that it was a good photo, which it was. Lots of memories in it. On that night in Hana they hadn't been newlyweds by any means, but there was something about the tropical air and the jungle solitude and the on-and-off rain that had worked a certain magic. Aside from eating and an occasional dip in the ocean after dark, they hadn't surfaced for three days.

He watched her slide the Hana photo into its niche among the other relics of their past, and then took the newspaper into the den, where he sat down and turned immediately to the weather page, something he did on weekend mornings, checking the five-day forecast, the ocean conditions, and the annual rainfall totals, which were only interesting if it had rained over the course of the week, which of course it hadn't.

It hadn't rained since February, according to the paper. There were 2.14 inches total for the year—worse than last year, which had been the second drought year in a row—and half an inch of this year's rain had fallen ten months ago, in July, for God's sake, a summer torrent with lightning strikes that had immolated the top of a queen palm two blocks down the street, a bang-up beginning to the rainy season, literally. After that no storm had dropped more than a quarter of an inch. The glory of that wet July morning seemed to Harper to be the recollection of a dream rather than an authentic memory. The photograph of Lana came into his mind, and he realized uneasily that he'd had this same sort of thought twice in a ten-minute span of time.

There were storm clouds in the little weather illustration for Sunday, but Monday was clear and sunny after morning low fog—typical May weather. A hamster could have predicted it, along with more of the same on into June. He found the travel section and laid it aside for Lana, who read every page of it, and then got up and crammed what was left of the paper into the trash. The rest of the news didn't concern him, or perhaps concerned him too much. Probably it was vital to know how many people had been murdered over the weekend and what parts of the world were annihilating each other or being annihilated, but he had no good use for the information. Like the weather or the passing of time, there was damn-all he could do about it. Thinking about it simply poisoned the air.

Lana appeared in the doorway. "Did you know that the sprinklers are on?" she asked.

"Probably a prank," he said. "It's those damn Palm Street kids again."

She nodded doubtfully. "They're predicting rain for this morning. A sixty percent chance."

"I don't find their percentages convincing," Harper said. "It's like predicting a man's chances of dying. You can't be wrong forever." He handed her the travel section.

"You're the only person I know who takes the weather personally," she told him. "Just don't think about it. If it doesn't rain then it doesn't rain. Who cares?"

"I guess I do. Like you said."

"Then let's walk down to Hosmer's and get some breakfast—some waffles to sweeten you up."

"All right, but no umbrellas," Harper said, forcing himself to sound enthusiastic. "We'll tempt fate." He got up out of his chair and the two of them went outside. Lana wore a sweatshirt, but he didn't bother with a jacket.

"Is that what's up with the sprinklers?" Lana asked. "It's some kind of challenge? Isn't that what they mean by sympathetic magic?"

"Completely unsympathetic in this case," Harper said. He bent over and shut the sprinkler valve off. The lawn and flowerbeds seemed grateful to him, no longer quite so exhausted. "Think of it as a poor man's way of seeding the clouds."

"You *know* it's crazy not to bring the umbrellas," Lana told him as they started off down the sidewalk.

"I hope so."

"I don't mind carrying one. The sky's *really* getting dark."

"Not half dark enough to suit me," Harper said. "Look, our shadows are still visible." A moment later, their shadows disappeared as if the sky were fixing to prove him wrong. A small breeze lifted a scattering of leaves and blew them down the street. They were nearing the corner now, and in another minute the house would be out of sight behind them. As soon as it was, Lana's obsession with umbrellas would fade. "Waffles sound good," he said, distracting her with food talk. "Waffles and a cup of coffee."

"Decaf?" she asked, looking sideways at him.

"Sure," he said grudgingly. He used to be able to drink coffee all day between naps, but nowadays things were different, and he hated lying awake at night, although as often as not he lay awake anyway.

"Here it comes," she said.

"What?" He looked down the street, but it was empty of cars.

"The *rain*. I just felt a drop."

"It's just a teaser to work up your anticipation. Then it'll back off and let you down again." They walked under the foliage of a big, leafy camphor tree. "Dry as a bone," he said, but he saw drops of rain on the exposed sidewalk ahead.

"It's going to *pour*," she said. "Let's hurry."

They picked up the pace, but he was damned if he was going to run. Hosmer's was two blocks away, at the edge of the downtown—no way they'd drown between here and there even if the alleged storm got serious, which wasn't likely. The drops were large, but were widely spaced. He looked up and a big drop hit him in the eye. "*Go ahead*," he muttered.

"What?" Lana asked.

"I said that we should go ahead and walk between the drops. That's how the Zen masters stay dry."

"*You* walk between them. I'll go get us a table." Lana started jogging on ahead, pulling up the hood on her sweatshirt. When she was fifteen feet away, she turned around and looked back at him, slightly incredulous now. "Are you *coming*?"

"I'll be there," he said, the rain picking up. "Get that table!" She turned around again and jogged off without another word. "Out on the patio!" he shouted after her, laughing out loud. He forced himself to walk at a comfortable pace, and by the time he got to the restaurant his shirt was soaked through and his hair was plastered to his head. Lana sat at a table in the window, watching him come up. She looked doubtful, so he smiled at her to show that he had a sense of humor about it all. He brushed his hair back with his fingers and picked up the menu just as the waiter appeared carrying two cups of decaf.

Hosmer's was full, and there was a pleasant clamor of noise and the smell of bacon and coffee. For a couple of minutes they watched it rain, drinking the hot coffee and waiting for their waffles. It wasn't a downpour by any means, but it might be the beginning of something. Harper realized again how much he loved the rain, especially when he was inside watching it fall. He winked at his reflection in the glass. "Chalk one up for me," he said, half to himself.

"You're such a skeptic," Lana said. "It's part of that thing you have for instant gratification."

"I'll be gratified if the rain keeps it up for an hour. You see how it's still dry under the tree out there on the curb? According to the *Farmers Almanac* it's not measurable rain until it gets down past the foliage. Same with the cars parked on the street. The rainwater's got to get the street wet enough so that it flows under the cars—no dry spots. Otherwise it means nothing."

The waffles arrived and they started in on them. Several minutes passed before Harper looked out at the street again, but by this time the rain had stopped. The sidewalk under the curb tree was dry and getting drier. They paid the check and set out for home. Already it was warming up, enough so that Lana took off her sweatshirt and tied it around her waist. The breeze had fallen off, and the clouds were breaking up like a retreating army, easily provoked and easily defeated. Despite Harper's elevated mood in the café, he couldn't find much satisfaction in his small victory.

Inside the house again he felt restless, as if the morning were waiting for him to act, and yet he didn't have the energy to do anything but sit in a chair. In the old days he would have been out in the garage early, accomplishing things, but he had lost most of his jazz in that regard, and anyway he couldn't think of anything that wanted doing. Lana had started up with the photos again, and she glanced up at him and smiled. He could pitch in and give her a hand, of course, if only for the sake of his image, but the very idea of it made him impatient. He would look through the album later, after Lana had sorted out the good photos.

He left her to her work and went out to cultivate the tomatoes, grabbing a little pointy-tipped hoe out of the garden shed. He cut out the scattered weeds and dragged the loose soil into dams around the plants, which had set on plenty of blooms. Because of the morning's rain, the ground appeared to be wet, but right below the surface it was dry. The clouds were returning—unenthusiastically, it seemed to Harper. Lightning flickered out over the mountains, too far away for him to hear any thunder, a dumb show of an impotent storm. He went to the spigot, turned on the water, and dragged the garden hose back over to the vines, flooding the well around each plant, picturing in his mind the droplets soaking in around the roots, drawn upward through the stems and out into the leaves, the blossoms swelling, the plants noisy with growth.

He made a circuit of the back yard then, watering the flowerbeds heavily, washing the dust off the garage siding and squirting down the walkway. He took a couple of big gulps of hose water, tasting the vinyl in it, and thought about trying to catch raindrops in his mouth when he was a kid. He gave the sky an appraising look, recalling bits from the *Farmers Almanac*—how it had been in the old days when the weather was real weather, when rain fell at the rate of three inches a day and the drops were the size of fifty cent pieces. He returned to the tomatoes to flood the wells again, and then he trained the hose at the sky, so that the water fell back down in big drops, a share of them blowing back in the breeze, showering his face and shoulders, soaking his shoes.

Lana came out onto the back porch, where she stood watching him. Out of the corner of his eye he saw that she was smiling, as if she were watching a child playing in the sprinklers. *So what?* he thought. This wasn't her fight; she couldn't be expected to understand it. He quit spraying the sky, though, and was surprised to find that the shower hadn't stopped. It was raining again, as if he had drawn the rain out of the clouds with the hose water.

"I was thinking of making some popcorn," Lana said to him.

The Dry Spell | James P. Blaylock

He went over to the spigot to crank off the water and then ducked up under the porch roof. "I was making sure the tomatoes got their fair share," he said. "If they get short-changed now, the blooms won't stick."

She nodded. "What about the popcorn? *Road to Singapore* starts in about ten minutes. Maybe you could call some sort of truce with Mother Nature for a couple of hours."

"Actually, I just called her bluff," he said, looking out at the rain. "But I'll give her some time to play her hand."

"I'll get out the Whirley-Pop," she said. "You're in charge of the Dr Pepper."

When Lana came out of the kitchen with the bowl of popcorn, he was standing at the window, dressed in a dry shirt, looking out at a mere drizzle.

"So it *was* a bluff?" she asked, turning on the television.

"An inept bluff. I was more convincing with the damned hose." He smiled at her to show that it was all in good fun, and then helped himself to the popcorn.

⋇

Later they ate enchiladas in front of the television, watching the weatherman yammer away, the doppler radar illuminating green patches on the map, out against the foothills. Supposedly there were clouds coming in off the ocean and a high surf advisory. Waterspouts had appeared off the coast and given everyone a thrill before they spun themselves apart. A film clip started up now, showing a cloudburst out in the desert, a real gullywasher. A family camping along the Mojave River had been forced to run for high ground when their gear was swept away. The husband had chased after the Styrofoam ice chest, though, wading out into the flood, where he had lost his footing and gone under. If it weren't for the ice chest, which had kept him afloat, he'd be swimming with the fishes now. His wife and three children stood by, the kids mugging for the camera, the wife looking peeved. "No way it was going to get my beer," the man said.

"Good man," Harper said to the screen.

"Low IQ," Lana said. "Maybe his wife looks angry because he didn't drown."

The weatherman promised more rain for tonight and tomorrow, virtually certain. "*More?*" Harper said. "More than *what?* What he means is more of the same." Lana glanced at him doubtfully, as if he might get worked up and throw his fork at the screen. "I'll pull up the drawbridge," he said tiredly, getting up and heading toward the front door. He flipped on the porch light as he did every evening, and then stepped outside and picked up the rain gauge from the seat of the chair. He held it up so that the sky could get a good look at its pitifully empty condition, and then tossed it onto the chair again. That was it for the rain gauge. He'd had it with the mockery. He went back into the house, shut and locked the door, and closed the blinds.

As usual, Harper awoke in the early morning twilight, listening for something—wind or rain, whatever had disturbed his sleep, but the room was ghostly quiet. After a moment he heard the lonesome wail of a train whistle in the west, the sound falling away and then resuming again until it dwindled in the distance, heading for parts unknown. He found that he was already wide-awake, his mind revolving around matters of unfinished business.

He climbed out of bed quietly, went around and pulled the blanket up over Lana's shoulder, and picked up his pants from the chair. After a moment's thought he dropped them again and stepped across to the dresser where he pulled out his swimsuit and a t-shirt. In the kitchen he took the canister of decaf out of the cupboard, stood looking at it for a moment, and then put it back. He rooted around in the freezer for authentic coffee, which these days they kept mainly for company. He spooned plenty of it into the cone filter and watched the boiling water sink through it, the aroma filling the room. It looked heavy, like used crankcase oil. "That's the stuff," he said, carrying the mug through the living room and out onto the porch. It was too cool outside for swim trunks and a t-shirt, but he didn't give a damn.

The morning sky was a clutter of unmoving clouds. Apparently they were waiting for him. He raised his coffee cup in a salute, feeling the wind through his shirt and the cold concrete on the soles of his feet. He set the mug down and walked along the carport to the garage, where he hauled out a bucket, carwash soap, a sponge, and a couple of terrycloth towels. The problem with pretend rain, among other things, was that it merely splashed the dirt around on a car's finish, magnifying the grime. That's what yesterday's contemptible sprinkles had amounted to—dirt splashers.

Out front again, he turned on the hose and filled the bucket with suds, then played the water over the grill and bumper, softening up the dead bugs and road grime before going on to spray the wheels and the paint. While the car soaked, he drank his coffee and watered the patches of lawn that the sprinklers didn't quite reach. Then he went after the car again, really making a job of it. He had the whole day in front of him. There was no reason he couldn't wash and polish both the cars and still be finished by lunchtime.

When it started to rain, he didn't look up, but simply kept working, soaping down the finish with the sponge now. The rain was like an irritating fly: if you couldn't swat it, then it was better to ignore it. Sooner or later it would get bored and go away. He rinsed the hood and squirted the whole shebang down again, then grabbed the soapy sponge, opened the car door, and stepped up onto the floorboard in order to reach far enough over the top of the car to get the roof. It was a real stretch, but on tiptoe he could just make it halfway.

Raindrops bounced into his face, and he squinted his eyes, working away with the sponge. There was a bright flash of lightning, close enough to be reflected in the paint, and then the crack of thunder—loud, but he was expecting it, and he didn't give the storm the satisfaction of reacting to it. "Flash in the pan," he muttered, reaching far out with the sponge now, stabbing at a distant spot of dirt that lay on the other side of the imaginary equator. In that moment, while he was off balance and leaning forward on one wet foot, a deluge of water fell from the sky and struck him square in the middle of the back. His foot slipped downward, he cracked his chin on the edge of the car roof, and quicker than seemed possible he found himself on his back on the lawn, lying in a puddle of soapy water that had spilled out of the bucket. The church bells down the street began to chime, as if counting him out, and he hurriedly climbed to his feet, shrugging his shoulders and neck to make sure that he hadn't crushed any vertebrae. His thigh hurt like hell where he had sat down hard on the edge of the bucket, but other than that he was okay.

"That was *it?*" he said to the clouds. Already the rain seemed to be letting up.

"Are you all right?" Lana asked from behind him. She stood on the porch in her bathrobe.

He waved the sponge at her. "No harm, no foul," he said, wondering how long she had been standing there. "Did you see what hit me?"

"It looked like a big crystal ball. It just fell out of the sky."

"*One big drop?*"

"As big as your head. Maybe you should give this up and come inside, Harper. It's no joke, with the lighting and all."

"The best time to wash a car is in the rain," he told her. "It loosens up the dirt and helps rinse away the hard water deposits."

She nodded, as if this made perfect sense. "They usually close down the carwash on rainy days, too," she said, "so you've got no choice, I guess. You've got to do it yourself or it won't get done."

"That's a hell of a good point," he told her, going after the trunk with the sponge. He wondered what she was up to. Irony?

"Maybe you should wear your old wetsuit," she said. "You'd be warmer."

For a moment he actually considered the wetsuit. Probably Lana was kidding, but it made perfect sense, really, except that it would take him an hour to find it. It was part of the mothballed fleet of old stuff hidden away in the garage—his youth, really, packed into a couple of cardboard cartons. He hadn't looked at it in fifteen years, since the last time he had gotten the wild idea of going to the beach. *The wild idea,* he thought, picking up the hose, and there came into his mind a picture of the man on last night's news, leaping into the river to save an ice chest full of beer.

Lana went back inside and shut the door, probably having given up on him. As if on cue, Sharon came out after the *Times*, hurrying along down her driveway. Doc stood on the side porch in his pajamas. He spotted Harper out on the lawn, barefoot in his swim trunks and soaked t-shirt. He noted the hose and the carwash debris, and waved heartily, his face lighting up. Harper waved back with the hose, swinging it like a lariat, ducking away when a loop of water splashed across him. The boy laughed out loud and ran out into the rain, dancing a jig on the driveway, his face turned toward the sky, his mouth open. Sharon hustled him back onto the porch, giving Harper an angry look, as if he were some kind of rain-drunk pied piper. The boy knew the score, though. Harper had seen it in his eyes.

Lana came outside again, wearing a bathing suit and flip-flops, her hair pinned up. She waved cheerfully at Sharon, who gaped at her, decided to say nothing, and hauled Doc into the house before he was infected with their madness. Harper gaped at Lana, too.

"Now it's *my* car's turn," she said, picking up the bucket and squirting fresh soap into it. "Don't just stand there." She grabbed the hose and started to fill the bucket. The rain came down harder now, getting serious. Lana's car was parked under the carport, so Harper backed his own car out and parked on the street and then backed hers into the open.

The sky had grown evenly dark, a low, iron-gray ceiling. The wind sprang up from the direction of the ocean. It was cold, but Harper didn't give a damn, and apparently Lana didn't either. He squirted her Toyota with the hose, but it wasn't really necessary. The rain was doing the work for him now. Probably it would want a tip when they were through. Harper laughed, trying to think of a way to convey the idea to Lana, but he gave it up and turned off the hose, then dipped a towel into the soapy water and helped Lana with the hood.

"You're right about the rain loosening up the dirt," she said. "You sounded like a crazy person, though."

"But I'm not, am I?"

"The jury's still out on that one." She kissed him. "You're soapy." She wiped her mouth with her arm. "You get that side and I'll get this one."

She bent over and disappeared from view, working on the rims. Harper did the same. He discovered that he was whistling the theme song from "Steamboat Willy," but he couldn't remember having started it up. He was right in tune, though, and so he raised the volume a little, stood back, and snapped the towel at a smudge of grit, cleaning it off in one blow like whichever Jack it was who had killed the flies.

Abruptly the rain got heavier, redoubling its strength in an instant, and he staggered just a little as the wind caught him. He recovered, steadied himself, and went on to the door panels now, soaping the hell out of them and then standing back a couple of feet again. "Go ahead and rinse it," he shouted at the sky.

"What?" Lana said. She looked at him across the trunk, shielding her face with her hand.

"I was talking to the rain," Harper shouted at her.

"Is it listening?"

"Seems like it!"

They both worked on the trunk and the rear bumper, although by now it was raining so hard that the dirt had been scoured off. They had to stand with their backs to the storm. Rain was driving down at an angle, surging through the air in heavy, blowing clouds, sweeping the soapy water off the car and down the driveway. Lana picked up the bucket and went out to the curb to dump out the dirty water while Harper grabbed the soap and sponge and towels. He dropped them into the bucket and Lana carried it to the carport, in no apparent hurry. He watched her happily, very happily.

She was on her way back down the driveway when there was a bolt of lightning so close that it enveloped them in a cosmic, white glow. Harper felt his hair stand on end, and there was a shattering blast of thunder that shook the car. It was a moment before he could see again, and then only dimly through the rain, which was torrential now. The curb trees waved frantically along the street, and the roses shed petals in a whirlwind of white that was driven down onto the lawn. Lana stood at the hood of the car, steadying herself with one hand, half-hidden by a white mist of shattered water. Harper shrugged at her, as if he had seen worse. Abruptly it did get worse, the rain slanting down in sheets. Lana shouted something and headed around toward him, but the wind snatched her words away.

"Now *that's* rain," Harper shouted when she was close enough to hear. He yanked the door open and she slid into the car, the wind nearly tearing the door handle out of Harper's hand. He hunched around to the driver's side and climbed in beside her. They sat together listening to the storm drumming away outside, catching their breath. He turned the key in the ignition and switched the heater and the wipers on.

"You really look phenomenal," he said to her breathlessly.

"Thanks," she said, kissing him again. Then she looked down at herself skeptically and hastily arranged her bathing suit top. "Why didn't you tell me that I wasn't ladylike?"

"Do you have to ask?" He winked at her. "What would Sharon say if we…"

"I was thinking we'd take a little Sunday drive."

"Now? Dressed like this?"

"Not exactly like this," she said, reaching behind the seat and coming up with her sweatshirt. "Your carry-on bag is behind you on the floor."

He turned around and looked. Sure enough, there it was. He could see the toes of his shoes beneath it, and his jacket was tucked neatly through the handles. Lana's bag was there too, shoved in behind the passenger seat along with her purse.

"When did you pack?" Harper asked.

"This morning," she said. "I sneaked the bags out the back door and down the carport. I was thinking about a hotel. Maybe that place just this side of Ventura, right on the beach there." She raised her eyebrows at him.

He pictured the hotel they'd stayed in on the first night of their honeymoon. It had been storming then too, the ocean a spectacular chaos of breaking waves, the sky full of tearing clouds. He didn't remember a lot about it beyond that. They hadn't spent a lot of time looking out the window. "Will we need a reservation?" he asked, shifting into reverse and backing out of the driveway.

"In weather like this?" she asked.

The rainwater was up over the curb now, the street a river. He swerved around onto the empty highway, suddenly anxious to get out of town, keeping to the center of the street, which wasn't flooded yet. The road was clear, the freeway dead ahead.

"What's that?" Lana asked as they drove up the onramp. She pointed out her window toward the west.

Harper stared past her at a dark blur in the distance, something that looked like a rapidly approaching squall. Suddenly it spun itself into the shape of a waterspout, rose into the air, and tore along above the rooftops, as if bound for their very neighborhood a half-mile away.

"A couple more minutes, and it'll know we ran for it," Lana said, apparently serious.

"Then it's a good thing we brought the umbrellas," Harper told her. Laughing, he switched the wipers onto high, checked the rear-view mirror, and accelerated into the fast lane.

He Who Grew Up Reading Sherlock Holmes

by Harlan Ellison®

A bad thing had happened. No, a "Bad Thing" had happened. A man in Fremont, Nebraska cheated an honest old lady, and no one seemed able to make him retract his deed to set things right. It went on helplessly for the old lady for more than forty years. Then, one day, she told a friend. Now I will tell you a story. Or a true anecdote. For those who wish this to be "a story I never wrote," have at it; for those who choose to believe that I am recounting a Real Life Anecdote, I'm down with that, equally: your choice.

Once upon a time, not so long ago…

A man in an 8th floor apartment in New York City lay in his bed, asleep. The telephone beside him rang. It was a standard 20th Century instrument, not a hand-held device. It was very late at night, almost morning, but the sun had not yet risen over the decoupage skyline of Manhattan. The telephone rang again.

He reached across from under the sheet and picked up the phone. A deep male voice at the other end said, very slowly and distinctly, "Are you awake?"

"Huh?"

"Are you awake enough to hear me?"

"Whuh? Whozizz?"

"Are your bedroom windows open…or shut?"

"Whuh?"

"Look at the curtains!"

"Whuh…whaddaya…"

"Sit up and *look* at the curtains. Are they moving?"

"I…uh…"

"*Look!*"

The man's three-room apartment was on an airshaft in mid-Manhattan. It was in the Fall, and cold. The windows in his bedroom were tightly closed to shutter out the noises from the lower apartments and the street below. The curtains were drawn. He slumped up slightly, and looked at the curtain nearest him. It was swaying slightly. There was no breeze.

He said nothing into the phone. Silence came across the wire to him. Dark silence.

A man, more a shadow, stepped out from behind the swaying curtain and moved toward the man in the bed. There was just enough light in the room for the man holding the phone in his hand to see that the man in black was holding a large raw potato, with a double-edged razor blade protruding from its end. He was wearing gloves, and at the end of the gloves, at the wrists, just slightly outstanding, the man in the bed could see the slippery shine of thin plastic food-service gloves. The man in black came to the bed, stood over the half-risen sleeper, and reached for the phone. Keeping the slicing-edge of the razor blade well close to the neck of the man imbedded against the pillow, he took the receiver with his free hand.

From across the line: "Just say yes or no."

"Yes, okay."

"Is he sitting up?"

"Yes."

"Can he see you…and whatever you have at his throat?"

"Yeah."

"Give him back the phone. Do nothing till I tell you otherwise."

"Okay." He handed the receiver back to the man quivering beneath the razor blade. The eyes of the man below were wide and wet.

Across the line: "Do you believe he's serious?"

"Huh?"

"All I want from you is *yes* or *no*."

"Who're…"

"Give him the phone." Pause. Again: "Give him the phone!"

The frightened man handed back the instrument.

"I've told him to say yes or no. If he says anything else, any filler, any kind of uh-huh-wha…can you cut him?"

"Yes."

"Not seriously, the first time. Let him see his own blood. Make it where he can suck it and taste it." The man in black said nothing, but handed the receiver back, laying it tight to the other man's ear. "Now," came the motionless voice out of nowhere, "are you convinced he's serious and can do you harm? Yes or no?"

"Listen, whoever the hell you are…"

The potato swept down across the back of the man's hand, from little finger to thumb. Blood began to ooze in a neat, slim line, but long, almost five inches. He dropped the phone on the bed, blood made an outline on the top sheet. He whined. It may have been the sound of a stray dog side-swiped by a taxi in the street far below, faint but plangent. The man with the razor-in-a-potato reached toward the pale white throbbing throat and nodded at the dropped phone. All else was silence.

Sucking on his knuckles, he lifted the instrument with a trembling, slightly-bleeding hand; and he listened. Intently.

"Now. Listen carefully. If you say anything but yes or no, if you alibi or try to drift in anything but a direct, straight answer, I have told him to get a thick towel, jam it into your mouth so no one will hear you scream as he slices you up slowly. And your brother Billy. And your mother. Do you understand?"

He began to say, "…uh…" The potato moved slightly. "Yes," he said quickly, in a husky voice, "yes. Yes, I understand."

The level, determined voice off in the distance said, "Very nice. Now we can get down to it."

The man in the bed, with morning light now glinting through the curtains and shining off the razor blade poised quivering near his throat said, "Yes."

"You hold a painting by a nearly-forgotten pulp magazine artist named Robert Gibson Jones…" The voice paused, but the man beneath the razor-blade knew it was merely a lub-dub, a caesura, a space in which, if he said the *no* or *I don't know what you're talking about* or *it's at my cousin's house in Queens* or *I sold it years ago* or *I don't know who bought it* or any other lie, his body would be opened like a lobster and he would lie in his own entrails, holding his still-beating heart in his fingertipless hands. Throat cut ear to ear. Immediately.

He said nothing, and in a moment the voice at the other end continued, "You have been offered three purchase prices by four bidders. Each of them is eminently fair. You will take the middle bid, take the painting in perfect condition, and sell it this morning. Is that clear?"

The man holding the phone, whose blood was now pulsing onto the bedspread, said nothing. The voice from Out There commanded, "Give the phone to…" He held the instrument out to the dark figure poised above him. The potato-blade man took the phone and listened for a few seconds. Then he leaned close enough to the other so the man snugged in his pillow could see only the slightly less-black line where the knit watch-cap covering the potato-man's head gave evidence he had eyes. No color discernible. "Is that clear?" Then he said into the phone, "Says he understands," and he listened for a few more moments. There was moisture at the temples of one of the men in the bedroom. The connection was severed; the razor blade sliced through the cord of the telephone receiver; the man in the bed was swiping at the back of his left hand, sucking up the slim tracery of blood. The figure all in black said, "Now close your eyes and don't open them till I tell you to."

When the bleeding man finally opened his eyes, a minute or two after total silence, even though he thought he'd heard a bump of the apartment door to the hall closing…he was alone.

An *haute couture* newsletter editor on *le Rue Montaigne dans le huite arrondissement*, greatly hacked-off at her third Editorial Secretary, demanded an appearance, *en masse*, of all her "verticals," the 21st Century

He Who Grew Up Reading Sherlock Holmes | Harlan Ellison®

Big Business electronic word for "serfs," "minions," "toadies," "go-fors," "vassals," "water-carriers," "servants." Slanguage today. She fired five of them. The wind blew insanely near the northern summit of Mt. Erebus in Antarctica.

Within the hour, one of two thin-leather driving gloves, black in color, had been weighted with stones from the East River and sealed with a piece of stray wire from a gutter, and had been tossed far out into the Hudson. Another glove, same color, filled with marbles from a gimcrack store on Madison Avenue, sealed with duct tape, went into the Gowanus Canal in Brooklyn. Items were dropped in dumpsters in New Jersey; a pair of common, everyday, available-everywhere disposable gloves used by food-handlers were shredded, along with five heads of cabbage, in an In-Sink-Erater in a private home in Rehoboth, Massachusetts. One of a pair of undistinguished off-brand sneakers was thrown from a car on the New Jersey Turnpike into the mucky deep sedge forty feet from the roadway. The other piece of footwear was buried two feet under a garbage dump in Saranac Lake, A day and a half later. But quickly.

But only three hours and twenty-one minutes after the closing of a door in mid-Manhattan, a man in an 8th floor apartment called a woman in McLean, Virginia, who said, "It's a little early to be calling so unexpectedly after what you said last time we talked, don't you think?" The conversation went on for almost forty minutes, with many question marks hindering its progress to an inevitable conclusion. Finally, the woman said, "It's a deal. But you know you can *never* hang it or display it, is that okay with you?" The man said he understood, and they agreed at what time to meet on the third stairwell of the Flatiron Building to exchange butcher-paper-wrapped parcels.

In a second-floor flat in London, a man removed one of three hard-backed books from a stylish slipcase. He took the book to a large Morris chair and sat down beneath the gooseneck reading lamp. He glanced to the wall where the overflow of light illuminated a large and detailed painting of a long-extinct prehistoric *lepidopteran*. He smiled, addressed his attention back to the book, turned a few pages, and began reading. In a shipping office in Kowloon, a young woman badly-trained for her simple tasks placed a sheet of paper from a contract in the wrong manila folder, and for days, across three continents, "verticals" raged at one another.

Sixty-five minutes after the exchange of parcels at the Flatiron Building in New York, a 70 lb. triangular concrete cornice block did *not* somehow unpredictably come loose from a construction pile being hoist on pulleys above Wabash Avenue in Chicago, but a white man whose collar fit too snugly did not, also, go to his office at the international corporate office where he was a highly-paid Assessment Officer: instead, he made a dental appointment, and later in the day he removed his daughter from the private pre-school she had been attending. Nothing whatever happened in the Gibson Desert in west central Australia; nothing out of the ordinary.

In London, a man sat reading under a painting of a butterfly. For every action...

However inconsequential it may seem...

There is an equal and opposite reaction in the River of Time that flows endlessly through the universe. However unseen and utterly disconnected it may seem.

Every day, in Rio de Janeiro, late in the afternoon, there occurs a torrential downpour. It only lasts a few minutes, but the wet, like bullets, spangs off the tin roofs of the *favellas* beneath the statue of Christ the Redeemer. On *this* day, at the moment nothing was happening in the Gibson Desert, the rain did *not* fall, the Avenida Atlantica was dry and reflective. Pernambuco had hail.

Later that day, a trumpet-player in a fusion-rock band in Cleveland, Ohio heard from a distant cousin in Oberlin, who had borrowed fifty dollars for a down-payment on a Honda Civic ten years earlier and had never bothered to repay him. She said she was sending a check immediately. He was pleased and told the story to his friend, the lead guitarist in the group. Four hours later, during a break in that night's gig, sitting in just a clue y'know, a woman unknown to either of them drifted up between them, smiled and inquired, "How are ya," and in the course of a few minutes' conversation both the guitarist and the trumpet player recounted the unexpected windfall of the stale fifty dollar repayment. They never saw her again. Never.

Even later that day, a hanging ornament from a 4th Century BCE Dagoba stupa originally from Sri Lanka, missing from a museum in Amsterdam since 1964, was mailed to a general post office box in Geneva, Switzerland stamped

STOLEN PROPERTY ADVISE INTERPOL

Stamped in red. Hand-stamped. At the Elephant Bar of the Bangkok Marriott, a Thai businessman was approached by the bartender, extending a red telephone. "Are you Mr. Mandapa?" The gentleman looked up from his Gin Sling, nodded, and took the receiver. "Hello yes; this is Michael Mandapa..." and he listened for a few seconds, smiling at first. "I don't think that's possible," he said, softly, no longer smiling. Listened, then: "Not so soon. I'll need at least a week, ten days, I have to..." He went silent, listened, his face drew taut, he ran the back of his free hand across his lips, then said, "If it's raining there, and it's monsoon, you will do what you have to do. I'll try my best."

He listened, sighed deeply, then put the phone back in its cradle on the bartop. The bartender noticed, came, and picked up the red telephone. "Everything o-kay?" he said, reading the strictures of Mr. Mandapa's face. "Fine, yes, fine," Mr. Mandapa replied, and left the Elephant Bar without tipping the man who had unknowingly saved his life.

Somewhere, much earlier, a man stepped on, and crushed beneath his boot, a dragonfly, a Meganeura.

The next morning, at eight AM, four cars pulled up in front of a bad-ly-tended old house in Fremont, Nebraska. Weeds and saw-grass were prevalent. The day was heavily overcast, even for a month that usually shone brightly. From the first car, a Fremont police cruiser, stepped a man wearing a Borsalino, and from beside and behind him, three uniformed officers of the local Police Force. The second car bore two Nebraska State Troopers; and in the third car were a man and a woman in dark black suits, each carrying an attaché case. The fourth car's doors opened quickly, wings spread, and four large men of several colors emerged, went around and opened the trunk, and took out large spades and shovels. The group advanced on the house, the Sheriff of Fremont, Nebraska leading the phalanx.

He knocked on the sagging screen door three times.

No one came to the closed inner door. He knocked again, three times. An elderly white woman, stooped and halting and gray, and dusted with the weariness of difficult years, opened the inner door a crack and peered at the assemblage beyond the screen door. Her tone was mid between startled and concerned: "Yes?"

"Miz Brahm?"

"Uh, yeah…"

"We're here with a search warrant and some legal folks, that lady and gentleman there…" He nodded over his shoulder at the pair of black suits, "…they've been okay'd by the Court to go through your propitty, lookin' for some books your son took to sell on ebay or whatever, for a lady back East in New York. Is Billy here?"

"Billy don't live here no more." She started to close the door. The Sheriff pushed his palm against the screen door, making an oval depression. "I asked you if Billy was here, Ma'am."

"Nuh-uh."

"May we come in, please?"

"You g'wan, get offa my property!"

At the same moment Miz Brahm was ordering the Sheriff of Fremont, Nebraska off her porch, in Mbuji-Mayi, near the Southern border between The Democratic Republic of the Congo and Zambia, a representative of Doctors Without Borders found his way to a small vegetable garden outside three hut-residences beyond a wan potato field. He carried two linen-wrapped packages, and when a nut-brown old man appeared at the entrance to the largest hut, he extended the small parcels, made the usual obeisance, and backed away quietly. Miz Brahm was still arguing with the Nebraska State Troopers and the men with shovels, and the duo in black suits, but mostly with the Sheriff of Fremont, Nebraska, nowhere near Zambia, There was, however, thunder in the near-distance and darkening clouds. The air whipped frenziedly. A drop of rain spattered on a windshield.

He Who Grew Up Reading Sherlock Holmes | Harlan Ellison®

The argument would not end. Inevitably, the officers of the law grew impatient with diversionary answers, and yanked the screen door away from its rusted latch. It fell on the porch, Miz Brahm tried to push the front door closed on the men, but they staved her back, and rushed in. Shouts, screaming ensued.

A hairy, unshaven man with three pot-bellies charged out of a back hall, a tire iron double-fisted behind his head; he was yowling. One of the State Troopers clotheslined him, sending him spawling onto his back in the passageway. Miz Brahm kept up a strident shrieking in the background; one of the attorneys—when attention was elsewhere—chopped her across the throat, and she settled lumpily against a baseboard.

※

"That ain't Billy," Miz Brahm managed to gargle, phlegm and spittle serving as consonants. "Thas his *broth*-er!"

One of the Troopers yelled, "Let's get 'em *both!*" He pulled his sidearm and snarled at the downed tri-belly, "Where's yer brother?"

"You ain't gonna take *neither* of 'em!" screamed the old lady: a foundry noon-whistle shriek; she was pulling a rusty hatchet out from behind a chifferobe. The Trooper kneecapped her. The hatchet hit the linoleum.

Four hours later two of the men with shovels, who had been stacking and restacking magazines, digging out rat nests and spading up rotted floorboards, found Billy hiding in the back corner of the last storage quonset behind the property. He tried to break through the wall, and one of the laborers slammed the spade across the back of his head. The search went on for the rest of that day, into the next, before the attorneys were satisfied. The weed-overgrown property was a labyrinth filled with tumbling-down shelves and closets, bookcases, cardboard boxes piled so high that the ones on the bottom had been crushed in: vintage pulp fiction magazines, comic books in Mylar sleeves, corded sheaves of newspapers, and the forty-seven pieces Billy had cozened out of the old woman Back East.

The next day, the entire family was in custody, and at the same time, but eight hours later by the clock, Greenwich Mean Time, the man in

London who had been reading "The Red-Headed League" closed the book, looked long at the wonderful painting of an ancient butterfly above the mantel, smiled and said, "Ah, so *that's* how it all comes together. '*Omne ignotum pre magnifico.*' Clever."

This story is dedicated to the memory of my friend, Ray Bradbury.

A Small Price to Pay for Birdsong

BY K. J. PARKER

"My sixteenth concerto," he said, smiling at me. I could just about see him. "In the circumstances, I was thinking of calling it the Unfinished."

Well, of course. I'd never been in a condemned cell before. It was more or less what I'd imagined it would be like. There was a stone bench under the tiny window. Other than that, it was empty, as free of human artefacts as a stretch of open moorland. After all, what things does a man need if he's going to die in six hours?

I was having difficulty with the words. "You haven't—"

"No." He shook his head. "I'm two-thirds of the way through the third movement, so under normal circumstances I'd hope to get that done by— well, you know. But they won't let me have a candle, and I can't write in the dark." He breathed out slowly. He was savouring the taste of air, like an expert sampling a fine wine. "It'll all be in here, though" he went on, lightly tapping the side of his head. "So at least I'll know how it ends."

I really didn't want to ask, but time was running out. "You've got the main theme," I said.

"Oh yes, of course. It's on the leash, just waiting for me to turn it loose."

I could barely speak. "I could finish it for you," I said, soft and hoarse as a man propositioning his best friend's wife. "You could hum me the theme, and—"

He laughed. Not unkindly, not kindly either. "My dear old friend," I said, "I couldn't possibly let you do that. Well," he added, hardening his voice a little, "obviously I won't be in any position to stop you trying. But you'll have to make up your own theme."

"But if it's nearly finished—"

I could just about make out a slight shrug. "That's how it'll have to stay," he said. "No offence, my very good and dear old friend, but you simply aren't up to it. You haven't got the—" He paused to search for the word, then gave up. "Don't take this the wrong way," he said. "We've known each other—what, ten years? Can it really be that long?"

"You were fifteen when you came to the Studium."

"Ten years." He sighed. "And I couldn't have asked for a better teacher. But you—well, let's put it this way. Nobody knows more about form and technique than you do, but you haven't got *wings*. All you can do is run fast and flap your arms up and down. Which you do," he added pleasantly, "superlatively well."

"You don't want me to help you," I said.

"I've offended you." Not the first time he'd said that, not by a long way. And always, in the past, I'd forgiven him instantly. "And you've taken the trouble to come and see me, and I've insulted you. I'm really sorry. I guess this place has had a bad effect on me."

"Think about it," I said, and I was so ashamed of myself; like robbing a dying man. "Your last work. Possibly your greatest."

He laughed out loud. "You haven't read it yet," he said. "It could be absolute garbage for all you know."

It could have been, but I knew it wasn't. "Let me finish it for you," I said. "Please. Don't let it die with you. You owe it to the human race."

I'd said the wrong thing. "To be brutally frank with you," he said, in a light, slightly brittle voice, "I couldn't give a twopenny fuck about the human race. They're the ones who put me in here, and in six hours' time they're going to pull my neck like a chicken. Screw the lot of them."

A Small Price to Pay for Birdsong | K. J. Parker

My fault. I'd said the wrong thing, and as a result, the music inside his head would stay there, trapped in there, until the rope crushed his windpipe and his brain went cold. So, naturally, I blamed him. "Fine," I said. "If that's your attitude, I don't think there's anything left to say."

"Quite." He sighed. I think he wanted me to leave. "It's all a bit pointless now, isn't it? Here," he added, and I felt a sheaf of paper thrust against my chest. "You'd better take the manuscript. If it's left here, there's a fair chance the guards'll use it for arsewipe."

"Would it bother you if they did?"

He laughed. "I don't think it would, to be honest," he said. "But it's worth money," he went on, and I wish I could've seen his face. "Even incomplete," he added. "It's got to be worth a hundred angels to somebody, and I seem to recall I owe you a hundred and fifty, from the last time."

I felt my fingers close around the pages. I didn't want to take them, but I gripped so tight I could feel the paper crumple. I had in fact already opened negotiations with the Kapelmeister.

I stood up. "Goodbye," I said. "I'm sorry."

"Oh, don't go blaming yourself for anything." Absolution, so easy for him to give; like a duke scattering coins to the crowd from a balcony. Of course, the old duke used to have the coins heated in a brazier first. I still have little white scars on my fingertips. "I've always been the sole author of my own misfortunes. You always did your best for me."

And failed, of course. "Even so," I said, "I'm sorry. It's such a waste."

That made him laugh. "I wish," he said, "that music could've been the most important thing in my life, like it should've been. But it was only ever a way of getting a bit of money."

I couldn't reply to that. The truth, which I'd always known since I first met him, was that if he'd cared about music, he couldn't have written it so well. Now there's irony.

"You're going to finish it anyway."

I stopped, a pace or so short of the door. "Not if you don't want me to."

"I won't be here to stop you."

"I can't finish it," I said. "Not without the theme."

"Balls." He clicked his tongue, that irritating sound I'll always associate with him. "You'll have a stab at it, I know you will. And for the rest of time, everybody will be able to see the join."

"Goodbye," I said, without looking round.

"You could always pass it off as your own," he said.

I balled my fist and bashed on the door. All I wanted to do was get out of there as quickly as I could; because while I was in there with him, I hated him, because of what he'd just said. Because I'd deserved better of him than that, over the years. And because the thought had crossed my mind.

※

I waited till I got back to my rooms before I unfolded the sheaf of paper and looked at it.

At that point, I had been the professor of music at the Academy of the Invincible Sun for twenty-seven years. I was the youngest ever incumbent, and I fully intend to die in these rooms, though not for a very long time. I'd taught the very best. My own music was universally respected, and I got at least five major commissions every year for ducal and official occasions. I'd written six books on musical theory, all of which had become the standard works on the aspects of the subject they cover. Students came here from every part of the empire, thousands of miles in cramped ships and badly-sprung coaches, to hear me lecture on harmony and the use of form. The year before, they'd named one of the five modes after me.

When I'd read it, I looked at the fire, which the servant had lit while I was out. It would be so easy, I thought. Twenty sheets of paper don't take very long to burn. But, as I think I told you, I'd already broached the subject with the Kapelmeister, who'd offered me five hundred angels, sight unseen, even unfinished. I knew I could get him up to eight hundred. I have no illusions about myself.

※

A Small Price to Pay for Birdsong | K. J. Parker

I didn't try and finish the piece; not because I'd promised I wouldn't, but because he escaped. To this day, nobody has the faintest idea how he managed it. All we know is that when the captain of the guard opened his cell to take him to the scaffold, he found a warder sitting on the bench with his throat cut, and no sign of the prisoner.

There was an enquiry, needless to say. I had a very uncomfortable morning at guard headquarters, where I sat on a bench in a corridor for three hours before making the acquaintance of a Captain Monomachus of the Investigative branch. He pointed out to me that I was a known associate of the prisoner, and that I'd been the last person to be alone with him before his escape. I replied that I'd been thoroughly and quite humiliatingly searched before I went in to see him, and there was no way I could've taken him in any kind of weapon.

"We aren't looking for a weapon, as a matter of fact," captain Monomachus replied. "We reckon he smashed his inkwell and used a shard of the glass. What we're interested in is how he got clear of the barbican. We figure he must've had help."

I looked the captain straight in the eye. I could afford to. "He always had plenty of friends," I said.

For some reason, the captain smiled at that. "After you left him," he said, "where did you go?"

"Straight back to my rooms in college. The porter can vouch for me, presumably. And my servant. He brought me a light supper shortly after I got home."

Captain Monomachus prowled round me for a while after that, but since he had absolutely nothing against me, he had to let me go. As I was about to leave, he stopped me and said, "I understand there was a last piece."

I nodded. "That's right. That's what I was reading, the rest of the evening."

"Any good?"

"Oh yes." I paused, then added, "Possibly his best. Unfinished, of course."

There was a slight feather of shyness about the question that followed. "Will there be a performance?"

I told him the date and the venue. He wrote them down on a scrap of paper, which he folded and put in his pocket.

⋇

The good captain was, in fact, the least of my problems. That same evening, I was summoned to the Master's lodgings.

"Your protégé," the Master said, pouring me a very small glass of the college brandy.

"My student," I said. It's very good brandy, as a matter of fact, but invariably wasted, because the only times I get to drink it are when I'm summoned into the presence, on which occasions I'm always so paralysed with fear that even good brandy has no effect whatsoever.

He sighed, sniffed his glass and sat down; or rather, he perched on the edge of the settle. He always likes to be higher than his guests. Makes swooping to strike easier, I imagine. "An amazingly gifted man," he said. "You might go so far as to call him a genius, though that term is sadly over-used these days, I find." I waited, and a moment and a sip of brandy later, he continued; "But a fundamentally unstable character. I suppose we ought to have seen the warning signs."

We meaning me; because the Master wasn't appointed until the year after my poor student was expelled. "You know," I said, trying to sound as though it was a conversation rather than an interrogation, "I sometimes wonder if in his case, the two are inseparable; the instability and the brilliance, I mean."

The Master nodded. "The same essential characteristics that made him a genius also made him a murderer," he said. "It's a viable hypothesis, to be sure. In which case, the question must surely arise; can the one ever justify the other? The most sublime music, set against a man's life." He shrugged, a gesture for which his broad, sloping shoulders were perfectly suited. "I shall have to bear that one in mind for my Ethics tutorials. You could argue it quite well both ways, of course. After all, his music will live for ever, and the man he killed was the most dreadful fellow, by all accounts, a petty thief and a drunkard." He paused, to give me time to agree. Even I knew better than that. Once it was clear I'd refused the bait, he said, "The important thing, I think, is to try and learn something from this tragic case."

A Small Price to Pay for Birdsong | K. J. Parker

"Indeed," I said, and nibbled at my brandy to give myself time. I've never fenced, but I believe that's what fencers do; make time by controlling distance. So I held up my brandy glass and hid behind it as best I could.

"Warning signs," he went on, "that's what we need to look out for. These young people come here, they're entrusted to our care at a particularly difficult stage in their development. Our duty doesn't end with stuffing their heads full of knowledge. We need to adopt a more comprehensive pastoral approach. Don't you agree?"

In the old duke's time, they used to punish traitors by shutting them up in a cage with a lion. As an exquisite refinement of malice, they used to feed the lion to bursting point first. That way, it wasn't hungry again for the best part of a day. I always found that very upsetting to think about. If I'm going to be torn apart, I want it to be over quickly. The Master and the old duke were students together, by the way. I believe they got on very well.

"Of course," I said. "No doubt the Senate will let us have some guidelines in due course."

I got out of there eventually, in one piece. Curiously enough, I didn't start shaking until I was halfway across the quadrangle, on my way back to my rooms. I couldn't tell you why encounters like that disturb me so much. After all, the worst the Master could do to me was dismiss me—which was bound to happen, sooner or later, because I only had qualified tenure, and I knew he thought of me as a closet Optimate. Which was, of course, entirely true. But so what? Unfortunately, the thought of losing my post utterly terrifies me. I know I'm too old to get another post anything like as good as this one, and such talent as I ever had has long since dissipated through overuse. I have doctorates and honorary doctorates in music enough to cover a wall, but I can't actually play a musical instrument. I have a little money put by these days, but not nearly enough. I have never experienced poverty, but in the city you see it every day. I don't have a particularly vivid imagination—anybody familiar with my music can attest to that—but I have no trouble at all imagining what it would be like to be homeless and hungry and cold in Perimadeia. I think about it all the time. Accordingly, the threat of my inevitable dismissal at some unascertained point in the future lies over my present like a cloud of volcanic ash, blotting out the sun, and I'm incapable of taking any pleasure in anything at all.

He will always be known by his name in religion, Subtilius of Bohec; but he was born Aimeric de Beguilhan, third son of a minor Northern squire, raised in the farmyard and the stables, destined for an uneventful career in the Ministry. When he came here, he had a place to read Logic, Literature and Rhetoric, and by his own account he'd never composed a bar of music in his life. In Bohec (I have no idea where it is), music consisted of tavern songs and painfully refined dances from the previous century; it featured in his life about as much as the sea, which is something like two hundred miles away in every direction. He first encountered real music in the Studium chapel, which is presumably why nearly all his early work was devotional and choral. When he transferred to the Faculty of Music, I introduced him to the secular instrumental tradition; I suppose that when I appear at last before the court of the Invincible Sun and whoever cross-examines me there asks me if there's one thing I've done which has made the world a better place, that'll be it. Without me, Subtilius would never have written for strings, or composed the five violin concertos, or the three polyphonic symphonies. But he'd already written the first of the Masses before I ever set eyes on him.

The murder was such a stupid business; though, looking back, I suppose it was more or less inevitable that something of the kind should have happened sooner or later. He always did have such a quick temper, fatally combined with a sharp tongue, an unfortunate manner and enough skill at arms to make him practically fearless. There was also the fondness for money—there was never quite enough money when he was growing up, and I know he was exceptionally sensitive about that—and the sort of amorality that often seems to go hand in hand with keen intelligence and an unsatisfactory upbringing. He was intelligent enough to see past the reasons generally advanced in support of obedience to the rules and the law, but lacking in any moral code of his own to take its place. Add to that youth, and overconfidence arising from the praise he'd become accustomed to as soon as he began to compose music, and you have a recipe for disaster.

Even now, I couldn't tell you much about the man he killed. Depending on which account you go by, he was either an accomplice or a rival. In any event, he was a small-time professional thief, a thoroughly worthless specimen who would most assuredly have ended up on the gallows if Subtilius hadn't stabbed him through the neck in the stable-yard of the *Integrity and Honour* in Foregate. Violent death is, I believe, no uncommon occurrence there, and he'd probably have got away with it had not one of the ostlers been a passionate admirer of his religious music, and therefore recognised him and been able to identify him to the Watch; an unfortunate consequence, I suppose, of the quite exceptionally broad appeal of Subtilius' music. If I'd stabbed a man in a stable-yard, the chances of a devoted fan recognising me would've been too tiny to quantify, unless the ostler happened to be a fellow academic fallen on hard times.

I got back to my rooms, fumbled with the keys, dropped them—anybody passing would have thought I was drunk, although of course I scarcely touched a drop in those days; I couldn't afford to, with the excise tax so high—finally managed to get the door open and fall into the room. It was dark, of course, and I spent quite some time groping for the tinder-box and the candle, and then I dropped the moss out of the box onto the floor and had to grope for that too. Eventually I struck a light, and used the candle to light the oil lamp. It was only then, as the light colonised the room, that I saw I wasn't alone.

"Hello, professor," said Subtilius.

My first thought—I was surprised at how quickly and practically I reacted—was the shutters. Mercifully, they were closed. In which case, he couldn't have come in through the window—

He laughed. "It's all right," he said, "nobody saw me. I was extremely careful."

Easy to say; easy to believe, but easy to be wrong. "How long have you been here?"

"I came in just after you left. You left the door unlocked."

Quite right; I'd forgotten.

"I took the precaution of locking it for you," he went on, "with the spare key you still keep in that ghastly pot on the mantelpiece. Look, why don't you sit down before you fall over? You look awful."

I went straight to the door and locked it. Not that I get many visitors, but I was in no mood to rely on the laws of probability. "What the hell are you doing here?"

He sighed, and stretched out his legs. I imagine it was what his father used to do, after a long day on the farm or following the hounds. "Hiding," he said. "What do you think?"

"You can't hide here."

"Overjoyed to see you too."

It was an entirely valid rebuke, so I ignored it. "Aimeric, you're being utterly unreasonable. You can't expect me to harbour a fugitive from justice—"

"Aimeric." He repeated the word as though it had some kind of incantatory power. "You know, professor, you're the only person who's called me that since the old man died. Can't say I ever liked the name, but it's odd to hear it again after all these years. Listen," he said, before I could get a word in, "I'm sorry if I scared the life out of you, but I need your help."

I always did find him both irresistibly charming and utterly infuriating. His voice, for one thing. I suppose it's my musician's ear; I can tell you more about a man, where he's from and how much money he's got, from hearing him say two words than any mere visual clues. Subtilius had a perfect voice; consonants clear and sharp as a knife, vowels fully distinguished and immaculately expressed. You can't learn to talk like that over the age of three. No matter how hard you try, if you start off with a provincial burr, like me, it'll always bleed through sooner or later. You can only achieve that bell-like clarity and those supremely beautiful dentals and labials if you start learning them before you can walk. That's where actors go wrong, of course. They can make themselves sound like noblemen after years of study so long as they stick to normal everyday conversational pitches. But if they try and shout, anyone with a trained ear can hear the northern whine or the southern bleat, obvious as a stain on a white sheet. Subtilius had a voice you'd have paid money to listen to, even if all he was doing was giving you directions to the Southgate, or swearing at a porter for letting the sludge get into the wine. That sort of perfection is, of course, profoundly annoying if you don't happen to be true-born aristocracy. My father was a fuller and soap-boiler in Ap'Escatoy. My first job was riding with him on the cart collecting the contents of chamber pots from the inns in the early hours of the morning. I've spent forty years trying to sound like a gentleman, and these days I can fool everybody except myself. Subtilius was born perfect and never had to try.

"Where the hell," I asked him, "have you been? The guard's been turning the city upside down. How did you get out of the barbican? All the gates were watched."

He laughed. "Simple," he said. "I didn't leave. Been here all the time, camping out in the clock tower."

Well, of course. The Studium, as I'm sure you know, is built into the west wall of the barbican. Naturally they searched it, the same day he escaped, after which they concluded that he must've got past the gate somehow and made it down to the lower town. It wouldn't have occurred to them to try the clock tower. Twenty years ago, an escaped prisoner hid up there, and when they found him, he was extremely dead. Nothing can survive in the bell-chamber when the clock strikes; the sheer pressure of sound would pulp your brain. Oh, I imagine a couple of guardsmen put their heads round inside the chamber when they knew it was safe, but they wouldn't have made a thorough search, because everybody knows the story. But in that case—

"Why aren't I dead?" He grinned at me. "Because the story's a load of old rubbish. I always had my doubts about it, so I took the trouble to look up the actual records. The prisoner who hid out up there died of blood poisoning from a scratch he'd got climbing out of a broken window. The thing about the bells killing him was pure mythology. You know how people like to believe that sort of thing." He gave me a delightful smile. "So they've been looking for me in Lower Town, have they? Bless them."

Curiosity, presumably; the true scholar's instinct, which he always had. But combined, I dare say, with the thought at the back of his mind that one day, a guaranteed safe hiding-place would come in useful. I wondered when he'd made his search in the archives; when he was fifteen, or seventeen, or twenty-one?

"I'm not saying it was exactly pleasant, mind," he went on, "not when the bells actually struck. The whole tower shakes, did you know that? It's a miracle it hasn't collapsed. But I found that if I crammed spiders' web into my ears—really squashed it down till no more would go in—it sort of deadened the noise to the point where it was bearable. And one thing there's no shortage of up there is cobwebs."

I've always been terrified of spiders. I'm sure he knew that.

"Fine," I snapped at him; I was embarrassed with myself, because my first reaction was admiration. "So you killed a man and managed to stay free for three weeks. How very impressive. What have you been living on, for God's sake? You should be thin as a rake."

He shrugged. "I didn't stay in there all the time," he said. "Generally speaking, I made my excursions around noon and midnight." When the bell tolls twelve times, there being a limit, presumably, to the defensive capacity of cobweb. "It's amazing how much perfectly good food gets thrown out in the kitchens. You're on the catering committee, you really ought to do something about it."

Part of his genius, I suppose; to make his desperate escape and three weeks' torment in the bell-tower sound like a student prank, just as he made writing the Seventh Mass seem effortless, something he churned out in an idle moment between hangovers. Perhaps the secret of sublime achievement really is not to try. But first, you have to check the archives, or learn the twelve major modulations of the Vesani mode, or be born into a family that can trace its pedigree back to Boamond.

"Well," I said, standing up, "I'm sorry, but you've had all that for nothing. I'm going to have to turn you in. You do realise that."

He just laughed at me. He knew me too well. He knew that if I'd really meant it, I'd have done it straight away, yelled for the guard at the top of my voice instead of panicking about the shutters. He knew it; I didn't, not until I heard him laugh. Until then, I thought I was deadly serious. But he was right, of course. "Sure," he said. "You go ahead."

I sat down again. I hated him so much, at that moment.

"How's the concerto coming along?" he asked.

For a moment, I had no idea what he was talking about. Then I remembered; his last concerto, or that's what it should have been. The manuscript he gave me in the condemned cell. "You said not to finish it," I told him.

"Good Lord." He was amused. "I assumed you'd have taken no notice. Well, I'm touched. Thank you."

"What are you doing here?" I asked him.

"I need money," he replied, and somehow his voice contrived to lose a proportion of its honeyed charm. "And clothes, and shoes, things like that. And someone to leave a door open at night. That sort of thing."

"I can't," I said.

He sighed. "You can, you know. What you mean is, you don't want to."

"I haven't got any money."

He gave me a sad look. "We're not talking about large sums," he said. "It's strictly a matter of context. Enough to get me out of town and on a ship, that's all. That's wealth beyond the dreams of avarice." He paused—I think it was for effect—and added, "I'm not asking for a *present*. I do have something to sell."

There was a moment when my entire covering of skin went cold. I could guess. What else would he have to sell, apart from—?

"Three weeks in the bloody bell tower," he went on, and now he sounded exactly like his old self. "Nothing to do all day. Fortunately, on my second trip to the trash cans I passed an open door, some first-year, presumably, who hasn't learned about keeping his door locked. He'd got ink, pens and half a ream of good paper. Don't suppose he'll make that mistake again."

⁂

I love music. It's been my life. Music has informed my development, given me more pleasure than I can possibly quantify or qualify; it's also taken me from the fullers' yard at Ap'Escatoy to the Studium, and kept me here, so far at least. Everything I am, everything I have, is because of music.

For which I am properly grateful. The unfortunate part of it is, there's never been quite enough. Not enough music in me; never enough money. The pleasure, emotional and intellectual, is one thing. The money, however, is another. Almost enough—I'm not a luxurious sort of person, I don't spend extravagantly, but most of it seems to go on overheads; college bills, servants' wages, contributions to this and that fund, taxes, of course, all that sort of nonsense—but never quite enough to let me feel comfortable. I live in a constant state of anxiety about money, and inevitably that anxiety has a bad effect on my relationship with music. And the harder I try, the less the inspiration flows. When I don't need it, when I'm relatively comfortable and the worry subsides for a while, a melody will come to me quite unexpectedly and I'll write something really quite good. But when I'm facing a deadline, or when the bills are due and my purse is empty; when I need money, the inspiration seems to dry up completely, and all I can do is grind a little paste off the salt-block of what I've learned, or try and dress up something old, my own or someone else's, and hope to God nobody notices. At times like that, I get angry with music. I even imagine—wrongly, of course—that I wish I was back in the fullers' yard. But that's long gone, of course. My brother and I sold it when my father died, and the money was spent years ago, so I don't even have that to fall back on. Just music.

"You've written something," I said.

"Oh yes." From inside his shirt he pulled a sheaf of paper. "A symphony, in three movements and a coda." I suppose I must have reached out instinctively, because he moved back gently. "Complete, you'll be relieved to hear. All yours, if you want it."

All my life I've tried to look civilised and refined, an intellect rather than a physical body. But when I want something and it's so close I can touch it, I sweat. My hands get clammy, and I can feel the drops lifting my hair where it touches my forehead. "A symphony," was all I could say.

He nodded. "My fourth. I think you're going to like it."

"All mine if I want it."

"Ah." He did the mock frown. "All yours if you pay for it. Your chance to be an illustrious patron of the arts, like the Eberharts."

I stared at him. All mine. "Don't be so bloody stupid," I yelled. "I can't use it. It'd be useless to me."

He pretended to be upset. "You haven't even looked at it."

"Think about it," I said, low and furious. "You're on the run from the Watch, with a death sentence against your name. I suddenly present a brand new Subtilius symphony. It'd be obvious. Any bloody fool would know straight away that I'd helped you escape."

He nodded. "I see your point," he said mildly. "But you could say it's an old piece, something I wrote years ago, and you've been hanging on to it."

"Is that likely?"

"I guess not." He smiled at me, a sunrise-over-the-bay smile, warm and bright and humiliating. "So I guess you'll just have to pretend you wrote it, won't you?"

It was like a slap across the face, insulting and unexpected. "Please," I said. "Don't even suggest it. You know perfectly well I could never pass off your work as my own. Everybody would know after the first couple of bars."

Then he smiled again, and I knew he was playing me. He'd led me carefully to a certain place where he wanted me to be. "That won't be a problem," he said. "You see, I've written it in your style."

Maybe shock and anger had made me more than usually stupid. It took a moment; and then I realised what he'd just said.

"Hence," he went on, "the symphonic form, which I've never really cared for, but it's sort of like your trademark, isn't it? And I've used the tetrachord of Mercury throughout, even quoted a bar or two of the secondary theme from your Third. Here," he said, and handed me a page—just the one, he was no fool—from the sheaf.

I didn't want to take it. I swear, it felt like deliberately taking hold of a nettle and squeezing it into your palm. I looked down.

I can read music very quickly and easily, as you'd expect. One glance and it's there in my head. It only took me a couple of heartbeats to know what I was holding. It was, of course, a masterpiece. It was utterly brilliant, magnificent, the sort of music that defines a place and a time for all time. It soared inside me as I looked at it, filling and choking me, as though someone had shoved a bladder down my throat and started blowing it up. It was in every way perfect; and *I could have written it.*

"Well?" he said.

Let me qualify that. No, I couldn't have written it, not in a million years, not if my life depended on it; not even if, in some moment of absolute peace and happiness, the best inspiration of my entire life had lodged inside my head, and the circumstances had been so perfectly arranged that I was able to take advantage of it straight away, while it was fresh and whole in my mind (which never ever happens, of course). I could never have written it; but it was in my style, so exactly captured that anybody but me would believe it was my work. It wasn't just the trademark flourishes and periods, the way I use the orchestra, the mathematical way I build through intervals and changes of key. A parody could've had all those. The music I was looking at had been written by someone who understood me perfectly—better than I've ever understood myself—and who knew exactly what I wanted to say, although I've always lacked the skill, and the power.

"Well," he said. "Do you like it?"

As stupid a question as I've ever heard in my life, and of course I didn't reply. I was too angry, heartbroken, ashamed.

"I was quite pleased with the cadenza," he went on. "I got the idea from that recurring motif in your Second, but I sort of turned it through ninety degrees and stuck a few feathers in it."

I've never been married, of course, but I can imagine what it must be like, to come home unexpectedly and find your wife in bed with another man. It'd be the love that'd fill you with hate. Oh, how I hated Subtilius at that moment. And imagine how you'd feel if you and your wife had never been able to have kids, and you found out she was pregnant by another man.

"It's got to be worth money," I heard him say. "Just the sort of thing the duke would like."

A Small Price to Pay for Birdsong | K. J. Parker

He always had that knack, did Subtilius. The ability to take the words out of the mouth of the worst part of me, the part I'd cheerfully cut out with a knife in cold blood if only I knew where in my body it's located. "Well?" he said.

⋇

When I was nineteen years old, my father and my elder brother and I were in the cart—I was back home for the holidays, helping out on the rounds—and we were driving out to the old barns where my father boiled the soap. The road runs along the top of a ridge, and when it rains, great chunks of it get washed away. It had been raining heavily the day before, and by the time we turned the sharp bend at the top it was nearly dark. I guess my father didn't see where the road had fallen away. The cart went over. I was sitting in the back and was thrown clear. Father and Segibert managed to scramble clear just as the cart went over; Segibert caught hold of Dad's ankle, and Dad grabbed onto a rock sticking out of the ground. I managed to get my hand round his wrist, and for a moment we were stuck there. I've never been strong, and I didn't have the strength to pull them up, not so much as an inch. All I could do was hold on, and I knew that if I allowed myself to let his hand slip even the tiniest bit, I'd lose him and both of them, the two people I loved most in the whole world, would fall and die. But in that moment, when all the thoughts that were ever possible were running through my head, I thought; if they do both fall, and they're both killed, then when we sell the business, it'd be just me, best part of three hundred angels, and what couldn't I do with that sort of money?

Then Segibert managed to get a footing, and between them they hauled and scrambled and got up next to me on the road, and soon we were all in floods of tears, and Dad was telling me I'd saved his life, and he'd never forget it. And I felt so painfully guilty, as though I'd pushed them over deliberately.

⋇

Well, I thought. Yes. Worth a great deal of money.

"More the old duke's sort of thing," he was saying, "he'd have loved it, he was a man of taste and discrimination. Compared with him, young Sighvat's a barbarian. But even he'd like this, I'm sure."

A barbarian. The old duke used to punish debtors by giving them a head start and then turning his wolfhounds loose. Last year, Sighvat abolished the poll tax and brought in a minimum wage for farm workers. But the old duke had a better ear for music, and he was an extremely generous patron. "I can't," I said.

"Of course you can," Subtilius said briskly. "Now then, I was thinking in terms of three hundred. That'd cover my expenses."

"I haven't got that sort of money."

He looked at me. "No," he said, "I don't suppose you have. Well, what have you got?"

"I can give you a hundred angels."

Which was true. Actually, I had a hundred and fifty angels in the wooden box under my bed. It was the down payment I'd taken from the Kapelmeister for the Unfinished Concerto, so properly speaking it was Subtilius' money anyway. But I needed the fifty. I had bills to pay.

"That'll have to do, then," he said, quite cheerfully. "It'll cover the bribes and pay for a fake passport, I'll just have to steal food and clothes. Can't be helped. You're a good man, professor."

There was still time. I could throw the door open and yell for a porter. I was still innocent of any crime, against the State or myself. Subtilius would go back to the condemned cell, I could throw the manuscript on the fire, and I could resume my life, my slow and inevitable uphill trudge towards poverty and misery. Or I could call the porter and not burn the music. What exactly would happen to me if I was caught assisting an offender? I couldn't bear prison, I'd have to kill myself first; but would I get the chance? Bail would be out of the question, so I'd be remanded pending trial. Highly unlikely that the prison guards would leave knives, razors or poison lying about in my cell for me to use. People hang themselves in jail, they twist ropes out of bedding. But what if I made a mess of it and ended up paralysed for life? Even if I managed to stay out of prison, a criminal conviction would mean instant dismissal and no chance of another job. But that wouldn't matter, if I could keep the music. We are, the Invincible Sun be praised, a remarkably, almost obsessively cultured nation, and music is our life. No matter what its composer had done, work of that quality would always be worth a great deal of money, enough to retire on and never have to compose another note as long as I live—

I was a good man, apparently. He was grateful to me, for swindling him. I was a good man, because I was prepared to pass off a better man's work as my own. Because I was willing to help a murderer escape justice.

"Where will you go?" I asked.

He grinned at me. "You really don't want to know," he said. "Let's just say, a long way away."

"You're famous," I pointed out. "Everywhere. Soon as you write anything, they'll know it's you. They'll figure out it was me who helped you escape."

He yawned. He looked very tired; fair enough, after three weeks in a clock tower, with eight of the biggest bells in the empire striking the quarter hours inches from his head. He couldn't possibly have slept for more than ten minutes. "I'm giving up music," he said. "This is definitely and categorically my last ever composition. You're quite right; the moment I wrote anything, I'd give myself away. There's a few places the empire hasn't got extradition treaties with, but I'd rather be dead than live there. So it's simple, I won't write any more music. After all," he added, his hand over his mouth like he'd been taught as a boy, "there's lots of other things I can do. All music's ever done is land me in trouble."

※

What, when all is said and done, all the conventional garbage is put on one side and you're alone inside your head with yourself, do you actually believe in? That's a question that has occupied a remarkably small percentage of my attention over the years. Strange, since I spend a fair proportion of my working time composing odes, hymns and masses to the Invincible Sun. Do I believe in Him? To be honest, I'm not sure. I believe in the big white disc in the sky, because it's there for all to see. I believe that there's some kind of supreme authority, something along the lines of His Majesty the Emperor only bigger and even more remote, who theoretically controls the universe. What that actually involves, I'm afraid, I couldn't tell you. Presumably He regulates the affairs of great nations, enthrones and deposes emperors and kings—possibly princes and dukes, though it's rather more plausible that He delegates that sort of thing to some kind of divine solar civil service—and intervenes in high-profile cases of injustice and blasphemy whenever a precedent needs to be set or a point of law clarified. Does He deal with me personally, or is He even aware of my existence? On balance, probably not. He wouldn't have the time.

In which case, if I have a file at all, I assume it's on the desk of some junior clerk, along with hundreds, thousands, millions of others. I can't say that that thought bothers me too much. I'd far rather be left alone, in peace and quiet. As far as I'm aware, my prayers—mostly for money, occasionally for the life or recovery from illness of a relative or friend— have never been answered, so I'm guessing that divine authority works on more or less the same lines as its civilian equivalent; don't expect anything good from it, and you won't be disappointed. Just occasionally, though, something happens which can only be divine intervention, and then my world-view and understanding of the nature of things gets all shaken up and reshaped. I explain it away by saying that really it's something primarily happening to someone else—someone important, whose file is looked after by a senior administrative officer or above—and I just happen to be peripherally involved and therefore indirectly affected.

A good example is Subtilius' escape from the barbican. At the time it felt like my good luck. On mature reflection I can see that it was really his good luck, in which I was permitted to share, in the same way that the Imperial umbrella-holder also gets to stay dry when it rains.

It couldn't have been simpler. I went first, to open doors and make sure nobody was watching. He followed on, swathed in the ostentatious cassock and cowl of a Master Chorister—purple with ermine trimmings, richly embroidered with gold thread and seed pearls; anywhere else you'd stand out a mile, but in the barbican, choristers are so commonplace they're practically invisible. Luck intervened by making it rain, so that it was perfectly natural for my chorister companion to have his hood up, and to hold the folds tight around his face and neck. He had my hundred angels in his pockets in a pair of socks, to keep the coins from clinking.

The sally-port in the barbican wall, opening onto the winding stair that takes you down to Lower Town the short way, is locked at nightfall, but faculty officers like me all have keys. I opened the gate and stepped aside to let him pass.

"Get rid of the cassock as soon as you can," I said. "I'll report it stolen first thing in the morning, so they'll be looking for it."

He nodded. "Well," he said, "thanks for everything, professor. I'd just like to say—"

"Get the hell away from here," I said, "before anyone sees us."

⇒)|(⇐

There are few feelings in life quite as exhilarating as getting away with something. Mainly, I guess, if you're someone like me, it's because you never really expected to. Add to the natural relief, therefore, the unaccustomed pleasure of winning. Then, since you can't win anything without having beaten someone first, there's the delicious feeling of superiority, which I enjoy for the same reason that gourmets prize those small grey truffles that grow on the sides of dead birch trees; not because it's nourishing or tasty, but simply because it's so rare. Of course, it remained to be seen whether I had actually got away with aiding and abetting a murderer after the fact and assisting a fugitive. There was still a distinct chance that Subtilius would be picked up by the watch before he could get out of the city, in which case he might very well reveal the identity of his accomplice, if only to stop them hitting him. But, I told myself, that'd be all right. I'd simply tell them he'd burgled my rooms and stolen the money and the cassock, and they wouldn't be able to prove otherwise. I told myself that; I knew perfectly well, of course, that if they did question me, my nerve would probably shatter like an eggshell, and the only thing that might stop me from giving them a comprehensive confession was if I was so incoherent with terror I couldn't speak at all. I think you'd have to be quite extraordinarily brave to be a hardened criminal; much braver than soldiers who lead charges or stand their ground against the cavalry. I could just about imagine myself doing that sort of thing, out of fear of the sergeant-major, but doing something illegal literally paralyses me with fear. And yet courage, as essential to the criminal as his jemmy or his cosh, is held to be a virtue.

The first thing I did when I got back to my room was to light the lamp and open the shutters, because I never close them except when it snows, and people who knew me might wonder what was going on if they saw them shut. Then I poured myself a small brandy—it would've been a large one, but the bottle was nearly empty—and sat down with the lamp so close to me that I could feel it scorching my face, and spread out the manuscript, and read it.

They say that when we first sent out ships to trade with the savages in Rhoezen, we packed the holds full of the sort of things we thought primitive people would like—beads, cheap tin brooches, scarves, shirts, buckles plated so thin the silver practically wiped off on your fingers, that sort of thing. And mirrors. We thought they'd love mirrors. In fact, we planned on buying enough land to grow enough corn to feed the City with a case of hand-mirrors, one angel twenty a gross from the Scharnel Brothers.

We got that completely wrong. The captain of the first ship to make contact handed out a selection of his trade goods by way of free samples. Everything seemed to be going really well until they found the mirrors. They didn't like them. They threw them on the ground and stamped on them, then attacked our people with spears and slingshots, until the captain had to fire a cannon just so as to get his men back off the beach in one piece. Later, when he'd managed to capture a couple of specimens and he interrogated them through an interpreter, he found out what the problem was. The mirrors, the prisoners told him, were evil. They sucked your soul out through your eyes and imprisoned it under the surface of the dry-hard-water. Stealing the souls of harmless folk who'd only wanted to be friendly to strangers was not, in their opinion, civilised behaviour. Accordingly, we weren't welcome in their country.

When I first heard the story, I thought the savages had over-reacted somewhat. When I'd finished reading Subtilius' symphony, written in my style, I was forced to revise my views. Stealing a man's soul is one of the worst things you can do to him, and it hardly matters whether you shut it up in a mirror or thirty pages of manuscript. It's not something you can ever forgive.

※

And then, after I'd sat still and quiet for a while, until the oil in the lamp burned away and I was left entirely alone in the dark, I found myself thinking; yes, but nobody will ever know. All I had to do was sit down and copy it out in my own handwriting, then burn the original, and there would be no evidence, no witnesses. You hear a lot from the philosophers and the reverend Fathers about truth, about how it must inevitably prevail, how it will always burst through, like the saplings that grow up in the cracks in walls until their roots shatter the stone. It's not true. Subtilius wouldn't ever tell anybody (and besides, it was only a matter of time before he was caught and strung up, and that'd be him silenced for ever). I sure as hell wasn't going to say anything. If there's a truth and nobody knows it, is it still true? Or is it like a light burning in a locked, shuttered house that nobody will ever get to see?

I'd know it, of course. I did consider that. But then I thought about the money.

※

The debut of my Twelfth Symphony took place at the collegiate temple on Ascension Day, AUC 775, in the presence of his highness Duke Sighvat II, the duchess and dowager duchess, the Archimandrite of the Studium and a distinguished audience drawn from the Court, the university and the best of good society. It was, I have to say, a triumph. The duke was so impressed that he ordered a command performance at the palace. Less prestigious but considerably more lucrative was the licence I agreed to with the Kapelmeister; a dozen performances at the Empire Hall at a thousand angels a time, with the rights reverting to me thereafter. Subsequently I made similar deals with kapelmeisters and court musicians and directors of music from all over the empire, taking care to reserve the sheet music rights, which I sold to the Court stationers for five thousand down and a five per cent royalty. My tenure at the University was upgraded to a full Fellowship, which meant I could only be got rid of by a bill of attainder passed by both houses of the Legislature and ratified by the duke, and then only on grounds of corruption or gross moral turpitude; my stipend went up from three hundred to a thousand a year, guaranteed for life, with bonuses should I ever condescend to do any actual teaching. Six months after the first performance, as I sat in my rooms flicking jettons about on my counting-board, I realised that I need never work again. Quite suddenly, all my troubles were over.

On that, and what followed, I base my contention that there is no justice; that the Invincible Sun, if He's anything more than a ball of fire in the sky, has no interest and does not interfere in the life and fortunes of ordinary mortals, and that morality is simply a confidence trick practised on all of us by the State and its officers to keep us from making nuisances of ourselves. For a lifetime of devotion to music, I got anxiety, misery and uncertainty. For two crimes, one against the State and one against myself, I was rewarded with everything I'd ever wanted. Explain that, if you can.

Everything? Oh yes. To begin with, I dreaded the commissions that started to flood in from the duke, other dukes and princes, even the Imperial court; because I knew I was a fraud, that I'd never be able to write anything remotely as good as the Symphony, and it was only a matter of time before someone figured out what had actually happened and soldiers arrived at my door to arrest me. But I sat down, with a lamp and a thick mat of paper; and it occurred to me that, now I didn't need the money, all I had to do was refuse the commissions—politely, of course—and nobody could touch me. I didn't have to write a single note if I didn't want to. It was entirely up to me.

A Small Price to Pay for Birdsong | K. J. Parker

Once I'd realised that, I started to write. And, knowing that it really didn't matter, I hardly bothered to try. The less I tried, the easier it was to find a melody (getting a melody out of me was always like pulling teeth). Once I'd got that, I simply let it rattle about in my head for a while, and wrote down the result. Once I'd filled the necessary number of pages, I signed my name at the top and sent it off. I didn't care, you see. If they didn't like it, they knew what they could do.

From time to time, to begin with at least, it did occur to me to wonder, *is this stuff any good?* But that raises the question; how the hell does anybody ever know? If the criterion is the reaction of the audience, or the sums of money offered for the next commission, I just kept getting better. That was, of course, absurd. Even I could see that. But no; my audiences and my critics insisted that each new work was better than its predecessors (though the Twelfth Symphony was the piece that stayed in the repertoires, and the later masterpieces sort of came and went; not that I gave a damn). A cynic would argue that once I'd become a great success, nobody dared to criticise my work for fear of looking a fool; the only permitted reaction was ever increasing adulation. Being a cynic myself, I favoured that view for a while. But, as the success continued and the money flowed and more and more music somehow got written, I began to have my doubts. All those thousands of people, I thought, they can't all be self-deluded. There comes a point when you build up a critical mass, beyond which people sincerely believe. That's how religions are born, and how criteria change. By my success, I'd redefined what constitutes beautiful music. If it sounded like the sort of stuff I wrote, people were prepared to believe it was beautiful. After all, beauty is only a perception—the thickness of an eyebrow, very slight differences in the ratio between length and width of a nose or a portico or a colonnade. Tastes evolve. People like what they're given.

Besides, I came to realise, the Twelfth *was* mine; to some extent at least. After all, the style Subtilius had borrowed was my style, which I'd spent a lifetime building. And if he had the raw skill, the wings, I'd been his teacher; without me, who was to say he'd ever have risen above choral and devotional works and embraced the orchestra? At the very least it was a collaboration, in which I could plausibly claim to be the senior partner. And if the doors are locked and the shutters are closed, whose business is it whether there's a light burning inside? You'd never be able to find out without breaking and entering, which is a criminal offence.

Even so, I began making discreet enquiries. I could afford the best, and I spared no expense. I hired correspondents in all the major cities and towns of the empire to report back to me about notable new compositions and aspiring composers—I tried to pay for this myself, but the university decided that it constituted legitimate academic research and insisted on footing the bill. Whenever I got a report that hinted at the possibility of Subtilius, I sent off students to obtain a written score or sit in the concert hall and transcribe the notes. I hired other, less reputable agents to go through the criminal activity reports, scrape up acquaintance with watch captains, and waste time in the wrong sort of inns, fencing-schools, bear gardens and livery stables. I was having to tread a fine line, of course. The last thing I wanted was for the watch to reopen their file or remember the name Subtilius, or Aimeric de Beguilhan, so I couldn't have descriptions or likenesses circulated. I didn't regard that as too much of a handicap, however. Sooner or later, I firmly believed, if he was still alive, the music would break out and he'd give himself away. It wouldn't be the creative urge that did for him; it'd be that handmaiden of the queen of the Muses, a desperate and urgent need for money, that got Subtilius composing again. No doubt he'd do his best to disguise himself. He'd try writing street ballads, or pantomime ballets, secure in the belief that that sort of thing was beneath the attention of academic musicians. But it could only be a matter of time. I knew his work, after all, in ways nobody else ever possibly could. I could spot his hand in a sequence of intervals, a modulation or key shift, the ghost of a flourish, the echo of a dissonance. As soon as he put pen to paper, I felt sure, I'd have him.

A Small Price to Pay for Birdsong | K. J. Parker

I was invited to lecture at the University of Baudoin. I didn't want to go—I've always hated travelling—but the marquis was one of my most enthusiastic patrons, and they were offering a thousand angels for an afternoon's work. Oddly enough, affluence hadn't diminished my eagerness to earn money. I guess that no matter how much I had, I couldn't resist the opportunity to add just a bit more, to be on the safe side. I wrote back accepting the invitation.

When I got there (two days in a coach; misery) I found they'd arranged a grand recital of my work for the day after the lecture. I couldn't very well turn round and tell them I was too busy to attend; also, the Baudoin orchestra was at that time reckoned to be the second or third best in the world, and I couldn't help being curious about how my music would sound, played by a really first-class band. Our orchestra in Perimadeia rates very highly on technical skill, but they have an unerring ability to iron the joy out of pretty well anything. I fixed up about the rights with the kapelmeister, thereby doubling my takings for the trip, and told them I'd be honoured and delighted to attend.

The lecture went well. They'd put me in the chapter-house of the Ascendency Temple—not the world's best acoustic, but the really rather fine stained-glass windows are so artfully placed that if you lecture around noon, as I did, and you stand on the lectern facing the audience, you're bathed all over in the most wonderful red and gold light, so that it looks like you're on fire. I gave them two hours on diatonic and chromatic semitones in the Mezentine diapason (it's something I feel quite passionate about, but they know me too well in Perimadeia and stopped listening years ago) and I can honestly say I had them in the palm of my hand. Afterwards, the marquis got up and thanked me—as soon as he joined me on the podium, the sun must've come out from behind a cloud or something, because the light through the windows suddenly changed from red to blue, and instead of burning, we were drowning—and then the provost of the university presented me with an honorary doctorate, which was nice of him, and made a long speech about integrity in the creative arts. The audience got a bit restive, but I was getting paid for being there, so I didn't mind a bit.

There was a reception afterwards; good food and plenty of wine. I must confess I don't remember much about it.

I enjoyed the recital, in spite of a nagging headache I'd woken up with and couldn't shift all day. Naturally, they played the Twelfth; that was the whole of the first half. I wasn't sure I liked the way they took the slow movement, but the finale was superb, it really did sprout wings and soar. The second half was better still. They played two of my Vesani horn concertos and a couple of temple processionals, and there were times when I found myself sitting bolt upright in my seat, asking myself, *did I really write that?* It just goes to show what a difference it makes, hearing your stuff played by a thoroughly competent, sympathetic orchestra. At one point I was so caught up in the music that I couldn't remember what came next, and the denouement—the solo clarinet in the *Phainomai*—took me completely by surprise and made my throat tighten. I thought, *I wrote that,* and I made a mental note of that split second, like pressing a flower between the pages of a book, for later.

It was only when the recital was over, and the conductor was taking his bow, that I saw him. At first, I really wasn't sure. It was just a glimpse of a turned-away head, and when I looked again I'd lost him in the sea of faces. I told myself I was imagining things, and then I saw him again. He was looking straight at me.

There was supposed to be another reception, but I told them I was feeling ill, which wasn't exactly a lie. I went back to the guest suite. There wasn't a lock or a bolt on the door, so I wedged the back of a chair under the handle.

While I'd been at the recital, they'd delivered a whole load of presents. People give me things these days, now that I can afford to buy anything I want. True, the gifts I tend to receive are generally things I'd never buy for myself, because I have absolutely no need for them, and because I do have a certain degree of taste. On this occasion, the marquis had sent me a solid gold dinner service (for a man who, most evenings, eats alone in his rooms off a tray on his knees), a complete set of the works of Aurelianus, ornately bound in gilded calf and too heavy to lift, and a full set of Court ceremonial dress. The latter item consisted of a bright red frock coat, white silk knee breeches, white silk stockings, shiny black shoes with jewelled buckles, and a dress sword.

I know everything I want to know about weapons, which is nothing at all. When I first came to the university, my best friend challenged another friend of ours to a duel. It was about some barmaid. Duelling was the height of fashion back then, and I was deeply hurt not to be chosen as a second (later, I found out it was because they'd chosen a time they knew would clash with my Theory tutorial, and they didn't want me to have to skip it). They fought with smallswords in the long meadow behind the School of Logic. My best friend died instantly; his opponent lingered for a day or so and died screaming, from blood poisoning. If that was violence, I thought, you can have it.

So, I know nothing about swords, except that gentlemen are allowed to wear them in the street; from which I assumed that a gentleman's dress sword must be some kind of pretty toy. In spite of which, I picked up the marquis' present, put on my reading glasses and examined it under the lamp.

It was pretty enough, to be sure, if you like that sort of thing. The handle—I don't know the technical terms—was silver, gilded in places, with a pastoral scene enamelled on the inside of the plate thing that's presumably designed to protect your hand. The blade, though, was in another key altogether. It's always hidden by the scabbard, isn't it, so I figured it'd just be a flat, blunt rod. Not so. It was about three feet long, tapering, triangular in section, so thin at the end it was practically a wire but both remarkably flexible and surprisingly stiff at the same time, and pointed like a needle, brand new from the paper packet. I rested the tip on a cushion and pressed gently. It went through it and out the other side as though the cloth wasn't there.

I imagined myself explaining to the watch, no, the palace guard, they wouldn't have the ordinary watch investigate a death in the palace. You know he was a wanted criminal? Quite so, a convicted murderer. He killed a man, then killed a guard escaping from prison. He was my student, years ago, before he went to the bad. I don't know how he got in here, but he wanted money. When I refused, he said he'd have to kill me. There was a struggle. I can't actually remember how the sword came to be in my hand, I suppose I must've grabbed it at some point. All I can remember is him lying there, dead. And then the guard captain would look at me, serious but reassuring, and tell me that it sounded like a straightforward case of self-defence, and by the sound of it, the dead man was no great loss anyhow. I could imagine him being more concerned about the breach of security—a desperate intruder getting into the guest wing—than the possibility that the honorary doctor of music, favorite composer of the marquis, had deliberately murdered somebody.

The thought crossed my mind. After all, nobody would ever know. Once again, there'd be no witnesses. Who could be bothered to break into a locked house on the offchance that there might be a candle burning behind the closed shutters?

I waited, with the sword across my knees, all night. He didn't come.

※

Instead, he caught up with me at an inn in the mountains on my way home; a much more sensible course of action, and what I should have expected.

I was fast asleep, and something woke me. I opened my eyes to find the lamp lit, and Subtilius sitting in a chair beside the bed, looking at me. He gave the impression that I'd been dangerously ill, and he'd refused to leave my bedside.

"Hello, professor," he said.

The sword was in my trunk, leaning up against the wall on the opposite side of the room. "Hello, Aimeric," I said. "You shouldn't be here."

He grinned. "I shouldn't be anywhere," he said. "But what the hell."

I couldn't see a weapon; no knife or sword. "You're looking well," I said, which was true. He'd filled out since I saw him last. He'd been a skinny, sharp-faced boy, always making me think of an opened knife carried in a pocket. Now he was broad-shouldered and full-faced, and his hair was just starting to get thin on top. He had an outdoor tan, and his fingernails were dirty.

"You've put on weight," he said. "Success agrees with you, obviously."

"It's good to see you again."

"No it's not," he said, still grinning. "Well, not for you, anyway. But I thought I'd drop in and say hello. I wanted to tell you how much I enjoyed the recital."

I thought about what that meant. "Of course," I said. "You'll never have heard it played."

He looked as though he didn't understand, for a moment. Then he laughed, "Oh, you mean the symphony," he said. "Not a bit of it. They play it all the time here." He widened the grin. He'd lost a front tooth since I saw him last. "You want to get on to that," he said. "Clearly, you're missing out on royalties."

"About the money," I said, but he gave me a reproachful little frown, as though I'd made a distasteful remark in the presence of ladies. "Forget about that," he said. "Besides, I don't need money these days. I've done quite well for myself, in a modest sort of a way."

"Music?" I had to ask.

"Good Lord, no. I haven't written a note since I saw you last. Might as well have posters made up and nail them to the temple doors. No, I'm in the olive business. I won a beat-up old press in a chess game shortly after I got here, and now I've got seven mills running full-time in the season, and I've just bought forty acres of mature trees in the Santespe valley. If everything goes to plan, in five years' time every jar of olive oil bought and sold in this country will have made me sixpence. It's a wonderful place, this, you can do anything you like. Makes Perimadeia look like a morgue. And the good thing is," he went on, leaning back a little in his chair, "I'm a foreigner, I talk funny. Which means nobody can pinpoint me exactly, the moment I open my mouth, like they can at home. I can be whoever the hell I want. It's fantastic."

I frowned. He'd forced the question on me. "And who do you want to be, Aimeric?"

"Who I am now," he replied vehemently, "absolutely no doubt about it. I won't tell you my new name, of course, you don't want to know that. But here I am, doing nobody any harm, creating prosperity and employment for hundreds of honest citizens, and enjoying myself tremendously, for the first time in my life."

"Music?" I asked.

"Screw music." He beamed at me. "I hardly ever think about it any more. It's a little thing called a sense of perspective. It was only when I got here and my life started coming back together that I realised the truth. Music only ever made me miserable. You know what? I haven't been in a fight since I got here. I hardly drink, I've given up the gambling. Oh yes, and I'm engaged to be married to a very nice respectable girl whose father owns a major haulage business. And that's all thanks to olive oil. All music ever got me was a rope around my neck."

I looked at him. "Fine," I said. "I believe you. And I'm really pleased things have worked out so well for you. So what are you doing here, in my room in the middle of the night?"

The smile didn't fade, but it froze. "Ah well," he said, "listening to music's a different matter, I still enjoy that. I came to tell you how much I enjoyed the recital. That's all."

"You mean the symphony."

He shook his head. "No," he said, "the rest of the program. Your own unaided work. At least," he added, with a slight twitch of an eyebrow, "I assume it is. Or have you enlisted another collaborator?"

I frowned at him. I hadn't deserved that.

"In that case," he said, "I really must congratulate you. You've grown." He paused, and looked me in the eye. "You've grown wings." Suddenly the grin was back, mocking, patronising. "Or hadn't you noticed? You used to write the most awful rubbish."

"Yes," I said.

"But not any more." He stood up, and for a split second I was terrified. But he walked to the table and poured a glass of wine. "I don't know what's got into you, but the difference is extraordinary." He pointed to the second glass. I nodded, and he poured. "You write like you're not afraid of the music any more. In fact, it sounds like you're not afraid of anything. That's the secret, you know."

"I was always terrified of failure."

A Small Price to Pay for Birdsong | K. J. Parker

"Not unreasonably," he said, and brought the glasses over. I took mine and set it down beside the bed. "Good stuff, this."

"I can afford the best."

He nodded. "Do you like it?"

"Not much."

That made him smile. He topped up his glass. "My father had excellent taste in wine," he said. "If it wasn't at least twenty years old and bottled within sight of Mount Bezar, it was only fit for pickling onions. He drank the farm and the timber lot and six blocks of good City property which brought in more than all the rest put together, and then he died and left my older brother to sort out the mess. Last I heard, he was a little old man in a straw hat working all the hours God made, and still the bank foreclosed; he's three years older than me, for crying out loud. And my other brother had to join the army. He died at Settingen. Everlasting glory they called it in temple, but I know for a fact he was terrified of soldiering. He tried to hide in the barn when the carriage came to take him to the academy, and my mother dragged him out by his hair. Which has led me to the view that sometimes, refinement and gracious living come at too high a price." He looked at me over the rim of the glass and smiled. "But I don't suppose you'd agree."

I shrugged. "I'm still living in the same rooms in college," I replied. "And five days a week, dinner is still bread and cheese on a tray in front of the fire. It wasn't greed for all the luxuries. It was being afraid of the other thing." My turn to smile. "Never make the mistake of attributing to greed that which can be explained by fear. I should know. I've lived with fear every day of my life."

He sighed. "You're not drinking," he said.

"I think I've got the start of an ulcer," I said.

He shook his head sadly. "I really am genuinely pleased," he said. "About your music. You know what? I always used to despise you; all that knowledge, all that skill and technique, and no wings. You couldn't soar, so you spent your life trying to invent a flying machine. I learned to fly by jumping off cliffs." He yawned, and scratched the back of his neck. "Of course, most people who try it that way end up splattered all over the place, but it worked just fine for me."

"I didn't jump," I said. "I was pushed."

A big, wide grin spread slowly over his face, like oil on water. "And now you want to tell me how grateful you are."

"Not really, no."

"Oh come on." He wasn't the least bit angry, just amused. Probably just as well the sword was in the trunk. "What the hell did I ever do to you? Look at what I've given you, over the years. The prestige and reflected glory of being my teacher. The symphony. And now you can write music almost as good, all on your own. And what did I get in return? A hundred angels."

"Two hundred," I said coldly. "You've forgotten the previous loan."

He laughed, and dug a hand in his pocket. "Actually, no," he said. "The other reason I'm here." He took out a fat, fist-sized purse and put it on the table. "A hundred and ten angels. I'm guessing at the interest, since we didn't agree a specific rate at the time."

Neither of us said a word for quite some time. Then I stood up, leaned across the table and took the purse.

"Aren't you going to count it?"

"You're a gentleman," I said. "I trust you."

He nodded, like a fencer admitting a good hit. "I think," he said, "that makes us all square, don't you? Unless there's anything else I've forgotten about."

"All square," I said. "Except for one thing."

That took him by surprise. "What?"

"You shouldn't have given up music," I said.

"Don't be ridiculous," he snapped at me. "I'd have been arrested and hung."

I shrugged. "Small price to pay," I said. Which is what he'd said, when he first told me he'd killed a man; a small price to pay for genius. And what I'd said, when I heard all the details. "Don't glower at me like that," I went on. "You were a genius. You wrote music that'll still be played when Perimadeia's just a grassy hill. The Grand Mass, the Third symphony, that's probably all that'll survive of the empire in a thousand years. What was the life of one layabout and one prison warder, against that? Nothing."

"I'd have agreed with you once," he replied. "Now, I'm not so sure."

"Oh, I am. Absolutely certain of it. And if it was worth their lives, it's worth the life of an olive oil merchant, if there was to be just one more concerto. As it is—" I shrugged. "Not up to me, of course, I was just your teacher. That's all I'll ever be, in a thousand years' time. I guess I should count myself lucky for that."

He looked at me for a long time. "Bullshit," he said. "You and I only ever wrote for money. And you don't mean a word of what you've just said." He stood up. "It was nice to see you again. Keep writing. At this rate, one of these days you'll produce something worth listening to."

He left, and I bolted the door; too late by then, of course. That's me all over, of course; I always leave things too late, until they no longer matter.

※

When I got back to the university, I paid a visit to a colleague of mine in the natural philosophy department. I took with me a little bottle, into which I'd poured the contents of a wineglass. A few days later he called on me and said, "You were right."

I nodded. "I thought so."

"Archer's root," he said. "Enough of it to kill a dozen men. Where in God's name did you come by it?"

"Long story," I told him. "Thank you. Please don't mention it to anybody, there's a good fellow."

He shrugged, and gave me back the bottle. I took it outside and poured it away in a flower bed. Later that day I made a donation—one hundred and ten angels—to the Poor Brothers, for their orphanage in Lower Town; the first, last and only charitable donation of my life. The Father recognised me, of course, and asked if I wanted it to be anonymous.

"Not likely," I said. "I want my name up on a wall somewhere, where people can see it. Otherwise, where's the point?"

※

I think I may have mentioned my elder brother, Segibert; the one I rescued from the cart on the mountainside, along with my father. I remember him with fondness, though I realised at a comparatively early age that he was a stupid man, bone idle and a coward. My father knew it too, and my mother, so when Segibert was nineteen he left home. Nobody was sorry to see him go. He made a sort of a living doing the best he could, and even his best was never much good. When he was thirty-five he drifted into Perimadeia, married a retired prostitute (her retirement didn't last very long, apparently) and made a valiant attempt at running a tavern, which lasted for a really quite creditable eight months. By the time the bailiffs went in, his wife was pregnant, the money was long gone, and Segibert could best be described as a series of brief intervals between drinks. I'd just been elected to my chair, the youngest ever professor of music; the last thing I wanted was any contact whatsoever with my disastrous brother. In the end I gave him thirty angels, all the money I had, on condition that he went away and I never saw him again. He fulfilled his end of the deal by dying a few months later. By then, however, he'd acquired a son as well as a widow. She had her vocation to fall back on, which was doubtless a great comfort to her. When he came of age, or somewhat before, my nephew followed his father's old profession. I got a scribbled note from him when he was nineteen, asking me for bail money, which I neglected to answer, and that was all the contact there was between us. I never met him. He died young.

My second visit to a condemned cell. Essentially the same as the first one; walls, ceiling, floor, a tiny barred window, a stone ledge for sitting and sleeping. A steel door with a small sliding hatch in the top.

"I didn't think there was an extradition treaty between us and Baudoin," I said.

He lifted his head out of his hands. "There isn't," he said. "So they snatched me off the street, shoved me into a closed carriage and drove me across the border. Three days before my wedding," he added. "Syrisca will be half dead with worry about me."

"Surely that was illegal."

He nodded. "Yes," he said. "I believe there's been a brisk exchange of notes between the embassies, and the marquis has lodged an official complaint. Strangely enough, I'm still here."

I looked at him. It was dark in the cell, so I couldn't see much. "You've got a beard," I said. "That's new."

"Syrisca thought I'd look good in a beard."

I held back, postponing the moment. "I suppose you feel hard done by," I said.

"Yes, actually." He swung his legs up onto the ledge and crouched, hugging his knees to his chin. "Fair enough, I did some stupid things when I was a kid. But I did some pretty good things too. And then I gave both of them up, settled down and turned into a regular citizen. It's been a long time. I really thought I was free and clear."

Surreptitiously I looked round the cell. What I was looking for didn't seem to be there, but it was pretty dark. "How did they find you?" I asked.

He shrugged. "No idea," he said. "I can only assume someone from the old days must've recognised me, but I can't imagine who it could've been. I gave up music," he added bitterly. "Surely that ought to have counted for something."

He'd taken care not to tell me his new name, that night in the inn, but a rising young star in the Baudoin olive oil trade wasn't hard to find. Maybe he shouldn't have given me that much information. But he hadn't expected me to live long enough to make use of it.

"You tried to poison me," I said.

He looked at me, and his eyes were like glass. "Yes," he said. "Sorry about that. I'm glad you survived, if that means anything to you."

"Why?"

"Why did I do it?" He gave me a bemused look. "Surely that's obvious. You recognised me. I knew you'd realised who I was, as soon as our eyes met at the recital. That was really stupid of me," he went on, looking away. "I should've guessed you'd never have turned me in."

"So it was nearly three murders," I said. "That tends to undercut your assertion that you've turned over a new leaf."

"Yes," he said. "And my theory that it was somehow connected to writing music, since I'd given up by the time I tried to kill you. I really am sorry about that, by the way."

I gave him a weak smile. "I forgive you," I said.

"Thanks."

"Also," I went on, "I've been to see the duke. He's a great admirer of my work, you know."

"Is that right?"

"Oh yes. And to think you once called him a savage."

"He's not the man his father was," he replied. "I think the old duke might have pardoned me. You know, for services to music."

"Sighvat didn't put it quite like that," I replied. "It was more as a personal favour to me."

There was quite a long silence; just like—I'm sorry, but I really can't resist the comparison—a rest at a crucial moment in a piece of music. "He's letting me go?"

"Not quite," I said, as gently as I could. "He reckons he's got to consider the feelings of the victim's family. Fifteen years. With luck and good behaviour, you'll be out in ten."

He took it in two distinct stages; first the shudder, the understandable horror at the thought of an impossibly long time in hell; then, slowly but successfully pulling himself out of despair, as he considered the alternative. "I can live with that," he said.

"I'm afraid you'll have to," I replied. "I'm sorry. It was the best I could do."

He shook his head. "I'm the one who should apologise," he said. "I tried to kill you, and you just saved my life." He looked up, and even in the dim light I could see an expression on his face I don't think I'd ever seen before. "You always were better than me," he said. "I didn't deserve that."

I shrugged. "We're quits, then," I said. "For the symphony. But there's one condition."

He made a vague sort of gesture to signify capitulation. "Whatever," he said.

"You've got to start writing music again."

For a moment, I think he was too bewildered to speak. Then he burst out laughing. "That's ridiculous," he said. "It's been so long, I haven't even thought about it."

"It'll come back to you, I bet. Not my condition, by the way," I added, lying. "The duke's. So unless you want a short walk and an even shorter drop, I suggest you look to it. Did you get the paper I had sent up, by the way?"

"Oh, that was you, was it?" He looked at me a bit sideways. "Yes, thanks. I wiped my arse with it."

"In future, use your left hand, it's what it's for. It's a serious condition, Aimeric. It's Sighvat's idea of making restitution. I think it's a good one."

There was another moment of silence. "Did you tell him?"

"Tell him what?"

"That I wrote the symphony. Was that what decided him?"

"I didn't, actually," I said. "But the thought had crossed my mind. Luckily, I didn't have to."

He nodded. "That's all right, then." He sighed, as though he was glad some long and tedious chore was over. "I guess it's like the people who put caged birds out on windowledges in the sun," he said. "Lock 'em up and torture them to make them sing. I never approved of that. Cruel, I call it."

"A small price to pay for birdsong," I said.

Most of what I told him was true. I did go to duke Sighvat to intercede for him. Sighvat was mildly surprised, given that I'd been the one who informed on him in the first place. I didn't tell the duke about the attempt to poison me. The condition was my idea, but Sighvat approved of it. He has rather fanciful notions about poetic justice, which if you ask me is a downright contradiction in terms.

I did bend the truth a little. To begin with, Sighvat was all for giving Subtilius a clear pardon. It was me who said no, he should go to prison instead; and when I explained why I wanted that, he agreed, so I was telling the truth when I told Subtilius it was because of the wishes of the victim's family.

Quite. The young waste-of-space Subtilius murdered was my nephew, Segibert's boy. I didn't find that out until after I helped Subtilius escape, and looking back, I wonder what I'd have done if I'd known at the time. I'm really not sure—which is probably just as well, since I have the misfortune to live with myself, and knowing how I'd have chosen, had I been in full possession of the facts, could quite possibly make that relationship unbearable. Fortunately, it's an academic question.

Subtilius is quite prolific, in his prison cell. Actually, it's not at all bad. I got him moved from the old castle to the barbican tower, and it's really quite comfortable there. In fact, his cell is more or less identical in terms of furnishings and facilities to my rooms in college, and I pay the warders to give him decent food and the occasional bottle of wine. He doesn't have to worry about money, either. Unfortunately, the quantity of his output these days isn't matched by the quality. It's good stuff, highly accomplished, technically proficient and very agreeable to listen to, but no spark of genius, none whatsoever. I don't know. Maybe he still has the wings, but in his cage, on the windowsill, where I put him, he can't really make much use of them. ━

The Truth of Fact,
the Truth of Feeling

BY TED CHIANG

When my daughter Nicole was an infant, I read an essay suggesting that it might no longer be necessary to teach children how to read or write, because speech recognition and synthesis would soon render those abilities superfluous. My wife and I were horrified by the idea, and we resolved that, no matter how sophisticated technology became, our daughter's skills would always rest on the bedrock of traditional literacy.

It turned out that we and the essayist were both half correct: now that she's an adult, Nicole can read as well as I can. But there is a sense in which she has lost the ability to write. She doesn't dictate her messages and ask a virtual secretary to read back to her what she last said, the way that essayist predicted; Nicole subvocalizes, her retinal projector displays the words in her field of vision, and she makes revisions using a combination of gestures and eye movements. For all practical purposes, she can write. But take away the assistive software and give her nothing but a keyboard like the one I remain faithful to, and she'd have difficulty spelling out many of the words in this very sentence. Under those specific circumstances, English becomes a bit like a second language to her, one that she can speak fluently but can only barely write.

It may sound like I'm disappointed in Nicole's intellectual achievements, but that's absolutely not the case. She's smart and dedicated to her job at an art museum when she could be earning more money elsewhere, and I've always been proud of her accomplishments. But there is still the past me who would have been appalled to see his daughter lose her ability to spell, and I can't deny that I am continuous with him.

It's been more than twenty years since I read that essay, and in that period our lives have undergone countless changes that I couldn't have predicted. The most catastrophic one was when Nicole's mother Angela declared that she deserved a more interesting life than the one we were giving her, and spent the next decade criss-crossing the globe. But the changes leading to Nicole's current form of literacy were more ordinary and gradual: a succession of software gadgets that not only promised but in fact delivered utility and convenience, and I didn't object to any of them at the times of their introduction.

So it hasn't been my habit to engage in doomsaying whenever a new product is announced; I've welcomed new technology as much as anyone. But when Whetstone released its new search tool Remem, it raised concerns for me in a way none of its predecessors did.

Millions of people, some my age but most younger, have been keeping lifelogs for years, wearing personal cams that capture continuous video of their entire lives. People consult their lifelogs for a variety of reasons—everything from reliving favorite moments to tracking down the cause of allergic reactions—but only intermittently; no one wants to spend all their time formulating queries and sifting through the results. Lifelogs are the most complete photo album imaginable, but like most photo albums, they lie dormant except on special occasions. Now Whetstone aims to change all of that; they claim Remem's algorithms can search the entire haystack by the time you've finished saying "needle."

Remem monitors your conversation for references to past events, and then displays video of that event in the lower left corner of your field of vision. If you say "remember dancing the conga at that wedding?", Remem will bring up the video. If the person you're talking to says "the last time we were at the beach," Remem will bring up the video. And it's not only for use when speaking with someone else; Remem also monitors your sub-vocalizations. If you read the words "the first Szechuan restaurant you ate at," your vocal cords will move as if you're reading aloud, and Remem will bring up the relevant video.

There's no denying the usefulness of software that can actually answer the question "where did I put my keys?" But Whetstone is positioning Remem as more than a handy virtual assistant: they want it to take the place of your natural memory.

It was the summer of Jijingi's thirteenth year when a European came to live in the village. The dusty harmattan winds had just begun blowing from the north when Sabe, the elder who was regarded as chief by all the local families, made the announcement.

Everyone's initial reaction was alarm, of course. "What have we done wrong?" Jijingi's father asked Sabe.

Europeans had first come to Tivland many years ago, and while some elders said one day they'd leave and life would return to the ways of the past, until that day arrived it was necessary for the Tiv to get along with them. This had meant many changes in the way the Tiv did things, but it had never meant Europeans living among them before. The usual reason for Europeans to come to the village was to collect taxes for the roads they had built; they visited some clans more often because the people refused to pay taxes, but that hadn't happened in the Shangev clan. Sabe and the other clan elders had agreed that paying the taxes was the best strategy.

Sabe told everyone not to worry. "This European is a missionary; that means all he does is pray. He has no authority to punish us, but our making him welcome will please the men in the administration."

He ordered two huts built for the missionary, a sleeping hut and a reception hut. Over the course of the next several days everyone took time off from harvesting the guinea-corn to help lay bricks, sink posts into the ground, weave grass into thatch for the roof. It was during the final step, pounding the floor, that the missionary arrived. His porters appeared first, the boxes they carried visible from a distance as they threaded their way between the cassava fields; the missionary himself was the last to appear, apparently exhausted even though he carried nothing. His name was Moseby, and he thanked everyone who had worked on the huts. He tried to help, but it quickly became clear that he didn't know how to do anything, so eventually he just sat in the shade of a locust bean tree and wiped his head with a piece of cloth.

Jijingi watched the missionary with curiosity. The man opened one of his boxes and took out what at first looked like a block of wood, but then he split it open and Jijingi realized it was a tightly bound sheaf of papers. Jijingi had seen paper before; when the Europeans collected taxes, they gave paper in return so that the village had proof of what they'd paid. But the paper that the missionary was looking at was obviously of a different sort, and must have had some other purpose.

The man noticed Jijingi looking at him, and invited him to come closer. "My name is Moseby," he said. "What is your name?"

"I am Jijingi, and my father is Orga of the Shangev clan."

Moseby spread open the sheaf of paper and gestured toward it. "Have you heard the story of Adam?" he asked. "Adam was the first man. We are all children of Adam."

"Here we are descendants of Shangev," said Jijingi. "And everyone in Tivland is a descendant of Tiv."

"Yes, but your ancestor Tiv was descended from Adam, just as my ancestors were. We are all brothers. Do you understand?"

The missionary spoke as if his tongue were too large for his mouth, but Jijingi could tell what he was saying. "Yes, I understand."

Moseby smiled, and pointed at the paper. "This paper tells the story of Adam."

"How can paper tell a story?"

"It is an art that we Europeans know. When a man speaks, we make marks on the paper. When another man looks at the paper later, he sees the marks and knows what sounds the first man made. In that way the second man can hear what the first man said."

The Truth of Fact, the Truth of Feeling | TED CHIANG

Jijingi remembered something his father had told him about old Gbegba, who was the most skilled in bushcraft. "Where you or I would see nothing but some disturbed grass, he can see that a leopard had killed a cane rat at that spot and carried it off," his father said. Gbegba was able to look at the ground and know what had happened even though he had not been present. This art of the Europeans must be similar: those who were skilled in interpreting the marks could hear a story even if they hadn't been there when it was told.

"Tell me the story that the paper tells," he said.

Moseby told him a story about Adam and his wife being tricked by a snake. Then he asked Jijingi, "How do you like it?"

"You're a poor storyteller, but the story was interesting enough."

Moseby laughed. "You are right, I am not good at the Tiv language. But this is a good story. It is the oldest story we have. It was first told long before your ancestor Tiv was born."

Jijingi was dubious. "That paper can't be so old."

"No, this paper is not. But the marks on it were copied from older paper. And those marks were copied from older paper. And so forth many times."

That would be impressive, if true. Jijingi liked stories, and older stories were often the best. "How many stories do you have there?"

"Very many." Moseby flipped through the sheaf of papers, and Jijingi could see each sheet was covered with marks from edge to edge; there must be many, many stories there.

"This art you spoke of, interpreting marks on paper; is it only for Europeans?"

"No, I can teach it to you. Would you like that?"

Cautiously, Jijingi nodded.

⋇

As a journalist, I have long appreciated the usefulness of lifelogging for determining the facts of the matter. There is scarcely a legal proceeding, criminal or civil, that doesn't make use of someone's lifelog, and rightly so. When the public interest is involved, finding out what actually happened is important; justice is an essential part of the social contract, and you can't have justice until you know the truth.

However, I've been much more skeptical about the use of lifelogging in purely personal situations. When lifelogging first became popular, there were couples who thought they could use it to settle arguments over who had actually said what, using the video record to prove they were right. But finding the right clip of video often wasn't easy, and all but the most determined gave up on doing so. The inconvenience acted as a barrier, limiting the searching of lifelogs to those situations in which effort was warranted, namely situations in which justice was the motivating factor.

Now with Remem, finding the exact moment has become easy, and lifelogs that previously lay all but ignored are now being scrutinized as if they were crime scenes, thickly strewn with evidence for use in domestic squabbles.

I typically write for the news section, but I've written feature stories as well, and so when I pitched an article about the potential downsides of Remem to my managing editor, he gave me the go-ahead. My first interview was with a married couple whom I'll call Joel and Deirdre, an architect and a painter, respectively. It wasn't hard to get them talking about Remem.

"Joel is always saying that he knew it all along," said Deirdre, "even when he didn't. It used to drive me crazy, because I couldn't get him to admit he used to believe something else. Now I can. For example, recently we were talking about the McKittridge kidnapping case."

She sent me the video of one argument she had with Joel. My retinal projector displayed footage of a cocktail party; it's from Deirdre's point of view, and Joel is telling a number of people, *"It was pretty clear that he was guilty from the day he was arrested."*

Deirdre's voice: *"You didn't always think that. For months you argued that he was innocent."*

Joel shakes his head. *"No, you're misremembering. I said that even people who are obviously guilty deserve a fair trial."*

"That's not what you said. You said he was being railroaded."

"You're thinking of someone else; that wasn't me."

"No, it was you. Look." A separate video window opened up, an excerpt of her lifelog that she looked up and broadcast to the people they've been talking with. Within the nested video, Joel and Deirdre are sitting in a café, and Joel is saying, *"He's a scapegoat. The police needed to reassure the public, so they arrested a convenient suspect. Now he's done for."* Deidre replies, *"You don't think there's any chance of him being acquitted?"* and Joel answers, *"Not unless he can afford a high-powered defense team, and I'll bet you he can't. People in his position will never get a fair trial."*

I closed both windows, and Deirdre said, "Without Remem, I'd never be able to convince him that he changed his position. Now I have proof."

"Fine, you were right that time," said Joel. "But you didn't have to do that in front of our friends."

"You correct me in front of our friends all the time. You're telling me I can't do the same?"

Here was the line at which the pursuit of truth ceased to be an intrinsic good. When the only persons affected have a personal relationship with each other, other priorities are often more important, and a forensic pursuit of the truth could be harmful. Did it really matter whose idea it was to take the vacation that turned out so disastrously? Did you need to know which partner was more forgetful about completing errands the other person asked of them? I was no expert on marriage, but I knew what marriage counselors said: pinpointing blame wasn't the answer. Instead, couples needed to acknowledge each other's feelings and address their problems as a team.

Next I spoke with a spokesperson from Whetstone, Erica Meyers. For a while she gave me a typically corporate spiel about the benefits of Remem. "Making information more accessible is an intrinsic good," she says. "Ubiquitous video has revolutionized law enforcement. Businesses become more effective when they adopt good record-keeping practices. The same thing happens to us as individuals when our memories become more accurate: we get better, not just at doing our jobs, but at living our lives."

When I asked her about couples like Joel and Deirdre, she said, "If your marriage is solid, Remem isn't going to hurt it. But if you're the type of person who's constantly trying to prove that you're right and your spouse is wrong, then your marriage is going to be in trouble whether you use Remem or not."

I conceded that she may have had a point in this particular case. But, I asked her, didn't she think Remem created greater opportunities for those types of arguments to arise, even in solid marriages, by making it easier for people to keep score?

"Not at all," she said. "Remem didn't give them a scorekeeping mentality; they developed that on their own. Another couple could just as easily use Remem to realize that they've both misremembered things, and become more forgiving when that sort of mistake happens. I predict the latter scenario will be the more common one with our customers as a whole."

I wished I could share Erica Meyers' optimism, but I knew that new technology didn't always bring out the best in people. Who hasn't wished they could prove that their version of events was the correct one? I could easily see myself using Remem the way Deirdre did, and I wasn't at all certain that doing so would be good for me. Anyone who has wasted hours surfing the internet knows that technology can encourage bad habits.

⸎

Moseby gave a sermon every seven days, on the day devoted to resting and brewing and drinking beer. He seemed to disapprove of the beer drinking, but he didn't want to speak on one of the days of work, so the day of beer brewing was the only one left. He talked about the European god, and told people that following his rules would improve their lives, but his explanations of how that would do so weren't particularly persuasive.

But Moseby also had some skill at dispensing medicine, and he was willing to learn how to work in the fields, so gradually people grew more accepting of him, and Jijingi's father let him visit Moseby occasionally to learn the art of writing. Moseby offered to teach the other children as well, and for a time Jijingi's age-mates came along, mostly to prove to each other that they weren't afraid of being near a European. Before long the other boys grew bored and left, but because Jijingi remained interested in writing and his father thought it would keep the Europeans happy, he was eventually permitted to go every day.

Moseby explained to Jijingi how each sound a person spoke could be indicated with different marks on the paper. The marks were arranged in rows like plants in a field; you looked at the marks as if you were walking down a row, made the sound each mark indicated, and you would find yourself speaking what the original person had said. Moseby showed him how to make each of the different marks on a sheet of paper, using a tiny wooden rod that had a core of soot.

In a typical lesson, Moseby would speak, and then write what he had said: "When night comes I shall sleep." *Tugh mba a ile yo me yav.* "There are two persons." *Ioruv mban mba uhar.* Jijingi carefully copied the writing on his sheet of paper, and when he was done, Moseby would look at it.

"Very good. But you need to leave spaces when you write."

"I have." Jijingi pointed at the gap between each row.

"No, that is not what I mean. Do you see the spaces within each line?" He pointed at his own paper.

Jijingi understood. "Your marks are clumped together, while mine are arranged evenly."

"These are not just clumps of marks. They are…I do not know what you call them." He picked up a thin sheaf of paper from his table and flipped through it. "I do not see it here. Where I come from, we call them 'words.' When we write, we leave spaces between the words."

"But what are words?"

"How can I explain it?" He thought a moment. "If you speak slowly, you pause very briefly after each word. That's why we leave a space in those places when we write. Like this: How. Many. Years. Old. Are. You?" He wrote on his paper as he spoke, leaving a space every time he paused: *Anyom a ou kuma a me?*

"But you speak slowly because you're a foreigner. I'm Tiv, so I don't pause when I speak. Shouldn't my writing be the same?"

"It does not matter how fast you speak. Words are the same whether you speak quickly or slowly."

"Then why did you say you pause after each word?"

"That is the easiest way to find them. Try saying this very slowly." He pointed at what he'd just written.

Jijingi spoke very slowly, the way a man might when trying to hide his drunkenness. "Why is there no space in between *an* and *yom*?"

"*Anyom* is one word. You do not pause in the middle of it."

"But I wouldn't pause after *anyom* either."

Moseby sighed. "I will think more about how to explain what I mean. For now, just leave spaces in the places where I leave spaces."

What a strange art writing was. When sowing a field, it was best to have the seed yams spaced evenly; Jijingi's father would have beaten him if he'd clumped the yams the way the Moseby clumped his marks on paper. But he had resolved to learn this art as best he could, and if that meant clumping his marks, he would do so.

It was only many lessons later that Jijingi finally understood where he should leave spaces, and what Moseby meant when he said "word." You could not find the places where words began and ended by listening. The sounds a person made while speaking were as smooth and unbroken as the hide of a goat's leg, but the words were like the bones underneath the meat, and the space between them was the joint where you'd cut if you wanted to separate it into pieces. By leaving spaces when he wrote, Moseby was making visible the bones in what he said.

Jijingi realized that, if he thought hard about it, he was now able to identify the words when people spoke in an ordinary conversation. The sounds that came from a person's mouth hadn't changed, but he understood them differently; he was aware of the pieces from which the whole was made. He himself had been speaking in words all along. He just hadn't known it until now.

※

The ease of searching that Remem provides is impressive enough, but that merely scratches the surface of what Whetstone sees as the product's potential. When Deirdre fact-checked her husband's previous statements, she was posing explicit queries to Remem. But Whetstone expects that, as people become accustomed to their product, queries will take the place of ordinary acts of recall, and Remem will be integrated into their very thought processes. Once that happens, we will become cognitive cyborgs, effectively incapable of misremembering anything; digital video stored on error-corrected silicon will take over the role once filled by our fallible temporal lobes.

What might it be like to have a perfect memory? Arguably the individual with the best memory ever documented was Solomon Shereshevskii, who lived in Russia during the first half of the twentieth century. The psychologists who tested him found that he could hear a series of words or numbers once and remember it months or even years later. With no knowledge of Italian, Shereshevskii was able to quote stanzas of *The Divine Comedy* that had been read to him fifteen years earlier.

But having a perfect memory wasn't the blessing one might imagine it to be. Reading a passage of text evoked so many images in Shereshevskii's mind that he often couldn't focus on what it actually said, and his awareness of innumerable specific examples made it difficult for him to understand abstract concepts. At times, he tried to deliberately forget things. He wrote down numbers he no longer wanted to remember on slips of paper and then burnt them, a kind of slash-and-burn approach to clearing out the undergrowth of his mind, but to no avail.

When I raised the possibility that a perfect memory might be a handicap to Whetstone's spokesperson, Erica Meyers, she had a ready reply. "This is no different from the concerns people used to have about retinal projectors," she said. "They worried that seeing updates constantly would be distracting or overwhelming, but we've all adapted to them."

I didn't mention that not everyone considered that a positive development.

"And Remem is entirely customizable," she continued. "If at any time you find it's doing too many searches for your needs, you can decrease its level of responsiveness. But according to our customer analytics, our users haven't been doing that. As they become more comfortable with it, they're finding that Remem becomes more helpful the more responsive it is."

But even if Remem wasn't constantly crowding your field of vision with unwanted imagery of the past, I wondered if there weren't issues raised simply by having that imagery be perfect.

"Forgive and forget" goes the expression, and for our idealized magnanimous selves, that was all you needed. But for our actual selves the relationship between those two actions wasn't so straightforward. In most cases we had to forget a little bit before we could forgive; when we no longer experienced the pain as fresh, the insult was easier to forgive, which in turn made it less memorable, and so on. It was this psychological feedback loop that made initially infuriating offences seem pardonable in the mirror of hindsight.

What I feared was that Remem would make it impossible for this feedback loop to get rolling. By fixing every detail of an insult in indelible video, it could prevent the softening that's needed for forgiveness to begin. I thought back to what Erica Meyers said about Remem's inability to hurt solid marriages. Implicit in that assertion was a claim about what qualified as a solid marriage. If someone's marriage was built on—as ironic as it might sound—a cornerstone of forgetfulness, what right did Whetstone have to shatter that?

The issue wasn't confined to marriages; all sorts of relationships rely on forgiving and forgetting. My daughter Nicole has always been strong-willed; rambunctious when she was a child, openly defiant as an adolescent. She and I had many furious arguments during her teen years, arguments that we have mostly been able to put behind us, and now our relationship is pretty good. If we'd had Remem, would we still be speaking to each other?

I don't mean to say that forgetting is the only way to mend relationships. While I can no longer recall most of the arguments Nicole and I had—and I'm grateful that I can't—one of the arguments I remember clearly is one that spurred me to be a better father.

It was when Nicole was sixteen, a junior in high school. It had been two years since her mother Angela had left, probably the two hardest years of both our lives. I don't remember what started the argument—something trivial, no doubt—but it escalated and before long Nicole was taking her anger at Angela out on me.

"You're the reason she left! You drove her away! You can leave too, for all I care. I sure as hell would be better off without you." And to demonstrate her point, she stormed out of the house.

I knew it wasn't premeditated malice on her part—I don't think she engaged in much premeditation in anything during that phase of her life—but she couldn't have come up with a more hurtful accusation if she'd tried. I'd been devastated by Angela's departure, and I was constantly wondering what I could have done differently to keep her.

Nicole didn't come back until the next day, and that night was one of soul searching for me. While I didn't believe I was responsible for her mother leaving us, Nicole's accusation still served as a wake-up call. I hadn't been conscious of it, but I realized that I had been thinking of myself as the greatest victim of Angela's departure, wallowing in self-pity over just how unreasonable my situation was. It hadn't even been my idea to have children; it was Angela who'd wanted to be a parent, and now she had left me holding the bag. What sane world would leave me with sole responsibility for raising an adolescent girl? How could a job that was so difficult be entrusted to someone with no experience whatsoever?

Nicole's accusation made me realize her predicament was worse than mine. At least I had volunteered for this duty, albeit long ago and without full appreciation for what I was getting into. Nicole had been drafted into her role, with no say whatsoever. If there was anyone who had a right to be resentful, it was her. And while I thought I'd been doing a good job of being a father, obviously I needed to do better.

I turned myself around. Our relationship didn't improve overnight, but over the years I was able to work myself back into Nicole's good graces. I remember the way she hugged me at her college graduation, and I realized my years of effort had paid off.

Would those years of repair have been possible with Remem? Even if each of us could have refrained from throwing the other's bad behavior in their faces, the opportunity to privately rewatch video of our arguments seems like it could be pernicious. Vivid reminders of the way she and I yelled at each other in the past might have kept our anger fresh, and prevented us from rebuilding our relationship.

Jijingi wanted to write down some of the stories of where the Tiv people came from, but the storytellers spoke rapidly, and he wasn't able to write fast enough to keep up with them. Moseby said he would get better with practice, but Jijingi despaired that he'd ever become fast enough.

Then, one summer a European woman named Reiss came to visit the village. Moseby said she was "a person who learns about other people" but could not explain what that meant, only that she wanted to learn about Tivland. She asked questions of everyone, not just the elders but young men, too, even women and children, and she wrote down everything they told her. She didn't try to get anyone to adopt European practices; where Moseby had insisted that there were no such thing as curses and that everything was God's will, Reiss asked about how curses worked, and listened attentively to explanations of how your kin on your father's side could curse you while your kin on your mother's side could protect you from curses.

One evening Kokwa, the best storyteller in the village, told the story of how the Tiv people split into different lineages, and Reiss had written it down exactly as he told it. Later she had recopied the story using a machine she poked at noisily with her fingers, so that she had a copy that was clean and easy to read. When Jijingi asked if she would make another copy for him, she agreed, much to his excitement.

The paper version of the story was curiously disappointing. Jijingi remembered that when he had first learned about writing, he'd imagined it would enable him to see a storytelling performance as vividly as if he were there. But writing didn't do that. When Kokwa told the story, he didn't merely use words; he used the sound of his voice, the movement of his hands, the light in his eyes. He told you the story with his whole body, and you understood it the same way. None of that was captured on paper; only the bare words could be written down. And reading just the words gave you only a hint of the experience of listening to Kokwa himself, as if one were licking the pot in which okra had been cooked instead of eating the okra itself.

Jijingi was still glad to have the paper version, and would read it from time to time. It was a good story, worthy of being recorded on paper. Not everything written on paper was so worthy. During his sermons Moseby would read aloud stories from his book, and they were often good stories, but he also read aloud words he had written down just a few days before, and those were often not stories at all, merely claims that learning more about the European god would improve the lives of the Tiv people.

One day, when Moseby had been eloquent, Jijingi complimented him. "I know you think highly of all your sermons, but today's sermon was a good one."

"Thank you," said Moseby, smiling. After a moment, he asked, "Why do you say I think highly of all my sermons?"

"Because you expect that people will want to read them many years from now."

"I don't expect that. What makes you think that?"

"You write them all down before you even deliver them. Before even one person has heard a sermon, you have written it down for future generations."

Moseby laughed. "No, that is not why I write them down."

"Why, then?" He knew it wasn't for people far away to read them, because sometimes messengers came to the village to deliver paper to Moseby, and he never sent his sermons back with them.

"I write the words down so I do not forget what I want to say when I give the sermon."

"How could you forget what you want to say? You and I are speaking right now, and neither of us needs paper to do so."

"A sermon is different from conversation." Moseby paused to consider. "I want to be sure I give my sermons as well as possible. I won't forget what I want to say, but I might forget the best way to say it. If I write it down, I don't have to worry. But writing the words down does more than help me remember. It helps me think."

"How does writing help you think?"

"That is a good question," he said. "It is strange, isn't it? I do not know how to explain it, but writing helps me decide what I want to say. Where I come from, there's a very old proverb: *verba volant, scripta manent*. In Tiv you would say, 'spoken words fly away, written words remain.' Does that make sense?"

"Yes," Jijingi said, just to be polite; it made no sense at all. The missionary wasn't old enough to be senile, but his memory must be terrible and he didn't want to admit it. Jijingi told his age-mates about this, and they joked about it amongst themselves for days. Whenever they exchanged gossip, they would add, "Will you remember that? This will help you," and mimic Moseby writing at his table.

On an evening the following year, Kokwa announced he would tell the story of how the Tiv split into different lineages. Jijingi brought out the paper version he had, so he could read the story at the same time Kokwa told it. Sometimes he could follow along, but it was often confusing because Kokwa's words didn't match what was written on the paper. After Kokwa was finished, Jijingi said to him, "You didn't tell the story the same way you told it last year."

"Nonsense," said Kokwa. "When I tell a story it doesn't change, no matter how much time passes. Ask me to tell it twenty years from today, and I will tell it exactly the same."

Jijingi pointed at the paper he held. "This paper is the story you told last year, and there were many differences." He picked one he remembered. "Last time you said, 'the Uyengi captured the women and children and carried them off as slaves.' This time you said, 'they made slaves of the women, but they did not stop there: they even made slaves of the children.' "

"That's the same."

"It is the same story, but you've changed the way you tell it."

"No," said Kokwa, "I told it just as I told it before."

Jijingi didn't want to try to explain what words were. Instead he said, "If you told it as you did before, you would say 'the Uyengi captured the women and children and carried them off as slaves' every time."

For a moment Kokwa stared at him, and then he laughed. "Is this what you think is important, now that you've learned the art of writing?"

Sabe, who had been listening to them, chided Kokwa. "It's not your place to judge Jijingi. The hare favors one food, the hippo favors another. Let each spend his time as he pleases."

"Of course, Sabe, of course," said Kokwa, but he threw a derisive glance at Jijingi.

Afterwards, Jijingi remembered the proverb Moseby had mentioned. Even though Kokwa was telling the same story, he might arrange the words differently each time he told it; he was skilled enough as a storyteller that the arrangement of words didn't matter. It was different for Moseby, who never acted anything out when he gave his sermons; for him, the words were what was important. Jijingi realized that Moseby wrote down his sermons not because his memory was terrible, but because he was looking for a specific arrangement of words. Once he found the one he wanted, he could hold on to it for as long as he needed.

Out of curiosity, Jijingi tried imagining he had to deliver a sermon, and began writing down what he would say. Seated on the root of a mango tree with the notebook Moseby had given him, he composed a sermon on *tsav*, the quality that enabled some men to have power over others, and a subject which Moseby hadn't understood and had dismissed as foolishness. He read his first attempt to one of his age-mates, who pronounced it terrible, leading them to have a brief shoving match, but afterwards Jijingi had to admit his age-mate was right. He tried writing out his sermon a second time and then a third before he became tired of it and moved on to other topics.

As he practiced his writing, Jijingi came to understand what Moseby had meant; writing was not just a way to record what someone said; it could help you decide what you would say before you said it. And words were not just the pieces of speaking; they were the pieces of thinking. When you wrote them down, you could grasp your thoughts like bricks in your hands and push them into different arrangements. Writing let you look at your thoughts in a way you couldn't if you were just talking, and having seen them, you could improve them, make them stronger and more elaborate.

Psychologists make a distinction between semantic memory—knowledge of general facts—and episodic memory—recollection of personal experiences. We've been using technological supplements for semantic memory ever since the invention of writing: first books, then search engines. By contrast, we've historically resisted such aids when it comes to episodic memory; few people have ever kept as many diaries or photo albums as they did ordinary books. The obvious reason is convenience; if we wanted a book on the birds of North America, we could consult one that an ornithologist has written, but if we wanted a daily diary, we had to write it for ourselves. But I also wonder if another reason is that, subconsciously, we regarded our episodic memories as such an integral part of our identities that we were reluctant to externalize them, to relegate them to books on a shelf or files on a computer.

That may be about to change. For years parents have been recording their children's every moment, so even if children weren't wearing personal cams, their lifelogs were effectively already being compiled. Now parents are having their children wear retinal projectors at younger and younger ages so they can reap the benefits of assistive software agents sooner. Imagine what will happen if children begin using Remem to access those lifelogs: their mode of cognition will diverge from ours because the act of recall will be different. Rather than thinking of an event from her past and seeing it with her mind's eye, a child will subvocalize a reference to it and watch video footage with her physical eyes. Episodic memory will become entirely technologically mediated.

An obvious drawback to such reliance is the possibility that people might become virtual amnesiacs whenever the software crashes. But just as worrying to me as the prospect of technological failure was that of technological success: how will it change a person's conception of herself when she's only seen her past through the unblinking eye of a video camera? Just as there's a feedback loop in softening harsh memories, there's also one at work in the romanticization of childhood memories, and disrupting that process will have consequences.

The earliest birthday I remember is my fourth; I remember blowing out the candles on my cake, the thrill of tearing the wrapping paper off the presents. There's no video of the event, but there are snapshots in the family album, and they are consistent with what I remember. In fact, I suspect I no longer remember the day itself. It's more likely that I manufactured the memory when I was first shown the snapshots and over time, I've imbued it with the emotion I imagine I felt that day. Little by little, over repeated instances of recall, I've created a happy memory for myself.

Another of my earliest memories is of playing on the living room rug, pushing toy cars around, while my grandmother worked at her sewing machine; she would occasionally turn and smile warmly at me. There are no photos of that moment, so I know the recollection is mine and mine alone. It is a lovely, idyllic memory. Would I want to be presented with actual footage of that afternoon? No; absolutely not.

Regarding the role of truth in autobiography, the critic Roy Pascal wrote, "On the one side are the truths of fact, on the other the truth of the writer's feeling, and where the two coincide cannot be decided by any outside authority in advance." Our memories are private autobiographies, and that afternoon with my grandmother features prominently in mine because of the feelings associated with it. What if video footage revealed that my grandmother's smile was in fact perfunctory, that she was actually frustrated because her sewing wasn't going well? What's important to me about that memory is the happiness I associated with it, and I wouldn't want that jeopardized.

It seemed to me that continuous video of my entire childhood would be full of facts but devoid of feeling, simply because cameras couldn't capture the emotional dimension of events. As far as the camera was concerned, that afternoon with my grandmother would be indistinguishable from a hundred others. And if I'd grown up with access to all the video footage, there'd have been no way for me to assign more emotional weight to any particular day, no nucleus around which nostalgia could accrete.

And what will the consequences be when people can claim to remember their infancy? I could readily imagine a situation where, if you ask a young person what her earliest memory is, she will simply look baffled; after all, she has video dating back to the day of her birth. The inability to remember the first few years of one's life—what psychologists call childhood amnesia—might soon be a thing of the past. No more would parents tell their children anecdotes beginning with the words "You don't remember this because you were just a toddler when it happened." It'll be as if childhood amnesia is a characteristic of humanity's childhood, and in ouroboric fashion, our youth will vanish from our memories.

Part of me wanted to stop this, to protect children's ability to see the beginning of their lives filtered through gauze, to keep those origin stories from being replaced by cold, desaturated video. But maybe they will feel just as warmly about their lossless digital memories as I do of my imperfect, organic memories.

People are made of stories. Our memories are not the impartial accumulation of every second we've lived; they're the narrative that we assembled out of selected moments. Which is why, even when we've experienced the same events as other individuals, we never constructed identical narratives: the criteria used for selecting moments were different for each of us, and a reflection of our personalities. Each of us noticed the details that caught our attention and remembered what was important to us, and the narratives we built shaped our personalities in turn.

But, I wondered, if everyone remembered everything, would our differences get shaved away? What would happen to our sense of selves? It seemed to me that a perfect memory couldn't be a narrative any more than unedited security-cam footage could be a feature film.

※

When Jijingi was twenty, an officer from the administration came to the village to speak with Sabe. He had brought with him a young Tiv man who had attended the mission school in Katsina-Ala. The administration wanted to have a written record of all the disputes brought before the tribal courts, so they were assigning each chief one of these youths to act as a scribe. Sabe had Jijingi come forward, and to the officer he said, "I know you don't have enough scribes for all of Tivland. Jijingi here has learned to write; he can act as our scribe, and you can send your boy to another village." The officer tested Jijingi's ability to write, but Moseby had taught him well, and eventually the officer agreed to have him be Sabe's scribe.

After the officer had left, Jijingi asked Sabe why he hadn't wanted the boy from Katsina-Ala to be his scribe.

"No one who comes from the mission school can be trusted," said Sabe.

"Why not? Did the Europeans make them liars?"

"They're partly to blame, but so are we. When the Europeans collected boys for the mission school years ago, most elders gave them the ones they wanted to get rid of, the layabouts and malcontents. Now those boys have returned, and they feel no kinship with anyone. They wield their knowledge of writing like a long gun; they demand their chiefs find them wives, or else they'll write lies about them and have the Europeans depose them."

Jijingi knew a boy who was always complaining and looking for ways to avoid work; it would be a disaster if someone like him had power over Sabe. "Can't you tell the Europeans about this?"

"Many have," Sabe answered. "It was Maisho of the Kwande clan who warned me about the scribes; they were installed in Kwande villages first. Maisho was fortunate that the Europeans believed him instead of his scribe's lies, but he knows of other chiefs who were not so lucky; the Europeans often believe paper over people. I don't wish to take the chance." He looked at Jijingi seriously. "You are my kin, Jijingi, and kin to everyone in this village. I trust you to write down what I say."

"Yes, Sabe."

Tribal court was held every month, from morning until late afternoon for three days in a row, and it always attracted an audience, sometimes one so large that Sabe had to demand everyone sit to allow the breeze to reach the center of the circle. Jijingi sat next to Sabe and recorded the details of each dispute in a book the officer had left. It was a good job; he was paid out of the fees collected from the disputants, and he was given not just a chair but a small table too, which he could use for writing even when court wasn't in session. The complaints Sabe heard were varied—one might be about a stolen bicycle, another might be about whether a man was responsible for his neighbor's crops failing—but most had to do with wives. For one such dispute, Jijingi wrote down the following:

Umem's wife Girgi has run away from home and gone back to her kin. Her kinsman Anongo has tried to convince her to stay with her husband, but Girgi refuses, and there is no more Anongo can do. Umem demands the return of the £11 he paid as bridewealth. Anongo says he has no money at the moment, and moreover that he was only paid £6.

Sabe requested witnesses for both sides. Anongo says he has witnesses, but they have gone on a trip. Umem produces a witness, who is sworn in. He testifies that he himself counted the £11 that Umem paid to Anongo.

Sabe asks Girgi to return to her husband and be a good wife, but she says she has had all that she can stand of him. Sabe instructs Anongo to repay Umem £11, the first payment to be in three months when his crops are saleable. Anongo agrees.

It was the final dispute of the day, by which time Sabe was clearly tired. "Selling vegetables to pay back bridewealth," he said afterwards, shaking his head. "This wouldn't have happened when I was a boy."

Jijingi knew what he meant. In the past, the elders said, you conducted exchanges with similar items: if you wanted a goat, you could trade chickens for it; if you wanted to marry a woman, you promised one of your kinswomen to her family. Then the Europeans said they would no longer accept vegetables as payment for taxes, insisting that it be paid in coin. Before long, everything could be exchanged for money; you could use it to buy everything from a calabash to a wife. The elders considered it absurd.

"The old ways are vanishing," agreed Jijingi. He didn't say that young people preferred things this way, because the Europeans had also decreed that bridewealth could only be paid if the woman consented to the marriage. In the past, a young woman might be promised to an old man with leprous hands and rotting teeth, and have no choice but to marry him. Now a woman could marry the man she favored, as long as he could afford to pay the bridewealth. Jijingi himself was saving money to marry.

Moseby came to watch sometimes, but he found the proceedings confusing, and often asked Jijingi questions afterwards.

"For example, there was the dispute between Umem and Anongo over how much bridewealth was owed. Why was only the witness sworn in?" asked Moseby.

"To ensure that he said precisely what happened."

"But if Umem and Anongo were sworn in, that would have ensured they said precisely what happened too. Anongo was able to lie because he was not sworn in."

"Anongo didn't lie," said Jijingi. "He said what he considered right, just as Umem did."

"But what Anongo said wasn't the same as what the witness said."

"But that doesn't mean he was lying." Then Jijingi remembered something about the European language, and understood Moseby's confusion. "Our language has two words for what in your language is called 'true.' There is what's right, *mimi*, and what's precise, *vough*. In a dispute the principals say what they consider right; they speak *mimi*. The witnesses, however, are sworn to say precisely what happened; they speak *vough*. When Sabe has heard what happened he can decide what action is *mimi* for everyone. But it's not lying if the principals don't speak *vough*, as long as they speak *mimi*."

Moseby clearly disapproved. "In the land I come from, everyone who testifies in court must swear to speak *vough*, even the principals."

Jijingi didn't see the point of that, but all he said was, "Every tribe has its own customs."

"Yes, customs may vary, but the truth is the truth; it doesn't change from one person to another. And remember what the Bible says: the truth shall set you free."

"I remember," said Jijingi. Moseby had said that it was knowing God's truth that had made the Europeans so successful. There was no denying their wealth or power, but who knew what was the cause?

※

In order to write about Remem, it was only fair that I try it out myself. The problem was that I didn't have a lifelog for it to index; typically I only activated my personal cam when I was conducting an interview or covering an event. But I've certainly spent time in the presence of people who kept lifelogs, and I could make use of what they'd recorded. While all lifelogging software has privacy controls in place, most people also grant basic sharing rights: if your actions were recorded in their lifelog, you have access to the footage in which you're present. So I launched an agent to assemble a partial lifelog from the footage others had recorded, using my GPS history as the basis for the query. Over the course of a week, my request propagated through social networks and public video archives, and I was rewarded with snippets of video ranging from a few seconds in length to a few hours: not just security-cam footage but excerpts from the lifelogs of friends, acquaintances, and even complete strangers.

The resulting lifelog was of course highly fragmentary compared to what I would have had if I'd been recording video myself, and the footage was all from a third-person perspective rather than the first-person that most lifelogs have, but Remem was able to work with that. I expected that coverage would be thickest in the later years, simply due to the increasing popularity of lifelogs. It was somewhat to my surprise, then, that when I looked at a graph of the coverage, I found a bump in the coverage over a decade ago. Nicole had been keeping a lifelog since she was a teenager, so an unexpectedly large segment of my domestic life was present.

I was initially a bit uncertain of how to test Remem, since I obviously couldn't ask it to bring up video of an event I didn't remember. I figured I'd start out with something I did remember. I subvocalized, "The time Vince told me about his trip to Palau."

My retinal projector displayed a window in the lower left corner of my field of vision: I'm having lunch with my friends Vincent and Jeremy. Vincent didn't maintain a lifelog either, so the footage was from Jeremy's point of view. I listened to Vincent rave about scuba diving for a minute.

Next I tried something that I only vaguely remembered. "The dinner banquet when I sat between Deborah and Lyle." I didn't remember who else was sitting at the table, and wondered if Remem could help me identify them.

Sure enough, Deborah had been recording that evening, and with her video I was able to use a recognition agent to identity everyone sitting across from us.

After those initial successes, I had a run of failures; not surprising, considering the gaps in the lifelog. But over the course of an hour-long trip survey of past events, Remem's performance was generally impressive.

The Truth of Fact, the Truth of Feeling | Ted Chiang

Finally it seemed time for me to try Remem on some memories that were more emotionally freighted. My relationship with Nicole felt strong enough now for me to safely revisit the fights we'd had when she was young. I figured I'd start with the argument I remembered clearly, and work backwards from there.

I subvocalized, "The time Nicole yelled at me 'you're the reason she left.' "

The window displays the kitchen of the house we lived in when Nicole was growing up. The footage is from Nicole's point of view, and I'm standing in front of the stove. It's obvious we're fighting.

"You're the reason she left. You can leave too, for all I care. I sure as hell would be better off without you."

The words were just as I remembered them, but it wasn't Nicole saying them.

It was me.

My first thought was that it must be a fake, that Nicole had edited the video to put her words into my mouth. She must have noticed my request for access to her lifelog footage, and concocted this to teach me a lesson. Or perhaps it was a film she had created to show her friends, to reinforce the stories she told about me. But why was she still so angry at me, that she would do such a thing? Hadn't we gotten past this?

I started skimming through the video, looking for inconsistencies that would indicate where the edited footage had been spliced in. The subsequent footage showed Nicole running out of the house, just as I remembered, so there wouldn't be signs of inconsistency there. I rewound the video and started watching the preceding argument.

Initially I was angry as I watched, angry at Nicole for going to such lengths to create this lie, because the preceding footage was all consistent with me being the one who yelled at her. Then some of what I was saying in the video began to sound queasily familiar: complaining about being called to her school again because she'd gotten into trouble, accusing her of spending time with the wrong crowd. But this wasn't the context in which I'd said those things, was it? I had been voicing my concern, not berating her. Nicole must have adapted things I'd said elsewhere to make her slanderous video more plausible. That was the only explanation, right?

I asked Remem to examine the video's watermark, and it reported the video was unmodified. I saw that Remem had suggested a correction in my search terms: where I had said "the time Nicole yelled at me," it offered "the time I yelled at Nicole." The correction must have been displayed at the same time as the initial search result, but I hadn't noticed. I shut down Remem in disgust, furious at the product. I was about to search for information on forging a digital watermark to prove this video was faked, but I stopped myself, recognizing it as an act of desperation.

I would have testified, hand on a stack of Bibles or using any oath required of me, that it was Nicole who'd accused me of being the reason her mother left us. My recollection of that argument was as clear as any memory I had, but that wasn't the only reason I found the video hard to believe; it was also my knowledge that—whatever my faults or imperfections—I was never the kind of father who could say such a thing to his child.

Yet here was digital video proving that I had been exactly that kind of father. And while I wasn't that man anymore, I couldn't deny that I was continuous with him.

Even more telling was the fact that for many years I had successfully hidden the truth from myself. Earlier I said that the details we choose to remember are a reflection of our personalities. What did it say about me that I put those words in Nicole's mouth instead of mine?

I remembered that argument as being a turning point for me. I had imagined a narrative of redemption and self-improvement in which I was the heroic single father, rising to meet the challenge. But the reality was... what? How much of what had happened since then could I take credit for?

I restarted Remem and began looking at video of Nicole's graduation from college. That was an event I had recorded myself, so I had footage of Nicole's face, and she seemed genuinely happy in my presence. Was she hiding her true feelings so well that I couldn't detect them? Or, if our relationship had actually improved, how had that happened? I had obviously been a much worse father fourteen years ago than I'd thought; it would be tempting to conclude I had come farther to reach where I currently was, but I couldn't trust my perceptions anymore. Did Nicole even have positive feelings about me now?

I wasn't going to try using Remem to answer this question; I needed to go to the source. I called Nicole and left a message saying I wanted to talk to her, and asking if I could come over to her apartment that evening.

—※—

It was a few years later that Sabe began attending a series of meetings of all the chiefs in the Shangev clan. He explained to Jijingi that the Europeans no longer wished to deal with so many chiefs, and were demanding that all of Tivland be divided into eight groups they called 'septs.' As a result, Sabe and the other chiefs had to discuss who the Shangev clan would join with. Although there was no need for a scribe, Jijingi was curious to hear the deliberations and asked Sabe if he might accompany him, and Sabe agreed.

Jijingi had never seen so many elders in one place before; some were even-tempered and dignified like Sabe, while others were loud and full of bluster. They argued for hours on end.

In the evening after Jijingi had returned, Moseby asked him what it had been like. Jijingi sighed. "Even if they're not yelling, they're fighting like wildcats."

"Who does Sabe think you should join?"

"We should join with the clans that we're most closely related to; that's the Tiv way. And since Shangev was the son of Kwande, our clan should join with the Kwande clan, who live to the south."

"That makes sense," said Moseby. "So why is there disagreement?"

"The members of the Shangev clan don't all live next to each other. Some live on the farmland in the west, near the Jechira clan, and the elders there are friendly with the Jechira elders. They'd like the Shangev clan to join the Jechira clan, because then they'd have more influence in the resulting sept."

"I see." Moseby thought for a moment. "Could the western Shangev join a different sept from the southern Shangev?"

Jijingi shook his head. "We Shangev all have one father, so we should all remain together. All the elders agree on that."

"But if lineage is so important, how can the elders from the west argue that the Shangev clan ought to join with the Jechira clan?"

"That's what the disagreement was about. The elders from the west are claiming Shangev was the son of Jechira."

"Wait, you don't know who Shangev's parents were?"

"Of course we know! Sabe can recite his ancestors all the way back to Tiv himself. The elders from the west are merely pretending that Shangev was Jechira's son because they'd benefit from joining with the Jechira clan."

"But if the Shangev clan joined with the Kwande clan, wouldn't your elders benefit?"

"Yes, but Shangev was Kwande's son." Then Jijingi realized what Moseby was implying. "You think our elders are the ones pretending!"

"No, not at all. It just sounds like both sides have equally good claims, and there's no way to tell who's right."

"Sabe's right."

"Of course," said Moseby. "But how can you get the others to admit that? In the land I come from, many people write down their lineage on paper. That way we can trace our ancestry precisely, even many generations in the past."

"Yes, I've seen the lineages in your Bible, tracing Abraham back to Adam."

"Of course. But even apart from the Bible, people have recorded their lineages. When people want to find out who they're descended from, they can consult paper. If you had paper, the other elders would have to admit that Sabe was right."

That was a good point, Jijingi admitted. If only the Shangev clan had been using paper long ago. Then something occurred to him. "How long ago did the Europeans first come to Tivland?"

"I'm not sure. At least forty years ago, I think."

"Do you think they might have written down anything about the Shangev clan's lineage when they first arrived?"

Moseby looked thoughtful. "Perhaps. The administration definitely keeps a lot of records. If there are any, they'd be stored at the government station in Katsina-Ala."

A truck carried goods along the motor road into Katsina-Ala every fifth day, when the market was being held, and the next market would be the day after tomorrow. If he left tomorrow morning, he could reach the motor road in time to get a ride. "Do you think they would let me see them?"

"It might be easier if you have a European with you," said Moseby, smiling. "Shall we take a trip?"

❋

Nicole opened the door to her apartment and invited me in. She was obviously curious about why I'd come. "So what did you want to talk about?"

I wasn't sure how to begin. "This is going to sound strange."

"Okay," she said.

I told her about viewing my partial lifelog using Remem, and seeing the argument we'd had when she was sixteen that ended with me yelling at her and her leaving the house. "Do you remember that day?"

"Of course I do." She looked uncomfortable, uncertain of where I was going with this.

"I remembered it too, or at least I thought I did. But I remembered it differently. The way I remembered it, it was you who said it to me."

"Me who said what?"

"I remembered you telling me that I could leave for all you cared, and that you'd be better off without me."

Nicole stared at me for a long time. "All these years, that's how you've remembered that day?"

"Yes, until today."

"That'd almost be funny if it weren't so sad."

I felt sick to my stomach. "I'm so sorry. I can't tell you how sorry I am."

"Sorry you said it, or sorry that you imagined me saying it?"

"Both."

"Well you should be! You know how that made me feel?"

"I can't imagine. I know I felt terrible when I thought you had said it to me."

"Except that was just something you made up. It actually *happened* to me." She shook her head in disbelief. "Fucking typical."

That hurt to hear. "Is it? Really?"

"Sure," she said. "You're always acting like you're the victim, like you're the good guy who deserves to be treated better than you are."

"You make me sound like I'm delusional."

"Not delusional. Just blind and self-absorbed."

I bristled a little. "I'm trying to apologize here."

"Right, right. This is about you."

"No, you're right, I'm sorry." I waited until Nicole gestured for me to go on. "I guess I am…blind and self-absorbed. The reason it's hard for me to admit that is that I thought I had opened my eyes and gotten over that."

She frowned. "What?"

I told her how I felt like I had turned around as a father and rebuilt our relationship, culminating in a moment of bonding at her college graduation. Nicole wasn't openly derisive, but her expression caused me to stop talking; it was obvious I was embarrassing myself.

"Did you still hate me at graduation?" I asked. "Was I completely making it up that you and I got along then?"

"No, we did get along at graduation. But it wasn't because you had magically become a good father."

"What was it, then?"

She paused, took a deep breath, and then said, "I started seeing a therapist when I went to college." She paused again. "She pretty much saved my life."

My first thought was, *why would Nicole need a therapist?* I pushed that down and said, "I didn't know you were in therapy."

"Of course you didn't; you were the last person I would have told. Anyway, by the time I was a senior, she had convinced me that I was better off not staying angry at you. That's why you and I got along so well at graduation."

So I had indeed fabricated a narrative that bore little resemblance to reality. Nicole had done all the work, and I had done none.

The Truth of Fact, the Truth of Feeling | Ted Chiang

"I guess I don't really know you."

She shrugged. "You know me as well as you need to."

That hurt, too, but I could hardly complain. "You deserve better," I said.

Nicole gave a brief, rueful laugh. "You know, when I was younger, I used to daydream about you saying that. But now...well, it's not as if it fixes everything, is it?"

I realized that I'd been hoping she would forgive me then and there, and then everything would be good. But it would take more than my saying sorry to repair our relationship.

Something occurred to me. "I can't change the things I did, but at least I can stop pretending I didn't do them. I'm going to use Remem to get a honest picture at myself, take a kind of personal inventory."

Nicole looked at me, gauging my sincerity. "Fine," she said. "But let's be clear: you don't come running to me every time you feel guilty over treating me like crap. I worked hard to put that behind me, and I'm not going to relive it just so you can feel better about yourself."

"Of course." I saw that she was tearing up. "And I've upset you again by bringing all this up. I'm sorry."

"It's all right, Dad. I appreciate what you're trying to do. Just...let's not do it again for a while, okay?"

"Right." I moved toward the door to leave, and then stopped. "I just wanted to ask...if it's possible, if there's anything I can do to make amends..."

"Make amends?" She looked incredulous. "I don't know. Just be more considerate, will you?"

And that what I'm trying to do.

※

At the government station there was indeed paper from forty years ago, what the Europeans called "assessment reports," and Moseby's presence was sufficient to grant them access. They were written in the European language, which Jijingi couldn't read, but they included diagrams of the ancestry of the various clans, and he could identify the Tiv names in those diagrams easily enough, and Moseby had confirmed that his interpretation was correct. The elders in the western farms were right, and Sabe was wrong: Shangev was not Kwande's son, he was Jechira's.

One of the men at the government station had agreed to type up a copy of the relevant page so Jijingi could take it with him. Moseby decided to stay in Katsina-Ala to visit with the missionaries there, but Jijingi came home right away. He felt like an impatient child on the return trip, wishing he could ride the truck all the way back instead of having to walk from the motor road. As soon as he had arrived at the village, Jijingi looked for Sabe.

He found him on the path leading to a neighboring farm; some neighbors had stopped Sabe to have him settle a dispute over how a nanny goat's kids should be distributed. Finally, they were satisfied, and Sabe resumed his walk. Jijingi walked beside him.

"Welcome back," said Sabe.

"Sabe, I've been to Katsina-Ala."

"Ah. Why did you go there?"

Jijingi showed him the paper. "This was written long ago, when the Europeans first came here. They spoke to the elders of the Shangev clan then, and when the elders told them the history of the Shangev clan, they said that Shangev was the son of Jechira."

Sabe's reaction was mild. "Whom did the Europeans ask?"

Jijingi looked at the paper. "Batur and Iorkyaha."

"I remember them," he said, nodding. "They were wise men. They would not have said such a thing."

Jijingi pointed at the words on the page. "But they did!"

"Perhaps you are reading it wrong."

"I am not! I know how to read."

Sabe shrugged. "Why did you bring this paper back here?"

"What it says is important. It means we should rightfully be joined with the Jechira clan."

"You think the clan should trust your decision on this matter?"

"I'm not asking the clan to trust me. I'm asking them to trust the men who were elders when you were young."

"And so they should. But those men aren't here. All you have is paper."

"The paper tells us what they would say if they were here."

"Does it? A man doesn't speak only one thing. If Batur and Iorkyaha were here, they would agree with me that we should join with the Kwande clan."

"How could they, when Shangev was the son of Jechira?" He pointed at the sheet of paper. "The Jechira are our closer kin."

Sabe stopped walking and turned to face Jijingi. "Questions of kinship cannot be resolved by paper. You're a scribe because Maisho of the Kwande clan warned me about the boys from the mission school. Maisho wouldn't have looked out for us if we didn't share the same father. Your position is proof of how close our clans are, but you forget that. You look to paper to tell you what you should already know, here." Sabe tapped him on his chest. "Have you studied paper so much that you've forgotten what it is to be Tiv?"

Jijingi opened his mouth to protest when he realized that Sabe was right. All the time he'd spent studying writing had made him think like a European. He had come to trust what was written on paper over what was said by people, and that wasn't the Tiv way.

The assessment report of the Europeans was *vough*; it was exact and precise, but that wasn't enough to settle the question. The choice of which clan to join with had to be right for the community; it had to be *mimi*. Only the elders could determine what was *mimi*; it was their responsibility to decide what was best for the Shangev clan. Asking Sabe to defer to the paper was asking him to act against what he considered right.

"You're right, Sabe," he said. "Forgive me. You're my elder, and it was wrong of me to suggest that paper could know more than you."

Sabe nodded and resumed walking. "You are free to do as you wish, but I believe it will do more harm than good to show that paper to others."

Jijingi considered it. The elders from the western farms would undoubtedly argue that the assessment report supported their position, prolonging a debate that had already gone too long. But more than that, it would move the Tiv down the path of regarding paper as the source of truth; it would be another stream in which the old ways were washing away, and he could see no benefit in it.

"I agree," said Jijingi. "I won't show this to anyone else."

Sabe nodded.

Jijingi walked back to his hut, reflecting on what had happened. Even without attending a mission school, he had begun thinking like a European; his practice of writing in his notebooks had led him to disrespect his elders without him even being aware of it. Writing helped him think more clearly, he couldn't deny that; but that wasn't good enough reason to trust paper over people.

As a scribe, he had to keep the book of Sabe's decisions in tribal court. But he didn't need to keep the other notebooks, the ones in which he'd written down his thoughts. He would use them as tinder for the cooking fire.

We don't normally think of it as such, but writing is a technology, which means that a literate person is someone whose thought processes are technologically mediated. We became cognitive cyborgs as soon as we became fluent readers, and the consequences of that were profound.

Before a culture adopts the use of writing, when its knowledge is transmitted exclusively through oral means, it can very easily revise its history. It's not intentional, but it is inevitable; throughout the world, bards and griots have adapted their material to their audiences, and thus gradually adjusted the past to suit the needs of the present. The idea that accounts of the past shouldn't change is a product of literate cultures' reverence for the written word. Anthropologists will tell you that oral cultures understand the past differently; for them, their histories don't need to be accurate so much as they need to validate the community's understanding of itself. So it wouldn't be correct to say that their histories are unreliable; their histories do what they need to do.

Right now each of us is a private oral culture. We rewrite our pasts to suit our needs and support the story we tell about ourselves. With our memories we are all guilty of a Whig interpretation of our personal histories, seeing our former selves as steps toward our glorious present selves.

But that era is coming to an end. Remem is merely the first of a new generation of memory prostheses, and as these products gain widespread adoption, we will be replacing our malleable organic memories with perfect digital archives. We will have a record of what we actually did instead of stories that evolve over repeated tellings. Within our minds, each of us will be transformed from an oral culture into a literate one.

It would be easy for me to assert that literate cultures are better off than oral ones, but my bias should be obvious, since I'm writing these words rather than speaking them to you. Instead I will say that it's easier for me to appreciate the benefits of literacy and harder to recognize everything it has cost us. Literacy encourages a culture to place more value on documentation and less on subjective experience, and overall I think the positives outweigh the negatives. Written records are subject to every kind of error and their interpretation is subject to change, but at least the words on the page remain fixed, and there is real merit in that.

When it comes to our individual memories, I live on the opposite side of the divide. As someone whose identity was built on organic memory, I'm threatened by the prospect of removing subjectivity from our recall of events. I used to think it could be valuable for individuals to tell stories about themselves, valuable in a way that it couldn't be for cultures, but I'm a product of my time, and times change. We can't prevent the adoption of digital memory any more than oral cultures could stop the arrival of literacy, so the best I can do is look for something positive in it.

And I think I've found the real benefit of digital memory. The point is not to prove you were right; the point is to admit you were wrong.

Because all of us have been wrong on various occasions, engaged in cruelty and hypocrisy, and we've forgotten most of those occasions. And that means we don't really know ourselves. How much personal insight can I claim if I can't trust my memory? How much can you? You're probably thinking that, while your memory isn't perfect, you've never engaged in revisionism of the magnitude I'm guilty of. But I was just as certain as you, and I was wrong. You may say, "I know I'm not perfect. I've made mistakes." I am here to tell you that you have made more than you think, that some of the core assumptions on which your self-image is built are actually lies. Spend some time using Remem, and you'll find out.

But the reason I now recommend Remem is not for the shameful reminders it provides of your past; it's to avoid the need for those in the future. Organic memory was what enabled me to construct a whitewashed narrative of my parenting skills, but by using digital memory from now on, I hope to keep that from happening. The truth about my behavior won't be presented to me by someone else, making me defensive; it won't even be something I'll discover as a private shock, prompting a reevaluation. With Remem providing only the unvarnished facts, my image of myself will never stray too far from the truth in the first place.

Digital memory will not stop us from telling stories about ourselves. As I said earlier, we are made of stories, and nothing can change that. What digital memory will do is change those stories from fabulations that emphasize our best acts and elide our worst, into ones that—I hope— acknowledge our fallibility and make us less judgmental about the fallibility of others.

Nicole has begun using Remem as well, and discovered that her recollection of events isn't perfect either. This hasn't made her forgive me for the way I treated her—nor should it, because her misdeeds were minor compared to mine—but it has softened her anger at my misremembering my actions, because she realizes it's something we all do. And I'm embarrassed to admit that this is precisely the scenario Erica Meyers predicted when she talked about Remem's effects on relationships.

This doesn't mean I've changed my mind about the downsides of digital memory; there are many, and people need to be aware of them. I just don't think I can argue the case with any sort of objectivity anymore. I abandoned the article I was planning to write about memory prostheses; I handed off the research I'd done to a colleague, and she wrote a fine piece about the pros and cons of the software, a dispassionate article free from all the soul-searching and angst that would have saturated anything I submitted. Instead, I've written this.

The account I've given of the Tiv is based in fact, but isn't precisely accurate. There was indeed a dispute among the Tiv in 1941 over whom the Shangev clan should join with, based on differing claims about the parentage of the clan's founder, and administrative records did show that the clan elders' account of their genealogy had changed over time. But many of the specific details I've described are invented. The actual events were more complicated and less dramatic, as actual events always are, so I have taken liberties to make a better narrative. I've told a story in order to make a case for the truth. I recognize the contradiction here.

As for my account of my argument with Nicole, I've tried to make it as accurate as I possibly could. I've been recording everything since I started working on this project, and I've consulted the recordings repeatedly when writing this. But in my choice of which details to include and which to omit, perhaps I have just constructed another story. In spite of my efforts to be unflinching, have I flattered myself with this portrayal? Have I distorted events so they more closely follow the arc expected of a confessional narrative? The only way you can judge is by comparing my account against the recordings themselves, so I'm doing something I never thought I'd do: with Nicole's permission, I am granting public access to my lifelog, such as it is. Take a look at the video, and decide for yourself.

And if you think I've been less than honest, tell me. I want to know.

A Long Walk Home

BY JAY LAKE

April 27th, 2977 CE [Revised Terran Standard, relativity-adjusted]

Aeschylus Sforza—Ask to his friends, such as they were—had camped deep in the cave system he was exploring here in the Fayerweather Mountains of Redghost. Well, technically assaying, but the thrill of going places no human being had ever before seen or likely would see again had never died for him. Planetary exploration was interesting enough, but any fool with a good sensor suite could assay from orbit. Creeping down into the stygian depths of water and stone…now that took some nerve.

Challenge. It was all about challenge. And the rewards thereof, of course.

Back at the Howard Institute, during the four-year long psychological orientation prior to his procedures, they'd warned Ask that ennui was a common experience among Howards. The state of mind tended to reach psychotic dimensions in perhaps fifteen percent of his fellows after the first century of post-conversion life. At the time, the observational baseline had only been about sixteen decades.

Pushing 800 years of age now himself, Ask had not yet surrendered to terminal boredom. Admittedly he found most people execrably vapid. About the time they'd gained enough life experience to have something interesting to say, they tended to die of old age. People came and people went, but there was always some fascinating hole in the ground with his name on it.

He'd discovered the sulfur fountains deep beneath the brittle crust of Melisande-3?. He'd been the first to walk the narrow, quivering ice bridges in the deep canyons of Qiu Ju, that rang like bells at every footfall. He'd found the lava tube worms on Førfør the hard way, barely escaping with his life and famously losing over two million Polity-IFA schillings worth of equipment in the process.

First. That romance had never died for him.

Here beneath Redghost, Ask was exploring a network of crevices and tunnels lined with a peculiar combination of rare earths and alloys with semiconductive properties. Considerable debate raged within his employer's Planetary Assay Division as to whether these formations could possibly be natural, or, to the contrary, could possibly be artificial. After over a millennium of interstellar expansion to a catalog of better than sixteen thousand explored planets, more than two thousand of them permanently inhabited, the human race had yet to settle the question of whether other sophont life now populated, or ever had populated, this end of the galaxy.

Ask recognized the inherent importance of the question. He didn't expect to run into aliens beneath the planetary crust, though. Beneath any planetary crust, in truth. So far he had not been disappointed.

And these tunnels… Many were smooth like lava tubes. Most of those interconnected. Some were not, jagged openings that tended to dead-end. All were lined with a threaded metallic mesh that glinted in his hand-light with the effervescence of a distant fairyland glimpsed only in dreams. Seen through his thermal vision, they glowed just slightly warmer than the ambient stone, a network like a neural map.

That resemblance was not lost on Ask. Nor was the patently obvious fact that whatever natural or artificial process had deposited this coating inside these tunnels was more recent than the formation of the tunnels themselves. His current working theory was that the smooth passages were the result of some long-vanished petrophage, while the rough passages were formed by the more usual geological processes. The coating, now, there was a mystery.

A Long Walk Home | Jay Lake

Ask sat in an intersection of three of the smooth passages, enjoying his quick-heated fish stew. Redghost boasted a generous hydrosphere that the colonists here had husbanded magnificently with Terran stock. And the smell of it was magnificent, too—the rich meat of the salmon, spicy notes from tarragon and false-sage, the slight edginess of the kale.

If he closed his eyes, held very still, and concentrated, Ask could hear the faint echoes of air moving in the tunnels. Atmospheric pressure variations and subtle pressures in the lithosphere made a great, slow, rumbling organ of this place.

A series of jarring thumps more felt than heard woke him from his reverie. Dust fell from the arch of the ceiling—the first time he'd observed that kind of decay while down here.

He consulted his telemetery. One advantage of being a Howard was all the hardware you could carry in your head. Literally as well as figuratively. Data flowed into his optic processing centers in configurable cognitive displays that he could chunk to whatever degree he liked. Like fireworks in the mind, though fractal in nature. Elephants all the way down, one of his early tutors had said, before being forced to explain the joke. Elephants, made of tinier elephants, made of tinier elephants, almost ad infinitum.

In this case, Ask's fractal elephants informed him that the subsurface sensors were jittering with tiny temblors, confirming in finely-grained technical detail what he'd already felt. The surface sensors were offline.

That was odd.

He also noted a series of neutrino bursts. Solar flares from Redghost's host star? That hadn't been in any of the forecasts.

The still-operating sensor cluster closest to the cave mouth started to register a slow increase in ambient radiation as well. Everything above that was dead, as was his surface equipment. It would be a long walk home if the rockhopper and his base camp equipment just outside were knocked out of commission just like the upper sensors.

Had someone let off a nuke? Ask found that almost inconceivable. Politically it was...bizarre. Disputes within the Polity weren't resolved by force of arms. Not often, at any rate. And even then, almost always via small-scale engagements.

Tactically it was even stranger. Redghost didn't have much that anyone wanted except living space and arable land. Who would bother?

Uneasy, he rested out the remainder of his body-clocked night. The radiation levels near the surface quickly peaked, though they did not subside all the way back to their earlier baseline norms. Hotter than he might like, but at least he wouldn't be strolling into a fallout hell.

April 28th, 2977 [RTS-ra]

When he reached the first inoperative sensor cluster, Ask peeled the nubbly gray strip off the wall and studied it. Ten centimeters of adhesive polymer with several hundred microdots of instrumentation. The only reason for it to be even this large was the convenience of human hands. With no camera in his standard subsurface packages, focal length was never an issue.

The failure mode band at the end was starkly purple from radiation exposure. The neutrino bursts must have been part of some very fast cloud of high-energy particles that fried the equipment, he realized. Instrumentation deeper down had been protected by a sufficient layer of planetary crust. Not to mention the curiously semiconducting tunnel walls.

A cold thought stole through Ask's mind. What would that burst have done to the enhancements crowding for skullspace inside his head?

Well, that spike had passed, at any rate.

He doubled back and dropped his camping gear, instruments, tools and handlights down the tunnels with the last working sensor. It seemed sensible enough, given that he had no way of knowing whether the events of last night would re-occur.

Once that was done, he approached the entrance with caution. Though the official reports he occasionally saw were far more complex and nuanced, the chief causes of death among his fellow Howards could be boiled down to either murder or stupidity. Or too often, both.

Whatever was happening on the surface seemed ripe for either option.

His outside equipment remained obstinately dead. Ask drifted to the point where reflected light from the surface began to make deep gray shadows of the otherwise permanent darkness. He should have been able to pick up comm chatter now, at least as garbled scatter.

Nothing.

There had been no more quakes. No more neutrino bursts. Whatever had taken place last night was a single event, or contained series of events, not an ongoing situation. Which rather argued against solar flares—those lasted for days at a time.

Stupidity? Or murder? Could those happen on a planetary scale?

Why, he wondered, had that thought occurred to him? Everything he'd experienced since last night could just as easily be local effects from a misplaced bomb or a particularly improbable power plant accident. Not that there were any power plants up in Redghost's mountains, but a starship having a very bad day in low orbit would have served that scenario.

It was the silence on the comm spectra that had put the wind up him, Ask realized. Even the long-wave stuff used for planetary science was down.

Quiet as nature had ever intended this planet to be.

He walked into the light, wondering what he would find.

⇥⫲⇤

The base camp equipment looked normal enough. No one had shot it up. Fried electronically, Ask realized. The rockhopper on the other hand, was…strange.

When you'd lived the better part of a thousand years, much of it exploring, your definitions of strange became fairly elastic. Even in that context, this decidedly qualified.

Really, the rockhopper was just an air car, not radically different from the twenty-fourth century's first efforts at gravimetric technology. A mass-rated lifting spine with a boron-lattice power pack around which a multitude of bodies or hulls could be constructed. Useless away from a decent mass with a magnetosphere, but otherwise damned handy things, air cars. The rockhopper was a variant suited to landings in unimproved terrain, combining all-weather survivability with a complex arrangement of storage compartments, utility feeds and a cab intended for long-term inhabitation. Eight meters long, roughly three meters wide and slightly less tall, it looked like any other piece of high-endurance industrial equipment, right down to the white and orange "see me" paint job.

Someone had definitely shot it up. Ask was fairly certain that if he'd managed to arrive somewhat earlier, he would have seen wisps of smoke curling up. As it was, sprung access panels and a starred windshield testified to significant brute force—that front screen was space-rated plaz, and should have remained intact even if the cab around it had delaminated.

Something had hit the vehicle very, very hard.

After a bit of careful climbing about, Ask identified seven entry points, all from a fairly high angle. He couldn't help glancing repeatedly up at the sky. Redghost's faintly mauve heavens, wispy with altocirrus, appeared as benign as ever.

Orbital kinetics. No other explanation presented itself. That was even weirder than a nuke. And why anyone would bother to target an unoccupied rockhopper off in the wilderness was a question he could not even begin to answer.

A particularly baroque assassination attempt, perhaps? He'd always avoided politics, both the official kind intertwined with the Polity's governance, and the unofficial kind among the Howards themselves. That particular stupidity was the shortest path to murder, in Ask's opinion.

As a result of the strike on the aircar, the power pack was fractured unto death and being mildly toxic about its fate. Nothing his reinforced metabolism couldn't handle for a while, but he probably shouldn't hang around too long. As a result of the neutrino bursts, or more to the point, whatever had created them, every independent battery or power source in his equipment was fried, too.

Someone had been annoyingly thorough.

He finally found three slim Class II batteries in a shielded sample container. They lit up the passive test probe Ask had pulled out of one of the tool boxes, but wouldn't be good for much more than powering a small handlight or some short-range comm.

The way things were going, carrying any power source around seemed like a bad idea. Unfortunately, he couldn't do much about the electronics in his skull, except to hope they were sufficiently low power to avoid draw-ing undue attention.

As for the batteries, he settled for stashing them with the surviving campsite equipment he'd left back in the caves with the last working sensor suite. He retrieved what little of his gear was not actively wired—mostly protective clothing and his sleeping bag—and went back out to survey his route down out of these mountains. His emergency evac route had been almost due west, to a place he'd never visited called the Shindaiwa Valley. A two-hour rockhopper flight over rough terrain could be weeks of walking.

Not to mention which, a man had to eat along the way. Even, or per-haps especially, if that man was a Howard.

May 13th, 2977 [RTS-ra]

Ask toiled across an apron of scree leading to a round-shoulder ridge. He was switchbacking his way upward. Dust and grit caked his nose and mouth, the sharp smell of rock and the acrid odor of tiny plants crushed beneath his boots.

Had the formation been interrupted, it would have been a butte, but this wall ran for kilometers in both directions. The broken range of hills rising behind him had dumped him into the long, narrow valley that ran entirely athwart his intended line of progress.

Over two weeks of walking since he'd left the rockhopper behind. That was a long way on foot. Time didn't bother Ask. Neither did distance. But the ridiculousness of combining the two on foot seemed sharply ironic. He'd not walked so much since his childhood in Tasmania. Redghost was not the Earth of eight hundred years ago.

At least he'd been out in the temperate latitudes in this hemisphere's springtime—the weather for this journey would have been fatally unpleas-ant at other times and places on this planet.

He had no direct way to measure the radiation levels, but presumed from the lack of any symptoms on his part that they had held level or dropped over the time since what he now thought of as Day Zero. His

Howard-enhanced immune system would handle the longer-term issues of radiation exposure as it had for the past centuries—that was not a significant concern.

Likewise he had no way to sample the comm spectra, as he'd left all his powered devices behind. But since he had not seen a single contrail or overflight in the past two weeks, he wasn't optimistic there, either. The night sky, by contrast, had been something of a light show. Either Redghost was experiencing an extended and unforecasted meteor shower or lot of space junk was de-orbiting.

The admittedly minimal evidence did not point to any favorable outcome.

Those worries aside, the worst part of his walk had been the food and water. He'd crammed his daypack with energy bars before leaving the rock-hopper, but that was a decidedly finite nutritional reserve. Not even his Howard-enhanced strength and endurance could carry sufficient water for more than a few days while traveling afoot. Those same enhancements roughly doubled his daily calorie requirements over baseline human norms.

Which meant he'd eaten a lot of runner cactus, spent several hours a day catching skinks and the little sandlion insect-analogs they preyed on, and dug for water over and over, until his hands developed calluses.

Two hundred kilometers of walking to cross perhaps a hundred and twenty kilometers of straight line vector. On flat ground with a sag wagon following, Ask figured he could have covered this distance in less than four full days.

The scree shifted beneath him. Ask almost danced over the rolling rocks, wary of a sprained or broken ankle. When injured he healed magnificently well, but he could not afford to be trapped in one place for long. Especially not in one place with so few prospects for food or water as this slope.

The cliffs towered above him. The rock was rotten, an old basalt dike with interposed ash layers that quickly—in a geological sense—surrendered to the elements so that the material sheered away in massive flakes the size of landing shuttles. That left a wonderfully irregular face for him to climb when he topped the scree slope. It also left an amazingly dangerous selection of finger- and toe-holds.

A Long Walk Home | Jay Lake

On the other side of this ridge was the wide riparian valley of the Shindaiwa River, settled thickly by rural Redghost standards with farmland, sheep ranches and some purely nonfunctional estates. Drainage from rain and snowpack higher up the watershed to the north kept the valley lush even in this drier region in the rain shadow of the Monomoku Mountains further to the west.

All he had to do was climb this ridge, cross over it, and scramble down the other side. And he'd find... People? Ruins?

Ask didn't want to think too hard about that. He couldn't think about anything else. So he kept climbing.

The river was still there. He tried to convince himself that this was at least a plus.

The ridgeline gave an excellent view of the Shindaiwa Valley. Though nothing curdled with the smoke of destruction, he also had an excellent view of a number of fire scars where structures had burned. There seemed to be a fair amount of dead livestock as well. A lot more animals still wandered in fenced pastures.

Nothing human moved. No boats on the river. No vehicles on the thin skein of roads. The railroad tracks leading south toward Port Schumann and the shores of the Eniewetok Sea were empty. No smoke from fireplaces or brush burning. No winking lights for navigation, warning or welcome.

Even from his height and distance, Ask could see what had become of the hand of man in this place.

He had to look. At a minimum, he had to find food. Most of the structures were standing. The idea of looting the houses of the dead for food distressed him. The idea of starving distressed him more.

He didn't reach the first farmhouse until evening's dusk. Ask would have strongly preferred to do his breaking and entering in broad daylight, but another night of hunger out in the open seemed foolish with the building right in front of him. A tall fieldstone foundation was topped by two stories of brightly painted wooden house that would not have looked out of place on one of the wealthier neighboring farms of his youth.

Ask wasn't sure if this was a deliberate revival of an ancient fashion of building, or a sort of architectural version of parallel evolution.

Chickens clucked and fussed in the yard with the beady-eyed paranoia of birds. Some had already climbed into the spreading bush that seemed to be their roost, others were hunting for some last bit of whatever the hell it was chickens ate.

Beyond the house, a forlorn flock of sheep pressed against the fenced boundary of a pasture, bleating at him. He had no idea what they wanted, but they looked pretty scraggly. A number of them were dead, grubby bodies scattered in the grass.

Water, he realized, seeing the churned up earth around a metal trough. They were dying of thirst.

Ask walked around the house to see if the trough could be refilled. He found the line poking up out of the soil, and the tap that controlled it. Turning that on did nothing, however.

Of course it wouldn't, he realized. No power for the well pump.

He sighed and unlatched the gate. "River's over there, guys," Ask said, his voice a croak. He realized he hadn't spoken aloud in the two weeks he'd been walking.

The sheep just stared at him. They made no move for freedom. There wasn't anything more he could do for the animals. He shrugged and walked back to the house, up the rear steps.

Inside the house was a mess. If he'd come on it in broad daylight, even from the outside he'd have noticed the cracked and shattered windows. Inside, the floors were dirty with splinters and wisps of insulation.

The lack of people was disturbing. So was the lack of blood, in a weird way.

They'd just walked outside, leaving the doors standing open, and vanished. Then orbital kinetics had plowed through the roof to disable the house's power plant, core comm system and—oddly—the oven. He figured it had to have happened in that order, because if anyone had been inside the house when the strikes hit, there would be signs of panic—toppled furniture, maybe blood from the splinters and other collateral damage.

With that happy thought in mind, Ask walked around the house in the deepening dark, checking every commset, music player, power tool and any other gadget he could find to switch on. The small electronics were fried, too, just like the equipment in his rock hopper.

It was if the old fairy tale of the Christian Rapture had come true, here on Redghost. Followed by the explosive revenge of the exploited electron? He hadn't so much as looked at a Bible in over seven hundred years, but Ask was pretty sure that there hadn't been any mention of a rapture of the batteries.

"Render unto Volta those things which are Volta's," he said into the darkness, then began giggling.

His discipline finally broke. Ask retreated to the kitchen to hunt for food and drink.

June 21st, 2977 [RTS-ra]

It took him five weeks to explore every house in this part of the Shindaiwa Valley. On the way, Ask opened all the pasture gates he could find, shooing out the cattle and sheep and horses. The llamas, pigs and goats were smart enough to leave on their own, where they hadn't already jumped or broken the gates, or—in the case of the goats—picked the latches.

Most of them would starve even outside the fences, but at least they could find water and better pasture. Some would survive. So far as he knew,

Redghost had no apex predators in the native ecology. Humans certainly hadn't imported any.

Give the dogs a few generations of living wild and that would change, though.

It was the damned dogs that broke his heart. The household pets were the worst. So many of them had starved, or eaten one another. And the survivors expected more of him than the farm animals had. When he slipped open a door or tore a screen, they rushed up to him. Barking, whining, mewling. He was a Person, he was Food, he could let the good boys Out. And the dogs knew they had been Bad. Crapping in corners, sleeping on the furniture, whining outside bedroom doors forever shut and silent.

In truth, that became the reason he'd entered every house or building he could find. To let out the cats and dogs and dwarf pigs. Finding a bicycle meant he could gain distance on those dogs that wanted to follow him. The cats didn't care, the pigs were too smart to try. He let the occasional birds out, too, and when he could, dumped the fish tanks into whatever nearby watercourse presented itself.

The more he walked, the fewer of them were left alive inside. But he had to try.

Thirty-nine days in the Shindaiwa Valley, and he'd visited almost four hundred houses, dormitories, granaries, slaughterhouses, tanneries, cold storage warehouses, machine workshops, emergency services centers, feed stores, schools. Even three railroad stations, a small hospital and a tiny airport terminal.

Not a single human being. Not so much as fingerbone. He'd even dug up both an old grave and a recent one to see if the bodies had been left behind. They had. Ask couldn't remember enough about Christianity to figure out of that was evidence for or against the Rapture. He did rebury them, and say what he could remember of the Lord's Prayer over the fresh-turned earth.

"Ten thousand sheep, a thousand cats and dogs, and me," he told a patient oak tree. It was wind-bent and twisted, standing in an ornamental square in front of the Lower Shindaiwa Valley Todd Christensen Memorial

A Long Walk Home | JAY LAKE

Railroad Depot Number 2. A sign proclaimed this to be the first Terran tree in the valley, planted by one of the pioneer farmers two centuries earlier. "You're a survivor. Like me."

But of what?

One small blessing of the railroad station was a modest selection of cheap tourist maps printed on plastene flimsy. Some people just didn't want to mess with dataflow devices all the time. On a relatively thinly-settled planet like Redghost the electrosphere was largely incomplete anyway.

Had been. It was nonexistent now, which was the utmost form of incompletion.

Ask shuffled the map flimsies. His knowledge of local planetography was poor—it simply hadn't been important. He'd been dropped by shuttle at Atarashii ʔsaka, the main spaceport and entrepôt for Redghost. He was vaguely aware of three or four other sites with support for surface-to-orbit transfer. And his assignment in the Fayerweather Mountains, for which he'd based out of Port Schumann after an atmospheric flight from Atarashii ʔsaka.

That was it. All he'd known about the Shindaiwa Valley was that this was his first line of emergency evacuation. All he'd known about Redghost was the semiconducting tunnels, and a notion of a bucolic paradise home to perhaps twenty million souls.

His next stop, he figured, would be Port Schumann. It was a city, at least by Redghost standards. Anyone else surviving on this part of the planet would have headed there.

In a bleak frame of mind, Ask figured that twenty million people would have about five million residences and perhaps half a million commercial structures. He'd managed an average ten buildings per day here in the Shindaiwa Valley. Denser in the cities, of course. Still, figure six hundred thousand days to check every structure on Redghost, plus the travel time between places. Fifty years? A hundred, if the buildings in Atarashii ʔsaka and the few other relatively large cities were too big to check so quickly?

Where the hell did twenty million people go? A planet full of corpses, he could understand. A planet empty of people…

The Best of Subterranean

January 4th, 2978 [RTS-ra]

The crashed airplane in the hills east of Port Schumann had caught his attention as he'd cycled along the rough service road paralleling a rail line. It was a fixed-wing craft with propeller engines—something fairly simply designed to be locally serviceable without parts imported from off-planet. The fuselage looked intact, so he'd gone to check it out.

Weapons hadn't seemed to be much of an issue, and most of what he'd found in that department had been useless anyway due to embedded electronics, but he was always curious what he might find.

This craft had seated six. Small, white with pale green stripes and the seal of the Redghost Ministry of Social Adjustment on the side. Planetary judiciary, in local terms. It was missing one door, he noted as he approached.

He looked inside to see someone in the rear seat.

"Shit!" Ask screamed, jumping back.

He'd been too long without company. He was starting to regret not bringing a few of the dogs from the Shindaiwa Valley with him.

Feeling foolish, Ask unclipped the aluminum pump from his bike and held it loosely like a club. Some of the Howards were killers, dangerous as human being who'd ever lived, but he'd never bothered with that training or those enhancements. He was strong enough to swing something like this pump right through a wall at need. At least until the wall or the pump shattered.

That had been enough.

Until now.

He approached the airplane again. Having already screamed, there didn't seem much point in secrecy now. Still, he didn't want to just march into the wreck.

The person was still there.

No, he corrected himself against the obvious. The body. Who the hell would stay seated in crashed airplane? For one thing, it was pretty cold out here at night.

A man, he thought. Handcuffed to his seat. Ask climbed into the cabin and crept close. It was hard to tell, with the flesh mummifying in the cold, but it looked like the prisoner had struggled hard against his cuffs.

Ask stepped up to the pilot and co-pilot's seats. Smashed instruments and windows, torn seat cushions. No blood.

They'd been gone from the plane, or at least out of their seats, before the orbital kinetics had struck the aircraft. In flight.

And the missing door? Had the pilot and guards just stepped out in mid-air? Ask imagined the prisoner, straining to follow whatever trumpet had called his captors away. Then shrieking in fear as the cockpit exploded in sizzling splinters, the engines shredded and died under the orbital strikes, and the plane had glided in to its final landing.

He hoped the poor bastard had died in the landing, but suspected he might have starved chained to the seat.

This also meant that people who had been unable to move from a position would not have been taken up by whatever had snatched everyone from Redghost's surface. Prisoners? The few jails he'd visited had stood empty and open-doored. The guards had taken their captives with them. Hospital ICUs? That explained the several medical beds he'd found dragged into gardens and on outdoor walkways.

Still, he knew where to look.

Ask went back for his bolt cutters and freed the dead prisoner. He didn't have a shovel and the ground was too cold to dig in anyway, but he spent two days making a rock cairn next to the airplane.

"The second-to-last man on Redghost," he said by way of prayer when he was done. His fingers were bruised and bloody, several of his nails torn. "You and I are brothers, though you never knew it. I wonder if you had it better or worse than those who were taken away."

October 11th, 2983 [RTS-ra]

On the sixth year of his hegira, Aeschylus Sforza entered the city of Pelleton. He had not found a living animal indoors in five years. He had not found a living animal penned outdoors in over four. He had not seen evidence of a human survivor other than himself on the planet at any time. He had found six bodies in various improbable circumstances. The hardest had been a little girl locked in a closet with a piss pot and a water bottle. She'd obviously been there a long time before Day Zero. And a long time after.

Ask devoutly hoped whoever had done that to a child had been taken directly to the lowest circle of whatever hell had opened up and swallowed the human race.

In any case, he'd buried them all. And he obsessively checked closets after that child. It took more time, but what was time to a Howard walking home all by himself?

Pelleton was located on an eastern curve of the Eniewetok Sea. It was the first city he visited with buildings over four stories tall. Some optimist had built a pair of fifteen-story office towers along the waterfront. By then, Ask had seen enough of the planet's architecture and development to understand most people wanted it small and simple.

Not so unlike the Tasmania of his youth. People who had wanted the big city moved to Melbourne or Brisbane or Sydney. People who wanted the big city here on Redghost had moved to Atarashii ?saka or taken up a line of work with off-planet demand.

He'd taken up the habit of visiting airports first, when it was at least sort of convenient to do so. Not just for the sake of any other trapped prisoners, though he'd never found another one of those. But rather, in hopes of finding something useful. Anything, really.

The gasbags of the heavy-lift freighters were all long since draped in tatters from their listing semi-rigid frames, but he kept wondering if he'd find a fixed-wing aircraft or a gravimetric flyer that hadn't been gutted by orbital kinetics. Not that Ask expected to build an engine or power pack with his bare hands, but it would have been a start.

Most of the cockpits were smashed or shattered. Too many electronics in there. Likewise power systems. And in most cases, the airframes as well. He'd amused himself for a while calculating the total number of separate surface targets that had been subjected to bombardment by orbital kinetics

in a single twenty-five point six-hour period—the local planetary day—
and how many launchers that implied. How much processing power in
guidance systems that implied.

Ask had concluded that no power in human space had the resources to
commit such a saturated attack. Not so quickly and thoroughly.

That of course raised several more difficult questions. The one
that concerned him most was whether this had happened to every
human-settled planet in the Polity, or just to Redghost. He almost certainly would not have known if a spaceship or starship had called here
since Day Zero. Short of catching a glimpse of it transiting in orbit, how
would he find out? Not a single comm set on the planet still worked so
far as he was aware.

Was he not just the last human being on this planet, but the last
human being in the universe? Ask couldn't figure out if that thought was
paranoia, megalomania or simple common sense. Or worse, all three.

By now most of the airframes had acquired layers of moss, grass and in
some cases, even vines. Another decade and there would be trees poking
through the holes in the wings. He clambered around Pelleton's airport all
day without finding anything novel, then sheltered inside the little terminal as the dark of the evening encroached.

The dog packs were getting worse all over. Sleeping outside at night was
no longer safe as it had been in the early times after Day Zero. The question of weapons had re-entered his mind. Especially projectile weapons.

June 6th, 2997 [RTS-ra]

On the twentieth year of his hegira, Aeschylus Sforza began to compose
epic poetry. His Howard-enhanced memory being by definition perfected,
he had no trouble recalling his verse, but still he took the trouble to refine
the rhymes and metre so that should someone else ever have call to memorize the tale of his walk home around Redghost, they could do so.

Over the years he had found and buried twenty-three people. None of
them appeared to have long survived Day Zero, as whatever confinement

had prevented their ascendance had also prevented their continued life and health unattended by outside aid.

The towns and cities were changing, too. Rivers in flood-damaged bridges and washed-out waterfronts. Storms blew down trees, tore off roofs and shattered those windows that had survived the orbital strikes. Plants, both native and Terranic, took over first park strips, lawns and open spaces; then began to colonize sidewalks, rooftops, steps, basement lightwells.

The edges that civilization draws on nature were disappearing into a collage of rubble, splinters and green leaves.

He'd spent the years hunting clues. He'd dug the payloads of the orbital kinetics out of enough wrecks and buildings to realize that he wouldn't know much about them without a lot of lab work. In a lab he didn't and could not have access to, of course, in the absence of electrical power. They appeared deformed, heat-stressed metalloceramic slugs about two centimeters in diameter that had probably been roughly spherical on launch. That left the question of guidance wide open.

Likewise the various bodies he'd found. None of them told Ask any more than the dead prisoner had. Every human being who was physically able to do so had walked outside the afternoon or evening of April 27th, 2977 and vanished. Presumably along with their clothes and whatever they had in their hands at the time. He'd found plenty of desiccated sandwiches on plates and jackets hung on chair backs indoors, but nothing equivalent on the sidewalks and in the back yards of Redghost.

The light show in the sky had subsided years earlier, though the occasional re-entry flare still caught his eye at night. He periodically found batteries and even small pieces of equipment that had survived both the orbital kinetics and the electronic pulse attack by dint of shielding either deliberate or accidental. So far he'd declined to carry those things with him, for fear that whatever it was might still be monitoring from orbit.

And that was it.

So one day he began to compose epic poetry. It was a thing to do while he passed the time hacking through vines and checking closets.

A Long Walk Home | Jay Lake

I sing of the planet now lost
Though still it spins through space...
Homer he never would be, but who was there to sing to, anyway?

April 23rd, 3013 [RTS-ra]

On the thirty-sixth year of his hegira, Aeschylus Sforza finally began to take seriously the proposition that he had gone completely mad. He wondered if this had been true from the very beginning. Was he trapped in a decades-long hallucination, something gone badly wrong in his Howard-enhanced brain? Or was even the passage of time a cognitive compression artefact, like the illusory and deceptive time scales in dreams?

Ask wasn't sure it mattered, either way. He wasn't even sure anymore if there was a difference.

He was exploring the town of Tekkeitsertok, on a largely barren island in Redghost's boreal polar regions. The journey to this place had required quite a bit of planning, and the use of a sailboat found intact due to its complete lack of electronics. Still, restoring the boat to seaworthiness had consumed over a year of his time.

Time. The work had been something to do.

Tekkeitsertok was a settlement of low, bunkered buildings, most of them with slightly rounded roofs to offset snow accumulation and present a less challenging profile to the winter winds howling off the largely frozen Northcote Sea on the far side of the island. Lichen now covered every exterior surface that hadn't been buried in wind-blown ice and grit. The insides of the buildings where insulation had not failed were taken over by a fuzzy mold, so that everything looked slightly furry. Where insulation had failed, the interiors were just a sodden, rotting mess.

Ask picked through the town, wondering why anyone had bothered to live here. Tekkeitsertok had probably been the most extreme permanent human habitation on Redghost. He'd decided some time ago not to worry about camp sites, research stations, and whatnot, so anyone who'd been out on the ice cap was on their own. Not that any ice station would have survived three and a half decades without maintenance. Even this place with its thick-walled air of permanence was already surrendering to nature.

Nothing was here, of course. Not even in the closets, which Ask still conscientiously checked. He'd never found so much as a footprint of the attackers, but had held some vague notion that evidence might be preserved in the icy northern cold. Even in summer, this place was hostile—built on permanently frozen ground, flurrying snow every month of the local year.

The moment of madness came when he was inside the town's mercantile. The windowless buildings meant he had to use an oil lantern even with the endless summer daylight outside. That in turn produced strange, stark shadows between the warmly glowing pools of light. Racks of merchandise ranging from cold weather gear to snow-runner wheels crowded the retail space. Ask was pushing from aisle to aisle, watching for useful survival gear as much as anything in this place, when he heard an electronic chirp.

He froze and almost killed the lantern. That was stupid, of course. Anyone or anything that might have been alerted to the light already had. Still, he turned slowly, mouth wide open to improve his hearing over the pounding of his heart. His blood felt curdled.

The noise did not repeat itself.

After standing in place for several minutes, he gave up on stillness as a strategy and headed for the sales counter. That was where any surviving equipment was likely to be.

Three and a half decades after Day Zero, and now there was something else moving on this planet?

Nothing.

He found nothing. Ask tore the sales counter apart, looking in all the little drawers, even. He opened the access panel behind to the long-useless breaker boxes and comm line interchanges. He turned up the dry-rotted carpet. He yanked everything out from inside the display cases. He grabbed an axe from the tools section, though there wasn't a tree within five hundred kilometers of this place, and chopped up the cases looking for whatever might be hidden inside them. He tried chopping the floor, but stopped when he nearly brained himself with the rebound of the axe.

Panting, sick, shivering, Ask finally stopped. He'd trashed the interior of the place. In all the years of his wandering, he'd never stooped to petty vandalism. For all the windows he'd broken getting in and out of places, he'd never destroyed for the sake of the pleasure of destruction.

Now, this?

It's not like they were coming back. Wherever they'd gone.

With that realization, he took up the axe and charged through the mercantile screaming. A long pole of parkas collapsed under his blows, their insulation spinning like snow where they tore. He smashed a spinner rack of inertial compasses. Tents spilled and tore. Useless power tools went flying to crack against other displays or the outside walls. When he got to the lamp oils and camping fuels, he spilled those, too, then transferred the flame from his lantern to the spreading, glistening pools.

After that, he retreated outside to the almost-warmth of the polar summer, that had cracked above freezing. Smoke billowed out from the open door of the mercantile. After a while, something inside exploded with a satisfying 'whomp.' He watched a long time, but the roof never fell in.

Finally Ask stretched in the cold and turned to wonder what he might do next. That was when he realized he had been surrounded by a patient dog pack. Furry, lean, with the bright eyes of killers, they had watched him watch the fire.

"Hey there, boys," he said softly. Though surely none of these remembered the hand of man. These were the descendants of the survivors, not the domestic escapees of the early years.

One of the dogs growled deep in its throat. Ask regretted leaving his guns in the sailboat. Deliberately archaic collector's items, they were all that worked anymore with the interlocks burned out on any rational, modern weapon.

Not that he had much ammunition, either.

And not that he had any of it with him.

Knife in hand, he charged the apparent leader of the pack. It was good to finally have something to fight back against.

The Best of Subterranean

November 1st, 3094 [RTS-ra]

On the one hundred and seventeenth year of his hegira, Aeschylus Sforza returned to the Shindaiwa Valley. He'd buried forty-seven bodies in the years of his wandering. The last of them had been little more than heaps of leather and bones. The cities, towns and settlements he'd visited had largely buried themselves by the time he'd been to every human outpost he could possibly reach on this planet.

He had not spoken a word out loud in thirty years. The epic poetry was not forgotten—with his Howard memory, nothing he meant to remember was ever forgotten—but he had not bothered with it in decades. The madness, well, it had stayed a long time. Eventually he'd grown tired even of that and retreated back to sanity. The track of that descent was marked in the number of burn sites across one whole arc of Redghost's northern hemisphere.

The dogs had failed to kill him. Wound infections had failed to kill him, though he'd come perilously close to dying at least twice. Even the ocean crossings had failed to kill him. Loneliness, that curse of the Howards, had failed to kill him.

Boredom might, though.

The Shindaiwa Valley had gone back to the land. Many of the houses still stood, but as rotting shells overgrown with weeds. Some things were more permanent than others. The railroad tracks, for instance. Likewise the plascrete shells of the hospital and the train stations.

Ask had time. Nothing but time. So he set about using it. He needed a place to live, near water but not likely to be flooded out when summer thawed the snowcap at the head of the watershed. He needed to catch and break some of the wild horses that haunted these fields and forests to draw the plow. He needed to log out trees in some areas, and find saplings young enough for the project that had been forming in his mind for the past decade or so.

He needed so much, and would never have any of it. Now that he was done walking home, Ask had nothing but time.

A Long Walk Home | Jay Lake

March 17th, 3283 [RTS-ra]

The demands of controlling the horses, not mention managing the pigs and goats he eventually took on, had brought Ask's voice back to him. He'd become garrulous over the long years with those patient eyes staring back at him.

He'd also been convinced he was the last man in the universe. In over three centuries since Day Zero, no one had come calling at Redghost so far as he knew. If the rest of the human race were still out there functioning normally, the planet should have been swarming with rescuers and Polity investigative teams in the first year or two. Or any of the decades since.

Someone might have done a fly-by then hustled away. Ask knew he wouldn't have been aware of that. But human beings could not leave a disaster alone. And Redghost, whatever else it had been, was definitely a disaster.

He even had a little bit of electronics, having at one point taken a pair of pack horses back to his cave and retrieved his surviving equipment. The passive solar strips used on so many Shindaiwa Valley rooftops were still intact, and he worked out a sufficient combination of salvage parts and primitive electronics to keep a few batteries charged. Space-rated equipment lasted, at the least. He had steady light by which to read at night—Shindaiwa Valley had boasted two hundred and eleven surviving hardcopy books by the time he'd gotten around to salvaging those. Four of them were actual paper printings from the Earth of his childhood, three in English that he could read. Their unspeakably fragile pages were preserved in a monomolecular coating as family heirlooms.

He'd read them all over and over and over. He could recite them all, and some years did so just to have something to say to the goats and horses—the pigs never cared so much for his voice.

Still, reading and reciting those words written by authors long dead was the closest Ask could come to speaking to another human being.

In the mean time, his project had matured. Blossomed into success, in a manner of speaking. He'd spent decades carefully surveying, logging and replanting, even diverting the courses of streams to make sure water was where he wanted it to be.

When that had grown boring, he'd built himself a new house and barn. Living in the hospital had felt strange. The weight of souls there was stronger. Having his own home, one that none of the people before Day Zero had ever lived or worked or died in, had seemed important for a while.

So Ask had built the house at the center of his project. Made a sort of castle of it, complete with turrets and a central watchtower. A platform for a beacon fire, just to make the point. It wasn't high enough to see his work, but when he climbed the ridge at the eastern edge of the valley—the one he'd first come down in those confused weeks right after Day Zero—he could glimpse what his imagination had engineered.

Eating a breakfast of ham and eggs the morning of March 17th, Aeschylus Sforza heard the whine of turbines in the air outside his home. Centuries of living alone had broken him of the habit of hurrying. He finished his plate a little faster than normal, nonetheless, and scrubbed it in the stone trough that was his sink. He pulled on his goatskin jacket, for the Shindaiwa Valley mornings could still be chilly in this season, and walked outside at a measured but still rapid pace.

Ask had realized a long time ago that it didn't matter who they were when they came. The unknown raiders who'd stripped this planet, the descendants of those taken up by the attackers, or his own people finally returned. When they returned, whoever they were, he'd wanted to meet them.

That was why his house sat in the exact center of three arrows of dense forest, each thirty kilometers long and spaced one hundred and twenty degrees apart, each surrounded by carefully husbanded open pasture. A "look here" note visible even from orbit. Especially from orbit. Who the hell else would be looking?

Outside his front gate a mid-sized landing shuttle, about thirty meters nose to tail, sat clicking and ticking away the heat of its descent. The grass around it smoldered. Ask did not recognize the engineering or aesthetics of the machine, which answered some of his speculations in the negative. It certainly did not display Polity markings.

He stood his ground, waiting for whoever might open that hatch from within. His long walk was done, had been done for over two hundred years.

Time for the next step.

The hatch whined open, air puffing as pressure equalized. Someone shifted their weight in the red-lit darkness within.

Human?

It didn't matter.

He was about to learn what would happen next.

Aeschylus Sforza was home.